Knight of Chaos

By

Dexter C. Herron

To: DHANWANTI
MAY THE ADVENTURE
NEVER END

1/31/04

ISBN: 1-4107-4777-8 (e-book)
ISBN: 1-4107-4778-6 (Paperback)

Library of Congress Control Number: 2003092933

This book is printed on acid free paper.

Printed in the United States of Amercia
Bloomington, IN

Cover Illustration by Michel Bohbot,
Copyright 2003. www. mbohbot.com.

1stBooks – rev. 07/01/03

To my brother, Dio;
Without your nurturing, constructive criticism and encouragement,
this book would not have been written.

To my beautiful, wonderful wife/bestest friend in the whole wide world, Hilary;
Without your dedication, devotion and unwavering faith and support,
this book would not have been published.

Prologue

In near darkness, he slipped from his wife's embrace. He skillfully untangled himself from her arms and pulled himself from under the layers of blankets, gently unhooking her tail from his ankle. His wife purred in her sleep, her arms wrapping around a well placed pillow. Slowly, gently, he leaned close and his lips found hers and in her sleep she returned his affection and smiled. *At least one of us is having nice dreams,* he thought as he rose from the bed.

He dressed silently, with only an occasional glance to his sleeping wife. He watched as the cat leapt onto the bed and found herself a place by his wife. He nodded, and the cat waved her tail goodbye as he crept out.

He took his Kabar knife from the mantle and shoved it into his sash. As he did this, the dog who had been sleeping by the warm hearth, opened one eye and then the other. The springer spaniel said nothing and only followed his master to the door, making sure that he did indeed take his sun hat and smoke darkened glasses.

The two made their way silently through the caverns and out into the bright light of day.

Through his dark glasses he gazed out into the valley. The sun had cleared the crest of the mountains, burning the morning fog to mist. The sky was blue, the mountains were black, and the land was green, with shadows shifting against the white walls and red roofs of the village that nestled in the valley. The air was crisp, the mist was gray and the wind blew sharp and steady from the north. He rarely saw the sun any more. He usually timed his travels for the sun to set before going out and to be in before it rose again. He hadn't realized he had missed it so. The sight of day was a beautiful thing when touched by the hand of God.

Or gods, he made himself remember. It was a bird god of the sun. *Kemoto.* There was a god *(or was it goddess?)* of the mists and fog, another for the wind and still another one for the dawn. *Swell. But no god for sunsets. There is a god for left turns, but not right turns. Go Figure.*

He shook his head sighing, and his dog looked up at him. He smiled at the dog. "Kemoto, the sun. Mistang, the mist and Shegatesu the dawn."

The dog wagged his tail and said: "Very good, master Craig. But by now, Shegatesu is done and gone from the sky."

Craig snorted a laugh and looked out into the valley again. He was reluctantly learning the culture. It seemed thrust on him by anyone who would talk to him. 'You don't know of Okshiru? Boy, a'fore he strike you down with his wrath, let me learn you proper!'

He angled his wide brimmed hat to block the light of the sun as he started walking the trail that ran along the lip of the valley, and his mind played back the stories. There was no real record, but thousands of clearly conflicting stories from every side, including the Orks who claim that the Supergod was an Ork. But sifting through the similarities of the stories, led to a few possible ideas. Craig had taken all that he had heard and compiled their common points into one legend that he could personally handle.

The legend of the Re-awakening of Time.

The world before, was a world of machines, and castles of glass and steel, and the lands were stone, and nothing grew. Across the face of the earth, there lived a trillion people some how stuffed into the cracks and cavities of the world. There were three extraordinary lords of science, and in their castles were the most wondrous machines of all. Their creations were so amazing that they could alter the courses of the stars by changing the elements of life itself! Changing lead to gold was simple. Making fish from loaves of bread was almost as easy.

Two of the lords remain un-named, least the power of their spoken names raise them back to the world. The last had been known to mortals as Lord Hammerstrike, but the gods knew him as the Supergod.

Their machines were so complex, to control them the three men used neural links, actually connecting cables directly into their minds, but in doing so took on the power later to be known as the "Poer Ther Of". Once the "Poer Ther Of" had moved into them, they no longer needed the machines. Their merest thoughts simply became reality.

Within no time at all, the three began to battle. First, it was limited to tiny arguments and disputes, but as thoughts and dreams ran rampant, the sky soon filled with childhood nightmares and monsters. Dragons flew high and became so numerous that the very sun was eclipsed. Myths and legends were fighting hand and foot with creations constructed by the darkest and most uncontrollable recesses of their god-infant minds.

The armies of the three were short lived, for the battle quickly escalated and the ground itself rippled like waves across the ocean, changing the shape of the land. Life and death were meaningless as the three brought the worlds from beyond the curtain of oblivion together in a furious clamor that sent cracks running through the very bedrock of the Earth. The sun was exploded and the moon was wielded as a weapon, jerked from above and thrown into the fray for good measure.

The Supergod realizing that existence itself was in danger as it splintered and fractured from the stress, reached up and grabbed the titanic chain of events and stopped time.

Then the real battle began.

It is said that the Supergod took his stand on the Arch of Time, throwing shafts of Light like harpoons. Of the other two, one made camp at the base of oblivion, wielding the cosmos like a whip, while the third stood with his back to the gates of hell and tossed balls of flaming Hate. Or so one story goes.

The only thing that everyone could agree on was that the Supergod, won.

He had used all of his power in an act of desperation and created a Thought that suddenly took the "Poer Ther Of" from their minds and memories and they all suddenly found themselves back on Earth. The three men, who had been slinging stars at each other, brawled with bare fists, rocks, and sticks until two lay dead.

But the Supergod had arranged for the "Poer Ther Of" to temporarily, (having learned that such power was extremely dangerous) return to him should he kill his enemies. He looked across the wrecked and shattered worlds, and with his hands, shaped them into Mortalroam. He took the generals from his armies and retired them to Worldsend. He gave each the responsibility to re-build what had been destroyed while he patched things up with the span of Time. Patches that to this day ripple across the face of Forever.

As Okshiru took his place as the god of sky and sea, the Supergod took the minions of his enemies and the remains of his cities and machines and weapons of old and, with a broad, sweeping motion of his hand, swept them off Mortalroam to a place he named Hel.

Then, with the "Poer Ther Of", quickly fading from his memory, he reached up and re-started time.

And with mortal eyes, he watched the Re-awakening.

There was a long, ringing silence as moments passed. A tinge of panic came to him as he believed that time would not re-start, when suddenly, dragons fluttered to the sky like flocks of birds. (thus the legend that when the last Dragon flies the world will end, began) Elves will say they were the first and others will argue it was the Dwarves, moving out of the earth to stand beside the Supergod.

And the Supergod took the title "Lord Hammerstrike", and went about his life as just another mortal, living in obscurity, with only one small after effect of godhood. He was immortal. This small after effect proved to be of great concern to the gods, as they feared the possibility of the Supergod regaining his Supergodhood. They trembled for eons wondering what to do until finally, Sharpe, the god of deep and provocative thinking, came up with a brilliant philosophical argument. When it was presented to the Supergod, (he, being the fair and understanding kind of guy that he is) had no choice but to leave Mortalroam. An argument, so complicated, so intricate, that it would kill a mere mortal out right.

And so, the Supergod retired to Worldsend, sitting just outside of the gods chain of command, studying concepts beyond mortal comprehension, waiting patiently for the world to end.

So the story goes.

Craig walked on, allowing the legend to roll about in his mind as he looked out over the valley, shaking his head in reluctant belief. *It rudely violates just a few fundamental laws of physics,* he thought, *but where a legend is needed, it will do.*

He shifted his cloak and sun hat and made his way down the twisted trail along the back side of the hill into the valley of Seeda Gully. From here he could see across the distance to the grassy and rising steps of Tashwalk, to the land were Lord Hammerstrike spent his final years on Mortalroam, the great city of Fanrealm. To the right, he could see the church of Ponsi, perched on a pimple of a hill. It was not a temple to any of the gods and no one went there. It is said that Lord Hammerstrike built the church and he alone went there on occasion. No one knew why.

Save one.

As Craig walked down the slope, he let his mind wander, going over the strange, almost creepy thought that always ran in his head when he passed the church of Ponsi. Lord Hammerstrike, the Supergod, creator of Mortalroam, Worldsend, Hel and a host of gods and demons, was a Christian.

Craig turned to the right, away from Fanrealm and continued along the side of the hill until it became a gap between Hill Number Six and Hill Number Five or commonly known as 5th and 6th Brother Mountains. He had a habit of calling mountains hills. It was one of the few things that he clung to from his time spent in the United States Marine Corps, in a land a world away. Perhaps a hundred years, perhaps a thousand, before Lord Hammerstrike plugged an RCA jack into his frontal lobe and awoke the great "Poer Ther Of", Craig had been abruptly yanked from the stream of time. After a hundred millennium had passed, he was re-inserted again in hopes that his power to command the great dragons could be used for skullduggery. Rudely plopped into a world he didn't fully understand, with powers he couldn't control, he now walked the land of Lord Hammerstrike as "The Dragoncaller".

The sun had risen higher as he approached the first gate. He didn't look up for fear of the sun's glare, but only spoke his name when the guard challenged him. "Craig Tyrone." *The Dragoncaller and his trusty sidekick, Onary, the neigh-beast.*

The watch knew him and bid him enter to Dragonrealm. It really wasn't Dragonrealm. Where he stood was a pavilion of temporary tents and shacks to house the Dragonslayer's armies while the real castle was being re-built. The real site was across a narrow river perched on a tiny island. It wasn't a real island either, but the calcified and petrified remains of a frighteningly huge sea going armadillo like creature, who had gotten trapped in the river thousands of years ago and died. Natashi, the black witch of the village, who's claim to fame was that she tangled with a dragon that bit off her left buttock and lived to tell the tale, swears that the creature yet lives and one day, the creature will awaken. The construction crews that have burrowed deep into the island have yet to make it all they way through the creature's amazingly thick carapace, so her story may prove true yet. So much so, that Roc canceled the plans for the sub, sub dungeons.

Craig looked across the water and could see the half built walls and the dwarves of WARCO, Wreck and Rebuild Company, with their magical golems, mixing mortar, building scaffolding, and setting bricks. Day and night, they worked, re-building the great castle of Roc the Dragonslayer. Craig had seen the plans for the construction and marveled at its ingenuity. He himself was a physicist, a rocket scientist to be precise, and as he stared wide eyed at the parchments and drawings, he thought about how it must have been for explorers to gaze upon the construction of the ancient pyramids of Egypt.

Craig moved past the rows of tents for the troops, over to the watch tower and handed a note to the signalman. The signalman turned and called the sergeant of the watch who was an elf and the sergeant, after reading the note, put his hands to his lips and blew the eerie melody of an *elfcall*.

With this done, Craig headed over to the tent of the Watch Commander. He passed another row of tents for the construction crew and then the tents for the officers. In almost the middle of things, its roof, half draped on the only standing building, was the tent of the Watch Commander.

He ducked under the flap and made his way past the planning dwarves who were arguing with the mining Gnomes, past a fat elf cooking lunch for the officers, and past the Admin counting coins in preparations for payday. Craig followed the maze of canvas walls to the far side, where the tent was connected to the stone wall. Facing the wall, Gorn brooded over his desk. He finally tossed his stylus onto the stack of papers and slouched into his chair rubbing his temples.

Craig approached casually. "Gorn, if your staring at…" The archer reeled, spinning in his seat and jumping to his feet. In the same motion he had snatched his bow from the corner and was prepared to use it as a club. Craig stood motionless, his hands were forward and his palms exposed in a gesture of peace. "the guard roster," Craig went on nervously, "I can do it for you."

"Blessid!" The archer swore. "Don't be sneaking like that!"

"I wasn't sneaking."

"Well then. You are going to have to make a bit of noise or I will die like an old man while I am still a young man." He set down his bow. "We go through this every time. Have you considered my idea?"

"About a cowbell? Yes, but it isn't very fashionable and the noise hurts my ears." He pulled off his hat and cloak as he approached the table and over looked the mess of paper. "Besides. I was making noise. I cleared my throat."

"Craig, what is thunder to an elf is a whisper to a man." Gorn leaned against the table, folding his arms. "Didn't I relieve you this morn? Isn't the sun up?"

"I had…business to attend to."

"Could have left it with me. Man, after an eight hour watch, are you not wanting sleep?"

"What is with the questions?" Craig snapped more than he wanted and tried again with a milder tone. "Dude, I just have to do some things."

Gorn nodded understanding that it was the business of the Dragoncaller and no business of his. "Is there anything I can do?"

Craig half shrugged. "I'm not sure." Then he motioned with his head towards the stone building. "Is his Nastiness in?"

"Nay. Lord Dragonslayer is in Cornerstone at last word."

"Keeping the world's beer population in check?"

"What else?"

Craig nodded, then looked up and very distant.

Gorn knew elves and the look they take when they hear something. "What is it?"

"Elfcall." Craig answered looking back down over the desk. "I would imagine it's from Fanrealm. I was going there this morning, but I changed my mind. I figured I could send a message and see elfzilla and kill two birds with one stone. I should have gone to Fanrealm." *I should have stayed in bed.*

"And the message?"

"I requested Lady Fantista to summon the House of Hammerstrike." He said casually.

A cold hand pushed through Gorn and the archer swallowed, slowly taking his seat. "Is it bad?"

"Yes...NO!...Hell, I don't know. When do I ever know what I'm doing?" Craig plopped down in a chair, throwing up his hands in frustration. "Damn it! I'm a rocket scientist, not a Mystic."

Gorn nodded suddenly seeing how tired the Dragoncaller was. "Your thinking on an empty head." Gorn shouted over his shoulder: "Koda! Hot mead for the Dragoncaller!" Then he looked back at the Craig. The dark elf's face was hidden in his hand. "And the reply?"

"I don't know!" He spoke into his palms, his anger again rising more than it should. He sighed, letting it escape. "Let me stop biting your off head."

Gorn shrugged. "Tis daylight, you're a Nih elf, I would expect a bit of head biting."

Craig looked up. "But I'm not a real elf. At least I wasn't always an elf and I don't speak Elfcall. It really isn't a language, it's a...tune of emotions that elves are raised with. Since I wasn't raised an elf, I don't grasp the lingo. Oh, they've tried to teach me…" He shrugged knowing the real reason was his stubbornness. He paused as Koda brought him a steaming mug of sweet mead.

"Doeth the Dwagoncaller have any pwefrentheth for lunch?"

Craig sipped his mead and burned his tongue. "What are we having?"

"Beef, pultwy and whice wrapped in seaweed."

"Translate that into: Leftovers. I'll have an amazingly small amount of beef the way I like it." Craig looked at Gorn. "I should be grateful that I can still at least eat red meat."

"One beef thamwith coming wright up." Koda chirped brightly.

"And I mean: Small!" He shouted at the cook's back. Then he looked back at Gorn. "His small will feed three of me."

Gorn smiled as the sergeant of the guard entered the tent. "Sir, The Dragoncaller requested…"

"Proceed." Gorn spoke quickly, cutting off the guard, but then held up his hand to stop him. He leaned over to Craig. "Do you want this in private?"

Craig shook his head and Gorn waved to the guard to proceed. "Lady Fantista replies that she will summon the House." The elf paused and listened. "I hear her summon them now."

Gorn rose to his feet. "It may be a few days before they all get here, but it is best it see to it that all is in readiness. I will check the lines. If you get bored, you can look at the roster if you like." Gorn realized that Craig wasn't listening, only staring blankly at the table. His mind was a thousand leagues away.

He didn't even hear Gorn leave.

He didn't move when Koda brought him lunch. He mindlessly took his Kabar and cut the sandwich in half, giving a share to Onary. He didn't touch the other half.

He was in the same place when Koda refilled his empty cup with more hot mead.

It went cold.

They have faith in you. He thought to himself. *She didn't even ask why. Which is good 'cause you don't know why. I was foolish to come here. I should go home.*

He didn't move.

He listened to the shouts of the guards as a wagon pulled up. He heard hellos of two of the Dragonguard. Then he heard the wagon squeak and a man being punched.

Roc was home.

Onary slipped under the table.

"Didn't I tell him that I want arms distance at all times?" Roc's growl was unmistakable. "Did I say that here?"

"He should have known, my lord." Sounded like Blade, Chief of the Dragonguard.

"Alright then!" Roc suddenly bellowed. "NOW HEAR THIS! ANYONE WITHIN ARMS DISTANCE IS FOOLISHLY RISKING THE CHANCE OF HAVING THE GREAT ROC THE DRAGONSLAYER THROW UP ON THEM. Think they got that?"

"Yes my lord."

Craig listened as the Gnomes, Dwarves, Cook and Admin quickly took precautions and secured everything movable, as Roc lumbered into the tent. Craig could see the tent walls tremble. He listened to Roc's footsteps come closer and he rose to greet him. Craig fixed a determined look on his face, forcing himself to be prepared. Roc was a leader, a king in his own right which meant he was a king who fought his own wars. Minstrels sang in chorus the tales of the Dragonslayer, leaping into battle, his mighty sword clenched in both hands, cleaving row after row of his enemies in twain.

His heroic style was not without penalty however, as the Dragonslayer tended to lead with his face.

Over the years the magically healed scars began to build until finally his face could handle no more (rumor had it that the healer was just sick of fixing Roc's face) and something unexpected happened. Roc could keep his rather handsome face, but when he was excited, or angry, or even showed too much expression, his face would twist, sometimes so badly that no one could face him. For this reason, Roc wore a mask most of the time.

Somehow Craig knew this wasn't one of those times.

"Craig!" Roc shouted rising to his full height. His head pushed into the canvas roof. He stumbled forward and Craig braced for collision, but Roc swayed backwards. With his legs spread and his arms apart, for a moment, Craig thought Roc was trying to surf on solid ground. "I'm alright." He regained his balance and placed a huge hand on Craig's shoulder. "Guess what?"

"What?" Craig said, not really wanting to know.

"I remember what you said." He whispered. He looked over himself for something. "Ah!" He pulled a set of keys out of his sash. "Here you go."

"Where is it?"

Roc looked around thoughtfully, then leaned down and looked at Craig, his eyes the color of meat. "I don't really know." He rose up again shrugging, then stumbled towards the steps.

Now is your chance. "Roc, I have to talk to you." Roc waved a hand at him without turning around. "Roc, I asked Fantista to summon the house." Roc stopped in his tracks. "She has."

Roc slowly turned, looking back over his shoulder. He knew there was a reason why he came home.

Craig came closer. "I had a dream. The kind that comes true."

Roc rose to his full height, again pushing into the roof of the tent. Sobriety was coming over him like a slow wave as he thought about it. Craig was close enough so he rested his hand on his shoulder for a brace. Craig looked so honest and so much wanting to help but unable to. *Poor Craig.* Roc shook his head. "You don't need me now, do you?"

"Roc, I…"

The giant elf shook his head. "No, you don't need me right now. I don't get this…" He lowered to Craig's height. Craig could see his watery eyes shifting back and forth in confusion. "Fucked up. Is that the word? Fucked? Am I fucked up now?"

Craig nodded. "Very."

"I don't get this very fucked up often. When was the last time?"

"I don't remember."

Roc nodded slowly, putting pressure on Craig to keep standing. "I didn't plan to get this very fucked up." He thought about why he did. "I just…couldn't sleep." Roc looked at Craig, blinking his eyes to get them to focus. "You have your dream, and I can't sleep." His eyes grew wide. "Could that mean something?" He swayed, taking a step back for balance. "No, no it doesn't. Nothing, nothing at all." He waved his hand to dismiss the thought. "I hope to hel not. I leave magic alone. You know what I mean? Don't you? I know you would if you could, but you're a shit magnet. Shit always happens to you. Poor Craig, the shit magnet. You are one of the few people who I can trust. I can't even trust Dwayne like I trust you. I love him to death, I mean, he is my brother, sort of, but, I love him to death anyway. But you are the only one who I can trust. I trust you with this. I trust you with everything." He rose, looking around. "CRAIG TYRONE THE DRAGONCALLER IS IN CHARGE!" He shouted to the tent walls and then looked back at Craig. "You're in charge. Call me when Dwayne, or what ever name he's using, gets here."

Craig nodded helplessly as the big elf staggered off to his stone hut, swaying as if he were on a ship in a rough sea.

Onary watched and flinched when Roc slammed the door and bolted it. "Rather! Well, at a minimum we got that out of the way. Right?"

Craig nodded backing up to the chair and sitting down again. "What am I doing?" He put his hand in his face again. Onary ducked under his other hand and pushed up against it. Craig petted his head. "Pal? Do me a favor? Go find that guard…" Craig glanced at his watch. "Damn, I've been here all day. He should be off post by now. Go to the communications tower and find somebody and tell them I want to be notified if any member of the House responds to the summons."

"Right!" He said brightly and stepped out of reality.

Craig looked around the tent. There was a time that Onary's vanishing trick was startling to say the least. But now it was as common as walking across the room. *Used to be that a talking dog was big shit.* He thought.

He felt alone and tired and he closed his eyes and saw flames.

Onary stepped back into reality beside him. "Message relayed." Craig reached down and scratched the Springer Spaniel's chest. "Oh! Thank you. And now the bad news." Craig stopped scratching. "Neeko is coming up the trail."

Craig moaned inwardly. "I left her a note saying that I was going to Fanrealm. She must have gone to Fanrealm and now come here." Craig looked down to Onary. "Is she mad?"

"I couldn't tell."

"She took the cart?"

"Yes."

Craig breathed a sigh of relief. "At least she didn't walk."

He rose and took up his cloak and made his way through the tent and waited for her in the shadow of the entrance. He followed her silently as she parked the cart. She was smiling and kissed him on the forehead as he lifted her down. "This isn't Fanrealm." She scolded playfully as her cat leapt out and on to the ground.

Onary glared at the cat. "Edia." He welcomed her with thinly concealed contempt.

"Dawg." She replied with no intent to conceal her loathing.

Craig ignored the two as he took his wife's hand. "Sorry about that, I changed course." He guided her towards the tent to get out of the afternoon sun. "You didn't go there, did you?"

"Blessid no. And you have Edia to thank for it."

"Ah can follow that dawg anywheres." The cat spoke up.

"How delightful!" Onary seemed quite charmed. "Why not follow me down to the new moat."

"Whut moat?"

"Precisely."

Craig led his wife silently through the tent to the Watch Commander's station. He sat her in a chair, mindful of her very pregnant status. "I didn't want to wake you. I know how you need your sleep." He knelt beside her and she caressed his face.

"My sweet husband." She purred and her green cat like eyes searched his face. "Only you could sneak out on a Ne-arri." Her tail rose up and hooked his arm. Her face grew concerned. "You had a dream, didn't you." He nodded as she played with his long, black hair. "My poor baby." She shook her head. "So many burdens, Dragoncaller. You want to sleep, but the dream won't let you." She put her hand under his chin and tilted his face up. She could almost see the trouble bubbling in his eyes. "We will find you a cot to lay down. And when you have slept, we will eat what ever Koda is brewing in the kitchen."

Craig shook his head. "I can't..." He whispered.

She smiled. "Hey, lover, I am a Chirurgeon. I can fix anything that troubles you. I can tell your Centre is troubled. Let me ease the pain. Share it with me."

Craig could feel her hand was warm even though the day was cold. It was time to tell someone, get it off his chest, but as he tried to form the words, he had nothing to say. He never did.

He kissed her hand and held onto it. He looked to her tender, beautiful face. With his free hand, he reached up and caressed her smooth, apple cheeks. Her wide eyes closed and she let out a purr. He tickled her whiskers and she smiled. Her cat ears, hollow triangular cones perched on the top of her head were angled towards him, ready to listen.

But how could he put it all into words. The dream was small, but yet spanned farther than he could see. It was going to happen, perhaps already happened, or was happening right now. There was so much that he didn't know, so many uncertainties. He had summoned the house out of a near panic. But somehow it felt justified.

"I saw," He began with a suddenly dry voice. "I saw a baby, it wasn't ours." He quickly added as he touched her swollen belly and she held his hand there. "I know it wasn't ours. But I don't know whose it was. It was shivering and crying and there was no one to help it." In his dream he saw an archeological dig, and in the lowest part of the dig, there were demons with pick axes and shovels, digging, and from out of the hole flashing steel claws were digging their way free, burrowing out of the ground where the creature had been buried. The demons were giggling with delight.

That was the dream. Craig looked at his wife, uncertain what he should tell her, what she would understand. There were things and meanings that went beyond the dream. The thing in the pit was the Iron Dragon, trapped years ago by the Dragonslayer, being freed.

The Dragon destined to slay the Dragoncaller.

On top of that, Craig could tell that the beast wasn't alone. There were others with him clawing to get free, meaning something else was amiss. But Craig knew that was not the central focus of the dream. Monsters crawling out of the depths of the earth, cursing his name with anger was nothing new to him. It was the baby. The crying baby that Craig could somehow see down in the pit with the Iron Dragon.

With a slow, heaving sigh, the words were found for him. "The baby," He whispered as tears welled in his eyes. "The baby was in hell." He leaned his head against his wife's knee, and silently wept.

Chapter 1

Kemoto, the bird god, spread his great fiery wings across Okshiru's wide blue sky. Although he beamed heavily, there was a coolness to the air, leaving it brisk and quick. The war horse of autumn stamped his hooves and shook his mane. Chinook, the snow biter, snorted and shivered in the cool wind that Hauge had brought him. He knew that Fikor was coming. The time for the god of winter was now at hand.

Hauge, the god of wind, dashed and danced down from the ridged northern peaks of snow and rock, across the open, windy steppes of swaying grass and woolly beasts, to the highlands of the elves and the spruce forests of Meleki. He left the elven mountains and sped clear of the deep forests to the southern ridge of foot hills that peered into the soft lowlands of the Glowing Valleys. From the height of the hills, the god of wind looked over the sun-drenched valleys of abundance. He gazed approvingly to the farms and nests that mortal men carved from the face of Mortalroam to claim for their own. The pastoral fields of grass and wheat, swept and waved to the whim of the playful wind, as he came down from the hills to the valley below.

Oustrand came down from his porch and walked the beaten path up the small, gently sloping hill. Through squinting eyes he gazed down along the path, taking in the cool, dry morning wind that Hauge brought him—feeling it play in his stringy blonde hair. He paused beneath the spread of the old Lone Oak. Its great boughs covered with leaves of gold, red and brown towered over him. Its massive roots pushed into the ground and its tall, twisted trunk grew painfully towards Okshiru's sky.

The Lone Tree had stood in its spot before Oustrand's grandfather had settled on the land. As a boy, Oustrand played in the tree as his grandfather watched him from the porch and Oustrand knew that one day, he would sit on the porch of his house and watch his grandchildren play on that old Lone Oak.

But now it was not the tree and its golden leaves that he stood on the hill for, but his wheat swelling with ripeness in the valley below. It was a small acreage compared to the land barons near by, but it was large enough for a goodly profit. He could see by the sweeping wave of the grain and the chill in the air that it would soon be time to harvest his

1

work. He thought about the near by help that would make themselves available for just that.

As he thought this, he noticed at the top of the road to the far side of the wheat field, the ruffle of tattered cloth. Distance masked its features showing just a post draped with rags, but when this post waved to Oustrand with arm extended, he realized that this post was some gaunt, tall, Tattered man! Oustrand waved back. It was an almost automatic reaction. The people of the town were always friendly, even with strangers, for they had no one, or reason, to fear.

But before he could wonder about this stranger, he heard his name and turned around to answer. He gave a sharp, bright 'Hoy!' to give his where abouts to the faint light voice of his daughter. Many years Oustrand as his wife had been childless and they thought the gods would not bless them children, but yet the spawn of he and his wife now came running out of the house, across the porch and up the path to the Lone Tree. She was a delight, a dream come true for Oustrand and his wife. She was full of charm and wit and sang to his thick, leathery heart. She had sung at the Season Festivals to the beaming pride of her parents and to the awe struck, jubilant faces of the town folk. On stage like a porcelain doll, with a dress her mother had made just for the occasion, her sweet voice floated out across the crowds and held them all in rapture. All the people of the town near by would readily confess that she had the grace, poise and voice of an angel—and in certain aspects, she was.

Oustrand stood as all fathers would—tall and unmoved, but he had to smile as she breathlessly told him that mother had returned from the pasture with milk from the cows and they were going to town to sell it, and then to the northern city to spend it. Her deep, dark eyes sparkled as she talked in detail about the things she would do when they reached Rendon. They would push through the bustling shops to buy a dress for sabbath and with what money was left they would buy some sweet sap and bake pastries for her Papa.

Oustrand's pride beamed through his hard, tanned face. He bent at the knee and swept his daughter into his arms. His dry calloused hands gripped her tightly in a deep hug. Her tender, creamy, white face scratched against his abrasive stubble.

He let her go and caught her tiny hand in his own as they turned to head towards the house, but something touched her hearing and she looked back. Her wide, brown eyes squinted at the sun hovering over the horizon, rising from the low ground. The long black shadows stretched across the reddish ground and golden wheat. As they reached the crest of the hill in the shadow of the Lone Oak, Oustrand turned to see what his daughter saw and saw the Tattered man standing by the gate leading to the house. It was a quarter of an hour to reach the gate from the road at a sharp stride, yet the Tattered man was there in scant moments. The Tattered man waved again and Oustrand saw the glint of a sword's hilt poking from out of the man's rags.

The Tattered Man called out in a heavy northern accent. "How fare wit ye?" The Tattered Man's face was dark and shaded with his back to Kemoto's rising light.

Oustrand knew him to be a man of the sword out to make his fortune by doing any job he could. The big man's daughter hid herself behind his leg. She didn't like him in the least.

Oustrand's hard dry voice returned the Tattered Man's call. "I and my family are fine. What brings you here?"

The Tattered Man took the bedraggled cover from his head. "I see ye hath wheat lookin' fer cuttin'. I be a fine man who does hard work fer a meal and a few pennies."

Oustrand again saw the man's sword hilt. It was not long ago when Oustrand was a man like him. A man with a sword to fight for any glory and bragging rights. The weight of gold laying heavily in his palm and its rattle that brought out the flagons of drink from the tavern master's casks, and the ladies of ill repute to win it with their charms. He could remember fighting evil magic with only a sword and a swear, choosing to side with the most gold or excitement.

That was long ago. He was a farmer now, with simple wants and joys like the laughter of a little child ringing in his ears and the smell of a warm kitchen in his broad, bold chest. The feel of a soft bed and a wife to hold him was what he wanted now.

He felt his daughter clutching at his leg. He could tell that she didn't like him. "My wheat won't need cutting until the end of the month. I'll hire out then. If you wish, head over the hill to Mas' Gregaer's stead. His land is bigger and it wants cutting now."

The Tattered Man bowed and bid a good day and turned up the trail to the road. Oustrand told no falsehood. His crop still needed more days to swell with sun and cold nights to harden its kernel. And although he was a swordsman, and traditionally not the most dedicated of laborers, he was a man obviously down on his luck and hungry. He should've hired him or told him to return in a few days and not send him away like he did. His guilt growled at him. He could have at least given him a bit of food for the road. But deep inside his heart, he felt relieved that he sent him away as he felt the clutch of his daughter loosen. He took his daughter's hand again and turned to the house. He could feel her fear still echoing in her. What frightened her so?

Hot lashing wrapped around Oustrand's throat and lifted him high into the air. His hands slid on the thin leather that held him aloft by his neck. His feet kicked and his body thrashed as his face began to swell. He was spinning slowly like tinsel on a tree. He saw the Tattered Man tying off the noose on the bough of the tree. The Tattered Man in the blink of an eye had ran a cord to the limb of a tree, around the big man's throat and hoisted him into the air. Oustrand knew it was Magic, evil magic. Evil magic that he saw too late. Gray fogged in his eyes and his ears rang with the roar of the dead. The Tattered Man looked at him, standing barely out of the reach of his heavy, groping hands.

"Hi." The Tattered Man wore a half smile on his cryptic face like he was born with it there. He admired his work, the big man dangling from a tiny line. He watched the weight grow on the Oustrand's waving arms until they raised no more.

He turned to the girl. He could see her tiny trembles as her heart felt for breath to scream. Her hands hid her face and her brown eyes stared in horror at the Tattered Man.

"Shall we play a game?" The Tattered Man asked the child.

She sparked to life as her legs turned to flee. Like a rabbit darting from hounds she dashed wide eyed without taking time for breath. She felt no pain and heard no sound. She only knew to run faster.

Her mother dropped the ceramic drums of milk when her daughter turned the bend. Her heart began to pound as she felt the tender child's fear. The woman had to stop her daughter's charge and hold her down. The little child quaked uncontrollably. The woman searched the child's pale face for what could have frightened her so.

The little child whined as she tried to slow her breath to catch her voice on it. The woman swept the child close to her breast and held her there. "Little darling…" Her mother cooed…"What is it?" She felt the child swallow and gasp as she tried to find her words. The woman pushed the child to arms length and brushed the dark hair from her white face. The girl's eyes widened as her mouth opened and her breathing stopped.

The woman stood with a jerk and spun around putting the child behind her. The Tattered Man's hand clamped smoothly and quickly over the woman's mouth. Her muscles clenched as her will was drawn out of her and into his icy touch. Her tears ran suddenly down her face and over the Tattered Man's hand. Her body stiffened at his command and her scream locked in her throat. She mustered her resistance and with waning strength, pushed her hand back, shoving her daughter away.

The child ran. She tore into the barn looking for a place to hide. She knelt and crawled into a small space against the wall behind some tools. Through a small crack, she could see the shadow of the Tattered Man still holding her mother by the face. He dragged her across the hay covered floor to the wagon parked by the wall. The little child's heart thundered in her slight body making her shake and quiver. The Tattered Man slammed the woman against the wagon. Her tortured limbs stretched apart at his will. Rope, beckoned to his silent, magical call and entwined themselves about her wrists and legs, twisting and writhing like snakes—tighter until her blood was twisted with them. A final cord lashed into her blond hair and pulled her head and shoulders over the gunnel of the wagon, pulling her shoulder blades out of her narrow back.

He stood back and admired her like some twisted pose for his art. He turned with a smile against his lips. "Come and play." He invited.

Magic leapt across the room and caught the tiny child. Slowly the girl's arms begin to bend. With spastic jerks she inched from her space, stood, and walked out to the center of the barn. Slowly, her muscles bunched and fought against her will as her mouth and lips came together.

And her eyes watched the terror.

The Tattered Man grabbed fists of the woman's dress and stripped it from her body. He flung the cloth away and it rustled like birds in the air as he eyed her shapely and writhing form before him. Her face and arms well tanned, but her wide bosom and hips had seldom seen the sun and were ridiculously pale. He snorted a laugh.

With a flick, he held a razor in his fingers. He brought it's silver sight to her body and a thin line slid into her flesh followed by a tear of blood. A hiss of pain escaped her lips as she felt the hot cut across her chest, down her belly and ending at her hip. His attention drawn to her handsome face, his blade softly touched her temple, slowly sinking into the skin, watching her reaction. His blade danced along the side of her face, across her cheek to the edge of her lip. It's taste was colder than the gleam of Ovam the moon, and her blood flowed hot, like the late setting sun. He touched her chin with the tip of the blade and her mouth opened but she was unable to scream. Blood dripped slowly into her open, gasping mouth.

He paused a moment, regarding her with idle fascination as she chocked on her own blood.

Then he smiled.

He pulled himself to her, his hands gripping on the sides of her face, smearing her blood. He began to shudder as his hands clasped over her eyes and blood began to spew from beneath his fingers.

He shouted as if in pain and flung his blood covered hands from her face sending a spray of blood into the air. His face glistened with sweat and fire from his wrath and spent fury as he stepped away from her.

He turned to the girl.

The girl stood locked and frozen waiting for him. He held the knife for her to see. She wanted to run and her legs were starting to move, but no more than that.

And her heart screamed from within her body.

She could see her mother, stretched against the side of the wagon. Her flesh pulled tautly over her shifting, panting ribs. She watched as he turned and slashed at the woman, carving a brutal gash like a flowing red ribbon into the woman's side. He began randomly slicing into the woman's body—slashing her face and neck with thin, torturous lines.

Finally, mercifully, he drove the steel into the woman's chest.

He jerked the blade free and held it parallel to the ground, carefully balancing the rivulet of blood as he stepped over to the little girl. Her eyes looked up to the dark, towering Tattered Man. He turned the point of the blade down and let her mother's blood drip into her face.

Then he brought the blade down.

"PARADOX! NO!"

His name tore through him as if it were hot steel in his belly. He slipped and twisted awkwardly about to face the open doors of the barn. His opponent stood as a silhouette in the rising sun. Spells and magic words collided in confusion as his mind raced with surprise. The Tattered Man quickly caught his bearing and instinct took over as he flipped his knife and let it fly. His confronter twisted and let it go by. Paradox drew his sword in a flash and two of them faced off, circling each other like animals in a cage. Sparks of steel clashed together, then again as the two combatants danced in and out. Paradox, the Tattered Man, thrust through, but a back hand fended him off. Again Paradox pushed but this time his opponent feigned and side stepped, stepping inside his arm to drive the sword into his hip above the bone.

Paradox screamed and leapt back. He stumbled and let his sword drop to the floor as he gripped his wound. His back slammed hard to the wood of the barn. Pain flushed his mind clear. Magic spoke to his lips and his right hand shot out. From his blood stained fingers came gleaming colors, flashing of the sky and sun and sea and space obscured by fat, drifting, white clouds and the shades of midnight, spanning the wing tips of dragons in flight across the lifting sway of sliding thunder rambling through bruised mists of war and pain from the height of mountains to the depths of worm holes spiraling through the dark earth in the green endless forest woods slick with dew dripping slowly and steadily to fill the blue oceans spreading across infinity fading to the edge of the earth.

Silence.

The swaying of the wheat caught in the tug of the wind swelling with the new warmth of the early morning sun. Leaves floating to the dew covered ground landing silently on the tall grass. Milk running out of broken drums and into the hard, brown dirt. Death bleeding back into the soil.

Paradox was gone. Hidden by his spell. His opponent waited. Listening to the sound of nothing. She flexed her grip on her hand-and-a-half sword, feeling its leather cushion as she waited for a sign that he might still be about. Her elvish ears pushed out but there was nothing to hear. She cursed herself for letting him trick her so. She could've defeated his magic, but she couldn't think straight. The sight of the assassin seemed to rob her of her skill as a Knight. Perhaps she was too cocky and confident. Her mistake.

She pulled off her dolman and let it fall to the floor. Her long, black hair cascaded around her shoulders. With a twitch of her head it slipped to where she wanted it.

Her sword, still clenched tightly in her hand, glistened as ice with Paradox's blood still running from it. Slowly she relaxed her grip and her anger with her self, ran it clean against her sash and sheathed it.

She noticed the tiny girl still standing there. She had heard her screams from high above the valley floor and at full gallop came to the rescue. When she saw Paradox, she forgot why she came.

7

Slowly the woman came to the girl and crouched down. She reached out but the child made no move. Slowly, clumsy uncertain arms went around the tiny child and held her lightly in a soft hug against her cold armor.

And the tiny child, daughter of brave Oustrand, stood as cold as winter.

Chapter 2

The mountains pushed high above the snow white fog sleeping in the valley. Shegatesu the dawn, stood on mountain number eight and with her paints of pastel and gold, filling the above with color. First she tinted the clouds with pink and stretched them still and flat on the dark blue sky. On this canvas, she quickly brushed with broad strokes fading lines of gold that would welcome Kemoto's new morning. With this done, she dashed down the mountain to Valleyview and the land of Fanrealm. As she passed over the walls and the stirring city below, she saw Mistang, rousing from the lowlands, looking up to the child goddess. "And what are you doing young lady?"

The dawn looked to the mists. "I hear that there is a new child in Fanrealm. Since Fantista is my knight, I wish to see what she is doing."

Spoiled brat. The mists mumbled. "And is your dawn finished?"

She looked to the east. "It is good enough for today, I must hurry before Kemoto comes." The little goddess looked to the Mistress of the Mist. "I will make tomorrow extra special to make up for today." She moved on towards the Manor. "Goodbye for now."

The mists hrrmphed and thought. *Little one, you have no idea what is going on.* She thought to herself knowingly and settled back down for a few moments more of sleep. In truth, Mistang didn't know what was going on either.

The little goddess flew over the fields to the Great wall and there, she dumped her colors of pink and gold into the moat so that its still waters shone with the dawn. She then passed over the last wall and into one of the windows of the Manor itself. She pushed through the gloom of the room. She waited for Kemoto's light and slowly, gently, it came.

Shadows of the night peeled away from the coarse, stone manor walls. On the Great wall, the watchman on his post stamped his feet and blew on his hands to warm them. He faced the east and his cheeks felt the warm rays of a newly birthed day. Inside the manor, thin pale streaks of light filtered through the leaded window from the early morning glow. It inched it's way across the stone walls and oaken door, lighting gently on the polished metal of the brass bed post where it fractured and flung itself onto the walls of the room. Shegatesu, the dawn, paused to behold the purity and beauty of the child that slept within the warm quilted caress.

In the darkness of the night's final refuge, a woman sat staring at the bed. She had held her vigil the entire night by the side of the child. Her thin fingers clutched the leather hilt of her hand-and-a-half sword with the flat of its cold steel blade pressed tightly against her leg. She listened, and watched. Each breath the child took the woman counted, as if they were few remaining. At the child's tiny whimpers, the woman braced and stiffened her back, tuning her tight elvish ears to any sound, any disturbance, ready to pounce on whatever may be.

The woman felt not the cold. Her thin, cotton cloth tunic and pant gave her little protection against the chilly air. The unearthly draft that swept from the cracks in the stone passed cruelly over her skin, but she didn't shiver or curse the cold, she only accepted it as is.

Shegatesu recognized Frita, Knight of Fikor, Knight of Winter.

The latch of the door twisted with a sudden jerk, dropping the bolt away. Frita slid from her chair to her feet whirling the sword, bringing the hilt across her knee and pointing the blade forward. How could this be? How could she not have heard the footsteps approaching in the hall, passing without sound or presence?

The door swung ajar and the woman tensed, switching the hilt across her body directly above her right shoulder, poised there in a low crouch for the deadly strike.

The strike never came.

The knight spun the blade and rested it's point on the stone of the floor, shifting her crouch to one knee and bowing her head. "Milady." She whispered.

The caller stood at the doorway with a tray in her hands and Shegatesu knew her. She was elven, and still very attractive, although to Shegatesu's eternally young eyes, she was an old woman, worn slightly from hard toil. She held her hair tied in a small bun set at the top of her head. Her gray gown draped in flowing gathers to the floor that kicked out when she walked. A four pointed silver star hung from her neck, glinting in the light from the middle of her breasts. The star of the House of Hammerstrike.

The woman said nothing as she set the tray on a table by the door and stepped into the room. She reached out and touched Frita's hands and they opened, allowing the woman to take the sword and lean it against the wall by the window.

Frita still did not lift her eyes to her. She only waited for permission.

"You are quick with your brother's sword Frita." She said fetching her tray. As she reached it, she noticed that Frita had not moved. The caller turned and touched the center of the younger woman's head, and gave her a silent blessing. "This is not necessary Denice."

"But thou art the Grandmaster, Lady Fantista." Frita spoke looking up.

Fantista said nothing as turned to fetch her tray. Frita could see that her reverence displeased the Grandmaster in some way but didn't know how to amend it. She only watched her sit on the edge of the bed and place the tray on the night stand. Frita thought vainly for something to say, but there was nothing.

With her open palms, Lady Fantista pressed gently on the underside of the little girl's jaw.

"Lady Fantista?" Frita asked. "Does the child fever?" Her words stumbled on her lips and felt as awkward as they sounded, but it was better than silence.

"No, Denice," Fantista answered. "How did she sleep?"

"Deeply," Frita's arms wrapped themselves about herself, as if to warm her against a cold she couldn't feel. "She hasn't spoke a word since I found her."

Fantista took away the cloth that covered her tray exposing a white washrag and a dish of warm water. She wet the rag and rung it tightly. She took the steaming cloth and pressed it to the girl's face and wiped it clean.

The girl's eyes opened wide but she made no sound or motion. She merely adjusted enough to allow the Grandmaster better access in her cleaning. "Child?" She called gently to the girl, but the little girl did not stir. Fantista continued, sighing to herself. "Any word of Dwayne?"

Frita glared at the floor. "He responded to the summons, and I left word with Max, but Lord Frito could be anywhere, Lady Fantista."

Lady Fantista looked at Frita and sighed, preparing to speak, but she thought better of it and turned her attention back to the child. She set down the cloth and removed the child's blouse and continued. "You have yet to tell me how you found her." Lady Fantista said without looking away. "You came to my door last night wet with rain like an orphaned kitten."

The Grandmaster pulled the child's blouse back on her, pinning the silk bow. The child didn't stir or react. Fantista turned and looked at Frita staring blankly at the child. Then she looked at the child staring blankly back. "This is your nightgown." Lady Fantista commented picking at the shoulders to get it to fall properly about the girl's frame. "I saved it from when you were her age." When Frita still didn't answer, Fantista looked back. "Denice? Frita?"

Finally Frita looked up. "Milady?"

"What happened? Denice, you haven't told me."

"I was responding to the house summons. When passing near the town of Rendon, I heard the child screaming. By the time I arrived, the child's father and mother had been slaughtered. The child was like this when I found her. My limited magic was of no avail. This was two days ago." Frita answered curtly.

Lady Fantista had long ago adjusted to Frita's abruptness. "Who did it?"

Frita turned and looked out the window, mindlessly clutching the silver star that hung around her neck. From there she could see the forward gate of the manor and the road leading to it. A horse in full gallop carried it's rider, a man of armor and steel to the gates.

"Denice?..." Lady Fantista called to her. "Did you see who did this?"

"No." She whispered to the window. "Friska is here."

Lady Fantista tuned her elvish ear and could hear the hailing guard bid him enter. She turned back to the child. "There are no scars on her, I can see no form of injury."

"The man who did this used magic and caught me unaware. I knew not until it was to late. The child was stiff and cold when I found her. I didn't know were to go, Milady." Frita continued to glare out of the window.

Lady Fantista took up a brush and began to do the child's hair— pulling the long, dark locks smooth. Gathering them into strands of three, she deftly braided them. "And what of the child's parents," The Grandmaster questioned without looking from her work. "Who were they? What clan?"

"The house of Oustrand. Human." Frita spoke to the window.

"Human?" Fantista paused in surprise. "Then the child is adopted."

"I knew them not, Milady."

Flustered, Lady Fantista set the brush on the bed turning to face her. "Denice? I am your mother. Not a stranger." Lady Fantista's eyebrows came together and her lines of age dug deeper into her face. "You speak to me as if I were not?"

Frita faced her but did not look at her. She shrouded her shoulders and covered her mouth with her hand. "I know." She whispered into her hand.

"Then what is it?" Fantista could feel her daughter's pain.

Frita shook her head slowly, her gaze dropped to the floor and her eyes began to search it as if it had the answer.

Lady Fantista turned back to the child who sat oblivious to everything. She pulled back the cover and slid sandals on her tiny feet. She coaxed the child out of the bed and taking her hand, guided her out into the hall.

Shegatesu the dawn looked to the window as Kemoto set on the edge of the world, preparing to fly across the sky. Her time on Mortalroam was gone. She passed through the window and out into the sky, finding her way to Worldsend.

Fantista, Frita and the little girl stepped into the pantry, passing the bellowing hearth and the copper pots to a small wooden table in the corner.

"Itsy pity chil." The fat cook said as she set a steaming bowl in front of her. "Shes wils liaks mea coogin." She smiled a toothless grin. Lady Fantista took a spoon and swirled the porridge. "Thank you Trisha. If you see Friska roaming about, send him here."

"Oah I shes hem ant I shent his." She waddled out the back door, leaving it open.

Friska poked his head through the shroud from the main dining room. "Is that fat sow gone?" His dark eyes flashed like the gleaming polished steel linked on his chest. He held his helmet tucked tightly under his arm. His dark braided hair bounced on his back as he came to the small table. "Mother..." He stooped and kissed her on the cheek. His mother reached up and patted him affectionately on the cheek. He looked at Frita. "My twin..." Her icy glare burned through his welcome. "How wonderful to see you..." His lips twisted to a half frown and his eyes avoided her penetrating glare.

He took his sheathed sword and hung it from one of the pot stands. "Well, this has been one of the warmest welcomes..." He rambled on as he set his dolman on the counter. "Who is this tiny child?" He said finally facing them.

Fantista took up a spoonful to the child's lips. Instinctively the child took it in her mouth and swallowed it.

"This is the Daughter of Oustrand." Frita answered her twin. "He and his wife were murdered two days ago."

"Any idea…"

"No." Frita answered before Friska could ask. "Mother has summoned Frito to…"

"What?" Friska stepped from the table. "Why not invite Thamrell into your home?" Friska's eyes narrowed at such an idea. "Dwayne! That murdering cur!" Horror flashed through Friska's mind. "No! I shall not allow him in this place. I swear on my father's…"

"No!" Fantista dropped her spoon and it clanged on the floor. "You shalt not swear your oaths in here." Her lips curled as heat came from her aged bones. Her eyes softened, as her flash of anger past. "What has angered you so? He is your brother."

Friska dared not answer his mother. He bowed his head and chewed on the inside of his mouth. "I won't stand for this." He spat his words low and to the earth.

"Friska?" Friska whirled around to see his brother standing at the back door. "What is the matter?"

Friska's sword leapt from it's sheath and magically slipped into his summoning hand. Whistling through the air the honed steel edge sliced it's way towards Frito, bracing for the attack.

"Friska!" His mother leapt with unimaginable speed as her creaking bones moaned, stiff as wire and her thinly skinned hand gripped at his arm. "You shall not!" Her voice stretched thin and hard in plead. "I summoned him here!"

Friska stayed his hand not taking his eyes from the man who stood calmly before him. The dark elf was draped in a heavy brown cloak that hid most of his dull, black armor. A strap ran across his right shoulder holding his blade-spear to his back. His gloved hands reached slowly to part his cloak and with a tug of leather strings, his blade-spear slid from his back, clanged to the stairs and fell outside.

Friska tightened his grip on his own sword not to be fooled by a demon's trickery. "Ninefingers, Devilslayer, Trid Dreath the third, Hauth, Lord of Lightning, what ever name you go by…get out of this house."

Frito shook his head. "Friska, there is nothing more that I can do to…"

"You can get out of this house, demon!" He bellowed pointing the blade closer to Frito's face.

Frito's dark eyes narrowed and his eyebrows lowered them even deeper. "Friska,...Daniel, I..."

"GET OUT DEMON!"

Frito grit his teeth, more impatient than angered. He looked at the blade pointed at his face and then to his brother. With a snap, Frito's hand whirled from beneath his cloak and the back of his fist smacked into the flat of Friska's blade knocking it from his face. The dark elf stepped into Friska's stance, gripping his arm and twisting the sword from his grasp. Driving his palm up, he struck Friska in the center of his chest with a shoving, stunning blow sendind Friska stumbling backward into the copper pots with a shambling clatter.

Lady Fantista stood between them with her arms apart. Her robe draped at the sleeves to form a large wall of cloth between the two. "NO!" She shouted, waiting until the fire burned lower in Friska's eye. "no." She whispered.

Friska picked himself from the pots. "Mother!" His voice rang of stern warning. "He is a murderer!"

"Daniel." She whispered. "He is my son."

Frito balanced the sword on the floor with the tip on the stone. With a touch, he let it teeter into Friska's hands.

Friska took up the sword, feeling the weight in his hands, eyeing Frito cautiously. He reached back and unhooked the sheath from the pots. He slid against the racks giving Frito the greatest berth possible. He stopped at the back door and slowly turned to face him. "Fine...Lord Ninefingers." His eyes burned as he spat the name in disgust. "My mother has intervened here in this house, but I swear..."

"What is it you want from me?" Frito's words cut off his brother's oath. "I've begged you to forgive me. I'll do anything you ask...What is it you want?"

Friska brandished his sword. "I want your blood stained on my blade!"

Frito reached out suddenly with his left, patch-worked hand and tightly gripped the end of Friska's sword. Frito clenched the sword tightly and shoved Friska into the door jamb with his right, holding him into it. "Now you have it..." Frito shoved him out of the door. Friska stumbled down the steps and landed on the walkway.

Frito waved a bloody finger at him. "No more! No more begging for you to forgive me. No more groveling for your damned grace, you obnoxious, self centered, vain,...I've tried Dan, with Okshiru himself as

15

my witness, I tried, but you won't let me. Then so be it, but please notice Friska, Knight of the Wind, I'll go on living without your grace."

Friska stared hard at his brother at the top of the stairs. Terror quaked through his body resisting all his will to hide it. He forced anger to flood it out, hatred to stop his shaking, fury to give him the strength to pick himself up and stand bravely at the bottom of the stair.

Frito waited for some response. Beats stretched in tense anger, like fine webs waving in the air, each one easily shattered by any motion. Friska took a step back, then waited. His chest swelled like a fighting cock before he turned and stormed off to the stables.

Frito turned from the door and latched it shut. He leaned against it scowling hard at the pots scattered on the floor. He didn't want to do what he did. He swore never to anger to the point of outburst, but he did and what hurt the most was the ease with which his anger erupted to wildfire. He looked to Frita still sitting at the table and the child sitting blankly before her porridge. His eyes wandered and locked with Frita's.

"Lord Frito...I mean..." Her strained deep voice held slightly above a whisper. "Dwayne, Friska deserved..."

Frito waved a sharp finger at her. No, Friska did what he himself might have done. Friska was one of the Knight's of Okshiru, defender of his realm. His mother, brother, sister, and once upon a time he himself, had been tied to the oath to uphold the lives of all who held life. Once, long ago, they were a family of knights. Once long ago.

He looked at his mother. Her back was to him and her arms and robe wrapped tightly about her. Her head was bent and he couldn't see her face, but he knew she was crying. He felt his heart rend and break as he knew that he had caused her more pain. She was the matriarch, the mainstay of the house of Hammerstrike. Her heart seemed to be a never ending well of strength. But how much could be drawn before even it would run dry? He had drawn too much before, and it pained him to do it again. He reached out and touched her shoulder. The hard bone shuddered underneath his touch. She wasn't angry at either of them. She had already forgiven them both for their senseless anger and was pulling it all into herself. It overflowed in the gentle tears that slid down the tiny lines of time on her beautiful face.

Frito took back his hand and cursed himself. He had no words, no gestures to ease something that couldn't be eased. He turned to the child, the reason for his being there, and stepped smoothly to the table to look at her. He gently gripped her chair and turned it around slowly to face him. His eyes probed into her own and he looked deep into her silent soul.

He could hear her screaming a life time away.

He stood over her thinking as he pulled off his gloves. He looked at his torn, blood stained left glove before he tucked them both into his belt and put his full attention to the mysterious little girl.

He passed his hand in front of her unseeing gaze. He gently eased her from out of the chair and stood her upright. Then he looked at blood still flowing from his palm and dabbed his finger into it. Carefully he drew the four pointed star of Hammerstrike on the child's pale forehead.

His blood left no mark.

He looked at it quizzically, then wiped it off on his robe and smeared fresh blood on his finger so it dripped. It slid off the child's skin as if it were oil and spotted her blouse. Frito sat back on his haunches. He took a handkerchief from his belt pouch and crammed it into his palm to stop the bleeding while he thought.

Slowly he rose to his feet. He stepped over to his mother who had turned to watch him. He gently reached up and caught her tear on his finger. Carefully balancing the tiny drop, he stepped back to the girl and lowered himself to his knees. With the tear, he drew the symbol again. It's wetness shined on her dry head like grimy sweat. They all watched as the child slowly swallowed—her first reaction to something other than instinct. Her eyes began to shift about and her lips began to quiver. The tear stain on her fore head began to sweat tiny balls of black tar. It quickly dripped down her face, against the side of her nose to her mouth. Frito stemmed the flow with his finger so it's foulness wouldn't reach her lips. It kept dripping down her face and her hands reached up to catch it from falling on the floor but Frito grabbed her tiny wrists to stop her. He pulled her forward and slightly off balance and let the blackness rain on the kitchen tile. The girl began to gasp as if she couldn't breathe, but Frito didn't let go until the tar stopped and her head was clear.

She screamed for her mother, like a child in the darkness, alone in terror. She screamed to be held, for arms of security to be around her. Fantista swept the child readily in her arms. The child melded perfectly to her bosom as if it were meant to be. She held her tight as the child wailed into her shoulder. Screaming in tears as the thought of her parents came to her.

Frito was stunned and had to catch his breath. He hadn't expected a reaction so emotional and it caused him to feel the pain swelling in his throat. A fear that he thought was long ago lost was suddenly reborn within him. The fear of being alone, the fear of abandonment, the fear of the dark and its hollow embrace. He looked for his sister Frita. Perhaps she too felt an emotion long ago lost.

She was gone.

Chapter 3

The heaving dark blue water crashed against the black rock. Each wave smashed into fine, white mist against the unyielding stone. Again it pounded only to recede back to the depths. Like a sleeping man breathing in and breathing out again, the waves crashed with a roar against the rocks. This was the will of Okshiru, god of the endless sea, master of each ripple, king of every fish and lord of every wave. As deep as the endless sea, Okshiru also ruled the sky. He held its thunder, gripped its clouds, and seized its storms. Okshiru, god of sky and sea, storm and wave, cloud and spout, rain and rainbow.

Paradox, the Tattered Man stood on the shore watching the sea before him. His black cloak wrapped and tugged at him as Hauge the wind, playful child of Okshiru, danced all around him. The wind took up the sea mist and flung it into his eyes until it stung. Paradox only waited.

He stooped down to a circle of stones he had arranged and added another bead of incense to the smoldering pot.

Kemoto, bird god of the sun, swelled and burned to an angry red as he dipped into the black sea. Columns of clouds, based above the water, held the sky aloft. Fishermen gathered their nets as the evening crept upon them.

After the sun submerged into the water, its fiery light burned the blue sky to red and purple. Neathina placed her evening star and it sparkled in the sky like a pinhole in the tapestry, white and hot, piercing the sunset. Paradox sat by his circle of stones.

Across a black sky Ovam's white light lay across the face of the placid water. A few of Neathina's brightest stars gleamed faintly in the sky against the will of the obese moon god. The clouds hung flat and long against the sky as Hauge slept and his winds dropped to a light breeze. Paradox sat in Ovam's white glow. His face was white and flat with out features. His lips quivered in the cold night and he drew his cloak about him tighter, until it could stretch no more.

Following Kemoto, Ovam began to dip into the sea. Neathina, child of stars, began to set out the rest of her tiny sparkles on the black curtain of Leatha's night. Paradox's incense had burned to ashes. He sat with his legs drawn to his body and his head on his knees.

"You sleep?" Light as the wind, her voice carried softly on the night air. It was sweet and playful, soft and alluring. It was a woman's voice, pleasing to the ear. It cut into Paradox like the cold of steel.

"I hear you." He said panting, blinking his eyes to fight the sleep still in them. "Oustrand and his wife sleep in hel tonight."

She stood like a silhouette with her back to the last light of the moon. She stepped easily to the rocks beside him. As she faced him, the light touched her, and Paradox could see half of her face, smooth and soft. Her lips were full and sensuous. Her long flowing gown wrapped about her long, sleek legs. But Ovam's light bent the truth and faded color. Her flesh was gray and her smile was black.

Paradox, The Tattered Man slipped his legs and with his hands to brace him, shifted to a kneeling position before her. "The girl yet lives."

"A swordsman of great skill. I have seen."

Paradox bowed his head in shame. As he looked up, he saw the woman's feet were bare and they stood as white marble on the black rock, the tiny nails glinted dully in the dimming light. She watched his fascination with her feet and smiled. "Who was this man?" She said to break his admiration.

"Man?" He looked to her face only to see that her hair now shrouded it in a veil of shadow. "What...Man?" He stressed the word 'man' carefully.

"The man who slashed your belly. Did you know him?" Just then, Hauge stirred her silken hair and it began to drift against her body. "Was it a knight? Whose?"

She could not see through the knight's veil of power. They could not see who it was. "I did not know...him." Paradox felt his heart beating faster. He looked away from the woman's penetrating stare. "The child holds within the House of Hammerstrike. The Ninefingers is there. He knows me and will strike me down."

There came a strange laugh from the woman's direction. "You need not worry. You may not have killed the child, but you pained her. Pained her beyond death. For that, we are pleased."

Paradox looked at the black outline against the sky. The wind pulled harder at her hair. Hauge had awakened. "What was this child to you?"

Again came the laugh, but this time, it wasn't from the woman. "Who slashed you? Did you see him?"

"She caught me by surprise. I used my magic to stun her whilst I escaped."

"She?" The woman scowled as the waves began to heave higher into the rocks.

Paradox felt caught in his lie, but he held calm to let it slip. "It was a she." He felt the warm air about his body and the chilling mist of the waves on his face. He could feel the woman scowl.

"You said you didn't see?"

Paradox looked up into her hidden face. "I didn't see him." He stressed the 'him' again.

Hauge moaned as he swept about the rocks. "Was it Achillia?" The woman didn't raise her voice above the wind, yet Paradox heard her none the less.

"It was." His heart pounded harder with fear as he lied a second time.

The woman turned and stepped from the rock. "Achillia, is marked." The woman said without turning around. "I grant the summons, use it wisely. It is a dangerous thing."

Paradox staggered to his feet against a gust of wind. "And what of the child?" He screamed over the torrid wind.

Thunder jolted his bones and it echoed across the sky. He turned to see Okshiru's anger against the world. The waves crashed against the beach and the black clouds rolled and swelled with the wind. Uko's lightning flashed white crooked lines, like cracks in heaven. Okshiru's fury trembled above and shook Mortalroam.

Paradox, The Tattered Man, stumbled in the howling wind as he made his way alone on the beach with laughter echoing in his bones.

Chapter 4

Lightning sparked and for an instant the room flared white without shadows. Frita sat her post with her sword pressed against her knee and her arms holding it rigid and ready. Her dark eyes glared at the child. She listened to her, watching her sleep. She listened to the storm rage outside. She listened to the manor and it's creeks and moans against Hauge's howling wind.

It had been hours of calming and soothing the child to get her even to hold down hot broth with out heaving it back up. It took even longer to get the child to rest. Even after Lady Fantista gave the child a command to make her sleep, she still moaned and tossed in nightmare. Lord Frito and Lady Fantista sat by her side until she finally drifted to sleep. Frita remained on guard, watching the child.

Lightning flashed white again and the child suddenly sat bolt upright in the bed. Her eyes blinded by the white light, she sat blinking to see as her chest heaved in pain. Frita slipped quickly across the room, laying her sword on the floor by her feet and took the child in her arms. Imitating her mother, she soothed and cooed to the child.

Gasping as the tears rolled quickly on her face, the child reached out and grabbed on to Frita with all her might. Sobbing, coughing, she tried to speak through her pain, but her words stumbled in her throat. "A beast!" She cried, "A beast under the bed!" She finally blurted out, burying her face into Frita's shoulder.

Frita felt awkward. She had no concept of what to do, what to say to the poor suffering child. "There is no beast under the bed." Frita tried to use her voice like her mother would, but it cracked awkwardly and didn't help at all.

The child swallowed hard and gasped again. "His name is Thumber! He is coming after me!" Her fingers dug harder into Frita's back as if she was never going to let go. Frita wanted to call for her mother, but she knew it would only upset the girl more. She gripped the girl's arms and pulled her away far enough to look her in the eyes. The child used the back of her hand to wipe away her tears as Frita glared at her. "There is no beast in this house." Frita said firmly. "You are safe here." Frita's words drove into the girl as the child held back her fear. "You had a dream, child." She brushed the child's black hair from her wet face. "A dream can not hurt you." Frita's words were clear and somber.

The little girl's lips bent downward as she tried to be brave. "bbu But…"

"But no." Frita tried a soothing voice like her mother again. "There is nothing under the bed." Frita could see the child's terror on her face. Frita held the child's tiny hand and leaned over the bed. Lifting the tick, she went to look under. The little child gripped the shoulder of Frita's shirt. Frita took both of the girl's hand in one, and caressed the girl's face. "There is nothing there." She whispered. "I will show you." Frita again bent over and the tiny child held her breath and watched her.

The lightning flashed and the thunder roared as Frita was jerked from the bed, her hand grasped the sheet and dragged it with her as she disappeared under the bed.

The little girl sat paralyzed with her eyes glaring wide, exposed to the thunderous storm that raged outside her window. Trying to scream out, her breath rasped in and out of her throat as her voice tried desperately to catch it.

The child screamed louder than the howling wind, louder than the storm, louder than Okshiru's fury.

The door flung open as Lady Fantista darted in, her elvish eyes burned silver in the dark, piercing the shadow to show the girl on her knees, her body lifting and forcing herself to scream. Lady Fantista swept to the bed, her arms swept out to comfort the girl.

"NO!" The girl screamed, "He will get you!" The tiny girl shoved at her, pushing her away. Lady Fantista gripped the fighting child into her arms and swept her from the bed into her grasp. The girl screamed into Fantista's shoulder, "He will get you! He will get you!"

Frito stepped out of the shadow. His face drawn, he scowled as he entered the room, tying his robe's belt. The tiny child's voice cracked in a horse whisper as she could no longer scream. "He's under the bed! He's under the bed!" Fantista denied this idea. Cooing to the child that it was a dream, the child wailed at her with angry fists. Frito looked at the bed, and saw the hand-and-a-half sword lying by it. He charged at the bed, shoving it across the room, sliding against the stone floor.

There was nothing there.

He dropped to his knees, his fingers slid across the rock testing it's surface. Like a hot coal he found it, sucking into the stone like a vortex. Lightning flashed and exposed the black blood bleeding out of the floor.

Magic!

Dexter C. Herron

He probed into it, using his arcane skills to identify it, but it was too late. He could feel it slip from his fingers, like dry sand in an hourglass.
And it was gone.

Chapter 5

Darkness welled in fistfuls of tangible clouds. It swirled and dipped around her as she fought to consciousness. Her eyes snapped open suddenly, but the absolute dark kept her blind in the cutting cold of oblivion.

Frita reached out, groping with her hand and brushing it against a stone wall. Her elvish senses were gone, as was her power of seeing through the darkness. She laid her hand flat on the stone for a solid point of reference, to still the black, swirling confusion that had enveloped her. The air was dank and moist from the tiny trickles of water seeping from the stone all about her in thin streams. Scurrying noises scratched the stone with tiny grunts, as little monsters crawled in the darkness. They were random and disorganized, roaming in their home far beneath the sun in the spiraling crypt of the ground.

One chanted, others chanted. Squeaking, cawing, moaning in unison, dancing like little demons in the blinding dark. A well planned chorus sang all around her, confusing her, frightening her—like bats in her hair, gnawing at her sanity, ripping away the fabric of what she understood. Her long, thin, white fingers dug into her black hair to block the sound from her ears, to shut out the black madness that assailed her. She chanted a spell of hope and light exploded silently beside her with a blinding awakening.

Creature's eyes of black pearl screamed and shut against the whiteness of Frita's magic. They dipped and dove to their tiny holes covering themselves from the cleansing white sun suddenly thrust into their coal dark world. Frita waited, holding her heart to hear the sounds of what was around her. Her lips parted slightly exposing her teeth as tiny winds whisked in and out of her body. She clutched the four pointed silver star that hung about her neck as her wide eyes glared at the slick wet walls that were around her. The black dots of tiny holes seemed to shift slightly in her magic light. It was more light than she needed for she was an elf, and elves need only the tiniest of sparks to see plainly, but it kept the beasts at bay.

She pushed against the wall to find her feet. Her body ached and twitched as she shifted. She examined herself, bunching her sleeves above her elbows to expose bruises, black and swelling, like stone mice sleeping beneath her skin. Dried, clotted, blood clustered in a recent

wound from thin, vicious claws. When she moved, pain popped against
the backs of her eyes. She knew she had been unconscious for hours,
rotting at the bottom of Mortalroam. Now, only a ball of light hung
above her head for protection against what was still about her.

Things crept behind the shadows of her light, crawling against the
sides of the cliffs high above her. They went about scratching the stone
with their tiny claws and randomly squeaking to themselves.

She looked around herself. Her sword was not any where to be
found. That was a material thing and she had been trained not to
depend on such things. She ordered her ball of light higher in the
caverns to shed its radiance for her to see. As it did, it plainly revealed
the labyrinth of stone, like a monumental cathedral to some mad god.
Its bowed and arched ceilings bounced every noise, distorting sounds
and their origins. Her white luminescence shed its glow, twisting all it
touched into deathly blue hues. Her white light plainly showed that
there were many ways to go, but none could lead her out.

A beast sat patiently, a mere ten paces from her.

Like a giant, furry toad it sat with scintillating eyes glinting in her
light. Warts and growths popped out of it's nasty skin without any
apparent cause. It eyed her curiously, waiting. Frita faced it, her hands
twitching and flexing. Her fingers could feel the sweat forming in her
palms against the cold of the crypt. Frita's dark brown eyes watched it
distrustfully, for it was a beast she knew not.

"I am Frita." Her voice was a whisper cracking against her hard dry
throat, but the sound echoed madly and danced about the cavern,
growing loud before dying to nothing. "Of the House of
Hammerstrike." She continued speaking, hoping wildly that this beast
would understand. The beast didn't alter it's posture. It still waited,
cocking an eye slightly over the other. "Do you speak? Perhaps I can
understand you." Frita waited, but it just sat there, also waiting.

Then without warning, it swelled suddenly growing half again it's
size as it's maw opened and it's massive fangs flashed in the white light.
It's stubby legs trampled and pounded the place where it stood as it
screamed a bestial scream. It wasn't a language that could be spoken but
it's meaning was very clear. Frita's arm from elbow to hand tightened
with muscles flexing and fingers exercising as she lifted her arm if to
strike. A buzz like angry bees flared from her heart to her hand.

It suddenly charged her, it's tiny disfigured legs ran in a awkward
rush at her. Frita tightened her fist hard and waited. At five paces,

Frita's hand leapt out and from the end of her two fingers came a sucking of air that swirled around her. With a flash of light and a crack of thunder the beast lay still and frozen in ice, it's mouth still open and locked in a horrid, silent scream.

Frita looked to the ceiling as her light suddenly screeched and cried. A thing with wings had touched it. The light gave no heat and the beast felt no pain but the light's angry wail caused the winged thing to leave it be.

Frita looked back to the frozen beast. She came closer, watching it carefully. Her heart pained as she realized it was just a dumb beast hoping for a meal. Her hand lightly grazed the surface of her ice and with a rumbling crack, it shattered, beast and all, into a thousand tiny pieces at her feet.

Frita jumped back from it aghast. She hadn't meant to cause it to break, it just did.

Then it began. A small snicker at first, then building to a mountainous crescendo of laughter, echoing from the walls and ceiling. Frita clamped her hands over her ears to shut out the horrid noise that came from the darkness itself.

It stopped.

Her ears rang in the sudden silence. Her eyes scanned the darkness for a source, but there was none. There was nothing for her to fight, nothing to dispose of with a spell of cold, nothing for her to confront.

"Well done my child." It's voice trembled like granite sliding on stone, black and cold, coming from the darkness itself.

Frita's fingers flexed again, "Show your self to me!" She shrieked her order. "I am the Knight of Fikor, god of Winter! Do not mock Me!"

Beats stretched in agony as Frita's ears stilled their ring leaving only a greater quiet.

"You know me." It finally answered with great assurance.

Frita shook her head. "I know you not. I know only that I wish to leave this place." Frita could feel it smiling at her from all about, stripping her clothes and leaving her bare and cold.

"What do you fear Frita?"

Frita's hands began to glow as mystical energy streamed to them. It was a trick question and not simply answered. "I fear what I fear.", she finally said.

"Wrong answer." It trembled. "You fear me."

Frita felt the fear that the darkness spoke of, but she was too well disciplined to ever show it. "Then who do I fear? Does my fear have a name?"

"It has a great name…simply called by man. Like the name of the power of light is, sight, and the force of all, is life. I am your fear, I am Thumber, keeper of your nightmares."

Frita turned a full circle eyeing the dark crevices carefully. "Can you confront me, Thumber?"

"Yes child, I can."

Frita felt the itch of tiny legs dancing at her shoulder. She glanced at it to see a spider about the size of her fist slowly crawling on her shoulder towards her head. "Frito fears spiders," She said taking it tenderly from her shoulder and setting it to run on the floor. "Not Frita."

"Your fear is what I see. You fear spiders but it is tangible. You can defeat tangibles."

A bloodcurdling scream fell from over head. The winged thing swooped from the ceiling with it's angry teeth bared in a macabre grin. Frita whirled and from the ends of her fingers light leapt out and the winged beast exploded in a blast of magic. Swords and axes poised to strike, came charging with men chanting for blood. In an instant Frita's eyes sparked and spears of ice filled the cavern, impaling their dried, cobweb filled bodies with a crackling crunch. Before their lifeless bodies crumpled to the cold floor, a monster of great height and serrated fangs leapt from it's dark hole at her. She gave a shout of magic and it bent over in agony and shriveled into a shuddering ball of prickly fur. Thousands of winged creatures swarmed the air at her. She pulled her arms to her chest and chanted the wind, calling her ice and snow in a whirlwind of frost. A blizzard of unbelievable might and biting cold raged wild against the cavern, tossing the winged beasts frozen to the ground. When it was done, the caverns glistened white with her magical snow, with out trace of the stone below. A giant stood behind her, his axe was worn and chipped but it's weight swung with fury. Frita ducked from its path and with blinding speed kicked the giant twice in the ribs and then threw a flurry of punches into its mid-section. The giant staggered back from the force of her blows, but it was a creature without feeling and merely shambled forward again. Frita suddenly grasped a sword and parried the giant's blow with great skill. She stepped back and the giant lunged forward dragging his axe behind him, using it's momentum to drive it to speed. Frita feigned and faked low with a sudden change. Stepping forward, she hyper-extended in a bow bringing the tip of her blade into the giant's skull.

It didn't bleed.

It just lay still in the frozen snow.

The darkness chuckled. "Your father's sword arm, and your brother's magic. Frita the cold." It taunted. "Is that because you are the knight of Winter, or is it because you are celibate?"

Frita looked from her dead foe with the sword weighing heavily in her hands, Her face twisted in frustration as she panted. A thin veil of sweat covered her face. "What madness do you ask me?"

"You find it all absurd?"

"YES!" She shouted at what wasn't there.

"Why do you follow Okshiru?"

Frita pulled back her immediate answer, trying to fit his madness together, then tried again. "For he works for what is fair and just."

"Is that what you do?"

"I serve him."

"You kill for good?"

His questions were coming too fast and too planned. Frita knew that this was a entity trying to trick her with words and she would not be so tricked. He forced her to exhaust her magic and now while her mind was numb, plagued her with questions. She would not be so tricked. "I kill when there is nothing else."

"So I see…" It paused as it re-aimed it's thought. "Do you pray to Okshiru?"

"Yes." Which was true, there could be no harm in the truth.

"When you kill, do you pray to Okshiru?"

"Yes."

"What do you pray for?"

Again she held back her answer as she tried to see through his questions. "I pray for forgiveness."

"Forgiveness for who?"

Frita's eyes looked at the sword in her hands. She never remembered where it came from only that she had it when she needed it, and she quickly relied on it. She looked at the giant who's blood never ran, but was now dripping from her sword's blade.

"Frita..." Darkness called to her. "Who do you pray for?"

...*Myself*...Frita let the sword drop into the snow. "Why?" She finally asked.

"Because you truly don't know what you fear. I am Thumber. I want you to fear."

Suddenly Frita began to tremble in a cold that she could not feel. Her blinding light left her in the center of a white world covered with the bright red blood of a giant who didn't bleed. She felt fear. A fear that caused her to stand plainly before what lurked in the shadow. "I do not fear you." She threatened in a hiss.

"You fear..." The shadows confirmed.

A woman's cry ripped through Frita. The knight turned to see a woman slip and fall on the hard ice, her arms flailing about helplessly as she tried to regain her footing. Frita darted without a second thought to the woman's aide. Her bare feet caught traction on her ice as she leapt to the woman's side and prevented her from falling again. The woman's dark hair shrouded her face but her moaning pain was enough for Frita to see the woman was hurt. Her hand clutched her belly, swollen with child. Frita's heart labored in her centre as she tried to calm the pained woman and her child to be. She didn't question why the woman was there, she was in need of her aid and that was all that mattered. Frita's hand touched the woman's hand that clutched her belly only to see that her own hand was covered in the giant's blood. *How could this be?* Her thoughts raced in confusion, *The giant didn't bleed!* But there was blood still warm on Frita's hand, blood that came from her own hand each time she touched the mother's belly. The knight gasped and retreated in horror. The woman looked up and for the first time Frita looked into the woman's face and saw her own.

Frita couldn't move, paralyzed by what she saw. Fear bored through her like shining metal shavings. The pregnant woman's lips twisted and she cried 'Denice', over and over again, reaching out to grab her. Frita pushed the bloody horror from her and turned to flee. Her feet suddenly lost their traction and she fell hard onto the reddened snow. Frita's fingers dug in and forced herself to rise from the ice. She ran, with what speed she could, to get away from the abomination still reaching for her. Thumber's laugh slammed into her like a solid punch to the sternum, and she buckled and fell onto her face. She bolted forth again, bursting into the golden afternoon sun. Her cold bones quickly warmed and stifled the sting of her pains. Her breath left her as she suddenly could not stand. With a gasping plea, she dropped again into darkness.

Chapter 6

Glinting steel axes, perfectly arrayed, their razor sharp blades reflecting the early morning sun. Helms of different sizes sat up on the shelf above several chest plates hung up on pegs. The swords of fine, hot rolled steel were held tightly in their racks with their jewel encrusted scabbards of rich materials. Behind the glass counter, there were shelves of small cubby holes stuffed with ancient parchments and yellowed paper. Four puppies lay in a pile sleeping atop one another in a basket high on a shelf on the left wall above the glistening shields.

This was Max's, The Adventures' Emporium. A potpourri of maps and magic, arms and armor, shields and shafts, swords and sorcery. It has been said, in the din of bars, where most story telling went on, that Max was a great wizard grown too old for battle. Some, a minority, believe, whispering in hushed breath with a sly, cautious eye, that Max is an old fool filled with stories, trinkets and charms for the gullible. Some swear that Max is an angel, and others swear he is not. Many say that he stood beside the Supergod at the Re-awakening of Time. All that is said, none can be quite sure, and all that is sure is that he is Maximilian Hammerstrike, keeper of the arms of Hammerstrike, god-father of all children of Hammerstrike, and boss to Orrin.

Orrin stood on a stool and took the sleepy puppies from the shelf. He was a slim, fine, handsome young man with the sharp, elven features of his race. His deep, dark brown eyes, off set by his sharp high brows, scanned the store front as he stepped down from the stool with the last puppy, still sleeping, in his arms. He gingerly set it in the corner with its brothers and went about his morning chores. He reached under the counter and took out his feather duster and began dusting the helmets on the shelf. He listened carefully as he heard the plodding footsteps of his master coming down the stairs. Orrin quickly stashed his duster under his arm and took a small covered pot from the shelf. He took off the lid and pulled out a soaked ball of cotton and began to swab it over one of the chest plates. His master came to the foot of the stairs, stepping carefully to be sure that the puppies left nothing for him to find. To his surprise, there was none. He grumpily trudged over to where his stool was usually set only to find that it had been moved by the counter. He grumbled and trumped over to it, and again, to his surprise, his mug sat steaming on the counter. With a quizzical look, he climbed the stool's special steps, designed for his height, to the counter where he could reach his mug, filled with brew. He sipped his coffee, finding it boiled with the right amount of beans, justa root, and cane. He sipped it again and enjoyed it's taste—then he realized.

"What are you doing?" He grumbled.

Orrin didn't turn away from his chore. "Polishing the ar-mor, eh?"

Max sipped his coffee again, hoping to calm himself. "I can see that..." He paused, "What are you doing up so early?"

"Cleaning". Orrin huffed the armor and wiped off the vapors to finish the shine.

Max buried his face in his hand and sipped his coffee. He looked around the shop and noticed that Orrin had dusted, swept, mopped, arranged everything neatly (including the dogs), and polished all the metals on display. He sipped his coffee and realized that Orrin had painstakingly tortured himself to prepare his brew exactly the way he liked it. Max pursed his lips and raised an eye brow. "What did you break?"

Orrin stopped cleaning the store front window long enough to look back at his master. "Break? I didn't break any-thing." He said earnestly and turned back to his work.

Max stroked his long white beard and sipped his coffee again. "You want another animal." He said glancing at the puppies beginning to stir.

"No...I have plen-ty, eh?"

Max knew that Orrin had nearly 20 animals roaming around somewhere. He sipped his coffee again and thought about sipping slower to save the flavor. Orrin stuffed his cleaning rag into his back pocket and stepped behind the counter and out the rear to the pantry. He immediately returned with a kettle and plate and set it on the counter. He poured Max a fresh steaming cup, set the kettle on the plate, and resumed his window washing. Max looked at the swirling black mixture with restraint. *Could it be?* He wondered as he sipped. It was true! An entire pot of his favorite coffee. "You met a girl?"

"Not, like, re-cent-ly." He said humming an ancient elf call. "Not that Stroirda would allow, eh?" Max knew this was true. The two were an inseparable item. Max shook his head and contented himself to watching. Orrin placed his hands at his hips and admired a job well done. The glass was so clear, that if it wasn't for the bold, but gentle, 's'xaM', (emblazoned backward so that people on the other side would read 'Max's',) written on the glass, he would've sworn that the glass wasn't there at all. "I'm just in a cleaning mood, eh?"

Max shook his head. '*Elves*' he murmured, they lacked the solid, dependable, predictability that his race of dwarves so counted on. Elves seemed too erratic and spirited for his taste. What Max never seemed to mind was the fact that the entire household of Hammerstrike, consisted of elves.

He reached to top off his brew when Orrin took up the pot for him and poured some into his mug with a fresh plume of its sweet steamed aroma wafting into the air, and took the kettle back into the pantry and hooked it over the coals to keep it hot. Max shook his head again in disbelief. "Has Frito been about?" He called back to the pantry. An unsure question. Max knew Frito from birth and he was the most unpredictable of all the elves.

"Yes sir, I saw him come from a-cross the street to the ta-vern, eh? I think he went to eat."

"Very well, then bring his…" Max paused as Orrin came from the pantry carrying leather saddle bags and dropped them on the floor by the counter.

"This is like, every-thing he ordered from last night, eh?." Orrin said as he smiled at Max with his favorite and incredibly friendly smile. Max really didn't want to cope with Orrin's smile that early morning, so he turned and grumbled incoherently to his brew. There was nothing wrong with Orrin's cheery smile, it was automatic and very open, but for Max, not enough time had passed from when he creaked out of bed to look at something that just chirped pleasantly, 'Happy to serve you.'

Orrin paused and his smile lost it's flex as his eyes seemed to drift. Max knew that Orrin had sensed something. "He is coming." Orrin whispered.

"Can you see him?" Max leaned closer, his eyes sparkled with Neathina's stars.

Orrin closed his eyes and concentration etched lines into his forehead. "No, but like, I can see through the eyes of others around him, and like, he is only a rip-ple, a wave ro-lling up the street."

Max raised a brow and sipped his brew. "Very good. To see Frito like that is quite an achievement. He normally can pass unseen to Kamri." Orrin smiled proudly. Max looked at him and then back to his brew. "I'd wipe that off if I were you, It's too early in the morn for the

Ninefingers to see such a thing." It was true, for no matter what side of the bed Frito rolled off on, it was always, the wrong side.

Orrin ducked quickly into the pantry as the bells over the door to the shop started to ring. There was a yank, and the ping of a nail giving way before the tolling, greeting door bells clanged and clunked across the dry wooden floor. Frito's wide frame seemed even wider with his back to the light and the heavy cloak over his shoulders. His haunting gaze, gleaming red, beamed through the room piercing even the dark spectacles he wore over his eyes. He slowly reached up and took them from his face and set them on the table. He blinked against even the small, dim light in the shop. Orrin quickly darted in with the steaming kettle, mug, and a plate of flat pastries balanced on a tray, and set them down before him. He quickly took up the mug and began to pour brew, but Frito reached out and took the kettle from Orrin's hand. "Is this your coffee?" He said as he brought it to his lips. Steam spilled from the corners of the dark elf's mouth as he quickly quaffed the contents of the pot. Max and Orrin watched in amazement as his swallows could be heard through out the shop. When it was empty, Frito took it from his lips and slammed it on to the table. "Blah! That stuff is horrible!"

"Its also like, piping hot." Orrin whispered in amazement.

"You didn't have to drink it." Max added as reached over and took up the kettle. He peered into the darkness and then turned it upside down and let dregs drip into his mug. Frito growled for the purpose of growling and gripped the counter as he stared at the pastries on the plate. "The tavern didn't have breakfast ready. What is this?"

Orrin smiled and quickly tried to hide it. "Oh, they're…"

"You make these?" He held up one turning it back and fourth in his fingers deciding whether or not to try them. He looked to him with a heavy glare.

Orrin's smile grew even wider. "Yes, I did."

Frito cocked his left brow. "I remember the last treat you wiped up."

Orrin's smile quickly pulled from his face as he remembered a major flaw in his plan. "NO, No there…"

"I mean," Frito cut him off. "This isn't from a recipe you found somewhere in the basement." He looked at the seemingly innocent pastry. "This isn't going to…you know…"

"No, its, like, okay, I know what I did wrong that last time, eh?"

35

Frito looked at him still not convinced. "I'm glad, it took us three hours to chain up the last one."

"No, this one is okay, like, I had some this mor-ning myself, eh?"

Max propped his head up with his hand and sighed. "That may explain a few things."

Frito raised both brows as he looked to the dwarf. "Do I dare?" He looked at the tart and then took a bite out of it. Orrin waited for some critical comment, but Frito only took another bite. As elves went, to take a second bite out of anything meant it was palatable. Few elves commented otherwise.

There was a bark and a howl from the pantry and Orrin knew the animals were waiting impatiently for their breakfast. Max turned to the young elf and watched as he backed toward the pantry. "Well, got other hun-gry mouths to feed so, okay, so like, G'morn, eh?" And quickly dashed through the curtain.

Max chuckled quietly to himself and sipped his brew as Frito broke up one of the tarts and ate it's pieces. Abruptly Frito stopped in mid chew as if he had bitten into something. He quickly glanced about the room as if it were the first time he had ever seen the place. "Wait a tic, something is different." He looked at Max. "You dyed your face? Right?"

Max pushed his snow-white beard forward and looked at it. "Not lately."

Frito looked around the room again. "Weren't the swords back there?"

"They were back there ten years ago. You've been here since then."

Frito leaned heavily on the counter and scanned the room with a frown on his face like he was trying to tie a knot with his mind. "This place is clean." He said uncertainly at first, then he sniffed the air and it confirmed it. "This place is clean! What's the occasion?"

"Beats me." Max said shrugging his shoulders. "Orrin spent the entire night cleaning the place, he even prepared the stuff you asked for from last night." Max thumbed to the end of the counter.

Frito squatted in front of the sacks and inspected them with a quick overall glance—it seemed to be in order. "There is enough food here to last six days," He said rising to his feet. "I asked for only three."

Max shook his head. "Well I'm not surprised, he polished the armor, fixed my coffee the way I liked it, said he didn't break nuthin'. I

think puberty is setting in finally. Kids that age are so unpredictable."
He sipped his brew and dwelled again on the fact that it tasted so good.

And then stopped.

He suddenly looked at Frito, his mouth was a black dot on his face
and his eyes were wide and round. His surprise quickly melted from his
head and Max buried his face in his hand. "You're not going!" He
shouted at the counter.

"But Max!" Orrin came out of the pantry wearing a riding duster
and carrying his walking staff. Frito sighed and pulled up a stool.

"No buts!" The dwarf roared that caused the place to tremble.
"You can't go!"

"Why not?" Orrin argued.

Max glared hard at the boy as he realized that Orrin had planned this
well and was not about to give up with out a fight. Max also needed the
precious seconds to think of a decent reason why not. "Because you're
too young!"

"Max, I'm se-ven-ty years old! Eh?"

"Sixty nine if you're a day." Frito added in as he ate another piece of
tart.

Orrin glanced at Frito and breathed draggingly. "I'll be se-ven-ty in
a week."

"You'll never reach that day!" Max countered.

Frito set his head on the counter and looked·at the Saint puppy
sitting at the end of the counter wagging it's tail. Frito reached out to
pet it but it turned and stepped out of reality. It was one of Onary's
litter, Frito concluded. Frito shifted his head and looked to the other
end of the counter where the puppy was now sitting.

"Do you know what's out there?" Max said wagging his stubby
finger. "Have you ever beheld a Basticore preparing to rip your face
off?" Max's thick fingers scratched at the air in front of Orrin's face.

"But I'll be with Frito!"

"What if your separated? It can happen!"

Frito held out his left hand to the puppy and slowly brought it
closer. He then slowly reached with his other hand, hidden against the
side of the counter, closer. As the puppy stared at Frito's left hand,
Frito's right hand came from behind and tapped the puppy in the back
of the head. The puppy froze for an instant and dashed out of reality.
Frito took another piece of tart and snickered to himself.

"And what of your animals, will you leave Stroirda to take care of them?"

"Rob promised to come in and care for them while I'm gone."

"Rob! It amazes me that he remembers how to wake up in the morning!"

Frito carefully set the third coin on top the other two, balancing them on their edges. It collapsed and rolled off the counter and on to the floor. Frito quickly put on his glasses and tried to look as if he hadn't done it.

"And did Frito say you could go with him?"

"He would want me to come along, my Kamri could be a great help!"

"Its not developed yet!"

"I'll learn by ex-per-i-ence, you said so your-self."

"You'll learn to be dead. Tell him Frito."

Frito dropped the hand axes he had been juggling, quickly jerking his feet out of the way. "Huh, yeah, right, absolutely."

Orrin tightened his lips as he switched to his next plan. "But you trained my Kamri, and Frito taught me to fight;" Orrin spoke quickly, ignoring Max's attempts to interrupt him. "Dragon-slayer taught me the art of war; Fantista taught me the Sho-Pa; Fryto, the woods and trees; Frita taught me dis-ci-pline, J'son and J'cob the way of stealth and con-cel-meant; Craig taught me the bow. Max, I've been trained to, like, see the world, why won't you let me see it, eh?"

Max twisted up his face in anger. "Because you're too young!"

Orrin seemed to flop slightly and slapped his arms loosely to his side. "Frito was se-ven-ty when he went out, and he went out alone."

"Frito was trained his whole life, you've been here only scant years! And to correct your history, Frito went out with Roc, he wasn't alone!"

"But I'll be with Frito, eh?!"

"No!"

"But..."

"NO!"

Orrin felt everything shatter as the walls of the shop pulled away from him. He fixed his jaw tightly and his head dipped as he took a deep breath and looked at Max from beneath his brows. "Yes sir." He looked away and headed to the pantry as he could not hold back the tears suddenly welling in his eyes. "I've got to see to the an-i-mals, eh?" He stepped quietly out.

Max dejectedly turned to his brew. He brought it to his lips, then didn't want it and set it aside. "The boy's too young!" He said to the counter.

Frito took off his dark glasses and set them down. "Look, Max, about what I said last night..."

"You had much more training," Max said waving a stubby finger. "Your mother had taught you Shoulin to perfection."

"Yeah, Max, that was then."

"He's too young, he would only get in your way."

Frito sighed, "Max, if you remember, I didn't ask permission, I was seventy, little older in mind and body than Orrin, and I would have gotten killed on the second day if it wasn't for dumb luck. Now, about that..."

"Rob to take care of the animals? Rob couldn't figure how to put dirt in a shovel."

"Max, about..."

"What got into that boy's head?" Frito put his head in his hand and sighed. "It's puberty," Max went on. "I remember it hit you pretty hard too." Max pounded on the counter.

Frito shook his head and slipped off the stool. He leaned over the counter and whispered into the dwarf's ear. "Tell him he can go."

Max pulled away and glared at the dark elf as he took his chair. The dwarf tugged at his beard and huddled over his brew. He frowned at it, then at Frito, a dim jagged line tucked in an alcove of hair. He glanced quickly over his shoulder to the pantry then back at his brew. He pushed out his leathery lips from his white beard and sipped at it.

"Hekengo." He murmured into the cup.

"All Right!" Came a voice from the pantry. Orrin came out of the pantry without his riding duster and staff, but with a big smile on his face.

"You will do everything that you are told without argument!" Max ordered. "You are not to pester Frito, understood?"

"Yes, Max! Like, Whatever you say, Max!" And he meant it.

Frito reached down and took up the three fallen coins and held them in front of Orrin. "Take these to the stables and tell him that you what the best horse and tell them that I sent you. They still owe me."

Orrin took the coins quickly. "ThankyousomuchFrito!"

Frito growled, "You're not gone yet?"

Orrin darted into the pantry and then back out. "Right, the best horse."

"Today boy! Today!" Frito howled. Orrin darted across the room stepping on the fallen bells. He quickly snatched them up and looked for a place to put them. Finding none, he dashed them to the floor and ran out the door.

Max watched him through the glass window running towards the stables at full tilt. Then he looked at Frito. "You bring him back in one piece!" He growled poking a finger into Frito's tunic, thudding into the armor plate underneath.

"Which piece do you want?" Frito said smiling.

"No jokes, I want him back." Max said as he slipped from his stool and plodded to the floor. "This isn't a trip to the ferry. Bad things are lurking about."

"I'll keep him far from trouble."

"You'd better. How long will you be gone?"

"Long enough for him to want a warm, soft bed again."

"Then I will fix his dinner." Max pushed the rolling ladder that hung against the far wall and when he reached his desired section, started to climb one step at a time.

"Max," Frito called after him. "Don't underestimate the boy." Frito took another piece of tart. "He has a fair knowledge of what to expect." Max selected one volume from out of several and carefully climbed down the steps. "There isn't a dragon behind every tree." Frito spoke to the dwarf's back. "In fact, if it wasn't for Craig, I don't think Orrin would have ever seen one in his lifetime." Frito place a hand on the counter and looked around the shop. "I remember," Frito watched a ghost of himself carrying loads of coal for the kiln. "When I worked here, a great amount of knowledge rubbed off on me."

Max walked over to the counter with the book. "You also nearly got your head traded in, you remember that?"

"But I only worked here for a few years, Orrin has worked here for twice that. He also has a far greater retention for knowledge than I ever had."

Max sat back up on his stool again and set the book down. "You can say that again. I only wished that he retained how to stay where it is safe. Now, I don't want to argue, just bring him back." He opened the ancient text and quickly thumbed through it. He stopped at one page and turned the book for Frito to read. "See here," He pointed to a certain paragraph. "Thumber, keeper of nightmares, the beast that lives under the bed."

Frito carefully picked up the manual as not damage it's delicate, time worn leaves and scanned the text. It was written in the ancient Thest language of higher scholars. A tongue designed to keep the commoner from finding knowledge to great for them. Frito however, was well versed in the script.

"Okay, it doesn't say much more than what I was able to get out of Onary and Edia. Thumber is an entity, a monster."

"But they can be major problems."

"In hel," Frito turned a page. "Not on Mortalroam."

Max nodded slowly. "Thumber is respected in his circles, but they are small circles. He can be called up by mortals and sent to plague people in their sleep, haunting their nightmares."

Frito pointed out a specific line. "What is 'Manga thu laurde'?"

"That is the special notation that means magic through grant. In other words, Thumber is powerless unless his summoner grants or bestows power on to him to carry out his mission. Every once in a while, he has gathered enough of his own magic to appear in a child's dream, his favorite pastime, and give the kid a real spook. But he has never been known to have enough power to incarnate and pull someone through a floor."

"We are talking about a lot of power." Frito said as he turned a page. "Enough power to penetrate the magic wards I had in the house, and enough to get her out of the house again without tripping the wards." Frito turned back to see if he missed anything. "Is this all there is?"

"Not quite," Max scratched the underside of his beard. "There are a few minor references to him in other texts, but that's the real bulk of it. He is considered a small time demon and relatively harmless as monsters goes. Somebody conjured him. Somebody powerful."

Frito closed the book. "It must have been the same one who killed Stephanie's parents. Frita mentioned something about him using magic. Did you know of Oustrand?" Max shook his head, no. Frito set his eyes on the cover of the book. "I'll head south, to the find the house of Oustrand and find out who killed him and why. Perhaps that will lead me to Frita."

"But what if he is going after the child?"

"The child is too well protected at Fanrealm, he won't strike there. I've strengthened the wards about the house and made them very specific in reference to her. Then on top of that, I summoned the Dragonslayer to house sit."

Max slapped his forehead with the heel of his hand. "Just as things were getting quiet."

"I've got to go, Max. I've got to find her." Frito toyed with the crumbs left from his tart. "It's driving me mad. He took her right from under my thrice damned nose." His fist clenched on the glass counter.

Max took Frito's hand, turning it over. "What is this?" Max squeezed at the bulge under the glove.

"Nothing." Frito said quickly trying to pull his hand back, but Max held it tighter, pulling off the glove and exposing the bandage.

"What happened to your hand? Haven't you mangled this thing enough?"

"Shaving accident."

"You have got to stop this new masochistic tendency that you have developed and don't look at me as if you don't know what I'm talking about! You're running yourself ragged and blaming yourself for everything."

"Max, I AM to blame for everything."

"No you're not!" Max's hand gripped tightly on Frito's wrist with strength. "No you're not!" The dwarf's white bushy eye brows lifted up into his hair line. "You should know better." Max looked at the hand, pulling away the bandage. "You're still mad at yourself." Max looked at the blood clotted gash. "You're trying to cause all the pain back on yourself for no reason. Just because you're doing penance doesn't mean you have to walk around like this. You're a Knight. You can heal this."

"I'm not, I can't." He said grimly. Max's black onyx eyes glared at him from beneath bristly brows. "I still have my magic." Frito's eyes played on the cut in his hand. "But Okshiru has left me." He felt Max's grip relax. "He hasn't forgotten." The dark elf smiled slightly. "and he's the one that counts, right? Fact is, I no longer deserve the name Frito. I am now only Dwayne."

Max tossed the bloody cloth to the floor as he slipped from his stool. "I don't believe it."

"But the good comes with the bad." Frito spoke as if he hadn't heard the dwarf. "I've learned so much in the last two years. I think we all have." Frito watched the dwarf open a drawer and take out a wooden box. "In my penance, I've seen so much more of Mortalroam. I have met with new races of people that seem to have sprung up over night. I can feel it in the magic. Its cleaner, more pure. Like snow." Max climbed back up to his stool and set down his box. "You're not listening."

"I don't believe you." He said stolidly, opening up his box.

"About what part?"

Max frowned as his hands grouped around in his box. "The part about not being a knight." Max took out a small, brass can and uncovered it. "Your mother let you out of the house like that?"

"Things were a little confusing." Frito said, flexing his hand. "What is there not to believe? I should know."

Max took hold of Frito's wrist again. "And tell me why? Okshiru knows more than anyone." Max pushed his index finger into the can, pulling out a brown paste. With his fingers he pulled open the cut letting fresh blood seep out. Then he worked the paste and blood into the wound. "How could we have known? If that is the case, then we all are at fault. It had to happen, the Calling was on and some one had to go to hel and stop Angus, the Trid Dreath." Max wiped his finger clean on his robe.

Frito clenched his teeth. "But I fell for it. No one else did."

"They aimed at you. No one else could fit the billet." Max took out a bottle of clear liquid and uncorked it, whiffing and making up his face as he did.

"And for all my vaunted power, I couldn't resist? Max, that was me...the whole time."

Max splashed some of the liquid over Frito's hand. "With the eyes of the Trid Dreath in your head—you didn't know you had done wrong until it was over...You, Roc, Craig, Achillia and Wendell went to hel to fight the devil. We assumed that hel would be against you. We assumed wrong. It was a perfect trap."

Frito took the bottle from Max's hand and took a swig. "It wasn't unavoidable." He said with a rushing gasp.

Max took back his bottle. "And what would you have done differently? If you hadn't gone to hel to stop Augus, the first Trid Dreath, he would have taken all of Mortalroam." Max took a swig and corked his bottle.

"We could have stopped him here."

"After he was organized? After his troops were formed? How?" Max took a roll of gauze from out of his box. "My point is, Frito, we didn't know. As a knight, you did the right thing. Okshiru can't punish you for that." He unrolled a length of gauze and wrapped Frito's hand.

"He can..." Frito watched him. "Perhaps he tried to warn me, I couldn't read the signs..."

Max stopped his wrapping. "Show me one! Show me a sign that he gave you—describe one! Hmmm? There where none. Perhaps he didn't know himself. He blundered and you are the scapegoat." Max's eyes flickered at the idea. "You wonder why people have trouble remembering the war? A whole damn war almost as big as the re-awakening happened only two years ago and people can't remember it? They blame plagues and storms for the dead and missing. Only those who were in the middle of the fracas know other wise. I bet that the rest of the knights don't remember it was you. Why? Why is that? Okshiru blew it, that's why. He sent you to Hel, playing the victory march before it began. When you won, we thought it was over but in the think tanks of Hel it was just beginning." Max looked past Frito to Orrin outside securing his horse to the railing. The elvish boy looked harried as he came in the door. "Max! Dragon-slayer is like, com-ing!"

"How far?"

"A half click at least but he is tra-ve-ling at an like, in-cred-i-ble speed, eh?"

"What do you see?"

Orrin closed his eyes and his breathing slightly slowed as he concentrated. "He's riding in a red wa-gon of steel. It is that car thing of Craig's, eh?"

"The Red Barchetta?" Max looked to Frito for confirmation and he nodded. "Shit." Max swore under his breath, then suddenly looked about the store to be sure no one else heard him.

Frito turned on his stool. "Orrin, get your things, we ride in two tics." Frito watched as the boy dashed behind the counter into the pantry then looked back at Max. "A half click away, that's good." He whispered.

Max shook his head. "Dragonslayer has a tendency to be known when he is coming. And that car? You are to blame for that."

Frito shook his head putting his hands up in defense. "It was Craig. When he saw it in Hel, he was a man possessed. He had to have it. I didn't believe it when he said he could make the thing run with out magic and still out run a horse." Max pulled back slightly, not believing the exaggeration. "Even a Chiron horse. Now I know that the lights in front are magic, Sungazer made them. But the rest is all machine-science. I would dare say that it works that same way the Hothering, Slothering, Wanderblest Beast complete with Horro-shred option. Its science. Craig tried to explain it once, but it was beyond me." He looked at his bandaged hand. "Far beyond me." Frito looked up. "Like a lot of things." He smiled. "I know one thing though, I'm going to get back my sister. As of now, the past is past. She is gone and I'm going to get her." His lips tightened and he looked out the wide clear window, blinking at the bright light. "I feel for the man that gets in my way."

"Then you'll need a sword." Max said as the dropped from his stool. "And do I have the sword!" Frito watched him step to the corner of the shop to something leaning against the wall. He was a salesman now, a merchant with something to sell. "I dug this out of storage last night after you left. This sword was made by my hands in the days when the rising coast was still rising. Kreshemir was the knight of Uko then and he called down the lightning from the sky to heat my furnace to forge the steel." Frito had heard Max's story a dozen times over, but it felt good to hear it again. "I pulled pure steel and rolled it to this." Max went on as he carried the cloth covered sword around the counter and held it up to the dark elf.

Frito knew it before he touched it. He knew its weight, its feel, its power. The magic recognized his hand and warmed to his touch. It seemed to swivel on the axis of the hilt with a precision balance. A crafted blade.

The cloth fell away and the steel was exposed. "What a weapon." Max went on. "Is it not the finest you have ever held? You can feel its balance, it sings in your hand, does it not?"

Frito smiled at its blade. It was nearly weightless in his hand. "It sings." His father had given him the sword on his 68th birthday. He trained with it, ascended with it. Killed the devil with it. A knight's weapon.

"Rumor has it that it has been blessed with magic." Max whispered coyly, carrying on with his charade. "Name your price and it is yours."

Frito shook his head. "No, not today." He said as the memories tumbled about in his head. He reached to the floor and took up its cloth. "Give it to a Knight." He rolled the cloth around it.

Max nodded grimly. "Perhaps then," Still the salesman, "Another, I have many…"

"I have the blade-spear you made me." He set the sword on the counter.

"And a fine weapon that is. An excellent choice." Max plodded around the counter. "I crafted it with you in mind."

"Dru liked it. She put a sinister kiss of magic to it." Frito thought about it, before he said: "I like it."

"Good." Max took his seat, "Good because…" Suddenly Max glanced out the window to see a flurry of people dashing through the streets. "Roc is here." He said calmly. They both watched as the huge gleaming car came screeching down the street terrorizing the horses and people. They watched him spin out and park it dead center of the road.

His massive black armored frame barely fit through the door as he stomped into the shop. "Frito, you nasty knight!" He said petting Frito on the head.

"I'm not a knight…" Frito said to deaf ears.

"Max you nasty dwarf you!" He said petting Max on the head.

"Just passing through?"

Dragonslayer looked at Max with a macabre grin that exposed all of his teeth at once. "No…I think I stay FOREVER!" He struck a stunning profile. "Orrin, quick! Come witness this horribleness!" Orrin darted out wearing his duster to see the giant Dragonslayer posing like a statue. The awesome fighter wore the frightening, twisted mask that covered from his hairline to his upper lip that prevented anyone from seeing his true face. "Well? Why aren't you quivering in fear?" Dragonslayer demanded.

"I've gone passed that, and like, I've tuned to jelly, eh?"

"That boy is smart." He turned to Frito. "Well what's your excuse?"

Frito slowly shook his head. "I have no excuse." He answered turning to Orrin. "Come on, we ride."

Chapter 7

Beyond the edge of the world, Kemoto, bird god of the sun, set smoothly on Okshiru's still waters as he came to rest from his daily flight across the face of Mortalroam.   Lapping waves licked at his gleaming feathers, blasting up rolling clouds of steam that swelled in Okshiru's pastel sky. Kemoto gave a final glance across the sea to the rocky beach of Mortalroam.

The fading light burned across the sand and crawled slowly up the cliff face. Twilight shadows crept higher against the walls of the house as he walked slowly up the small road. Crumbling mortar and brick were held together by the great brown vines that clung tightly to the stone, their leaves rustling in Hauge's gentle wind. The leaves were old, dry and brittle now—a year's length too old, and were brown too, like the dust they sprang from, waiting to return.

Paradox paused and watched the setting sun dip into the sea. He could see from the top of the hill the cliff that started from the manor's edge and ran all the way to the black rocks and white salty foam far below. Hauge's wind brought the smell to him, a good smell. A smell that he couldn't fill his lungs enough with.

He could also smell bread baking in the oven, its fragrance billowing out of the tall chimney of the house. A warm hearth on the inside, but on the outside, the walls of the manor were black and cold with shadow, its windows, save one, were dark holes in its surface. A light burned in the window. A lantern to guide him in.

The dead leaves in front were crackling as they tumbled over themselves and tripped over his feet as he stood in the path that lead to the front door to the mat that said Welcome.

Welcome to the Home by the Sea.

He walked to the far side of the house. Shielded in the darkness he scanned the walls to find a good point to climb. He couldn't use the front door, that wasn't the way. The front door was too simple, too dangerous. He was too tired for danger.

He brushed the sand from his hands before he gripped the vine. It had been an difficult walk from the inlet to his home. It was a long, lonely walk along the beach exposed to the elements. The wind had thrown stinging sand in his face and brought to him the rotting smell of

Okshiru's waste washed along his shore. He was a man hated by the gods. Despised by all save one.

He climbed, swiftly, silently, like a shadow against a mist. Calmly he moved. Twenty five feet to the window he was beginning to breathe a little harder. Past the sill, what was in the darkness? On the floor? By the wall? He slid passed them. No traps. He hadn't set this window, and neither did she.

She did set the hall. A thin string gleamed in the dying light. He went to step over it and the thin cloth that covered his feet felt the tiny thread beneath it. Even before he could apply pressure, he pulled back. Clever, a thick string to trick setting off the second. She had improved.

Past the first door, nothing there. Past the second, still nothing. Past the third, nothing. Nothing but darkness. Nothing but shadows.

The shadow moved at him, speckles of shining metal leapt at him, slicing the darkness with their sharp, silent, furor. She didn't set these, she couldn't. He had set them, set them to trap himself.

His own sword was in his hands and thrust smoothly into the darkness before they could strike again, but he was a fool stabbing at phantoms. Shadows with no substance in the shape of men surrounded him, to kill him. His steel warded their's with a ring that sang in his ears. There was something he was doing wrong. Again a sword thrust to his side and he shifted from it's bite only to tear at another recent wound, to stir at it like coals of a fire, stirring to flame.

Flame.

He dropped to the floor and rolled beneath the axe slashing for him. He darted down the hall with the pursuit of the darkness upon him like ants in the fine hairs of his neck. He dove past the stairs to the fourth door and with a kick, it was open.

Light poured out as it cascaded instantly into the hall. With silent screams, the hall lay empty, weapons dropped on the aged carpet. He looked into the room, barren wooden floors devoid of all furniture save a tub of copper and a table by the window with a lamp sitting on it.

This was a good trap, one he set. One he couldn't remember, or didn't want too.

He crept down the long winding stairs, his feet feeling each tattered hole in the faded carpet. He felt the creaks before they creaked and passed them silently by. To the stairwell, following the dim light that reflected down the hall. Against the walls he silently slipped past the torn and hanging draperies, past the smashed and shattered statues, past the chandelier lying on the floor, to the glowing light of the hall. The main dinning room shifted with haunting shadows that danced in the buttresses from the flickering light of the candles dotting the main table. Wines, poultry, beef, bread, food on shining silver, glistened in the light. Candle flame sparkled in the wine, glittered on the crystal and gleamed on the glazed hens shrouded in green parsley. She sat at the far end of the table stiff and still like a porcelain doll. A tight, white, satin corset gripped her narrow waist. Long satin gloves painted to her skin, ending right before the elbow. Her long auburn hair tied in a bun perched at the top of her head. Her soft white skin with taint of rouge on the soft of her cheeks warmed to the firelight before her. Her innocent eyes of green sparkled behind her long black lashes. Her lips painted red with blood darkened in the dim unsteady light.

She didn't move, she nearly breathed, she only waited.

He came closer, walking smoothly, calmly out of the shadows, his arms swinging loosely at his sides. This was her trap, what could it be? He gazed into her deep seemingly unseeing eyes staring blankly at the chair at the other end of the table.

Sit down.

Too simple, too complex, what could this be? He stepped to the end of the table. The tattered cloth of his sleeve dangled as his hand passed the air for any invisible lines. None. His magic leapt beyond sight and searched the room for anything to see. There was none. He was perspiring. Was it too hot? He shouldn't be sweating. He removed his tattered robe and slung it over his arm as he stepped around the chair. He looked to her, still staring.

Sit down.

He looked into the shadows of the ceiling, what could be there? His magic saw nothing. He looked at the chair, nothing, the table, nothing. Still she stared.

Sit down.

He was still sweating. Too much sweat.

Sit down.

Too warm. This was her trap to challenge him, to kill him if she can. He must challenge it, to risk it.

Sit down.

Too warm.

Sit down.

He looked to the candles on the table, they had been burning for quite some time as they burned close to their bases, one of them burned into the wax spilling over into the stand. He scanned the candles, his magic saw nothing. He scanned her. Her sweet tender face, her breasts pushing gently into her gown, her eyes of a child, shining dark and green like a jungle leaf wet with rain.

Sit down.

He suddenly tossed his cloak onto the table directly before the chair and with a sweeping motion stood in front of the chair, in front of her gaze.

Sit down.

Slowly, gently he did. Carefully sliding between the high arms of the chair, letting his weight slide evenly into the flat cushion of the until all of his weight was on the seat. Still she stared, not moving a muscle, not an expression, not a thought.

Sit down.

This was a joke! To drive him crazy! To have him search like a fool! He folded his arms and leaned back into the tall, flat, back of the chair in triumph of figuring out her game.

He fell back, off balance, his arms flailing in the air grasping nothing. His legs reflexively raised up and kicked the underside of the table upsetting the decanter, spilling it into the candle, and with an igniting roar, flaming rum rushed to meet him like the sea does the shore. He was trapped, the chair back was too high to roll and the arms blocking his dodge—no where to go.

The waves splashed against his tattered cloak and went no further.

She smiled.

Lucky man he was. His magic didn't see how she sawed the legs of his chair, or propped the rum on a pea, or burned the candle to its height, pulling at its wax to spill it just so. His magic didn't notice how the table was slightly slanted towards him. It was a good trap. A very good trap and she would be rewarded.

He crawled out of the chair and walked away from the burning end of the table towards her. He sat in a chair beside her and took up a plate. "Very good, my Lady."

"Thank you my Lord." Her voice was soft and light in the air.

"How long did it take you to concoct that?"

"It was all I thought of in the months you were gone." She glanced at the wine in her glass, then slid it over to him. "Your mission was fulfilled?"

"Almost. I had some problems."

Her eyes deepened trying to understand. "Was it Achillia? You had trouble with her before."

His teeth tore at the roasted pheasant. "No, it was Denice...Excuse me FritA." He stressed the 'A' heavily. "Bloody knight...I can't see how she knew. There were no screams, no way she could have known." He gulped his wine and set it down and resumed stuffing the bird into his mouth. "I couldn't fight her with sword." He impulsively pounded the table with the pheasant wing in hand. "Damn it! The bitch appeared from nowhere! My luck was a surprise of magic that blinded her." He voraciously tore into his meal.

She sat silently, watching the sparkle of the wine. She breathed deeply and went to speak.

"Did you bring the girl?" His lips spoke around his food. He wasn't watching her, he didn't know she had something to ask. She lowered her gaze and whispered yes. "How old?" He demanded.

"Eight, seven."

"Pure?"

"Yes. I checked. I bought her at an orphanage for two gold, six silver."

He nodded his head with approval as he sheared off a slice of beef. "A bit pricey, but if she's pure, its worth it. Is all prepared for the cacodemon?"

She nodded. "Is this for Frita?"

"No, my new target is Achillia, I had anticipated that, that's why I prepared you for the summoning." He continued to eat while she stared at the smoldering clothes on the far end of the table. Her hand glanced at her left breast, as if to feel its smoothness, to be sure it was still there. She sighed and went to ask him again. "Where is the child now?" He spoke again without looking at her. "I wish to see her. She must be right for the summoning."

Her eyes flashed in question as her brows came closer together. "My lord, what is a cacodemon?"

He stopped his meal and looked at her. He had forgotten to tell her, or just didn't bother. "Well, its really simple, Ura has graciously granted me the knowledge and power to tap into the sub planes of Hel and call up a demon. A rare thing indeed because demons are so damn hard to control. They tend to turn and eat you unexpectedly. I plan to send it after Achillia and kill her long distance. I'd rather be there to see it, but it's the next best thing to being there." He went on dabbing his lips with his napkin. "Achillia is too good a knight and I have tried umpteen times to kill her. I dare not try her again. My hope is to send in the demon." He rose from his chair and slapped down his napkin. "I'm sure that'll be lots of fun, but right now, lets greet our guest, shall we?"

She took up a candle from the table and stepped slowly to the stairs with him close behind. Up to the second story and down the left wing. The halls flickered from the unsteady light and loomed at them strangely. They moved on past the first door wherein the lantern waited, to the second. She stood at the door and opened it with a key.

He took her candle and stepped in and closed the door behind him, setting the tiny candle flame on the stand by the door. Its light cast gently on the bed where a little girl laid sleeping, surrounded in warm quilted linen. Gently he sat on the bed and watched her sleep until the light from his candle threatened to burn itself out. Then he licked the end of the ring finger of his right hand and made three gentle lines on the girl's forehead. He leaned towards her and lightly kissed her on the lips.

He blew out the candle and stepped out, locking the door behind him. He turned left and walked slowly to the third room. Light now fell from its door and he knew it was where she waited. She had lit several candles and stood in the center of the room at the end of the bed in front of the large trunk that sat there. She had changed from her corset and now only wore a light cotton sleeping gown. The fire in the place glowed an angry red, warming the room, but she shivered with cold none the less. "She will do." He said. "She is perfect."

She smiled and gazed dazedly at his feet. "My Lord?" She looked up to him. "Will you share my bed this night?" And at this invitation, she parted her robe exposing her left breast, perfect and smooth, a good hand in size with a tart, pouting nipple. Her green eyes seemed to plead in innocent want.

He stepped over to her and closed her robe. He flipped his fingers in the air and all the candles in the room, save one, magically snuffed themselves leaving great darkness lying about. His hand slid to her shoulders as he sat her down on the large trunk. Again her hands went to her robe to expose her left breast, but he forced her arms away and to the sides. He parted her robe and exposed the right.

She shuddered as his hand waved over the scared area. She gasped hotly as he caressed gently at the spot where her right breast had been. It was gone, leaving several cruel and jagged scars each with different ages. She was no archer. He had cut off her breast years ago on a whim. He delighted returning to it on occasion and her scars indicated that the occasion was often.

He squeezed and the most recent cut opened like a tiny mouth and seeped blood. She began to moan as the pain pulled at her chest. He gripped her suddenly and savagely. Like rough sea on the rocks she bit her lips to hold the scream in her throat, then moaned quietly as the wave of pain flowed back like the tide of the sea.

She had done very well, and would be rewarded.

Chapter 8

The frigid breath of Fikor, the great snow dog of winter, rolled down from the white northern mountains and draped the forests with the chilling blanket of frost. Leatha the night, held still and silent as Hauge the wind slept. Meleki, goddess of woods, crept through her forests and checked her sleeping children, being sure that each one was bundled warm and ready for Fikor's season. The snow dog was coming south and soon, very soon, she would tuck her children in for the winter.

Cold air rested on his young, elven face as his eyes fluttered open and began to glow with molten gold. His vision cut though the veil of shadow revealing the forest beyond. He had been sleeping in the soft moss between the draw of two gigantic roots of a towering oak tree. Peering out to the forest before him, Orrin's elvish eyes searched quickly through the dark. He could see the great trees about him, the ferns and grass squirming to push free from its enormous wooded feet. Through branches, hundreds of paces in the air, he could see patches of a star filled sky.

He slowly arose, gathering his robes about him and stepped out of his camp to the forest floor. He sniffed the cold air, then listened, using his elvish skills as he had been taught. He scanned the forest and knew he was alone. His Kamri pushed out. Gentle waves of thought rippled through the air as if it were a still lake, bouncing from the tiny mice and moles to rabbits and squirrels, searching for another thought like his own.

He called it back. He had instinctively sent out his Kamri to find someone that Kamri was blind to. He began to turn in a circle whistling an elf call, letting it gently resonate off the trees in the clear night air. A call beyond the range of human senses, a call for elves and their clan.

An echo? He thought as his sharp pointed ears perceived. No, an answer. Quickly he darted over the rocks, to a small knoll that over looked an open field. At first he saw nothing, but the elf call in his ears directed him to the center of the tall grass, to a large object perched on a rock. Orrin clutched his robes tighter. Feeling the four pointed star of Hammerstrike against his skin warmed him, knowing it was there. He stepped out, parting the tall grass with his staff as he headed to the center of the field.

"I didn't mean to wake you." Frito said without looking back.

Orrin scrambled up the stone and found a place for himself. "You were not be-side me. I grew frigh-tened." Orrin's warm golden sight looked up to the dark elf. At first Frito's face was a black mask of shadow, but then his eyes began to glow with blood as his elvish power cast itself at the boy and studied him before fading out once again. "I will never leave you."

Frito again gazed to the sky. Orrin felt a stone roll about in his centre. The oath nerved him. He looked away, not knowing why, then also looked to the sky. "What do you see, eh?" he asked.

"Do you see the North arrow?" Orrin knew his stars to find something as obvious as that. "Follow it south," Frito continued, "Tell me what you see."

Orrin's eyes stopped their glow as he scanned the heaven. There was nothing there but stars, from the base of the arrow to the sash of..."Ninefingers!" He exclaimed in a whisper, "It moves, eh?" He watched the single star, moving slowly in a steady pace toward the sash of Neathina. "What is it? Like, what could it be?"

"It is the remnant of a long ago world, Orrin. It is a satellite, a machine of science."

"I know of sci-ence." He replied, "Like, Rob and Craig showed me. But this sci-ence I do not know, eh?"

"I do not know how to put this..." He took his gaze into the ground to ponder. "Do you know of the Eye of Rasham Harugh?"

"It is like, the Eye that stands at the Wove of the worlds and wat-ches the world, eh?"

"Yes, but what is it."

"An eye mag-i-cally cre-ated to do its masters bi-dding, to watch over the world and like, tell him what it sees, eh?"

"Good," Frito looked skyward again. "This is hard to explain without being technical."

"What is 'tech-ni-cal'?"

Frito put his hands to his face then waved them in the air as if to erase his words. "Forget that, lets get back to the eye, okay, before the reawakening of time, men...humans, lacked the skill of magic, so they built an eye of steel," He gestured to the rock they were sitting on, "about the size of this rock. Do you remember the rocket that Craig built for your birthday?"

"Yes! It like, went up into the air and ex-plo-ded. Boom!"

"Okay, but this one didn't go boom and it was the size of the red dragon. They put the metal eye in it and shot it into the air so high, it wouldn't come down. To this day, it floats up in the sky watching the earth."

"Where are its mas-ters, eh?"

"Gone. Dead. Now the eye sees for no one. No one told it to come down."

"Oh," Orrin answered earnestly. "So like, what is 'Tech-ni-cal'?"

Frito laughed breathlessly. "Technical is a Kay Why one seven-Dash-McDonald and Douglas weather satellite as the payload for the Atlantis shuttle-craft launched into a free floating orbit from Cape-Canaveral with a nuclear fusion power plant sending thirty three thousand computer generated graphic images per second to a now nonexistent terminal station in Houston Texas." Frito leaned and stood on his feet, his wide frame blocking the sky. "There is an even more technical term for it, would you like to hear it?" Orrin sat silently. "Well, we really don't have time right now anyway and besides, you will have to ask Craig for it. There is much I don't understand myself." Frito scanned the horizon in the east, looking for signs of morning. "We must ride farther south." He looked to the boy getting to his feet. "Come Orrin, Shegatesu is coming soon, so let us meet the dawn."

Shegatesu awoke and filled the sky with her warming blush. Her twin sister, Neathina, pulled her stars from Leatha's cloak, as the night pulled it back to unveil Okshiru's great sky. Mistang, the sleeping fog, roused and crawled from the higher lands to hide from the coming light as Kemoto, the flaming bird of the sun, spread his wings preparing to take the sky.

The sun swollen grain jerked and fell to the steel of the scythe sweeping back and forth in the hands of the autumn harvesters. Chinook, the giant Clydesdale stood off and away, stamping his heavy hooves. The god of autumn felt Hauge bringing the gift of Fikor and knew winter was upon him. His reign of autumn was ending as the gold filled grain fell to the men and their tools below.

Frito and Orrin watched from the crest of the hill as women followed behind the men, rolling the straw into bushels and standing them up in the cleared field. Dust clouded the air in a mist and clung to the bare backs of the men. Kemoto burned brilliantly and warmed the field despite the on coming call of Fikor.

"Aye," The fat bishop said nodding to the workers in the field. "The child has no claim to the land."

"Well that bites, eh?" Orrin mumbled. Frito glared at the boy and them back to the priest.

"The wheat shall be sold, and the land auctioned." The priest went on.

Frito gazed into the orchard at the two newly dug graves. "Who did this?" He asked quietly.

The priest continued to watch the workers in the field as he replied. "The Devil." He said very simply.

Frito glared at the clergyman taking his answer in stride. "Why? Money? Land?"

"No," He shook his head as he stepped closer to the ridge over looking the old tree and its two graves. "Oustrand was a man of other wealth. All he had was his wife and daughter and the blessing of Okshiru."

Frito continued to watch him. Two years ago he could have seen the blessing, but now all he could see were two cold graves. "Blessed? How so?"

The priest smiled laying his hands on his wide belly. "For years his home laid empty until came the sound of Stephanie, his daughter. She is a blessing." He chuckled to himself shifting his mass as he did. "A child of the Gods."

Frito looked the cleric then to the men in the fields. "What of his past, had he enemies?"

Again the priest chuckled. "No, he was a grace to the land and a friend." The priest looked back to the fields. "Since the legion he has been a simple farmer." The priest squinted at Kemoto's early light and gazed at the road beyond the field. He could see the image of a rider and horse moving briskly along the trail. "Who is this?"

"He was in the legion?" Frito questioned ignoring the rider.

The priest looked back to him and shook his head. "Yes, but the Legion has been gone since the reign of Dragonslayer."

Frito looked out over the fields to the workers there. "And them? The men were also in the legion?"

"Most of them."

Frito studied them. Each one taller than two paces and the tallest nearly three. They were all blond, and broad, tanned with sun. Frito looked to the holy-man beside him. A mountain of a man standing where Frito reached the center of his chest. His long blond hair braided to a single lock draped down his back. Frito lifted his dark spectacles long enough to gaze into the azure blue of the priest's eyes. "The child? She was adopted?"

The priest cocked his head slightly and laughed softly. "No, I birthed the girl myself." He held out his large, cupping hands as if to hold an infant.

Frito pulled at his small beard. "And Oustrand the father?"

The priest's laugh faded quickly. "My lord, adultery is death by stoning." He smiled and his eyes softened with tiny wrinkles in its corners. "No lad, they were of love. Oustrand was the father."

Frito now looked out over the field as if to see an idea standing there. There wasn't, but the rider was now trotting past the gate to the field. "Orrin." He called. "Who is that?"

Quickly Orrin reached into his hip pack and produced his spy glass. Stretching out its brass sections he put it to his eye, and smiled. "It is Achillia!" He exclaimed.

"The order summoned her. Had we known that the House of Hammerstrike would inquire into this matter, we would not have bothered." The priest explained. They watched as she trotted up the road to the hill. Her black and gold trimmed armor glistened in the early sun. Her long black hair cascaded across her shoulders and draped over her face as she ducked below the hanging boughs of the old oak tree. Her long sword slapped time against her leg as her horse trotted along. She nodded to the priest and halted abruptly. With raking fingers, she combed her fingers away from her strong, handsome face. A single lock of winter white hair could be seen. She seemed ghostly pale in comparison to the priest's baked skin. From her mount she addressed the two with a nod. "I am Achillia of the house of Avenger." Her tone was kind and gentle but her voice was rough and rusted. Her flashing steel eyes were piercing and unyielding as she scanned the vicar critically. "I look to father Fostric."

"And you find him." He extended his arms in welcome. "And this is lord..." He glanced to his right to find that he was alone with Orrin. "Why he was right here?"

Orrin looked about and sprinted off towards the barn. Achillia watched him go with a start. "Orrin?" She whispered, hissing at herself for not paying attention to the boy. "Father? was that Orrin?"

"Yes." He stumbled. "I think that's what he said his name was."

58

She spurred his horse and trotted after the boy. "By your leave, Father." She shouted over her shoulder as she trotted off.

She came to the large, open doors of the barn and dismounted. She dropped the reins of her horse and stepped in, letting her eyes adjust to the sudden loss of light and her nose to fill with the warm smell of dried grasses. There, in the center of the barn, a dark figure sat on its heels digging through the strewn hay. "Frito, of the House of Hammerstrike." She announced. "Lord of lighting, Devilslayer, Holy Archknight of Okshiru, complemented to Dru goddess of Death. The Ninefiners himself."

"Not any more." He mumbled as he rose and ran his fingers along the wheel of the wagon now black with blood. "Not any more. The name is Dwayne, now. Just, Dwayne."

"Then it is true." She said coming closer. "You have left the faith?"

He turned from the wheel back to the blood in the hay. "I'm not going to get into that right now. We have this problem."

She glanced back to her horse faithfully grazing at the door, then back to Frito with something he found in the straw. "And what is that?"

"The murder weapon." He handed the dirk to her. "This is becoming an unusual murder."

A shadow crossed in front of him and the dark elf followed it to the priest standing at the door. "So here's were you've run off to." He said pleasantly waddling in. "What have you found?"

"Enough I hope. Close the door." The dark elf rose and the priest shot a curious glance at the tall female knight who only shrugged her shoulders. The priest turned and pulled shut the doors with a squealing clatter.

Glowing shafts of sun shot through cracks and spaces of the barn's walls and spilled Kemoto's light on the grass covered floor. Tiny flicks of dust slipped silently down warm poles of light that fell from the ceiling. Orrin found a large square of sun that beamed through the barn window, and sat himself down. Like a lurking panther, Frito moved darkly around him in the shadow. He crouched low, and found his place beside the boy outside of the light.

The fat priest moved softly on the shifting dry grass and through the shafts of light to stand beside the woman knight. "My lady knight," He began in a whisper.

"You may call me Achillia." She looked to the priest who was a finger width taller than she.

"What are they doing?"

Orrin gently laid the blade in his lap and closed his eyes. With hands on his knees, he sat bolt upright and looked straight ahead.

Achillia leaned closer to the priest and whispered back. "Orrin is of the mind—of the Kamri. He is putting himself into the blade, to find its owner."

The priest bit his lower lip not liking this deviltry, but if a knight stood accomplice to it, then he contented himself to watching.

Frito hovered like a shadow over the boy watching with glowing red eyes. "Watch your breathing." He hissed a breath under a whisper. "Smooth it out...better." Frito's gloved hands were like black spiders as they slid smoothly over the boy's shoulders and firmly massaged his stiff and trembling body. Through his leather gloves the boy felt like a bag of wires.

Orrin began to bend, and then melt. Sagging slowly, his head dipped and lowered and then suddenly snapped back. His eyes fluttered open, white as paste.

The fine hairs against the priest's neck rose as he felt his breath grow shallow. He could fell the Kamri fanning out in the room. He could taste it on his moist tongue, along the backs of his teeth. He stepped back nervously, trying to put Achillia between himself and the boy. Achillia smiled within herself at the priest who was only more cautious than afraid. She then looked to the boy who was now mumbling to himself.

"Boo." Orrin grumbled through his numbed lips. "Insects!" He hissed. "Run...from me...can't run...don't run." Orrin's head lulled and rolled about his shoulders.

Frito leaned closer, breathing on the line of shadow and sun. "Who are you?" He whispered.

"No shouting..." Orrin said. "Stop your crying." A tear fell from his eye.

"Who are you?" Frito repeated.

"I am nobody." Orrin frowned. His white eyes gazed out into the darkened barn. "I am such a lowly worm." He smiled at the thought but for only a breath. His eyes closed as expression slid from his face. "Ready for this?" He spat though clenched teeth as his body tightened and his fingers dug into his knees.

"Who are you?" Frito spoke loudly and clearly. "Tell me your name!"

"Who calls me?" Orrin's head snapped suddenly to the side. "Blessid Ura! How? How could she have found me? There were no screams! Damn you Denice!"

"Who Are You?"

"I must kill her quickly!"

"Who are you?"

"I must kill her now!" Orrin crumpled without bones into Frito's hands. He cradled the boy's head and only waited.

"What?" The priest whispered, but Achillia motioned him silent with a hand.

Orrin's eyes sprang open burning with gold before melting into gentle brown. He found himself and slowly fought to sit up. He looked back to Frito who sat on his heels. "Like, how did I do, eh?"

"Real good." Frito said curtly. "A name?" He coached.

Orrin looked away. Inadvertently, his eyes found the blade now lying in the hay. "He didn't have a name. He ne-ver did."

Frito cocked an eye. "He had to have something?"

"Its hard to re-me-mber, eh?" His voice trembled. "I didn't look too deep. I didn't want to. I was, like, a-fraid. I think…" His brown eyes looked into the shadow were Frito was. "I think he hurt her, I'm sorry, I couldn't look."

"Who called him?"

"Denice." Orrin said strongly.

"Not Frita? Her knightly name is Frita." Frito pressed him. "She called his name. What was his name?"

Orrin tightened his lips. "I can't re-mem-ber…" He looked away, "I don't think he ever had a name. Not a real one any way."

Frito clamped a firm hand on the boy's knee. "You did good."

"But…" Orrin looked flustered as the spinning pictures quickly swirled from his head like a bad dream. "She called him, eh? I heard it." In his mind he could see Frita, her mouth shouting a silent name.

Frito shook his head. "Don't push it."

Orrin looked at him determinedly. "I know…" His dark brows came together. "Para…Para-keet? Parrot? Para…She said it, she said…" Suddenly the boy's face broke into an award winning smile. "Para-dox!"

Achillia drew a deep, tight breath. "Unholy knight of Ura, goddess of Chaos. It explains everything."

"Almost." Frito said looking to the grass. "We gotta find him."

61

"He has to answer for this!"

Frito nodded, slowly rising to his feet. "Where has he gone? How do we find him?"

Achillia nodded to Orrin. "Can the boy?"

Frito shook his head. "He's probably too far away, but we'll have to try later. Orrin must rest."

"I can try now, Eh?" Orrin protested.

Frito looked down at him. The boy was so full of strength, so full of ambition that it reminded Frito of himself. But Frito was also of the Kamri, he knew its limits and the price of over taxing oneself. "We will try later."

"If I may?" Fostric the priest stepped forward. "Many years ago, before my time, there was a temple to the goddess of Chaos. It was torn down long before the town was ever built. Its remains are not far from here. A half days ride."

Frito frowned thinking it over in his mind. "All right, we'll hit town and draw some more supplies. We've got very few options and this is our only clue." He looked up at the knight. "What about you Achillia?"

"I follow your lead my lord."

Town failed to compare to the city of Cornerstone. The shops were small and several were no more than tarps for merchants spread heavily along the lone short street. Among the sparse wooden and stone dwellings, the one keep store stood out proudly. It was larger than most of the other places and every inch filled with goods. Blankets, lanterns, candles, oil, flour, grain, rice, dried wine, jerky, furs, and skins, were all stuffed about using every available space.

"Tar, wax, twine," The shop keeper scribbled illegibly on his pad. "Rice wine, jar of licorice..." Frito looked at the entire jar of licorice sitting on the pile. He reached in and took two strips from the jar and stared at Orrin as he put the jar back. Frito then smacked him with one licorice whip and gave it to him, eating the other. "Two licorice." The shop keeper scratched more on his pad. "21 bits, will it be good?"

Frito frowned as he opened the string of his pouch. "Keep it." He slapped a coin on the counter.

Faster than a mouse on a kitchen floor, the man's hand snatched it from the counter and stuffed it in his purse. "Bless you my lord." He said.

"Bless you my lord" It repeated in its wicked voice.

"Well all right!" Orrin exclaimed as he looked up at the large black bird in the cage. "It talks, eh!"

"Well all right" It repeated.

"G'morn, eh?"

"G'morn eh"

Frito scraped the sacks from the counter. "Let's go Orrin."

"Well, g'morn." Orrin said as he turned to leave. The bird flapped its wings, almost as if it were afraid of losing its audience, and began to sing—not the squawks and clicks of birds, but the song of a child's voice. Orrin looked back at the bird.

"Who taught the bird to sing?" Achillia asked thumping a sack on Orrin's shoulder. "Its beautiful." She glared at it entranced.

"Oh," He chuckled. "Its not for sale."

"Great, lets go." Frito headed for the door.

"Oustrand's daughter taught that bird to sing." The shop keep went on. "Sad story. Child of the gods she was. Sad to die," He looked down in reverence and shook his head. "Sad to die."

"Fear not." Achillia soothed. "The child…"

"Is dead!" Frito hissed, spinning on her quickly. "Now we will go." He turned and the bird chanted at his back.

"Child of the gods she was…sad to die, sad to die"

As he hit the door, Frito stopped and glared at the black bird on its perch. It was mocking his glare. Frito grit his teeth to himself and stepped outside.

The dark elf squinted painfully at the bright light as he slapped the sacks to his horse. Achillia followed after with Orrin close behind. "I apologize my lord."

"Forget it. It's my fault for not telling you." He said strapping on the bags. "I don't want any attention drawn to us and with the assassin still about I don't want word to…" He stopped in mid word. "What the…" He looked to the dirt road running through the center of town. He stepped from behind his horse and closely inspected the road. Two, sometimes three or four large strips of upturned dirt waving equidistantly through the street, leading to a large crowd of people. Frito, Orrin and Achillia headed into the crowd, cautiously making their way to see shattered wood strewn on the street and a newly burrowed hole in the side of the blacksmith's shop where the tracks led into. From the dark of the tunnel came a rumbling as two tiny white lights gleamed in the darkness.

"The Red Bar-chet-ta…" Orrin whispered the instant before Frito grabbed him and dragged him out of the way of the shining car barreling backwards out of the shop. It wove erratically in the street before coming to a rest. The engine revved and the car heaved slightly. Dragonslayer leaned back in the front seat and casually tossed an arm against the passenger head rest. "I'm ready for my next driving lesson." He said revving the engine again.

Frito let go of Orrin and walked up to the car examining the damage to the hood as he did. He leaned on the hood and glared at the giant elf behind the wheel. "Your next lesson is: The use of your rear view mirror. It is to see behind you and not to watch yourself while your driving!"

Roc shut off the engine and adjusted the mirror. "I thought it was too small." He looked at the mirror and gritted his teeth at it.

"Thanks Roc." Frito said quietly. "You just called a lot of attention to something that I didn't want attention called to."

Roc lifted up out of the seat and rested on the back. He scowled at the people who had gathered in awe of him. "I AM ROC THE DRAGONSLAYER!" People recognizing the name shrieked in horror and scattered aimlessly about in a flurry of panic. Those few who didn't know the name scurried about in the same flurry of panic because it seemed to be the thing to do. In seconds the streets where empty. "Look at that." He said folding his arms across his broad chest. "They've all run home to tell their friends that I'm here."

"G'morn My lord." Orrin said with his smile.

"Either you wipe that smile off your face or I'll wipe your face off that smile." Orrin bashfully looked to the ground as Roc turned to Frito. "Your mother is a charming woman. But my ego couldn't handle it. I Am Roc The Dragonslayer, conqueror of nations, lord of realms, master of dragons, slayer of any one who gets in my way, or looks like they might get in my way, or thought about getting in my way, or knew someone who might get in my way. Milk and cookies is too humiliating in front of the troops."

"Troops?"

"That's right. I moved three divisions (which is all that is left) and the Dragonguard around your castle (which is nicer than the camps we are in)."

"You got bored?"

"Out of my skull. Your mother filled me in and I thought it would be fun to tote another sword." For the first time he glanced to Achillia. His tone, voice, changed and he scowled. "Another Knight. I hate Knights." He turned back to Frito. "I'm glad you gave it up. Lets get wasted."

"I'm busy." Frito replied. "We've got work to do."

"I bet you a coin I can put you on the floor."

"What?" Frito lifted off the hood and put his fists into his hips. "I can out drink you any day."

"What are you doing now?"

Frito folded his arms and looked at Dragonslayer skeptically. "Are you coming or not."

"Of course I am coming." He leaped out of the car. "Let me get changed. My armor is in the trunk."

"Your not going to park it here?" Frito pointed to the car.

"Well I don't think the blacksmith would want it back in his shop."

"We can park it somewhere. I'll send an elf call for Craig to come and pick it up." Frito looked about. "Here, Orrin, help Dragonslayer with his armor and get it out of the trunk. I'll park the car over there some where. Achillia, buy a horse for his nastiness. Have you money? Good. We haven't the time to spare."

Chapter 9

Kemoto lifted high into the distant blue of Okshiru's sky—his light faintly warming on the pale dry sand. The chilling breeze of Hauge swept salt from Okshiru's sea, to the open air. He dashed across the rolling waters, leaped over the waves, to the shore and the beach beyond. Thin reeds lashed at the legs of the god of wind as he rushed by. Fat white clouds formed fantasies in the blue sky as they slid slowly over head.

Fumbling, stumbling, rolling down a reed swept hill and crashing to a halt in a pile at the bottom. She slept, hiding in the darkness of the earth, until her bone's aching pain woke her once again. She drunkenly rose to her quivering legs and thrust herself forward once again, shambling aimlessly. She dashed her legs against the sharp rocks that pushed out of the sand that she did not have the strength to avoid. Plodding mindlessly until she fell, rising and falling again into a tangle of noisome reeds with her face buried in the sand.

"Hammen das shelfuel!" Cried the tiny girl's voice as she dashed across the field. "Hammen das shelfuel!" She ran quickly through the flashing reeds to the body that lay still in the sand. She poised in fear of coming to close and her young mind tried all of its options to understand. She turned and cried to the wind. "Das Vendel! Kathreen!"

Kathreen doggedly ran through the grass until she came close enough to call back. "Buffet! You mustn't run so, stay by me!" She came trudging through the grass.

Buffet turned and shouted again. "Vendell! Kathreen! Doufel hammen das vendel!" The woman in the sand stirred and slowly looked to the child standing over her. She moaned as she tried to stand again and Buffet stepped back afraid. The little girl turned and saw Kathreen running towards her. Knowing that help was on the way, the child turned back to see the woman rising to her knees, uncoiling like a snake, glaring at her. Buffet took two steps back and waited. The woman reached out to Buffet and fell to her face in the grass. Moaning, she rolled to her side and bleakly tried to shield the sun, but her fingers lacked the strength to hold the light and it leaked on her bruised face like water through a sieve. She blinked and squinted at the sun as she tried to see.

Kathreen shoved Buffet aside and quickly knelt at the woman's side. "Blessid!" She exclaimed as she lifted the woman to her knees. Her head hung sickly to her shoulder and her long black hair draped like a tangled spider's web across her face. "You are bleeding!" Kathreen cried, taking the woman's arm. The woman blearily looked at her arm and mindlessly placed her three fingers along the three even slashes. Blood clung to the bottom of her fingers where it had seeped through the sand clogged in the wounds. Kathreen removed her sash and quickly bound the wound.

Supporting her, Kathreen lifted the woman to her feet. "Buffet, fetch the basket." The girl looked at her strangely until Kathreen pointed with her free hand to the basket full of dried wild flowers.

"Ter gunt loumfta!" She shouted scooping up the basket. Kathreen ignored the child as she helped the woman back to the manor. They made their way slowly up the long sloping hill to the dirt packed trail running the lip of the cliffs high above the water. She half dragged the woman past the gate and down the small path. She walked the extra distance away from the front door glancing at it momentarily. It was a simple door complete with a simple welcome mat.

Welcome to the Home by the Sea.

The woman's feet banged as Kathreen dragged her up the three wooden steps and into the pantry. Kathreen set her limp body down on the bench and gently leaned the woman's head back to rest against the wall and brushed the hair from her battered face. "My lady, do you hear me?" The woman mumbled something in response. Kathreen left her and quickly snatched up a washing cloth and took it to the pump.

The woman slowly lifted her head and glared at the child before her. "Wiesen der altherman." The little girl said with a curtsy. "Good mornik mine Lard. Mine Name Iss Boffet." Again she curtsied.

The woman blinked.

Kathreen stepped beside Buffet and took her damp rag and began to swab the woman's face. "This is Buffet," she explained as she worked. "I am learning her words. She is Karanin." She wiped away the sand and mud from the woman's face and neck.

"This…" The woman said painfully, "is your daughter?"

"No…" She laughed gently, not stopping from her task. "She is…adopted." Pulling the woman's tunic revealed tiny dried scars about her throat. "Blessid woman, thou art harmed."

The woman only gazed hypnotically at Buffet. "Good mornik mine Lard." Buffet began again. "Mine name Iss Boffet."

The woman smiled and sat limply as Kathreen stripped her tunic from her body. "Your child is beautiful." She whispered weekly. "Buffet?...My name is..." The woman's face went suddenly blank. Her eyes began to shift around the room as lines drew into her head. Her breath shortened as if her chest couldn't draw air. "No...I..." She blurted trying to form words that her mouth couldn't utter.

"Rest lady. Thou art safe." Kathreen placed a hand on the woman's shoulder, restraining her to the bench. "Stay down you must!"

The woman clutched at Kathreen's shoulder and held back her hand. "No...No...Who can this be? Who is this...Why do I not know her?"

"Her?" Kathreen looked to the woman, searching her pain stretched face, trying to understand her.

"Me!" She screamed with sudden strength! "Who am I?" Kathreen held back, unsure of what to do. Little Buffet was now in the far corner of the kitchen sitting timidly. The woman's grip of pain relinquished as her body could no longer hold the energy. Her eyes dropped and tears ran freely down her face.

Kathreen's arms dropped neatly about the woman's shoulders and the embraced her tightly. "Cry not my lady." She whispered holding the woman tighter. "Cry not." Kathreen suddenly hissed and broke away. Kathreen felt herself bleeding and she lightly touched a spot where her blouse had stained with blood. It was small and she was used to her old wounds opening up from time to time so she let it bleed as she reached over and undid the bandage on the woman's arm.

The woman grabbed Kathreen's arm and looked at the tiny red spot on her blouse. Kathreen paused, trying to figure out the woman's actions. When the woman, reached out and touched the spot, Kathreen hissed again and drew back but the woman's grip would not let her. "Woman, you mustn't!" Kathreen squirmed but the woman held her with astonishing strength. Again she reached out and as Kathreen tried to interfere, the woman smacked her hand away and touched the spot again. "Blessid!" Kathreen cried in surprise and then froze. Her heart began to quicken and her breath rushed away as she felt a wave of relief ripple from the woman's touch. She leaned back against the table as the woman slowly began to stand.

She reached past Kathreen and braced herself on the table with one hand. She then released Kathreen's arm and began to unbutton her blouse. Still dazed, Kathreen watched the woman's face concentrating on her task. She popped the first three buttons and gently slid her hand into Kathreen's shirt. Her touch was smooth and cool against Kathreen's scared chest. Her hand softly caressed were Kathreen's breast should have been, gliding over scars, smoothing out the older ones, and sealing the new.

Kathreen felt numb and filled with warmth as the woman removed her hand and slowly sat back down. The woman's dark eyes drifted to the floor and stared into nothingness. Kathreen tried, but her voice was lost. Her jaw opened and closed several times before she found her voice rolling about in her mouth. "Woman?" Kathreen spoke slowly and softly as she was speaking to a spirit. "Art thou a Healer?"

MURDERER

"No." She answered in a empty, hollow moan, her eyes still lost on the floor.

"A holy knight? A paladin?"

BLASPHEMER

"No." She whispered.

"A witch perhaps. Lama or holy dragon?" Kathreen had heard of traveling witches who appeared to need help when they only sought to give it.

SINNER

She shook her head. "I am...Dennis? Yes I am Dennis." Her eyes looked up and she smiled weekly and hopefully.

Kathreen found her mouth was hanging open and closed it. The woman before her was smiling with a bruised and darkened face. Her cheeks were lopsided from swelling and her pale lips were split with darkened lines of blood. She shook her head as she remembered her task. She took up her cloth again and dipped it into the bucket of water. "I have never heard such a name, my lady." She took up the woman's arm and the woman winced as Kathreen began to clean the blood from her. "It is...a nice name."

The woman didn't think it was. He expression deepened as she looked into herself. It was dark and empty and in the void of her mind, the name Dennis didn't belong. She didn't like Dennis. She preferred, Denice. Yes, it is. "Yes!" She answered clearly. "I am not Dennis. I am Denice. This I know. I am Denice." That name fit. She blinked twice and looked into her wound as Kathreen finished.

Kathreen smiled. "I have never heard of Denice, but I think it much nicer. Come Denice." She coached. "We will have to bathe the rest of you."

As Kathreen helped her up Denice thought in her empty head: *I have never heard of Denice either, but I prefer it to Dennis.* She didn't know why and it hurt to think any deeper, so she left it alone.

Once on her feet, the two walked leaning against the other through the hall, carefully avoiding the shattered pieces of the chandelier lying on the floor and up the creaking steps to the second floor. Denice looked down the right wing of the manor. Its darkness and shadow flawed only by the glimmer of light falling from worn holes in the ceiling on steel axes and swords lying in the hall. They turned to the left hall. "Where is the master of the house?" Denice looked back over her shoulder towards the right wing down the hall.

"The master meditates." She said turning to the first room they came to. The room was brightly filled with the light of Kemoto's sun and it beamed as large shafts of gold falling through large open windows. Wooden ribs of walls exposed through the mortar and boards torn from the floor exposed the support beams beneath. In the center sat a large brass basin dulled from use. Kathreen guided Denice over the beams to a solid part of the floor and sat her down on a low stool. "Take off those things." She said stepping over to the fireplace. The woman watched as Kathreen took a wooden stick and shifted the still hot embers to the center of the pit. She then took up a faggot and popped the thread that held it together. Taking several from the pile, she snapped them and tossed them on to the coals. In moments, with careful fanning, the twigs crackled to flame.

Buffet stood out in the hall peeking in. Her blue eyes watched the room quietly as Denice tossed her clothes to a pile on the floor. Unseen, unknown and unnoticed by the two women, the closet door opened a tiny bit and two dark eyes peered out.

Kathreen took a black cauldron and swung it over the flames to warm. She turned to see Denice sitting in the tub and the bit of water already within.

Startled, Kathreen sprang from the hearth waving her hands. "Oh No! Denice, I wanted to put a robe on you while I heat the water! That water must be near frozen!" Kathreen knelt by the woman who seemed not to hear her. Although it was cold, Denice did not shiver, but sat contentedly in the water that only covered her waist. The tub was small, so she had to keep her knees pulled into her body. Amazed, Kathreen reached for a wash towel and slowly began to bathe her. "Are you elf?"

"No…" The woman hung on the question. She really wasn't sure. "Yes," She decided. "I am hiran." She finally answered. "My father was human." *My father was a god.* She looked to Kathreen and knew right away that she was human.

"Where do you hale?"

Denice instinctively reached between her breasts as if to find something only to realize that it wasn't there, only tiny scratches in its place. "I do not remember." She said dreamily. "From the north." Why did she say north when she didn't know if she were south?

The cold water began to hurt Kathreen's hands, so she handed the cloth to the woman and let her bathe herself. She slowly rubbed the wash cloth across her arms and her neck, moving her hair to the side to wash her back. She washed the tiny scars on her chest and her small, firm breasts. She was such a beautiful woman, Kathreen thought, in face and body. Who would want to hurt her so badly that she wouldn't remember her own name? Kathreen reached to the place where her right breast should have been. It felt strange to not feel pain in its absence. Not strange, good. She couldn't understand why she felt flustered as she went to the kettle. She tilted the water into a pan and brought it over the tub and poured it into the bath. Denice looked to the faint traces lining Kathreen's arms and slowly began to realize the her host had scars of her own. "What cut you so?"

Kathreen looked to Denice where her legs came from the gray white water and could see as the water rippled down her smooth, tan skin, that it never had a scar before. "My scars are old." Kathreen said setting down her pan. "Yet you have only new."

Denice inspected herself. She ran her hand along the scar where she tore open her leg climbing a fence chasing her brothers. There was another scar on her hand, given to her by Donald during a mishap with sword practice. There were burns on her arms from Zashwhind, the blue dragon.

There were no scars, there were no memories. *Who were these people?* A beautiful woman with shining eyes gently and painlessly lifted off her scars, old and new. She was always smiling, always loving. Other faces came into focus, names drifted with them. Dexter the eldest. First born, first dead. Dwayne, little dark one. The dark blood runs in him. Donald the fire. J'son, twin to J'cob. Daniel, twin to…*Me? Not me. All of them my brothers? Why do I not know them?*

"Denice." Kathreen called softly holding out a large towel and draping it over the tub. "You healed me. Could you not heal yourself?"

NO

Denice stood into the towel and dried herself stepping out of the tub with Kathreen's steady hand to help her step free. Kathreen then used another towel and dried Denice's hair.

More thoughts rolled in the wide spaces of Denice's head. Donald healed the scar on her leg. Dwayne healed the one from the sword. The burns…*Myself? Why could I then, but not now? How could these others heal?*

Kathreen dressed her in a gown of her own and put wooden shoes on her feet. Denice's eyes watched her, but only saw the beautiful woman and her shining eyes. Dwayne, Donald, they could only close the wound, take away some of the pain, this but woman could clear them away easily. She could see them shrink on her skin and vanish. The woman looked familiar. The others had names, why doesn't she? *What is her name? What is it? Mother? Is that your name?*

Kathreen led her out across the hall to another room. "This is my bed. You will sleep in it this night." Kathreen said as she pulled back the sheets. "Come." She slowly guided her into the bed and pulled the heavy covers about her. "Sleep now. I will wake you in a few hours to supper with Buffet and I."

Back in the hall, back in the room with the dull, brass tub, Buffet watched with frozen fear as the closet door swung open on its own and a wicked woman slowly crawled out. Her pale white eyes glared at the tiny girl at the door. Buffet didn't know the woman was Howerer, the monster of the closet, now out of the closet. She was blackish green with moldering flesh and her black, hanging hair draped across her vile, scarred face. Her green, sharp teeth crawled with bugs as a withered green hand with a crooked black claw rose to her crooked black lips. "Shhhhhhh."

Buffet didn't move.

Howerer's emaciated body crouched and pushed through the pile of clothes on the floor. A bit of metal tinged as it slipped free of the pile and hit the floor. She touched it, and a painful hiss, like the sound of water on a hot coal, followed. She quickly took up the tunic and bundled up the white gold star in it and tucked it under her arm. She looked at the little girl still at the door. Her shriveled breasts moved as her visible ribs slid beneath them. Her moon white eyes squinted in the sun that she was so unaccustomed to. Her twisted finger again rose to her lips. "Shhhhh." Then quietly slipped back into the closet, closing the door behind her.

Buffet heard the tiny click of the latch and could hear no more. She waited, her breathing quickening as fear finally rose within her. Her head vibrated with the sound of her screaming. It was unfortunate that Kathreen couldn't understand Karanin, for by time she arrived and the little girl showed her the closet, it was empty and Kathreen had no idea what the little girl was trying to say.

Chapter 10

Black night began to spread, growing, from the east as Kemoto, bird god of the sun, rested his head in the west to sleep on blankets of soft glowing orange and robes of fading royal purple. Cool breezes lifted in the woods along the narrow dirt road they traveled upon. Flashing sparks ignited tar and burst into flame. Torches pushed the night back, to hide behind trees, glancing at them, waiting for them to pass and take the road again.

Orrin pulled his staff from his horse's saddle and from its tip billowed a plume of light. "Max's magi-cal field staffs." He smiled proudly.

Frito turned away from its light. "Orrin, save that, we have torches."

Orrin looked at it. "Oh, like, it'll last all night and re-charge in the sun, eh?"

"Well save it anyway, I can do without it."

Orrin doused it and slipped it back under his saddle.

Achillia looked up. "Why does Dragonslayer ride amidst?" Torrid fire from the torch burned above her head like wind in blonde hair.

Orrin explained. "Like, we can see far-ther with out tor-ches, eh?"

Achillia moved her torch down and shadow quickly filled its place. "But without it, I can not see. I can not ride blind."

"And neither can the horses." Frito turned to her. "I am glad you are along."

"Then why can you not tell me what you know? Why does Dragonslayer, King of all from sea to mountain and Dwayne Hammerstrike, The Ninefingers, slayer of Trid Dreath the first and second, seek after a simple murder."

Frito removed his dark spectacles and looked back to her. He shielded his eyes from her torch. "There is no simple murder here. I thought I had explained." He pushed his spectacles into a side pouch and looked out onto the road.

"Yes," Achillia switched hands with her torch to keep it from Frito's eyes. "You explained that this murder has no motive, but still, if you have left the faith and no longer serve Dru as I serve Uko, why would you be out here? An act of kindness? Kindness from Dragonslayer as well? Roc is not known for his acts of kindness."

Frito looked up ahead and watched Dragonslayer's horse round a bend. He knew the Slayer could hear her, but chose to ignore. "We need something to do in the off season." Frito answered simply.

Frito and Orrin halted their mounts abruptly. Achillia stopped only after they did. She went to speak, but Frito bade her not with his hand. "Elf call." Orrin said. Achillia listened intently, but heard nothing. "Dra-gon-slayer has found a trail, it may be the one we're loo-king for, eh?" Orrin tapped his horse to motion.

They moved to the bend and followed Frito's lead. He ducked a low, thorny bush and pushed his way off the side of the road. There was a trail, seemingly untouched for a stretch of years. The hard packed earthen road was cracked and pitted—broken apart by the wooded green of Meleki's persistent fauna, now drying and yellowing from the reign of Chinook the Snowbiter. The wagon ruts ran deep from the rains of Danshu. Saplings pushed their way out of the road making it impassible for wagons of any sort.

Roc had dismounted and now led his horse along. His large bulky frame pushed his way through the over grown branches and used the blade of his buckler like a machete. He was making no considerations to stealth—he was the Dragonslayer, he had no need for stealth.

Frito passed as Nih elves always did. Even with full armor under his tunic and pant, he was near silent and he moved through the thicket. He let go the reigns of his horse and Horse watched him slip into the woods with Orrin close behind him carrying his field staff. Achillia looked back at the heavy horse standing there as she brought her's past. He was looking back at her. Achillia knew the peculiarities of Frito's horse. It was a contemptuous beast. A true mount for a knight.

They pushed on. Over head, Leatha, goddess of the night spread her dark cloak over the world. Meleki's woods were dark and challenging with the giant trees standing their thousand year guard. Roc's elven eyes were dark, but his elven sight pushed out as he made his way. He paused and looked at the earth at his feet. He touched something then moved on. The woods parted and Roc made his way into the clearing, wading his way through the dry, knee high tall grass. His elven hearing cast out like a fisherman's net for any sound. His lungs drew in air and expelled it softly, testing it, tasting it, feeling it. "Someone has been here recently." He spoke to the ruined stone chapel before him. It's shattered walls sank into the moss covered earth. Vines, stripped by Hauge and Chinook of its leaves, clung to the stone like an age old spider's web. It had no roof, and only one wall stood higher than Roc's chest. Large carved stone blocks lay scattered and hidden in the tall grass. Roc eyed it sharply and then the surrounding ring of trees. "I smell a fire. Some one isn't far off."

Frito stepped around him. "Wonderful." He mumbled. Frito found what seemed to be the entrance and stepped in. Vine stems lined the floor. Thin, breeze ridden reeds pushed from the cracks in the stone. There was no furniture, no pews. There was no sign of inhabitants save for a lone imprint on the far standing wall.

Shadows loomed and fell to the floor as Achillia's torch was brought around. She stepped beside Frito and looked at the mark on the wall. "Ura, goddess of Chaos." The knight outlined the shape with her hand, outlining what Frito already saw. "This is her symbol. Obviously it was imprinted on this wall, probably in silver." She approached it looking it over. "Stripped by looters after the temple was destroyed."

Roc growled. "Tell us something we don't know."

Frito put out a hand to quiet the Dragonslayer. He looked to Achillia hoping that she would continue. "What the looters probably didn't know," She said as she drew her long sword. "Was this." She tapped the tip of her sword to the stone floor at the foot of the image and it rang like a bell.

Roc moved forward looking at the square of stone in astonishment. "And how did you know about that?"

Very politely Achillia bowed with a nod. "My lord, I am a knight of Uko. The magic bars protecting that cache attracted me like a load stone."

Frito smiled. "Roc, Achillia is probably the second best source of information on Ura."

Achillia looked offended. "Second?"

"Don't forget our boy, Paradox." Roc growled.

Achillia shook her head. "I would believe that he would be the least informed." Frito paused a moment and could only agree.

Roc tapped the stone with his foot. It sounded dull and prosaic. "And what is it, a secret tomb?"

"That, I do not know; However, I don't think it is very big."

"Can you open it?"

"I think that yourself, my lord, would prove more suited for that." She nodded reverently to him.

Roc snorted and looked at the space. He motioned with his arms for more room for swinging space and withdrew his heavy hammer. He glanced at Frito who was staring intently. Frito suddenly broke his stare and looked at Achillia. He then turned his back. Roc glanced at Achillia who was oblivious to what Frito was up to. He straightened to his full height and looked at her. "Are you sure about this?"

"Sure about what?"

"Smashing my way in here."

Suddenly Achillia looked rather insulted. "My lord, what your saying is…"

Roc held up a large gauntleted hand remembering the discussion he had earlier with Frito about arguing Achillia. "I'm just mentioning the idea that It would be just like the followers of Ura to…"

Achillia smiled politely. "My lord Dragonslayer. I have dealt with several temples of Ura. Some are trapped and some are not. Some I can foresee and circumvent, others I could not and with the blessing of Uko I was able to handle the situation. I have already broken the two wards that protected that stone. I will admit they were of considerable potency. If there is anything else in there, it is beyond my powers to detect." She cocked her head and dwelled on the small space. "However, there may be something in there that they may be trying to protect, or merely an elaborate trap."

Roc looked rather annoyed and appealed to his cousin. "Dwayne, do you want in?"

Frito glared out into the darkness. Achillia was a knight and a proud one. For Roc to question her and Frito to intercede was an insult to her and her god of the highest order. *However,* He thought, *this is my quest. I have to see it my way.* Slowly he turned to his cousin. "Roc, I have already gotten what I needed to know." Then he looked Achillia. "My centre pulls me to open that space and destroy whatever icon there may be in there. But it is no crime to worship the goddess of Chaos. Unless the cult broke some law then it was wrong of Father Fostric's predecessor to run them off. We have no evidence to say the temple broke the law. I say leave it be…for now. I know your hate of Paradox, Achillia, but I know that your are a knight true to justice."

Achillia nodded in agreement. "You speak true." Behind her, Roc threw up his hands and she glanced back to him. "Lord Frito is correct. We have learned much."

Roc looked to Orrin hoping that he might have caught it. He didn't.

Frito turned and looked back into the dark woods. "This temple is fully active. They may have destroyed the house, but not the temple. So now we figure out how to find the members of the temple."

Roc took a deep solid breath understanding. "Okay, that is something that I can do."

Achillia looked at him. "Do you know where to find them?"

Roc smiled showing all of his teeth. "They shall come to me."

Roc turned and dropped to one knee. He felt the weight of his hammer in his hand. He looked at the thickness of the stone floor and tried to judge the amount of force he was going to need. He didn't want to pulverize it in fear of possibly damaging what ever was underneath. Two blows, he thought. Two short, sharp blows.

He raised his hammer quickly and Frito called to him. "Roc, be careful."

Roc looked up to the dark elf still watching the woods. He shrugged off the idea and brought his hammer down. He was the Dragonslayer, careful was not his way.

Magic hammer impacted with magic bars with a off tone clang. Roc's elven ears rang with a piercing wail that made his teeth ache. He squinted and ignored it and raised his hammer for its second blow. The stone was glowing red from the angry magic of Roc's hammer. It sparked white as the hammer came again and clashed against stone with a piercing tone. A spider's web spread instantly across the stone face and the angry glow seemed to seep into the cracks, outlining the spider's web.

The stone hissed and spat steam, missing the Slayer's face by a breath—his elvish speed saving him. Roc reeled, jerking back from the plume that erupted from the stone spun web and stood quickly to his feet. His eyes blazed green at the shattered stone. Its plume wavered, faltered, and then died.

Achillia unfolded her arms. "Relax Lord Dragonslayer." She said off handedly. "It is a ruse tactic. Harmless."

Roc looked up at her with a twisted snarl. "Why didn't you warn me?" He barked.

"There was nothing to warn." She said simply. "Now that you've broken it, let us open it."

Roc glanced at Frito who was gazing mindlessly out into the dark. "And what are you doing?"

Frito looked back over his shoulder. He went to speak and then thought better of it and resumed watching the woods. Roc shook his head and looked back to the stone. He knelt down and tried to gingerly pick out the shards with gauntleted fingers, but the steel couldn't grip the stone. He made up his face and mailed up his fist and punched through with a crunch. With a twist, he wretched his hand free and large black spiders flowed from the hole after.

Roc jumped to his feet and back peddled with a gasp. Achillia lowered her sword. Frito whirled about and froze where he stood.

Frito didn't like spiders.

Roc suddenly realized that it was only spiders the size of a fist and lunged forward.

"Roc! No!" Achillia screamed. "Don't step on them!"

Either she was too late or Roc ignored her as he came crashing down with his giant foot on top of one. Almost magically, the spider shifted with impossible speed out from under Roc's foot, over to the side avoiding the terrible stomp and leaped neatly and smoothly to the top of Roc's foot. Roc quickly shook it free and it flung to the far side of the room. It bounded against the low wall and charged at Frito who still hadn't moved.

"Avoid them!" Achillia shouted to Roc stepping out of the way. "Don't fight them!"

"What in blazes an I supposed to do?" Roc did a quick two step and bounced around the crawling horrors. Roc reached under his sash to a secret pouch. "I'm gonna try this!" With a sudden draw he pulled free a red crystal.

Achillia pointed the tip of her sword at a spider heading right at her and a lick of lightning leapt from the end and turned it into a crisp eight legged lump of carbon.

"Flaring castles of burning king's thrones," Roc chanted and his left fist burst into flame. "Feel the heat of the my Fire-stone!" A cone of fire leapt from his hand and left a burning path with its touch. The spiders danced out of the flames, unscathed.

Frito still hadn't moved and a lone spider silently and swiftly charged from behind him, stepped though him, and kept going.

Roc snapped forward with a sudden stomp and caught a spider unaware. "Ha!" He shouted at the glitch that remained.

Orrin sat perched on a short wall as three spiders climbed their way to him. Frito suddenly moved. With a hollow, echoing voice he shouted at Orrin and the young elf responded. He jammed his pole into the floor and levered himself over into Frito's catching arms just as he became solid form. The spiders turned, sensing Frito's sudden presence and converged on him.

Frito really, really hated spiders.

Frito couldn't phantom walk with the boy in his arms and for love nor money could he remember the spell that was good for killing spiders. He chanted the first spell that came to mind and a ring of fire spread around him but the spiders stepped through it as if it wasn't there.

Roc suddenly lunged forward, stomping on spiders who paid him no mind. Achillia did the same, but the spiders moved forward, trained on The Ninefingers.

Frito closed his eyes and chanted. He felt his lungs vibrate and his teeth rattle. Air pulled into his nose and the spell was ready.

A spider was on his pant leg.

Frito bellowed with a horrible noise that shook the walls. The spiders fell back, rolling into little hairy balls. Frito didn't move, and neither did the spiders.

The tip of Achillia's sword touched one and it was indeed dead. She looked at the hole where the spiders had crawled from and then to Frito. "I am sorry."

Frito blinked and looked about, breathing normally as he relaxed slightly. He looked at her as he set the boy down. "Why?"

"I should've checked more carefully."

Frito looked to his pant leg were the spider had crawled. There was a hole the size of a coin where it had bitten him. "How? What was there to check?" He gathered up the pant leg and exposed the armor underneath. "I didn't know and neither did Roc." He rose to a stand and looked out into the forest.

Achillia straightened. Knights could not lie, or be lied to.

Frito realized his mistake and turned to her. "I..." Was all he could get out.

She shook her head in near shame. "You wanted to let me make my mistake." Knights shamed quite easily.

"No!" Frito glared at her. "I suspected something, yes," That was true. "Mostly paranoia. We're dealing with Ura, her favorite pastime is playing games with knights." That was also true. "Do you think I would've let Roc stick his hand in there if I knew there were...[ICK], spiders in there?" Obviously true. "I told you, that the murder of Oustrand and his wife was not a simple one. We have to be extremely careful." He looked out to the woods again. "However, Roc's plan worked. There was an alarm on the vault. We have company coming."

"What?" Roc moved forward and listened. "Wardogs." He cursed. "Quicker than I thought."

Achillia listened but heard nothing "Can you hear them?" Roc nodded. He could almost hear them transforming from simple, stupid farm dogs and sheep dogs into beasts of hel as they ran through the woods. "How many?"

"Lots." Roc turned, taking charge. "Orrin! In the corner. Stay near by." He looked at Frito. "Anything?" His Nih sight scanned the heavens. "They see us."

Achillia looked up at the circling Joncrow and then to Frito. "A temple of Ura, right under the noses of the people of Rendon."

Frito cocked his head still watching the bird. "Maybe."

Roc looked at it as well. "How long has it been watching us?"

"Just flew in."

"Down it."

Achillia glared at Frito as he stooped over and pushed his fingers into the grass. "Are you saying these people knew?" Achillia felt her centre filling with anger. "These people...were part of the temple?"

Frito took up a small stone. "Maybe." He looked up at the Joncrow weighing the stone in his hand. "I'm saying some might have known about it, supported it. These people are nearby. Oustrand was well known." Frito thought a moment and then said: "The whole town knows about the daughter and Fostric remembered the details of this place a little too readily. I don't think he was part of the temple, but he might have suspected it and feared trying to oust it a second time. He probably hoped we would wipe them out for good. Others ignored it, didn't know...or insulted it."

"Is that what happened to Oustrand?" Achillia's centre was cooling. Her anger still there but now more defined. "He insulted the temple, so they killed him?"

"I doubt he knew they existed." Frito looked at the stone. "That's why I want to talk to these people."

"I'm glad of that." Roc cut in sardonically. "'Cause they're getting closer. If your done flapping your lips, nail the bird. The less they know the better."

Frito looked to the circling Joncrow. "In a tic." He said touchily. Frito put the stone in his mouth, rolling it about on his tongue for a beat and spat it back into his hand. He whispered to the stone a magic secret and leaned back slowly cocking his arm with the stone perched between his thumb and forefinger. With a snap of his arm, it flew with an unerring arch and caught the Joncrow in the head. Its silhouette circled with dead locked wings and crashed into the shadowed forest.

"S'nice." Roc nodded, them looked back to Orrin. "You, get out of sight."

Orrin had already thought of that and had just been waiting for his cue. He huddled in his corner with his field staff running through his legs and opened up his Kamri, his power of the mind, and sent out a simple suggestion. An idea rippling in the air, that he was merely, not there. This trick for all practical purposes, was complete invisibility. Roc looked to the horses who were beginning to sense the presence of the wardogs and started fidgeting. Roc motioned to Frito who nodded.

"Horse!" Frito called and the war-steed stepped into reality. "Get them out of here." Wardogs were notorious for eating horses.

Horse complied, scooping up the reigns in his teeth of each of the other horses and stepped out of reality with them. Frito nodded.

Roc only wished that Horse could take Orrin with him but knew it was impossible. "Achillia..." He cut off abruptly, quickly checking the sky for more spies. Finding nothing, he resumed. "Achillia, you stop the dogs. I will stand here, you to the right and Dwayne, you to the left. With our backs to the temple, they will be forced to face us here, in front." Roc looked back to where Orrin should have been. "Orrin keep tabs on them as they approach. Tap into me and let me know." Orrin nodded. "You be ready." Roc pointed at his cousin. "Achillia will get you your moments to talk."

Frito nodded and called magic to his will. He felt his hand charge with power as he readied himself. He tried to look casual, aloof and not too worried. He didn't want to pose a threat. He wanted them to concentrate on Achillia and Roc who were certainly looking the part.

Achillia could hear the dogs rushing closer. She felt the weight of her sword lighten and warm in her hand. It sensed the coming dogs and welcomed them. Her sword was Ou'cry, the Skycracker, a knight's weapon. It was vibrating softly in her hand, humming with power, listening to the heavy foot falls of the Wardogs.

The dogs came.

They suddenly leapt from out of the bushes barking. They held back until the last minute and then let the full force of their howling, fearsome bark be known. Their hanging forked tongues dripped with caustic foam. Their black, puss bleeding eyes glistened in the torch light. Their massive wet shiny bodies thundered into the field with their spiked tails lashing behind them.

Achillia jerked back her immediate motion and waited the half beat until all the dogs were in sight. Her eyes flashed with lightning as she raised Ou'cry above her head with a shout and she burst with white, paralyzing light. "In The Name Of Uko And The Might Of Okshiru I Order You To HOLD!"

The dogs suddenly reared up and bowled over backwards from the sudden flash. They rolled and found their feet and stood their places, shying from the white light, wanting to push forward, but unable. Achillia's light faded and only torch light remained, but the dogs held their places.

Roc's ears perched as he heard Orrin's invisible voice of Kamri whisper into his ear. "Straight on, eh? Four are sli-ding about to the rear to check out what might be there. There are like, twen-ty one in all. One angling to your left is the one to talk to, eh?" And then the young elf was silent and again not there.

Three men stepped from the woods with torches in their hands held above their heads. They weren't dressed for fighting. One had thrown a padded shirt on his back and an old footman's helm on his head. He stood on the right and brandished a foot man's pike, twirling it in his hands as he spoke. "You are not welcome here." He spoke quietly, in a deep voice that rumbled from his large body. He was a local, standing almost two and a half paces in height with long uncombed blond hair draped over his broad shoulders. "This is holy ground." He and the other two held their place at fifteen paces from Roc.

Roc looked at the one in the center. His barrel chest was covered with heavy blonde curly hair like a rug. His long hair skirted around the bald spot of his head. He was lifting and weighing his sword for fighting. Roc ignored him and looked to the one on the left. The others were panting from the run up. They were wired, waiting to fight, but this one, dressed in a simple throw robe and silver chain belt was quite calm. He held his axe with both hands across his waist. A rest position, not an attack position. Roc snorted and sneered. "This ground is my ground." He said contemptuously to the one on the left. "Who says it is not?"

The two wanting to fight motioned forward, but the one on the left spoke and when he did, the other two held their place. "And who says this? My lord."

Roc knew then that Orrin was correct. "I am Roc, the Dragonslayer. This is my realm." Roc lifted his hammer. "Do you challenge my authority?"

The three visibly paled. This wasn't their plan. The spiders were to soften up their opponents if not kill. The dogs were to take care of who was left. According to theory, all they had to do was to loot and desecrate the bodies. But the man on the left quickly resumed his calm. His eyes flashed about. This was Roc and there was no doubt to that. But where was his vaunted Dragonguard? The two beside him? What could he want? "A blessid pardon my great lord." He bowed and the others followed his example. "We did not know. We beg your grace."

"Denied." Roc said sharply. "I have none. I should wash your mouth out with my fist for saying so!"

The man on the left bowed again. "My apologies my great lord."

Roc raised an arm. "All of you! Come out. You cannot hide!" He scanned as one by one, fourteen men and three women stepped out of the bush. "You!" He pointed. "Come out as well. I speak to you all!" Reluctantly, a small face peered out and then stood to his feet and crawled out.

Achillia's centre sang. It was a boy! Ura recruits children!

The third again bowed as he spoke. "I am Ethrod. I am your servant. You, my lord are welcome as always, but the knight is not."

Roc glanced at Frito and then realized he was talking about Achillia. "The knight is with me."

"Please my lord. My mistress is disturbed at the acts of this knight (His voice was not contemptuous for fear of Roc's wrath) desecrating her ground."

Achillia's centre flared and she spoke with anger. "How dare you!" She forced her centre to calm and refrained herself.

"As you must know, my lord," Ethrod spoke to Roc. "We are humble Children of Ura, and wish no trouble."

Roc stepped forward and Ura's children stepped back. "No? No trouble?" Roc said snarling, closing the gap. "It's a bit late for that." Roc eyed each one. Roc stepped closer and snatched the footman's pike from the first man's hands faster than the man could react. "Your existence annoys me."

Ethrod looked about and then to Roc. "My great lord, (Contempt tingled in his tone) following Ura is no crime."

Roc's burning green eyes fell on him. "No?" Roc eyes shifted to the shaft in his hands. Its smooth wood slid beneath his fingers as his hands spread out across it. "No crime?" The shaft splintered with a sudden crack as Roc snapped it in half. "Did I say there was a crime?" He threw the pieces to the footman's feet.

Orrin's tiny voice spoke to his ear. *"Roc. He is thin-king of chal-len-ging you, eh? Like, he sees no guards and might try to take you. He knows magic, eh?"*

Roc stored this bit of information and stepped closer to Ethrod. The blond man was taller than Roc by a breath but the Dragonslayer, still looked down on him. "You anger me."

"An explanation is what we ask my great lord."

Roc tilted his head and his eyes softened their green and they melted to their deep dark brown. "I need not explain myself, but answer this question: A man and his wife has been murdered, what do you know of it?"

Ethrod stepped back but didn't take his eyes from Roc's. "Nothing my lord."

Frito's voice rang suddenly sharp and clear. "You dare lie to The Dragonslayer with a knight present!"

Roc glanced back at Frito and then to Ethrod. "What say you to that?" He said gently. "Penalty for lying..." Roc's hand balled into Ethrod's robe and pulled him from the circle and tossed him easily to the ground. "Is Death!" Roc seethed, drawing his buckler and hammer. "Answer me, feck!"

Ethrod laid back in the grass propped on his elbows. He looked up to Roc with spitting disdain. "Who are you to challenge my mistress?"

"Roc, he's go-ing to cast!" Orrin whispered. "Behind you, they move!"

Roc whirled brandishing his hammer. "I! I challenge!" The closing circle pulled back still afraid. Roc looked down at Ethrod. "It appears that you challenge me."

Ethrod's voice trembled with power. "You over step your bounds, Roc." He spat. "Your realm ends at Ura's feet." Ethrod looked at him. "You dare accuse me? You know not what you do!" Anger swept with power and his unholy magic came to being. Ethrod floated magically to his feet. "You will not tempt Ura!" Power swirled with magic and twisted the air with sound. Ethrod lifted a pace in the air on his magic. His hair sprawled wildly and his eyes burned with hate.

Frito raised his hand and there was silence.

Ethrod's eyes were cooled. His hair dropped limply to his shoulders. The magic swirling was gone. "Yes I do." Frito smiled at him, unimpressed by his display of magic. "Allow me to introduce myself. I am Dwayne, of the house of Hammerstrike. I am the Ninefingers." Frito's smile faded. "I am the Devilslayer." Ethrod sank to the ground. "This is Achillia. Of the house of Avenger, the Goblinslayer."

Frito finished introductions and Ethrod's centre howled. *Why would Roc bother with puny guards if he walks with Achillia and the Ninefingers?*

"You lied to Roc." Frito went on. "Bold face." Frito stepped closer. "Your life is forfeit as of now by law." Frito's crimson eyes of Nih seemed to open as his interrogation began. "Your flock..." Frito's hand presented them. "They are accessories to the crime." Ethrod felt a tremble as his centre filled with fear. Where was Ura? Where was her knight? Frito went on. "Dragonslayer asked a question. There was a murder. You knew about it."

"No my lord." He whispered quickly.

"You knew!" Frito howled, his crimson eyes flaring at the words. "You knew who did it!"

"No." He whimpered.

"You saw him, you met him!"

"No, I did not." He pleaded. "I am innocent."

"You knew his name!" Frito stepped at him and he stepped back. "You met him, spoke to him, knew he was coming, knew his mission and even gave him directions!" Frito's hands flashed and gripped Ethrod's robes pulling him down to his height. "You know me! You cannot lie to me!" Ethrod sobbed in Frito's hands. His knees buckled and he sank, melted at Frito's feet. Frito suddenly wanted nothing more to do of him. The man was filth. Frito could see him talking to the assassin before the deed with a smile. Nodding his head with conspiracy. Sleeping well knowing the deed was done. But Frito felt his pain. Ura had left him. He was a man suddenly abandoned by his god and Frito knew the feeling too well. But Ura left him because he was weak. If Ethrod had held his faith and not given to fear, Ura would not have left him. Frito could imagine Ura bestowing a full range of powers on the simple servant just for laughs, but even the goddess of Chaos would not have just dropped him if he had shown some spine.

He released him, not wanting to touch him any more and Ethrod crumpled to a weeping heap. Frito looked around him to the Children of Ura. They were broken and afraid. The toys that Ura had given them were to handle other locals, not the Dragonslayer, not the Devilslayer, not the Goblinslayer. Frito looked at the man at his feet. His Nih eyes of red cooled leaving only his silhouette to the torch light. "Why?"

Ethrod looked up. His face was pale and wet and his eyes rimmed red with pity. "My...my lord?"

"Why?" Frito repeated.

Ethrod suddenly looked to the grass as if he had almost forgotten. But he knew. "The girl." He said dreamily to his hands in the grass. "The girl." He looked expecting Frito to understand. He didn't. Ethrod looked to his flock milling about with their heads bowed in shame. The dogs were sitting, staring at him with intensity. "The girl." He mumbled. "Her voice...it was," He looked into Frito's shadow hidden face. "Beautiful."

They had to silence the voice. They had to see an end to it. Child of the gods, Frito thought. Okshiru had blessed them. For all the others forgotten by the god of sky and sea, those living ordinary lives couldn't go on with a little girl who walked their streets with the great god of sky and sea beside her. Instead of looking within themselves for their own blessings, they turned to destroy another's. They prayed for an answer. Ura gave them hers. "Where is he?" Frito said gravely.

"South...I know not where he came."

Frito bent at the knee. "Not good enough."

"I don't know...I swear." Ethrod pleaded, hoping to redeem himself with someone, some how.

Frito shook his head. "Where..."

Ethrod took a long breath. "Brewster...our sister temple." and that was all.

Frito turned and walked back to the temple. He looked at Roc and Achillia. "Lets get out of here." He said quietly. Roc looked to Achillia for an answer. Her face was still and set. If she knew, and Roc thought she did, she wasn't telling.

Horse suddenly stepped into reality leading the reigns of the other horses. Horse glared at the wardogs still sitting about. The dogs paid her, and the other horses, no mind. They only gazed intently at Ethrod, still on his knees. Ethrod watched Frito mount. "My lord." He called out, reaching for a hand. "What of me?"

Frito looked at him stolidly. *Thinking of yourself?* "You're a dead man. You will be dead within the hour by Ura's own hand for your failure and weakness in her faith. She didn't fail you. You failed you. You should have looked within yourself before looking at others. A lesson learned too late." Frito felt his centre spilling over with pity. "I feel for you." He said compassionately. "You follow a cruel mistress." *As do I,* he thought. Frito, immune to Kamri, glanced back at Orrin, still for all practical purposes not there, and watched him mount his horse. He then looked to the children. "Your fate lies in the mercy of your Mistress. I would imagine her sparing some of you." *If only for kicks.* He thought as he spurred his horse and trotted on. Roc, Orrin and Achillia followed in line.

There was quiet in Meleki's forest. Only the soft hiss of the trees swaying to Hauge's gentle night winds disturbed her woods. Frito listened to the sound of Horse's hooves on the hard earth. He concentrated on the methodical plod the shoes made. When the sound of wardogs tearing human flesh came to his elven ears, he tried to block it out with the sound of his horse's trot.

"You plan worked My Lord." Achillia spoke over the screams that she could hear.

Frito glanced back at her. His angry, elvish eyes glared back at her. "Don't be facetious." He hissed.

"My intent was not to challenge you my lord." She quickly explained. "That is not like me."

Frito looked back to the road as his eyes cooled. No, it wasn't like her. "I am sorry."

"I have to comment on your handling of the situation." She spoke on oblivious to the screaming and the howling. "You handled that like a ranking Archknight."

Frito glanced back at her. She wasn't kidding. She doesn't kid, ever. "I picked up a few tips from the job." He mumbled.

Orrin's horse bumped his leg. He looked at the boy cringing at the screams. Frito reached out and gripped the boy's arm. Orrin didn't ease his white-knuckle grip on the reigns.

"That is not what I'm trying to say." She went on.

"Achillia," Frito began. "I am not a knight."

"You knew Ethrod was lying."

"That was obvious."

"Was it?" She pressed him. "You're telling me my business."

Frito looked to the road. The screams had quieted down and all he could hear was a lone whimper. Frito looked back over his shoulder at the tall woman knight. "What are you trying to say?"

Achillia cocked an eyebrow. "I'm not trying to say anything."

Roc stopped his horse abruptly. "I smell a fire." He grunted. "Not far." He had been listening to the conversation and felt it time for a change. He had smelled this fire for some time and only now decided to announce it.

Frito was quietly relieved. "What do you think?"

Roc shook his head. "I doubt if it has anything to do with the Children of Ura. They came from the east. This is west."

Frito looked sharply, testing the air and nodding. He glanced to the woman knight. "Achillia?"

She decided to play the game. "Let us see this." She spurred her horse quickly and galloped off with Orrin closely in pursuit. Roc and Frito lumbered along with their giant clydesdales. The heavy horses thundered, building momentum to catch up to the lighter, faster horses. Horse seemed to suddenly burst with speed and slowly moved along side of Achillia, but she only smiled and took the lead again. Having proven whose horse was the fastest, she slowed to a trot.

Frito pulled on his reins and brought his horse to a canter and then trot. He breathed deeply, taking in the air around him and let it out slowly. "Not far." He whispered, stopped and then dismounted.

Roc snorted as he dismounted. "Why are you whispering? He heard us coming." Roc took up the lead to his horse and lead him off the side of the road. The undergrowth was small and sparse and Roc had little trouble moving through. He fettered his horse and moved on. Achillia followed his example. Roc's wide hand waved at her torch to douse its light before moving on. Achillia took a heavy wax cloth and wrapped the head of the torch to snuff it. Suddenly she was in darkness. She moved forward slightly, crouching low to feel her way. She felt Frito's hand under her arm to guide her a bit easier through the wood. Roc was almost silent as he moved. Passing quickly with out a motion of the pine covered forest floor and only a slight clink from his heavy amour he disappeared into the quiet night. Achillia had lost him, as did Frito. She looked at the Nih elf beside her and whispered every so slightly. "What is he doing?"

"It is a game we are playing. We can smell the fire but also we can smell the fire builder. Achillia caught on as Frito rose to his full height, pushing aside a branch as he did. "C'mon up." He said out loud.

Achillia rose glaring at him as she did. "What are you doing?"

"Old trick." Frito mumbled as he kicked up the small twigs and pine needles. "You'll see." He smiled. "We did it when we were younger." He looked back over his shoulder. "Common Orrin, don't hang."

"Frito, there is some-thing Roc should know, eh?" Orrin announced coming forward. "I know who is around the fire."

Frito nodded, looking through the trees. He could see the glinting light of the fire. "Who?" Frito challenged, already knowing.

"Like, your bro-ther, eh?" Orrin smiled. "Fryto, the flame."

Frito smiled. "Lets go see. Frito made no moves to quiet his approach, walking straight towards the fire light. Achillia caught a glimpsing shadow of Roc's giant armored body slipping past—sliding across the fire site to the rear. Frito was the distraction, tramping loudly from one side while Roc prepared to attack from the other. Achillia came closer, kicking up flurries of pine needles following Frito's example. She could see the fire in its clearing and a figure moving about it. Armor glimmered from its polished shine. The figure pointed to the east with great theatrical poise, and then pointed to the west with the same over acted exaggeration. He seemed oblivious to their approach and even more so to Roc the Dragonslayer crouched behind a sodded log. She looked at the man prancing about his fire and recognized him as Frito's younger brother, Fryto, knight of Meleki.

Roc lifted from his position and slowly slithered towards the fire. "Fire of life, fire of death," Fryto spoke as if in a trance. "Spark to light, wood to burn. Give to me your warm breath. Glowing my heart that I did earn." He danced around his fire and it danced to his stupid song.

"You don't know it…" Dragonslayer said raising to his full height. "But you're no poet."

"What?" Fryto realized that he wasn't alone and shrilled as he dived to a pile of equipment lying on the ground. "Come at me you nasty and taste my burning axe!" With a singing of steel his great war axe leapt out into the air. It glided in his hands and in its wake left a banner of crackling flame. It crashed into Dragonslayer's own steel buckler. "Aha. take that." He drew back and slashed again and again. "Take that, that and especially that!" Dragonslayer growled and carried his attack, pushing into the fiery knight with his might and ferocity. The man only retorted. "Think you could creep up on me! Well, wrong you are!" He kept stepping back and Dragonslayer continued to step forward.

Frito listened to the sound of steel ringing together as he led his horse out from the low hanging branches and sat himself several paces away from the fire raging at least seven paces in the air. Achillia and Orrin followed him.

"You beast!" Fryto chortled. "You can't take nay for an answer eh?" He shifted and blocked the Dragonslayer's blows. "Then have at ye then!" He shouted and continued stepping back.

"Look out for the fire!" Orrin shouted, but it seemed to late as the flaming knight backed away from the Dragonslayer's buckler and hammer and into the fire.

"Hahaha!" He laughed from within the flames. "Come get me! I wave pig guts at your ancestry! I wipe nose snot on your undies! Is that your face or are you wearing a dog's ass on your neck?" His form could be seen from within the raging flames.

Dragonslayer growled and charged into the flames—a beat later, he charged out, tripping and stumbling over the logs of the fire. Scores of sparks, smoke and steam flowed from the creases of his armor. "If you can't stand the heat, get out of the kitchen! Are my flame's embrace too tight for the Mighty Dragonslayer? Come! I smear curdled milk on the walls of your horse stables! I fill your home with loving kittens! Watch as I taunt you with lurid gestures! I pucker my asshole at your leftovers! Come and fight Fryto the flame, ward of Hammerstrike and all around nice guy!"

"It is I you oppose." Roc bellowed over the crackle of the flames. "Taunt me if you dare!" Dragonslayer slid his hammer to his sash and slipped the harness from his back and let if fall to the ground after sliding out his great sword. "For anger sings my prose!" He shielded his face with one hand and wielded the sword with the other and stepped as close to the raging glow as he could stand. With a slow swipe, he let the five foot blade slip into the flames. "Now you face The Dragonslayer!"

The mad man screamed and leapt from the flames, stumbling into the grass with a crackling hiss. "Whoa, I've gone and pissed him off now." He sat up and limply laid his war axe across his lap. He hooked his thumbs along the edge of his dolman and with a pull slid it from his head. "I'm not one to fence with a lyrical slaughterer." He smiled, panting though his grin. "My Lady." He bowed slightly to Achillia and she returned his gesture. "Orrin?" He said looking at the boy. "Isn't this a school night?"

Orrin smiled his beaming charm in a reply of "G'night."

Fryto turned to his older brother. "Well Frito, or Dwayne?" He brushed his hand against his nose. "What goes with you."

"Trouble." He answered simply.

"What else is new? Were ever you go, trouble follows. Look even now the Dragonslayer stands behind you." Roc sat with a clash beside Frito. "As I can see it, it is little coincidence that Roc the Dragonslayer, ruler of all he sees, and Achillia, from the house of Avenger would ever share the same spot unless it was a time of crisis or mutual heat. So since it is not the end of the world and they are both wearing yards of steel, then it is of another matter entirely. So, I am correct in stating that you know about Friska?"

"What would that be?" Dragonslayer grumbled as he took a boda from Orrin and popped the stopper with his thumb.

"I was on my way to Fanrealm to respond to the summons of the house when I heard about Friska the wind." He said gazing into the fire. "He has caused great trouble yesterday, and Chiron, of the house of Morrin has asked me to look into it. Seems he and several other followers raided the shire of Sugartown."

Achillia leaned forward. "That is my providence. What has he there?"

"What it was had little to do with good." Fryto went on. "Seems he got into a heated argument. Declared that everyone in the town knew nothing but lies and went about to prove his point. He burned the temple for what he said was their own good. When the priest tried to interfere, his followers gave him a good beating." They all looked to him aghast save Dragonslayer who drank his wine. "They say he was headed this way and I hoped to cut him off. My question is, what is he doing around here?"

Frito mentally drew a line across a mental map. "Following me…Sugartown is in the way."

Achillia looked drawn as her eyebrows formed a ridge across her eyes. "But why there? Why in Sugartown?"

"Does not your memory serve you?" Fryto went on. "A double handful of years, ten years to be more numerical, when we used the grand treasure of Agiath and rebuilt the great halls of Sugartown? They hailed it in the name of Frito, and he being, at that time, the modest senior knight present, placed it in the loving, but well disciplined care of Achillia?"

Frito nodded not taking his eyes from the flames. Achillia looked up and watched the light play on the dark elf's face. "My lord," She called him. "The halls still echo your name." Achillia spoke quietly, realizing what must have happened.

Frito looked suddenly at Dragonslayer and then to Fryto and Achillia. "But Roc was there ten years ago. In fact it was he who slew Agiath, not me."

"But you gave them the money." Roc looked at him carefully. "Against my advice. That's what they remember. We should have kept it."

"And done what with it?"

"Horde it and look at it, like the big red dragon looks at his gold. Sleep on it, silver for my feet and jewels for my head!" Dragonslayer stretched out in the grass and closed his eyes.

Frito hissed like the wood in the fire. "That maniac..." He grimaced and then looked to Fryto. "And he heads south." Frito muttered to himself and Fryto nodded. "Shit." He cursed under his breath. Could it be that Ura had planed to use his brother as her knight? What a lovely sight, the Knight of Hauge the wind, battling his brother in her secret temple before her flock! How sweet a victory!

"I do not understand." Achillia spoke out. "Has Friska left the faith too?"

"No." Frito shook his head as he spoke. "He has embraced it. He believes that Okshiru has empowered him to slay me."

"This is madness! Okshiru could not ever be so cruel as to pit brother against brother."

"None the less. Friska comes for me."

"But why?"

"For my sin." He said quietly and gazed the field about him. "This would be a good place to fight him."

"Would you fight him?"

Frito looked ruefully at Achillia and shook his head. "Perhaps I can fight him with words."

"Words words words..." Dragonslayer growled. "Bust him in the teeth."

93

"And what makes you so sure that he will find you here?" Fryto asked.

"He'll know." Frito could almost hear Ura calling him. "This would be too good for her to pass up." Frito looked up and felt the cool breeze on his face. Was Hauge, the fickle wind, even aware that his knight was being led by another god?

Fryto nodded and looked at his fire. "Then camp here and sleep. I will hold watch. I have quite a bit of work to do before the night is out."

"Forget it." Roc grumbled. "I've seen your watching."

Achillia leaned forward. "And just what is it that you're doing?"

"My penance." He said proudly. "I must hold a giant bon fire in tribute to my mistress. When I was the knight of Kemoto, I burned the forests Dwemoner with my carelessness. Now that I am the Knight of Meleki, as a tribute, I must burn in her forests and not harm a single tree."

Simple justice. Frito thought.

Chapter 11

"Can Frita come out and play?"

The wind howled about her shivering body and she clutched tightly at the thin robes she wore. Elves felt not the cold and shivering was a new thing for her. *Why am I cold?* She had no one to ask. *What has happened to me?* Air flowed through winding worm holes, wrapping smoothly and insanely through the stone tunnels that lead to nowhere. Her dark eyes searched the caverns and into the darkened holes. One of them called to her. "Answer me! I shall command you and you shall comply."

"I know you not." Her voice leaked out of her in a tiny whisper.

"Surly you jest." Said the voice with no body. "Am I not Thumber? If not, then who?" The girl shook her head. The laugh ripped at her soul and stripped her centre bare. "Frita, you please me."

The winds howled again, blowing against the tunnels and causing them to moan in agony. "Who calls me?" She shouted not realizing the warmth on her cheeks were her tears running on her face. Her centre swam about inside of her as her thoughts raced in circles. "Why do you frighten me?" There was no answer save the moaning of dark caves about her. She shivered uncontrollably—her jaw clashed against her teeth and her knees clenched tightly to each other. "Thumber," She pleaded. "Where am I now? Where is it you have taken me?"

"To the gates of hel." He said quietly.

"Then why is it that I am here?...If you cannot tell me such, then I beseech you to tell me who I am!" The tunnels moaned at her again. Suddenly she felt alone. The voice was gone and no longer had she the company of a tormentor. She felt her bruises and wounds like lumps of ice beneath her skin. The cold winds lashed against her bones and the cotton of her gown lightly danced against the bare of her legs. She closed her eyes and couldn't tell if they were closed. She opened them again and knew it didn't matter. She was locked in the nightmare realm from which she had no means to escape. Not knowing what to do or where to go, she turned and walked slowly into the first tunnel beside her. Her tiny white feet shuffled and slid against the stone as she stepped into the darkness. Puff balls of warm air billowed about her and she welcomed it. The stench of grimy sweat assailed her and burned her skin. She coughed at the smell that she could almost see. A smell of death.

She shuffled on into the warmth of the darkness for it was better than the cold. Her arms slowly lifted from her body as she felt her way along. Her fingers stumbled over the skips in the stone and her toes tripped over the cracks in the rock.

Her name glided to her in a whisper, gently sliding to her ear. It lead her, and she followed. She could hear tiny creaks of wood, straining and stretching with age. She could hear tiny moans against the wind, grunting from beyond. A tiny, flickering glow of a candle wrapped from around the bend. She slowly inched towards it and peered around the wall.

His body was thin and gaunt with his skin stretched taut on his ribs, exposing each one to sight. The muscles of each arm wrapped tightly about the bones, pulled and flexed with pain. Ugly and twisted steel spikes pushed into his wrists and feet, driven through his limbs into the wood beyond. His head bobbed feebly on a neck too spindly to hold it up. His eyes, swollen and shut, fluttered as his body began to stretch. His lips moved not as he moaned. His body was nailed to the two doors to hold them shut and each time they began to open he murmured in his pain. "Abandon all hope…" He gasped in a tiny whisper that came so readily to her ear as his head bobbed up from strain. "ye who enter here…" And again the doors lost their heave and his neck hung feebly again.

His black blood slowly trickled to the floor forming a small puddle beneath his feet. A thin tongue lashed like a whip beneath the door and continually lapped it up. "By the time of history passes." He whispered sickly. "Of long ago of what I've seen soon to occur." His head held up a moment and he gazed beyond the shadow of the candle. "Be the truth you seek little sister, for it is what I can tell. If it is a lie, then that too is what I have told. And being that neither is accepted as either is believed dwells greatly on your point of perspective." He gasped and moaned as the great door that he held together again tried to open and failed. "I know what plagues you mother…I have dwelled on this time again and discovered the horrid answer to your question." His head fell to his chest and he held still.

Slowly Frita stepped from the darkness and sat beside the candle. She eyed the man and watched his pain for a great time saying nothing. She noticed beside him sat a bucket with a ladle. It had not been there before, but she didn't question its appearance. She took up the ladle and dipped it with water and set it to her lips. In her mouth, it tasted stagnant, but it took the bite from the dryness of her mouth. She dipped it with water again and set it to his. "You quench the eternal desert and I hold your tender soul to my heart, my wife. I grant your boon. The answer rings truth to those who hear lies and to others they fail to hear." His eyes opened slowly and his flat, gray, clouded sight was cast upon her. "I babble uselessly and I make sense to only those who can't understand. You do understand my daughter."

"No." She whispered to his whisper. "I don't understand."

"Then it would seem that all I've said makes great sense to you." She closed her eyes and shook her head, but he went on. "To sleep is horror, for you are most exposed, so you pull covers and quilts about you and hide." He tilted his head and gazed into her eyes with his blind sight. "I see the answer to the question I can't hear. You fear to ask for I shall drive you to the light fantastic and the soft room of screams in eternal madness. Confused…good, then I have told of what to be, is and never will."

"You are mad."

"I am not mad. Not even angry, mother. I am mad in who that sees me mad. Fact is, oh best beloved, as the great hot glow burns high in the bonny blue—the brightest day will cast shadows. You stay because you know not what to do and where to go. I shall not torment you my pretty and I ask you not to pluck out my liver. I have become quite fond of it. I am Quegrestor Thudrested the Weird. Supreme of supreme, dancer of the fine wire and lock of this door. I am the great whisperer of secrets. I am called Weishap. I know everything there is to see and not to see. When you see everything, all at once as I can, you get a mite strange.

"I have a great secret that you know and it is what has been told, and no one remembers because they don't want too. You will ask me who you are because you can't remember, but I tell unto you that you can remember who you are, but you wish not to be it anymore. So you pack your scrambly mind in a pillow and hide in your sleep. This message was sponsored by the dweller of nightmares. Now if you ask me, if you dwell in the muck of a mind, you will go very crazy.

"Don't ask who I am because I will tell you. I know every thing. Plain and simple. That makes me mega cool and ultra amazing. I'll tell you who you are my bride. You are Denice Hammerstrike, daughter of

Lord Hammerstrike the Supergod, one of the original three. You are Frita the cold, knight of Fikor the Snowdog and sister of Dexter, Frito, Fryto, Friska, J'son and J'cob, and cousin to Roc the Dragonslayer. Dexter, the eldest and the first dead; Dwayne/Frito, the once and future Archknight, Knight of Dru; Donald/Fryto, Flaming Knight of Meleki; Daniel/Friska, Inquisitor Knight of Hauge." She shook her head in confusion. "To solve your problem sister, I must go to its source. You call me mad because I show my insanity. I call you mad because you hide it with in you. Your madness is your silence. You're cold because you pull your guilt within you. You are wrapped with guilt.

"I am confusing myself. I will spin a lie of truth for you to misinterpret. When the spectrum of gods came to be, after the great war of your father and his brothers; when dragons were new on the earth and magic was awakened to open eyes—the gods fought and haggled for a place in Worldsend. I came to birth from the spiral of the universe. I was summoned to a body as the gods wished knowledge and appointed me as the answer man. I answered their questions and they used my answers to fight each other and gain their place in heaven. Those who used the most correct answers in the most correct questions received the best place.

"I thought that I was so great, but I had no questions of myself to ask and therefore no answers to place me in Worldsend. I floated for all of eternity. (about two million years give or take, who is to say). I have a body that I cannot use. I am a puppet and no more.

"I looked to Hauth. Great Hauth. He knew the times of long ago from the diary of your father the Supergod. Hauth was a master of all he did. Hauth knew the blade and magic. He knew the Sho-Pa of his mother. He took his power from Okshiru himself in the ranks of his great knights. He was perfect. I summoned him. Hauth unknowingly answered and came to Hel to battle with Augus Trid Dreath, the first devil, and slew him. Hauth was my road to Worldsend.

"But Hauth was not yet ready so I went to Fobotec and gave her my aid. I told her my secrets and she took all of Hel and sat on the throne as Trid Dreath the second. I again summoned Hauth and I betrayed Fobotec for I knew she was too weak for my plans. Hauth slew the second Trid Dreath and unknowingly became the third Trid Dreath. But Hauth was a knight who could not rule the evil he was to destroy, so he left Hel and went home. But I had already planted the seeds of hate in his brain. They grew before his eyes and he saw with a devil's vision.

He raved, ranted, raped his wife and beat his sister. He returned to Hel to rally his troops and took them where Fobotec was too weak to take them; above ground to Mortalroam. The army of Hauth came across your world like the black tide of the sea. Monsterbelly, king second only to Dragonslayer, fell in a fortnight. Dragonslayer was no fool and rallied his forces at the great crystal tower and its impenetrable walls. But Hauth was no fool either as he used my answers like a master, and rained fire from the skies and destroyed the dragons and armies of the Dragonslayer. He took the broken body of the Dragonslayer, tied it to a banner and carried it across the world.

"He crossed the great waters and released Kiupquixdaviduom, the Moaltoian Meca demon, and bound it to his will. Then with his army, he stormed Worldsend.

"It wasn't easy. Even with the right answer, there were too many wrong questions. Many gods sided with Hauth to follow the new order, but many fell against him. There was the new Dragoncaller who even now stands outside of the cosmic balance. His existence is outside of even my answers. In a maneuver that befuddled my best answers, he took Hauth's hand and led him through Worldsend. Okshiru didn't fight at all but only permitted the Dragoncaller to lead Hauth to the Supergod. Then on the wings of the World-dragon, the three crossed alone without me into the gate above all gods, to the god's God.

"And I waited.

"Then the light came. The great white light that opened the dark, green clouds and poured onto the ruined Mortalroam and healed its wounds. Dragonslayer stood reborn and rallied his dragons and men as they awoke from death. Cities built themselves and the people rose from the blood of war and went on living. The armies of Hel were sent back and I was nailed to this door to hold them.

"The Tower, the great castle of Dragonslayer, and the manor of Hauth, still remain destroyed as the light failed to reach them. The Meca demon was again imprisoned and almost everything else turned wrong was made right.

"But why, is what you ask. Why did my plan fail? I didn't fail. I did it all to gain the righteous place. Hauth ruled everything. He ruled the heavens but I put him there. I was the god responsible! I was on top. Hauth was a puppet of the puppet. He didn't use me, I used him. I still am on top. You see a man broken and defeated, But I see a man who is feared beyond all heavens. I gained the attention of God. How many people can say that?

"But now your question is what happened beyond the gate of the gods. It was you father, Lord Hammerstrike who sired you, your five brothers and one who is now dead, met with Hauth and said, 'We're busy right now, come back next week Thursday after ten o'clock.' That is not true, but the lower demons all like to think it is true. But what actually happened was that Hauth was face to face with an entity higher than the Supergod. The one that he simply called, God.

"Hauth ruled Worldsend and Mortalroam and Hel and all points between. But they were worlds fashioned by the hands of man (and woman) and ruled man (and woman) and lived in by man (and woman). You see, after all of that, after ruling the entire heavens, he still was nothing in the eyes of the god's God. A mere pittance beneath His gaze.

"Suddenly Hauth could see clearly. He had been defeated even before he started.

"And you sister, you waited loyally for his return and you forgave him and kissed him and called him brother, because after all of his sin, it didn't compare to yours. Yes! Hauth is Frito, is Dwayne, is the Ninefingers, is the Lord of Lighting, is the Devilslayer, is the Archknight, is Trid Dreath the Third, is a whole slew of other titles that I shall not go into and you were not one to judge him. But you can't remember your sin. You didn't then and you can't now and if I told you, you still wouldn't know because you don't want to know, so I'm not going to bother."

He fell quiet as his narrative ended and her ears rang from the sudden silence. "How kind." She whispered after a long pause. "But then, what sin have you committed to have you nailed at the door to Hel? Surly answering a question is no sin."

"In the eyes of the right question, it is harmless. In the hands of the wrong question. It is death. But that is not your question. You cannot hide from he who sees all. You wish to ask why has Thumber, twister of dreams and crier of the night brought you to this place. Surly it is not to keep me company. I have me for that. He wishes for me to show you your sin. He wishes to hurt you beyond pain and such a small request I shall grant. There is a child behind this door. This child cries for you. You scream to ask: How can a child commit sin to go to Hel? But the crimes of the father, are the crimes of the son."

The giant door heaved again and Weishap moaned and strained against its push. Fingers wiggled like worms through the wedge to find a grip to push wider. Weishap's blood trickled faster as the doors spread wider. A tiny arm wiggled out of the space and a tiny girl's voice cried out for her mother.

Denice screamed hard and lunged from the bed. Lithe arms wrapped about her and held her close, swaying her back and forth as a mother coos a child, stroking her hair and pacifying her fears. "Be quiet my child. Thou art safe." Kathreen whispered in her ear. "I heard you crying in your sleep and I came to see. T'was a bad dream you were having and no more."

Denice relaxed, blinking tightly against the glow of the dim lantern beside her bed. It cast a soft light on Kathreen, leaving her tender face, all the softer. "My lady..." Denice sobbed as her eyes filled with tears. "What frightened me so? What was it?"

"Child, t'was a dream, a phantom." Denice griped Kathreen's arm as she leaned against the bedhead. "Fear not." Kathreen went on. "I shall stay with you." She smiled gently and wiped Denice's tear away with her hand.

"Kathreen, you are so sweet to me. You know me not."

"And you know you not. And if I did know you, thence I would love you and care for you the same. Thou soothed my pain this afternoon." Her hand passed lightly where her right breast should have been. "That tis all I need to know." Her hand reached out and slid lightly to the side of Denice's head and into her black silk hair. "Thou art friendly elf folk." Her hand brushed lightly against Denice's ear and tickled her.

Denice reached up and touched her other ear. The distinctive point it came to made her race obvious. "I wish I could say from memory that I was," Denice said. "But it seems that I discover as you."

Kathreen reached out and took Denice's hand from her ear. "Then this is what we discover." She said examining the woman's hand. "Your wounds hide your hands. I look at them now and see they are hard and calloused as a man's." Kathreen lightly stroked the back, "And they are strong and defined. Thou art a swordsman, perhaps a knight. They heal as you did me." Denice shook her head unknowingly. Kathreen continued her probe. "Your nails are cropped. That says that ye work as a man." Her soft gentle hands slid up Denice's arms, caressing them. "And your arms are strong as a man's. True, thou art a woman, yet you lead as a man."

"But I am no knight, of that I am certain." Denice spoke firmly.

Kathreen smiled slightly and placed her hands beneath Denice's chin, cupping her face. "And how can you be so certain, when there is nothing you know." Kathreen made a face, "And you feel a slight fever." Kathreen's eyes widened as she noticed the tear at Denice's gown. "And this?" She said pulling the tears wider, exposing eight scars leading from the bone at her neck, down towards each breast. "Thou weren't scarred so this afternoon!"

Denice's hands traced the faint red lines on her white flesh. Her eyes filled with horror as they searched into Kathreen's concerned face. "I am frightened." She barely squeaked. Kathreen's arms slid neatly into Denice's and they held each other tightly. "Don't let me go, I am so afraid."

"Hush child." Kathreen cooed. "I will sit by you." They pulled apart, each looking to the other; Kathreen's round sweet face, Denice's sharp handsome features, in the glow of the warm flame. Kathreen slowly moved closer to Denice and kissed her, lightly brushing her lips. They parted and Denice's confused eyes scanned Kathreen's warm face. Denice moved forward slightly and paused, and Kathreen completed the distance and they gently, sensuously kissed again.

Chapter 12

Dawning hues of Shegatesu's misty blush tainted the eastern sky far above the blackened mountains that pushed through Mistang's blanket of fog. Bits of dew rained from the yellowing leaves in light random drops onto the wind blown piles of leaves already fallen. Warm steam floated from heated embers and pushed back the cooling waves of nipping frost.

Snug blankets of wool wrapped him tightly by the smoldering fire. His wide eyes watched the changing flickers of red in the flameless fire. He could hear the cooing sound of an elfcall. He had been listening to it for quite some time. Watching the others now beginning to stir, he waited for what seemed to be the right moment. He tried not to wish for his feather bed in his dry room back at home, but instead be thankful for the soft moss to sleep on. He really didn't want to leave the warm embrace of his bed-roll after trying so hard to find a comfortable position, but the night was gone and the morning slowly began to creep into the sky as the autumn mists began to rise. His long arm snaked from his covers to his sack and dragged it closer. Rising to a seated position, still wrapped in wool, he rummaged in the leather sack for his jahlava. He tugged it over his head and covered the hood before climbing out of his roll. He lifted the blankets from the ground and hung them over a broken branch to dry. He watched Roc still trying to sleep and knew that if he was awake he would say, 'Boy, come here so I can beat you good morning.' He smiled to himself and followed the sound of the elf call.

Frito sat on the wet grass and stopped playing as Orrin came near. Frito laid his white gold flute in his lap and looked up at the boy. The boy's eyes were still swollen with sleep. Frito gestured and Orrin sat by his side. He extended his cloak and draped it across the boy's shoulders, drawing him near, and kissed him lightly on the head.

"Good mor-ning, eh…" Orrin rumbled in a strangely deep voice. He rubbed his eyes and leaned into Frito's shoulder only to find him still in his armor.

"Why not sleep some more?" Frito said. "You look like a rough night."

"I hurt too much from sleep, eh?" Orrin lifted the flute from Frito's lap. "I am like, un-a-ccus-tomed to sleeping on the ground, eh?" Orrin put the tube to his lips and blew a soundless note.

Frito had no concept of how it was to be a lone child, an orphan to say the least. He had always Dexter and Roc who were close to his age. Orrin had no one, not even a father. Max was a lousy parent at best. The man was a child so many centuries ago, he couldn't remember how valuable it was to have some one show him something new. "Here…" Frito turned the flute slightly, "Blow over the hole, like that." Orrin made a whisper of a whistle from the flute, but tried again and Frito watched him. Everyone had adopted Orrin in a way, but strangely, it was Roc who held him under his wing the most. Roc also made a poor parent but fortunately, Lady Fantista made up the slack. "Don't spit." He coached. Frito didn't take his arm from Orrin and Orrin seemed content there. Strange, he thought, how his own family was becoming, and deservedly so, estranged to him. Frita was lost to all and Friska was coming to kill him.

Orrin stopped playing. "It's like, I can not hear your thoughts," He announced. "But I can hear your thin-king, eh? It's Friska, is he coming?"

Frito's lip slightly curled to a smile. Had the boy unknowingly tapped deeper than he thought he could, or was it a lucky guess? "Yes, he answered this morning before sunrise. He has twenty men with him." Orrin continued to play a strange run of notes and then stopped. "So, will you kill him?"

Frito shook his head. "No." He whispered, "I will not fight him."

"And like, if he fights you?"

"I mustn't let it come to be."

Orrin put the flute to his lips and continued. Frito had been thinking all morning about how he intended to stop Friska. If it were true, and he had burned the temple in Sugartown, then what was to say he still had a rational sense.

"Stop right there!" Frito and Orrin turned to see Dragonslayer pushing out of the bush. "What are you two doing?" Frito looked to Orrin who was equally innocent. Roc eyed them both suspiciously and then relaxed. "All right, I'll let it go this time." Frito smiled at Orrin who was trying to hide his own. Dragonslayer ambled over. He shifted his weapons belt, plopped down beside Frito and took the flute from Orrin. He waved it in the air and it made slight whistling noises. "This must be a bitch to play." He dropped it in Frito's lap and leaned over to glare at Orrin. "Boy, come over here so I can beat you good morning." Orrin smiled in spite of himself. Roc looked at him and then looked away again. Then he looked up and his pointed ears began to stiffen.

They listened to the elfcall that came through the forest. The song sang that J'son and J'cob had heard Frito's call and were en-route.

Frito lifted his flute to his lips and answered the call. He played gently into the soft mist of the fall morning, a tune of swirling carousels spiraling though the majestic oaks of the turning forest. He played to the shivering drops of rain in the warming sun, and the gentle sway of rustling leaves soon to drop. He played to the gray clouds and the thunder rolling in them, the sweeping winds pushing them on. His tune sang to the fire, burning bright through the night and then to the frost, creeping up on the morning light. He played of peace, and of calm, of rest, and of play. He played for better times from past and to be. He played to love, and family, to joy, and wonder, to moon, to stars, to life and to all.

His tune lifted through the trees and its echo hung mystically in the air as a dream fading from memory. "I bet you thought only J'son had talent." Frito chided Orrin who seemed to be sulking, staring harshly at the wet grass before him. "Orrin?" Orrin slowly turned, then suddenly looked up in to Frito's dark, Nih eyes. He looked away to the sound of his name. It was Fryto in need of a water bearer. "Go." Frito whispered as he pulled back his cloak. Orrin braced his hands into the grass to push off and scrambled back to the site.

Roc watched him go. "Will he be alright?"

Frito nodded. "He's worried about Friska coming here. Everyone is worried and he keeps picking up their thoughts and compounding his own fears." Frito spoke to himself more than to Roc. "He's got to learn to control that. He's young. He will learn. I did."

"You did?" Roc glared at him. "Learn what? Your Kamri is nothing compared to his."

Frito raised one brow looked at his cousin. "I have one mental Kamri. Immunity to other mental Kamri. Not much to learn." He lifted the flute in his hand, tightly clenching it in a fist. Suddenly, it slipped from his hand, as if it wasn't there. "As for my one physical Kamri of Phantom Walk, that I had to master."

"Big deal." Dragonslayer mumbled.

Frito smiled. "It is to me."

"We'll see." He said. "And what about Friska, have you thought about him?"

"I have thought all I can." He shook his head with uncertainty. "I have an idea or two, but other than that, I'll have to play this all by ear."

Dragonslayer shook his head disapprovingly. Frito glared at him, but Roc dropped the subject. "And what of Stephanie? That…" Roc stopped what he was going to say and interjected: "child back at the house." instead.

"I cannot figure her out. Her family is Tethern. You know, blonde hair, blue eyes and two or more paces in height. But she is Hiran, born of her Tethern parents."

"Mixed breed." Roc said simply. Frito looked at Roc rejecting the idea, shaking his head. "Why not?" Dragonslayer went on. "It takes one elf to interbreed. Remember the Hiran/Nerin alliance and the cross breeding afterwards. Our Great-great-grandmother was born Hiran/Nerin. Then a war with the Nih came the rape of that woman and the birth of our great-grand-mother. She was Hiran yet had two offspring that were Nerin. The line remained a random choice between Hiran and Nerin with no signs of Nih, until the marriage of Lord Hammerstrike, your father, a human, and Fantista, your mother, a Hiran with hidden Nerin traits and a forgotten Nih trait. That created the mixed up family of yours. None of you resembles the other. Frita and Friska are twins, yet one is Hiran and the other is Nerin. Dexter was human. No one had shown the traces of Nih from our Great-grand-mother, but four generations later, you, a Nih show up. What does Dwayne mean in Nih?"

"Little dark one." Frito whispered. Frito cocked his head and looked at the Slayer. It always surprised him when Roc the Dragonslayer produced intelligent thoughts other than how to silently fondue a sentry. Still Frito shook his head in doubt. "She is Tethern. Her father fought in the legion three decades before your reign. The war of Purity. To oust the mecca of Cray folk. No, interbreeding doesn't hold up. Only elves retain the pure line. A Nih may be born of a Hiran, but humans won't keep the trait like that."

"Of course you know what this means."

"Back to square one." Roc nodded as Frito went on. "Brewster is our only lead."

"The Red Barchetta would be faster."

"And call too much attention."

Roc shrugged. "No matter, not enough go juice."

"How much left?"

The Dragonslayer scratched the stubble on his twisted chin exposing his lower teeth as he did. "Enough to get it back home from Rendon."

Frito suddenly looked into the grass. He reached for his flute and fingered its keys. The Slayer leaned forward and looked at him. "What?" Roc glared at him. "The fuel? Craig has already commissioned the Monks of somewhere-or-another to distill another fuel that the car can run on." Frito turned and stared into the grass again. Roc looked away shaking his head. "Its not the car your worried about, is it? Your worried about Friska and Frita and everyone in between. Your sitting there blaming yourself for everything."

"No, I was just thinking when we found that car." Frito smiled weakly. "Craig thought he had seen a ghost."

Roc looked at his cousin with steady, level eyes. "Must I get Orrin back here to tell me otherwise?"

Frito looked away from his cousin's stare and mindlessly fingered the keys of his flute. "Is it that obvious?" He laughed breathlessly. "Its hard not to think of it when my brother is coming to kill me." He pushed his fists into the ground and pushed to his feet. "Who am I kidding? I'm running around like a chicken with out a head pretending I still have one."

"Dwayne..." Roc voice bent in an unusually gentle tone. "Stop this. Don't put yourself through it." Roc leaned forward and lifted his bulky form from the grass. He flexed his back. "I don't want to hear it." He said sternly "And neither do you." Roc made a face as he stared into Frito's back. "Hey!" Roc pushed him into a tree. "I'm talking to you!" Frito struck the wood with a clang and stumbled back towards the Slayer. Roc leaned forward and charged with his shoulder into Frito's side. Frito reeled and struck the ground hard, rolling over to his back. The Dragonslayer's rush carried him into a bush and onto the ground as well.

Frito rolled and caught to his feet. Roc pulled himself from the dirt and went after him again. Frito shifted his weight to his back leg and twisted suddenly, engaging the Dragonslayer's thrust knocking him towards the ground. But Roc gripped Frito's leg and pulled him to the ground with him. The two rolled in the dirt pounding into each other with closed fists. Roc rolled over on top with his knees pressed into Frito's arms pinning them to the ground and bellowed, pounding his breast plate. Frito only smiled and the wind whipped from the woods like a battering ram and lifted the Slayer off of his chest and flung him like a sack into the soft moss.

"You cheat!" The moss shouted.

"I cheat?" Frito shouted lifting himself from the ground. "Magic isn't cheating, thank you." He extended a hand to help Roc up from the moss. Roc suddenly pulled him in and the two laid there panting. "Since my return," Frito said staring at the clearing sky, "Everything is…" Frito paused in mid thought as he heard an elf call. It was Fryto calling them to breakfast. He shrugged his shoulders and followed the Dragonslayer.

Chapter 13

Dark shadow crouched—shielded by the rocky cliffs from Kemoto's bright light. The cold, stone castle walls that were carved from the hard, cliff rock glared at the valley and watched as it filled with golden sunlight. Fikor's cold darted in gusting drafts through the spaces of the stone and Hauge howled and moaned as he ran through the dark filled rooms.

With white, drawn, trembling hands, he poured his brandy. It ran like oil in his mouth and burned the back of his throat. He snorted and felt its warmth in the long hairs of his nostrils. He took up the poker and with quick, deft strokes he sent scores of sparks up the flue. He tossed on another log and teased it to flame.

He shouldered his heavy wool blankets and puttered around in the cluttered room. He skittered across with tiny shuffling steps to his desk and with withered hands scooped up fistfuls of crackling, yellow paper and shuffled back to the fire. With a casual toss, they were ablaze with brilliant flames.

He snorted at it, feeling its sudden burst of warmth, and headed back over to his desk. As he past the shuttered window, thin lines of Kemoto's light gently touched his hand as if the bird god of the sun was trying to call his attention. He looked at his hand with the spot of clean, white light on it, and then to the window pasted shut with spider webs and dust. His feeble hands clutched at the rusted latch and with a tiny grunt, it opened. With a thrust the shutters flung open and Kemoto's light poured in with Hauge's winds. The old man squinted at the light as the bitter morning cold made him tear. His long stringy beard flicked in the breeze and he could hear sheaves of paper take to flight in the room behind him.

Light had filled the valley. His glazed and jaundiced eyes looked to the moat below. It was drained years ago and now was a garden for the local villagers. They left a basket at his door and took what ever else they grew. It was empty now, save stakes and drying vines. *Alone, barren and dying*, he thought, *like everything else.*

A sudden chill behind him, a wind colder than any draft caressed the back of his neck. He knew who was there before he turned around.

"Welcome, Thamrell." He muttered. "Thank you for coming."

Thamrell hovered a pace from the floor. His black, wide brimmed hat hid his haunting face. "How could I refuse such an invitation." He spoke to the fire with a voice of sarcasm. "I really have nothing more pressing, Jon."

Jon shuffled closer to the god of despair. "I...I've made my decision." He nodded, brushing the top of his bald head. "I'm going to do it."

The god of depression turned slowly as if he hadn't been listening. "What was that, Jon?"

The old man straightened, as his face drained. "You know...we spoke about it."

"Yes Jon," Thamrell answered tiredly. "We spoke a great deal about a lot of things." He lifted his gaze and his empty, draining eyes looked out to him. "And that is all its been, Jon. Talk."

The elderly man shifted and licked his lips with a dry tongue. "I thought about it. And I want to do what you think is best."

Thamrell lifted slightly higher and began to slowly glide around the room. "What I think?" He paused and faced him. "What does it matter what I think? Jon, I am the god of Human Introspection. I am to show you what you think." The god of despair floated closer. "It is what you think, Jon. You."

Thamrell turned away and continued his slow slide across the room as Jon bowed his head. He then looked up and sighed. "Yes Thamrell, its what I want."

Thamrell paused looking out the window. Where Kemoto's light touched his dead gray flesh, he faded becoming transparent. "Are you sure this is the right thing, Jon?"

The old man almost gawked. "You said..."

Thamrell rose quickly into the air and hung above the old man. "I said...I said...yes, what I said! Jon, Jon, you're not listening. It is what you said. It is what you wanted to say and I said it for you. I spoke the words that you were to weak to speak." Thamrell lowered and then turned away.

Jon looked towards the window and shuffled over to it. In the far village he could tell that the men were beginning their trudge to the mines. "Why have you summoned me here, Jon?" Thamrell called to him.

Jon turned from the window. "I...wanted to tell you."

"So you've told me." Thamrell said quickly. "I'll add it to the pile. Is there anything else?"

Jon felt anger begin to fill his centre. "I'm going to do it!"

"And what do you want from me? To push you? I won't push you, Jon."

The old man's eyes lowed. "I know…" He said quietly as his anger drained from him. "Its just that…there is so much pain."

"Yes, I know."

"And, my eyes, they're losing their sight." He looked back out the window. "Can you see them? Out there?" He pointed towards the town. "I can't, but I can tell you exactly what their doing, as they have done for my whole life." He looked down to his rag wrapped feet. "I gave them so much."

Thamrell sighed as something rattled about in his hollow lungs. "I know, Jon, but that was a long time ago."

The old man didn't hear him. "I banished a dragon for them! Drove the beast away with my magic!" He looked up beaming.

"And it waited for you to grow old and came back. It ate a bunch of people and it took the Dragonslayer to get rid of it forever. The people didn't blame you for it, you did the best you could. The elders remembered the first time though, they remembered you in your prime. But the elders have all but died. And now, Jon," Thamrell's words cut easily through the old man's static pride. The old man's face sagged on itself as Thamrell sailed closer. "And now, Jon?" He prompted the old man to finish the sentence.

His jaundiced eyes followed the god's tattered robes. "And now its a bag of vegetables at my door. They'll be sorry when I'm gone."

"And your work?" Thamrell pressed.

The old man glanced up and then at the desk, littered with paper. "It failed."

"It failed?" Thamrell came closer. "Did it?"

"I failed." The old man was near sobbing. "I could have changed the face of Mortalroam."

"You were asking too much."

"Was I?" The old man's voice came back with strength. "Was it? I was so close."

Thamrell shook his head. "And what did close get you."

The old man's head lowered and his voice drained. "It was near completion. But…"

"But what, Jon?"

"The pain." He said sadly. "I got sick."

"Was it the pain?" Thamrell lifted higher. "Was it your wretched body that failed you? Or were you searching for naught."

"I was so close!" The old man pleaded.

Thamrell sighed and turned away. "Yes Jon, you were."

"Where are you going?" The old man reached out for the specter.

"There is nothing for me here." Thamrell said floating towards the wall.

"No! Thamrell, wait!" His old voice cracked and strained over his dry tongue.

The god of despair paused and looked back over his shoulder. "For what, Jon?"

"I don't want to be alone," The old man was panting. His voice was a high whining whimper. The spirit of desolation looked back down at him and Jon bowed his weak head. "When I do it." He whispered in broken words.

"Are you?" The ghost came closer. "Going to do it?" Thamrell asked unconvinced.

"What have I to live for?" The old man begged.

Thamrell shook his head. "You tell me." His dark eyes leveled peering through the old man. "But asking the god of despair to keep you company says much, don't you think?"

The old man looked about the room and slowly nodded.

He shifted and pushed the chair from his desk to the center of the room. He pulled rope from a chest in the corner of the room and gathered it in his hands. He tossed it up to the rafters and it fell back down on his head. He tried again but lacked the physical strength to get the rope over the beam. He took a deep breath, holding back the twist in his lungs to cough and tossed with his waning strength and the rope fell on him again.

Thamrell condensed, the air filling with skin-crawling tension as he temporarily, partially came into reality. He lifted the rope from the broken, sobbing, old man and lofted it over the beam. Slowly the old man tied one end to the hook rod by the fire place. He looked at the other, hovering above the chair in the center of the room. He had it measured from last night. The knot already tied.

With heavy leaden steps, the old man climbed onto the rickety chair and looked at the rope. The noose framed his face and he looked at the dark walls of his room through it. At his last moments of life, he felt nothing. He was empty, used up.

"Have you left a note?" Thamrell called over, startling him.

The old man looked at him. "A note?"

Thamrell shrugged his bony shoulders. "As I see it, someone is eventually going to notice that you are gone. At least by time Frandrell the spring dragon returns. You should leave a note."

The old man glared out the window, trying to focus on something. "I've nothing to say to them."

Thamrell frowned. "Nothing? And what will they have to remember you by?"

The old man looked at the god of despair now floating at his height. The yellowed eyes widened. "I know." He nodded slowly. "I know!"

The old man dropped from the chair with renewed strength and hobbled over to his desk. He touched the wall behind his desk with the inside two fingers, and in response, a small space, about a hands breath, shifted. The old man flustered at the fact that this simple spell of opening was failing. The man's wrinkled, sallowed hands pawed at the smooth rock, pushing it only slightly. Thamrell again concentrated his essence and partially entered reality as his dead, grey hands joined the old man's and swung the space open.

The man gripped the worn leather bound book and pulled it from the space and slapped it onto his desk. "There..." He said firmly. "You think they will see that!"

Thamrell nodded. "They can't miss it."

The old man nodded looking at it. "My life's work." He caressed it with ill feeling fingers. "They'll see that and know how wrong they've been."

"I'm sure they will, Jon." Thamrell turned and floated back from it as if the book meant nothing to him.

The old man turned to the god of despair, watching him slide across the room. "Thamrell, I'd like to thank you."

The god stopped and rotated. "For what?"

"Well, for..." The old man groped. "For everything!"

Thamrell nodded in acknowledgment. "Would you like me to wait?"

The old man felt his heart for the first time in years begin to pound. "Yes." He uttered soundlessly.

The rope still hung in the center of the room waiting. The drafts made it sway.

Its rough hemp scratched his fleshy face and neck as he pulled it over his head. He paused and as a second thought, pulled the knot tighter about his neck. His hands fell to his sides and he stood stock still.

Thamrell floated lower, almost touching the floor. He watched the old man, standing at attention on the chair with the rope around his neck. The man was sweating in the cold morning breeze.

He nodded to the god of despair, and the chair shot out from under him.

Thamrell watched as the old man feebly clawed at the rope for air while his thin gaunt legs kicked out like he was trying to run.

A hulking, green scaled monster walked behind the struggling, gurgling old man. "For me?" He gestured to the old man. "Thamrell, you shouldn't have."

Thamrell shook his head slowly not looking at the monster. "Thumber?" The god of despair spoke retrospectively. "I wonder, if mortals will ever realize that suicide is not a viable option for dealing with problems." The god of depression shook his head.

Thumber stepped around the old man, now kicking out spasmodically. "And then what would you do for laughs?" Thumber laughed at his own joke. When Thamrell only stared at him he coughed nervously. "Well I'm here. If it wasn't for this..." He jerked a thumb at the dying old man.

Thamrell beckoned him with a nod. "Here, I want you to take this." He pointed to the book on the desk.

"And what is it?"

"Its the spell of Babble. Its original plan was to enable mortals, all mortals, to communicate with each other not unlike an elfcall."

"Huh?" Thumber questioned picking up the book.

"I'm sure we can work out the problems. At least enable us to communicate short ranges."

Thumber shrugged his shoulders. "And?"

"And, we will use it to control the forces from a central point. I'll be able to direct the army personally."

Thumber nodded. "So then, everything is a go?"

Thamrell smiled, dust crackling on his leathery face. "And what have you to report?"

"We have Denice Hammerstrike."

"Frita? Then you were successful." He concluded. "Where is she?"

"You'll never guess."

"No, I won't." Thamrell said tiredly. "Where?"

"Guess!" Thumber encouraged.

"Thumber!" Thamrell scolded, rising up.

The monster from under the bed smiled broadly. "In the house of Ura's knight!"

Thamrell's empty eyes widened. "How in Trid's name did you manage that?"

Thumber held up a hand to show its simplicity. "Hey, that's my job."

"What else?"

"We have her star."

Thamrell turned away, mindlessly floating higher. "This is working too well."

"What are you going to do?" Thumber stepped closer.

Thamrell turned with a simple look of innocence. "Do? I now have Friska to drive against his brother. By colliding the two, I can't lose. Frito will not raise a hand against him. Friska will kill him."

"And Roc?" Thumber reminded him. "Roc will kill Friska." Thumber pursed his lips at the thought. "Roc will knock the bejesus outta Friska." He decided, trying to imagine the gore.

Thamrell dismissed the idea with a wave of his hand. "I can do away with Friska now that I have Frita and her star."

Thumber tilted his head from side to side. "I don't know about that, chief. We can't touch the star let alone approach either gate. I have enough of a time getting about in this form even with the Magna Thu Laurde."

Thamrell looked at the green scaly monster. "A technicality." He tossed off the idea. "No, this is going to work." He motioned. "Now go. And keep an eye on her."

Thumber nodded, tucking the book tightly under his arm. He carefully stepped around the dead hanging man in the center of the room and walked past the clutter to the unmade bed.

The monster looked back. The god of despair was mindlessly circling the top of the room. Thumber felt the weight of the book under his arm. He sighed, slipped under the bed and was gone.

<u>Chapter 14</u>

Muffling mist curled and withdrew as Kemoto awoke with a rustle of flaming feathers. Mistang pulled back her quilts and crawled slowly beneath the cover of the trees to hide from Kemoto's sight. Orrin trudged and the wineskins slapped against him to the beat of his gait. He had filled each one at the running stream and now carried them back to the site.

He paused and wiped the light sweat from his brow. He knew he wasn't to go far out, but he had moved lightly upstream to a small water fall where the water pooled at the bottom. The water was clear and fresh and the bottles were easy to fill there. The others over-worried. He thought: *I can, like, sense another person approaching for clicks, eh? What is there to fear?*

His foot snagged suddenly and sent him sprawling to the ground. Wet leaves clung to his face and hands as he pushed himself from the cold dirt. *Bright, eh? He thought. I can sense anything for click, but can I see a root under my own foot, eh?* He paused suddenly, his sharp pointed ears tapping into the air to hear it again. No, it wasn't, just a…again. His name riding the mist, a long trailing whisper ringing in his ears over and over again. He looked around him and there was no one. "Who is there, eh?" He called into the mists, but only silence heard him. He shouldn't have gone so far, he shouldn't have left sight of the camp as he was told. He puckered his lips and quickly gave out an elfcall but the ring howled in his ears and cut him short. His heart pounded and his brain sparked into power. Kamri energies housed in his head bled to the surface, massing to fight. He looked around, slowly bringing himself to his feet. His eyes searched the woods and white fog for signs of any one.

An elfcall pushed into his ears and he knew it to be Frito calling after him. He went to answer when he saw it ripping in the wind. Tattered rags like banners fanned from a leafless tree above him. Braced against the fog was a girl, perhaps twelve years, clinging to the branches. Her face had no features. Her eyes had no sight. Her frazzled dark hair danced in the still wind. Her voice was only a whisper.

Orrin stared blankly, afraid to answer. His fist clenched on the silver star pendant hanging over his heart beneath his shirt.

"Give it to me…" The phantom said. "Tell me, I beg of you."

Orrin clenched the pendant tighter. He must not give up the star of Hammerstrike, it was his token of right. She couldn't want that. What could this be? What did it want? Thousands of withered, aged pages of ancient texts and volumes flashed through Orrin's mind. What could this be? Has Max a reference to this?

Yes he does.

"Tell me, please!" It cried more pitifully than before. It reached out with one hand hoping to bridge the gap between them. But Orrin knew better. Although the tree she was in was in arms reach, he had no intention of touching her, let alone getting closer.

"It is...Mary." Orrin said quietly.

The girl smiled in hollowed grace as if pain was suddenly lifted from her torment. Her hand withdrew to her face, touching herself as if to convince herself it was no dream. "Mary..." She whispered in a tender soothing voice. "Mary." She repeated as if she hadn't before.

The clouds parted and light streamed from Kemoto in bright golden beams. Warming sun striped the tree where the girl had been, leaving tattered ribbons in it's branches.

Tiny twigs crushed beneath hard boots and steel plates clashed against each other in a frantic hustle. Orrin turned to see four figures dashing through the woods. "Frito! Roc! I'm alright!" He cried. "I'm alright, eh?." He suddenly found tears welling in his eyes as his throat balled itself. His hand still clutched his pendant.

Frito gripped the boys shoulders and held him. "What happened?" He spoke with such urgency it frightened him.

Fryto stood beside his brother and waved a finger at the boy. "Did I not tell you to stay near the camp?"

"What the Hel is this all about?" Dragonslayer said dejectedly when he found there was nothing to kill.

Orrin looked back and forth to each one until his tears over ran his face and he wiped them away with the backs of his hands.

"Alright," Frito said. "Just relax and tell us what happened." Frito relaxed his grip. "We heard half an elfcall and then you didn't answer. I had visions of you being swallowed whole."

Orrin looked up to Frito through his tears and dirt streaked face, smiling. "It was an Ad-jat, and I killed it, eh?"

"An ADJAT?" Dragonslayer roared. "You found an Adjat and didn't leave anything for me? I thought we were friends! I never killed an Adjat before...what's an Adjat?"

117

Orrin tried to suppress his smile. "An Ad-jat is, you know, like, the ghost of a child that, like, died at birth with out being blessed or named." Orrin wiped his face again to stem his runny nose. "Okay, so, their spir-it floats and gets caught in trees, and they like, beg to be named, eh? They age slow-ly so like, they a-ppear as chil-dren hun-dreds of years after their death. To put them to rest, all you must do is like, bless them or name them, eh?"

Dragonslayer grunted and headed back towards the site. "I don't wanna kill one of them."

"Are these the child's swaddling clothes?" Achillia said examining them.

Orrin shrugged. "I don't know, eh? Could be like, rags that the ad-jat gath-ered for like, clothes, sort of any-way. Like, some-times, de-pen-ding on their strength, they can escape the trees and haunt their par-ents or rel-a-tives. Also de-pen-ding on their power, their touch can blind, or like, you know, kill." Orrin recited text from Max's beastology.

Fryto clenched his shoulders and grimaced. "Ick." He said not wanting to touch anything. "Ick. Ick" He said as a signal to head back to the fire.

Chapter 15

Kemoto's flaming wings of red silk and yellow satin rose higher into the air shedding his brilliant glow across the blue of Okshiru's sky. Kemoto's blazing light burned into the leaves of every tree now reflecting speckles of gold, amber, scarlet and rust to fill the bed of Chinook, the snow biter.

Okshiru's waves and Hauge's winds clashed against the sea torn rocks as Kemoto lifted gently in to the sky, stripping back Auger, the shadow, from the cliffs high above the waters. Kemoto rose higher and his light found its way through little cracks in the shutters and cast his delicate feathers into each room of the manner. Light pranced upon her sleeping face in warm tender strokes. Her green eyes flashed quickly in the morning light as she awoke and swept to her window. Her hands banged suddenly at the shutters and thrust them wide with the bark of a dog and let Kemoto's light, shining from high above the mountains edge, set the room to glow. She ignored the sudden brisk of Fikor's chill as she quickly turned and dashed to the far end of the room and pushed open the shutters to the roar of Okshiru and his never ending waters far below.

Welcome, she thought to the glow.

Welcome to the Home by the Sea!

She turned from the window, feeling the crash of the waves against her bare back as the warm sun god filled her heart. She dashed back to the east window feeling the sungod's call and heated embrace. She pirouetted and began to dance in delicate leaps and sways to the sungod's whim. Soft, slow, swimming motions of grace as she swept the room with her arms and legs in the golden light. Her dreams blinded her sight as she could see her audience, awed by her repertoire, deep in her mind. A silent orchestra of strings and tiny chimes played for her. The song of a flute sang to her, and the heart of Kemoto made love to her.

She turned and fell panting into the bed. Between each breath she felt laughter quake her soul. Her laugh was uncertain, as if stiff from disuse. She watched the ceiling and the shadows creeping to hide from Kemoto. Again she laughed, though she didn't know why.

She rose from the bed and dressed for the day. A warm slip followed by a heavy cotton dress of autumn brown. She took up a silken cloth and stuffed it into her bosom where her breast should have been. She peered into her reflection to ensure they were even.

Out into the hall she walked silently over the worn faded carpeting. At the head of the stairs she paused and peered down the right hall. Every thing was as it should be including the axes and long swords lying on the floor. She came down the creaking stairs watching carefully for the pit falls of the broken steps. She passed the hall and the broken statues and torn paintings in the main room. She didn't even cast a glancing look at the burned table as she pushed her way into the pantry.

She stood at the door gazing into the bright, sunlit kitchen smelling the boiling ham and baking bread.

"Good morning Lady Kathreen, how are you?"

She looked to the little girl before her. "I am quite well Buffet. And how art thou?" Kathreen smiled at the little child smiling back at her.

"I am well." She answered with a curtsy.

Kathreen waited long enough to determine that the child's new vocabulary had reached its full extent. The little child took the woman's hand and led her to the morning table where she had set it for breakfast. Buffet pulled back a chair for her to sit.

"Thank you Buffet." The woman said once seated.

The child became suddenly hesitant as she could not remember the proper response. "You are welcome Lady Kathreen." She replied with an exasperated smile.

Kathreen patted the girl on the head. "Well done child...well done" She turned to the sound of the back door opening. Denice came in with a sack of wood and set it by the stove. She then took up a pail and began to crank the pump for water. "Your strength is returning." Kathreen spoke over the sound of the water.

Denice paused her pumping and turned around. "Slowly." She breathed. "For that I have you to thank."

Kathreen looked away slightly embarrassed and Denice resumed filling her pail. "Buffet is learning well." Kathreen spoke up after Denice finished with the pump.

Denice turned wiping the sweat from her head. "She only repeats...she does not understand what we say." She took her pail and filled a pot on the stove. "She will learn soon." She took up a tray and set it on the counter by the stove. "I will prepare a tray for your master."

Kathreen slowly rose up in her chair. "Say thou hast not been down the hall. He is meditating."

"No…I have not been by the hall." Denice answered with out turning from stoking the stove.

Kathreen slowly lowered in her chair to a relaxed position. "He will not be eating. He is fasting."

Denice closed the metal hatch and latched it shut. "Surly he will need water?"

"I will be responsible, please, let it be as such."

Denice nodded and took a covered tray from the counter to the table. Setting it down, she lifted Buffet into a chair and took her place.

Breakfast went quickly with Buffet identifying all the food, condiments, flatware and silverware. Once past breakfast, they cleared the table and cleaned the kitchen and dinning room.

Denice's strength easily hitched the horses to the wagon and lead them from the stables. They were poorly cared for and Kathreen had professed her lack of equestrian knowledge and blamed herself for their mis-care, but Denice found it simple to soothe their swollen knees with binding cloth and 'Nick's salve' made from a fungus found growing under the house. She had bathed, groomed, fed them and by noon, the horses were ready for travel.

"They were such a sight." Kathreen stood at the door to the stable with a basket hooked on her arm. "I knew not to care for them." She stepped to the first one and stroked it's mane. The horse's large eyes stared mindlessly ahead. "You did not sleep well." Kathreen spoke without looking. "Thou weren't in the bed this morning."

"Take no offence my lady." Denice came closer with the brush in her hand. "I had never shared my bed with another woman and never enjoyed another's company so much, but…" Her eyes began to drift, setting a gaze out the doors to the hill. She could see the field where Buffet played. "My dreams were frightening." She looked down to the hay strewn floor.

"Do you think you can remember them?"

"Aye, that I can." She looked back at her. Her elvish eyes caught into Kathreen's green eyes. Kathreen leaned over to Denice and lightly draped her hand over her shoulder in a gentle hug. "I was riding my horse…" Denice started. "In a woods that I could not remember. There was snow and mist on the ground. I came to a river and dismounted. I set my hands into the clear, cold, water and washed my

121

face. The water was fetid and spoiled and I cast my hands from it and dried my face with my tunic. I went to mount my ride again when I saw a woman across the way on the opposite bank. She was upstream several paces and I could not see who she was. I called to her, but she could not hear. It was then I saw her cast a bundle into the water. I watched the bundle sink quickly and was gone. I thought nothing of it and went to mount again when I heard the screams of the woman! She was in the water and swept by the current! I stripped my boots and dove into the water after her. I swam closer and passed the floating ice to reach her. As I came closer, it was no longer a woman, but a child, no older than Buffet. I got to the child but she sank out of my grasp. It was then I realized that I could no longer see the shore, and I was lost, swept by the river and tossed by the waves. I went down in the black rancid water and started to drown, as I did, I awoke, beside you in the bed."

Denice finished her story. The silence stretched leaving only the squeals of delight as Buffet chased her ball. "I still do not know who I am, and where I am from. I hear names in my sleep and see places that are strange to me and they confuse me…and torment me."

Kathreen reached up and cupped the woman's cheek in her hand. She caressed her shoulder as she stroked her face. "Little sister. You want to remember, and soon you shall, there is time for such things. Thou art a knight for you hold the strength of a man and you hath soothed my pains like none other. Thou hast loved me, and found a way into my heart. I can only pray that you too shall find the peace that I have found with you." She took her hand and lightly kissed the palm. "I ask you to reconsider your decision." Kathreen said still holding her hand. "Tis an entire days ride to Brewster and you'll be traveling at night. Tis dangerous."

Denice smiled faintly and weakly, and she took Kathreen's hand and kissed the back. Then she quickly stepped up into the wagon. Kathreen took up her basket and placed it in the wagon.

"Will you find what you look for in Brewster?"

"You say it is a large town. Surly I came from somewhere, Perhaps there."

Kathreen nodded. "Perhaps. I shall send my hopes with you." She took out a small pouch from the pocket in her skirt. "This, I also send with you. T'isn't much, but tis what I can send." Denice opened the string and examined the pennies inside. Several from different kingdoms from the markings on the face. She felt the weight of the metal in her hands before slipping it under her tunic.

"I shall return at the next day after. I shall only spend a night and an afternoon."

"Then speed to you." Kathreen stepped from the wagon.

With a click and a lash, the horses leaned into their harness and the wagon pulled from the shelter. The rumbling wheels warbled and waved on warped axles. Squealing wood and squeaking metal, rolled along on the hard packed dirt road. Buffet ran down from the hill waving after the wagon.

The trees and woods shaded the road from the sun and made the trails all the lonelier. Sun light filtered in beams of gold through the gaps of leaves above. Kemoto's great wings spread out over the sky and his feathers danced in bright gentle sweeps over Denice's shoulders and legs as she moved along in the rickety wagon. Slowly and steadily the horses pulled along. She listened to the steady beat and sway of the cart as she moved on. Birds of Meleki filled the air with song as they sang to Kemoto's great light. They fluttered about Denice and lit on the gunwales of the cart and rode some ways with her before lifting to air again. Meleki's great trees lifted high above and their sun yellow leaves fluttered to the road, riding gently on Hauge's thin rising wind.

But the woman rode straight along the road, neither turning to the side or behind. Her sharp ears listened to the sliding leaves and shrilling birds, but her eyes stared at the road before her and her face held solid in concentration. Her hands held the reigns tightly, as if prepared for the horses to suddenly bolt and lurch away. They were tired mares, too old for bolting; however, she held them tightly just the same.

Kemoto's great wings folded as he took his perch in the west just below the cliff beyond sight. As Auger the shadow of the night crept along the road, creepers and night-things and crawlers of the shadows began their cries and croaks, moaning to Leatha's approach. Soon, Ovam's great white light began to glow in the blackening sweep of Leatha's robe.

Steel chipped hot flicks of flint to soddened cloth and light burned from a lantern wick. A glowing ball of light pushed into the thin mist that formed in the cooling dark air. She hung her light on the post attached to the side of the wagon so that it hung over her head and gave the horses light to see.

She traveled on, neither feeling the cold in the air nor hearing the moan in the wind.

A woman plodded along on the road before her. A long brown shawl was pulled tightly around her shoulders and her coat tails dragged behind her in the dirt. She clutched tightly in the nook of her arm, a large woven basket with a hinged lid to cover it. She moved along like a beetle in the grass—slow, steady strides with each one a determined step.

As the wooden cart came along side of her, Denice turned her attention for the first time to the woman. She was stooped over, with her hood shielding her face. The woman glanced for nary an instant to see who was riding along side of her before turning back to her walking. "Will you ride with me woman?" Denice asked with a rasped voice. The woman stopped and looked up, straightening her back as she did. She defensively clutched her basket with both hands. She nodded and took her lantern and set it in the cart by Denice's feet. Still clutching her basket, she reached up to the gunwale for a firm hand hold and with old withered bones, began to pull herself into the cart. Denice reached over, holding the reigns in one hand, caught the woman's arm to support her and was amazed at how emaciated the woman was. Long strands of white wire hair frazzled out of place. The hand clutching her basket was shriveled thin flesh wrapped around bones. The woman's odor caught her sharp, elven senses. Hauge's wind swept it from her before, but now so close it could not be avoided. The woman reeked of uncleanliness.

The woman sat herself in the seat with her basket in her lap. Her hands laid lightly over the lid. Denice drove back the brake and clicked the horses on. They leaned forward and with a slight lurch they moved on.

"Where art thou from?" The woman suddenly spoke. They had rolled along the road a four click in silence. The woman never lifted her gaze from the lid of her basket.

Denice looked at her, listening to her question. It suddenly frightened her and she didn't know why. "Where do you think I come from?" She answered with a question after great thought.

"Elf-folk." The woman grunted still not looking up from the basket. "There tis be none elf-folk about this place."

"And you are from here? Brewster?"

"Nay, I tis not."

Denice looked at the woman with a glare of skepticism. "Then how do you know that elf-folk are not in these parts?"

"I know." Was all she answered before dropping into silence once more.

An eight click of the road crawled beneath the wheels of the wagon with silence. Then, with out provocation the old woman said: "There are no knights in Brewster." She mumbled under her breath.

Denice suddenly reached for the center of her chest, her fingers only clutching into cloth and nothing beneath, but still she held the spot as it were there. "And what would I have with knights?" She spoke clearly, using the power of fear to amplify her voice above the moaning and creaking of the pulling wagon. The woman didn't answer. She only stared at the lid of her basket. Denice released her tunic and took up the reigns in both hands. "Do you think me a knight?"

The woman suddenly looked up and glared at Denice. Her withered, drawn face twitched at the deep, sunken eyes. Her lips drew tight to a thin scraggly line across her face. "I know." She said in a harsh whisper. She looked back at her basket. "I know."

"You know what, woman?" Denice felt her heart begin to shutter from the touch of fear. Her hand slowly went back to the space on her chest. "Do you know me?"

The woman smiled knowingly and her cracked, yellowing teeth showed in the dim glow of the lamp light. "I know." She laughed breathlessly, patting lightly at the lid of her basket. "I know."

Denice looked at the basket then back to the road. She then looked as far down the road the dim lantern light would go. Then she looked back to the woman. She was no longer smiling, but still patting the lid to her basket.

"Tell…Me…" Denice said staring at the basket. "What you know."

The woman stopped patting her basket and laid both hands over the opening lip. Her shriveled face turned and looked at the young woman's face. Her thin lips bent in glee. "I know you, Frita the Cold."

Denice jerked hard on the reigns pulling the horses to a sudden halt. The horses jostled and stamped the cold ground waiting. Her breath dragged shallowly in her lungs in long steady pulls. Her eyes narrowed beneath her brows. "I know her not."

"I know." The torrid woman cackled "I know."

"Who are you?" Frustration sparked to anger. Denice's fists clenched and wrung the leather reigns. The young woman threw them

125

down and snatched the lantern from its post and held it close to the woman's face. "I grow tired of your riddles. Cease them or I shall cast you to the road!" Her voice waned and rasped in her dry throat and her hands shook uncontrollably. "Who are you?"

The woman's face was flat and yellow from the lamp light. Only her eyes seemed shadowed, casting back emptiness. "Who are you?" The witch said. "Do you know? I know."

Denice waned and almost pleadingly cried to the woman. "Tell me!"

The woman looked away, casting her empty eyes on the basket in her lap. "You are the woman who lives the life of another who is not. I cannot tell you." She laid both hands on the lid of the basket. "I can show you..." She turned to the glow of the light and her empty eyes drained the last bits of strength from Denice. "But will you look?"

Slowly the old witch opened her basket.

Denice's quick eyes shot from the woman's face and gazed into the dark cove of the basket. She looked at the woman again. Nothing had changed. Her eyes looked into the basket again. Slowly she brought the lantern close to the edge, but the light wouldn't enter the basket. Denice looked at the woman with confusion filled eyes. "I cannot see..." She said dumbly.

"You cannot see, because you have not looked. Are your eyes all that you see with?"

Denice eyed the woman again and then the dark basket. "These are your tricks..." She glared hotly at the woman. "I will have none of them!"

"Then..." The woman said closing the lid to her basket. "You will never know." She laid her hands complacently on the lid and looked ahead to the road and waited for her journey to continue.

But Denice stayed affixed to the basket.

The witch smiled, as she knew her spell was done. The young woman's hands slid along the lid of the basket and the witch moved her hands from the lid to allow access. Denice looked at the woman and then again to the basket. Slowly, she opened it.

Inside, was a rag doll.

Dressed in a frilly mismatched gown of tattered bits of cloth it was sallow and rotted with age. Its eyes were two black shiny buttons of polished black wood. Its mouth was only a tiny thin line of red thread embroidered into a smile.

Slowly and gently Denice lifted it from its place. Its arms and legs flopped back and hung from its stitched joints. Denice looked at the old woman who only gleamed in satisfaction. She looked at the doll again. Its black patchy hair stiffly hung in place as she turned the toy to its side to examine it. She allowed its arms to flop about from side to side and then up and down.

The doll suddenly wailed.

Denice flung it to the floor in surprise and it hit the wood with a solid thud. It laid there with its stuffed arms flopped about.

Dead.

Denice broke her startled fear and looked for the woman, but she and her basket were gone. Denice was suddenly confused and frightened as she slowly stood up in the wagon. Her left hand clutched the lantern, holding it higher to shed its light against the road and into the trees along the side. They stood cast in light and shadows like a solid wall of wood and a black shadowed roof. It followed the road like a tunnel. She cast her eyes as far as the could see and the woman was beyond.

The woman was gone and Denice was alone and the doll laid dead on the floor of the wagon. The horses stamped their feet and flicked their tails as horses did. Denice's lips came together and tightened. A trick, she thought. A trick. She again looked for the woman along the sides of the wagon to see if she was hiding along its side in the shadow of the lamp light. She wasn't there. Denice hooked the lantern again and took her place. She quickly snatched up the reigns in her right hand and lifted them to snap the horses into the motion.

She paused.

Blood ran in a thin red line to her elbow. She quickly traced it to her hand. She looked closer to see its source, but there was no wound. Slowly she stood and examined her body. There was only few drops on her tunic, but no tear or scratch. She unhooked the lantern and looked about the wagon to see from where it came from.

The doll lay on the floor of the wagon in a pool of blood.

The lantern slipped from her hand and crashed at the horses back legs igniting one of their tails. The flames shot up suddenly and the horses bolted, trying to escape it. The wagon lurched and threw Denice to the floor. It rambled out of control and tossed her about in the back. The wood jolted against her body and thundered about her ears. The blackness of the Leatha's night quickly blinded her as the horses left the burning lantern behind on the road. The horses charged on into the night as the cart banged and tossed along the hard packed road, not knowing that the fire had snuffed itself and that Denice had fallen out and lay in the road behind.

New bruises burned against old, sealed scars opened again, seeping steaming blood in the cold air. Stinging pain scoured her cheeks with tiny bits of hard dirt. The knuckles on her hands were torn and bleeding as her fingers clenched into tight fists. Her large eyes opened and looked into the darkness against the night. "Thumber..." She cried in less than a whisper. "Please, Thumber...help me..."

With Hel for a cloak about his shoulders, he swept her into his arms, and she welcomed him.

Chapter 16

Fire tore the night with sheets of gold and blood. Heat pushed the dark cold to hide in the forest. Fryto sat closest to the edge of the pit, glaring into the heart of the fire. He listened intently to the hiss of the air and the crack of the wood. He could hear the symphony play to him, the glow seduce him, the fire call him. Slowly he reached into his fire and the flames caressed his hands. He turned his hand slowly until his palm was flat and open, and in it, was a small flickering flame, dancing in his palm.

Directly behind Fryto the flame, far back in the shadows cast by the light, stood Roc the Dragonslayer. His dull armor caught tiny flecks of firelight. He watched the blurry reflection dance along his metal arm for a short moment and then looked to the knight sitting at his fire. Roc snorted and turned his body from the light and stood in the direct shadow of the tree. His elvish ears pushed themselves forward as they filtered the sounds about him. His eyes cast back the night and gave him sight into the darkness and shadow. There was nothing there that was not there before. He flexed his hands, feeling the weight of his hammer. His left hand tugged on the leather wrapped tightly about the handle while his right supported the stone end. His eyes searched above into the trees and instantly he found J'son sitting comfortably in the crook of two boughs ten paces from the fire. He held his bow in his hands, pulling along the string as if to use the natural oils of his hands to wax it. Roc turned back towards the fire as his eyes began to burn green, then cooled to brown again. He caught sight of Achillia sitting cross-legged by Orrin's side. Her face was half lit by the fire and shadows showed the definition in her hands and face. Strong sharp features such as hers were unusual in the human breed. It made her rather attractive.

He flushed the thought from his mind and looked to the young boy, Orrin, his face wrapped in trance. Orrin was 69 years old, more than twice that of Achillia. His elvish race would allow him to out live her long before he reached middle age. He was as all boys his young age of 69, amazed at a world so vast and wondrous. But unlike boys his age he was willing to work and didn't complain or whine like a child. Orrin was growing into a man faster than anyone could control. He seemed to be filled with an endless array of impressive surprises.

129

Before the boy, sat Frito. The former knight stared intently at the boy in his trance. His hands reached out and caught the boy as he began to waver. Roc tuned his ears to what the boy had to say.

"I could...not." Orrin blinked several times to clear his head. His large brown eyes finally focused on Frito. "There was some-thing in the way. I could not see." Orrin tilted his head and looked apologetic. "I am sorry."

Frito's attention seemed to stray and then came back long enough to say, "There is nothing to be sorry about."

Achillia's hand gently stroked the boy's arm to reassure him. She looked at Frito. "What could be blocking his Kamri?" Achillia was only vaguely familiar with the rare gift of the mind.

Frito again was pulled back. This time he shook his head at varying speeds as it seemed his attention had difficulty settling in one spot. "A spell, perhaps."

"I'm sorry." Orrin again apologized. Achillia gave him a light assuring squeeze and Frito looked at him.

"No, you may do it yet." Orrin gazed at him in hope. "We must do it together, if you're willing."

Orrin was too pleased to help, that's what he was there for. Frito reached up and took Orrin's right hand and placed it firmly on his shoulder. He then reached up with his scared, left hand and gently placed it against the boy's temple.

Achillia watched intently, only glancing over her shoulder at Fryto, still playing with his fire, watching little puffs of flame flutter about his head. She looked back to Frito, who was intensely staring at the boy. Then she felt it, an itch at her shoulder that wasn't there. She reached back but there was nothing, then she turned around and noticed the Dragonslayer sitting a few paces behind. Roc shifted nervously and began to admire his hammer as he turned back to the shadow of the tree.

"Frito?" Orrin's voice called her attention and she looked back to see Frito's eyes roll up into his head and his grip on the boy loosen.

Roc The Dragonslayer took gaping strides toward him but as he arrived, Frito resumed consciousness. He glared at the boy before him and then glanced slowly all around him as if to confirm where he was. "Wow..." He whispered. "How long was I out?"

"A fleeting moment, my lord." Achillia answered. "A breath and no more."

"blessid…" Frito looked at Orrin as if he were trying to read the boy's mind through his eyes. "What you got in that head."

Orrin was quite confused. Unsure of whether to accept it as a compliment or not, he remained silent. Roc knelt beside Frito and took his shoulder. "Did you find Friska?"

"I found him." Frito shook his head quickly to clear it.

Achillia waited before asking the obvious question. "And where is he?"

Frito looked at her surprised that she didn't know as he did. "Near, but that's not the main problem." Frito said nonplused. "Thamrell rides with him."

Fryto suddenly turned from his fire sending a flurry a fire puffs scattering about. "Thamrell!" He exclaimed as he scrambled to his feet. His armor clanked together as he sat close. "Thamrell? Did you say, Thamrell?" Frito nodded his head. "But…that's impossible!"

"'Tis true." Achillia confirmed. "Holy knights are immune to his possession."

"None the less, he rides with despair." Frito spoke grimly.

Roc rose to his feet. "Then we prepare. J'son and J'cob stay in the trees, Fryto can hide in the fire. Achillia will take Orrin into the woods and hide him while Frito and I stand here and wait for him."

"That won't work." Frito shook his head. "He knows we are here. He was blocking against Orrin, specifically. He had not anticipated my using Orrin's power and therefore didn't block against me. He is too close anyway." Frito fought to his feet and gave an elf call. He waited and J'son came from his post. J'cob appeared from the other side of the camp. The twins stood together and waited. Frito nodded and stepped ten paces out, turned, and walked the perimeter of the camp mumbling to himself. Then he stood at the top of his circle and walked across to the other side. He changed directions at the circle's edge and paced off another invisible line. Fryto recognized the pentacle Frito was forming. Once his fifth and final line was paced, he stood at the center, closed his eyes and summoned power.

Roc drummed his fingers impatiently. Nothing had happened, or seemed to be happening. Just a waste of time. Chanting invisible words on flaky bits of hollow and unreliable magic. They should be preparing for an assault, not a seance.

Frito parted his arms and suddenly lights flickered about the circle. A gentle, warm wind blew lightly from all sides and wrapped itself around Roc. He watched the lights flashing themselves randomly in the circle. Then suddenly, one of them ran across the line within the circle. Soon others followed, lashing about the pentagram in frenzy. Roc reacted unexpectedly as one of the lights lifted into the air, arching over and diving back to the circle like a holiday firework. A second, quickly followed by a third, did the same. Each one living only for a bright instant before diminishing.

The wind began to blow with greater urgency as the lights increased intensity and brightness. They were flashing all about the arch, forming a dome with their fading trails of light. Faster and more random they flew, bouncing into each other and flowing onward towards the ground and bounding up again. The fire, still roaring in the center of the camp, also joined in as Fryto's the little puffs of flame leapt into the sky and joined the lights dancing across the invisible dome. Each one, burning itself out as it reached the circle, but then leaping up again, with renewed brightness, back across the dome.

J'cob leaned closer to his brother and nudged him. His twin didn't look, but nodded in response.

Frito turned his eyes from the bright light of his own magic. His sensitive eyes could not hold the splendor as the light seemed to now bend in a solid sheet of scintillating colors.

Then it was gone. The wind and light vanished as simply as blowing out a candle. Frito looked up and all about the perimeter, satisfied.

"Will it work?" Achillia was the first to break the silence.

"What was it?" J'cob said stepping closer to his older brother. "What did it do?" He looked about and saw nothing different.

"It will keep Thamrell out of this site." Frito said calmly. "Friska will walk through the dome, but Thamrell cannot." He looked at Achillia. "And it should work." She nodded in approval. "And free of Thamrell's influence, we will be able to find out what happened." He turned to face Roc to see his approval.

Roc looked around the perimeter, lightly rolling his hammer in his hands. He tested it's weight before sliding it into his belt. He stepped over calmly to his horse still looking about. All eyes were on him, watching and waiting for his response. He ignored the eyes as he stripped his helm from his horse and drew out his great sword. "This will call for my number six answer." He felt it slide about the air as he readied himself for battle.

Roc felt Frito drawing a breath to speak and spun about faster to cut him off. "What do you want me to do?" The Dragonslayer shouted. "I see nothing!" He scanned the perimeter before looking back. "How can I invest against Thamrell with nothing!" Frito started but the Roc cut him off with a sharp wave of his blade. "No! I don't want to hear it. We will do it your way. I will stand fast—right at your side." He removed the scabbard from the horse and slipped the sword back into it before strapping it on his back. "I will wait before I move." Frito nodded, knowing that it was Roc's plan all along. "Now listen!" Roc called everyone to order. "When I do move, so will you. That will not be Friska who I move against. Do not parry or play with him. Is that understood?" Achillia nodded solemnly. The rest looked down, away, or into the fire. Roc's eyes, blazing green glared at Frito. "You understand, Dwayne?" Frito looked up. He knew too well what Roc spoke of. "That isn't your brother coming." Roc told him. "You'll have your say. But remember, he has sworn to kill you and even Friska the Wind does not give oaths lightly. Do everything in your power to sway him. No matter what happens, it ends this night. On my honor, it will be over before the dawn." His green eyes sharpened as his eyes narrowed. "We are in agreement on this." He spoke as an order. Frito nodded submissively. Roc's eyes cooled as did his tone. "This isn't the first. We've had our fights. Remember the worst beating we ever got, Dwayne. Your father caught us slugging it out by the shed. He beat you for knowing better and then he beat me for winning."

Frito shook his head. "This isn't the same..." Frito glared at him. "We didn't take swords to each other."

Roc cut him off with a sharp twist of the head. "True! True! But a petty argument sparked us both to fight. We are older. We have moved to bigger arguments."

Frito cocked his head contemplatively, his eyes never lost sight of the Dragonslayer. "This isn't an argument. He is driven by Thamrell."

Roc's eyes cast out their green and took in Frito as the thought rolled in his head. *You think me blind, or are you that blind, cousin. No matter, it is time to awaken you.* "No, Thamrell only guides Friska's hate for you. He hates you. He hated you before you left and hates you more now that you have returned. He's always hated you. He has tried his whole life to hide it, change it, be something else. Now, Thamrell has taken that mask away. Stopping Thamrell will not stop him. You were different. I saw it in your eyes. When you were Hauth you didn't hate, you were just driven. A puppet. Cut the strings and it ended. It won't work like that this time." His eyes cooled to brown. "I will be watching him. I will know. You knights claim to be able to look into a man's centre," Roc thumbed his chest. "I can look into his centre as well." Roc nodded to himself and peered out into the dark wood.

Silence dragged on with the sound of crickets chirping in the forest. Fryto nodded at nothing particular and sniffed the air as if to test it. He then turned and looked to Orrin. "How much time?"

Orrin looked lost for a moment, before looking up. "They're here." He said to Fryto before turning to Frito. "Not far. Twenty men, heavily armed. Two spell casters and Friska in the lead. A few mo-ments away." Orrin paused. "He has dropped his defenses. He knows I'm here and wants me to see him."

Fryto looked to Roc and then his brother Frito. "Well?"

Roc turned slowly breathing out like a dragon hissing before it strikes. "No reason to hide. He knows, doesn't he? Orrin stay with Achillia. Stay with your back to the fire. You three," He pointed to Fryto, J'son and J'cob. "Flank her. Dwayne and I," He looked at his cousin. "Dwayne will do the talking." He looked back to Orrin who was visibly nerved. "Which way?"

"South…" He whispered pointing.

Roc looked about in surprise. Friska had been circling them, watching them. He finally turned to Frito. He walked over to him and looked down to him. "You best not fail, cause I won't."

"You know, if I fail, I will be dead." Frito said simply stating fact.

The Dragonslayer tightened his gaze. "If you fail, so will your brother."

Frito looked away. He watched as Horse nudged at his fellow horses and step out of reality with them. He then turned and watched as Roc readjusted his great sword on his back. Frito stepped behind him and held it as he tightened it in place. He could feel it's weight and solidness. Deep beyond its steel he could feel the ancient magic living within. A sword of power, giving man the power to slay the great dragons. A sword falling by right into the hands of the Dragonslayer. Frito stepped back and looked him over. The Dragonslayer was frightening indeed. The wide armored shoulders and narrow waist fit his form perfectly. The patches of barbed spikes that ran from his neck to his gauntlets, across his belly and down his thighs was designed to emulate the terror that was Roc himself. Frito bent and scooped up

Roc's helm. Roc grunted, flexing himself to insure that everything was properly in place. Frito cocked his head to the side and eyed the Dragonslayer. Then he tossed him the helmet.

Frito sighed, then raised his hands to his lips, and gave an elfcall.

Achillia looked around as she waited. The Dragonslayer stood a pace behind Frito with his buckler in his left hand, and his hammer in his right. "He is calling Friska." Orrin whispered to Achillia knowing that humans could not understand the elfcall. "Friska has replied. He is here."

"Good Evening." Came a shout from off in the distance. Men tramping through the dry, dead brush could suddenly, be clearly heard. Friska dropped all of his shields and no longer gave pretense to stealth. "Be there room by your fire in which one could rest his cold bones?"

With his back to the fire, Frito realized how cold it was. As an elf, he felt not the cold and Achillia was not the person to mention it. Fikor's winter was coming. Frost stuck to his face and everything seemed sharp and keen in the cold's darkness. The tree's outline cast pure shadows, shifting suddenly, flickering like the fire that cast them. "Come Friska…" Frito shouted. "Come see me." Frito was trembling beneath his armor. His centre sat unstill and his fingers felt swollen as he flexed them.

"Do you still think to command me?" Wind whipped hard, swirling the leaves and lifting them to dance in mad circles. "You are no longer one to command!" The fire's light cast upon him and the others moving closer. "Okshiru has cast out the unclean!" He came closer and stood right before the pentacle. He searched the area with a quick glance. "I heard your elfcall from a thousand clicks away. You summon your doom!" His face was withered like an old man. The yellow glow of the fire lit upon his face leaving it drawn and shriveled. His eyes were wide and white with the gaze of hel. "Fryto!" He yelled across the pentacle. "You stand on the opposing side of Okshiru. Stand by him. Stand by me."

Fryto shook his head. "No Friska, it is you who are wrong." Fryto glanced to Frito who was staring intently at Friska. "Come, my brother, you and I." He called to Friska. "We shall talk."

Friska smiled broadly. "He has lied to you. Come with me." He turned and looked to Achillia. "And Achillia, you too stand against Okshiru? Have you fallen from Uko as my elder brother once had? If so, then stand by me, welcome him, again!"

"I am the servant of Uko who is the servant of Okshiru. That is where I stand." She announced plainly.

"You stand beside the Ninefingers. You stand with Hauth." He read her confusion and turned to Frito. "You didn't tell her? Don't tell me, it just never came up in conversation."

Frito tightened his lips, and glanced back to Achillia. "Its true…" He said facing his brother again. "But it has passed and all done wrong has been set right again."

"LIAR!" He screamed drawing his long sword–losing all composure. "All is wrong! Nothing was saved!"

"Friska…come, talk to me." Frito held out his hand.

"You hold out your hand in friendship with the Dragonslayer in battle array standing beside you? Oh, have I failed to mention? Dragonslayer, you too have been a thorn in the side of my lord and I'm here to kill you as well."

"Then come do it!" Roc coaxed.

"Friska…" Achillia called him. "I stand with Uko, and I stand with Frito." Frito glanced over his shoulder and Achillia nodded back.

"Hear me Friska…" Frito began.

"I shall not listen to the master of Hel. But I implore you, let the boy go."

Frito shot a quick glance to Orrin hiding behind Achillia. "Hear me…" Frito went on. "The time for death is over. Okshiru taught you to forgive. There is no longer a call for death but only a call for life. Please, Daniel, end this death."

"You blasphemy! I shalt not hear it. I planned words to sway you brother, I did not want your death, but it calls to me and my words escape me. The time is over. In the name of Okshiru, I will slay you."

Roc crouched, ready to fight. Frito held his hand out to keep him in check. "Okshiru would not put brother against brother? Why you, Friska? Why not Milo, or Achillia? Why you, my brother?"

"Because all have fallen to your spell. Even Achillia. But I stand immune." He stepped across the pentacle.

Roc stepped forward but again Frito held him in check. "It didn't work!" Roc hissed but Frito still held.

"No Friska…hear me." He glanced over at Friska's men standing about. Friska had planned that they would not interfere unless needed. "What you hear is not Okshiru…But Thamrell."

"Knights are immune to Despair." He stepped forward and Frito stepped back, signaling again to hold the Dragonslayer.

Faster than Roc could move, Friska struck. His sword whistled in the air and thrusted deeply into Frito's chest. "You didn't forget I could do that?" Frito asked calmly with an empty, hollow voice.

Friska slashed again and again at the Frito who was not quite there. Friska bit into his lower lip as he pulled away. He stepped slowly back. "Come back here and let me kill you."

"You and I…" Frito went on. "We can go to mother, together, she is the Grandmaster, she will know what is right."

"You bastard!" He screamed through his teeth. "You hurt her. You're not her son!" Again he swung through Frito's intangible body. "Stop that!"

"Friska…don't you see? You are possessed, break the spell!"

Suddenly winds swept from the south. Giant gusts hurled stones and leaves everywhere. Blinding bits of sand were thrown by the billowing cold night. Fryto's fire toppled like a great tree and snuffed into darkness, the fire-master himself stumbled against the wind and like a toy was thrown to the line of the pentacle. There he held fast as if pinned to a wall. Achillia, Orrin and Roc himself, moved like puppets and also pressed into the invisible wall. J'son and J'cob tumbled like clowns into the wall. Wind whipped around the pentacle and held them all fast in place.

Frito stood unmoved as did Friska and his men who still stood out side the pentacle. "Let them go." Frito hissed.

"Fight me."

Frito lowered his eyes as they began to burn red. Friska was not a spell caster and Frito knew it. He had to of spent a fortune to purchase one this powerful. "How long have you planned this? You had this in the works when we met at Fanrealm, didn't you? You just weren't ready. You did the fracas at Sugartown to find me. You knew it would bring us together. How many people died in that fire, Daniel? How many injured?"

"Fight me."

"Were their lives worth it? Can you over look the blood you have spilled? And what will you get out of this…"

"Fight me."

"Who will respect the man who slew his brother!"

Orrin screamed as the wind lifted him higher into the air.

"STOP IT!" Frito screamed.

"Fight me, Ninefingers!" He spat the name in contempt.

Orrin screamed again and the blade-spear magically hurled itself into Frito's hands.

Edged steel bit into the wooden shaft of the blade-spear as Frito parried the blow carried by his younger brother. Frito quickly lifted the butt and jammed it into Friska's chest forcing back his attack to defense. Frito then braced the butt into the ground and using the haft, shoved into Friska, sending him to the floor.

Quickly Friska rolled to his knees only to have Frito's boot slam into the side of his head. He faltered and rolled hard into the side of a stump. His armor clanged and again he fought to his feet, but Frito slid the haft between his legs and tripped him to the ground.

"Look up, Daniel." The fire was gone and light was lost. Friska's elven eyes looked past the darkness and gazed up into the honed edge of the blade-spear. "Okshiru does not fight with you! You've lost in less than twenty beats!" Friska lifted his sword and waved off Frito, rolling to his feet. They squared off again. Friska, this time more carefully, stepped into his stance, using the blade to do the work. He thrust and forced Frito to the defensive. He spun, driving the blade up, but Frito deflected the blow easily away. Friska stepped forward, but Frito held out the blade-spear forcing him back. Friska turned and lunged, his blade danced close to Frito's head, but Frito side stepped and let him pass. Frito twisted back, driving the butt into Friska's spine as he drove by. Again, Friska clashed to the ground, but this time he was on his feet quickly.

They faced off again. "Daniel!" Frito called him as their weapons clashed again. "Let this go, its your anger the Despair wants!" And again they clashed. "Can't you see this is wrong! He's using you!" And again. "Look how you are beaten!" Frito stepped closer dropping his haft. He drove his armored elbow into the side of Friska's head. The younger brother recovered quickly and swung out his sword to keep his brother at bay, but Frito again stepped closer and muscled his brother, shoving him back. Friska swung wildly and Frito ducked. With his younger brother off balance, he brought the haft into the side of his head with a loud crack. Through his ringing ears he could hear his brother shout. "That could have been the blade, I don't want to fight you!"

"You want to pull me over." Friska couldn't hear his own voice over his rattling teeth. "I'm more use to you as a servant of evil. I'll hear no more of your lies." Again his blade shot forward and Frito parried it away. He glanced quickly about as Friska squared off again. Roc was still pinned to the invisible wall—squirming to reach his hammer. Fryto held along with Achillia, fighting to get free. Orrin slightly higher, reached fruitlessly towards his field staff, also pinned to the wall.

Friska's sword called his attention. Drawing his guard up as Friska brought it down, but Frito was faster and kicked out and back, catching Friska slightly behind his knee bringing him down again. "Daniel...everyone has forgiven me." Frito panted as his brother crawled to rise.

Friska sat on his knees as his rasping voice ripped his lungs. "They haven't...forgiven you..." He spat out. His eyes slowly rose until they met his brother's. "They only fear you."

The words had spilled from Friska's mouth in Friska's voice with Friska's tongue, but it was Thamrell who spoke.

Friska's words tore into Frito's centre. No, it wasn't true. It couldn't be true. They forgave him out right. He couldn't hurt them any more. They knew it. They loved him. They did. They didn't want him to hurt them any more.

Friska suddenly lunged forward, springing from his knees, his sword tip pushing into his brother, punching through his robes and armor beneath. A pace of steel lifted Frito from the ground and Friska screamed in triumph, holding his brother aloft for fleeting beats, impaled on his sword.

Thunder cracked as Frito crumpled to the ground. Friska turned in scant time to see that Roc had finally broken free. But his sword was too slow and the Dragonslayer's hammer came to kill.

The first blow lifted him from his feet and sent his helmet twisting from his head. The ground lifted and the earth betrayed him as it tossed him down. "From the pits of hel I come." The Dragonslayer growled as he came closer. Friska tried to center his vision and keep his sword in his hand. "Awakened from my lair." Friska lashed out and glanced off the edge of Roc's shoulder. Roc returned the blow, swinging his hammer in both hands into Friska's shoulder. "I'll drag you back when I am done." Friska screamed as his sword flew, spinning from a numb hand, into the bushes. The blow flipped him to his belly. He felt the bone swim in his arm as he crawled on his knees to hide. "So swears, Dragonslayer!" His hammer sang the air but twisted at the last moment and veered from its path.

Roc lifted from Friska's body, and with a brush of his arm, snapped the crossbow bolt in his side. Men were rushing from the woods. Plucked strings of whistling arrows, invisible against the sky, found their mark and the first two of Friska's minions fell from the hands of J'son and J'cob's lethal arrows. Roc was already moving. He ducked his head and charged at the closest one. His shoulder drove into the minion's chest, forcing him back and off balanced. Roc's hammer followed and slammed his head too far to one side.

The others now were moving towards Roc. They shuffled, almost stumbling with awkward and unfamiliar weapons into the welcoming arms of The Dragonslayer. "Come to me!" He shouted as they came at him. "Meet your defeat!" In fury he tossed his hammer back and forth. Its power struck each one with a glowing might that threw them to death as they struck the ground with their bodies shattered. "Its Lord Dragonslayer!" Roc's hammer caught another and he too fell quickly. "The one to beat!" He looked around and discovered, he didn't have enough to kill. "How can I send you to Trid Death, with your chest filled with breath? Get up again, your not quite dead. Come again and I shall lay you to bed!"

Light struck his side with a burning blow that nearly toppled him. The Dragonslayer staggered and turned to face one of the wizards. He stood beside a tree with a swirling power ball in his upraised hand. Roc was above human magic, immune to it by sheer will. But it annoyed him beyond imaginings. He saw the power ball coming and blocked it with his hammer. The spell caster had hoped for a kill, putting more power into his magic and the impact only knocked Roc to ground.

Fire tore the earth and the spell caster screamed as he ignited suddenly. Fryto stood over his brother Frito with his flaming war-axe, giving light to the area. "Fires pit and warming glow." Roc mumbled as he rose to his feet, giving a quick nod to his cousin. "Adding glamour to the show." He clenched his hammer as he looked about for someone else to kill. "I've seen magic get things done." At four strides a minion squared off with him. "But magic ain't half as fun." Roc tossed his hammer and let it bounce off his opponent's head. Roc leaped and landed on him before he hit the ground, and beat him to death with his spiked gauntlets.

Battle blood roared a dragon's song in Roc's head. His flashing green eyes looked out and saw Friska's white enamel armor, crawling in the rough and Roc ignored the screams behind him. His eyes were set on Friska.

Friska was staggering away, trying to get his bearings. Voices screamed too loudly in his head to think as the earth still swirled around him.

"Oh, little Friska, you've made a mistake." Roc stumbled in the soft ground and fought to his feet, finding his hammer as he did. "You've taken a gamble with your life at stake." Roc took no time in covering the distance as he came at him. "But now its time to pay the player." Friska was empty and exposed without his sword. His hands were open, grasping in empty air. His sight filled with Roc charging at him like a bull. His vision centered, spiraling into a tunnel with Roc the Dragonslayer thrusting through. "And the collector is the Dragonslayer!"

Friska turned to run. Pain tore his sides and breath failed his lungs. His vision trembled. Fire light caught the gleaming hilt of his sword pushing from a dead stump and it winked mischievously at him. Trees loomed before him like a marching throng as he reached for the sword. He could hear the cynical rhymes of Roc behind him. Friska's hand went for Fellcannor, his holy blade. As he turned to face him, he gripped his sword and drew it out. It slid from the stump as if it were coated with heavy lard. It laid cold in his hand and pulled to the earth with a great heaviness. With waning strength, he took up Fellcannor and with a trembling hand, held it out. Hammer clanged against sword as stone does biting steel. The heated glow of magic hammer never faltered as it cleared its blow. Fellcannor shuddered and rang like tolling bell as it fell into the leaves. Friska fell back, trying to pull away, but the Dragonslayer backfisted him, the hammer catching his chest guard and sending him hard to the ground. Loose dirt and leaves enveloped him, caressing his head and back where he laid. There was no pain, no feeling, only the tiny tingles in his hand where Fellcannor had been. There was no hurt, no cold. There was no night or darkness. There was only Roc the Dragonslayer, standing much taller, darker and nastier.

Roc held his hammer in both hands, his fingers flexing the haft. For the first time, he hesitated, uncertain whether to carry out his final blow. He looked down at Friska, helpless in the dirt. The Dragonslayer's limbs grew suddenly cold as the heat of battle lifted like the fog of the dawn. This was Friska, Daniel, his cousin!

His arm jumped automatically into motion. Something moved suddenly from behind him and instinct drove the back of his fist against the side of Frito's head. "Blood is blood and water is not." Frito stumbled awkwardly, trying to clear his head from Roc's blow. He could fell a trickle of blood running from his temple. Roc's eyes widened as he realized. Frito was not dead.

Not even a little.

Frito stumbled forward and the two leaned against each other to get to their bearings. Roc's hand ran across the spot on Frito, were Friska had indeed run him through. There was not even a scratch. Dragonslayer's question held back as the sound of steel still clanged in the air. Flashing flame weaved the air with a lustrous flag of gold. Fryto the flame wielded his axe of fire against the last of Friska's minions as if it were a class on fencing. Slashing sword skidded against Fryto's armor as the flat of a shield shoved him back. But Fryto quickly shuffled his feet, feinting with the flaming head of his axe. His opponent raised his shield to block the blow but thought too late about the other end. Fryto swept the flaming butt hook low, turning at the upswing and caught him tightly at the point were knee met leg.

His leg buckled and gave out beneath him as a scream tore his lungs. His shield arm dropped to protect his wound, again forgetting that the war axe had two ends.

Fryto reversed his swing in the same motion—twisting his own body to curve the track of flame and caught his opponent beneath the chin.

Seconds passed as air laid thick in his chest, slowly hissing from his open throat. Silence rang when his rasping stopped. Not even Hauge dared to stir the still leaves above in the trees.

Light beamed from Orrin's staff in a billow of magic. Frito turned and shielded his eyes. With his back to Orrin, he stepped around to face his brother lying in the dirt. Frito cast a long, sharp shadow across him. Friska peered up to see the pure holy glow surrounding the shadowed form.

Frito stooped over and snatched Fellcannor from the dirt. Then, with it in hand, he bent to one knee at his brother's side.

"You...live?" Was all Friska could gasp. Frito ran his hand along his brother's arm. Roc had hit him solidly. A hammer's crushing blow is by far worse than a blade's. Friska's armor was bent severely at the point of impact and his arm beneath was contorted as well. Frito knew well that the bone was shattered and his little brother would lose the arm, if he lived long enough. Blood was pooling quickly and that would take his brother's life before the dawn.

Gently, Frito took up Friska's elbow and braced his shoulder. Fryto stepped around and knelt at Friska's head and used his hand to support the arm itself. Achillia knelt at the other side and held Friska's body still.

"This is bad." Fryto said as snatched off his gauntlets. He ran has hand along the armor. "Blessid." He cursed.

"But can you?" Frito asked.

"I doubt it." Fryto shook his head helplessly. "It must be broken in four places at least. Splintered as well and perforated the blood vessels." Fryto looked to Achillia and without asking, he knew that it was beyond her power as well. He looked to the dark elf. "Frito, you must. Achillia and I together are not enough."

He had been.

Frito felt the weight of the sky settle on him. He had been Archknight, appointed with great powers of healing wounds and sickness.

He had been.

He looked to his brother dying before him. He couldn't see a crazed self claimed zealot—only his little brother.

He had been.

He would be again. He closed his eyes and began to pray.

"I felt you..." Friska babbled above his brother's praying. "I felt you die..." Fryto freed one hand and deftly undid the buckling straps that held Friska's arm guard to the shoulder. "You were there..." Friska moaned in despondency. "not your game of...phantom...but there...I saw you die..."

Shadows shifted and moved as Orrin held his light closer to help show the way, but Frito turned his head and interrupted his chanting. "Fryto..." He called, give us some light."

Fryto the flame lifted one hand and pointed, not even looking, and a column of fire rose swiftly into the air from the fire pit, nearly half the height of the trees.

Friska pleaded with his brother with whimpers and whines of a tiny puppy suffering desolate agony. Frito only ignored his tears and chanted on. "By the great awe of the life giver..."

"Blasphemer..." Friska moaned.

"By who's light we see day…"

"Sinner…" Again he moaned.

Frito clenched his teeth. He never had to heal any one against their will before. It wasn't working. "Friska, listen to me." Frito bent low and whispered into his ear. "You will die if you fight me."

"And sit at his throne side…" Friska quoted.

Frito grit his teeth again as he looked up to his brother Fryto who was as lost as he was. Achillia held sympathy in her centre, but knew not the words. Frito then glanced up to Roc who leaned casually against a tree. Roc turned and looked down. Frito couldn't read his face. Roc looked away to the fire, and then back. "Well?"

Frito grit his teeth. "I am trying."

Roc pushed off the tree, his hammer hung from its strap around his wrist. Roc set his jaw and his green eyes flared. "Well try harder!"

Fryto looked up and his eyes locked with Roc's. "If you hadn't…" Fryto felt his hard restrained temper begin to unravel. "For Okshiru's sake Roc! You nearly killed him."

"I was trying to kill him!" Roc snapped.

"Roc!" Fryto felt his cool slipping. He suddenly remembered his own penance about losing his temper, and forced down the urge to damage Roc back into his centre.

But Roc responded quickly, stooping over and jamming a finger into Fryto's face. "No, don't Roc me! You're the knights! Fix him!"

"Again Lord Dragonslayer turns to Gods he shuns."

Roc turned fast on Achillia. Anger quickly flashed to fire as his mailed fist tightened for the blow that he some how held in check. The exposed bottom half of his face was twisted in a harsh growl. "It's the god I shun who sent him here to kill Dwayne." Roc waved a wagging finger at her. "Am I supposed stand around and watch?" Roc shook his head slowly. "No." He looked up to Frito who sat still watching his dying brother. "Dwayne, I'd kill for you. Damn, I'd die for you and you know it. If it came to a trade between you and Daniel, by my mother's grave I would rather slit my belly then have to choose…" Roc leaned back and finally stood. "But if I had to…" Roc turned and began to walk to the fire. "But if I 'had' to…" He stopped and looked back to Friska lying in the dried, autumn leaves. He twisted his lip in a Roc fashion and headed towards the fire.

Frito felt suddenly spent. He had forgotten that his dependency on Roc was equaled by Roc's dependency on him. But that wasn't the issue at hand.

It was Friska who was now chanting. Quoting the ancient script. "Steel your body and mind, shield strong from sin…" His head turned and focused on Frito. "My sin his made me shrivel like the leaf." His throat choked as he tried to swallow but lost the strength. "Okshiru appointed me his servant,…but my sin has failed him."

"Sin…What sin?" Fryto glared at him. "Friska, look at me! It wasn't Okshiru. It was Thamrell! He deceived you. He is in you now, wanting you to die!"

"Okshiru has sent me to die at the hands of Hauth for my sin." He slowly lifted his other arm to shield his eyes. He suddenly shuddered and started to cry.

There were no tears.

"Then repent your sins!" Fryto leaned and coaxed him. "Lift onto him an unladen heart."

Friska stopped sobbing and with gasping strength he mewed loudly. "Okshiru…Lord of Sky and sea…See your son…here on Mortalroam…I accept your judgement…I sinned at the hands of Hauth, so I shall die by the hands of Hauth…"

Fryto's mouth sagged open and he shrugged his shoulders from futile efforts as he realized his plan had failed. He had no idea of what sin Friska was talking about, however; Frito did.

"No…Daniel." Frito argued quietly. "I am no longer Hauth. He is gone from me." Frito took Friska's uninjured arm. "See the wound you gave me." Frito guided his brother's arm to the spot. His hand feebly touched the armor plates. No hole, no wound. "He has healed me…Okshiru has healed me…He caught me moments from death and I am now reborn the Archknight! He wants me to heal you, you must let me…let him!"

Friska's head bobbed and lifted to see where his hand was. Then he let it drop back to the ground. "Lie…Lies…"

"Listen not to Thamrell's whisperings in your ear. In your heart you know I speak true." Frito picked up Fellcannor. He took Friska's hand and held it with his own on the grip. "Feel your own blade and know it is true. Do you feel it's heat? Do you feel it?"

145

Friska could feel the warming surge of the holy blade and it's warmth grew in his cold hands. He could also feel the large warm hands of his brother on his own. It was a good feeling.

Whistling leaves lifted and skittered about. A tiny breeze swept over him—a warm wind that he knew was from within himself. Friska, the wind.

Fellcannor suddenly flared to brilliant light, radiating white brightness that lit the site with purity. A holy knight's light, shining out evil and illuminating good.

Fryto and Achillia reflected its glow as did Friska himself. Frito was glowing on his own. The truth was known.

"He..." words failed Friska. "He had forsaken you..."

Frito's hands pulled away. "I turned from him." Frito took up Friska's elbow and shoulder. "He never turned from me." Like flowing water in a stream, Friska's armor straightened and locked into place with the combined power of Achillia, Fryto and Frito.

With wide, glowing eyes Friska looked towards Worldsend, and slipped into unconsciousness.

Frito sagged and slouched back as the white light faded away. Fryto carefully examined his unconscious brother. He laid his hand beside his nose, then to his forehead. "Bravo..." He nodded in satisfaction.

Frito suddenly sat erect. He quickly glanced around, then fixed on Orrin. He reached back and snatched the boy's arm roughly. "Steel yourself...shield your mind." Orrin looked at him quizzically and then remembered.

Thamrell, the god of Despair.

"Where?" Frito whispered as if trying to hide his voice from someone who could be right next to him. He looked up to Roc who sat unaware on a large boulder. He mindlessly tapped his hammer on the rock, and with each tap, the stone heated with a blush of red magic, then faded leaving a dry brittle spot. With the second tap, the spot crumbled away. Roc seemed content with his aimless task of chipping the boulder to sand until he noticed everyone was staring at him. His green eyes burned as his face drew low, amazed that they dare look at him. "What?"

Slowly Frito rose to his feet. "Roc, its Thamrell..."

"So?"

"He is free of Friska..." Now Fryto and Achillia were on their feet. "He's around here somewhere."

Roc glanced behind him to see if the lord of Despair was behind him. "I'd like to see him try!"

"Perhaps he is gone?" Fryto said as he hefted his axe.

Frito turned about and searched for some physical response from the entity, seeing none, he turned to Orrin. Orrin took the unspoken hint and used his Kamri to search out the ghost. "I see him, he is still about..."

"He's waiting for us to drop our guard!" J'son exclaimed as he took out his staff and readied himself. J'cob followed the same example and stood at the ready with one sword in each hand.

"Well? What is he waiting for?" Roc bellowed, twirling his hammer as he rocked forward on his feet. Frito's sharp ears listened to the silent night as his eyes focused on Orrin's thousand mile stare. Frito felt silly looking for a physical response from an entity who wasn't physical, but after possessing a knight, the god of Despair could be capable of anything.

"I'm losing him." Concentration dug into the boy's face as he sought out the god. "He's leaving...he's gone." Frito crouched back down to his brother lying on the cold ground. He motioned to Fryto and Achillia and they gently lifted his body and carried him towards the fire. With care they set him down on the blankets that Orrin ran to set out. Pulling on straps and undoing buckles, they stripped him of his armor and wrapped him in the blankets.

"What do we..." Fryto looked nervously about. "You know."

"Do with him?" Achillia asked the question. "His soul needs repentance. He had fallen with Despair. It was the trouble in his heart that caused this." Achillia went on. "Sin does not make one weak physically, as he had thought. It breaks down the will with guilt."

"And Despair entered dressed as an angel." Frito finished. He nodded as he thought. "I can only think of one person who can help him now." He looked to Fryto and he confirmed the idea.

"You speak of Lady Fantista." Achillia spoke approvingly. "Then that is what is to be done. She will know what to do."

"Mother knows best." Fryto kidded.

Achillia turned slightly to her side and took Orrin's arm and instructed him to find Horse and have him bring back the horses. She followed him with her eyes as he dashed off. As he passed behind the Dragonslayer, her eyes set on him standing aloft from the group. He hadn't moved an inch since Thamrell left. She could see his jaw

147

clenching on itself and his breathing, long and sharp, almost hissing. He was coiled, ready to strike. She called to him gently, almost trying to calm him. "Lord Dragonslayer, the danger has passed, come sit with us."

Roc seemingly ignored her as his concentration was else where. Suddenly he turned and with a rasping voice, called Orrin back. Achillia rose to her feet searching the area. "My Lord? What is it?"

When he didn't answer, she turned to Frito and Fryto who only reflected her questioning look. Orrin trotted back up obediently. Roc leaned back and whispered over his shoulder. "Stay here."

"What is it?" Again Achillia asked. This time Roc turned to her, and then to each member of the group. "Something, is definitely…wrong." He said still looking about. His tight elvish hearing listened to the night. "Dwayne's horse would have brought the other horses back on his own." Roc fingered the grip on his hammer. "Something is wrong."

Fryto stepped over to where the Dragonslayer was standing to add his senses to the search. There was a sudden hacking cough. And all turned towards it. Slowly the Dragonslayer took steps towards the sound. One of the fallen minions was stirring. He coughed again as he lifted his head and tried to shake it into consciousness. "My job is not yet done." Roc was taking large, quickening strides towards him. "And the battle is not yet won." Fryto went after the Dragonslayer. He reached out and grabbed his arm, but Roc shrugged it off. "So come with me, and you shall see. Just how Roc has his fun."

The minion was on one knee and lifted an arm as Roc came closer. Fryto's cry of stop fell to the sound of cracking bone as the minion flipped over from the blow. Roc watched him shiver on the ground until he shivered no more and only the sound of the fire could be heard in Meleki's woods. He then turned and headed back towards the fire. Fryto knew that any words he had to say would fall on deaf ears. He only had a glare of disapproval for the Dragonslayer as the large elf passed by. A glare that turned to horror.

Roc stopped and turned to see what Fryto saw—and froze.

The minion was getting up again.

Frito was on his feet, his eyes still watching him as he fought to rise. Frito reached out and clutched Orrin's cloak and the boy needed no coaching as he stayed closer to the dark elf's side. The minions were all regaining their feet and clutching with thick fingers for their fallen weapons. Roc grit his teeth and growled as he suddenly charged at one standing and delivered a terrible back hand that twisted its head over its left shoulder. It paused for an instant before turning to face Roc again. Instinct drove his buckler to glance off the sword thrusting by. Roc shoved out his hammer to hold it at bay and then brought the blade of his buckler back around with a blur; catching it in the center of the throat. Steam and blood spilled from its neck like a glass overflowing. It coughed and hacked and choked on its own blood then took no further notice of the wound and made no move to stem the flow. It only grinned. Spasmodic coughs spewed up blood as it stood mockingly before Roc. A gap in its throat opened like another mouth. It didn't die.

Roc lifted his foot and shoved the abomination to the ground as his left hand slipped into a leather holster. His fingers slid easily over the smooth stone that warmed to his touch. As the minion again fought to its feet, Roc had the fist sized stone in his hand. "Burning flames of roasting bones...feel the glow of my Firestone!" A jet of flame came from his hand and instantly set it afire.

"Roc! Get back here!" Came Frito's order and Roc gave no argument and backed his way towards the group. They were circled and fighting back the attack of the other minions. J'son and J'cob parted, allowing Roc to join the group. As he did, the one he set afire, came charging at him and leapt at him at the last instant. With burning hands it gripped at Roc's mask and tore it free. Roc turned as J'son used his staff as a lever and wretched the minion free. J'cob hacked at it to no avail. Mortally wounded it still sought to fight, swinging its dead, cumbersome arms like a laundered shirt in the breeze. The Dragonslayer pushed forward swinging his mighty hammer. The magic hammer sank into its shoulder, crushing the bone. The force of the blow drove it to the ground with a broken fall, but it only sought to its feet again. Fryto lifted his axe and jets of fire and brimstone flared from the ends, setting another to flame. Achillia swung her sword and deftly chopped one between its neck and shoulder. Licks of lightning traveled the blade and into it, causing it to quake violently and fall to the ground. It only coughed twice, before rising up again.

Frito stood beside Orrin in the center of the circle with his blade-spear in hand. His summons of magic power lifted from the tip of the blade and lashed out in great glowing red tendrils of light. The flash struck one with a searing fury and sought to strip it of all flesh. It shook

149

and twisted as it was tangled in the twisting vines of burning magic and the stench of rotting flesh filled the air. As the light finally faded, only bits of smoking skin clung to the black bones. It still came forward.

"YO! DWAYNE!" Roc cried as he kicked off a bodiless hand that had grabbed his ankle. "Would you call this a perilous situation?"

"Yes." Frito gagged from the stink as he sent the fleshless horror shattering to bits with an invisible wave. "I would definitely call this a perilous situation."

"Then I think…" Roc stomped on the hand as he swung at the body it came from. "that you should think of something!"

"Me?" Frito whined. "How is it me?"

Roc bent down and smashed the hand under his foot with his hammer. "As I recall, it was my turn last time."

From Frito's patch-worked hand came two sparks that quickly grew to the size of flaming boulders. They hurled sporadically in the air before colliding head on with one of the minions caught between. The resulting explosion blasted it to smithereens.

"Good strike my lord!" Came from Achillia.

Frito hissed as he saw the smithereens quickly crawling to reassemble themselves. Frito turned hotly to Roc who was preoccupied with the disembodied hand crawling up his arm and J'cob trying to chop it with out hitting him. "Are you sure?" Frito called.

Roc pulled the crawling hand from his face. "Yes I'm sure, do you want me to stop and check my log book or are you gonna trust me?"

"Yes, Frito." Fryto said calmly as he let the length of his axe reach over and chop a forehead. "This is getting ridiculous."

A minion gripped tightly at J'son's staff and yanked him from the circle. They suddenly leaped at him with clawing hands as J'cob and Roc quickly fell after and leapt into the fray. Fryto, Achillia, Frito and Orrin, slowly shifted their circle to aid in protecting J'son. Roc was tossing them left and right to free him. J'son shoved one free and into the flaming wake of Fryto's axe. He smiled at his clever maneuver, but looked to late at an oncoming spear.

It pushed through his mail and sank a half finger deep into his belly before Roc could stop it.

With a rising snap of magic, Frito suddenly forced minions flying back with a stunning wave of light. A simple delaying tactic at best, but he needed time to cast a bigger spell. Frito was wearing down, as were the others, but Friska's minions weren't. He cursed and called down lighting from the sky with a bellowing cry that rattled his lungs and centre. Forks of light struck with thunder from above, through the trees into each minion. They jumped and bounced and rolled, thrashing in the dirt, flailing and kicking their arms and legs. Their screams were only bested by the assailing, retching, smell of roasted carrion. The lightning didn't stop until their shivering did.

"Hail! Lord of Lightning!" Cried Fryto, but his joy was too soon spoken as Friska's minions again fought to stand.

"Of course you realize..." Roc said as they reformed the circle again. "That since that idea didn't work..."

"What?" Frito stopped his prayer of healing for J'son and looked up. "That's not fair."

"Fair is fair and rules are rules."

"I wanna see the rules!" He grumbled as he laid a warming, healing hand over his brother's wound.

Roc twisted aside and let a spear pass. "You want me to stop and show you?"

Fryto screamed and crumpled to the ground. Achillia's sword flashed with streamers of lightning at a minion again and again until it fell back. She stepped aside to stand over the fallen knight and glanced down to see if he lived. He was rolled into a ball chanting an ancient call for life to heal himself. She turned back to fight. She could feel moisture clinging to her body beneath her armor and she was not sure weather it was blood or sweat, or whose. Not that it mattered.

J'son had returned in time to aid his twin brother who had taken a severe blow to the lower arm.

"Dwayne..." Roc called again. "I haven't got all stinking day!"

Frito stepped in front of the circle, bringing Harbinger, the blade-spear into play. It lashed and swept with a keen fury leaving nothing in its wake. But for every limb it severed, another took its place. He heard Achillia shout and knew that Orrin was behind her. If anything, he had to protect the boy. He glanced back to see her still standing and fighting before turning back. Flashing steel shone before him and only his mastery of Sho-Pa allowed him to keep his eyes in his head. His blade-spear again swept and with it came a head. It landed beside him, blinking its pale clear eyes.

Roc was beside him now and the two fought back to back, bringing the concentration to them and away from the others. Orrin was now fighting, swinging his staff as he had been trained. Tight fury clenched on the boy's face as he stood at Achillia's side.

"I do hope you're thinking!" Roc said as he slammed another only to have it come back again.

"I thinking that I'm going to hit you next!" Frito answered as the tip of his blade sliced its way into a face. No blood came from its torn head and no register of pain came from its clear, empty eyes.

And then he knew.

"Orrin!" He screamed. "Give me light! Give me light!"

A white plume of light blossomed from the lad's field staff at full power. Its light billowed brighter than the torrid flame that Fryto had conjured. Light blinded Frito with pain and he was forced to turn away. Max's magical field staffs were made for non-magical people. The staffs were charged by laying them in the sun and at night, when commanded, they burned with pure sun. Sun that Nih elves hated.

The minions screamed at first, trying to shield themselves from the light. Then they crumpled and fell hissing to the ground. Even the Dragonslayer stopped in awe as he watched them burning in the light, dissolving into green smoke.

"Roc!" Frito cried. "I can't see!"

Roc reached back and took his cousin's arm. "Their fading away!" Roc informed him.

"No…" Frito said. "Beware them! They're Shog Tie!" Roc only took his cousin's warning in time to see the smoke begin to form in the shadows of the trees above. Mouths filled with beastly, crooked fangs screamed as arms pushed out from under their chins. They swooped and dove, and struck. They first dove at Orrin, but the light forced them back. Another lashed at Achillia with raking talons at her face. She swiped at it, but it lifted higher out of the range of her sword. Another lashed at Frito, but Roc's firestone scorched it to nothing with a simple blast. Another blast sent the one buzzing around Achillia screaming into the woods. With his back to Orrin's light, the Frito hurled his blade-spear whistling through the air. It struck its target with lethal aim disbursing it into green whiffs of smoke.

"We've got them on the run!" Roc shouted as he unleashed his column of flame again. But this time, it fell short as the magic of its charge was draining. The Shog Tie saw it fail and circled around quickly and dove for Roc. With a howl, it's sharp talons sparked against his buckler. It finished its pass and again circled around for him, but

twisted slightly in flight and aimed for the unarmed Frito. It swirled the
air with a echoing scream of death as Frito braced himself for the attack.
From behind, Harbinger, the blade-spear, disbursed it to nothingness as
it magically returned to it's master's hand.

Roc was swinging at them as they swarmed him like giant wingless
flies. Each one in fear of coming to close to the path of the flailing
hammer stayed teasingly out of reach. Frito was now wielding bolts of
lightning, sparking the air in a shield that held them at bay. Roc's
crashing hammer lashed out and passed through its target, harmlessly.
Frito saw this and extended his band of lightning to include Roc in its
grasp. He glanced over his shoulder to see Orrin fighting with his staff,
its billowing flame shrinking in size and power as its charge was spent.
The field staffs could run all night, but not at full power. As it died, the
Shog Tie grew stronger, able to pass their way and still attack. The
Dragonslayer had now dropped his hammer and withdrew his great
sword. His body twisted and flexed as he heaved the heavy blade
through the air. It lashed through the electric barrier and cleft another
to dust, but others were now passing through as the staff continued to
dim. Fryto was now on his feet but barely able to protect himself. His
flaming axe gave only enough power to singe them. It held the Shog Tie
back for only moments before they realized they had not been harmed
and circled again.

Frito felt his own barrier was weakening as a Shog Tie sailed
through. He had hoped that the magical field staff would be strong
enough to kill them but it wasn't and now his spell was also failing. His
unplanned, unprepared spells were faulty and weak—but he needed the
time. He dropped the curtain of light as he summoned another spell.
He changed his tactics, lashing out bolts at individual targets, only to
find them passing through the enemy, harmlessly.

It was time for another idea.

He shifted tactics for he no longer had the strength to maintain the
bolts. He had to stand his ground, using his blade-spear to fend them
off. Only it and The Dragonslayer's great sword would send them to
nothing. Achillia's sword and Fryto's axe would pass through them,
fading them, but nothing more. They would fall back, reform and attack
again. J'son and J'cob were nearly defenseless. They stood closest to
Orrin's flickering light where its power made the Shog Tie weakest.
J'son used his quarterstaff and J'cob used his swords. Orrin only shoved

the waning light to back them away and tried desperately not to think of Max and broadcast his fear into every head around him.

Orrin's light suddenly sputtered, spat and died.

The Shog Tie howled and laughed and came for the final kill.

Frito charged at Orrin. His breath drew in air as a spell came to his lips. He reached the boy and gripped his shoulder with his right hand and held him fast. He dropped Harbinger, held forth his left, patchwork hand and with a sudden fist, came the thunder from his lightning. It trembled the earth and shook the trees, and with the assault of a crashing wave, cast the horrors tumbling over themselves backwards towards the trees. Again he swept his hand and the thunder again exploded with the sudden crack as if the sky itself had split open at his command.

He needed the time to conjure a final spell. If he was fast enough, they could escape. Transport spells were risky, even dangerous, but there was no choice. He felt the last bit of his magic drain from his body like breath from his lungs as he called for the Wove of the Worlds to open and accept them.

The Shog Tie were regrouping again but Frito felt the portals to the Netherworlds open and its sucking wind to haul them away.

The Shog Tie bellowed and charged to follow but it was too late and the gap was open.

And he stopped.

Friska.

He was still lying there unprotected and unconscious. If they were gone, surly the Shog Tie would tear him to shreds in anger and frustration. No, he would not leave him.

They were swarming again. Roc's great sword swung again and another faded to the air as he backed towards the magical opening. Frito only stood his ground, lashing out towards them. "Achillia!" He screamed and glanced back as he shoved Orrin towards her. "He is your life!" He shouted. Orrin screamed his sudden fear and argument to deaf ears as Frito shoved them both through the portal. He turned, looking up to the Shog Tie. "IF YOU BASTARDS WANT ME...COME GET ME!"

And they did.

Racing through the air they came. Each piercing and impaling themselves on the waiting blade-spear. They wanted Frito and they were dying to get at him. From behind, one snatched his arm holding it fast as another soared in and clawed deep into his breast plate. Razors burned like hot steel as they slashed open his exposed hands. They grabbed onto his kicking legs and held fast to his wailing spear.

Flashing steel rang as a war cry filled the forest and the Dragonslayer sailed though the air. His leg was cocked and his sword was brought across his body as he attacked in mid leap. His blade sliced mere inches from his cousin, causing a Shog Tie to fade to oblivion. He landed on his feet with a clatter of armor and a grunt from his lungs. His arms waved in circles for balance, but quickly recovered as his wild eyes flared green searching out the next horror to kill.

"Is my math that bad?" The Dragonslayer grunted as he lifted his sword once more. His arms were soft lead and shook with sweat. His fingers were too numb to grip the sword as it fell heavily to the earth. Claws dug into his back followed by the nick of steel as Frito's own blade-spear came too close with disposing of the Shog Tie. Frito looked up and realized what Roc had said. No matter how hard he disbursed them, they were reforming.

This was going to get difficult. He had planed to escape alone when the others had gone. He should have known that the Slayer would not leave him, but then again, it didn't really change his plan for he didn't have one. It was time to plan. A miracle would be nice but knights knew better than to count on one.

Still, a miracle would be nice.

And a small miracle came over the east.

Frito's heart leapt and jumped as he screamed. "Hey Boys! Do you know what time it is?"

The leading Shog Tie lifted out of the way of Roc's lumbering sword and turned to the east. Its eyes filled with the blue of a thousand blues casting out wider than it could behold. Shegatesu the Dawn peered out from the thick foliage in specks and shadows among the black wood. She filled it with the rising of ten, ten thousand, risings as she had done since the re-awakening of time and shall forever do.

It bellowed in it's twisted, nasty language and shot into the forest. The others went screaming and howling in different directions.

Rasping breath and steaming sweat held the morning at bay. The sudden shrill of a morning bird finally gave welcome to Shegatesu, the tender blushing child of the dawn. Frito reached back, his patch-worked hand tried to grip the Dragonslayer to no avail as he slid slowly to the ground. Roc tried to keep his cousin on his feet but only managed to join him on the ground. Panting, leaning back to back, the two prepared for any assault. "I hope they come back…" Roc tried to grunt. "I'm ready." His sword laid heavily across his lap. He could feel Frito's head nod in agreement. "How…did you know?[swallow]" Roc tried to remove his helm, but decided that leaving it on would be easier.

"I…knew them." Frito gasped. "They were minions from Hauth's [ach] army." Frito wiped his nose with the back of his hand but only succeeded in smearing blood over his face. "He promised [sniff] to give them bodies. Then he betrayed them…"

"He?…" Roc leaned back his head. "You…make it sound [gasp] as if you where two different people.[snort]"

[ach] "We are, now." [ach, ptou] "Thamrell…must've recruited them…[ack] and gave them bodies…[sniff] in exchange for their…loyalty to [ack, haaccck, ptou] my unsuspecting brother."

Roc tried to fight to his feet. Frito only slipped off and landed in the dirt. When Roc's energy expired, he too fell supine in the dirt.

"Why didn't you leave with the others?" Frito spoke to the sky. "I wasn't sure if [sniff] I could have pulled [ptou] it off."

Roc tried to sit up again but failed. "I had a choice of letting Achillia rescue me…or stay and fight to the death. I'm still thinking it over." Roc tried to toss an arm over his eyes, but his armor didn't stretch that way. "Besides, I knew you had another idea."

"I did, but I left it with my other armor." The two lay in silent exhaustion as the sounds of the forest began to rise and Kemoto the sun god rustled his feathers preparing to fly across the sky.

"Wait!" Roc exclaimed in a whisper. "I think they are coming back!" The Dragonslayer and The Ninefingers grunted and strained to fight the gravity of their armor and sit up. With flailing, grasping arms and hands the two fell back to the ground.

Roc lay beside him motionless. "Of course you realize, its your turn to come up with a good idea!"

"Lord Frito! Dragonslayer!"

"Oh, no, its worse than I thought!" Roc moaned. "Please Dwayne, put me out of my misery."

Achillia dashed over followed closely by J'son. J'son stood guard, watching the woods as Achillia knelt to aid. She went to Frito first for Roc was only moaning his disgust at her presence. She took up Frito's bloodied hands, held them both to her breast and turned her head towards Worldsend.

Slowly, the bleeding stopped.

When she had finished, she held his hands and took up a boda of Slivobitsa and poured it on Frito's hands, and then to the Archknight's lips. Then supporting his head, she lifted him to a seating position. She judged him fit and then turned to Dragonslayer. He had rolled to a seating position as he readied himself for her knightly first aid. She reached over and with effort, removed his great dragon helm. For the first time, she took a good look at his face.

Not a scratch or scar, not a whisker of mole. He was in fact...handsome.

Roc looked at her surprised expression and turned away as he quietly grinned to himself. When he did, Achillia could see that when he stretched his face, it contorted, and twisted (though unintentionally) into something...horrible.

He pulled back his arm and tried to stand. She gripped him and with great care, lifted him to his feet. Frito was already standing. The Archknight could feel the acrid healing burn of the Slivobitsa make its way through his body and on his hands. He breathed deeply and flexed his hands to ease its pain.

Running feet pounded as Orrin came from the trees. His long elven hair pulled behind him as he leapt into Frito's arms. The boy gripped him tightly and cried deeply into the Archknight's armor.

Frito didn't know why.

__Chapter 17__

Fikor, the great snow dog, stepped down from the north. His eyes of wet tar gazed across the face of Mortalroam and knew it was time. He shook his thick, white coat and snow flittered down like puppets prancing on the air. His shattering bark rode Hauge's winds and his mighty breath swept winter across the mountains. The great snow dog was angry and hungry as he howled in the morning light. Chinook, the Snowbiter, crept away to her stable and cringed from the cold, stamping her hooves in reverence to the god of winter. Chinook, the God of Autumn, had reigned too long and now the bells on Fikor's heavy collar rang as he came down from the mountains.

Black bark wrapped the cold, twisted limbs of the tree. Her hands trembled in the morning cold as she looked at the ground too far below. White frost salted the hard packed road. Mist and vapors curled from her shuddering mouth as her thick fingers worked in the rope of her robe. Above, the sky was blue and endless as faint lights of Kemoto's wings lit in the east. Fikor's winter stung the air as Hauge's wind dashed over her bare legs.

Above her, Okshiru's clouds swept from the north like a darkened army preparing to invade. She paused and wrapped her arms about herself to cease her shivering long enough to complete her task. She was not cold, for her breed felt not the cold, but she shivered uncontrollably just the same.

Her eyes looked to the North. Her teeth chattered together as she watched Okshiru's wave of darkness slide across the world. In the east, Kemoto's great wings began to spread his light across the land. It's warmth touched her like the hand of love and its light touched the cold tears in her eyes.

With the back of her hard, white hand, she brushed her tears aside and wiped away the run in her nose. Again she worked at knotting her rope—tugging at its loop.

Fikor growled from the north as he rode the clouds of Okshiru. He held Hauge to his winds and lashed across Mortalroam, twisting the world like a leaf in the wind. His bark boomed asunder and jarred the tree with suddenness. Her rope fell from her hands as she threw her arms about the bough of the tree. She looked to see her rope hooked on the branch below, spinning like a marionette dancing on stage.

Fikor looked down from the height of the world to the gray, green earth below and saw the white, tattered robes of his knight. The knight appointed to him by Okshiru was a good knight, a faithful knight. He loved her and cared for her as a proper god would for their knight.

Hauge charged by and the tree swayed side to side. Fikor howled and the world shivered. Kemoto bowed his head and folded his wings as Okshiru's clouds moved across the world.

With one hand gripped onto the limb above her, she gently eased herself from the branch she sat upon. Her foot extended lower and her toes clamped onto the rope tangled in the branch below. The tree shook and she gripped the branch tighter. Hauge dashed on and the tree stilled. She then slowly eased herself back up to the branch and took the rope from her toes. She almost laughed at her fear of falling.

Brown, red, and gold leaves leapt from their twigs and skittered on the frozen ground. The ground hissed with the frantic army of dead, dry leaves moving across the hard packed road. Her hands ached as she wrapped her rope about the limb above her.

Some one was coming.

Her wide, brown eyes searched the road but saw nothing. It was Hauge's wind, Fikor's bark, her heart.

Okshiru's thunder.

She looked to the north and watched as the great snow dog swept across the world, turning the new morning into night. Her eyes blurred with frozen tears as the rope from her robe scratched her neck.

Wagon wheels twisted and moaned in frozen ruts of dirt. Hauge squealed in delight at Fikor's cold breath. The world shivered in a cloak of dark clouds as Kemoto refused to shed his light. The branches waved feebly to the wind. The ground was too far away.

Fikor looked above and called to Okshiru with anger. The game was going to far and asked permission to interfere. Okshiru didn't move.

Her legs had stopped trembling as she gripped the branch she sat on. Hauge filled her ears, Okshiru's clouds blinded her eyes, and Fikor's breath filled her lungs with ice. Her eyes looked to Worldsend. Okshiru looked down to her. She felt her face burn with cold and her tears run with pain and her body quake with fear. His giant hand reached down across Mortalroam with a wave of calm. The winds halted and the cold ended and the howling died away.

Okshiru looked down on his tiny daughter. The god of sky, god of sea, ruling body of all gods said to her: No, my daughter. No.

Her eyes could not behold him. His sight was to great for her to see. She looked from him and turned from Worldsend and looked to the ground too far away. She slipped from the branch.

Denice, only daughter of Lord Hammerstrike, the Supergod; Frita holy knight of Okshiru, drifted in the gentle winds like a puppet with tangled strings.

Chapter 18

Steel rang against steel with trembling power as slick, black blood began to flow through channeled veins and red copper wire warmed to glow. Grinding cogs gritted in gear as vulcanized wheels tore the earth into billowing puffs of dust. Images twisted and bent in the polished gaze of chrome. Rumbling clouds of smoke were spat in balls of gray at the road it left behind. Grill teeth grinned defiance to the howling wind. Dry leaves crumpled and scattered beneath its thundering roar.

Spinning wheel in his one gripping hand, the leather ball of the stickshift in the other, he drove with the earth lifting beneath him and eight hundred fiery horses before him. Green fields melted like water beside him while thunder trembled within him.

The Red Barchetta rounded a bend and the road opened before it. Gears buzzed in his right palm as the wheel in his hand writhed like an electric cable. Branches snapped as it lunged by, whipping and waving in its wake. Feet sank pedals in motion as gears responded in rhapsody. Metal rods pulled as lifters lifted. Cylinders dropped when plugs exploded. Warming oil flowed faster as bearings spun about. Another gear leapt to power and the engine leveled off to a plateau. Needles flickered nervously behind glass shields. He felt the rumbling symphony in his heart as the sloping lands unreeled around him.

The engine was running unusually well for the trouble it had been giving previously. He found himself smiling at the idea that he had finally worked the quirks out of the engine. *Now if those monks made the fuel and Rob made that catalytic converter. We will be good to go.* He thought looking out into the cold, gray sky. *Now all we need is better weather and a tape deck.*

Fifth gear went with out a grind and the Barchetta responded with glee and lust for the road. It wanted to run. Like a Pegasus kept for the winter, it wanted to fly.

He looked out the window to the dark clouds looming closer. A storm was brewing. Winter was on its way finally. He reached to the dash board and pulled on a lever. It had only been two weeks ago when he had found a way to re-hook the heater. He rolled up the window and removed his dark glasses. As he felt the warm air sweep over him he suddenly remembered, he didn't feel the cold. Not any more. *But the windows still needs a defroster.* He thought as he turned on the headlights to push through the storm whipping around him.

The clouds blanketed the world and darkness came across the land, but the Barchetta only enjoyed the turmoil. The Barchetta only wanted to run.

His face grew concerned as a buzz came to his ears. His heart moaned and filled with slush as he listened closer to the engine for the origin of the sound. That didn't seem to be it. He looked about and into the rear view mirror. Nothing he could think of would make that noise. Perhaps a branch caught under the chassis? That wouldn't be a problem. If he had made a mistake while rebuilding the thermostat and the car was overheating, that would be problem.

He slowed the car and pulled off to the side of the road. He stepped out and listened to the purring engine. He looked under. It was not leaking oil or any fluids. The tires were sound and nothing was underneath. Then what?

He felt his chest itch, and he knew.

He pulled his cloak about him as he pushed against the wind back to the car. Which god was responsible for wind? He had been briefed on gods and immediately dismissed the entire idea—especially about Onda, god of left turns. How absurd! And no god of right turns, *what's the deal here?*

His skin quivered as his forearms began to itch. Sharp pins raced down his wrists and massed in his palms. Automatic response to stimuli, he thought, still holding his calm. He looked to the sky, there was nothing. He looked to the fields around him, nothing but swaying wheat as far as could be seen, but inside, he felt them coming. Flashing black shadows filled with hate and anger sailing over the mountains a thousand miles away headed right towards his position. *Not good.* With a shift, the Red Barchetta started off with force. He hissed at himself for leaving his armor back at Dragonrealm. The pain in his chest and arms were gone, but he knew that was only the warning stages. As he shifted gears and took hold of the wheel, he could see the mark of the Dancing Dragons on the inside of his forearms. Tattoos that only appeared when his was in trouble.

The Barchetta ran the road.

He knew they were closing. *One, no two…no, Lord! There are more! This is going to be bad.* He leaned forward and looked out his windshield. Where were they? There.

Seven.

Black.

Seven black dragons flying in a WWII bomber formation.

Fuck me. Monday, right?

He pulled a lever next to the ignition and started the second engine. Its main job was to operate the showy, but superfluous rocket/jet boost and the very important nitrous oxide thrust primer deceivingly named *atomic turbo drive.* Once he heard the engine buzzing behind him, he shifted to 'Drive'.

'Ralph.'

The road bent and he couldn't see them any more but he knew they were still there, circling overhead. His eyes searched the road and up ahead was a clump of trees. Cover! He needed cover, and then a plan.

'Yo, Ralph' The Barchetta bounced as winds lifted the car into the air and thrashed it down again. Tight, black leather wings folded about him, sweeping the air as it did. The dragons were playing, teasing, delighting in their game. They knew who he was.

He down shifted and took a hill then shifted again and waited for a second pass. He took the wheel in his right hand and held his left over his lap. Suddenly, magically, a bow appeared in his hand. A bow of his home world made of bizarre metals and unusual compound alloys. It had wheels and pulleys for its strings to ride smoothly, gracefully upon. The bow, as well as the car, were toys of his world, but inlaid into the grip of the bow were three ancient gems of this world. The three gems of the Dragoncaller.

But he was going to need more help than that. He was going to need...RALPH.

'Where are you? You're supposed to be flying escort!'

In his rear view mirror he saw the roof sag as black fingers, the size of his legs, pushed through the roof. The windshield exploded before him spitting tiny squares of glass in his face. The car skidded and the world suddenly spun around him as tan gravel splashed around him. A dragon's scream tore his bones with fear.

The roof was gone and wind now pounded him. To see, he pulled back on his dark glasses to shield the wind. The dragons floated about him like kites hundreds of feet in the air above him. He knew dragons could drop to scant inches above the ground and then suddenly rise, almost instantly, to where the air was too cold to breathe. He could see them laughing. He could see one beginning his bombing run as he folded and fell from the pack. He counted the three seconds...The engine screamed as he dropped to third and the dragon suddenly fell behind. Darkness swallowed him for scant seconds as a clump of trees gave him precious protection. His foot was to the floor and both engines were on redline.

The Barchetta was running.

He was in the open again and the dragons were looming closer. Leathery demon wings mastered the air easily, sloping and sweeping the hard air. Their tails passed to and fro to rudder their pass.

'Ralph, either you show in the next thirty seconds or so help me you're luggage!'

Craig looked over his shoulder to watch them behind him. His hand mechanically shifted to fifth and his foot floored the pedal. He looked back to the dash, at 75 miles per hour he could shift to sixth gear. Not bright on a dirt road, but desperation was setting in. He needed only a few seconds to reach it. The road bent suddenly too far to the left and vulcanized wheels skidded across the hard packed road. Equations danced in his head telling him one of the basic laws of physics—specifically the law that said the Red Barchetta, cruising at nearly eighty miles an hour would not make the upcoming left turn, unless there was an extra sixty pounds of compensating force per square inch applied to the right side of the car.

He could see the valley below as it approached him. There was only the time it takes a man to scratch his nose to act.

Not enough time. He was being chased by seven black dragons, going to sail off a hundred foot cliff and Roc was going to kill him for scratching the Barchetta. He could at least rest in the fact that he did indeed look exceedingly cool in his dark glasses for when he hit the valley below.

He knew, with out a doubt, that this, was indeed, Monday.

The transmission screamed as the Barchetta slipped into third. Gravity shifted as the world slanted to the right. The tires tore loose gravel and the driver looked out his right window and saw a beautiful view far below.

The Barchetta ran.

Road waved before him as the motor slipped into fourth and he tried to think of a good way to thank the god of left turns.

A strange euphoria fell over him as the wind suddenly died away. Balance came to him as a gray shadow dropped on him like a theater curtain. He glanced up and the white scales of a dragon's belly loomed above him as perfect enamel plates of armor. Its wings shielded him from the wind, and locked his car from turning. Slowly, smoothly, its great wide head dipped and looked down at its victim. Upside down white fangs gleamed in his face.

'*Times up Ralph!*'

The Black dragon smiled.

It erupted in flames.

The rolling ball of fire fell behind, bouncing on the road sending spits and clumps of flaming dragon flesh as it went. Scales flew like shrapnel and cracked standing trees with force. It didn't even know what hit it.

Craig was looking all about and could only see six black dragons suddenly rise into the air.

He dropped down to second gear and drove to the top of a hill. By a grove he stopped and looked to the sky. A tiny slit hung in the gray morning. It covered the span of the sky too quickly to see. It dipped and rose and flew with full, open sails. Far below, the Dragoncaller sat up on the back of the seat and smiled. He pushed the thumbs up sign to the sky..."*Good shooting, Ralph! Now, were the hell where you?*"

Ralph's giant blue wings swept low to the earth and with a flap took him faster than the eye could follow into the heavens. He held the sky before him, holding steady in the raging gray. With a cocked riding wing, he swung across and looked down to the green earth below. With a small dragon paw, he waved to the Red Barchetta below.

Fire from above. Ralph pulled up and let it by. He swept higher, his giant claws climbing the air as a black dragon swept down to meet him. Ralph laughed as they collided, their tails intertwining and writhing about. Ralph was nearly twice the size of the yearling black dragon and nonchalantly tore the flesh from his foe and sent him spiraling to the earth in sections.

Four black dragon's danced the air, sweeping like vultures around the giant blue. Ralph roared and whitefire responded to his call. A yearling black exploded with crackling static and dropped from the sky.

Air so thin, air so cold, spit drooled from his seething fangs and froze against his scaly mane. Frost cracked as his wings bent and gripped the air. Three black dragons lunged at him, their talons tearing. The leader spat his brimstone but Ralph's great sweeping wing angled itself and set it aside. From behind one seized his wings, from in front, another grappled with him. They pulled and held with flapping, beating wings, but Ralph's strength pushed them both aside.

Fire tore his wing. The third's bellow had caught him unaware and now blazed against his wing. The other two swung about and caught him again while the third sailed higher to catch the wind and gain power for a kill.

A black streak lined the gray sky hitting a black target in a black eye. A dragon roared and screamed as black caustic blood spilled down its black face and froze along the white of its neck. The third dragon forgot about Ralph as it ripped the thing from its eye. It was a mortal arrow, from the mortal below. *How could this be? No mortal could reach high enough to shoot down the sky!* Another pushed into the bone of his wing and it cracked and splintered and pain shot down its stalk and into its side. The dragon turned to the earth. The human had dared to attempt a dragon! *The human will die!*

It was a foolish thing for the yearling dragon to think for it was a dragon that was already dead—taking its time to fall. Winds swept about it as the earth came closer and it could see the tiny print of a man on a hill. It saw the black trail of the arrow line the gray sky with a black line, but it ended suddenly in it's shoulder. It wailed and shifted its flight. It was getting harder to fly. Its wing had grown numb with pain. It was flying awkwardly. It didn't know why. It could not fly this way, its chest was sticking too far out.

It looked down at it's own chest and could see the tiny feathers of the tiny mortal arrow. *A mortal arrow cannot hurt a dragon's hide, how could this be? A mortal arrow through a dragon's heart?* The dragon looked to the ground again. It was wider than he could see. The dragon looked to the sky. His brothers were getting higher into the sky, farther away. 'Brothers' it cried. 'Brothers, *how can this be? Why are you flying away? Why have you forsaken me?*' It looked to the quickening sky above. '*Mother, what is this? Am I not your child?*'

And the green hills of the earth swept around him and the brown clay of the ground sent him to darkness.

Craig Tyrone, the Dragoncaller, could not see where the dragon had fallen nor did he want to. He had listened to the dragon's cries as it fell. He took no pleasure in what he did.

He looked to the sky again and drew back his awesome bow to get a clear shot above. Ralph was hurt and fighting two dragons at once, but...*Wait a minute, two? There is one missing! Where the hell is he?*

Running on instinct, he leapt from the seat of the car and into the dirt. The giant roar of the wind swept at him as 75 feet of black lizard soared scant feet over him. Craig looked from the dirt to see the black horror turn in flight. A yearling dragon could miss a sweeping pass once...but not twice. Craig could hear the idling engine of the Red Barchetta call to him. '*Lets move Kato.*'

Craig swept over the door. Levers slid to places and pedals slammed as far as they could go.

The Barchetta took the road.

Fourth gear and the earth's landscape blurred beside him. Fifth gear went with a roar and his hands were slick on the wheel with sweat. There was no cover around him—only open road. He glanced in his mirror.

White teeth...*Whoops*...Craig took his hand calmly from the wheel. His muscles tightened and his arm whipped around and backfisted the dragon in the snout.

The Barchetta howled in delight as his sixth gear came to play. Craig looked behind him. The Dragon had been playing and not expected Craig to belt him across the chops. It had fallen back somewhere. Craig looked ahead. A covered bridge! This had to be done right, he tried to calm his heart and plan his physics. At this speed with a dragon behind, thinking wasn't a simple task. He knew that the dragon could pull up even at the last second and miss the bridge. Dragons could defy physics and maneuver the air too quickly. This, he had to plan.

The Barchetta hammered.

Craig looked at the dash.

Atomic turbos to speed...Rear Thrust at full charge...Seat belt on...*Oh, Yeah!*

He listened to the dragon's thoughts and knew what it was going to do. It was angry. He and his brothers had come to destroy the legend that was the Dragoncaller. *It is full of tricks.* It thought: '*But it is mortal and frail and I shalt take it apart a piece at a time!*'

Craig didn't like that thought as he looked up ahead. He needed more time to reach the bridge. He tried to think of a good distraction as he looked up into the mirror and saw the giant claws sink into the trunk.

Fire exploded behind him and the world was engulfed in it. The Rear Thrust spat hell in the bloom of the morning sun. His head was pushed into the head rest as the Nitro kicked in and the darkness of the covered bridge swallowed him.

Wood exploded over the roar of the engines. Splinters pricked at his face and danced on his arms. Light passed over him and the trees that lined the road fell like dominos to the sheer force. Hundred year oaks split asunder as they gave way.

His hand fought the dash board against the G's and pulled out a button. Twin circles of silken sheets blossomed behind him, catching the wind. The engine moaned in ecstasy as it fell from its high.

Craig sat gripping the wheel and the Barchetta trembled around him. He lifted with heavy limbs out of the car and looked to the road behind him. One dragon, stretched out over a mile of road.

Craig panted and tried to catch his breath. The yearling didn't expect the rocket boost in the back. It was blinded and plowed snout first into the bridge, and the road, and the trees. Craig stepped in front of the Barchetta and looked to the sky. Where was Ralph? Did he make it? Why couldn't he answer his call? Craig felt the wind blow again. The storm was closing. He was out in the middle of nowhere, alone and exposed. He had to reach Cornerstone and safety.

He looked to the Barchetta and its four head lights looked back. Twigs and branches stuck in its front grill like the remains of a tree it had eaten. The Barchetta panted and tried to catch its breath before it finally spoke. *'I'm ready, lets go at it again.'*

Craig looked to the sky and Ralph wasn't coming. The dark elf looked around as paranoia filled his veins. *I can't wait for the knuckle head. He can be a million miles away by now.* Craig slowly slipped behind the wheel. *A million miles or not, he should answer the dragoncall.* He thought as he looked across his gauges. He listened to the two engines and finally decided to shut off the second. He hadn't the fuel to waste on both. *'If you can hear me pal, go to Cornerstone, I'll meet you there.'* He called, staring blankly through the shattered windshield. *Last time I play parking valet for Roc, that's for sure.* He thought as he shifted into gear and headed north. *Shit magnet, indeed.*

Chapter 19

Thunder trembled in his bones and quivered in his centre as the angry rumbling in Worldsend woke him with a start. He lifted his heavy head from his blankets and with eyes squinted almost shut, looked about the brightly lit room. A small body rustled beside him. He looked to the boy, then he looked about him again. A wooden shack of sturdy logs with a warm fire in the fireplace, complete with a steaming pot of something on a hook. Achillia and Friska knelt in the corner, their heads bent in prayer. Roc sat against the door glaring at nothing in particular. Fryto sat beside him.

Frito propped himself on one arm and looked to his brother. Fryto leaned forward, rolling to his knees. He swirled the ladle in the pot over the fire before scooping out the warm broth and filling a tamake. He turned and held it out to his brother. Frito's trembling, patch worked hand reached for it and his brother's own guided him to it. Then, with the two hands to guide it to his lips, Frito drank deeply. Fryto took back the bowl as Frito rose to a seated position. His head was pounding from within like an anvil bouncing about gleefully on a steel floor. He was Nih elf and they didn't feel the cold, but this morning, he shivered.

He took the fist sized piece of Roc-bread from his brother and began to pluck out the soft inside with his fingers. "So how long do you plan to keep us in suspense?" Fryto asked as he filled the tamake again. "I mean, we find this cottage and you stroll in, toss your roll on the floor and you and Orrin crash with out a word." Fryto handed him the bowl. "I learned along time ago never to wake you up unless it was of dire emergency." Fryto cocked his head and watched his brother drink. "An emergency meant that you were personally on fire and I could not put out the flames without waking you. I know you must have been exhausted from Magic drain. In fact, I am amazed that you walked here on your own power." Frito continued to slurp. "Am I talking to much for you?"

Frito pulled the bowl from his lips. "Yes." He growled.

"Good. I do think we deserve an explanation."

"For?"

"Green, screaming, hard to kill things."

"Shog Tie." He said simply. "Enlisted in Hauth's army as spies and messengers." His voice grumbled and ground in his throat and he paused to clear it. "For their loyalty," He went on. "Hauth promised them permanent, material bodies. They never got them. Most of the time they are harmless."

"Harmless?"

"More or less."

"Harmless?"

"What he means…" Dragonslayer spoke with such a definition that it roused Orrin from his sleep. "That Shogs delve into bits of magic, but mostly have no or little effect on this plane of reality."

Fryto looked to Roc and then back to Frito. "Is that what you call harmless?"

"No." Frito answered.

"Then?" Fryto asked waiting for more.

"Then what?" Frito answered.

Fryto sighed sternly as his patience thinned. "Then how come they had the power of possession, dead-walk and resolvtion."

"Resolvtion? Is that a word?"

"It's moot. How did they do it?"

Frito shrugged his shoulders. "Got me."

"What?"

Frito looked at his brother. "I Don't Know." He pointed each word.

Fryto leaned back and his lips slightly parted. "You don't know?"

Frito shrugged his shoulders humbly.

Roc unfolded his legs as he leaned from the door. "Why not?" He hissed. "Why Not?"

Frito glared at him. His eyes watched him tightly. "What are you asking?" He spoke carefully.

"I'll spell this out for you." Roc counted on his thick, long fingers. "One, they used to work for you, two, they hate you, three, you're hiding something. I can tell you're hiding something. Knights can't lie. I don't know where you've learned it, but you still can't lie to me."

Frito's mouth dropped as his eyes bent. "Roc…" He whispered.

"DON'T ROC ME!" He roared as he shifted to his knees, coming closer.

Orrin suddenly looked up from his sleep. He blinked quickly through his swollen eyes. Roc went on, ignoring the boy and scrambled awkwardly to his feet, banging his head on the low ceiling. "Don't you dare 'Roc' me. It drives me nuts when you put on the bloody puppy face of yours! Stop it! I don't know where you got THAT from either, but knock it off! I makes me want to clock you in the head!" Roc slapped him in the head and Fryto leapt to his feet.

Frito took his brother's hand and tugged him back with a notion. Frito cocked an eye and rolled his jaw about as he looked at his cousin.

"Get up here." Roc growled.

Frito leaned forward and rose to his feet, standing comfortably in the low ceiling. His eyes locked with Roc. "Good." The Dragonslayer hissed. "That is the first time in two years that you looked me hard in the eyes. You're terrified, aren't you?"

Frito glared back harder. "Of what?" Some how, his voice hid the tremble in his centre.

Roc looked at him in disbelief. "You're asking me? You know!" Roc howled. "You know!"

Frito did. "Do you know what I hate?" Frito asked threateningly. He felt his heart pound on his centre like a drum.

"You hate being slapped up side your head. Hated it your whole life."

"I hate being slapped upside my head." He went on ignoring his cousin.

Roc leaned closer, towering over him. "And you're pissed. You're always pissed when ever you wake up. Its the Nih in you." Roc stepped closer, touching his chest with this older cousin's. "And what are you going to do?"

Frito slowly dropped his head and looked to the floor. His ears burned with fire and the sound of fury deafened him. He felt the sting where Roc had slapped him and it burned. Burned deeply.

He suddenly jerked forward, rising up on his toes and head butted Roc in the teeth. Roc stumbled from the surprise and Frito cocked his arm back and belted him.

The giant elf tumbled backward onto the floor of the cabin. Frito stood motionless as Roc put this hand to his lip to stem the flow of blood. Frito shot a hot eye at Orrin, who had quickly dove out of the way, and then back at Roc who was trying to stifle a laugh.

Fryto had stepped between the two. "Stop." He said quietly.

Roc shook his head. "Don't stop him. He's doing fine."

"I said, Stop." Fryto said with more authority. "I have one brother in the corner, I'll not have two."

Roc eyed Fryto and then Frito. "You done, Dwayne?" Frito's eyes of crimson cooled. He didn't know when they started glowing. Frito looked at his cousin and nodded. "Yeah? Good!" Roc announced sliding to his knees and sitting back on his feet. "Then sit down."

Slowly, Frito did.

Fryto looked at the two of them. "Will someone tell me what is going on?"

Roc motioned for him to sit. "He's been terrified at letting his temper rise. See?" Roc made a perky face. "I'm a good guy now." Roc resumed his nasty self. "Crap."

Frito glared at him. "Fuck you, pal."

Roc's eyes widened. "Bless you, Sir! Might I another?" Roc leaned closer. "It is why Friska beat you. It was Okshiru's plan all along to force you to hurt your bother knowing that you would retake the mantle of the Archknight to save him. You are allowed to be pissed off! Hauth is dead and gone. You losing your temper will not bring him back. Stop pussy footing around. You are Frito, Knight of Dru! You are the Ninefingers! Stop trying to act like him. Just be him." Roc waved a wide hand at him as he changed the subject. "I want to know the story." He lifted and slipped his long legs around as he leaned back against the door again. "'Tis not every day Dragonslayer grants and audience." Roc waved his hand again to proceed. "When did you learn to lie?"

Frito's ears still rang with anger. "Just now. When did you learn to spot it?" Frito asked quickly trying to cool his anger.

Roc shrugged. "I'm good. Plus, your lies are entertaining—especially the one about learning to lie just now. I thought Knights couldn't lie."

Frito slumped back as he thought about it, trying to calm down. "So did I." His eyes wandered over to Orrin still sitting propped in the corner wrapped in his blankets. Frito took up his tamake and passed it to the boy.

"Tell me about the Shog Tie." Roc pressed him. Frito watched the boy a bit longer before turning to Roc. His face burned from his cousin's glare. Roc didn't move. "What?" Roc leaned from the door. "What can be so wrong that you can't tell me."

Somewhere, somehow, Frito found the words. "I have an idea." His voice waved with uncertainty.

"Go on."

"Long story time."

Roc leaned on the door again and became comfortable.

Frito felt the heat lift from his cheeks. "We went to hel to battle Trid Dreath. You remember?" Roc nodded. "We met Weishap, told us about a lot of stuff that made no sense. He spoke about the Poer. You know about the Poer?" Frito glanced at his brother who seemed a bit lost. "The Poer is the essence of everything. We get our magic from its mere existence. It runs like cracks through Mortalroam and Worldsend."

"Go on." Roc growled. "He knows, he was with us."

"Shut up." Frito snapped quickly. "This is my story time. I'll tell it my way." Roc twisted his lip and remained quiet. He shot a glance and Fryto who still looked as if he was hearing this for the first time. Roc looked at him in surprise. "He also told us things that helped us defeat Trid-Dreath the first, right?" When both Roc and Fryto nodded, Frito felt more at ease. "We left Hel triumphant. But there is something that you don't know. The day that Weishap told us about the Poer, was the day I became Hauth, Trid-Dreath the Third."

Roc leaned forward.

Frito glanced at Orrin before going on. "Just my knowing that the Poer existed put it in my control, even though I didn't know it."

"Wait. I was there." Roc said. "We were all there, why didn't we get it?"

"It was the way his answers came." Frito breathed a sigh of relief as he spoke. "When Weishap speaks, he always answers correctly, though you might have the wrong question."

Roc nodded quickly. "I remember that part."

"Well I don't." Fryto pleaded, hoping someone would explain it to him.

Frito nodded understanding his brother's confusion. "We met with Weishap, the god of answers. Ask him questions and he gives you the correct answers. But you had to be careful, because you might have the wrong questions to his right answers. He was selecting special answers for me that at the time had no meaning to me. They floated around in my head and soon I found that the answers went to questions that I had deep in my mind. Concepts that my father hinted at, but never spoke of. Weishap knew this, being the god of answers you know everything. But I didn't know that his answers connected with my questions, until later—after we returned to Hel to slay Trid Dreath the Second. Questions that I had yet to properly form, but with the introduction of the answers, the questions assembled themselves."

Roc tilted his head as he took it in. "When the questions assembled, the answers made sense and became usable. Knowledge became power, so much so that it altered not only your brain, but your physical body as well and you became Hauth, the Beast with backward knees." Roc nodded. "I see. Then you were set up. Just like Friska." Roc nodded, agreeing with himself as the idea rolled about in his head. "We have been told a lie for so long we assuredly believed it true but now we know otherwise. Knights are not immune to the tricks of monsters. You were the direct target and none of us could see a plan so diabolical." Roc snorted as he smiled. "For all of our arrogant boasts, we are naught but mortal fools."

Fryto looked at the both of them. "I don't follow this."

Frito felt his heart skip with gaiety as it was relived of its burden of guilt. He looked at his brother and forced himself to go on with his story. "Once I realized that the Poer existed, everything became antiquated, second place to it. I had to have it. I realized that there was a way to take up the Poer and wield it as my father had. I felt it was my destiny. I didn't know I had the Poer already until after Monsterbelly had fallen and my armies were rolling towards Cornerstone, bent on destroying Mortalroam." Frito leaned closer. "Fryto, I wanted to reshape the earth. I wanted to destroy it and build a new one."

Roc grinned and looked at Fryto. "He didn't know what he was doing. Outlandish impulses became his will and then reality."

Fryto's eyes grew wide as plates as they filled with horror. "What ever for?"

"To be like Lord Hammerstrike, the Supergod." Roc answered, fixing his eyes on the Archknight. "Must be a bitch trying to live up to that." Roc's eyes fell and looked about. "You had nowhere to go." He looked at himself sitting on the floor. "Who am I kidding. Look at me and tell me that I escaped the influence of the supergod. He raised me as one of his own and it is irrefutable that he was successful." Roc shifted as he changed the subject and looked up quickly. "When did you notice what you had done?"

Frito's head swam. He never guessed that Roc knew so much. It was as if he had a view into his head. "When I was in Worldsend." Frito found his heart pounding and his hands sweating as he remembered the view of the earth as he looked down from heaven. He flushed that from his mind and focused on Roc. "How did you know? Craig wouldn't have told you."

Roc's eyes took on a gentle glow that leaked through slits as he uncontrollably smiled, squinting and twisting his jaw as he did. "I am Roc." He answered with smugness.

Frito glared at him and could only smile himself. It had been two years since the war. A year since he found the courage to return to his family and ask for forgiveness. They had all thought him dead—killed in Worldsend save for Craig who was with him and Frita who had waited at the bottom of Worldsend.

Her face flashed in Frito's memory of the day he returned to Mortalroam. He asked her, 'Why are you here?' She looked up at him with her battered, smiling face and said, 'Waiting for you, my brother.' But he could not look upon her. He could not accept her love and forgiveness and he fled into self exile. She and Craig kept his secret, allowing the family to continue to believe him dead. Did Roc think him dead too, and only searched for answers to soothe his ruffled curiosity? Or did Roc some how know that he lived and only waited as his sister had?

Frito had traveled Mortalroam in penance, a nameless stranger performing miracles in the name of Okshiru. Roc searched for the stranger, suspecting his identity all along. Frito had tried so hard to be anonymous, but perhaps not hard enough.

Frito eyed Roc carefully. *So, Roc? What am I telling that you don't know?*

Roc's eyes cooled as he pulled his smile under control. Smiling was bad for the image, Frito thought as he looked at his cousin with surprise and admiration. Why was he surprised? Was it not Roc himself who proclaimed on more occasions than necessary to 'Never Underestimate the Dragonslayer'? Or perhaps he didn't proclaim it enough.

Roc lifted his head in confidence. "When you lost, the gods showed you?" He spoke more as an answer than a question.

Frito shot a look to Fryto, and then Orrin. He took a breath and shook his head trying to focus on the fact that Roc didn't know everything. "I didn't lose." His centre balled and rose in his throat. "I won. I had them. Right where I wanted them." Frito's eyes were softly glowing again. "And my father looked to me and said, 'And what have you done?' and I looked...and...and I wept." A tear suddenly ran down his cheek and he wiped it free with his hand. "I wept in my fathers arms in shame. He had become the supergod creating, I had become the supergod, destroying." Frito looked over to Orrin who glared intently back at him. "I couldn't be in his presence after what I had done and I swept out of Worldsend. I used the Poer and tried to fix everything. As much as I could."

"And somewhere the Shog Tie snagged a bit more power for themselves."

Frito shook his head. "The Shog Tie did nothing." Frito's mouth opened, to speak, but the words caught in his throat and only air rushed out in a long tired breath. He realigned his thinking and tried again. "I tried to use the Poer to rebuild all that I had destroyed." Roc leaned forward and Frito went on. "Keep that in mind for a moment. Everyone has a connection of some sort to the Poer. Through practice and development you can condition yourself to use the connection in magic or" He looked at Orrin. "Kamri." He looked back to Roc. "But it all comes from the Poer and everyone has it. Even you, Roc. You are immune to most forces of Magic same as Craig is. You have unknowingly used it your whole life. Only your drive, motivation and will power has allowed you to unconsciously tap into it. I believe that 'Man' has had this connection for all time, but due to illuse we became jaded and the Poer faded within us. But at the Re-awakening of Time, it was awakened in us all. When my father started the wheels of time again, he became the supergod. In that act, everyone re-gained a touch of that Poer to become...'gods'. But it slowly began to drift off into sleep again in the millions of years since the Re-awakening." Frito leaned forward, gesturing as he spoke. "We already had the Poer. When I used it to fix everything, I woke it up again." Frito leaned back, resting his hands on his knees. "Remember, Roc, when I said that things were different? They aren't. They're just awake. Craig reports a increase in Dragon births. That is the strongest evidence I have. Dragons were nearly extinct. For generations we have been ignorantly bringing that about not realizing the disaster it would have caused."

Roc dwelled on Frito's words. It was many years since he had to stop slaying dragons because they were so few. As legend spoke, the day the final dragon falls from flight, the wheels of time will stop forever. Roc had not believed that such a thing would happen, but Craig with all of his atheistic prattle was a staunch believer in the myth. Staunch enough to stop the Dragonslayer from slaying dragons. Roc looked up, thinking of the good that came from it all. "Okay, now the Shog Tie."

"You summon them, you give them power to do a job, but they can't use it for themselves." *Like some one else I know,* he thought.

"Friska summoned them?" Roc asked. "He is not a wizard."

Frito weighed the idea. "Probably summoned for him by Thamrell, you don't need magic to give them. Sheer will Poer could do it."

"You think Friska even knew what he was doing?"

Frito shook his head. "No, he didn't know that he summoned anyone. The Shog Tie were hiding in borrowed bodies and had to have them destroyed in order to escape and fight which tells me that the Shog were hiding from Friska. He is not a spell caster. He wouldn't have noticed a change within himself and that the Shog were living off of him. He has a weak Kamri, but that would not have told him. He had Poer to spare and Thamrell siphoned it from him without his knowledge."

Fryto held up his hands and disagreed. "No," He spoke up. "He knew...something. I've spoken to him." He looked at Frito. "He hates you. He has always hated you."

"I know." Frito spoke grimly. "But he never admitted it to himself. That hate and his connection to the Poer summoned Thamrell. Thamrell used it to get into him." *That and a few other things.*

"Just like Weishap used your hate for the Trid-Dreath and your curiosity of the Poer to get to you." Roc made the connection. "Weishap wanted Worldsend. What does Thamrell want? Revenge for the Shog Tie?"

Frito shook his head.

"What?"

"I don't know." Frito said simply.

There was a soft rap at the door and Roc slid to the side, reached up with his long arm and unbolted the door. Stinging wind blustered into the room as J'son stepped in. He turned quickly, putting his shoulder to the door and closed it, bolting it shut. "Fikor is here!" He announced. "And so is Hauge."

"J'son?" Roc asked him. "Look around you. What is missing?"

J'son regarded the Roc, then looked around the room.

There was another soft rap at the door.

J'son whipped his fingers twice. "Oh!" He turned and opened the door, holding it against the force of the wind. "Hi, me! What a pleasant surprise! Come on in."

J'cob shouldered his brother out of the way, shoving his bucket of water at him. He crouched by the fire, and fought Orrin for his tamake of broth.

J'son forced the door closed again. "Jay! Glad you could join us."

"Jay'," J'cob paused with his wrestling. "You hit me in the nose with the door."

"Sorry about that, Jay'"

J'cob shoved Orrin away. "Get out of here, kid." He looked up to his twin as he cradled the tamake in his hands. "Did you tell them?"

"You said you were going to tell them."

Roc leaned back on the door. "Tell us what?"

J'cob went to speak, but J'son spoke first. "We're being watched."

J'cob looked at J'son. "Jay', I was going to tell them."

"So, Jay', what are you waiting for?"

"Watched by who?" Roc persisted knowing that they could go on for days.

"Elves, nomads, about ten of them." J'cob answered quickly.

Frito put his hand to his beard and tugged on the tiny hairs. Then he looked to the boy at his side. "Orrin, who are they?"

Orrin tried to hide his automatic smile as he used his Kamri. "They are Kemli elves, eh?. They were like, head-ing west when they de-ci-ded to, you know, set-tle a lit-tle ways from here. They think we are stran-gers and watch..." Suddenly the boy's eyes rolled into his head.

Frito clutched the boy's shoulder. "Orrin!" He hissed.

"There is Y'day...He is not with them." Orrin spoke with only white orbs for eyes. "He knows of us, eh? He is of Kam-ri. He sees us all and, like, ack-now-led-ges us and calls us friends, eh? He hails gree-tings and begs grace of Roc the Dra-gon-slayer-pah." Orrin blinked and his brown eyes looked up to Frito. "He doesn't see you, eh? Like, he can't see who we are tal-king too. He is con-fused."

Frito relaxed his grip. He was almost embarrassed by his lack of confidence in the boy and his sudden panic. He shouldn't have been surprised at all, and with a controlled breath, pushed it from his tired mind. Too much going on, he thought as he released the boy and looked to Fryto. "We will go to meet with Y'day of Kemli." Frito was glad for the distraction. "Its time we left here and headed on our way." He had already thought too much and still had much more to think about.

Chapter 20

The still, sweaty air sat across the valley like a blanket of oppression. One hundred crusty, dusty, chipped, human skulls arrayed neatly in rows, carpeted the hill with their eyeless vision staring across the motionless weeds in the muddy, waterless river. Long clumps of moss hung from the gnarled branches of dead, twisted trees that lined the river. The rusted steel of smashed and torn machines lay bent and broken on the ground. Swords and shields were placed in macabre designs that from the air spelled, 'Ow! My Fucking Balls!'

His heavy scaly feet left prints in the mud. He casually strolled over the broken bones and walked his way through the piles of dead, kicking his feet as he did. Splinters of dry yellowing bone stuck to his mud covered, scaly feet as he made his way to the road. He paused as he came to the lip of the road and looked behind him at the long trail he had made from the caves of Juan-tavous. It had been a difficult journey in oppressive weather. The mosquitoes made the only wind as they danced about his skin and the biting flies circled his head before they landed on his exposed back. Buzzing with passion as their mad patterns changed at whims, green/black, metallic flies dotted the freshly dead at his feet.

He didn't like it here. Then again, he didn't like the caves of Juan-tavous either. In fact, there was nothing at all that he liked about anywhere.

But that was to be expected in Hel.

A tearing wail caught his ear. A child sat on the road a little out of his way. He slowly, silently made his way over until he could see her clearly. She was a tender girl, sweet and fair with her hair pulled back into braids. She wore a yellow sun dress that opened into a circle as she sat on the road. At first he hadn't noticed, but as he came closer he saw that she had one small defect.

She had no eyes.

They had obviously been torn from her head long ago for she had been issued a guide dog, which lay dead beside her, to help her get about. Bloody tears fell from her empty eye sockets as she tugged on the dog's harness seemingly unable to understand why the dog wasn't moving. Her tiny hand brushed away the ants that crawled in and out of the empty spaces on her face as her other hand began to probe the

179

carcass of her dog. Her fingers stumbled over the deep tire tracks that rolled across the dog's spine.

Her attention was fixed on the dead dog and she seemed unaware of (or simply ignored) the gnats growing fat on the flesh where her eyes used to be. Slowly the idea that her dog was dead crept across her face and her lips trembled as she began to cry. Her voice bent and stumbled as she sobbed.

Her one hand never left her life long companion as the other felt the hard ground beside her. He watched as her hand crawled towards a long, thin, white stick. He reached out with a clawed foot and moved it out of the way of her probing hand. "Who is there?" She cried. "My lord, pity me and aid me?" He cocked his head slightly as he looked into her hollow eyes. He could see the maggots wriggle mindlessly in the spaces in her head, fattened on the tissue of her brain.

He concluded that the dog had been alive when it was issued to her. He doubted that she would've been so attached to the thing if it had been otherwise. He then concluded from the tire tracks criss-crossing over the dog's body that she had met with the Demon Bikers and they had made target practice of the dog. They hadn't touched her. If they had, there wouldn't be much left. They probably felt they could do more harm to a blind girl by leaving her alone. They were right.

Normally he didn't evolve himself in charity work, but even with torn out eyes, she seemed rather cute as chicks in Hel went and pity tugged at his centre. He bent at the waist and picked up the stick from the ground. He smiled and snapped the stick in half and placed the shorter end in her probing hand. He cocked the other half under his arm like a swagger stick, tilted an invisible hat and stepped on his way down the road.

Perhaps the place is not so bad after all.

He wiped away the grimy dirt from the back of his neck and hurried his way down the road, swinging his stick as he did. He had an appointment and didn't want to be late. He hurried his way past the burned villages and the massacred armies and only paused to admire the impaled, pregnant women that lined the road for nearly a mile. One of them he was certain that he had met at a party, but then he decided that it would be best to be mistaken and hurried off. From the top of the hill, he looked down to the fork in the road. He didn't bother to wonder why there was a fork lying in the middle of the road, only at the side road that lead off to the main highway.

Black tar ran like a stripe across the world. Yellow broken lines ran the center of the highway for no reason what so ever. His eyes followed along the highway until it ended almost at the edge of the horizon, mere feet from The Great Curtain of Oblivion. His hand shielded his eyes from the swelling sun in the north and looked to a small shack in the distance. Against one side of the shack was a sand storm, a swirling cloud of fury funneling from the earth. On the other side of the shack was the place known as Argra. It was thus named after the first person to explore the strange world of darkness. He had stepped in and screamed something like, Arrrge, but that would have been a silly thing to name a place, so it was hence forth named Argra. Most people thought of it as nowhere. Some called it the eternal shadow. He knew it best as Mef, and that was a private joke. It was the Great Wall of Oblivion—nothing more, nothing less.

The black river of Therd ran before the shack. Gray foam crested the rolling waves as the heaving, black water crashed on the rocks of the bed. The sinking sun burned gold in the water of death. A simple, solid concrete bridge spanned the wild waters, connecting the black tar road to the parking lot directly to the side of the shack. Vapors of heat twisted and distorted the shack in the far distance. He knew the place by reputation since he was never invited and knew better than to crash. The words Paradise Lost Truck-Stop were scrawled brightly in neon blue above the entrance. He couldn't make out the smaller sign in the window, but if he could, it would have told him that Cold Beer was served there. The truck-stop was perched against the edge of the world with the storm of passion on one side and oblivion on the other.

Parked in its place beside the truck-stop appeared to be a tiny speck in the haze, but the gleam of black enamel was unmistakable. It was a truck. A 22 wheeled Kenworth. It meant, the boss was home.

He shook his head and headed down the road away from the truck-stop. He knew that the proprietor didn't like people hanging around within sight of his place and he knew that well.

He continued down the road until the plains turned to hills and then to mountains and he could see the walls of the great stone city of Madagar. The darkening sky gave no relief to the sweaty air as he trudged up the long ass hill to the main gate. The tall, gray, stone walls rose high above him. Brown limbs of thick vines scaled the walls and seemed to hold together the cracks that threatened to throw the walls into the ground. The sagging towers of stone only stood in the dark shadows of the approaching night.

He walked boldly to the open gates of Madagar and only paused to look for the guard. He peered into the small wooden shack and the shaft of light that spilled on the ground from the tiny, single window. He wrinkled his lip wondering why there was no guard to greet him.

He walked on.

"Haly oh! Stop-ed and non ambulation! Freeze, Pally!"

He turned in surprise at the guard standing behind him. A crossbow was pointed at him.

"Haly He!" The guard chanted again. "Who art, What art and Why art?"

He looked at the ramshackle guard. His rusting chain mail was torn and hung in strips of brown rings. His bow was warped and splintered under its own tension and most of all, not even loaded. Grey bones were visible beneath his flesh with muscles that pulled like wires beneath the thin skin of his smiling toothless face. But he was ready to fight. His knees were cocked to spring and his sharp eyes glistened in the dimming light.

The scaly beast folded his arms across his chest and stood his tallest to let his wave of royalty and fear spread before him. "I am Thumber. Keeper of Nightmares and Beast Under the Bed! I come under the will of Thamrell the Despairer."

This was all a trivial matter of etiquette. To have the guard give a hard time to any one who entered Madagar was policy established shortly after the re-awakening of time. "Haly who?" The guard cackled. "Haly who? I have heard naught of thou? You here to break the peaceful sanctum of Madagar?" He aimed the bow a little higher.

Thumber's will and temper began to crest. The beast held out a scaly clawed finger pointed at the guard. "I will count to three and then I will break you into tiny bits regardless of what you do. Just thought I'd let you know."

"Haly hay!" The guard motioned with his bow. "Then have at it. You seem not like a beast big enough to wrestle a sack of shit let alone Mally, the gate guard."

"Mally? Is that your name, Mally?" Thumber asked. "Then I shall carve it nicely in the center of your forehead to give the taker a name for his books." Thumber stepped forward and with broad, burly arms and black, sheen talons he reached for the spindly guard as Mally lifted his bow in defense. Laughter and cheer held back Thumber's hand. The whistle of steel and snap of bone drew his attention in the direction of the inner citadel. "And what is that?" Thumber asked still poised to strike Mally.

"Haly ho, that is none but the family executions."

Thumber turned with out a word and headed in the direction of the festivities.

Mally waved with his bow goodbye. "Have a nice day!"

Thumber paused and looked behind him with a sneer then rushed down the darkening streets, passed the legless denizens and ugly painted whores. He pushed his way through a mugging and slugged someone standing on a street corner for no reason other than the fact that he was standing there. In the town center, where the streets of Garotte and 6th met in Grand Square, was where he found the crowds. People of Madagar all mobbed around the wooden platform, each vying for a better view. Thumber's height held him above the crowd as he watched a heavy set man dragged from the crowd by bigger men in black hoods. He was pushed to the wooden floor and his head laid flat against the block. The two hooded men worked the thick leather bands quickly to strap him into place.

In the center of the stage stood an obese executioner. His thick arms bled sweat as he raised them to get the attention of his audience. His multiple chins shook like jelly as he spoke and he constantly tugged at his too small mask to insure that it was still there. "Well, wasn't that a wonderful display of flogging by Ratwhip and his all iron lash?" He clapped loudly and his rolls of cellulite quivered. The crowd gave shouts of approval and waved their fists and cheered. "Well, moving right along, our next executioner has been with us for only a short time but he has found his way into our hearts. Lets have a warm welcome for The Unpredictable, Vengeance!"

The crowd went wild as women pawed the stage while executioners on the floor, locked arm in arm, held them back. From the left side a man stepped up the stairs of the stage and twin spotlights melded into one bright disk and targeted him in a circle of brightness. He was small compared to the gigantic fatness of the other executioners, but he was well proportioned and obviously had hidden strength. He stood casually on the stage, in his black silken tuxedo and white linen shirt complete with a thin black tie neatly tied about his collar. A black hood covered his entire head. He never spoke a word as his flickering steel eyes scanned across the crowd. Women swooned at the sight of his eyes of ice. Slowly, steadily, he took it all in before finally fixing on the sweaty, whimpering man strapped to the block. He turned casually, stepped over to the axe rack and carefully thumbed his way through the selection of armaments. This was merely a bit of theater, for he had already selected his weapon and placed it on the rack to use. It was a special day for him and he was going to make it good. He selected a long haft concealed in black cloth and dragged it out to the middle of the floor. He dropped away the cloth to reveal a club. It reached to the tip of his chin when balanced on the floor. Save for the length of his forearm at the top of the club, for him to grip, the entire club was studded with tiny brass lumps embedded into the wood. Shining iron spikes pushed their way periodically through the club with the largest and longest ones near the end. This was a brutal weapon. A new one that the crowd had never seen and they quivered with anticipation to see its effects. He twirled it on its end and let the blue/white light from the spotlight reflect off the silver spikes and splash on the wild faces of the crowd. Simple, yet refined. A trademark.

He stepped back from the block, looking into the eyes of his victim. They were wide, terror filled eyes draining of tears from red rimmed sockets. Vengeance judged his distance and length of the club. He put an invisible mental mark at the perfect spot where his feet should be when he brought the club down. If he stopped right there, and used a smooth, natural swing, then the longest spikes would catch at the right space. It was a delicate science for if he missed, or caught his victim at a bad angle, the outcome could prove quite embarrassing for him.

He looked up to the audience and held up his hand as the people began to cheer him on. He held up a single finger.

One?

No, more.

Two?

Two would be good. A large part of the group voted for two.

Three?

They seemed much more content with three.

Four?

They seemed to lose cheer for four. It would be too messy, too much of minced hamburger. Two was not enough, three would be good. Very good.

He stepped back again and stopped at the edge of the stage. There, he rolled the club behind him and looked out over the audience.

Ready?

They were ready.

He looked to his victim.

Ready?

The glazed looked of death covered his moon white face and bloody red eyes. A moth stuck to the sweat of his wet neck.

He was ready.

Vengeance stepped towards him with a quickening pace, the club dragging behind him. Faster he came, stretching his stride and the club in both hands. His feet reached the mark and he stopped suddenly, using the momentum in the swing to bring his heavy club up, about and home.

With the sound of cracking bone as a signal, the audience cheered with admiration. The victim's reflexive wailing howl only fed the fever of the crowd.

"Thumber!" The beast turned only one eye aside to see who called him keeping the other on the stage as Vengeance geared for his second throw of the club. "Thumber, I thought I told you…"

"Hold!" Thumber hissed hurriedly, letting his eye return to the stage. "Watch this."

Vengeance went at it again.

"Thumber…" Darkness suddenly grew about the beast. Darkness of loneliness and empty dreams, darkness of rejection and unfilled love, darkness of lies and cruel tricks, darkness of oppression, embarrassment, abandonment, hollow promises and broken toys. Only the cheer of the crowd brought Thumber from falling away. He felt the heat about him and the miserable, constricting crowd around him. He was suddenly uncomfortable and itchy. He looked down at Thamrell, floating below him. He never realized how short the God Of Human Introspection really was.

"I apologize my Lord. I am not one to tempt you."

"This is below me," He floated higher to see Thumber on an even keel. "mingling in the streets." He snorted.

"Lord Despair," Thumber said turning again to the stage. "You should lighten up." He pointed to the stage. "Who is this guy? I like him."

"He is new. Innovative. Inventive. I'm a traditionalist myself. I'd prefer a good racking."

"But you must admit, he has style."

Despair watched as Vengeance stood over his victim still twitching on the block. He lifted the heavy club into the air perpendicular to the stage. The audience chanted and cheered as Vengeance held the seconds above his head.

With the scream of excited children, he brought the club down in the third, crushing smash. The long spikes buried deeply into the wood with a solid, welcoming thunk. "Style he has." Thamrell said stroking his chin. "He handles gore with great skill."

"A crowd pleaser." Thumber said turning from the stage. "My mission was a complete success."

"How so?"

"Frita is dead!"

"Dead?" Despair whispered as his empty eyes fell open.

"Dead, died, defunct, over and out, bought the big one, kicked bucket, the last hurrah, regards to Broadway, pushing up daisies, renting dirt space, cashing in her chips and tuning up her harp." Thumber plucked imaginary strings on an imaginary harp. "Worm food, coffin stuffer, deep six, and carry me back to Ol' Virginny."

Thamrell's hands, like gnarled twigs, clutched at the space before his face. "You Idiot!" Thamrell hissed to hide his voice from the crowd.

"What?" Thumber stood aghast, interrupted in his list.

"How could you do that! I told you we needed her!"

"You said we needed her control of the Poer!" Thumber replied. "I have it!"

"What?" Thamrell reeled. "How can you?"

"She gave it to me."

Thamrell blinked. "Impossible."

"Yet, I have it."

"Are you assuming she gave it to you?"

"She must have since I have it and she is dead. I do not have to be summoned and issued Poer for a task. I can function on my own."

Thamrell glared suspiciously. "And you saw her die?"

"The 'ol neck stretch."

"Killed herself?" He squeaked in unbelief, thinking the act impossible for knights. "You saw this?" Thamrell asked again to confirm.

"Hung by the neck until she was dead, dead, dead, dead, buried under the ground dead as opposed to dead, dead, dead, dead, walking around dead."

"You *saw* this?" Thamrell repeated not getting an answer to his question.

"Yeah, sort of." Thumber's voice trailed off.

"What does that mean?"

"I didn't actually witness it. Its hard to stay in Mortalroam beyond the dawn. But she did it."

"I think not." Thamrell breathed in relief and looked to the stage and watched as Crusher demonstration his multiheaded axe-o-matic much to the audiences' delight. "You could not still have her Poer were she dead. The Manga Thu Laurde would end. It is a fragile bond."

"I am quite sure that she is dead." Thumber said.

"How so, who saw her?"

"Howerer..." Thumber said with less than an overwhelming reply. "Howerer said she died."

"Howerer?" Thamrell glared at him in abhorrence and distrust. "How can you trust her? I am surprised that you are still seen with her." Thamrell looked up to the stage to watch the boot torture.

Thumber seemed hurt. "She's always good for a laugh."

"Thumber..." Thamrell faced the beast. "She is a whore. Everyone knows that. The Beast Who Hides in the Closet and Keeper of Screams has a tendency to give her loyalty to any one." His white stare carved into him. "You are only fool enough to believe her. She will tell you what you want to hear."

A scream tore the night as the boot splintered and crushed a woman's foot much to the crowd's relish. Thamrell cast his gaze upon the stage. "Look at this." His dark voice rang. "Cheering for pain. Blindly following the whims of gods. Suffering the agonies of purgatory to find their way to the Steeples. A redemption for a god's game. What a waste of will. Those who make it only serve as slaves to the gods. It's the same as being here, only different clientele."

Thumber moaned. "Thamrell, you're depressing me." The beast crossed and uncrossed his arms over his chest trying to loosen the weight on his hearts.

Thamrell looked to the beast and smiled. Flecks of rotted enamel flashed silver in the dim light. The gaze of his empty eyes fell solidly upon him and a dim glowing light began to burn, far back in the hollow spaces with fainting glee. "I get you down? I? Get you down? Can't you see that we had the key to Worldsend? Not the Palladium, Not just Steeples, Worldsend! Out of the muck-dwelling Hell!" His smile vanished as his hot whisper rushed out cracked and broken while the words lifted the air with steam. "Away from the drudgery. We would be the ones pulling the strings. Manipulating the slime of mortals like so much clay! Us! Thumber…You and I!" Thamrell's head tilted aside as he watched the beast's reaction. "But we can forget it now. There is nothing left…"

"What?"

"Everything revolved around her Manga Thu Laurde. Our only hope was her."

Thumber felt the weights about his chest again. "Surly there is someone else? There is Friska."

Thamrell laughed breathlessly as he looked upon the stage. "Friska was our weapon against the Dragonslayer and the Ninefingers. With his defeat, I have lost his Manga Thu Laurde. Frito was even able to correctly guess how I did it." Thamrell shook his head. "No, it is all over…all my dreams, machinations, plans of lifting out of the darkness. It was in my grasp." His long bony fingers flexed as if to grab hold of the steaming night air. "And now it is gone." His hand opened exposing nothing.

"Thamrell…I"

"No…" Thamrell put out his hand to block the beast. "No, it is my fault. I put too much on you. I was wrong in my judgement."

Thumber was spinning in darkness. He could fell his centre sink, pulling his demonic soul with it. His was gasping suddenly, almost pleading. "Perhaps she's not dead!" He said too loudly.

A voice came from the crowd, 'I think she's dead.'

The monster and the god looked up to the stage at the unconscious woman in the boot. The executioners looked her over and nodded to each other before going about reviving her. Thumber turned back to Thamrell and spoke in a much greater controlled voice. "As you said, the Manga Thu Laurde wouldn't work if she were dead."

"That is my hope." The dark one spoke as he bowed his head. "But hope is only a fickle tease."

Thumber's red eyes rolled into his head. "Aww Jeeze! Thamrell, you were fucking with me!"

Thamrell cocked a bony brow. "Was I?"

"You damn well know you were and you had me going. Knock that shit off will ya? Anyway, what is it that is so dependent on her?" He turned and followed as the god left the executions. "Why is she so important?"

"She will be the tool to free Weishap."

Thumber stopped abruptly and reached out with a heavy scaled hand and tried to catch Thamrell by the shoulder, but only passed through his ghostly form. "How is this? How can she free Weishap?" Thamrell turned at him, offended that the beast had tried to touch him.

"Her sin makes her weak. Out of all the knights, her sin makes her defenseless."

"That is so." Said Thumber catching up with him, "But we cannot even approach the doors where Weishap is."

"The Ninefingers is powerful, but in his own way. We as demons and monsters cannot approach the doors of Hel, but she can."

They turned the corner and headed down the alley. Thamrell's steady, purposeful drift, made Thumber's keeping up with him difficult. "And what of your encounter with the Ninefingers?" Thumber called ahead as he stepped over the trash in the streets.

"I had greater expectations. I had hoped for Friska to kill a guilt wrapped Frito and a berserk Roc to kill Friska and get rid of two knights with one rock." He paused at his weak pun and went on. "But that was not to be. It seems that I have not damaged the Ninefingers in the least. Friska is out of the plan for now, however; I may be able to use him still." Thamrell suddenly stopped in his tracks. He peered down the ally and listened carefully.

"What is it?" Thumber looked over and down the ally, but saw nothing.

"Get back!" Thamrell's ice cold hands solidified and shoved at the beast and pushed him into a door way.

"What is it?"

"Be quiet! He will hear you!"

Thumber held his question as he gazed down the ally. His ears could hear shrieking and shouts of pain. People were pulling themselves from out of the ally and into what niches they could find. Thumber's wide head peered around the edge of the door way to see down the ally. "Who is that?" He whispered.

"That is…" Thamrell whispered the name filled with dread. "Teddy."

Teddy stood a proud height no higher than a mortal's outstretched hand. His soft limbs bent and walked with an aimless jaunt and his shinny button eyes gleamed with purity. His tender innocent smile shined with glee at all the wretches that admonished his presence.

"Oh heck." Thumber said stepping from the alcove, "He ain't shit!" Thamrell's long spiny fingers gripped like a smith's wire and pulled at the hulking beast. Before Thumber could react, Wounk came out from one of the buildings. Wounk's giant balloon feet slapped and bounced as he walked on his emaciated legs. The god of stubbed toes looked down the alley and saw the back of Teddy. The god's face suddenly crossed with mischief as he crept with unexpected silence with his bloated feet. He paused a step away from the cute, adorable Teddy and raised back one massive round foot. "This will be good." whispered Thumber. But the two watched carefully as Wounk suddenly popped and flashed in blinding white the instant as his gigantic toe touched the back of Teddy's head. His smoking skeletal remains held as a statue— his skull warped in horrific surprise. The fuzzy little bear only turned around to see what all the commotion was about and looked up to smoldering, bony figure. "Ooooh" was all it said in innocent wonder. Its attention was then caught by a strange fluttering moth and it ran off to catch it.

Thamrell let out a long breath of relief. Thumber's jaw hung open. "That was Teddy." Thamrell explained as he drifted from the door way. "He is the god of Innocence Lost. He was sent directly from Okshiru to piss us off. He will be the first of the gods I kill when our mission is accomplished."

"Now that is an idea." Thumber said as he looked over the still smoking remains of Wounk. Wounk tilted and slowly staggered his way down the street. The bones in his giant feet clicked as they rubbed together. He stopped at a dumpster. His now, blank, black, thousand mile stare fell on the box of trash. With the expression of horror still on his face, Wounk, the god of stubbed toes, climbed the dumpster and threw himself in. Thumber cast a final look back. "Yeah, a real good idea."

Chapter 21

Wind whipped and stung at Craig's face and he cursed at the fact that he couldn't remember the name of the god of wind. The Red Barchetta rumbled and roared down the long, main road towards the town of Cornerstone. As he passed the large, stone columns that welcomed travelers to the town, he turned the key and shut off the engine. He floored the clutch and took the car out of gear and let it coast down the center of town. Without the engine, the power brakes were like rocks as he pulled in front of Max's. He pulled himself from behind the wheel, holding tightly to the cloak about his shoulders. He paused only to look back at the giant car. In the dark clouds of the storming morning, it appeared dull and abandoned. The gouges in the trunk and shattered windshield looked worse than he had thought. He could hear the ticking of the motor and see the chrome front grill. The Barchetta gritted its grill and whispered in a breathless voice, 'No sweat.' but Craig didn't hear it. After all, the Red Barchetta was a car—an inanimate object. Inanimate objects didn't talk.

Craig made his way to the door and the door, sensing his presence, opened for him and closed behind him. He stepped in, feeling the floor sway beneath his feet. He faced the counter and stood teetering in the middle of the floor.

Max came from the pantry and climbed his special stool. "Welcome Craig. How's it going?" Max looked at the dark man before him. "Rough night?"

Craig moved with slow, precise motions and looked to his watch. "It's ten A.M., that means enough of this day has gone by to declare it a bad day."

"Why do you always dwell on the bad side of things?"

Craig rested his head on the counter. "Look out the window." He said to the glass.

Max stretched as much as he could and looked out. "Ooooh, I'm impressed." He resumed his seat. "How did you do it?"

"Seven black dragons in a B-25 "V" formation." Craig continued to talk to the glass.

"My, that is terrible. Now, what really happened?"

Craig reached under his cloak and pulled out a large black dragon scale and dropped it on the counter. He looked up as Max took up the scale. "Some people have one of those days. I have one of those lives." Craig watched the face of the old dwarf examining the scale. "I study for years in school, survive four years in the Marines, get a masters degree in physics at Cornell University in the same space as a bachelor's only to become a dragon chew toy in the land of the miss-filed. This isn't fair."

"Yearlings." Max said setting down the scale. "Born this spring. Probably just learning to fly."

"Well they were flying pretty good this morning. They hurt my blue dragon."

Max ignored Craig. "That is unusual. Dragons births have declined over the last few centuries, its unusual to see one, let alone seven."

Craig waved his hand in Max's face. "Yo Max, I'm the Dragoncaller remember? I know this. And Dragon births are on the up swing. The Blue Dragon?"

Max didn't seem to be bothered. "He'll find his way home. What I want to know is why the yearlings attacked you."

Craig set his face in his hands. "They were young and didn't understand. They sensed me and their destructive nature took over. I also sensed that they were bred. They had the mentality of watchdogs. I'm going to dwell on it as soon as the migraine in my head either quiets down or swells up and kills me." Craig set his head back on the glass and rolled it back and forth. "You do know that its Monday."

"Relax, it's the storm. Fikor has come down from the hills."

Craig looked up and glared at Max. "This storm is caused by a low pressure cold front sweeping south from Canada and playing havoc with the settled southern high in this region. This storm has nothing to do with anything."

Max stepped from his stool and stepped into the pantry. As he disappeared from sight, Craig could hear his voice. "You're the one who can talk to dragons, why is a snow dog so hard to conceive?" Max reappeared with his pot of coffee and two mugs. "Why not give sacrifice to the god of Monday and get him off of your back. What does he like?"

"Fucking with me." Craig mumbled.

Max reached up and set the pot on its ceramic plate and the two mugs on the counter. "You're the only one who has Monday's every week. I think its confusing that way." Max climbed the steps. "Perhaps the god of Monday is pissing on you because you invoke his name every week. Or you evoke it on the wrong day." Max filled the mugs. "Tis too early for mead. Drink this." Max pushed a mug at him. "Tis not only Monday on your brain. I can look at you and see there is more to this than meets the eye. Its one of your dreams, isn't it?"

Craig ran his fingers through his long, black hair and looked up to Max through the steam rising from the brew. The glinting eyes of the aging dwarf gleamed back at him. Craig knew that Max could see right through him. "It's too many names to remember." Craig said quietly, giving in to the dwarf. "Flashing visions, nothing solid. Perhaps if Orrin were here he could pull them out of my head and make more sense…"

"But he isn't, and you're so protective about them we will do without." Max said pouring his brew. "Come, clear your head. Tis why you can't hear your blue talking."

"There isn't anything to tell…" Max glared at him. "Okay, uh…" Craig leveled. "Its Ferris, the Iron Dragon."

"That's not good."

"I keep seeing him in dreams. I don't know what he's up to."

Max leaned back. "Doesn't have to be up to anything."

Craig looked at him firmly. "Except kill me." Craig sipped at his brew, testing the heat. "Do you have any sugar?"

Max looked under the counter. "I'm sure he has a lot of people to kill, probably be a while getting to you. Will sweet sap do?"

"I've survived the Demon-dragon Witch Queen during PMS, why not that." Craig pushed his mug forward and continued. "But he's not the point of the dream. There is something else going on. And it keeps changing. I can't keep it straight. When I try to focus on it, everything gets…weird." Craig's voice drifted off as his eyes slowly rolled into hie head.

Max's short, stubby arm shot out and gripped Craig's cloak. The dwarf braced his legs against the counter and held the dark man, easing his fall. Craig's body flowed like jelly and slid to the floor. Max leaped from the counter and lifted Craig to a sitting position.

"Coming across Modo highway." Craig spoke in a strange voice. "The wind all about and wing is hurt. Feel it not. Wing no fly. Can't land good, need big space. See Cornerstone not."

Max looked into Craig's blank eyes and couldn't see anyone home. "Rob!" Max shouted over his shoulder. "Rob!", The dwarf looked back to the man at his feet. "Craig, where are you?"

"Where Craig?" Craig repeated. "Craig safe? Did Ralph do right?"

Max leaned back as Rob stumbled down the steps. "Hey, what's up?"

Max looked over to him. "Get me glow balls. There is a basket in the cellar."

Rob stooped to the floor and pulled up the iron ring in the floor. Giant lashing tendrils flailed suddenly at him. The boy slammed the door shut and stomped on it until the tentacles pulled themselves back in. "Max, like, Mobie slipped his chain again."

Max had no time to waste. "Then go into the back room and bring me…never mind. Stay here with Craig." The little Dwarf moved with surprising speed into the back room while Rob took his place.

Rob brushed his platinum hair across his forehead as he squatted beside the dark elf. "So what's the story, eh?"

Craig's unseeing eyes didn't look. "Where Ralph is? Ralph not know. Ralph need big space to land. Wing hurt, hurt, hurt."

Max ran back into the room with a box tucked under his arm. As his fingers undid the strings that held it closed, he looked to the boy by him. "Get your duster." Max watched as he ran to comply. "Ralph!" He called to Craig. "Go to mountain 8."

Craig cocked his head. "See not 8. Gone for cleaning."

Max clenched his teeth. "Do you see the farm of Zorraxe?"

"Yes."

"What about Riles pass?"

"Yes."

"You are headed too far east. Bank to the left and head North. Can Ralph see the water?"

"Yes. The river of Kay."

"Follow the river and watch the left bank." Max glared hard into Craig's far off gaze, hoping to see some hint of where his lost dragon was. Rob came up behind him wearing his coat. The dwarf handed him the box. "Stand up the street and wait for my signal." Max shooed him and the boy dashed out the door with the box under his arm. "Ralph, where are you now…" Max shouted at Craig.

Craig's eyes focused and looked at the dwarf. "Huh?"

"Craig? Are you alright?"

"The Iron Dragon is awake and…Did I black out?"

"Relax Craig, what about Ralph? He is headed here and we have to guide him in. If he blows the landing, he could wipe out Cornerstone! Where is he?"

Suddenly the door burst open and Rob stumbled in with the box under his arm. "What do I do at your signal?"

Max nearly exploded with words. "Open the Box!" Rob quickly went to open the box. "Not now!" Max roared. Rob gave the thumbs up sign and dashed out the door. Max turned to Craig who was fighting to rise to his feet. "Where is he now?"

"How did you know his name?" Craig pressed.

"He told me—it doesn't matter. His secret is safe, now where is he?"

Craig glared through the window to the street outside and the gray sky above. "Too high. He'll have to make another pass. He is blinded by the clouds. He'll never find the town. He's in tremendous pain. I'm going to guide him out into the woods." Craig fumbled in his pockets for the key to the Red Barchetta.

Max grabbed his arm. "No, he will never find anywhere else. He's hurt and confused and will kill himself if he hits the tree line. The main street should be big enough."

The door burst open and Rob stepped in. "What's the signal?"

Max headed out the door grabbing at his emerald green cloak. He grabbed at Rob and pulled him out the door. Fikor's storm had risen in fury and Hauge lashed about in vengeful madness. Craig's cloak pulled and tossed about him as he looked to the angry sky. "He's coming around. Turning from the north." Craig said. Max turned to Rob and pointed him to the north. "He's passing the strait of Hols. He's completely blind. He's following my word. But I can't see either. I can't really guide him."

Max grimly nodded and Rob went on his toes and opened the box. Craig screamed.

Feathers from the wings of Kemoto lifted out of the box. Shafts of warming sun gleamed out of Rob's arms. The bright light pushed back the dark clouds and bent the wind with bands of gold. Max reached over to Craig and lifted him to his feet. "I'm sorry Craig, I should have warned you."

"I'm sorry too. I forget that I can't hang out on the beach anymore. What the hell is that?" Craig said as he reached under his cloak and took out his sun glasses.

"A little box of sunshine."

"Sure, just what I need. Sunshine." Craig pulled his cloak and tried to shield more of the light. Then he noticed. "He can see it!"

"Can you guide him in?"

"I can see through his eyes. Through them I can see the sunlight and it won't fry my brain. But I can't fly for him." Craig looked to the sky, subconsciously rubbing his arm. "He's on his own."

A tiny black line danced on the sky. Wings unfolded like a parasol. Flipping and flopping slowly, and gently in the now calmed winds of Hauge. Craig watched the sky. His voice whispered commands as his Dragoncall spoke to the flying blue beast. *'Stretch it out, watch your rudder, your banking too far, watch your nose.'*

Ralph glided, coming lower. The clouds were clearing away from the powerful beams of light from the box of sunshine. Ralph spread his wings and aimed for the light.

'Pull in your landing gear, you're still too high.' Craig whispered. *'Wait. Now, let them out again, they will help slow your air speed. Good. Stop looking at your feet they're in place. Get your stupid nose up.'* Far below, Ralph could see the sun. And beside the sun he saw Craig. *'Stop waving you moron, I see you. Yaw to the left 4 degrees, give a little lift. Slow down. You're too fast. Get your nose straight, stop looking around, sight-seeing is later. Get your nose up! Your Nose is on the other end! Slower...too high, lower, good, too low. Keep your wings up and glide now, one flap and the town will be smushed. Rudder right, too much, your nose, get it up, up the other way, that's up. Wipe that stupid smile off your face and concentrate. Pull in your wings, they're too big for the street. More! Put your feet back down, now pull your wings in again. Your NOSE!'*

The shining blue dragon glided lower and lower. Dirt and dust suddenly erupted beneath his belly as the street tore itself. His legs lowered to touch the ground.

His numb wing wasn't stopping right, he was too fast, too sudden. He pulled back but he felt the wing tear and pain shot though his side. His other wing draped too low and struck the roof of the tailor/undertakers, tearing off most of its shingling. The ground was a flashing brown smear beneath him. His hips were the width of the street and he struggled to keep a straight path. His rear claws screamed into the hard, cold earth and Craig screamed something about his nose.

Flashing azure screeched into a ball of shining blue. Scales shot out in all directions and dirt and dust clouded the air as he cleared the end of the street. Craig dashed across the road. He skidded to a stop, not sure of what to do first. He slowly and gently pulled back a leathery wing looking for Ralph's head. The dragon moved. He shifted his body and twisted it about, trying to shake his brain into working. His deep, blue, multifaceted eyes flashed and looked at Craig. A stupid smile crept across his face. *'Well that's it!'*

'Ralph, you had me scared shitless.' Craig threw his arms about Ralph's snout and hugged as much as he could. Ralph used his good wing to hug him back. Then he lifted his burned battered wing and showed it to Craig.

'Kiss it?' Craig pushed it away. But then he held it and looked at it, running his fingers over the scars knowing that was the best way to ascertain the damage. It was burned nearly to the bone and a hole through the membrane. It could be healed with time. Neeko was getting proficient with healing dragons. This would be good training.

'You'll be alright.'

'But hurts...' Ralph moaned piteously.

'You big, blue baby.' Craig reached up and scratched Ralph by his ear hole and the dragon began to purr.

Max waddled up and watched a boy and his dragon. "Look, the box of sunshine is draining. We can move Ralph to the barn. It's a little cramped, but it will have to do. I think we can fit most of him there. After the storm, we can get him to the river and he can swim upstream to his home."

Chapter 22

Elven calls hooted and whistled in the frosty, stinging air. Men moved between the trees as light as Mistang's dew—leaping from branch to bough as quietly as her fog. Horns of wood blew long, monotone notes of welcome and warning as Roc the Dragonslayer came into view. Orrin watched with large brown eyes as the men in the forest moved above him. They were tall and lean. Their skin was fair and smooth. Their clothes were of cotton and wools—leather and hide were nowhere to be seen. Their hair was black as silk and splashed upon their shoulders as they dashed across the trees, leading and following the party along the trail. Bows and shafts of black, oiled oak rode strung across their shoulders and thin small swords were concealed at their sides. Each one the same but yet different as if custom made. All were hand carved or personally wrought to fit and suit the user.

Silently they moved about—watching and allowing themselves to be studied as a token of mutual trust. They spoke not, as if their gentle grace of motion made words clumsy and awkward.

Roc sat tall in his saddle as they rode into the village. Orrin beheld the nomadic home. Huts of straw and mud were interlaced with webs of woven rope strung like nests to the trees. Elven children ran across connecting ropes as easily as Orrin could run down a set of stairs. Elven babies slept in sacks on their mothers backs. There were no fires, no smoke, No external sources of heat.

Roc stopped at what seemed to be the center of the village. He set aside his horse's reins and slowly eyed the place. He made a fist with a spiked gauntlet and then relaxed it. "I am Roc the Dragonslayer!" He announced in a mighty tone. His voice rang the trees and lingered in the cold air. Orrin looked upon the wonder of the silent people. Their eyes were wide at the what must be the strange noise that Roc was making.

Frito turned in his saddle and whispered sardonically, "Appropriate."

One of the elves that had followed silently along, stepped before the Dragonslayer and bowed in reverence. He motioned a complicated series of dexterous signs with his hands and hoped that his meaning had not been lost.

It wasn't. Frito pulled back his hood and Orrin felt all eyes shift to the Nih elf. It was unusual for any one to see a Nih elf in this part of the world and especially a dark Nih. Frito ignored the strange looks and signed in return the house of Hammerstrike and then showed them the four pointed star of Hammerstrike, the elven silver sign of family that all members of the house wore about their necks. The elf who had signed to Frito, identified himself as the captain of the guard and pulled back his black hair to expose his Crystal-silver tiara.

Orrin brought forth his Kamri, gently as he had been taught, and fanned it out to touch thoughts that he found. The captain signed of the house of Kemli and, for what Frito could make out, their temporary settlement in Dragonslayer's realm. They welcomed anyone who came in peace.

Frito nodded and dismounted. He reached out and imitated the captain's sign of peace and then bowed in mutual respect. Fryto dismounted and helped Friska who was still in silent penance. Orrin felt the eyes of wonder as Achillia dismounted and stood by her horse. She was human and her height was a head and shoulder taller than the tallest of the Kemli. Dragonslayer dismounted as well. They had heard tales of the Dragonslayer, but in person he was devastating. He stood a breath taller than Achillia and looked as mean as he could bear.

Frito took up the reins for his horse and Orrin's and followed the captain. Orrin pulled back his hood and looked to the children above him in the trees. Their warm brown eyes in the cold winter air only looked back at him. Slowly, he reached out with his Kamri.

Something touched his robe. He looked down to a woman at his side. Her eyes looked up to him in wonder. He looked about and saw all eyes were upon him. He looked to Frito and Frito looked back. Orrin suddenly realized, they were all nihra elves like himself.

Frito shrugged his shoulders and followed the captain. He lead them to an elven tree house that was stretched across three trees. The captain signed to the tree house for Frito and Orrin. He signed to another large tree house.

Roc leaned over to Frito and whispered to him. "Well?"

"There is the wise man of the Kemli tribe in this hut and he wants to see me. Something about holy ground." Frito pointed to the second hut. "I'll join you there in a moment."

Roc looked to the hut. "And if I feel like standing out here?"

"There is no one who could move you, so?"

"So." Roc said folding his arms and looking steadfast.

"So." Frito said as he turned to the rope ladder. He paused as he slipped the sash from his shoulders and tossed down his blade spear. It balanced itself on its end and waited. "Stay!" He ordered it.

Orrin watched as Frito shifted his size through the tiny hole into the nest beyond. He looked to the captain beside him and understood the gesture to follow. Orrin dashed up the ladder with as much speed and dexterity as he could muster. He knew the eyes of the other boys his age were on him. It was a thing of puberty.

He ducked as he pushed his way through the tiny cloth hole. Warm dry air surrounded him in the cluttered hovel. His eyes burned gold as they adjusted to the dark. He looked about at the strange plants in jars and colored glasses packed neatly in boxes. Buzzing glass crystal flew by his head. He ducked into the giant fuzzy quilts and accidently buried himself. He poked his head out of the feathers just as they zoomed past again. Dragons, no larger than a flower bud, lifted to the air, buzzing like bees. Their tiny eyes of rainbow brilliance winked at him as they circled about his head. Deep in his mind, he wondered if Craig knew about these. He reached out, but they weaved in the air out of reach.

He let them be and looked over to the blood red glow of Frito's elven eyes watching him. He crept over the wads of hay and sat beside him.

"Welcome Orrin-pa." Came a voice to his head. It wasn't of mouth or throat but of the Kamri.

Orrin seemed bashful at first and timidly answered in Kamri. "Thank you Y'day." Orrin looked up to the venerable man before him. Long, silver hair fell from his head. His gray, clouded eyes dead to sight still glistened. His skin was cracked and wrinkled. They slid and lifted as he smiled.

"Do you like my little home Orrin-pa?"

Orrin nodded. "Yes sir." Orrin's eyes wondered about the tiny nest. His ears listened to the buzzing of the tiny glass dragons and the horrible squeal of…it. Orrin looked to the cage and the creature within. Its long, shimmering tail scales coruscating with color like a blackbird's feathers, flexed and opened with out reason. Its hind paws hopped about its cage while its tiny hands picked up the dried slices of Hanna and nibbled at them. "What is it?" Orrin spoke through his Kamri.

"It is a peeve." Y'day said.

"You like, keep it as a pet?"

"Hey." Frito's voice shocked the air. "I'm a little out of the loop, here."

Orrin looked at him not understanding. Y'day spoke to him though Kamri. "Orrin-pa, there is a slight problem of communication. Frito-pas can hear my Kamri, but I cannot hear him. I cannot speak. It has been so long since I had need of my voice. I cannot see, I had no need for my eyes. Orrin-pa, I need you to translate for me."

"Okay." Orrin said looking to Frito.

"Its easy Orrin. I will speak, as you hear my words, you will project them so Y'day can 'hear' them." Orrin nodded.

Frito faced Y'day. His red eyes glared at him. "You know why I came?"

"I found the boy through his Kamri. Through him I learned your purpose. You seek your sister. I will find her through my Kamri." He unfolded and folded his legs.

He nodded to himself. "I search for Frita, I look across the plane. I reach up to the eye of Rasham Harugh, I ask it…it has seen her. But not recently. Others have heard of her but have no idea where she is now."

Frito leaned closer and hissed at him. "She is gone from the face of the earth?"

Orrin relayed.

"I see her not…Orrin-pa? Add your Kamri to mine. You know her."

Frito watched as Orrin's gold eyes turned to white orbs. "I see her! She calls herself Denice, she calls you Dwayne. She is in a house on a farm. I see not where. She is not a-wake, I can see her dreams. She, like, dreams of a child. Of Hi-ran de-cent. The child is an in-fant, in like, swad-dling clothes, eh?"

"Who is the baby?" Frito asked, but Orrin was lost in the Kamri.

"She is bury-ing the baby."

Frito raised an eyebrow.

"This is not Frita." Orrin mumbled. "She is too young to be Frita."

Frito glared at the boy. "Is the dream a memory? Is it now or past?"

Orrin ignored him. "She has taken the star of Ham-mer-strike and placed it about the baby. She has cov-ered the hole and she like, pla-ces stones about."

Frito cursed at the lack of his own Kamri. He was beginning to lose track of what was going on.

Y'day blinked his gray orbs flashing. "I saw a man. She called him paradox."

"Paradox. What is she doing with Paradox?" Frito was very confused and looked to Orrin to translate and saw him still in Kamri. "Orrin?"

"I see Fanrealm! There is fire!" Orrin shouted."

"What? What are you talking about?"

"I see Lady Fantista and a demon called Ha-rroc the son of Hate! He is try-ing to kill her!"

"Orrin! Where are you?" Frito turned hotly to Y'day. "What is going on?" He looked to the lost face of the ancient elf to realize that he couldn't hear him. The ancient elf had depended too long on his Kamri that his natural senses had shriveled and crumbled away.

Frito squeezed his large, heavy frame through the tight cluttered nest to the small opening. He poked his head through only to pull it back in. He fished for his dark glasses and placed them on before attempting the same stunt. Dragonslayer stood at the ladder as he had before. He saw the urgency on his cousin's face and started up the ladder. His size and weight of his monster armor caused the nest to sag. Frito stopped him with a hand. "No, what I need is Friska. I need his Kamri of the mind!"

Fryto pushed his head from the other large nest. "What?"

"Friska! I need Friska!"

Fryto didn't need to ask as he crawled back into the hole. Seconds stretched too long before Fryto's head reappeared. "He's gone!" Roc quickly looked about, using his elven ears. He targeted something and went to find him. Frito pulled his head back into the nest and went to Orrin's side.

"Craig is figh-ting Ha-rroc!"

Y'day could hear the boy as he drifted back into Kamri. "I see this naught. I search out Fanrealm. I see it now." His old feeble arm reached out and waved in the air. Frito took the arm and set Y'day's hand to the side of his own head. Y'day sent the pictures, and Frito received them.

"So will this work?" Max said as he sat on the hood of the Barchetta.

Craig sloshed a fluid around in a glass beaker. "If the Monks of Artus followed my formula, this should work."

"Well they are known for their liquor."

"Well, this stuff won't give you a buzz. It'll kill you." Craig looked from the beaker. "Well maybe not you but…" He waved his hand in the air. "Forget it."

"Now explain this…The Barchetta will run on alcohol."

"Gasohol, Max…I've devised this to work like gas."

"Why do you need two types?"

Craig lifted one of the kegs and braced it against the bumper with his leg. "Because the larger twelve cylinder engine uses a lead base as a lubricant for the moving parts."

"Lead?"

"Right." Craig said as he pulled down the New York license plate and unscrewed the cap. "While the second needs a detergent to keep it clean."

"Soap?"

"Sort of…Now that the catalytic converter that Rob designed is in place." Craig glared back at Max to insure the dwarf caught his inflection. The dwarf only mumbled sipping his brew dismissing Rob's ingenuity as a fluke. "The engine can take it." Craig went on, lifting the keg but he stopped. "Do you feel that?" Craig set the cap on the trunk and rolled up his sleeve. The tattoo of the dancing dragons were beginning to form.

"The feeling you were being watched?" Max said as he sipped at his brew. He made a face and tossed it into the hay of the barn.

"Snort!"

"Sorry, Ralph."

Suddenly the scene changed and Frito saw his mother. She stood in Sho-Pa pose. Battle, one of the dragon guard stood next to her, a mirror to her moves. Obviously, a training session in Sho-Pa. He saw the child Stephanie sitting off to the side watching carefully. Frito could see the four sided silver star about her neck.

And that scene melted away as well. "You see?" Y'day's Kamri said. "Your home is quiet."

Frito was holding Orrin. The elven boy was sweating and quivering in his arms. "Then what happened to him?" Y'day didn't hear him. Frito silently cursed the Kamri that made him invisible to the mind. He looked at Orrin who began to blink as consciousness came to him.

"But it was real." He said to no one in particular.

"It happens with Kamri." Y'day explained to him. "Images can be distorted, dreams and nightmares bleed in. One must learn to hold a clear Kamri."

Frito searched over the boy with his eyes and couldn't see any harm on him. "Stay here." Frito made his way through the nest. He jutted his head through the hole and looked below. Achillia was standing there surrounded by a flock of tiny elven children. Achillia looked up to the dark elf and helplessly shrugged her shoulders.

"What happened?" Frito barked as he pushed out of the nest.

"Friska made off some how." She said. "Roc, Fryto, and the twins have gone after him."

Frito made a face as he reached the bottom of the ladder. "How did he take off?"

"We, didn't see."

"You weren't watching him?"

"He was still and we were distracted. The children have never seen a human before and Roc's freakish size, no one was sure if he was human as well." The female knight bowed her head. "I apologize, Archknight. I have not served you well this Quest."

Frito shook his head. "It's not you." Frito looked up to her. "It's this Quest itself. This is the most screwed up…" Frito paused his words as he heard his brother pushing through the woods. "Fryto!" Frito called to him. "You find him?"

Exhausted and with heavy breaths, Fryto looked up. "No!"

"Where did he go?"

Fryto stepped from the tree line pulling a small branch from his shoulder. "Tell me and we'll both know." Fryto walked over to his brother. "He's running at a full tilt." Fryto held up the shin guard of Friska's armor. "He's shedding his armor as he goes. Roc and I can't even pretend to keep with him. I hope that J'son and J'cob have better luck."

Roc made his way to the nests. The trees snagged and clung to the spikes of his armor. With a bouldering shrug, he freed himself. "Here." He said holding up Friska's sword. "He tossed this too." Roc handed the sword to Frito.

Frito took the blade and felt the cold weight in his hands. He felt his heart sink in his centre. The sword was dead. No longer did the will of Okshiru move through it. Frito looked to Fryto. His brother's dower face confirmed it. He also shared the pain of losing the will of Okshiru. "It can be regained." Fryto said.

"But we have to find him first. I suspect that he is making a straight line to Fanrealm. Orrin had a Kamri nightmare or something and must have projected it by accident into Friska's head." Frito said looking up the ladder.

As if on a silent cue, Orrin nuzzled his head out of the nest and weakly climbed down the ropes. Roc stepped forward and in a strange act of kindness, reached up and took the boy in his giant arms and cradled him.

Y'day followed through the hole. He gently floated through and floated lower and lower until he hovered over the heads of everyone. "I see your brother running through the woods." His Kamri announced. "He is not running away, he is running to."

Roc looked to Frito hoping for an explanation. Frito had none. Orrin suddenly shuddered in Roc's arms. Frito quickly stripped off his cloak and draped Orrin with it. Orrin's hands clutched at the cloak and pulled it closer. "I'm al-right, Roc." He mumbled sleepily. "I'm al-right, eh?." He repeated as Roc lowered him to the ground. "Like, my head hurts." He announced putting his hands to his face.

"I cannot see what he is running to." Y'day went on oblivious to what happened about him. "I must see into him. He is of the Kamri. I must look into him." And he remained floating in the air.

"Now what?" Roc snarled, still panting from his run.

Frito held Orrin to his side and looked up to Y'day. "We wait."

"This is foolishness!" Roc hissed. "We can't depend on this venerable fool!"

Achillia touched Roc on the arm. He took her cue and looked about him. The entire tribe was now watching. Their eyes were trained on Frito.

"It is evident," Achillia whispered. "That although these are friendly people, they trust strangers only to a point."

Roc understood her unspoken words not to get exited. He curled his lip. He didn't like being told anything, and least of all by her. But he swallowed his bile and waited. Frito stood impatiently. He reached up and rubbed his forehead roughly, then ran his fingers through his long hair, scratching as he did. Fryto stepped over to him and spread his own cloak over his brother's shoulders, letting the hood fall across his head. "I know how the sun tears you up."

Frito looked at him through his dark glasses. "I'm alright." He looked to the sky above. "Okshiru's dark sky is clearing, but it is enough to save me from Kemoto's light." He pulled the hood lower to shadow his face. "Thanks."

"I see in him." Y'day spoke and all eyes turned towards him. "I see his Kamri before me. He sees a Cacodemon!" Y'day's eyes widened as pain swept his face. "I see...this is no dream!" His voice rose in pitch to a tiny squealing whine. "I see Fanrealm!"

Y'day dropped from the sky to the frozen earth. Frito swept to his side. The old man clutched his heart as if to rip it from his chest. Phlegm crawled on his lips and on his face as his gray eyes grew dull and empty. Frito felt the rattle of ghosts and the bells of Dru, goddess of death, brush his shoulder as she passed by him.

Y'day was dead.

Frito looked up and the captain was looking back down at him. The elf suddenly pushed at Frito to move him from out of the way, but Frito's bulk was not easily moved and the smaller elf pushed again at the dark elf to move him away. Frito took the hint and moved away on his own. Frito watched as the captain cuddled Y'day's head in his arms. Tears ran his face as he looked up to Frito with anger.

"Frito." Achillia called to him. Frito looked about him and saw the women and children were gone. Only the men stayed behind.

"That was quick." Fryto mumbled to no one in particular.

"We didn't mean this to happen!" Frito shouted to deaf ears as the air filled with whizzing shafts of wood. Frito shielded Orrin as arrows bounced off of his armor. A few arrows found their way into his armor but did him no harm. Fryto held up his axe and a circle of flames surrounded the party to hold back the rushing tide of angry elves.

Frito cast a spell to the air and the second breath of shafts bent and broke before they passed the ring of fire.

The captain set Y'day's head gently to the cold ground and took up his sword. Dragonslayer stepped before him almost as if to caution him, but the elf was not to be cautioned. The captain fainted and tried to lure the Slayer off guard as he thrust with his sword, but Roc raised a mighty fist and cracked it against the side of the captain's head with simple ease, knocking him unconscious.

Achillia withdrew her sword and cried aloud to the elven clan. "In the name of Uko, god of lightning, I call you all to HOLD!"

And they did.

They didn't understand her spoken words, but her holy glow of white force was clear. Fryto reflected the light, and Frito basked in it as the Archknight.

"Good move." Fryto said.

"With you and Frito holding off the horde, it was all I could do." She said as the glow faded.

"Now what?" Fryto said watching the angry elves in the trees around him. Frito was stooped over the captain. The elf's head was bruised and bleeding, but intact. Frito reached over and took Orrin's arm. "Orrin…" Frito called to him. "Use the Kamri, tell them it was not our fault."

Orrin nodded and he bowed his head. Frito could see the pain sweep the boy as he tried to use his Kamri. It was plain to Frito that the boy had overtaxed himself somewhere along the line. "Never mind." Frito said consolingly. "I'll think of something."

Roc stepped beside him. "Ninefingers, the natives are getting restless. I give you thirty beats to think of something, or I go a Bashing Brigantia."

Frito knew Roc's idea of peace negotiations was crushing the enemy into passivity. He quickly looked about. They were surrounded by all sides. Even if it were possible to make it to the tree line, they wouldn't be able to out run the nimble, swift elves. It was true that Frito, Fryto and Roc were elves themselves, but with heavy armor—Orrin was quick, but hurt, and Achillia was human and lacked elven speed. They could fight. Their combined might with Roc in the lead was strong enough to lay waste to the entire tribe. But genocide over a mistake?

The word of Uko was wearing off and would not work again. The elves were slowly approaching. Roc was fingering his firestone. How was he to explain? He couldn't.

"Roc!" Frito shouted. "Buy me a moment!"

Roc heard the words and braced himself for an attack. Roc knew his enemy. They would attempt a frontal assault since the arrow barrage failed completely. He watched as the elves drew near. He held up his hammer in his right holding back his stone of fire.

A silent cry somewhere sparked the tribe to action. A dozen elves leaped Fryto's circle of fire and charged the party. Roc's firestone sent a column of flame carving into the dirt at their rushing feet. They skipped and stumbled in suddenness. Roc shouted, brandishing his hammer. His voice alone, discouraged them. Achillia stood at his side. Her sword feinted and threatened, but didn't strike out. Fryto raised his axe and the wall of flames grew higher and held back the second wave.

Suddenly, Fryto began to grow. His armor melted away and black flesh was exposed from beneath. Fire shot from his eyes and ears as his hands grew to barbed talons. His mouth widened with fangs of blood and seething foam. His scream of anger shook the trees with fear. His new height loomed over the ring of fire and all the elves could see the horrible transformation. On his chest were the words written in the elven runes...'Elf eater.'

In one breath, the entire area was cleared.

Fryto whistled. "Huh?"

Roc stood, waiting for something to happen. He turned to Frito almost upset that he didn't get to slaughter everything. "Illusion, phantasm," Frito said getting up from his knees. "Combination of spells." He looked about. "HORSE!" He cried and his horse stepped into reality in response, dragging the reins of the other horses. "Right now we've got to go."

Roc wasn't happy, then again, never was. "You mean go?"

"Yes." Frito said putting Orrin up on his horse. "They won't be frightened for long."

"No!" Roc commanded. "They attack me in my own realm? They will pay with their lives!"

"That isn't the purpose of this Quest. You can come back later with an army, right now I have to worry about Orrin. Max will have my head if he finds out I broke they boy's brain."

Roc looked to the boy and grunted, then turned to the trees and shouted in his most menacing voice. "Hear me now and always Kemli, and understand my words that I, Dragonslayer will return to this wood and I shall slay every man, woman, child, relation, witness, bystander, or passer-by that I find here in the most agonizing, terrorizing and harrowing way that I can devise, conjure and invent, without mercy, regret or prejudice!" His words faded into the trees. "I shall return!" He added for good measure.

"Right..." Frito whispered as he took the reins of his and Orrin's horse and quickly led them out of the camp.

Chapter 23

Fikor's anger settled in the west as the storm was swept clean from the sky by Leatha, the night, mother of the moon, stars and dawn. Hauge slept quietly, exhausted from his day. Ovam perched on the edge of the world preparing to shine his pale sight to give light to the Twelve Shadow Walkers, guardians of the dark. Fikor's frost lingered against the ground as Mistang blanketed the fields already stripped of their yield. The animals lay in their hay, their sounds stopped in silent respect for Leatha.

Cinders of dark red burned in the place. Purples and blues danced on the black coals and the dim fire light. A black pot hung from its hook steaming its vapor slowly into the cooling air.

She lay wrapped in warm thick quilts. Her eyes burned silver as her elven sight pushed back the dark. She did not know this place, but lacked the strength to move. Her pointed ears listened to the sounds down the stairs—a farmer, his wife—several workers already in their beds asleep. The farmer and wife spoke about her, but their words were foreign to her. She listened as clumping foot steps came up the stairs. She rose in her bed and felt all her strength leave her. The effort of attention was exhausting, but she forced herself to at least sit up. A door in the floor lifted and light spilled in the loft. A woman slowly came up the steps and into the room. She stood bent in the low ceiling and stepped over to the bed. "Child, you wake?" She knelt at the bed. She set her lantern by the bed side and laid her gentle hands at the girl's shoulders. "But now you must rest." The woman's voice was heavy with accent. Her face was old and wrinkled with time. With motherly care, she tucked the young woman to bed.

"Who are you?" The young woman asked and found razors in her throat. The young woman clutched her throat and only found a heavy bandage.

The woman pitied. "You must not talks, child. I am Agatha, wife of Hormand. We are farmers. It was Hormand who founds you and broughts you here."

The young woman thought about this. Then she said with a small, sticky voice: "I am Denice, of the house of..." Denice reached to the center of her blouse to clutch for something that wasn't there.

Agatha leaned closer. "What is it?"

"I have lost something, a necklace." Denice answered weakly as pain in her throat forced her to silence. "What is this?" Her fingers touched her bandage.

"When Hormand founds you, some had trieds to do you great harms, but the, Lord of Lucks was with you. The rope they tries to hang you with brokes. But you should not worry abouts that." Agatha said as she pulled about the covers. "You are safes heres. You must sleeps. You wills be well in the morning."

Denice laid in the bed staring out the small window towards Worldsend. The rope was too thick to break, she knew that.

Chapter 24

Stepping out of Argra, the curtain of Oblivion (called the eternal shadow), and heading in a direct line to the east along the river of Therd, streaking past the Paradise Lost Truck Stop, over the dismal swamps and the long-ass stretch of highway known as The Road to Nowhere (because it does indeed lead to nowhere in either direction), will lead to the ghettos of Juan-tavous. Crossing this, and the swamps of darkness, through the valley of thunder, and the sea of fire will take you to the outer walls of Hel itself and the Barren Wastes beyond.

The Barren Wastes end suddenly at the great ocean of the east. Still heading east, but now in a backward direction (due to the distortion of leaving Hel) and passing through the great Wove of the Worlds, which circles all of Mortalroam like a protective/retaining belt, you would wash up on the east coast of Mortalroam. It is along this coast, from the peninsula of Conquistador, to the ice walls of Fjords, where most of the mortals go about. Mankind, and it's kin, live here with the grace of what ever god is looking out for them. The population fades on the other side of the Long river until it ends abruptly at the other side of the great Wove of the World which guards/guards against the Other Barren Wastes, that lie before Worldsend.

To make things simple, the barren wastes that lead to Hel are known as 'The Barren Wastes' and the barren wastes that lead to Worldsend are known as 'The Other Barren Wastes'.

From the border of the Other Barren Wastes is a stunning view of Worldsend and its unscalable mountains. Not that actual direction matters. Everything is a distortion of what the thinker is thinking, and any direction faced is the direction wanted. Whether it is Worldsend to the West, East, or North by South South East, it doesn't matter.

The gods will claim that no mortal has ever seen Worldsend. Legends, however, linger from mighty men who say they have scaled the unscalable mountains, or claim that it isn't necessary to scale them. Whether they actually saw it has never been properly documented.

"But, Hargor? Did ja' actually see the Great Mountains?"

"Wha'? Yew old fool! Ah was thare! Ah clambed to the toop! Now geve me ah-nuther bruw and let meh goo on with muh story."

And so it goes.

211

It is the same claim for Hel, with those who claim there is a tunnel leading under the great sea and swimming it is unnecessary. Basically, if it's a half decent story it will fly, and since no one can really dispute any half decent story, the legends still stand regardless of what the gods claim, even though they are the ones who would know if anyone had ever swam or climbed their respective boundaries. A half decent story teller can easily wave this by.

"And yur dum enuff ta believe them? Doo ya think thale admit to havin their precious mountain scalled by a mere mortal? Now looks hare, ma bruws gone flat an nearly done and muh story's goot mare tellin to it."

"Aye Hargor. Bar keep! Anoother roond!"

Then there is Craig Tyrone, who claims that the great sea isn't there and Hel is really in a cordoned off section of Mortalroam known in the past as New Jersey. However, the unscalable mountains are for real and they are not only unscalable, but unescalatorable. It's the Great Distortion that makes the two not really where you think they are. If you want them to be there when you get there, you have to get directions before you leave.

Craig is a peculiar guy. He was peculiar in his old world and peculiar in this world as well. In fact, he could be peculiar anywhere, which, in itself, is kind of peculiar. Legends claim that he was riding on the back of a dragon one day when he got himself lost and then found himself circling over Worldsend. He dropped a water balloon on the head of Quartertaker, the great god of video-games. The great god didn't see the humor, especially since it screwed up his high scoring game, and caused him to lose to Arcadia, the god of pinball. Furious, Quartertaker cursed Craig to be a Nih elf.

If there is any distortion anywhere, it's in that story. He had left his home and joined the Marine Corps to gain enough gold to enable him to seek the great knowledge of physics and become a rocket scientist (his true dream) when a strange accident (depends on who you ask) happened and he wound up in Mortalroam to claim the title of Dragoncaller.

Why? He doesn't know.

It was a simpler story of luck, when a Ne-arri child was found by Ameri, the Queen of Dragons, and raised the child as her own. That stepdaughter, Neeko, was as rambunctious as her cat race could be and sought out her fortune only to find the Dragoncaller and fall in love with him, and he with her.

It is suspected, that there is a direct connection to the chance that the Dragoncaller would find and fall in love with the Princess of Dragons, but neither Craig nor Neeko really want to know what.

Thamrell turned from the clear water of the scrying pool and drifted across the floor twice before he stood and looked rather depressed at the floor.

Ura swept into the room. She draped herself around one of the tall, white, cracked marble columns that stood by the door and watched the god of depression stare at the floor. She stroked, slithered and caressed the column with her leg, but Thamrell didn't look up. "You are early." She sighed with a light, disappointed air as she stepped around the stone couches and into the room.

"I should have been late, I wasted time either way."

"You seem depressed." She said as she sat by the side of the pool.

"Not really, just all of my plans are shifting into frazzled ends as they come to the surface." He opened his fist and spread his withered fingers to demonstrate. "I should have stayed in bed for all of last year."

"Mine or yours." She said stroking the tile of the pool. She outlined the Ammonite frozen forever in the Moroccan marble.

"Yours of course, where else would be best to prove that sex is a hollow deluding escape of love and merely an act of mutual masturbation."

The goddess looked sadly into the water. "I thought we were more than that."

"We were, but I wouldn't want to depress you with what it was."

"And what of love and caring?" She looked up at him almost hopefully.

"There is no such thing as love and caring, there are only degrees of pain and suffering. We name them different things to make them more palatable." He finally looked at her. "All that pain for a few fleeting, elusive moments of love." He pursed his withered lips. "Why bother? Just suffer and be done with it, at least that's consistent."

"What is dragging you?" She moaned, tiredly turning her back on him.

Thamrell sailed about the room, fading as he moved through the columns that weren't there for him. "It seems that a few factors have occurred that I hadn't anticipated."

213

"Those are."

"One: In a bright, blazing stroke of brilliance, Thumber snatched Frita right in front of the Ninefingers. I had hoped to let her disappearance go undiscovered for a while, but now I have the Ninefingers actively looking for her. To complicate matters, to make up for his glowing point of success, the fool lost her. Now, no one knows where she is. Two: Friska has failed to kill his brother. Three: Who is this?" Thamrell waved his hand over the pool and images rippled of Fanrealm. The water shimmered and couldn't focus on the manor itself, but in the outside courtyard was Lady Fantista locked in a pose of Sho-Pa and Battle, the Dragonguard, a mirror to her smooth, flowing movements, training beside her. Watching on the side was a child.

Ura peered into the pool at what Thamrell pointed at and curled her lip into a snarl. "The Brat. She is Stephanie. Daughter of Oustrand."

"Who is she?" Thamrell glided over the water and knelt by Ura's side. "Why did you have Paradox try to kill her?"

The goddess turned from the water, pulling her knees close the her body as she did. "She was an annoyance. What is she to you?"

"She was an annoyance?"

"Okshiru had a special interest in the girl. She was born of her parents, but actually of Fikor." She glared at him from beneath lowered brows. Thamrell read her unspoken comment about gods not interfering in mortal affairs and Fikor's seemingly unchecked violation of said rule. "Her voice would sing a song of grace," She poetically sang before her voice dropped to a despising hiss. "that only made my skin crawl." She looked with wide eyes to Thamrell. "And you know how I hate when my skin crawls." She pouted and ran her hand along her arm. "Again I ask, what is she to you?"

"Nothing." Thamrell said looking at her image in the water. "I hope. Then there is this one." Craig Tyrone flashed on the water. It was night, and the dark elf sat in the field of Fanrealm watching the stars. His wife, Neeko, swollen with child sat beside him. The two were bundled for the cold and cuddled in each others arms.

"He is the concern of Draca, The Demon Dragon Witch. Not yours." Ura answered.

"He is responsible for seven of my dragons."

"What happened?" She sat up, looking half concerned.

"They escaped and headed to Mortalroam. They came across the Dragoncaller, probably attracted by his aura and attacked him. He took them from the sky with a bow."

"That is the Tc-mock, bow of dragons."

"What worries me is that in the final battle, the Dragonslayer will use his dragons. Tyrone will lead them."

"Are you worried about the final battle now?"

Thamrell soared across the water and around the room. "YES!" He shouted. He looked about the room to insure no one heard him. He hovered a little higher and spoke with greater restraint. "Yes." *It is only days away, remember?* "I will only be able to bring a portion of the army out of Hel to take Cornerstone. We have a chance if the Ninefingers does not discover our plot. The Slayer's allies are still in disarray from Hauth and would be easily crushed. If I fail in keeping the Ninefingers busy and he exposes us, we lose the advantage of surprise. If Roc can rally his troops, and I suspect he can, and with Craig Tyrone and his dragons, we would be well matched." He turned from her. "Too well matched."

She suddenly took notice fully of what the god of Depression was saying and perked up, thrusting out her huge breasts as she did. "Matched?"

He turned back to face her, drifting back to avoid her melonous bosom. "Be careful, you can hurt someone with those." Thamrell looked at her breasts and the hard nipples pointing from beneath. "We are still perfecting the spell of Babble. Until it is ready, I will have trouble with Command and Control. Roc is tricky and is nothing short of devastating as a war general. He also has the Ninefingers who is still a hero due to the fact that no one remembers that he was Hauth." He paused as the non-interference rule boiled again. "He poses a psychological plus for the Dragonslayer." He looked to her, insuring that he was explaining so she understood. "Oh, look, it's the Devilslayer! Okshiru is fighting with us! Charge! That sort of thing. With all these considerations, I would imagine the balance in his favor." He held his breath in dry lungs as he waited for the idea to seep into her spongy brain. "I need the Iron dragon."

She smiled and flashed her eyes at him. "I have already summoned him for you." *You think I don't know what's going on, do you.* "You worry to much oh, god of despair." *I'm not that stupid. I want this as much as you.* "You're such a pessimist."

Dexter C. Herron

"No, I merely see the truth in matters, that is my curse. Are you sure that your boy, Paradox will summon Harroc the son of hate?"

"Give a mortal a weapon and he will use it. Especially against Achillia."

Thamrell glided along the floor to the pool side. "Your sending him to kill Achillia? Why? It would be better to have him kill Fantista."

"Fantista? I would have thought you would want Harroc to take out Frito."

"Frito, Roc, Fryto and Achillia are together. Three knights that close together will sense Harroc coming for clicks. Roc could have a trap set up and wipe out Harroc and his whole crowd with little trouble. Fantista wouldn't run, not from Fanrealm."

"And the barriers?" She leaned closer, amazed that Thamrell could have forgotten something like that.

"I have found a way around them, but you wouldn't have known that."

She tilted her head with a smile, congratulating him. "Why do you want Fantista dead?" She looked at him absurdly. "She's a grandmother."

"Harroc has a chance to kill her and she holds the sanity for the Ninefingers. The Archknight will be swept easily into despair along with his brother Friska."

She scoffed at the idea. "She is too loved by Okshiru. He would never allow anything to happen to her. No one save Uko will notice if Achillia is gone—and besides;" She said poutingly. "Uko and I had a spat."

He tilted closer. "So this is cheap revenge?" *You stupid cunt.*

"Revenge isn't cheap and a cacodemon isn't easy."

"I still think that move should have been planned better." *Don't get mad, Thamrell, and don't get her mad. Scold her gently, playfully.* "You are too whimsical."

The goddess fought to her feet, her boobs swaying and tossing her off balance. "Whimsical!"

"No, you're not whimsical. You're a bimbo." Thamrell said casually over his shoulder.

"I AM NOT A BIMBO." The goddess rose above the canopies and floated over Thamrell. "I am the goddess of Chaos!"

Thamrell looked up to the goddess over head. "Especially from this view. I haven't forgotten that."

216

"Then what do you mean?" She spoke in anger as she sank down to him.

"I didn't mean anything." He tilted his head so the brim of his hat covered his grin. "It so much fun to piss you off."

"Well stop it." She said hotly sitting by the pool side again.

"You're mad at me now?" He said floating over to her. "Or at yourself for being so weak as to be manipulated by a bodiless god."

She glared at him, seeing plainly the fine web of despair he was weaving. She reached out at touched his withered face. With a soft hand she stroked his neck. Her eyes relaxed and closed as she kissed him passionately. "I need you as you need me." She stroked him again. "Okshiru forbids me from directly interfering in Mortalroam, but not you." She kissed him on the cheek and whispered in his ear. "Lets fuck."

"Lets not." He said coldly as he pulled away. "I need to find Frita."

"I can't see why, she would never fuck you." She turned her back on him.

"I need her. Thumber can get her to free Weishap. If we cannot free Weishap, then we cannot open the doors of Hel and release the army."

She looked back. "How can Thumber do that?"

"By playing on her guilt. Her sin."

"Which is?" The goddess smiled like a gossiping vixen.

"He won't tell me, but I don't think he knows." Thamrell said circling the pool. "His nightmares are touch and go, he tries a button and if that works, he can do it."

"Is she the only one?"

"None of us, not even we gods, can approach the doors. But she can. She is the only one." Thamrell floated towards the window. "Thumber got heavy handed with one of his nightmares and the poor girl went overboard." He put his head though the curtain that wasn't there for him and looked out the window. "It will be dawn on Mortalroam soon."

"Then Harroc will be free this eve." The goddess floated over to him. "He will be able to bring several Led Captains with him. Achillia will be dead by the morrow and Harroc will be free of the summons and loose on Mortalroam. He will be able to serve you."

"If he can get Achillia alone and not get himself or his army killed off." Thamrell turned from the window and found himself in her arms.

He looked down to her petite young face, her stunning blue, almond shaped eyes slowly opened and closed. "I wonder." He said floating straight up out of her reach. "Where is Friska?" He glided over to the pool. The water showed him the knight running through the woods, stumbling, collapsing in the cold dirt. "Its such a shame to see a knight fall from grace." He turned and found himself in Ura's arms again.

Chapter 25

The black sky of Leatha, goddess of night, gave way to her daughter, Shegatesu the dawn. She took burning feathers from Kemoto's wings and flew to the edge of the east and set the sky to flame. Okshiru's black waves crashed the shore as if to climb the black rocks above. Waves pounded the cliffs as if hoping to cause them to crack and crumble, then waiting, a giant, watery maw with white foam like gnashing fangs to catch the falling house that sat alone at the top of the rocks.

Vines clung painfully to the sides of the house, barren of leaves. Fikor's cold poured in through the cracks in the shutters and under the spaces in the doors. Hauge the wind was still silent and didn't stir the dead leaves that lay scattered about the front of the house. He didn't touch the sagging wooden gate. He didn't move the sand along the walk to the front door. He dared not disturb the quiet of Shegatesu's morning.

Kemoto's light began to spread with the radiance of his fiery wings. He leapt to the air and with a single flap, was over the edge of the world. His light radiated out in bands of gold through the gnarled, dead trees. Shafts of warm sun splintered through the naked branches that hung nervously, like a witch's fingers, over the front yard. Warm, tangible light shone across the carpet of dead leaves in the yard, slowly crawling over the sagging gate and inching it's way across the front walk to the door. An ash covered, crumbling door complete with a rotted mat before it that said, Welcome.

Welcome to the Home by the Sea.

Kathreen stepped lightly through the cold halls of the house. She tipped lightly to Buffet's door and peered in. The tender child slept buried in blankets of wool. Kathreen silently passed through the room and to the window, where she closed the curtains and shunned Kemoto's light.

Back out into the hall, Kathreen took the key from Buffet's door as she locked it.

She hurried as quietly as possible down the stairs to the kitchen. The fire was dead in the fireplace and Fikor's winter was waiting. Kathreen pulled her robe about her as she crouched over the wood pile and selected a thick, double split, log—flat, like a wide, short plank. She watched her gaunt, spidery hands as they flashed across the logs, white and fragile, against hard, dark wood. She then stepped to the cupboard where she fetched a flat satchel. She stacked the satchel atop the log and it clunked with a bony, metal sound.

With nervous urgency, she hurried back up the stairs. She darted down the hall and stepped over the swords and axes that had been laying there from days past. She set the log and flat satchel before the door and beside a glass bowl of water already set there. She then knelt beside them and waited.

She had the easy part.

Her cold hands trembled as she wrung at the nape of her robe. She looked at her hands clutching in her lap like naked, cold, angry rats. She held them open and looked at them. Bloodless, they stung from the cold morning. Slowly, cautiously she reached up to where her breast had been. The place were such pain was always present, but Denice had taken away her pain with a gentle touch.

She gasped suddenly as the door opened before her. Vapors curled about her lips as she looked up into her masters face.

The Cacodemon had drained him. Drained the flush of his cheeks and pulled it tight against his bones. His hazel eyes had retreated into his head leaving rings of swollen darkness. His soft, auburn hair was a scramble of wires on his head. His lips were thin and split. Dried blood spotted his chin where his lips had bled. His lips parted just enough to expose his front teeth.

Her hand pressed into the spot where her breast had been at the sight of him. She bowed away from him to hide from his accusing stare.

Paradox opened the door a little more and sloughed back into the room. He leaned heavily against the wall and slid down until he sat on the floor. With a blank, seemingly unseeing gaze, he watched as she darted in the room with the glass bowl of water. She set it in the center of the room and darted out. She fetched the log and satchel and set them beside the bowl. She finally got up and closed the door.

As a second thought, she locked it.

She had the easy part.

He spent four years researching, studying and planning for the summoning and controlling of a demon. He followed Ura's seemingly playful hints until he discovered all that was required to do the deed. Then, for the last three days he spent every hour chanting for the Cacodemon. He had studied ancient, unknown texts for proper grammatical syntax to enable him to recite bizarre, mystic languages. He sang long hours of words that came hard to his lips, repeating phrases that were foreign to his mouth. Shouting a summoning until his voice grew brittle and soundless.

She knelt in the center of the room, and gathered the things about her. She reached into the pocket of her apron and pulled out two thongs of leather and laid them beside her. With trembling hands she reached up and took a bone bobb from her hair. In her nervousness, she dropped it then snatched it back up for some reason, holding it until the room's silence returned, and then placed it down neatly, beside the leather thongs.

She had the easy part.

He had spent every hour of the last three days scripting for the Cacodemon. Writing verses of unfamiliar text on the walls, ceiling, across the floor and on his body. Some pieces, as simple as a single letter several feet in size, with others consisting of entire volumes written on the skin of a single, chicken's egg.

She glanced up at him for an instant. His face was empty and he was still panting through the space in his parted lips. Short blasts of his breath could be seen in Fikor's cold. He seemed as impervious to the cold as an elf. She shuddered.

She went about her task, as she bunched up her sleeve and took up the leather thong and tightly wrapped it twice around her wrist and knotted it with the aid of her teeth. She then took the bobb and inserted it into the loops and knotted it again. She then turned the bobb, again and again, tightening the leather. Her fingers, then hand began to burn as tingles became needles and needles became skewers. She tightened the leather and her hand fell cold and the skewers melted like icicles. She wound until the pain stopped.

She took the second thong and tied the bobb to her arm.

She had the easy part.

He had spent every hour of the last three days gesturing for the Cacodemon. He had studied long movements and pranced about the room with fluid motions imitating choreographed dances. Some gestures were as small and dexterous as the playing of a lyre. His fingers fluttering in the air much like the flurry of a bird's panic flight.

She undid the satchel with her right hand and exposed the clever within. She lifted it and felt its weight as she tested its balance. It was much too large for her one hand as she waved it in the air. She suddenly drove it into the block. Almost letting the weight of the clever do its work. It stuck cleanly into the wood. With the clever still in the wood, she pulled it between her knees. She wretched it out of the wood and held it tightly in her hand. She then took her left hand, pale and paralyzed, and placed it flat on the block. She shifted it slightly until it was centered. It no longer felt like a part of herself.

She looked at Paradox. He seemed too exhausted to move or even show concern. She lifted the clever suddenly over her head. Its weight pulled itself down over her back, but with a rising snap she brought it back down into the block. She shouted and jerked her left hand out of the way and the cleaver missed its intended target.

She looked at him again, panting with her own surprise. He only licked his torn lips as he finally seemed to be watching her.

She had the easy part.

She wrenched at the clever again and pulled it from the wood. She let it lay limply in her hand as she caught her breath. She could feel her heart pound, awakening the pain where her breast should have been. She felt warmth lift from her face as her cheeks blushed with blood. She stared at the swollen hand sitting numbly on the block.

She had the easy part.

She jerked up the clever and brought it down with a sudden jerk.

Nausea twisted her belly and the room swirled around her. The clever had fallen from her grasp at some point but she didn't know when or where. Her eyes filled with tears as she took up the bloody hand from the block and quickly dropped it into the water beside her.

She looked at Paradox as pain constricted her face. She raised her left arm out to him as if to reach him. "I love you." She said as she crumpled to the floor.

He raised an eyebrow as he watched bright, red, blood slowly ooze out from her wrist and drip onto the floor. He then stared at the hand in the bowl, the clear water growing darker with blood. He grew fascinated as the water began to swirl, and then boil. He watched it a little longer and it was steaming furiously and foaming over. Slowly it began to cool leaving a wretched shriveled hand in a puddle of black water.

He slowly pulled from the wall and crawled to her side. He reached over her and took up the bowl in his arms. He rose and moved to the door and unlocked it. Without looking back, he opened it and slowly shuffled out of the room, closing the door behind him.

Chapter 26

Craig stood by the high wall of the main tower. He watched as the guards came and replaced themselves and the new watch take over. They marched in line, saluted one another, reported their posts, and passed on special orders, secret signs and counter signs.

The men seemed happier now that they were at Fanrealm. Living in the ruins of Dragonrealm was hard for them, as the destroyed garrison caught wicked, chilling winds from off the water and tents were not sufficient protection from them. Fanrealm's huge sub halls were easily converted into perfect winter barracks. The troops showed their improved morale by the snap and pop in the trivial matter of duty change.

Craig pulled further into the dark shadows to avoid the stare of sunlight. He had never felt that he was a "Day" person. As far as he was concerned, nothing should ever happen until after one in the afternoon. But now, there was no choice. To Craig, the sun was harsh and cruel and in short hours, direct light could kill him. It never really bothered him for the most part, he just stayed out of the sun and was careful to not be caught out in it. The people of Cornerstone, however; talk about a Nih thief that they caught and in a rage of vigilantic passion staked him spread eagled in a field. They say he saw the dawn, was blind by mid morning and dead by late afternoon. The ordeal was not at all pleasant, as the bards and minstrels sang of his demise. They include the gory details of how his azure blue eyes slowly smoldered and smoked in his skull and his pale, white flesh crinkled and became black, flaking off in the winds.

The word Vampire came to mind but Craig shook the idea from his head with a shrug and adjusted his gray, smoked glasses as Gorn came up the stairs.

"Ho, My lord. A quiet night?"

"Like the night before Christmas." Craig answered darkly. It was the first time that he had spoken to anyone for hours and it surprised him how somber it sounded. *Thinking of gloom again,* he sighed to himself.

The human cocked his head as he peered into the shadow. "Evil is brooding with you my lord."

"Can you tell?" Craig asked. "I don't know, just something is not right. Like getting a letter saying a convict who got life while you were on jury duty just escaped, but not without getting your address. Or like standing alone in the subway. You know what I mean?"

"No."

"Okay, how about finding a letter to the IRS that you were supposed to mail three months ago still in your briefcase?"

"No." He sighed, smiling at the Dragoncaller's strange attempt at mirth.

"How about relieving me so I can go to bed."

"Aye."

Craig darted easily down the stairs and into the main courtyard. He leapt over the door of the Red Barchetta, and with a few pumps of the pedal, started it. He let it warm up a bit and thought about how to properly reward Rob's brilliance for the new catalytic converter.

He shifted into gear and set out through the main gates. He drove quickly into the forest and parked by a tree. He leapt over the door again and walked fifty yards into the woods. There he found several large rock formations and at the crevice between two large boulders, a hole.

He ducked in quickly and followed the network of tunnels under the earth. His elvish sight pushed through the darkness showing the caverns as plain as day. Up head, he saw Onary waiting for him. "It is well enough time that you finally arrived." The springer spaniel said. "I was beginning to freeze."

Craig's transformation to a Nih elf had left him immune to the cold. "Then why didn't you wait inside?"

"You know how it is." Onary said as he stretched and yawned. "Dog/master relations. Traditions to be up held and all that." He waited with a wagging tail as Craig opened the door. He quickly pushed his way into the warm room. "Yes, it is very important to maintain these traditions, unlike cats who just do not care."

"Hmmm" Edia mumbled as she lifted her head from the mantle.

Onary circled the rug in front of the fire place before seating himself. "Nothing Edia, it's not dinner."

"Oh, so your back, dawg." Edia chortled. "Cold too much for yew?" She spoke in her long drawl.

"No, I was longing for your stimulating conversation." Onary laid his head on the rug watched as Craig peeled out of his armor.

"Are you feeling any better?" Craig asked without looking up from removing his leg guard.

"Yes. The food poisoning from the rancid mouse that Edia slipped in my food…"

"Ah did no such thing!" She howled looking up from the mantle with a start. "You just had one of those dawg diseases."

"As I was saying—my stock was able to shrug off the cat's feeble attempt at my life. I will be on post with you this eve."

"If Ah wuz trying to kill you, dawg, I wouda just tossed your food in the river and watch you drown trying to get it."

"I, Edia, unlike you, can swim."

Craig sighed as he crossed the living room and walked into the kitchen. He set his glasses on the table and watched as his very pregnant wife came in from one of the subcaverns. He quickly crossed over to her and took the pail of water from her hands and closed the door behind her. "What are you doing awake?"

"I couldn't sleep." Her warm, green, cat eyes smiled at him. "I couldn't roll over and I woke up." She leaned forward, lifting on her toes and hugged her husband, rubbing her cheek against his in Ne-arri fashion before kissing him gently. "Oh, oh." She said.

"What is it?"

"My tail won't reach." Try as she might, she couldn't reach her tail around to hug Craig with her stomach in the way. It finally settled to hook lightly on his ankle.

"Looks to me that you could give at any moment."

She shrugged her shoulders. "Nih elves are 18 months while we are 6 months. Humans are 9 months and Dragons are three years. I have no idea which one we fall under."

"Well its been 12 months." He said setting her in a chair. He turned and emptied the pail of water in the kettle on the stove. He suddenly stopped as he watched it.

"What's the matter?" When Craig didn't answer she pushed out of the chair and stepped over. She peered over his shoulder and looked at the water.

"Look at the water." He said. "Its spinning counter clockwise. Anything on this side of the equator should go clockwise." He made and clockwise motion with his finger.

"Okay…" Neeko said slowly. "So…"

"So, this is breaking a law of physics that was working yesterday." He took up the pot and poured it back into the pail. "See, its counter clockwise." He poured it back into the kettle.

Neeko watched him and saw that he was pouring the water the same way each time but now, it was spinning clockwise. "Now its going the other way." She read the concern in his dark eyes. "This is really something, isn't it?" She reached over to his sleeve and pulled it up. The Dancing dragons were forming. She touched his chest and through his shirt she could feel rising heat. "This is something."

Craig set the pot on the stove. "Onary? Edia?" He called. The dog pushed his way through the door. "Yes? You have a sick yearling and want me to feed it Edia?"

Edia followed him in. "No dawg, I'm sure its about who turned over the garbage."

"Edia, would you want to play a new game? Puss in the pond?"

"Onary." Craig cut him off. "Have either one of you felt something strange?"

"Like something not setting right in the pit of your centre?" Onary asked.

"Yeah."

"Sounds like tapeworm to me, Suh." Edia put in.

"Cat," Onary lectured. "If you cannot carry on an intelligent conversation, and I know you can not, then run along and play with an old barley sack down by the river."

Craig put up his hands to stop them from bickering. "Have you felt something strange?"

Edia looked about guiltily. "I did, Suh. A moment ago."

"Like a door in another room." Onary said. "Opening and closing."

"Or a portal." Craig said. He pulled back his sleeves and looked at the tattoos fading.

"What is it Craig?" Neeko asked taking a seat in the chair beside him.

"I don't know." He said. "It's like we're being...watched."

Neeko hung on to each word and listened about her. The feline ears on her head swivelled back and forth to pick up any tiny sound about her. Suddenly she let out a shriek.

"What?" Craig grabbed at her. She looked down to Edia.

"Ah am sorry, Mum. But your tail was just swishing about!"

"My lady." Onary said. "I will take Edia and quietly boil her in oil."

"Are you sure you have the recipe for boiling, dawg?"

"One pot, one stone of oil, and one cat named Encyclopedia!" He lunged at the cat, but she was too quick as she bounded out of the room.

Chapter 27

Mistang's final morning vapors lifted as Shegatesu returned the feathers of flame to Kemoto who now crossed Okshiru's sky. The gentle light filtered through the trees to the leaf covered ground below. Frito sat by Fryto's fire with Soulseng, the flute, to his lips. The sound was sweet and soft and lifted with the mist. Orrin sat beside him listening to the elfcall. He could hear the response of J'son and J'cob who where still in pursuit of Friska. If what they were saying was correct, the errant knight was on a direct course to Fanrealm.

Achillia and Dragonslayer emerged from the woods. They waited quietly until Frito was done. "Lord Frito, that was lovely." Achillia then asked: "Did you receive a reply?"

Roc stepped from behind her. "Yes he did." Roc went over to his horse and took some roc-bread from his saddle bag.

"And it said," Achillia prompted.

Frito knew that humans could not understand the elfcall. "Friska has run at full tilt since last night. J'son and J'cob are falling behind."

"But he is still headed for Fanrealm?" She asked him as she sat at the fire.

Frito nodded. "Yes, it falls together. His Kamri must have detected the same thing Y'day did before he died."

"And maybe he didn't." Roc said returning to the fire side. "I don't trust the old fool." Roc sat by the fire handing half of his Rocbread to Achillia. "Besides, we can't abandon Frita."

Achillia looked at Roc and the Rocbread in her hands. She didn't believe it.

"I'm not." Frito said taking his flute apart. "That is why Fryto is requesting a forest walk from Meleki."

"It's taking too long." Roc mumbled as he broke his bread.

"The longer you prepare, the safer it is." Achillia said as she broke up her bread.

Orrin looked up. Frustration and anger spread across his face. "But what I saw…" Orrin said. "Was like, so real."

"And what do you see now." Frito asked him.

Orrin lost his attention for the moment. "I see Gorn at post." Orrin's eyes looked to the Frito. "All is quiet."

"Does your head still hurt?" Frito could read the pain in the boys words. "Then rest your head for awhile." Frito was still amazed at the seemingly unlimited range of Orrin's Kamri.

Achillia looked at Roc only to find him looking back. Then the two looked to Frito. "And what is this...Cacodemon?" She asked. "I can hardly pronounce it."

"Okay, so like, a Ca-co-demon is the, like, sum-mon-ing of a demon from Hel to Mor-tal-roam, eh?" Orrin answered reciting from privileged texts. "It can, like, only be gran-ted through a de-i-ty."

"So Friska is trying to stop one at Fanrealm?" Achillia asked Orrin.

"Get real." Roc said. "No one at Fanrealm could or would cast one. Plus my army is there."

"Also, there is a barrier of magic about it." Frito added.

"Anything like the last one?" Roc pushed.

Frito remained quiet as he remembered when Thamrell broke his last one. "Friska allowed him through."

Roc nodded. "But your sending Fryto and Achillia just to be certain."

Yes, he thought. *To be certain. Orrin could have had a bad vision, or read someone else's and then broadcast it unintentionally. Friska never had the range to detect Fanrealm from here. What ever Orrin had, it was sent to Y'day and Friska. What was it? A distortion, an intentional ruse by Thamrell, or perhaps...*Frito looked down at the boy. *Is he now having dreams that come true? Like Craig? Or did Craig have one and Orrin tapped into it?* Frito pursed his lips as he thought. *And if Harroc is going to Fanrealm, are Achillia and Fryto enough to stop him? Is the re-enforced magic barrier strong enough to hold out Harroc? Thumber broke in and out of the last one at Fanrealm. How are they breaking my barriers?* Frito nodded, hoping to change the subject. "I will attempt another forest walk to Brewster. I think I can do it."

"And if not." Achillia asked before taking another bite of Rocbread.

"Then we walk." Roc said.

Everyone could read Roc's more than usual hostility.

"So what is it?" Frito finally asked.

Roc swallowed his bread. "This is all too confusing. You need a lady of the lists to track the enemy." Roc stuffed more in his mouth and slurped more coffee. "In the old days, you smashed up a castle, slapped around a beast or dragon, raped a maiden in distress and finished off with a beer."

"Rape?" Achillia looked at him in shock.

"No thanks, it's a little early in the day don't you think?" Roc answered.

Frito nodded, focusing on the subject at hand. "I know. Right now, there are too many factors. I can feel it. I suspect that everything that has happened points toward a greater play."

"Greater, as in gods?" Achillia asked him.

"Yes. Normally they do not interfere in mortal lives. But this time I think they are up to something."

"And we are the pawns." Achillia finished.

"Sounds like a personal problem to me." Roc growled in his characteristic way. "You knights allow yourselves to get tied up in the hangups of gods."

"You're just as involved, Lord Roc." Achillia smiled at him.

"Shit no!" Roc seemed to anger. "I hate them all equally."

"But don't you see," Achillia explained. "Okshiru uses you like Frito. The house of Hammerstrike is mostly what?"

Roc made up his face. "Craig, Neeko, Orrin, Max, J'son, J'cob and Me!" Roc counted each one off on his fingers. "Verses, his mom, him," Roc pointed at Frito. "Friska, Fryto, and Frita." Roc added up his fingers. "That's seven verses five." Roc gleamed with the satisfaction of stumping her.

"But what is the house known for?" She asked. "Knights." She answered for herself. "And although you do some violent things, you still do it with Frito. Frito does it for Okshiru."

Roc suddenly remembered the treasures of Agiath. Although it was he who slew the demon, it was Frito and Okshiru who received the credit. "No!" The Slayer exclaimed. "This isn't fair!"

"Don't take it personally." Frito cut in. "The gods manipulate everything. You, me, Hauth. All part of the game."

"Well I'm not out to play anybody's game." Roc scrambled to his feet. "I am ROC THE DRAGONSLAYER. Do you hear?"

"Everyone did." Frito said.

"I don't play games." Roc growled.

Frito tried to soothe him. "Look if you're going to storm off and burn down an orphanage just to give Okshiru a hard time, don't. Just to out smart one god you fall into another's plans, and if you do out smart them all, then they change the plan so they win after all. It always works out."

"Shit." Roc shook his head. "There has got to be a way out."

"Follow your heart." Achillia said. "Just do what you always have done. Be yourself." She smiled at him. "That is the biggest insult to all the gods—ignore them."

Roc sat back down. "Then I'll ignore them."

"I seriously doubt they will ignore you." Frito went on. "You're too big an elf to ignore." Frito laughed to himself. "You know, I wouldn't be half surprised if there was a god writing this all down for someone to read."

They all laughed to themselves and looked back to the fire. Slowly, one by one they all looked to woods around them—to the trees above and into the sun that filtered through the branches with mist swirling up transparent poles of brass. Then they all looked to themselves. Frito adjusted the dark glasses on his face as he looked to Roc.

Roc made up his face. "Nahhh."

They each breathed a sigh and a chuckle and looked into the fire.

"Yo! People!"

"Fryto!" Frito cried trying to calm his heart beneath his armor. He composed himself before going on. "You're back."

Fryto looked him self over. "What about my back?"

"A Craig Tyrone joke." Roc mumbled.

"I'm ready with the forest walk." Fryto came closer.

Roc looked up to Achillia only to find she was looking at him. He then turned to Orrin. "So how do you feel?"

Orrin looked up and an automatic smile came to his face. "With my fin-gers! Eh?" He exclaimed in laughter and Fryto joined him.

Roc mumbled again about it being another stupid, Craig Tyrone joke.

"Frito, do you want me to take Orrin?" Fryto asked.

Orrin looked up pleadingly to the Ninefingers shaking his head no. Frito wasn't looking at him. "No." Frito said simply. Orrin smiled to himself.

"Okay." Fryto said not surprised. "Achillia?" He turned and walked off.

Achillia rose and bowed to Frito. "Lord Frito," Then she faced the Dragonslayer. "Farewell, Lord Roc."

"Fare thee well." He answered.

She turned and joined Fryto. Without a word, they mounted and together, rode out of reality.

Once they were gone, Frito whipped his fingers several times.

"Do that again and I'll break them all off." Roc threatened. "You're the one who said be nice."

"I know, but it looks so strange to see it in real life."

Roc frowned at Frito and glanced down at Orrin. Orrin was looking dejectedly at the ground. "Boy, did I beat you yet this morning?"

Orrin looked up to Frito. "What hap-pened to Friska?"

Roc placed a large hand on him. "Orrin, Friska has gone stark raving mad and you won't see him any more. But well get you a new one, just like the old one, except this one won't be bonkers."

"Roc!" Frito scolded him. He shifted about and faced Orrin fully. "Orrin, Friska is confused right now. He went through some bad things—you saw it."

"Like, how you be-came Hauth?"

Frito felt his Centre swirling. Roc only looked away. "Yes. Something like it."

"Was it his, you know, sin?" Orrin remembered when they were talking about him in the Roam.

"Sort of."

"Sort of what?"

Frito was underestimating the boy. "Friska had done something that he couldn't live with. The guilt was eating him up inside."

"So don't ever feel guilty for what you do." Roc said and Frito glared at him. "I never feel guilty, and I don't go running through the woods without clothes."

Frito looked down and tossed a stick on the fire. "Roc is right in a way. Friska felt that he was right in his actions. He felt it wasn't a sin and it wasn't."

"But what was it that made Friska bug out?" Roc now demanded. "You just said he never felt guilty for anything he had done before."

Frito looked away. He had truly wanted to avoid this. "It was back in the invasion with Hauth." Frito glared at the fire. "Each one of you confronted Hauth," He suddenly found himself fighting to draw his breath. "confronted me. Including Friska. But he didn't fight. He dropped to his knees and begged for mercy. A coward."

Roc leaned back as he understood. "Oh, So," Roc started. "Hauth, knowing full well that the guilt would rip Friska up more than anything physically could, let him live." Roc said nodding, agreeing with himself. "And Okshiru did the same to you, letting you return to walk the world knowing the guilt would tear you up. He knew when you came back to undo all the bad you did, you would work a hundred fold harder at it and do it in his name and boost him many points! Have a nice day!" Frito nodded glumly and Roc went on. "He had the same plans for Friska, didn't he?"

"He still might." Frito said quietly.

"Well that sucks." Orrin said. "Like, its not fair."

"But it is." Frito said, straightening up. "I wanted it. I wanted a chance to fix everything that I had screwed up. No one put that idea in my head. If Okshiru can get points out of that, so be it."

Roc suddenly didn't like Frito's tone, it sounded dangerously familiar. "But it was the gods that started the Hauth thing."

Frito cocked an eye at his cousin. "Did they?"

"I was there." Roc felt the hand of fear touch his heart. "I saw. They had you so confused you couldn't even make a complete sentence."

Frito suddenly realized that he had forgotten that. The memory of trying to speak with what felt like three tongues in his mouth came back. He gently rolled the one tongue over his teeth. "That may be so. But not now."

"And Okshiru?"

"To Hel with him."

The hand of fear in Roc's centre clenched to a fist. Knights of Okshiru don't tell their gods to fuck off.

Frito leaned closer, feeling Roc's fear. "Their affairs in Worldsend have gone on since the re-awakening of time and will go on until it sleeps again." Frito touched Roc's knee. "Don't you see? What has that to do with me? I now know that there is only the here," He pointed to the ground. "the now that we have to worry about it. What are Okshiru's points to me? A week ago, I was on my own doing what I wanted. Okshiru saw this as an opportunity and latched on to me to get his points. He proved it by not allowing Friska to kill me. Perhaps his plan is to save Friska, Frita and myself for his own use. So what has that changed save that I now have a little power granted to me to help in doing what I want to do? Right now, our paths are the same. I want to re-build, heal, help. But the moment our paths divide, he doesn't want something fixed, or doesn't like who I help because they don't like him or follow him, he will drop me in a heartbeat with little or no warning leaving Dru pissed, but helpless to interfere." Frito sat back. "Okshiru and I have a relationship of convenience."

Roc felt the hand in his centre relax its grip. "And where does that road you are on lead to."

Frito waved his hand over the fire and it snuffed itself. "To find my sister and brother, and then my wife. After that?" He shrugged. "I think the nearest tavern. We've been here too long." He rose to his feet. "Horse." He called quietly and in response, his horse stepped into reality. "Its time we headed to Brewster." He mounted and took up his blade-spear from the ground. In the day light, he could not see the tiny flecks of green magic in its metal, but he knew them to be there. Its always present magic was like the glare of Worldsend. He clenched the reins of Horse and headed off into the woods with Roc and Orrin behind him.

Chapter 28

Kemoto's morning light filtered through the cracked, dirty windows of the house. Dust flitted into the air as her bare feet slowly descended the stairs. She looked about in a sudden motion over the house. A simple dwelling, one large room divided into pantry, bedroom and dining room. The master and mistress were buried under folds of blankets. The master snored like the mighty red dragon, while the mistress shifted about beneath the covers.

She descended the stairs completely and entered the pantry. She stopped at the stove and turned the iron handle to open it's door. With her hands, she scooped out the cold ashes and dumped them into a bucket. She looked at the wood ready to burn stacked neatly beside the stove. She took up a small log and held it in her hands. She knew there was something that she could do but couldn't remember. Something that Donald would do. In her mind, she could see him, slowly rolling the log in his palms with his fingers outstretched and the log would suddenly burst into flame. He held the burning log in his hands, himself, unburned as he showed her how, but now she couldn't remember how or if she could ever do it.

She couldn't remember his face.

She looked into the stove again and noticed a single line of smoke rising from the remaining ashes. She deftly stripped the bark from the log with fingers that worked like shears. Then she peeled the inner bark into paper sheaves, then to paper strings that curled in her fingers. She set the curling filaments to the smoldering cinder and with gentle blowing, it was soon aflame.

With kindling and larger sticks she fed the fire. She pulled a small log from the pile and set it against the flames and laid sticks along it to tease the fire to catch the log. Once it was going, she closed the hatch on the stone stove and brushed her hands against her trouser leg. She set a pot on the stove and left it to boil as she looked into the cupboard for what was there to eat.

In mid rummage, she paused. *How rude! Pawing through some one else's kitchen! Why am I doing this?* She wondered as she closed the closet door. She stared blankly at the door as a finger of hunger pushed into her, like a cold, hollow bone against her centre.

Sound came to her ears. Creaking boards and heavy footfalls. She noticed the absence of snoring. She reeled and turned about with a gasp.

"And whats have we heres?" The burly man asked with a rumbling voice that vibrated the morning air. "You feels well this morning little kitten?"

The woman found her self grasping at her blouse for something that wasn't there. "You frighten me my lord." She gasped breathlessly, immediately scolding herself again at her own rudeness. "Good Morning, my kind lord."

"No needs to fears in my house woman." The burly man set his fists into his waist. "Those who tried to harms you, won't harms you here."

"Bless you my lord." The woman released her blouse. "I am Denice. I am lost." That seemed the safest thing to say.

"I am Hormand and I knows exactly where you are. But heres isn't important, it is where you are from that I wishes to knows."

"I come from the house by the shore, about a days ride." Denice said quickly.

"The old house by the shore?" The farmer said stroking his beard. "No one lives there."

Denice looked away as if to see the answer elsewhere. She then looked up to him with her large, brown eyes. "It appears as if no one lives there, but I assure you, there is. That is where I took my horse and cart.

"The man laughed and rocked to and fro as he did. "Twas your cart that leads me to you. I thoughts it was strange to sees it there unattended."

"I was on my way to Brewster..." Denice lost her words as she tried to remember.

"When brigands befell you?" The farmer prompted. He was rough and without tact or merely didn't use it.

Denice looked at him, trying to remember. It seemed difficult and hazy. "No, it was a witch."

The farmer pulled at his beard. "I knows not of any witch along these parts." The farmer turned as his wife came out of the bed.

Still wearing her cap, she pulled quilts about her as she shuffled to the stove for warmth. "By the howl of Fikor!" She gawked. "Are you nots cold, child?"

The farmer laughed. "Agatha, can't you sees, she is of elven stock? They feels not the cold."

Denice hung at that idea. "Yes, that is true. I was headed to Brewster to find such kind as myself."

"There are no elves in Brewster." Agatha said as she pushed by to the cupboard. "We haves meat." She said to the shelves, but she turned back to Denice with a smile. "But I wills have fresh bread and cheese for you." Suddenly Agatha fixed on the girls neck. "Glory, glory! Wills you looks at this."

Denice became self conscious and put her hands to her throat.

"No need for thats." Hormand grumbled. "Lets haves a looks." His big first fingers gently pried away Denice's hands, careful to avoid contact of his rough hands and the delicate skin of her neck. Denice relaxed in their trust and stood stock still to be examined. Hormand raised his head and peered down is nose squinting. "Glory!" He whispered.

The girl looked to each one without moving her body. "What is it?"

"There were ugly scars about you last nights." Hormand said. "Seems that is nots the case this morn." Her hands touched her neck. The light, lines of scars burned in annoyance of her probe.

"Seems that Agatha's brew was wells with you." Agatha snorted happily as she turned back to her cupboard.

Denice fixed her gaze at the woman as she pulled a large black pan from the cupboard. "I thank you. I am much in your debt. I know not to repay you."

"That is nots required here." Hormand shrugged off the idea as he sat at the table.

Agatha pulled a flour sack from a box against the wall and Denice watched her. "There are no elves here, yet you know we do not eat meat."

The farmer pulled out a chair and waved for her to sit. "There are tribes and merchants who comes through Brewster." The farmer pulled over a plate and waited for his breakfast. "Your kinds are not unknowns to us."

"Though I must say." Agatha turned to face them. "I gets cold to sees you with only a shirt and pant. Are you sure your nots a little bit cold?"

Denice suddenly smiled and it felt strange. "No mistress. I am not cold." Then to Hormand she said: "I must go to Brewster. I must see if I may find my own."

The farmer shook his head. "Fikor has comes down from the North. The Tribes are set. You shalt not finds them until Frandrell returns in the spring."

Denice suddenly knew this to be true. "Then I must return to the house by the sea." She said thinking about Kathreen. "I know a woman there."

"If that is wheres you got your cart from." The farmer looked to his wife at the stove. "But nots before breakfast."

Chapter 29

Forest of evergreen woods spiraled around them. Needles of pine laid a blanket on the earthen floor. White tiny feet tread gently, leaving not a trace in their wake. Her gown of spun spider silk flowed smoothly about her as she walked through her woods. Meleki, goddess of the forest, watched her woods with care. She watched the Knight of her service and the Knight of Uko flash across her woods, seeming to pulse in and out of reality. The horses moved leisurely, yet their speed was nearly immeasurable. The pulsing affect seemed to slow and the riders slowed as the forest walk ended at the edge of the tree line. He seemed lost and confused, looking to the tall woman beside him who had followed him. "This does not look like Fanrealm." Fryto said looking about. "This might be bad." He slid from his horse.

"It is fortuitous that we made it anywhere." Achillia said calming her horse. "That storming wave in the Neighplane could have killed us."

Fryto laid his hand aside of a tree and seemed silent for a moment as he introduced himself to it. "My apologies." He spoke to her without turning.

"You could not have prevented it." Achillia answered. "Where are we?"

Fryto patted the tree. "Not as far off as I thought. This tree says we are about two and a half clicks outside of Fanrealm." He took up the reins of his horse. "If we hurry, we can get there before dawn tomorrow."

Achillia turned her horse. "The storming wave, what brought it about?"

Fryto patted his horse's nose. "The storming wave? Could have been anything." He curled the reins in his hands. "A glitch, an eruption on the Material, a nearby open portal to the Neighplane from the Wove of the Worlds."

Achillia's face grew taught. "As a demon entering Mortalroam?"

Fryto paused as his face went blank. "Can you…"

"No," She anticipated his question. "Uko does not grant forest walks." Achillia's centre suddenly filled with dread. She knew that Meleki would not grant him another so soon. Even if she had, the strain would tear him to shreds. It was only a miracle they were spared from the storming wave. "What do we do?"

Fryto leapt with ease into the saddle and without a word, kicked to a gallop with Achillia close behind him.

<u>Chapter 30</u>

The morning light of Kemoto's flames cast strips of golden light through the cracks in the shutters and drew bright lines across the floor and walls. Wisps of steam appeared only in flashes as they rose between the lines of Kemoto's light.

Dust and age fell from the windows as they were flung open to the air and Fikor's cold quickly flooded the room. Paradox stood at the window, gasping for the cold to fill his burning lungs. Tears rolled down his reddening checks as Fikor's breath stung his face. From this window, he could see the waters of Okshiru's sea rolling far below. He watched the smooth waves beating against the shore. He followed each wave sliding across the beach to the sea wall to smash against the craggy rocks. The trail caught his eye. The winding trail that ran the lip of the sea wall and weaved back and forth, disappearing behind the ascending cliffs to finally reappear as it lead around the house to the old, rotted front door complete with a crumbling mat that said, Welcome.

Welcome to the Home by the Sea.

He turned from the window and again looked to the stove and its steaming pots. He stoked the coals in the boiler and watched them for a bit.

Good, he thought.

With the back of his hand, he wiped away the discharge from his nose and looked over to the table nearby. The rabbit sat in its cage as rabbits do, with its paws tucked underneath and its head drawn tight in a snobbish, almost regal manner.

Paradox reached into his pocket an pulled out a large kerchief and wrapped it about his nose and mouth. He then stepped over to the table. He looked at the rabbit and it didn't move, nor acknowledge his presence. But he knew that the rabbit was watching him as he adjusted the rag over his face and cinched it tightly.

He took the lip of the cage and opened it up. Then, he took a firm hold of the rabbit by the scruff of the neck and lifted the squirming animal quickly into his cradling arms. He caressed the soft rabbit fur. It's smooth, glistening fur is said to be a gift to the rabbit from Meleki, goddess of woods and forest. The goddess had taken a lock of her own hair and gave it to Gozoo, the rabbit god, and told him to give it to rabbits as a gift of his special and dedicated service to her.

Paradox stood there thinking about the story as he stared at the stove and its steaming pots. Gozoo had taken the hair and being the kind of god that he was, gave it all to the rabbits and left none for himself. Paradox wondered what a hairless rabbit god would look like as he took a deep breath and walked right up to the stove.

Everything was laid out for him. There were four pots on the stove, but the only one that concerned him was tightly covered with special valves set in the lid for steam. The ingredients for his concoction were lined up on the counter to the right, so he could quickly grab each one in order. On the counter to his left sat the crystal bowl half filled with black brine and Kathreen's withered hand.

Holding the rabbit with one arm, its front paws clutched in his fingers, he unlocked and removed the special lid from the first pot and set it on the counter. With a pair of tongs, he reached into the bowl by the stove and took out the shriveled hand from the black water. He shook it to allow the final drips to fall free and set it aside. He then took up the bowl and poured the foul water into the pot and set the bowl back. Almost in the same motion, he took up the rabbit by its scruff and held the kicking rodent over the vapors for only a breath. It kicked once more and hung limply in his hand.

Paradox quickly covered the pot, folding over its lever to seal it closed, and stepped calmly, but swiftly to the back door. He flung the rabbit to the steps as he quickly headed out of the kitchen. The rabbit landed with a splash as if it held no bones and lay dead on the step where it landed.

He tore the mask from the his face and just let it fall. His centre twisted within him as his brain shuttered in his head. His eyes crossed and blurred and he felt the steps as they seemed come up to him. He sat there with his eyes closed so he wouldn't have to look at the steps rolling up at him but had to open them up again to confirm that he wasn't spinning head over heels. He didn't remember sitting, only that he was sitting.

It worked, was the first clear thought in his head. Someone should have warned him to cover his skin. They warned about breathing the vapors, but not a word about it being absorbed into the skin. *Make a note about this*, he thought, wondering if he would ever have to do it again.

Groggily, he looked at the rabbit lying on the step below him. Its mouth hung open and its large, yellow teeth were exposed. Its eye was sealed tight and its ears went straight back.

He touched it with his foot. It slid off the step and fell to the stone walk. Rigor mortis had already set in and now it was as if the creature had been stuffed. He could see its other eye was open, rolled far back so it showed as a white, crescent moon like Ovam's night of the blade in Leatha's black sky.

What do you see? He thought to the rabbit. *Can you see me looking at you? The Cacodemon needed to breathe. It took your last breath to breathe for its own.*

His bones swam as he pushed himself from the steps. He bent and fetched his mask and as he did, the rabbit seemed to glare at him. *So what do you see?* Paradox snorted and picked it up, hard and cold, and tossed it aside. He then went into the kitchen, putting his mask in place as he did. He stepped to the stove, watching the sealed pot for any change before pulling open the special lid. He quickly poured the contents of one pot to another and stepped away. He waited a few moments and waited again for another few. He then went over to the stove and looked in. He grabbed a rag and wrapped it about the pot to protect his hands from heat as he moved it to the counter. He took up a wooden spoon, carved from the heart of a ten thousand year oak tree, and began to stir, adding his ingredients as called for: the weep of a Lyrical Mushroom, the nightmare from a dreaming, a chocolate frog, the kiss of a virgin's death and the bite of a lone wolf's hunger. He tossed in a pinch of a child's broken hope and a sprinkling of a dying dragon's tear, crushed by the thigh bone of a bowlegged fairy prince (ss, can't really tell with them fairies) with the dried, black blood of a Boy Scout killed in the middle of his daily good turn. In went the ear bones of a holy Ethereal Shaman and the retina of a hazel eyed infant gnome, barely one hour old sprinkled with a touch of cinnamon for taste.

Stirring was easy at first, but the concoction soon became thick and hard to mix. He braced the pot against his body and cranked it as it congealed. He took out the spoon and with a sudden snap, slapped a small brown glop of paste onto the counter. He scooped another and slapped it on the counter the same way. He set down his spoon and used the palm of his hand to roll the two globs into balls.

He took the mask from his face and wiped his hands on it before dropping it to the floor. He reached into the cabinet and took out a large silver tin. He took off the lid looked inside. It was what he wanted.

He turned the tin over, and dumped a pile of brown sugar onto the counter. He took his two brown balls and rolled them in the sugar until they were completely covered.

He took the withered hand from the counter and pushed it into his pocket. He then took the two balls, set them on a cracked plate and headed into the hall, passed the dinning table and burned chair. He went straight to the stairs and moved slowly, painfully up them. He turned to the left and stood for a moment at the second door before trying the knob. It was locked.

"Kathreen!" Came a voice from beyond the door. "Kathreen! Ter dren greten!"

Paradox listened to the little girl for a moment pulling at the knob. He reached down and from the top of his boot, his nimble fingers found a thin, long, metal tool. With a twist in the lock the door was open.

Buffet's smiling face opened the door. "Sproken din greten." She said as she opened the door. Her face fell to fear as Paradox stood before her. She nervously stepped back. She bowed her head but her eyes never left him. "Good morning my lady…my name is Buffet." She said with uncertainty.

Paradox smiled slightly as he stepped into the room. "Hello, Buffet, my name is Paradox." He said gently as he closed the door behind him. "You are a pretty girl."

Buffet stepped away from him. His dirty clothes reeked of sweat and his hands were discolored with paints and pastes. His breathing was shallow and his breath held an odor that was bitter. His voice was soft, but his stare was hard.

Paradox stopped. He smiled a little more. "I have a present for you Buffet." He bent at the waist and held out the two sugar covered balls.

She did not move.

Still smiling, he took one of the balls and popped it into his mouth. His cheeks puffed as he chewed into it.

Buffet smiled, but covered her face with her hand. She twisted her body back and forth as she looked at the sweet he extended to her. Slowly she reached, but suddenly, snatched it and put it in her mouth. It was sweet and good and she quickly swallowed it. "Thank you my lady." She said with a courtesy.

Paradox lost his smile as he spat the ball from his mouth to the floor and walked out of the room.

Buffet's wide eyes of surprise looked at the sweet on the floor. He hadn't chewed it at all! He tricked her!

Paradox closed the door behind him and locked it with his tool. He could hear tiny Buffet's gurgling noises grow deeper as the Cacodemon was complete.

Chapter 31

"I hate this place." He mumbled to no one in particular. Cublatack the Small Mouthed Monster From the Basement squirmed in the cracked leather chair and chewed on the child's bone he had found. "I mean, I really hate this place."

Former sighed and fondled the heavy candle stick he had taken from the burned out church. The man said, 'If it ain't nailed down, take it, and remember: if you can pry it loose, then it ain't nailed down'. *Good words to live by*, thought the Monster From the Attic and Thing That Went Bump in the Night. He felt its cold, solid, weight in his hands as he looked over at Cublatack and decided if he said: 'I hate this place' one more time, he was going to get it and get it good.

"Does that fan work?" Cublatack asked.

Formor's first instinct was to hit Cublatack anyway, but he lulled his head back in frustration and rolled his eyes in his head instead as he shouted: "For the last damn time...NO!" Formor stood up on four of his eight legs, slapped the candle stick down on the table and walked vertically down the arm of the couch to the floor and across to where the small mouth monster sat. "The fan doesn't work, I don't have a quarter, I don't want to buzz sheep and I HATE THIS FUCKING PLACE TOO!"

Cublatack cocked his head and looked down at him with one eye. "Something eating you pal?"

Formor rolled his eyes again and paced about the room making a strange, long, howling noise as he did. He circled the floor, walked around the walls, circled the ceiling and finally dropped in a chair across from the Small Mouthed Monster From the Basement and stared at the window screen and the black flies that danced their patterns on the inside of it.

Cublatack watched him for the moment before asking. "Do you know why we are waiting here?" He hadn't asked this question before.

"No." Formor answered simply, curtly.

"Is there anything to eat?" Cublatack asked tossing the clean child's bone over his shoulder.

"No." Formor again answered simply, trying to hold his cool. He had asked that question several times before.

Cublatack looked about. The soda machine stood tall against the wall beside the record machine. The soda machine didn't work and the record machine only played 'The Impossible Dream.' Cublatack sighed and rest his head on the seat. "I hate this place."

Formor suddenly looked around for the candlestick, but he had left it on the table out of reach. He glanced at the Small Mouth Monster and gave him a 'you're lucky' look and leaned back in the chair and covered his eyes with his hands. "Go to Hel, pal."

Cublatack looked at him. "We're already in Hel."

Formor rolled his eyes. "For a monster, you're a real asshole."

"I'm an asshole?" Cublatack took defense sitting up. "I'm an asshole?"

"You said it, pal." Formor said turning at him hotly.

"I'm a monster!" He said proudly. "I'm supposed to be an asshole!"

Formor stopped pointedly surprised as he realized that Cublatack, for the first time in an amazingly long time, was quite right. The Monster From the Attic and Thing That Went Bump in the Night nodded slightly as he weighed the idea in his tiny brain and rested back in his chair.

Cublatack stared at Formor who stared at the flies. He wiped the grimy sweat from his brow and wiped it on the furniture. He slouched lower in his chair and watched a large roach walk up to the refrigerator, open it and stand before it in disgust before slamming it closed. Cublatack sighed. "I hate this place."

"Formor!" Thamrell's voice cut the hot air like ice. "Put down that candle stick!"

Formor's eyes were wide in mock surprise as he looked at the bloody, beaten body of Cublatack as if he didn't know how he got that way. He looked at the candle stick in his hand and then back at the body as if he was trying to put the two together in his mind. "A mosquito landed on his shoulder…" Formor explained.

"Never mind that," Thamrell glided into the room. "We have a guest." Thamrell poised in the room. "This is Harroc, Son of Hate."

The great seething demon stepped into the room. His long black arm twisted with muscle and bent at multiple elbows as he reached up and wiped away the foam from his mouth. "Hi."

Thumber followed behind and went directly to the soda machine. "Coke?"

"You got Pepsi?" Harroc asked.

What a monster. Formor thought dryly.

Thumber pounded on the side of the machine and a bottle dropped out of its chute. He popped the cap with his thumb and handed it to the demon.

"Hel of a climb you got there." His head motioned to the stairs outside the door as he took the Coke. "Thanks."

"I suspect they add another step each day while we're not looking." Thumber smiled, but wasn't kidding.

"I know your busy," Thamrell started. "So I'll get right to it. I know that a portal has been opened in the Wove and you're going to Mortalroam. I want you to take some people with you."

"What for?" He took a swig from the bottle, it was warm and flat, but the best to be expected in Hel.

"They're going to be my contacts on Mortalroam. That's all."

The demon took another swig, rolling around the taste in his mouth as he warmed up old thinking tubes. "How do you think I can go about that? I've got my entire entourage to worry about."

"A few more won't matter to one such as you." Thamrell waved the idea off causally. "Besides, they're on autopilot, won't have to give them a second thought."

"And what will the contacts do?" The demon pointed his bottle as he spoke.

"Gather news, fetch and run errands, just typical lackeys." Thamrell said off handedly.

The demon finished his drink and tossed the bottle aside. Formor scampered across the wall and snatched it in mid-air before it hit anything. "And what do I get out of this?" Harroc went on, oblivious.

Thamrell pointed to the television set and gestured for Formor to turn it on. Like a blur, the little monster dashed to the case for the empty soda returns, scooted up to the top of the towering stack, dropped the bottle in, leapt to the floor, crossed the worn, filthy carpet in a blink, climbed up the side of the set and punched the 'Power' button. On the screen through the snowy picture, Fantista could be seen walking outside the great wall with the orphan, Stephanie. "I happen to know how you can get to Lady Fantista. Would you like to get Lady Fantista?"

Harroc swallowed his slobber at the thought and held back his eagerness. Instead, he folded is arms several times bending at the multiple elbows. "How can you do this?" He glared suspiciously.

"Don't worry about that. I can get you there." Thamrell cast him a side glance. "Agreed?"

"Agreed. I'll take your boys to Mortalroam if you can guarantee that you can get me through the Ninefinger's barriers."

Thamrell gestured and Formor turned off the set. Then waved again and the little monster scurried down the set to the VCR. With a small paw, he pressed the 'On' button, then the 'Eject' button and with a painful, mechanical whine, it pushed out a thin, bone case from its front slot. This, he carried carefully to Thamrell and presented it.

"In this valise," Thamrell explained, "is a silver Star of Hammerstrike. This particular star was made by the Ninefinger's own hands. It will allow you to pass the magical barriers and enter Fanrealm" Formor turned and presented the case to Harroc. The Son of Hate played with Thamrell's words in his tiny brain before he agreed. "Remember, touch not the star on this world. When you manifest on Mortalroam, you should be able to touch it freely since it falls under the 'Item that you bring through customs' rule'." Harroc took the box and tucked it neatly under his arm. "Good!" Thamrell exclaimed almost cheerily, "Then all is set and you'll meet my people at the Wove of the Worlds." Thamrell saluted. "Go, and may the Trid Dreath look upon you with contempt."

They watched the demon as he walked down the hall and out of sight.

"His asshole's so big," Thumber started.

"I'm surprised his guts don't fall out." Formor finished.

Thumber looked to the god of despair. "Are you going to explain him?"

"Yes." Thamrell waited until he could see the Son of Hate on the street below from the window. "I need him to take Ethel and Edith to Mortalroam. Since I have lost Friska, they will be my point and allow me to pass to Mortalroam in a physical presence. Once there, I can find Friska and use him to open the portal in the Wove, a flavorful ironic twist. At the same time, you get Frita to open the gates of Hel and send our army out." He cast a hard look at Thumber. "You can find Frita, can't you?"

"No sweat." He smiled. "She's gonna call me." He said confidently.

"Don't screw this, Thumber."

"Unscrewable. To close the deal, I'm gonna check the 'eye' tonight. What about Harroc? Think he can wax the ol' lady?"

Thamrell turned and looked to the beast. "Harroc's fate is not my concern. In fact, I wish him dead and out of the way." Thamrell looked away as he spoke and floated about the dirty, cluttered room. "He is such a back stabber. I am sending him to Fanrealm to cause as much trouble and confusion as possible with the hope that his battle with Lady Fantista will leave him weak enough so Ethel and Edith can kill him and I can assume control of his entourage." He then thought: "If Fantista doesn't kill him out right."

"The grandmother is that good?" Thumber said in amazement.

"It is apparent that you haven't seen her in battle." Thamrell answered. "She is the Grandmaster of Knights."

"I thought it was an honorary title. So the grandmother can kick ass?"

Thamrell stopped and looked at Thumber. "What did you call Fantista? Grandmother?

"Thumber thought about it for a moment. "Yeah, we all call her that." Thumber looked to Formor who was poking the candle stick at Cublatack. "All the lower monsters and beasts call her that." Formor looked up and nodded in agreement.

Thamrell poised and thought about it. "She isn't one. None of her children have offspring." He looked at Thumber. "Do they?"

Thumber thought about this. If there was a child anywhere, he would know about it. After all, he was the infamous terror of all children. He shook his head. "Well, if Frito had a kid, we would all know about it. Friska has been fucking that Sheol for so long and we all know that nothing can result from that."

Formor looked up. "What about Fryto, J'son and J'cob?"

Thumber again shook his head, "Not that I know of...They fuck around a lot, but elves are hard to conceive." Thumber looked to Thamrell. "Nope."

Formor dropped the candle stick on Cublatack and headed for a chair. "Does it really matter?"

Thamrell looked down to him. "It really doesn't. I just want to be sure that I have covered everything."

"Maybe…" Formor proposed as he slithered into the old rotted chair, "we call her that because she's the Grandmaster. See, Grandmaster, Grandmother?" He held two of his hands as if he were weighing the names. Thamrell floated in silence.

"Speaking of thinking." Thumber suddenly spoke, "What about Hauth."

Thamrell didn't look at the beast as he spoke. "I fear not Hauth."

"Why?" Formor asked sitting up straight.

Thamrell cast a haunting glare at the Monster From the Attic and Thing That Went Bump in the Night, but let it go. "For one thing," Thamrell floated to the window. "To know of the Poer, there of, is to possess the Poer, there of. But when the Ninefingers, or Hauth or Frito or whoever descended from Worldsend, he put a block in his own head to insure that he could never properly envision the concept again. The Ninefingers can never be Hauth again." *Or so Weishap cheerfully babbled about.*

Sensing that there was more, Thumber and Formor leaned closer to listen. "Second…" Despair went on. "He no longer has the alliance of Hel as he had before. He turned against them. He promised them everything and they got nothing. They now side with me. Not even Dragonslayer's army will be able to stop us."

"But Thamrell…" Thumber quickly jumped in, "What of Cornerstone, You say we can take it, but even Hauth and the might of Hel turned from it. Can we do it? Perhaps Hauth knew something about Cornerstone that we don't."

Thamrell floated in thought and took a deep breath before he answered. "I don't think so. I think he turned from Cornerstone because Roc would have defended it to the last man. His war would have been over too quickly. He enjoyed chasing Roc all over Mortalroam, prolonging the agony. He wanted to destroy Roc at the base of Worldsend, at the Crystal Tower and use the wreckage like a stair to heaven."

"Yeah," Formor remembered, "he built that escrolater thingy."

Thamrell floated higher in the room and spoke as if to an audience. "But we haven't the time to waste. We must sweep across and step directly to Cornerstone and use its secrets to gain Worldsend."

Thumber felt energy spark lightly in his centre. Never before could Depression speak so inspirationally.

"Not to piss on the show or anything," Formor interjected. "But what about the big guy, the Supergod. Won't he get a little ticked about what is going on?"

Thamrell turned slowly, impressed by the little monster's grasp on the big picture. "Lord Hammerstrike the Supergod is in a precarious position. I am confident that he can again take up the powers of the Supergod, but to do so may very well destroy the world that he has tried so hard to save. He is still mortal and it is a power far beyond even his grasp to handle. He will not raise his hand unless it threatens reality. Its how the gods were able to force him to leave Mortalroam and go to Worldsend."

"They forced him?" Formor looked surprised. "I thought that Sharpe, the god who thinks all the time, out witted him."

"A rumor carefully spread by Okshiru. Public relations, that sort of thing. However, in our conquest, we have to be careful not to trigger the Supergod. This will also keep us below the notice of..." Thamrell paused suddenly, listening for who else might be listening. Thumber and Formor glared wide eyed at the god of Despair wondering if he would dare speak the name of..."the god's God." He mumbled in less than a whisper.

No one moved, hoping that in voicing the name they wouldn't attract His attention.

"But that is yet to come." Thamrell went on, breaking the silence as he swept across and lower to the floor. "What we must worry about is the Ninefingers. He is the only one that could foul things. We must hope that Harroc distresses Fanrealm to the point that it forces him to abandon his quest for his sister." Thamrell faced Thumber. "And you must find her."

"As soon as Kemoto's light drains from the sky to rest." He answered calmly.

"So!" Former began. "Lets see if I got all this." Thamrell looked at him and the monster folded his arms behind his head. "Harroc kills Achillia for the shits, Harroc then kills Fantista or vice versa. Edith and Ethel kill Harroc if its verse visa. Frito gets pissed and runs home to kill an already dead Harroc while we snag the wonder twins Frita and Friska to open the gates and raise all kinds of Hel." He smiled and looked at the god of Despair. "Right?"

Thamrell nodded, impressed. "Couldn't have said it better myself."

Chapter 32

Mistang crawled in the low space by the Great wall and nestled in the grass. She felt herself slowly sliding down the sloping hill and feeling it inevitable, let it go as such. She looked up and could see the towering wall of Fanrealm and its flying banners perched at the top. She stretched and with a final thrust, lifted into a pluming spire and looked about.

Fanrealm was perched with its back to a cliff and looked out over the valley of Tashwalk. The river Seeda Gully wandered and flowed through the valley, crossed by the single stone bridge that, during times of siege, could be lifted, and carted behind the Great wall or, in hurry cases, dropped and fished from the river later. The bridge was guarded by two stone rooks the height of three men and connected to the first wall that ran the perimeter of Fanrealm. The first wall also ran along the cliff face at the back of the manor where it flared out to a treacherous over hanging lip, chiseled smooth so no hook nor hand could grip.

The road lead on, into the second, higher wall and the second gate. The second gate consisted of a giant arch and five portals. The first portal was heavy, iron bound doors that were always bolted shut at sunset. To pass this was treacherous, for above, archers could shower the road and the hill with their shafts and oil could be poured down directly before the doorway itself and then ignited. The second set was another pair of doors, but in the space between the two, pikemen could stand above and run giant, fixed, sliding lances through small holes in the ceiling, raining spears of death. Break through here and a steel cage is next, dropped and locked just as the door collapses. More pikemen and more archers from above and now the front and sides as well. Then two more heavy doors and more of the same.

From here, Fanrealm begins. Small farms, and shops and markets flourish here. Business is very good for the traders come in their flat bottomed rafts, from their great ships anchored on the piers of the main river. Free from pirating, they trade and sell intensely under the governing body of the Manor.

Then, the Great Wall towers over the rest, protecting the homes and residences of the people of Fanrealm. Wide and smooth the wall is inlaid with arrow slits and the main line of ballistas and large catapults. Its imposing gate has seven portals, adding two steel cages along the line and spikes that rise from the floor in a sudden thrust and draw back again.

The Great Wall has other features including; a reinforced berm, a hook proof, over hanging lip, and a catapult overhang to minimize flying rock damage. Only a direct hit could ever damage the wall; however, to get a catapult big enough to damage the Great wall in range is doubtful, due to the rough terrain and the outer walls it would have to get over.

Rumor has it that one of Fanrealm's best features is the underground tunnels that interweave below the walls. It is said that these tunnels are more treacherous than the walls themselves.

Behind the Great Wall lies the city of Fanrealm, now the sixth largest city on Mortalroam. Monsterberg, formally the second to Cornerstone, and the Crystal Spire, formally third to Cornerstone no longer exist, due to the war with Hauth, the beast with backward knees, which pushed Fanrealm from eighth to sixth. The city of Fanrealm now contains five major temples, Okshiru, Kemoto, Hauge, Dru, and Fikor. It was years ago the sixth exploded and burned when Uko, in a fit of rage at Frito's arrogance, struck it from above (no injuries reported, however, a cat did go blind). Frito was then accepted immediately as Dru's Knight (if she planned it that way, no one is telling) and the temple count became five. There is however, a small mission for Uko located on the original spot as the temple, run by Cleric Thurlow under the protection of Achillia from the house of Avenger. There are several other smaller missions, including a school to the twin daughters of Okshiru, Shegatesu the dawn and Neathina the stars. There is no cleric and Fantista herself runs the school.

There is a wide, final wall that rings the Manor itself—The house of Hammerstrike.

No one has ever taken Fanrealm. Only one has ever dared try. It lay rich and overflowing for pirates and hoarding armies, but the walls are far too intimidating to attempt. Crossing the river puts anyone in range of the second wall ballistas and the Great Wall's main catapults. Then attempting to move up the open hill under the rain of arrows from the second wall that was constantly resupplied from the stores in the tunnels is suicide. Forget the Great Wall and forget the cliff side which starts from the river and goes straight up. Great catapults can launch flaming rocks to sink any vessel in the river for nearly a quarter click.

The one attempt was the great army of Flamthongs-shook. Goblins. Their awesome, and well respected amongst military communities, general Horroglance Foebiter (so the name he choose in elven tongue), marched four fighting battalions of 65,000 strong, four companies of calvary, two companies of engineers, a company of support groups (Cooks and supply) and forty war ships with full accompaniment, to seize Fanrealm.

They anchored down stream and disembarked their great war machines and wall breaking devices and painfully rolled them to the north. Their calvary was in the front, their black horses prancing proudly with glistening leather saddles and polished buckles of silver. The army followed, marching in column singing a throng of spooky, goblin chants in time with the great tornado drums mounted on giant wagons pulled by 18 heavy horses. The war machines came next rambling along with the cooks and their wagons behind.

The main fighting force of Dragonrealm was out conquering the western borders and the Flamthongs-shook were uncontested as the came along the well maintained highway. They had suddenly appeared, using the cover of Mistang's great fog (magic was suspected and rumored but unconfirmed) to hide the ships as they sailed north in the night. They were off loaded and on the road by dawn and standing at the river of Seeda-gully by early evening the next day.

Their lightning move was quoted by military experts as "Brilliant!" and "...their [Flamthongs-shook] organization was purely amazing, giving barely enough warning for Fanrealm to smash the chains and drop the stone bridge into the river". That evening, as the catapults were put into place, a note was sent to the Manor requesting an immediate and unconditional surrender of Fanrealm and all the occupants within. Within the Great Walls, as the last of the farming community moved behind the Great wall, Lady Fantista scribed a well crafted note of a **conditional** surrender. Goblin's were too well known for eating mortal flesh before, during, and after raping it. Her sworn responsibility to protect those within her walls required her not to unconditionally give up.

Four times she offered a king's ransom of cash and other wealth and three times they outwardly refused. The fourth time, they responded with a demand for twice the sum and in addition, an order for 3,000 young slaves with at least 2,000 being female. Fantista refused.

Moments before Shegatesu arrived to Mortalroam, the goblins attacked, their calvary leaping the low fence to the river were the engineers had set up bridges across the waters. Troops followed next, moving swiftly behind. Exchanges of flaming balls of tar criss-crossed the dark air and two of the four bridges fell into the water. Invisible lines of arrows inter-crossed. Goblin forces stormed up in mass as the defenders of the first wall retreated to the second. Fanrealm's catapults, using the advantage of height from the Great wall, launched with unerring accuracy, forcing the goblins to pull back their remaining hardware to prevent their destruction as their troops claimed the first wall.

They remained there the day, crouched behind the first wall to shield themselves from the never ending barrage of bolts and arrows from the second. Unable to find any entrances to the tunnels, the goblins waited for the cover of darkness to attempt a second attack. Horroglance could not risk a prolonged siege due to possible reinforcements from Cornerstone. They massed and reorganized in their positions and watched with seething eyes as Kemoto slowly dipped in the west. At twilight, literally moments before the renewed attack, a note came from the Mistress of Fanrealm. Her delicate hand had penned a single, eloquent sentence.

Your ships are burning.

The attack was stayed and messengers were immediately sent to the rear. They came running back with wild eyes of terror reporting that their ships were indeed burning and that Dragonslayer had returned with a full compliment of his forces and the Dragonguard from their campaign in the west. They reported that both the Lord of Lightning (Frito, then in Uko's charge [no pun]) and The Flame (Fryto, then in Kemoto's charge) were with them. Children of Hammerstrike summoned home by their mother. Their ships, blown with magic, traveled ten days in one and were now en route to the Manor.

Horroglance Foebiter ordered a complete withdrawal and sent an ultimatum to the Manor. Horroglance demanded that Roc the Dragonslayer allow him passage to leave or his forces would over run Fanrealm. Four requests were sent and three replies returned in her gentle hand writing stating that she could not make that decision for Roc. The fourth reply from Fanrealm was in Roc's own crude, brutal script.

No.

Horroglance and his forces fled north, the only way to go, abandoning their machines and siege devices and cooks and supply and, by accident, a company of engineers who were ultimately slaughtered for nubie practice by the Dragonslayer's troops. Three notes were sent to Roc's forces in pursuit and three responses came back the same.

Surrender what?

Finally, as the disheveled, crumbling army of Horroglance the took a final stand in the high north, shuddering in the icy breath of Fikor the dog of winter, the forth and last note was sent to Roc.

The reply was: **Yeah, alright.**

The exact details to the surrender are unknown. To date, that was the only major insurgence at Fanrealm.

Kemoto rose higher and the ground became warmer and Mistang faded slowly into the air, listening to the rumbling engine of the Red Barchetta.

The gate signalman waved his green banner with a white square in the center to the Great wall and in response, horn blowers perched on the front high towers, drew their shining brass horns in calculated, well rehearsed military cadence and blew 16, smooth, magical, musical notes in perfect tone and nasal resonance to the blue of Okshiru's sky. While the signalman waved, The gateman ran quickly down his spiral stairs, passed heavy doors to the gear room. He quickly threw the bolt and cranked the heavy wheel lifting the steel cage from the door. Its heavy, greased pulleys and wheels slid with little effort, winching the oiled chains to the spool. Once the cage was lifted, he threw back the bolt and called down to the doorwatch to stand at the ready.

At the high tower of the Great wall, Gorn stood at the watch with his bow laid casually beside him. He watched with interest as the billowing cloud of dust charged its way down the main road. He wondered what could be amiss—It certainly was the Red Barchetta and the only three people who could hold its reins were the Dragonslayer, Ninefingers, and Dragoncaller.

Behind him, the First reached the top of the steps and waited for his commander to acknowledge him. "The Spy eye recognizes the Dragoncaller." He spoke simply as Gorn would have expected. "He brings with him his wife."

Gorn's only response was a quickly cocked brow. This was unusual. Craig's shift as watch commander was done until the next evening. Craig was also Nih elf and Nih elves hated the sun and light. Gorn looked to the sky above. It was clear. The First, sensing the question, answered. "Spy eye detects no dragons about."

Gorn pursed his lips and stroked his chin. Almost absentmindedly his second hand was lightly stroking his bow. "Take the watch, First." Was all Gorn said as he headed down the steps towards the court yard. They were on alert because of the disappearance of Frita. *Be ready for anything*, he thought.

The gate keep gave a shout and the giant wooden doors swept open only long enough for the Barchetta to sweep in past the final walls to the Manor yard. Once safely inside, the doors shut and the cage dropped in place.

Gorn watched as Craig leapt over the door and circled the car. "Let me help you." Craig said as he twisted and lifted at the door to force it open.

"Is there a problem?" Gorn said as he approached.

Craig didn't look at him as he undid his wife's seat belt. "The door sticks. I think it happened from the attack yesterday." He gently placed his arms about his wife and half lifted her out of the car.

"My lady Neeko." Gorn said with a bow. "Your beauty grows with each day."

Neeko smiled as she leaned on her husband for support. "You mean my belly grows with each day." She gained her balance and took a satchel from Craig. "I think I'm about to give birth to a grown up." It wasn't before Neeko smiled until Gorn knew it to be a joke.

Gorn looked to Craig who fumbled with a large pack from the back seat. "Is everything well?"

Craig looked to the watch commander and read his words to mean '*I know you wouldn't be here unless it was serious, so what is the matter?*'

"Everything is fine." Craig said with a smile. "Neeko kinda owes Lady Fantista a visit." Which to Gorn translated to '*Yes there is something seriously wrong, but not in front of my wife. Not in her condition, anyway.*'

Gorn bowed and took the Lady Neeko's arm. "Then it is my position to lead you to her. I believe she is upstairs."

The three turned and headed towards the Court doors. Three children, two boys and a girl dashed over from seemingly nowhere and begged quite politely to take Craig's luggage. These were the children of the Temple DawnStar. They were Orphans and fosterlings in the care of Lady Fantista, under the house and banner of Hammerstrike. Craig knew full well that to turn them down was an insult and serving, for the fostered children, was a great honor. He stopped and gave a bag to each one and some how convinced them that each piece was of equal importance as to end any chance of envy or greater honor.

As he gave up the luggage, he noticed that Onary and Edia were not around. Surly the two would be bickering, especially with Onary back on his home turf. He looked back to the Barchetta. The springer spaniel sat by the open door waiting for something. "Onary!" Craig shouted. "Let Edia out of the car."

Onary perked his ears and faced his master. "But sir..." He said in his typical obnoxious British tone. "I'm not doing a thing. Its her."

Craig gave a glance into the manor and waved Neeko on before calling back to the car. "Edia? What is it?"

The response was a belch.

"If I may translate..." Onary offered. "Edia is quite sick."

Craig sighed and headed over to the car. He looked into the back seat where Edia was sitting in a crouched position with her head hanging over the seat. Craig scratched his head. "Car sick?"

"Sick, sick, suh," She said.

Onary poked his head closer. "My, what a shame, and we were having filet salmon glazed in white cheese sauce and cottage for lunch."

Edia slowly lifted her head and sluggishly extended her paw with her claws exposed. "A little closer, Beagle Brain!"

"Onary," Craig folded his arms. "Does this have anything to do with the mouse in your dog bowl?"

Onary seemed offended at the idea that he would extract cheap revenge. "Surly I am more diabolical than that."

Edia lifted her head with half closed eyes. "Ah ain't put no mouse in his food!" She squealed. "Musta died of natural causes whilst it wuz stealin his dawg food." The cat mumbled.

Craig shook his head and carefully scooped the cat up into his arms. He then looked about and noticed that children had gathered about to watch the talking dog and the talking cat. Craig summoned them over with a nod of his head and then pointed to the trunk of the car with his toe. "Please, take my armor out of the back of the trunk...Its open." Craig watched as they probed where he pointed and struggled with the large, clunky duffle bag from the lid less trunk. "So how do I write this on my insurance?" He said turning to the Manor.

Onary skipped closer. "Tell them the truth, you were driving about and were brutally and without provocation attacked by seven black dragons who tore off the roof and lid to the trunk."

Slowly Craig crossed the courtyard as not to jar Edia in his hands. "And what do I tell Roc. He loves that thing."

"Lie through your teeth." Onary quickly said. "Tell him Edia was driving."

Edia quietly moaned. "Choke on a hair ball, Dawg."

"Come now Edia. Surely you're dying, go out with a bang. Or when dealing with Roc, a splat."

Craig came to the door and watched the four children fighting with his armor. "Get inside!" Craig ordered when they waited for him. "Its cold out here." The warm fires inside felt good even though he really hadn't felt the cold. Fantista and Neeko paused in their light talk and looked to him as he entered.

"What's the matter?" Neeko said as she stepped over to her husband. "Is Edia alright?" She lightly stroked the cat's back. "Did she get car sick?"

"Sick, sick, Mum." Edia moan piteously, enjoying the attention.

"Now I'm getting sick." Onary mumbled, then pretending to take no note of the cat, went right up to Lady Fantista. "My most gracious mother," He bent reverently, "How are you."

Fantista smiled as she bent at the knee and scratched him right by the ear. "What is the matter Onary? Edia getting too much attention?"

"Oh please..." He said drolly, shrugging the preposterous idea with a casual wag of his tail. "A little higher." He couched her scratching. "By the center."

Without breaking her scratching, she looked at Craig. "Well, my Lord Dragoncaller, it is so rare I see you in the day." She gave Onary a final pat and stood up. "Just a glance at dawn and you're off."

"Well," Craig said off handedly. "I'm not one for the sun."

Lady Fantista stepped closer and placed a hand gently on Neeko's belly. "Any day now." She said confidently.

"Are you sure?" Neeko said rather surprised.

Fantista smiled knowingly with a wink in her eye. Craig felt something welling in the pit of his stomach. Lady Fantista recognized it right off. "Nothing to worry. It will all be well, Craig. You'll see. Would you like a Boy or Girl?"

"You mean there are two kinds?"

Fantista smiled and turned towards the stairs. "Come out Stephanie, don't hide." Craig stood a little taller. Since his becoming a Nih elf, his hearing had become so acute that no one could come that close without him knowing. But the little girl who stepped from out of the stairwell had taken him by surprise. "Craig and Neeko Tyrone, this is Stephanie. She is staying with us." Craig knew right away the child was deathly afraid of him. The odds were that she had never seen a Nih elf before, but her instincts told her to beware.

Neeko knew enough about elves and the relation to each other and quickly stepped in between them. She bent as well as she could to the little girl's height. "Hi Stephanie, I'm Neeko."

Stephanie took her eyes from Craig long enough to be polite to Neeko and return her greeting.

"Uh, huh." Craig said as he stepped over to Lady Fantista. "Since the baby is due and you always nag us to come and stay..."

"And you shall stay!" She announced turning to her runners. "My hands and feet," She addressed them. "Will you kindly take the Dragoncaller's things to Dwayne's room?"

"Lord Frito, Mum?" One asked brightly.

When she nodded the children moved to their task.

"Thank you, this does mean a lot to me." Craig said.

Fantista's smile warmed him. "You are now my son." She reminded him.

Craig instinctively reached up and touched the center of his chest where he felt the silver Star of Hammerstrike that hung about his neck. Losing words to say, Craig turned slightly and listened to Neeko and Stephanie.

"Stephanie is a pretty name," Neeko said. "Did you know Lady Fantista's name is Stephanie?"

Craig leaned to Fantista and whispered. "I didn't know that."

The little child looked when she heard him and glared.

"This is Edia." Neeko went on, breaking the girl's stare. "She isn't well."

Edia looked up with puffy eyes and moaned for pity. "Sick sick." She said.

Stephanie's eyes grew wide. "She talks!" The girl exclaimed.

"She walks" Onary teased. "She wets and she closes her eyes when you put her down...in the ground...and cover her with dirt."

"Onary," Lady Fantista called to him. "Why don't you go see the puppies, I'm sure they miss you."

"A novel idea!" He cried and quickly stepped out of reality. Stephanie had heard the dog speak, but he was gone by time she looked up.

"Where did he go?" She asked.

Neeko shrugged. "One of his tricks, I guess."

"I like your cat Lady Neeko." Stephanie said. "But..." The girls voice grew timid. "You're a cat too."

Neeko smiled, "I am Ne-arri, the cat people. See? I have a tail." Neeko brought her tail around for the girl to see.

"Neeko?" Lady Fantista called to her. "Why don't you and Stephanie go to Dwayne's room and get things settled."

Balancing Edia in one arm, Neeko took Stephanie's small hand. "Would you like that?" She asked the child. When the little girl nodded, the two headed towards the stairs following one of the runners.

Craig watched them go. "Well, that went well." He said dryly.

"What made her behave so?" Gorn spoke as he came closer. "She has never done that to any of the other guards before."

Craig leaned his back to the wall and stared at the floor, saying nothing. Fantista looked at him for a moment and then answered Gorn. "Hiran elves always react to Nih elves that way. It is blood."

"She must have done the same to Frito."

"No..." Craig spoke not looking up from the floor. "Frito is a knight and exempt from that." Having said that, Craig again fell into his silent mode.

Fantista gave a half nod and decided to change the subject. "How is Neeko doing?" Fantista spoke frankly. "Is she moody?"

Craig looked up abruptly, then sighed. "Its to be expected. Right now she has enough hormones running through her to power a Buick. A bit more than I anticipated, but then, isn't everything?"

Fantista's near invisible brows went up. How strange of a man to understand the moods of women with child. She looked at him, leaning against the wall. His long, satin hair hung in a pony tail over his shoulder. His chocolate skin was dusted from driving on the road. He was stocky, and built, more than when he first arrived. He looked much more now like a high land elf with his powerful arms built from swinging a sword and cinched waist from climbing the high peaks and riding his dragons. His knife at his side and the chain to his pocket watch beside it tucked into his black sash, was simple and functional as the custom highland elves.

Her centre sighed as she again realized his resemblance to Dwayne—not so much in the face, but in build. Both where dark Nih. A rare combination for most Nih are pale from lack of sun. Both were passionate and both were caring and both pulled their hearts inside. She wanted to take him and hold him as she would her own sons, but she held back. Four years since his arrival in this world and now with the coming of his child was he beginning to come around to accepting and understanding his new home. She looked for his eyes but his dark spectacles hid them. He had not taken them off as he habitually done indoors. Nih elves made all people nervous and when they shielded their eyes it was more so. But Stephanie caught him unawares. Fantista could still see into him as knights could and she saw him still wrestling with the Nih blood that flows in his veins. She looked further and found more. He came to the Manor with a worry swelling in his centre, and this display with the young child didn't help matters.

"What's the matter Craig?" Lady Fantista asked him so curtly, that it snapped him out of his revery.

"What?..." He fumbled his words. "Nothing."

She stepped from the wall towards him and her cold hands flashed smoothly and deftly and snatched Craig's wrist. She pushed back the sleeve on his shirt so quickly he hadn't the time to flex a muscle to stop her. She didn't look down at his forearm nor did he. They both knew fully well of what was there—swollen tattoos of the prancing dragon, the mark of the Dragoncaller. Tattoos that formed across his chest and arms only when trouble was near. Craig relented and relaxed as she let go of his arm. "Everybody has been doing that recently." He looked at his arm. "I can't hide anything anymore." He snorted. "I'm not really sure." He said earnestly, shaking his arm to allow his sleeve to fall back into place. "Its really just a gut feeling."

"A what?" Gorn asked.

"Gut feeling?" Craig repeated the question, "You know, like ice at the pit of your stomach." Craig tried again as Gorn drew a blank. "You know, your uh..."

"Centre." Fantista answered. "Your middle of being."

Craig nodded his head. "Anyway, it won't go away. The dragon's are sleeping and its so hard to wake them if I need them and with the baby on the way..."

"You thought here would be safer?" Fantista finished.

Craig bobbed his head from side to side as if he couldn't answer yes or no. "But I have this feeling that what ever will happen, will happen here. I'm not really sure what, but something." Craig looked up from the floor and into Lady Fantista's knowing eyes. Her face held the tiny lines of time. Elves age ever so slowly and show their age so well that it was hard to tell, but Craig could see the wisdom of the ages in her eyes. He could see her faith, confidence and underlying strength. With her smile, his fears eased, and with a glance, she read his soul, and smoothed them over with a touch. "I owe you so much, and I feel that my duty is here, to do what I can. I also feel better with Neeko here…with you."

Fantista smiled delicately, and then tilted her head slightly. "You had watch last night did you not?" Fantista lightly took his arm. "You and Neeko are night people and you must be begging for bed. I'll have Trisha bring you some of her hot cocoa."

Suddenly Craig felt sleepy and had the want of nothing more than to be with his wife. It was no spell or words of control, just her sense of correctness. She had looked into him and knew it. After all, she is the Grand Master of Knights.

Chapter 33

The low swelling of his heart grew in his chest. Hauge's winds whipped around his frail body as Fikor's cold rattled his bones within his drained flesh. The sand beneath his bare feet was as cold as the steel blade in her hands. She was so beautiful, her face so white. Her soft baby cheeks were smooth and round, and her lips were full and red with blood. Her teeth glistened bleached white as she smiled. The dress of crimson silk clung to her tight body as did the black gloves.

A thing of beauty. She stood against the shore. A thing of beauty that he must have. He would beg for her and grovel for her and serve her to make her happy. A thing of beauty, this Ura, Mistress of Chaos, woman of pain. A thing of beauty for his torn soul.

With a gloved finger beneath his chin, she lifted him from his knees and to his feet. She suddenly slashed at him with the blade, tearing into him. His hands instinctively thrust in the way but the blade slashed through them.

There was no blood, no wound.

Only pain. He was confused, and stumbled but she grabbed him by the back of the neck and pulled him down to her lips and he fell into them. He was lost in the warmth of her love. His hands glided over her tender body. Cold seeped through the cloth to his fingers and made them sting. Her lips were difficult to feel though his numbed senses no matter how roughly he kissed her. It was hard to see, hard to feel. What was that? What could that be?

Warmth ran freely down his legs and blood splashed on the walk.

He looked to the walk and the blood pooling. His eyes followed the walk to the door and the mat at the foot of the door that said Welcome.

He could hear the pounding of the waves about him and the tide swept him to the door. Closer and faster he came. There was no way around or away as he swam wildly in the air. The door flung itself open and beyond it was the oblivion of darkness. His hands flailed the air uselessly as he sailed along the walk and over the front step and over the mat that said, Welcome.

Welcome to the Home by the Sea.

A dream.

"GET UP!"

Morning and afternoon where only seconds apart. There had been a moment of laying in bed and then awake. At first he couldn't tell if any time had passed, but as his senses fixed themselves, he could feel that the room had grown cold. The fire in the place had burned to ash and the shadows moved from one side of the room to the other. There was a giant, snarling demon standing at his bed post that wasn't there before. There was white hot pain popping behind his eyes and what felt like a crew of gnomes with an earth drill slowly, laboriously boring their way out of his skull through his forehead. His bones cracked as he moved and his skin itched with dry grit, as if he had slept with sand in his sheets.

He felt the dream swirling out of his head through a hole. He couldn't remember what it was or was about, but it didn't really matter, he sighed, dreams were meaningless.

He looked at the demon seething at the foot of his bed and suddenly remembered what and why he was. The task had not yet been completed as the dream lead him to believe.

"You, Paradox?" The demon spoke.

"You, Harroc?" Paradox answered.

"Me, Harroc." The demon replied. "You food."

"You don't plan to eat me." Paradox said unmoved from the bed.

"Yeah, and not only that, I'm gonna do it slowly, with relish and mustard, and curse your name as I do it so your cretinous soul slithers into Hel where I have a bunch a friends lined up to give you a real, hard time."

"Why?"

"'Cause I'm sick and tired of the folly of man trying so hard to control demons. It's just not their place. Nothing personal, but I'm making an example out of you."

"I would rather you not."

"You are not one of the more interesting foods that I've found."

"I've got something that might interest you."

"Well, it better be a slice of cheese cake. I'm having a craving for a slice of cheese cake." Paradox shifted his blankets enough to show Harroc the hand. "That's not what I think it is." Harroc said eyeing the thing carefully.

"Yes, does it interest you?"

Harroc narrowed his eyes. "Yes, it most certainly does!" Harroc suddenly grabbed at the blankets but Paradox quickly clenched the hand

and it made a fist on its own. The demon doubled over writhing in agony. "It BURNS!" Harroc howled. "Its burning master. Please, no more!"

Paradox continued to hold up the hand as he spoke to the demon. "You will serve me in my task!"

"Yes!" The demon screamed in pain.

"You will accomplish my task completely!"

"Sure!" The demon cried. "Anything, just turn it off!"

Paradox loosened his grip slightly and the hand relaxed. "I have your demonic oath."

"On my cousin Lester's grave or be buried in marshmallow fluff."

Paradox was not sure if that was an oath and had no idea what marshmallow fluff was, but he could not lose momentum now. He was amazed at how physically draining the cacodemon was and was too exhausted to think straight. "I wish you to seek out the one named Diane of the house of Avenger. She is the holy Knight of Uko, god of lightning, and goes by the name of Achillia. When you find her, give her no reason or explanation, just slay her."

The demon looked up from the floor to Paradox. "What?" He said in disbelief.

"Did I stutter?" Paradox asked him. "Kill, Achillia!"

Harroc's tiny red eyes blinked. How easy! But demon's school first lesson is: Don't make anything seem easy. "It is a great task you call me upon. The slaying of a Knight and none less than Achillia!" He looked up at the ceiling, stroking his chin with exaggerated contemplation. "It shall take years!"

"Dawn." Paradox said simply. "As Shegatesu colors the sky and Kemoto rises over the edge of Mortalroam the knight of Uko will be dead."

"It can't be done, there is weeks of red tape alone." The demon whined. "I don't even know where she is!" Paradox held up the hand a little higher. "But, we can cut some of that tape and I'm sure she's listed in the white pages under holy pest."

Paradox glared hard at him and waved the hand towards him. As he did, the finger pointed. "Now go!" Paradox shouted at him like chasing away a dog with the hand. "Do as you are told!" He shooed, angrily.

Harroc shied away from the hand. He actually wanted to kill the accursed knight and was looking forward to his assignment. Paradox had left the command without specifics. He could not only bring his entourage, but their lackeys as well. A whole army running rampant on Mortalroam! The havoc! To make matters worse, Paradox had forgotten to give him commands of what to do after the job. He would be free, for the hand would only work once. He would return to the house and turn him into carrion cakes and then he'd be free to hunt down Fantista and...He stopped as he envisioned her beauty and realized he was foaming again. He wiped away his slobber and looked quickly about the room for the way out. He stepped to the full mirror against the wall and slipped out as easily as he had slipped in.

Chapter 34

Hauge danced on his winds to the voice Frito played through his white-gold flute, Soulseng. Leaves of red and gold leapt from their twigs and littered gently to the ground. Fikor's breath lingered through Meleki's great trees, but not their roots. She stood off to the side, gone from sight watching her woods. Her squirrels and rabbits and chipmunks had all found their holes and dens to sleep for Fikor's winter. It wasn't them whom she worried. It was Frito, Roc and Orrin who rode placidly on their horses through her forest.

"Are we there yet?" Roc growled.

Frito took Soulseng from his lips and glanced at him. "Being that I am not certain of the exact location of Brewster, I called my forest walk a little short."

Orrin turned from the trees and looked at the dark knight. "You mean we, like, did it al-ready?"

Frito nodded. "How do you think we covered fifty clicks in an afternoon?"

"I missed it some-how, eh?." Orrin said. "It, like, wasn't like the last one."

"I'm getting better." Frito smiled at him.

Roc suddenly stopped without warning. "A caravan." He said quietly. "Three full wagons, many mules, beasts, horses and men. I don't hear enough metal to make out warriors with armor."

Frito strained and listened and could hear them too. Orrin closed his eyes and let out his Kamri. He could see the merchants with their wives, and children up ahead. There were a few hired workers, less with swords longer than a foot and a half. Orrin sent out his Kamri so Frito could also see. "This is good." He said to Roc. "We can go with them. Surly they are going to Brewster."

Roc nodded and spurred his horse on. Frito turned to follow, slipping Soulseng into his saddle bag. But Orrin stayed behind, his eyes widening in sudden fear. "What is it?" Frito called back.

"Ban-dits!" Orrin whispered hotly. "Like, ready for an am-bush up by the turn, eh?"

Roc turned and reached for his hammer. "Great!" He reached down and took up his great helm. Pulling it on, he covered it over with his hood. "Hang back a little. Give us a shout if you need us."

"No farther than my throwing arm." Frito said pulling off his hood and pulling on his helm. Roc looked up at him, but Frito ignored him and turned his horse to the road, bursting to gallop.

Colors of aged autumn flashed about them. With deft speed their great horses leapt fallen trees and onto the road itself. Steel shod hooves skidded into the hard packed dirt as they galloped by the caravan, ignoring the shouts and swears of its members—quickly reaching the front and halting the procession.

"Mad are you!" The fat man shouted from his wagon. "Out of way!" He flipped his reins and his horses stepped forward. Roc glared from beneath his hood at the beasts and they stopped, refusing to budge. The fat man in the wagon glared in confusion for the moment then shook his fist. "Hoodlum! Get away!" But Roc didn't move.

Frito faced the quiet road ahead and quickly dismounted with his blade-spear in hand. He scanned at the trees hanging over head and the large thick bushes on the side of the road. Perfect for an ambush.

Two caravan members who had ridden up front as scouts, moved back towards Roc and Frito, again passing beneath the tree. One drew his sword.

Roc pointed an armored finger. "Put it away or eat it, don't make me choose for you."

The horseman looked at the giant frame beneath the cloak and lowered the sword. "Begone." He said with a nod of his head. "We not want with you." He flexed his grip on the sword.

Roc looked him over. A sword, but no arm. He could filet him with ease, but the great Dragonslayer shook his head and turned his horse to Frito and trotted to him. Roc looked at the over hanging trees. "I can smell them." Frito could smell them too. He nodded his head and Roc took the silent cue. He placed one hand to his mouth and cried out. "Olly olly oxen free. Come out! Come out! Trusted, busted, and disgusted."

Frito looked at him with a side glance. "Trusted, Busted, and Disgusted?"

Roc didn't look from the trees. "I got it from Craig." He whispered. Frito only pursed his lips and looked ahead.

Silence.

Roc sighed feeling the eyes of the caravan on him. "Look boys, I'm not going to stand out here all day. You've been caught. Come on out…"

Again silence.

Roc drummed his fingers on the pommel of his saddle, then looked down to Frito. "I think there are chestnuts in that tree, roast 'em."

Frito held up his patch worked hand. With a flick, magic exploded from his fingers and smashed into the over hanging tree. The blast knocked one from the tree. It was a rough landing, but not fatal.

Roc kicked his horse to spring into the fray as men rushed from the woods with flashing steel blades. Archers in the trees dropped their bows and took up their swords as they too dropped to the fray. Roc leapt from his horse, stretching his armored body in flight. He aimed for one thief and crushed him with his sudden weight.

Lightning and heat flashed behind him and immolated a thug. Roc knew Frito was back there, protecting his flank. A sword glanced off his shoulder. There were more brigands than he thought. They were also more coordinated than they should be. He had to concentrate, he had to rhyme.

"A dragon's heart beats with fire." The Dragonslayer pushed out with his buckler for room as he rose to his feet. "Okshiru's waves beats with flood." His hammer whirled to the air, blocking the blade coming at him. "The takers drum beats with death." His fingers opened and the hammer slipped through, catching it at the long thong of leather at the end. "But The Dragonslayer beats with blood!" The hammer whirled like a flail, suddenly longer and flying faster, smashing into bone and flesh as it passed by.

Frito took his stance as two rushed him. He held up his blade-spear and waited for them. His Sho-Pa training sprang forth, as he spun out the butt end first, catching his first opponent directly in the throat, crushing his wind pipe and stopping his charge. In almost the same motion, he spun around on the ball of one foot, using the counter force of his first blow to drive home the blade into the belly of the second.

Roc waded through the crowd of steel around him. His body seemed to worm like a wraith and their light swords merely glanced off of his monster armor, never getting a solid blow. His bladed buckler flashed too quickly to follow. They would duck past the great hammer only to taste the blade of his shield. Roc jammed back his elbow and caught a face with his blow. He let go of his hammer letting it swing on his wrist by its strap and reached back and grabbed his foe. He pulled him around and shoved him forward into one of the many thrusting swords about him, letting his team mates inadvertently stab him to death. "Furnace fires, smelting steel." His hammer drove forward slamming into a head. "Building might for man to wield." He drove forward shoving his shoulder through the pack. "But iron is nothing, useless and cold." He turned with his bladed buckler catching a temple purely by accident. "But in my hand, it burns foretold!" His hammer came down with the whistle of Hauge's wind. A shield of wood splintered along with the bone beneath it from the sheer force of the blow. Again Roc whirled his hammer. He caught the eyes of one foe before him and read the fear behind them. He cried aloud: "He is demon, eyes don't lie, he is invincible your head calls, he is man your heart denies, he is Roc and he is all!" Again he dropped his hammer to let hang. He reached out and snatched at the rogue's face, his fingers digging into his eyes. With a quick downward snap, he easily tore the skin from his head.

Frito downed another without pause. His speed was as calculated as his moves. Changing in pitch and tone like so much song. His blade-spear was a part of him, shielding swords from him and sending them back. One to his left, another straight ahead. There were five moves that came immediately to mind. One would kill both instantly, two, three, and four would kill both in days and five would kill only one and incapacitate the other.

He fainted at the one on the left. His blade swept straight down to his head with obvious intent. His foe raised his shield to block, but the blade-spear weaved against laws of right and universe. Faster than sight it shifted left, followed down low then up, carving up below the shield and into a mid-section. Without pause, he spun about, twisting the blade in his hands and bringing up the butt end to fend off the other outlaw with a confusing flurry of speed. He freed his blade-spear and drove its haft to his right with an upward swing cuffing his opponent in the chin. To finish the job, Frito gave him a blow to the side of his head with the wood of the weapon.

Frito watched him panting on the road. Puffs of breath curled from him as he laid there twitching. He turned to Roc who was finishing the last one by spinning him about by the feet stepping closer and closer to a large tree.

"Roc." Frito called to him. "That'll do, we're done." Roc looked up and his grip slipped as his foot skidded into the earth. The thug flew from his hands and rolled suddenly into the dirt. He quickly fought to his feet, running towards the tree line. Roc lifted his hammer and tossed it to follow. The thug found the trees and plunged into them. Roc's hammer also found the trees, and plunged into one.

Roc watched as the last thief, nimble and free of heavy armor, ran faster than he could follow. Roc turned hotly and quickly charged at Frito. "We must stop him. You must stop him." Roc ordered.

Is he part of the guild that we must find? Frito wondered as he cocked his arm, aiming his blade-spear. *He might be in league with the killers that we are looking for. Should he return and warn the rest, they could hide where we will never find them and then we will never know who killed Oustrand and his wife. Our only lead to finding my sister. Perhaps they might ambush us again. That would prove a dangerous problem.*

Frito hurled his Blade-spear.

The thief dodged through the trees, ducking and moving through the brush trying to put as much substance between him and the road. He paused, catching his breath, listening for pursuit.

A hissing buzz came to his ears and he turned as the noise grew in his head. His eyes caught a brief glimpse of something flashing back and forth through the trees. He raised his small, round shield instinctively to block but never saw the Blade-spear until it buried in the wood, pushing through his arm and bone. The blade writhed and twisted in his arm, as if alive. It began to grind and wriggle as he desperately tried to grab it somewhere and pull it free. It was spinning now, drilling and pushing with its eerie buzzing-hiss as it did. It forced his back against a tree and punched completely through his arm and shield and bored quickly through the soft of his leather and the soft of his stomach before his scream of agony escaped his lips.

But the goddess Dru had mercy, and claimed him quickly. The Blade-spear however, continued to bore until it jammed itself into the tree.

Frito trotted up as the Blade-spear wriggled to free itself. He grabbed it and pulled it free. He didn't look back as he headed towards the road. It was a thing of honor to kill in battle or to fight face to face, not zap people at a distance. But Brewster could be a fortress of thieves. Once warned, there could be a army waiting. He wanted and needed obscurity to work. *Who ever took Frita mustn't know that I am looking for her. If they find out, they might run. Or simply kill her.*

He looked at the blade and the streams of blood running along its edge. *Yes, Dru likes this new toy of mine.*

Roc bent over his captive. He half lifted, half dragged him to a sitting position and leaned him against a large rock by the side of the road. He could feel the eyes of the caravan behind him. "Go on." He ordered quickly. "Be about your way!" He spoke louder turning around. The fat man in the lead wagon looked to the others around him, then urgently clicked his horses on. Slowly the creaking wagons and sleepy mules moved through the carnage of broken bodies. Frito stopped at the edge of the road, watching them as they passed along. From the corner of his eye he watched them head along the road and around the bend.

Orrin stood directly behind him. He had been close by the entire time, using his Kamri to deny every one around him knowledge of his presence.

Everyone save Frito. "Come here." He whispered to the boy. Orrin knelt beside the battered, unconscious body. Without guidance, Orrin slowly reached out with his hand and touched the sweating, bloodied face. Dirt and grit rolled beneath his fingers as he did. Tattered, unshaven face—the unclean human smell—his hoarse, rasping breath dragged from his open, foul mouth. His warm, flowing blood was rich with cheap wine.

Slowly the boy reached out with his Kamri and touched the cutthroat's mind. He pushed his way through the darkness of unconsciousness. There were no surface thoughts, he was dreaming nothing. He pushed deeper.

The rogue awoke with a start.

Frito gripped him suddenly by the neck. His armored fingers quickly pinched a cluster of nerves and the rogue lay in too much pain to move. Roc now stood beside Frito and knelt by his side, his hammer at the ready.

Orrin was still trying to focus his mind. He had pushed too quickly, his own Kamri seemed too distressed and frayed to properly wield. He had woken the man and set off flashes of thoughts and fears like popping bright lights, blinding his Kamri.

Frito looked at Orrin. His eyes were hidden by his dark glasses but Orrin read into them. He knew Frito wanted him to try again.

Orrin reached out again and touched the man's face. The thug tried to pull back, but Frito held him in place. Orrin focused his Kamri. He looked past the thief's wide terrified eyes and into his centre. His Kamri filled with thought—foreign thought—words of different tongue—

gestures were unfamiliar, but Orrin could perceive a true meaning of what he saw. He tabulated and computed and re-arranged the mismatched array of mental inspiration into a simple flow of understandable motion.

In less than two beats, he was done and took back his hand. The thief laid limp in Frito's hand.

"Is that it?" Roc whispered, in fear of disturbing something, but Frito looked to the boy for an answer.

"I put him to sleep." Orrin said quietly.

Frito looked at the young elf, wavering and unsteady. His inner strength was gone, his bright, cheery self was glazed, empty. Frito pulled off his gauntlet and felt the boys cheek. It was hot to his cold fingers. Frito's own Kamri could feel the strain that was on the boy. He didn't understand. It was a simple mind walk, and then a simple suggestion to sleep. Frito himself lacked the proper aligned Kamri to accomplish this himself, but Orrin shouldn't have had any trouble.

Frito scooped the boy in his arms and Orrin fell limp. Frito walked quickly into the wood-line out of the sight of the road and set him down. His horse stepped calmly over to him as if from some silent command and stood there waiting. Frito reached up and took a blanket from the saddle and wrapped the boy.

Roc followed with the thief over his shoulder and leading his and Orrin's horses. "What is it?" Roc asked dropping the thief like so much trash. Frito shook his head. Roc pointed anxiously, uncharacteristically worried. "You're the one with Kamri!"

Frito again shook his head. "My Kamri is of the body. His is of the mind."

Roc stepped around him and looked to the boy who was sleeping peacefully. He knelt in the leaves by him. He pulled of his left gauntlet and carefully tucked the corners of the blanket about the boy's face.

Orrin open his eyes a small crack. "He didn't kill Ou-strand. But he's, like, part of the pur-ple horde, eh?" He murmured.

Frito stroked the boy's cheek. "Rest."

Roc tilted his head. "Purple horde? What is he talking about?"

Frito set his lips. "He's taxed himself. Strained his limits."

"You said he had none!" Roc whispered harshly.

"None in the sense that I could measure." Frito paused as he tried again. "If I came to a wall, just because I could not see the top, doesn't mean it goes on forever. It must have happened with Y'day. Something hit them, and Friska too. Strong enough to kill the old elf and drive Friska farther out of his mind."

"And the boy?"

Frito shook his head. "His natural strength protected him, but he is taxed."

"Alright, I understand that." Roc said. "But what do we do?"

"We have to get him to Brewster."

Orrin opened his eyes. "S'not far…" He mumbled. "'n hour or so, eh?. Safe there. The horde was dri-ven out by a Knight."

Frito scooped up the boy and turned to his horse. With an un-given cue, Horse knelt and leaned to one side to allow Frito to easily place Orrin in the saddle. The Archknight quickly followed.

"Hold on." Roc said as he lifted the thug up and threw him like a sack on to Orrin's horse. He coughed as his belly hit the hard leather but didn't wake. Roc quickly bound his arms and legs. Roc would have rather slain the man then and there, but public trials and executions were a far more effective deterrent to further burglaries of traveling caravans. If there was a Knight there, there was law and order. If the Knight was still there. "Lucky for him, Brewster's not far."

Chapter 35

Meleki's forest of spruce and pine soon gave away to the sand of Okshiru's sea. Fikor's cold swept about with the tides itself, teasing the ocean's mist with Hauge. Sea birds cried as they sailed above in the cold air, their great wings gliding, swooping and dipping, their talons splashing quickly with shimmering rainbows for its food.

He walked on his large heavy feet along the coast, following as close to the woods as possible. He listened with his large hanging ears, but there was only the hiss of dry, dead leaves in Hauge's wind. His nose, ever moving, ever twitching, sniffed the cold air, but could only smell the grinding salt from Hiroki, the old hermit at the bottom of Okshiru's great water. It is said that the old man lived during the reawakening of time, grinding his salt and grain in the abyss of the desert. It was there, that Okshiru wished to place his sea. He asked the creatures living there that if they did not wish to live in the ocean, they could live elsewhere and he gave all them lovely places to go. Those that wanted to stay were given fins to swim in the new ocean. Okshiru offered Hiroki a beautiful place to live, but the man wanted to be where he was with his tiny mill. Okshiru then offered to give him fins and the choice to rule the fishes of the oceans, but Hiroki refused that offer as well with a mocking gesture. "Put it elsewhere." Hiroki rudely ordered the great god.

"There is no where else, Hiroki." Okshiru patiently told him. "It must go here. You can grind your salt anywhere."

"I ground salt here while you battled your brains out and I will grind here until time sleeps again!" The old hermit cursed. Okshiru became mad and told him to move, but the hermit became stubborn. Okshiru trembled with his skies, but the old man took up a fist of ground salt and flung it at the god of the sea and sky.

Okshiru would not stand for such insurrection. "Hale well, Hiroki and grind your salt where you stay." And Okshiru took up his great ocean and set it right upon the house of old Hiroki.

He wiggled his nose and went along his way. It was a good explanation as any, he thought. His long, lean body stepped higher along the cliff sides to where he could see the large manor perched on top. He lifted an ear and listened. Nothing but the sea and Meleki's birds of white skimming the foaming water. He went along the trail that led to the front of the house and stood at the old sagging gate. He looked with gigantic brown eyes to the front door complete with a mat that said Welcome.

Welcome to the Home by the Sea.

He had no business with the front of the house, so he stepped with long bent legs over the low wooden fence and walked easily to the rear. On the stone steps at the kitchen door he stood over his mission.

The rabbit lay there on the step, dead.

With clawed hands he reached down and picked up the rabbit. As it reached the cradle of his arms, the rabbit's stiffness eased and it became supple in his hands. He stroked it and it grew warm and slowly began to breathe. It's ears flexed and twitched as did it's nose. Its eyes opened and it sat alert in his arms.

He looked down at the dead rabbit on the step and it began to shrivel and dry. Its bones appeared and crumbled to white dust. Hauge's winds soon scattered away all traces of it.

He looked at the rabbit's soul alive his arms.

"Hale Gozoo."

He looked at the rabbit in alarm! "You speak!"

"No, Gozoo." She said laughing. "I am here."

He turned and looked down to the girl before him. "Goddess Meleki…" He said with a bow. She walked smoothly to the giant hairless rabbit god and reached up to stroke his giant forehead. He bent and closed his eyes as she did. "I wish…" He whispered when she stopped. "To petition Okshiru. I have seen what has taken place in the last days and I wish to put an end to it."

Meleki looked into the deep eyes of the hairless god of rabbits. He was intent, an idea blazing within him. She only blinked in mild surprise.

"I know I can't do much." He said before she could speak. "But at least I can do something."

Meleki thought about what he said.

"Ura works through Thamrell," He again spoke before she could. "Surly Okshiru will let me do something."

Meleki glared at him. "I…"

"And that Harroc! Surely there is something to be said about that!"

"Yes, well…"

"And Fikor is furious at what has transpired with his knight. He cares so much about her."

"As do we…"

"And we mustn't forget Ferris! Blessid! The Iron Dragon! No one is safe!"

Meleki's brows bushed and her bottom lip pushed out as she thrust her fists into her waist and scowled.

"Oh, excuse me, you were about to say something?" The hairless god asked her.

"Yes!" She pushed out although he didn't try to stop her. "Okshiru's rule plainly states that gods are not to interfere with mortals. Thamrell and Thumber are bodiless and exempt from the rule."

Gozoo was prepared and smiled in a rabbit way. "And so the same applies to Chritchfeild." He held up the rabbit in his hands. Her innocent eyes searched his giant face. "A rabbit's soul is reincarnated as all the other animals." He explained away her confusion. "Chritchfeild here is...between jobs right now."

She shook her head. "He will say no." Gozoo bowed his head and then looked hopeful. "And we will have to ask him." She said anticipating his question. Gozoo sighed and bent down to set Chritchfeild free to find another body. Perhaps a deer or something a bit sturdier, like a wolf. That would be a change of pace.

"But," Meleki stopped him. "I'm sure he's busy right now." Gozoo slowly stood back up with the rabbit still in his hands. "I don't think we have to ask him...right away."

<u>Chapter 36</u>

His feet skidded on the hard, frozen earth while rocks and stones seemed to push out to obscure and block his way. Leafless branches lashed out at his open skin like so many lashes of a whip. Thorns and burrs in his feet stung him and bruises dressed his shins and knees from falls beyond counting. Blood flowed from his open wounds, some from his falls, most from his own hands.

Again he fell headlong to the earth. Friska, Knight of the Wind was now cast from the sky. The mother earth was unyielding to him and her ground was hard, cold and unsympathetic to the fallen knight. His sweat clung to his battered body as steam rose in Fikor's wintery air. He lifted himself slowly to his feet. His muscles screamed the pain his lungs were too weak to voice. He tried to run on but his legs refused to move. He couldn't lift them high enough to clear the root of a tree and had not the strength to stop from falling again.

"Okshiru..." He pleaded to the sky. "You mustn't leave me." He swallowed, but there was nothing to swallow. "Father...forgive your son!" His eyes turned to cry, but there were no tears. "Hauge..." He breathed and whispered to the wind. "Okshiru bade me to serve you, save me now!"

There was no wind. The forest loomed over him in silence.

Something moved about in the trees above him. Small leather wings spread and cupped the air as it gently floated down to his side. Her hands were soft and gentle. Her wings wrapped him in warm embrace as her kisses took the sting from his face. "My love." She whispered. "Show me the beast who did this on to you and I shalt slay him this hour!"

He shook his head. "There is no beast." His voice strained to speak. "There is only me." His eyes covered with mist as he looked into her simple, homely face. "I have fallen from Okshiru's side. But as he cast me out, he showed a vision unto me." He gasped. "Fanrealm was burning, my mother fighting with the Son of Hate! Thamrell deceived me and led me from my home." His voice faded to nothing.

Her arms swept him easily from the ground and her wings lifted them smoothly into the air. She glided through the heavy woods and out of the glade itself. She paused at the tree line. Brush and twigs ended in a small field of tall, heavy briar. Thick boughs of thorns twisted painfully about, laid dark and brown for the winter. She looked carefully around and shot quickly over the field. She circled once about and dove through a small break in the bramble and into her hole.

In her tiny hovel she laid his body down in her bed, quickly wrapping him in quilts. She dashed over to her fire and fanned it to flame. She tossed in two thick logs to get it hot.

She sat by his side. Her wing lightly covered over him as if to protect him. His eyes opened and closed. He knew where he was, he had been there before. In the den of a demon.

"Okshiru has forsaken me. He has thrown me from his sight." He moaned. "You too must cast me from your sight. I must not darken your soul."

Fear filled her centre. "This is not true!" She cried. "It was you who brought me from the flames of Hel. You redeemed my soul and bought it back for me. You lifted my heart and blessed it by the waters of Okshiru's sea. You will never be from my sight. You cleansed me." She touched the tunic that she wore. "You gave me clothes for I had none, and taught me to wear them. You taught me the word of Justice for I didn't know it and taught me to speak it. You gave me your heart, for I had none, and taught me to love."

He didn't open his eyes as he spoke. "But now it is I who is stained with sin."

She gripped the blankets about him. "Then I shall cleanse you!"

He shook his head. "Okshiru has forsaken me..." He mumbled as he drifted out of mind.

"'Tis not so." She argued. "It was your father's voice that carried Okshiru's message to me through Hauge's wind. He has not forsaken you. He shall never forsake you. You must not forsake him."

He didn't hear her.

She pressed her hand against his chest and could feel his heart. She felt him shiver and she curled up beside him, still with one wing draped protectively over him.

<u>Chapter 37</u>

Frito pulled his arms closer about Orrin's body. He looked at the sleeping boy and shielded his face from the stirring of Hauge's wind. He looked ahead to the stone pillars that signified the entrance to Brewster. He glanced at Roc riding slightly before him. "Bigger than I thought."

Roc glanced over his shoulder. "There is a gate man ahead. I will talk to him."

"Be polite." The Ninefingers reminded.

Roc looked him over. "You don't think you're asking a bit much do you?"

"Yes."

"Don't start me." He went along in silence. As they approached the guard, Roc shrugged his cloak to fall over his armor and the great sword strapped to his saddle in a vain hope to appear less threatening. He looked to the gate keeper. Human, perhaps in his twenties. *Its hard to judge the ages of humans,* he thought to himself. *This one seems more of a boy. Look at him. So proud to wear that mail shirt. He probably thinks he could lick the world with that pig stabber of a sword at his side.* Roc wanted very much to pound him hello just so he would stop looking so 'happy to serve you.'

The guard stepped from his little wooden house and waved a merchant and her tiny cart along. It was obvious that he recognized her from another time. His clean shaven face faltered and faded away as Roc loomed over him. "What brings you to Brewster, my Lord." The guard took a cautious step back as he eyed Roc's mask of terror.

Roc motioned with his head. "The boy is ill." He said plainly.

The guard cautiously stepped closer to Frito and looked Orrin over. "We have a surgeon." He suggested.

"No surgeon." Frito said quickly.

"I don't need any witch doctor cutting open the boy." Roc growled. "Just a bed."

The guard looked back and forth between the two now trying to judge their purpose. They didn't appear friendly with their dark armor and weapons, but it looked too much like a ploy to slip into the city to be for real. No one would look that obviously ready for war and try to sneak in. He stepped back, still regarding them and glanced over his shoulder towards the barracks further down and off to the side. There were two guards, processing writs of entry. One looked up and signaled the other. He in turn signaled into the barracks itself.

Roc whispered in elf tongue low enough for only an elf to hear. "This does not look like a guild's town."

"Not at all. Just the opposite." Frito watched as four guards came from the barracks, adjusting their weapon belts. One of the guards from the desk led them.

"Now what?" Roc hissed. "Beating these guys up wouldn't even be interesting."

"Tell them who you are."

Roc looked at this cousin. "You! Lay some knight stuff on them."

"Go on, your better at it than I am."

"Hey, were talking negotiations here, you're the statesman!"

"Excuse me!"

Roc looked to the guard below him surprised that he dare interrupt him. "What?"

"I asked if you would be staying in Brewster?"

"If I feel like it, maybe." Roc clenched his teeth as the idea of pounding him became more interesting.

"Do you have a writ of entry?" The guard was still polite but his voice began to drip with impertinence.

Roc curled his lip. "Do I have a writ? Oh, I have a writ for you alright."

"We are under the hand of Dragonslayer." Frito suddenly spoke up before Roc did something harsh.

The guard changed color. "The Dragonslayer! Why didn't you speak up before, man? Show me your device and enter."

"You want to see my device?" Roc tightened his fist on his horses reigns. "My device, Huh?" Roc's eyes caught Frito's look of, *just show it and we will enter.* Roc snarled as he pushed back on his saddle, sliding his hand from his gauntlet. "My device...Huh, Here!" Roc showed the gauntlet and the device was stamped on the wrist.

"Great and noble sirs, you are guests of Brewster! The corporal will escort you to see our knight, Milo."

Roc dropped his head. "Milo!" He moaned.

Frito looked closer. "Where can we find him?" He said anxiously.

"We don't need him." Roc growled.

Frito ignored him and leaned closer to the guard. "We would like to see him."

The guard, now confused looked to Frito. "He might be at the court house. The corporal will lead you on. Allow me to pipe your presence." With that he took a small whistle dangling from his neck by a cord and started blowing short, sharp notes.

Roc leaned over and snatched the whistle from the guards lips and wadded the metal in his hand like so much paper and handed it back to him. "We'll find him." Roc then leaned back pointing to the horse behind him. "I even brought a house warming gift." Roc stripped the blanket from the horse and exposed the thug. "He and his party attacked us on the road. He was the only survivor."

The corporal now stepped forward. "He is of the purple horde. He will swing for his crimes."

Well, alright! Roc thought. "Cut him down and he is yours." Roc watched as they did. The thug awakened and seemed to panic as he recognized the guards of Brewster. He knew what was coming. Roc only hoped that he could be there to watch. He kicked his horse forward and waded through the guards uncontested with Frito close behind him.

"You shouldn't have done that." Frito said.

"Done what?"

"Mash up his whistle. He seemed so proud of it."

"He was an asshole, and besides, I made his day. He's gonna go home and tell all his friends that something interesting happened."

Frito looked around at the shops and stores that lined the narrow street. Merchants were selling off the last of their wares and closing their shops. The smithy's ring fell silent as he hung up his hammer and covered his anvil. Carts pulled along the well made road to their homes as lights began to appear in the windows.

"This isn't what I expected." Roc said. "I was hoping for a real scummy place."

"Well, if Milo is here," Frito said.

"He's here. I can smell a knight at a hundred clicks." Roc turned his horse towards the middle of the main street. If Milo was anywhere, it would be in the center of things.

A mule's bray and the holler of a man's voice caught his attention. He turned his horse about and looked down the side street.

The giant stood at the height of the second story windows. His huge hands lifted a work mule into the air and held it there while it's owner pleaded for him to put it down. The ogre must have smashed through a lesser protected, isolated gate. Militia now mustered to deal with him. "Things are looking up." Roc chirped as he spurred his horse into the fray.

Frito watched Roc chase after the giant. The crowds were gathering around at a safe distance to watch the spectacle. Guards swept around the giant with their spears pointed at him, hoping to force him back and away, but he tossed the mule to the ground crushing a guard as he did. He laughed with a thunderous roar as the guards pulled their comrade out from the crippled mule. The giant stepped forward into the guards, swatting them aside with the sweep of his hand.

"Fe fi fo fum!" Roc shouted as he dismounted. "You seem to be pretty dumb." Roc pulled his great sword from his saddle sheath. "Fum fo fi fe." Roc charged at him, ducking the giant's sweeping hand. "Now come and fight, ME!" Roc lunged forward, his blade thrusted beneath the cap of the giant's knee pushing up towards the thigh. The giant howled in pain and stumbled back.

"So liddle man, you come to fi' me." The giant shouted. "I will smath you flat!" The giant limped awkwardly forward with a flat hand but Roc was faster and swung his sword up and with a swipe took off the giant's nose. "Doe Dhit!" He exclaimed limping back again, his hands coming away from his face red with streams of blood. "Do tut by dose off!"

"Times like this, I do savor." Roc rhymed. "For this time, I've shown you favor. From your face, a growth removement, and looks to me a vast improvement!"

Frito sighed and looked at the crowd around him. Humans all, save a few scant elves and one dwarf, his head popping up out of the crowd periodically, jumping up to see. They seemed too intent on the fight to worry about him.

A second commotion began as the crowds suddenly split and allowed several people through, the lead of the procession was Milo. Frito could see his aura before he could actually see him. His nappy, black hair popped up and down above the crowd as he trotted quickly through. "MILO!" Frito shouted and the knight turned and tried to peer over the taller crowd. Frito carefully made his horse wade through the people over to him.

Milo squinted and waved back. He quickly dashed through the people to Frito's side. "My lord!" He exclaimed as he reached Frito.

He gripped Frito's leg in a friendly gesture. "Is that Roc?" When Frito nodded the dark knight smiled broadly. "Well then, I'm not needed."

"Orrin isn't well." Frito said pulling his cloak to show him. Milo looked at the boy and with a gentle hand touched the boy's leg. Orrin was awake and looked at the Knight.

"Hi, Milo."

"Hi yourself." Milo looked to Frito. "Come this way, Brewster is at your disposal."

Frito looked over his shoulder to Roc dancing around the giant. "Tis so queer to be without an ear!" The Dragonslayer turned Giant killer sang.

Frito pursed his lips and blew an elfcall to get his attention.

Roc heard him.

"Thanks for coming, that's our show." Roc leapt forward and with a heaving swipe his great sword chopped halfway through the giant's hand and bone. "I hate to leave, but its time to go." Roc wretched the sword quickly and with a sudden jerk yanked it out. "Good luck, good night and with God's prayer." Roc swung the sword in a low sweeping motion before bringing it back over his shoulder. "Brought to you from Dragonslayer!" With all of his great might he whipped the sword around and lopped off the giant's head.

The crowd cheered as Roc walked across the still breathing chest of the giant. "IT IS LORD ROC THE DRAGONSLAYER!" Someone shouted and the crowd went wild. Roc glared sharply at them and the cheering crowd only seemed to cheer louder. "Milo said he would come!" Another shouted.

Roc didn't like this at all. From the giant's chest he could see the Frito make his way away from the crowds. He hissed to himself. What was he to do? Some woman timidly stepped over to him. She was bent in curtsy as she laid wild flowers at the giant's side. She slowly backed her way from him into the crowd. Another came fourth laying a few pennies down while yet another brought a small braying lamb. They were gifts for him. How could he handle this?

He thrust his great sword into the giant's chest which only pleased the crowd more. He put his hands to his mouth and blew and elfcall. His reply came simply.

"Be yourself."

Back at Dragonrealm he would be rude and abusive. People seemed to enjoy being abused by their lord holder, but this wasn't Dragonrealm.

He crossed his arms and shouted. "I DIDN'T SLAY HIM FOR YOU! I DID IT BECAUSE I FELT LIKE IT!" The people applauded and one at a time in an orderly manner, began to place gifts reverently before him. Roc made a face of panic. He hated people being nice to him. He could handle aggression but kindness was too much. "I DON'T WANT YOUR GIFTS!" He shouted into the crowds. "YOU WORMS AREN'T WORTH ENOUGH TO GIVE ME GIFTS." He stepped off the giants chest and took up a wildflower that was laid there and tucked it into the shoulder guard of his armor. "GO BACK TO YOUR MEAGER HOMES AND TO YOUR MEAGER LIVES AND NEVER FORGET THE GREAT DAY THAT I FELT LIKE GIVING YOU THE BENEFIT OF SEEING MY GREATNESS." He pushed his way through. "Go! Get away from me you maggots!" He pushed people to the ground. "I want arms distance at all times." He knocked a few more over.

One of them shouted: "He touched me! He touched ME!" as he picked himself off the ground. Others reached out to touch the man who was touched by Roc, the Mighty Dragonslayer.

Roc rolled his eyes and looked towards Worldsend. As he did, he noticed over one of the buildings was the banner of the fighting dragon, his banner. And beneath it was the banner of the pierced silver crescent. The banner of Milo, Knight of Okshiru, Knight of Ovam. He cursed the god of sea and sky under his breath and turned back towards the dead giant. "YOU!" He shouted pointing a armored finger. "Yes, You!" People scampered out of the way as not to be the one Roc was pointing at, but the target was unmistakable. It was the guard from the gate. He was either relieved from post or came to see what the trouble was, but it was him and was still wearing his mangled whistle by a cord around his neck. "Fetch my sword and bring it by." Roc turned his back and walked through the sea of people that parted for him. Another crowd was forming around to touch the man who touched the sword that Roc had touched.

Roc blustered to the main street trying to find where Frito went, but the crowd was following him. He turned at them and bellowed. "GO HOME!" They backed away, some left, but enough remained to still be a problem. Roc was angry now and he snatched off the mask that hid his face and grimaced. He could feel the folds of flesh slide about as muscles twisted and the inner skin of his cheeks puffed and swelled with air giving his eyes the appearance that they were sinking into his head.

At the same time he drew his face into a Dragon's grin, exposing all of his teeth at once which looked more like fangs in a dragon's maw than an elf.

They wanted a show, they got one.

The first row fainted dead away. Those still conscious fled at full speed, dropping what they had in their arms. The rest, further back, retreated away in repulsion. The streets were clear in a matter of moments. Roc placed back his mask in utter glee.

He looked at the one man remaining, hanging on to the shred of discipline in his lame, military body and the great sword in his hands before him. He was in the rear of the crowd and missed the full effect of the sight, but still he stood motionless with fear. Roc snorted and waved him on. He felt his face relax and re-arrange it self as he started down the street.

Milo came riding over on horse back leading the Roc's horse. "The Ninefingers is headed over to my house, will you join me?" Roc quickly mounted his horse. He bent over and took his sword from the gatekeeper and placed it back in the scabbard of the saddle. "It isn't far." Milo looked down to the gate keep. "Return to post. You've done well." The gate keep nodded to Milo and bowed to Roc before he trotted back to his gate. Milo started his horse to a light trot and Roc followed him. "What do you think?" Milo asked as Roc came abreast.

"I hate it." Roc answered.

Milo knew him well enough to know that meant he liked it. "I thought you had turned us down."

Roc looked at him curiously. "For what?"

Milo looked back at him confused at the Dragonslayer's questioning stare. "For statehood. Isn't that why you're here? We sent you several letters."

Roc looked ahead of him and squinted at the setting sun. "I've been away from my desk." He looked at the town for the first time in a lordly manner. It was clean, orderly, prosperous and populous. All of the characteristics of a good city. "I don't know if I like the idea." Roc said. "I've never had a state join voluntarily."

"Would you feel better if you sent a brigade to take it."

"But you wouldn't fight. What's the fun in that?"

Milo smiled and looked at the people who were lining the streets to watch them pass. "I came here after Hauth was defeated. There was a guild here, this entire city was governed by the hand of an assassin named Adjh. I defeated him and chased them out. Since then, I've been sort of a sheriff."

Roc made a face for no reason. "So why do you want to be a state?"

"Protection, there are many wandering tribes and hostiles. Also, the guild has reformed into a group called the purple horde. They raid through and I can't stop them. They also provoke what ever lurks out in the woods and mislead them here. I would not be surprised if that were the case with that ogre you slew."

"Raise an army."

"I'm not good at that. You are."

Roc rubbed his chin. "So the people were expecting me?"

"Aye, that they were. And you lived to every inch of their expectations. Even the giant running amuck. Your timing was perfect."

Or Okshiru's. Roc thought. "I don't know if I can take on such a project. Brewster is too far away. My home is still in disarray from Hauth. The castle destroyed and all."

"Dragonrealm fallen?" Milo was surprised at first but it melted from his face. "Oh, yes." Milo remembered. "You took the brunt of the attack."

Roc clearly remembered Hauth. It was a strange matter of how things happened. After Hauth was defeated, he used his last bit of power to restore most of what he destroyed. But the people who survived didn't remember or soon forgot. Even those who were there in the center of it all found themselves forgetting. A whole war! This had to be an act of Okshiru.

"Yes it was a great day when you and the Ninefingers destroyed Hauth." Milo went on.

Roc grimaced. Was this the distorted memories they held? Roc and Frito fighting for the will of Okshiru? He suddenly felt sick. In truth, Roc had laid beaten, and Frito...

"Will you not consider us?" Milo asked him.

Roc felt trapped. He really couldn't say no. "Tell them they are on trial. I want a tenth tithe each quarter." It sounded as if he had just leapt with both feet into Okshiru's plan. "I will decide this time next year. Until then, I will investigate this," He waved his hand regally at the nuisance, "purple horde thing."

Milo nodded with satisfaction.

Roc brooded at himself. Was he playing Okshiru's game or merely being paranoid thinking he was playing Okshiru's game. Would it be best just to ignore him? Remain blind to his machinations?

Damned if you do.

Damned if you don't.

Through another gate, Brewster finally petered out to the forests. On a smaller but heavily traveled side road, Milo turned and a little distance away sat his house. A small, but well built house of brick tucked away in a grove of evergreen trees. It was a simple dwelling in design and construction. One room for eating and sitting and the other for cooking with a loft for sleeping. A single chimney for heat. Roc grunted as he dismounted. He knew that Milo had given away his treasures, to live in the simple light of Okshiru. Roc personally had better beliefs. *Is it not better to take the gifts about you?* Frito was smart. He gave everything to his mother, but in solid things. The castle, servants, horses, land, things she couldn't give away on the streets. Being a knight herself, she would probably live like Milo if Frito would let her. But she lived with orphans and the poor within her walls. *Why? If things were reversed, would they take her in? No.*

Past the wooden door and into the main room, smells of fresh bread came to his nose and he filled his lungs with it. He had forgotten about the fair Lady Kaisu. She had to be the living incarnation of the word, wife. Her manner, cooking, and living were in complete devotion to her husband, his work, and his guests.

She quickly paid homage with a proper bow and a loaf of her baked bread in her arms. The second best thing in the world to give the Roc the Dragonslayer, was food. She set the bread on the table to cool and, without a word, she guided him to the wash basin in the corner of the room. With deft, nimble fingers she removed the Slayer's monstrous helm and mask and set them aside. His face was almost back to normal now so she was in no danger. She would not react to his power of fear anyway, for that would have been rude and unacceptable, unless of course, if Roc had wanted her to be frightened and then she could feign terror completely and convincingly.

She took off his gauntlets and set them with his helm. She was human, but she knew of the elven rituals of cleanliness before each meal. She took up a cloth with cleaning sand and washed Roc's hands and face. She dried him and then guided him to the table. Set before him in simple crockery was a steaming bowl of rice. Then fanning in a circle between the three men were small wooden bowls of uncooked and cooked fish, then steamed roots and starches—then an inner row, a block of cheese, whole bread, a chilled block of butter, and fresh garden vegetables (probably the last for the season). Set at the Slayer's left hand was a flagon of beer.

This was a meal! Dragonslayer held himself to only inhaling the aroma about him. The small primitive house began to melt away and the richness of a thousand kings came to mind. *What could be better than what Milo had? A warm house, good food and a loving wife is more than any one needs.* The simple things, Roc thought to himself. Strangely how he found himself missing the simple things of life. *Like, a home to come to, a loyal beast, quiet, warm nights, the last word at every conversation, ultimate revenge against all enemies, all the money in the world and its people groveling at my feet, painting the sky with a brush and chalk, shaping the face of Mortalroam like so much clay—the simple things.*

"You alright?" Frito said from his place across the table. "With you its hard to tell the difference between smiling and constipation."

Roc put his hand before his face and looked away. "And the boy?" He grunted.

"Out. Fast asleep."

"Is he alright?" Roc looked at him.

Frito nodded. "He needs rest." Frito rose to his feet as Kaisu, Milo's wife took her seat at his left. "This is a feast." Frito said as he resumed his seat. "It smells scrumptious." Kaisu smiled timidly and bowed her head. Milo clasped his hands and silently blessed the table. Roc sat quietly and waited for the word.

Frito nodded, and Roc took up the flagon of beer and gulped it empty. He wiped his mouth with the back of his hand and reached for the rice.

"This is quite a spread." Frito said taking up the tamake of rice. "I wasn't expecting…"

"No." Milo said with a wave. "Please, Frito, you honor my house. You are the Archknight and Roc is the Lord of Dragonrealm, the largest kingdom in the known universe. You do my house great honor."

Roc paused long enough to have his tamake filled with more rice.

"This is no trouble?" Frito asked.

"My lord, Kaisu is the Knight of Aldis, goddess of the home. You do her honor."

"Enough honor." Roc interrupted boisterously. "Eat already." He took up his flagon and bits of beer spilled. He looked to Kaisu. She had somehow filled it while he wasn't looking.

Frito took about him and ate without fetter. He drank beer and ate fish until he was quite stuffed.

Kaisu cleared the table quickly and Frito leaned back in his chair. "Oof" Was all he could say.

"Milo," Roc said as he lit his smoke. "You my friend, got it made."

Milo nodded watching as his wife disappeared into the kitchen. He then looked at the Slayer. "So if it wasn't my letters that brought you, how may I be of service?" Milo glanced over to Frito and then back to Roc.

Roc savored the taste of tobacco in his mouth before he let it out. "We search for a temple of Ura."

Milo waved it away quickly. "Burned. Destroyed years ago when they rose up."

"Anything left?"

"Not even ash."

"Could they have gone furtive?"

"They did and I found them up to their old tricks and drove them out along with the assassin Adjh.

Roc hissed. "How hard would it be to find them?"

"Hard!" Milo said turning to him. "I believe that Adjh is with The Purple horde now and keeps them moving. My only hope is that they will set in one place for Fikor's reign. I hope to find them then."

Frito looked rather distraught, before he looked up again. "Have you ever heard of the name, Paradox?"

Milo's dark eyes glared in fury at the name. "Have I!" The knight rose to his feet. "If I find him, I shall kill him outright!" The knight turned and spat into the fire.

"Paradox?" Roc grew with attention. For a knight to swear death on anyone was interesting. "Who is Paradox?"

Milo calmed himself and sat back down. "He is the Knight of Ura and a very sick individual. How came you by him?"

Frito seemed lost in thought as he tugged on his beard. He seemed to drift his attention back to Milo. "Orrin had a vision. The name came up." Frito sighed as he tried to think.

Roc leaned forward, letting out a stream of smoke as he did. "Getting back to Ura, when they went underground, where was that temple?"

Milo shook his head. "There is no one there."

"Where is it?"

Milo jerked his head back. "A little ways from here, about a days ride."

Frito seemed to drift further away in his thought. Suddenly the drift stopped and he looked at Roc understanding what his cousin was getting at. "Roc, get ready to roll." He looked at his brother knight. "Milo, where exactly is the meeting place?"

The knight spoke rising as the Archknight did. "What is it?"

"Past experience with Ura's temples."

"It is an old manner off the main road, I can lead." Milo followed him as Frito stepped over to the stairs, "I shall come with you."

Frito patted Milo on his good arm. "I want to carry this myself."

"As you wish my Lord."

"I ask a boon."

"Anything."

"Never," Roc cut in as he picked up his helmet. "ever, say: 'Anything.'"

Frito shot an off glance at Roc. "Take care of Orrin for a few days?"

"Certainly."

Frito turned and headed up the stairs. His eyes began to glow red in the low crouch of the loft. He bent and crawled over to Orrin's bed. He touched the boy lightly and he awoke. His eyes burned gold through tiny slits as he looked up. "Time to go?" His fists rubbed at his swollen eyes.

Frito rubbed the boy's belly. "Orrin," He said sternly. "I want you to stay with Milo."

Orrin's eyes opened wider as his face bent to argue. Frito's eyes of red hardened. "Do I as ask you." Frito relented. "Please, you need the rest."

Orrin felt his argument fading into the softness of his sheets. "But,"

"No." Frito said solidly. "I can't stop just yet. I'm too close. It's a day out, a day there, and a day back. I'll be here for you then. I want you to rest because I'll need you at full power when I return."

Orrin found himself fading into sleep. "What is it?"

"Things," Frito answered. "Like Hauge's soft winds warmed by Kemoto's heart. The shimmering skirt of Arua against Leatha's black sky. Ovam's white moon across Okshiru's great sea." Orrin was fast asleep.

Silent as an elf could crawl, Frito slipped out of the house and onto the road.

Chapter 38

Kemoto lit on the western edge of the world, dipping his wings beyond the hills. Leatha, wife of Great Okshiru, crept from out of the east slowly following Kemoto. Hauge stirred slightly, bringing Fikor's chill with him.

High in the watchtowers, the spyeye looked out over the land. He noted each of the woodsmen as they returned from the forests, dragging their loads behind them. He watched the ladies bringing home the sheep from the pastures, shooing them with the aid of Neigh hounds, stepping in and out of reality, their bark keeping the flock together. He watched the teacher bring her students from the school building, marching them in rows of two down the to the Manor. He signaled to the gateman with a flag and the doors were opened.

Kemoto's light faded from the face of the sundial. The spyeye lit his signal fire with a simple spark of flint. It was the night hours and times of challenging. The gatekeeper dropped down the great locks and lowered the steel cage over the door. Fires climbed the darkening sky as each of the watchtowers took to lighting their fires.

Jose Sungazer walked his final inspection as the watch commander, waddling over to the forward point. He climbed up to the lip of the wall and scanned the land before him. The brown, dried fields grew dark with night, as did the road and trees in the west. The great mountains beyond stood as they always did, holding up Okshiru's sky, the sentinels of the world. The mountains number eight and number seven cradled and held the last light of Kemoto as his flight came to end. Sungazer nodded in satisfaction. A quiet watch leading off to a quiet evening. He was a man of magic, not of war.

He climbed from the lip and looked up to the man standing before him. He bowed to Bloc, the Dragonguard. One of Dragonslayer's personal guard. Trained in all arts of warfare and glory. Loyal only to Roc the Dragonslayer and to his command. The gnome turned over the watch command to him as per orders and the Dragonguard nodded his head in reply. They turned to their lieutenants and bade each one to escort the relief to each post and relieve the watches.

Sungazer watched as each post was relieved. He wondered why the Roc ordered them to guard Fanrealm. Nothing ever happens here. Perhaps because it's such better housing for the men for the oncoming of Fikor's reign? The Manor was big enough to house them. Keeping watch would keep them from getting soft whiles a new castle was built for them.

He looked up at Bloc and went to ask him but then changed his mind and didn't bother. The Dragonguards were trained to only think in the absence of orders. His orders from Roc were to guard Fanrealm.

The post was relieved and the lieutenants marched the off going posts into the barracks. His job for the day was done. He bowed again to Bloc and headed in for the evening.

Chapter 39

Sharp bells tolled against the bruised and battered sky which echoed with flashes of heat lightning. The piercing ring sang to the black mountains. Dark clouds of Hate surrounded the world as flashes of anger tore the sky. Fury rumbled about the disk of the sky in discontent and growing impatience. The shadow of fear grew like a black flare from the center of the earth. It formed, and took shape, reaching out with ghostly wings. Its head peeled away from its chest, lifted and looked to the tormented sky. Its voice lashed thunder as spit bled from its mouth burning like lava. Trails of hot blood ran lines of fire across its black body.

Its eyes of glistening silver cut easily from its black head. Its polished steel teeth glinted as it smiled with malice.

The bell tolled louder. It's sound rippled through the great mountain sentinels that held the sky above. The shadow of fear roared the dragon's roar, a scream of death, colder than the ice of Fikor. The sky above and its ceiling of clouds began to fold and roll as he bade them to sweep across the sky. The cloud ceiling opened a ring in the sky and only a greater darkness spilled forth and rained down.

In the darkness, its true shape was seen, silhouetted black against black. Its head of might was a mace of war. Its body flexed beneath its armored scales of Iron. Arms of might held in prayer. Wings of flight closed about its body as if to guard itself.

The tolling bells shook the sky. The ringing song crept across the black earth, seeping into cracks with the touch of fear. Light was pushing its way from beneath it. Bars of white light pried its way from between its wings of metal darkness. It raised itself and spread its wings apart and the light poured forth like the torrential waves of Okshiru's sea. Light splashed like a flash flood, and the white river flooded into Cornerstone.

The light of darkness, the light of Hel, The light of Doom.

The bells tolled.

The soot flaked from its metal body. Ferris, the Iron Dragon laughed with freedom and Hel rode on his wings. He sat in the great smelting furnace from whence he had been born and glinted at the sound that echoed around him.

The bells tolled, hammers ringing, singing against an anvil. The forge flared as hot steel flowed. The hammers rang against the will of life as Karbon, the Steel dragon formed.

And Ferris spoke: "Hear the will of the Iron Dragon. I will suck the soul from your bones, Dragoncaller, and breathe life into my new brother, the Steel Dragon. Behold! I show you your Doom!" Ferris opened his wings and in the space was not the dragon's body, but the tunnels of Hel.

His eyes burned red into the dark room. Sweat dripped from his shivering limbs into the cold air. His heart quaked in his chest. His lips and mouth were dry. His ears rang with the tolling bell as the dream slowly drained out of his head.

He concentrated on the real about him. The oaken paneling and solid stone behind them. Cold walls, like the cold of his skin.

Onary sat beside him looking distraught, his dark eyes staring at him. Edia leapt up to the bed and looked at him. His elven vision could see the cat's green eyes in the dimness. Neeko's hand moved across his chest. He didn't react when she embraced him and held him close. She tried to will him to feel her and be comforted by her presence.

He was.

He slowly reached up and touched her silken hair. He lightly stroked her ears as he pulled the darkness about him as only night and nothing was in the dark.

Or so his parents had always told him.

Monsters don't live in Brooklyn his mother told him. There were no truth to the legends of the thunder bird—the Indian dragon. Craig didn't believe her and she smiled and sighed, "What are the odds," she then said, "of the monsters picking you out of the 300 million people in the United States?" That was something Craig could accept.

He was always comforted with that idea, but this wasn't Brooklyn, nor the United States and there was growing evidence that there was indeed something under the bed and the way his luck had been running recently, the odds were in his favor that it was his bed the monsters were under.

But there was the entire Dragonguard outside with walls, wizards, and war machines to defend the manor. Nothing could get in. So why was he so afraid?

He kissed Neeko on the top of her head. "I'm alright." He said in a voiceless whisper. "A bad dream." He had to remember to cool the glow from his eyes. It had no effect on his night vision but they glared when he was anxious and he had to control them. He wondered why elves could do such a thing. It only seemed to make others nervous.

He had slept all afternoon. He was nocturnal, so there should be no panic at waking up in the middle of the night. So why was he panicking?

Neeko pulled slowly from him. Her green cat eyes looked up to him and he looked away from them only to see Edia still on the bed. He hadn't told her to get off as was custom. She knew it was more than a bad dream. Her hand reached up and felt his chest. She then took the blanket from his hand and pulled it away. The Dragon tattoos on his forearms were swollen lines and the giant tattoo across his chest was throbbing from his heart pounding against his ribs.

He couldn't hide from her. She knew. She knew his fear. She knew his anger. She knew it all. It was a dream.

The kind that came true.

He didn't say a word as he swept from the bed. He stepped past Onary as he went to the tallboy. The cold air meant nothing to his elven flesh as he bent to the drawers and searched for his clothes.

There was a soft rap at the door. "Craig?" Came Lady Fantista's voice "Are you alright?"

Craig cut a glance to his wife. *'How could she know?'*. His wife's response was a slight shrug. "I'm fine." He lied. "A head call."

"A what?"

"Bathroom, latrine, out house, larry, john, cat hole." Both Neeko and Edia looked at him with suddenness. He glared at them with a look of *'Just an expression'*.

His elven ears listened but he couldn't hear her leave. He motioned and Onary crept to the door and sniffed. He nodded his head that she did leave. He continued getting dressed. He glanced out the window. Outside was only stars and the fires of each watch command. It was quiet outside.

The latch on the door slid and dropped.

Onary scampered from the door in a start. How could anyone sneak up on him? The bow of Dragoncaller instinctively flashed into Craig's hands with an arrow knocked at the ready.

"You always need your bow for the toilet?" Lady Fantista said. Her silver eyes scanned the room and then cooled to brown.

Her eyes of silver had cut through Craig and his lungs skipped their pace. Craig tried to cover, laughing breathlessly as the bow vanished from his hand. "I couldn't sleep," He lied almost choking. "You know how us Nih elves are, slaves to the night-life."

Fantista smiled warmly as the touched the lamp on the mantle and it lit in response. "You speak the truth." She looked at him. "But I would like all of it." Her face was softened by the gentle glow of the lamp. Her lips drew lightly to a smile.

There was nothing he could hide from her. Craig had so many secrets to keep, it was difficult for him to remember which were actually secrets and which were not. To be sure, he kept everything a secret. Neeko had gotten better at finding his secrets. Fantista could see though them. Craig heard of Okshiru's knights only through Onary. The dog spoke of them casually, save for lady Fantista who's name he whispered in only reverence. She was the Grandmaster of the Knights, she could not deceive nor could be deceived.

Craig's eyes adjusted as the room grew with the light of the lamp. He pulled on his gambeson to hide the tattoo across his chest. "It was a dream. The kind that comes true." Fantista bent and tossed several logs into the warm hearth. He could tell she was listening. "I'm not sure what was. I saw Ferris."

"The Iron Dragon?" Neeko whispered as she stepped beside him. She wrapped her arm about him and held him close.

Craig knew she was cold. She wasn't elf but Ne-arri, the cat people. The Manor was cold. He had devised a central heating system in the caves where he lived, but Fanrealm had no such luxury. He could only try to give her his elven warmth.

He looked back to Lady Fantista who stood before him. "I can't tell you what it was, I'm not sure myself. Its just this gut feeling. The more I think about it, the more I feel like something is going to go down tonight." Craig glanced at his watch. "This morning. Sunrise is in six hours. I can anticipate something in the pre-dawn hours. What ever happens will happen then."

"Then I shall defend my home and its people." Fantista swore easily.

Craig looked at her in amazement.

Fantista cocked an eyebrow. "I may be a grandmother, but I shall fight for my home!"

"I will fight by your side!" Neeko said sternly gripping his arm tighter.

Craig made his face and went to speak and stopped, then started again. "Look…" He said with an open hand as if to stop everything. "First thing. You!" He pointed to his wife. "Your job is this." He laid a hand on her belly. "You are to stay undercover." Then he turned to Lady Fantista. He quickly thought of every tactical and delicate way he could say 'stay out of the way'. She was a Knight and Knights could not think in troop leading modes. She would lead a reckless, suicide charge for right and let Okshiru sort the dead. That's how every knight Craig had met acted, to including Fryto who seemed to be the worst of all. Knights made rotten generals. Frito could think for himself. Perhaps the Archknight had that power. Could also the Grandmaster? *Best not to find out now.* "I need you to gather the people and bring them behind the main wall. Also bring the children to a safer place."

"Yes," She nodded, reading Craig like an open book and knowing his reasoning as best. She never had to lead troops in her youth. She didn't know now.

"Good!" Craig said thinking how simple that was. "Tell them it's a fire drill and they can go back to bed later." He glanced at his watch. "There isn't much time."

"Is it that bad?" Neeko's green eyes looked up to his. She was frightened. He had never seen her frightened like this before. For the first time in her life she was deeply afraid. She could always fight and defend herself but now with the baby, she had to depend of Craig. She trusted him, but still it was a new feeling.

He took her hand and brought it to his chest. She could feel the tattoos cooling. "I'm going to contact the Dragons. Give me a second." Craig said as he closed his eyes.

Lady Fantista nodded and left the room quietly to fulfill her task.

Craig relaxed his body and opened his mind. To link with dragons was a simple task in its own. The only difficulty was to wake them.

Breaker One Nine, breaker one nine, do you copy? Over.

There was static.

Hellooooo!

More static.

WAKE UP!

Yo! What? Was his answer.

Kugerand! Get to the flight deck and roll, who's with you?

Ralph here. Came an answer from Ralph.

'Ralph,' Craig ordered. *'I need you to stay behind and guard the house, you're the only one I trust.'* Actually, he was the only one wounded.

'Okey dokey.'

'Hey, like, man,' Kugerand asked. *'What's the story, Cory?'*

'I need you at Fanrealm, where is Brezhnev?'

'Bog, and no one is gonna wake him when he's like this.'

Craig knew when the big red slept, he slept. *'Then get Mojo, Boxy and Windshmere.'*

'They're, like, gonna be tweaked.'

'So sue me.' Craig shouted. *'You've got an hour.'*

'Plenty of time.' Was Kugerand's final reply.

'We'll see.' Craig cut off his signal. He turned to his wife who had gathered up a blanket and wrapped herself in it. She paused when she saw him staring at her so. "What is it?" She asked him.

"Do you hear that?" He said as his pointed ears bent slightly to listen more carefully.

"Hear what?" She asked as her ears rotated, trying to lock on to a sound.

Onary lifted his and dropped them again. "It could be an elfcall, only elves can hear it."

"Well," Craig said fastening the straps to his shin armor. "Isn't that good to know. It might as well be in Spanish. After seven years of Spanish one, all I can say is, Yo hablo." He started the second shin guard and stopped suddenly.

The itch in his arms started again. Like a quick ant scurrying on the inside of his skin where no scratch would reach. But it focused, concentrated ahead of him.

Twin silver eyes gleamed back from the darkness of the doorway at him. His own eyes flared red with surprise and his vision leapt passed the darkness and pushed back the shadow. "Stephanie," He said hiding the fear in his heart. "Come here."

Slowly she stepped out of the darkness. She rubbed her eyes and shuffled in her steps. Her fear of Nih elves had lifted. She knew to trust him. She padded over to him and reached for his outstretched hand.

Craig felt static electricity snap in his fingertips. His hand only jerked for an instant. The pain wasn't in his hands, but in his heart. He took her small hand in his and pulled her closer. He was reacting to her, the Dragoncall was thundering in his ears as the blood flushed in his face. What was this now? Why could he feel it?

He should talk to her, but his mouth was dry and lacking of words. What words could he say to her? "Couldn't sleep?" He said hoarsely. She nodded her head. "How come?"

She rubbed her eyes and yawned. Then she rubbed her eye again. "I can't find Lady Fantista." She yawned again.

The child had shared the Lady's bed and her absence must have frightened her. Craig looked up to Neeko. "Take her to the dining room and get ready for the rest of the kids to arrive." He looked back to Stephanie. "Lady Fantista is downstairs. Neeko will take you."

She nodded and took Neeko's hand. As Neeko passed out of the room, she turned and looked to her husband. Her eyes grew bent to tears as if she would never see him again. Craig smiled and hoped to wipe out her fears. He coaxed her on with a wave. "Everything will be fine, I'm probably overreacting." He assured her. She nodded, smiling weakly. He listened as the two headed down the hall with Edia.

"Edia!" Onary called to her. "Come here!"

The cat pushed her head back to the door. "Whut?"

"I need to talk to you." The dog said. He looked up at Craig who was taking up his chain mail. "What happened? Are you alright?"

Craig bent at the waist and slipped on the light chainmail shirt that Lord Arok had given him. "You saw it?." He stood up and let its weight pull down.

"No, but I guessed that something happened." The dog watched him carefully, looking for anything out of the ordinary. "Again, are you alright?"

"I hope. I still function."

Onary looked at the cat. "And what did you see?"

Craig looked at Edia who sat down looking rather concerned. "Ah couldn't say, suh." She looked up to Craig. "There was a bit of the magic about her. Ah saw it leap on to yew."

Craig looked at her. "What are you talking about?"

"Craig," Onary tried to explain. "cats can see the color of magic. They see its aura and can read it."

"You can?" Craig exclaimed. "Why didn't you say so?"

"Yew didn't ask, suh."

"They are nauseating like that." Onary coughed.

Craig tightened the belt that held on his thigh guards. "Then what did you see?"

The cat looked rather ashamed, curling and uncurling her tail. "Ah can't say, suh. It was nothing Ah have seen."

Craig knelt beside the cat. "Was it good, bad, radioactive, contagious, florescent, what?"

The cat tilted her head which was the feline equivalent to shrugging its shoulders.

"Your worth is dropping." Onary said sternly.

Craig pushed at the dogs snout to shut him up. "Edia, I want to know."

"But, suh," The cat denied. "Ah just don't know."

Craig tightened his lips as he looked about the room for an idea. And there was one.

He took up the cat in his arms and took her to the window. "Look at the sky, what do you see."

Edia pushed her nose to the window. "Stars...?"

Craig rolled his eyes and sighed. "Think: Cat Throw Rugs. Look again."

Edia hissed at the dog, then looked again. "Ah see the clouds of Okshiru, suh. There is also magic building up about the walls, suh. It is protective magic."

Craig looked out into the clear night sky. Swell, he whispered. Frito's patented magic barriers are kicking in. He set Edia back to the floor. "Find your Mistress and stay with her. Onary?"

"Yes!" The dog sat at attention wagging his tail.

"Stay with me, I'll need you." He didn't have to say that. There was nothing that Onary would have preferred. Beyond the fact that he could speak twelve languages fluently, read twenty and basically understand twenty five; beyond the fact that he was a grand master at chess, math and now thanks to Craig, quantum Physics, he was still a dog. He had a basic need to please.

Craig pulled on his breast plate. It had a strange way of fitting him well. He hadn't worn it in nearly a year but yet it felt comfortable, safer. It was not only an armor of extraordinary construction and metal, but there was the magic to be considered. A theme that he couldn't understand, or didn't want too.

He paused as he attached the arms to the shoulder guards. He looked at his right upper arm. He couldn't see any scratch or dent in the metal. Max had fixed that. There was no scar on his arm either, Neeko and Frito had fixed that with their touch of whatever voodoo they do. But still he felt the tinges of something as he flexed his arm. The thought of a sword edge biting into his arm and his arm hanging on by only a bloody bone came to his mind.

He flexed his arms again. He made it work and focused past the phantom pain. It felt good. He shook the feeling of the past off of his shoulders like so much dust. He took up his gauntlets and hung them from a hook on his belt. He took up his K-bar and stuffed that into its sheath and headed to the door. At the door, he snatched his dolman and tucked it under his arm and headed up to the watch with Onary in close pursuit.

Chapter 40

Clouds of bubbling purple and black stained the bleeding sky. Splashes of gold and fire outlined the levels of clouds looming above. Lightning flashed white hot like a crooked line in the crimson sky. A hot wind swept from the valley and stirred the dust from the ground. Billows of arid smoke choked the hot air as it rose and settled between puffs of Hauge's breath. Dust rested on the broken steps and tumbled columns. Dirt darkened the shattered walls and cracked brick. It covered the cobblestone walks only to have the winds of Hauge uncover them again. Steel posts stood rusting, swaying in the wind. Machines crushed beneath their own weight lay in distress about themselves.

Harroc walked calmly, assuredly, past the ruined buildings. He stepped over the broken glass and around the machines. He looked up at the trembling sky and knew Okshiru was indeed furious at something or someone. Either that, or he was getting creative. He did that at times in Hel. Red skies in Mortalroam would terrify men into doing the dumbest things. Okshiru usually held red skies and the such for special occasions on Mortalroam. But in Hel, it was just another day.

He walked up the cracked steps to the main doors. Columns still stood strong and loomed over his head as he passed them by. He followed the passage way through the high rubble and around its many bends. He weaved knowingly past the false turns and dead ends; following the maze plan to the letter. Glowing eyes, peering out from the cracks in the rubble, lit his way along. His path began to widen and as it did, light began to grow from a different source. He came to the clearing and paused. The rubble had been pushed away to form high walls in a circle around the pool. Light from the great pool beamed up beyond the roofless hall into the bleeding sky above.

Harroc, Son of Hate, folded his arms at the multiple elbows and stepped boldly to the edge of the pool set in the floor. He gazed for only a moment at its mirror reflection before he went to speak.

"May I help you?" Came a tiny voice from across the pool.

Harroc looked up slightly startled. He shielded the pools light from his eyes as he looked across. "Who are you?" He rumbled.

"I am Chritchfeild." Came the voice as it moved around the pool. "I am here to help you." The rabbit rose to his hind legs as he came within a man's length of the Son of Hate.

"I am not here to speak to you." The Son of Hate said impatiently.

"It's a new policy, The Eye is busy watching the world right know, so it sent me to answer your question."

"What nonsense is this?"

"The new S.O.P. Standard Operational Procedure."

"I will not speak to any rabbit." The Son of Hate growled as he looked again into the pool. "I, Harroc Son of Hate…" He began.

"You're wasting your time." Chritchfeild said sing-song, lowering to all fours. "I know that your destiny awaits at Fanrealm, a tic before dawn."

Harroc glared at the rabbit who was now cleaning himself. "I grow tired of you." He mumbled, "Perhaps, I will eat you." He said wagging a finger. "Prepare to be stew."

The rabbit paused. "Why, I'm not a stewing rabbit, I'm a fricasseeing rabbit. Besides, I'm just skin and bone," The rabbit looked up at the great demon with one eye. "I haven't been well lately. In fact, I've just been…dead."

Harroc folded his arms across his wide shiny black chest. Not long ago Thamrell had given him the power to enter Fanrealm. Was there a coincidence? "And how do you know my mission?"

If Chritchfeild had shoulders, he would have shrugged them. Instead, he only cocked his head. "The eye sees your mission, Achillia is at Fanrealm. That is what you seek, is it not?"

Harroc frowned before turning away and finding his way through the maze again. Chritchfeild listened until he could no longer hear the great demon before he moved a muscle. He then looked to the shining pool. "Oh eye of wonder, time and space, hear me Rasham, answer my question." The shimmering pool of light bubbled slightly and became smooth again. Its light flickered for a moment and became steady again.

Then it rose.

Smoothly, slowly, the great eye rose, round and white, its pink retina dangling beneath it, dripping steaming water back to the pool. It gazed about the room and up to the blood red sky before focusing down on Chritchfeild, the rabbit. "Oh Great eye," Chritchfeild began in a trembling rabbit voice, "I beseech of you and ask a question." The rabbit paused as he waited for some response. When he figured that there was none, he went on. "Oh great eye, I search for two knights of Okshiru, one, Daniel Hammerstrike, son of Lord Hammerstrike the Supergod. He is known as Friska the Wind, complemented to Hauge, god of winds." The rabbit paused, thinking of any more information that he could give to the eye. Details had to be specific or the eye would not respond. If there were two of the same, and the requester asked for only one, the eye would not answer.

Chritchfeild waited patiently. Watching the eye as it stared back at him. Chritchfeild had never done this before. Rabbits in nature were not ones to beseech and ask questions. What if the eye didn't recognize him? What if he asked wrong? What if the eye becomes angry and does something...hostile?

The pool began to flicker and Chritchfeild suddenly felt a warm breeze sweep from the water. His ever twitching noise smelled a human, no! An elf! And, a woman, a demon. He heard the crackling of a warm fire and the smell of burning wood. He smelled fresh dirt of a tunnel and the strong odor of fowl being roasted. He looked into the pool.

Friska slept in a restless sleep while a leather winged woman sat beside him, patting his head with a wet cloth.

The field shimmered and a great briar patch was shown to him. Chritchfeild knew the patch. There wasn't time. "Oh great eye," The rabbit looked up to the great eye still looking over him. "I look now for his only sister, Twin of the womb. She is Denice Hammerstrike, Daughter of Lord Hammerstrike, the Supergod. She is the Knight of Okshiru, given on to Fikor, the Snow Dog. She is known as Frita the Cold."

The sound of heavy steps came to his ears and he eagerly looked into the pool. The water shimmered and blurs slowly came into focus. He looked deeper into the picture as trees and a dirt road came to view.

But the foot steps were coming from elsewhere.

He looked up. Someone was coming from the maze! He turned and fled instinctively as rabbits do and dashed into a crack in the rubble. His shining eyes peered from beneath the crack.

A demon stepped from the rubble, a little smaller in size and girth than Harroc. His flesh was scaled as a lizard, and appeared wet at all times. His hands were large and black talons hung from each finger. His teeth jutted out of his bottom lip and pointed closely to each of his tiny blood red eyes. His tail switched back and forth as he stood at the pool's edge and addressed the eye. "I Thumber, Keeper of Nightmares and Beast Who Lives Under the Bed, beseech and..." Thumber suddenly noticed and glanced down into the pool. "What service!" He said as he looked into the water. "There you are Frita, heading to the house by the water's edge. Hah! This is too good! She returns to the house of Ura! I've got you right where I want you." He reached down to the water and lightly touched the water's surface.

A wailing shriek tore though the building. Chritchfeild laid back his ears and squinted. Thumber put his large hands to his ear holes. The eye lifted about a breath before plunging back quickly into the pool without another sound or splash.

"Hmmm." The demon piqued. He rose from his haunches and walked to the maze. Chritchfeild listened until he was gone from hearing. He crept slowly from his hole and tipped quietly to the pool's edge. It was a shining opaque, almost like Harroc's hide. Chritchfeild wondered if it would be best to ask, but the eye might be angry. He looked up to the ceilingless roof above him and noticed the sky changed to white as if its fire was snuffed suddenly with a puff of Hauge's breath. What could that mean? Did it have a meaning? Chritchfeild shook his head and headed for the maze.

Chapter 41

The wind blew from the west in a steady stream. It was caught and tangled in the golden hair of the watch fires. From the east, the horizon grumbled with distant thunder. The sky was clear and the stars above were very bright. The belt of the Milky Way could be seen curved along the crest of the world with a speckled stripe of silver.

The guard at each watch fire stood close by the flame to gather it's heat. The spyeye's glowing green eyes cast down from the high tower searching the land and forest below, watching the cobblestone road and the rolling field of crest grass that spread out from the Manor. It's eye projected out over the small river off the east wall and to the other side. All seemed quiet.

Craig watched the flicker of sheet lightning and counted the seconds before he heard the thunder. He glanced at his watch. He had listened to the storm for the last twenty minutes, it hadn't moved. Storms don't stand still.

He frowned. Things were coming to play.

He looked at the walls. Along the cat walks, all of the Dragonguard sat below the top of the walls. From anyone coming from a distance, they would only see the watch fires and a few guards—business as usual. Craig caught a glimpse of Onary as the dog popped in and out of reality as he carried messages between each watch command. He suddenly appeared at Craig's side. "Gorn is at the ready, all the men are in place. Sungazer wants to know what to expect and the spyeye wants to know what he is looking for." The dog wagged his tail for a reply.

Craig leaned forward on the wall. He stroked his beard as his red eyes cast out to the road. "I don't know." He said quietly.

Onary tilted his head. "That is what I had told them."

Craig nodded. "That's good." He looked up to the sky. "I had to send the dragons back. There is a freak jet-stream in the atmosphere. The dragons can't keep a holding pattern with it there."

"Will that be a serious factor?"

Craig shook his head. "I hope not. I felt better with them up there." He looked down to the dog. "What of Lady Fantista?"

"She's held up in the main room." Onary answered. "The children are quiet and have gone back to sleep." Onary paused and looked about before looking back. "Neeko sends her love. She wants to be at your side."

"I know." Craig said to no one in particular. "As do I."

"That is what I told her." Onary answered.

Craig smiled and looked again out to the black field before him. Silvery branches glistened with moisture like the Milky Way above him. Shadows stretched from the tree lines like rows of men drifting silently along the road. Craig looked to the spyeye above and to the men around the castle walls. They were cold. He could see his own breath before it was snatched by the wind. He looked to Onary, sitting at his side, peering diligently through an arrow slit for any signs that he could perceive. The dog was shivering. He too was cold. Craig knew the temperature was well below freezing. But he was an elf now. Elves didn't feel the cold, or know the dark, or need to stand by fires.

The fires were out.

Craig looked about suddenly. The fires were out. His night vision didn't notice the lack of light, but shadows by the trees? He looked above to the clear star sky. Craig calculated the lunar pass for this time of year. The moon would have set at about 10:00pm. It did.

He looked about at the men, they hadn't seemed to notice the lack of light. In such cold, they would have known. Onary would have known.

Onary?

Craig dropped suddenly to his knees and gripped the dog's collar roughly and shook him. "Onary?" He felt the ice form in the pit of his stomach as the twitch trembled in his arms. He didn't need any cat to tell him it was magic. Magic of stillness, of quiet. A spell of silence. The kind that needed a handsome prince and a sleeping beauty. But Craig was no prince. He cursed any god that might have been standing about and summoned his bow.

It was there as if it were all the time, gripped firmly in his left hand. The string touched to the three fingers of his right hand with an arrow touched between the tips. He gave a last look at Onary, still watching through the arrow slit. The three gems of power inlaid in his bow began their glow. Like the light of the moon they burned with the ice of winter.

Craig knew his bow. It was part of him, part of his soul. Its power came from his will, his compassion, his anger. He didn't need to believe in its magic, it only had to believe in him. It did as he wanted, regardless of whether he knew it or not. But this time he knew what he wanted.

What is so fragile that it can be broken with a single sound?

The wheels of his compound bow silently rotated as he drew the string to his cheek. His pointing finger touched to his lip and he was ready. He aimed below to the horses sheds, to its empty rain barrels.

The bow sang its single note, loud and low and it trembled the still air. Its black arrow streaked the silver hair of the quiet air and hit its target.

Craig wanted sound.

The arrow exploded in a flash of white snow glowing in florescent light. It's blow shattered the barrels with the boom of car backfire. The horses cried and pranced in their stables. Lamps took to their glow as the fire burned into the black night to warm the men standing about them.

"So how much longer?" Onary looked at him seeing the bow. "What are you doing?"

Craig didn't answer, he took up his lantern, opened its shield, waved to the spyeye, and then set it roughly by his feet. He watched the spyeye's light wave and listened to the men shuffle to readiness. Crossbows were cocked, catapults were set, ballistas were readied. Craig leapt up to the wall and walked along its lip. He glared with his glowing eyes of blood down at the men. It frightened them. Humans and elves had a natural fear of the Nih elves. It was inbred. Craig wanted them frightened. He knew the cold had stiffened them, stolen their light. He wanted fear to warm them, to pump their hearts.

He looked at one of the bowmen. He didn't know his name, but knew he was no older than one of his sophomore students back in high school. It very well could be his first fight. Craig watched him as he fumbled with the bow and dropped his shaft. His squad leader hissed at him and he dropped it again.

It was senses beyond the touch of sight—the boy knew he was being watched. He looked to the wall and two orbs of red set in a shadow beamed back at him. Craig could conceal his eyes, stop the glow with only a bit of concentration. But he didn't want to hide them. "Fear will kill you." Craig hissed harshly. "Fear will destroy you before the battle begins." He set his crimson gaze along the wall at the bowmen. "You cannot avoid your fear, only a fool will try." He set his stare to the sodermen with their pots of molten tar. "You must use your fear as power and use that power as your strength." He looked at the young archer. "It will carry you if you let it, but you must guide it." Craig's bow of Dragoncall appeared in his hand. "You've done this a million times before, this is no different." He pointed to the shaft on the floor. "Pick it up." He ordered.

Slowly, the boy bent and took it up. Craig looked all along the wall. "Nock arrows. Lock on all stations and stand by." He looked to everyone along the wall. "Dragonslayer sent us here, he knew that this would happen. He also knows that he doesn't have to be here to see his wishes done. When he arrives, we WILL, set a victory at his feet." He again looked all along the walls. "You will give it to him." He stopped at the young bowman. "You will give it to him."

Craig turned his back and looked out over the land before him. He wasn't one for leading troops. All the tactical defenses he knew was from what he didn't sleep through in history 101. He also wasn't good at motivating troops. Rousing cheers would be inappropriate at this time. It wasn't part of the plan. In fact, everything he had said, was mostly word for word from his high school swim coach.

"The bridge?"

"Dropped, as per your orders." Came Onary's voice from below the wall.

"Pull back non-essentials to the second wall and seal the tunnels. He will be here in a few moments."

"Who?"

Craig didn't answer. "Civilians?"

"The bulk of them had been moved behind the second wall when Frito locked down Fanrealm. As per your orders, they are being moved into the sub caverns and the rest are being moved now."

Craig took up his spy glass and peered out over the valley. It was three quarters of a click to the first wall and it was a bare line in the distance. His elvish sight peered through and he watched as the last of the night shadows suddenly bled into the river.

"First line!" Craig shouted over his shoulder to the signalman. "Weapons free!"

Craig watched through the spy glass as fire, arched like a red thread thrown with a rock, lifted from the first wall and beyond. Then the river rose in a sheet of flame.

And along the wall where Craig stood, the men began to cheer.

Craig lowered the spy glass. "Onary?" A line of light rose in the darkness. "Tell Fantista that we have guests."

Fire works exploded along the first wall, illuminating targets for the ballistas to launch their shafts. Craig could see lines of fire from shafts coated with napalm, zooming out like tracer rounds. There were screeching missiles, their only evidence were tails of white light.

"Sir!" An elf called from bellow the Dragoncaller. "Elfcall! The front line says its demons!"

Craig glared at him. Demons! He looked back out over the valley. He had damned the river and flooded it with napalm, an ecological nightmare, with hopes of making soup out of the enemy's front line. "Any effect at all?"

The boy seemed to listen and then reported. "They are climbing up the shore in flames and climbing up the first walls. Some are dying—roasted." The man smiled, still trying to hold his discipline.

It wasn't the fire, but the heat from the napalm. A new concept for fireproof demons. "Good. Get that first wall clear, full evac. Don't waste time. Inform the Second wall not to spare any of their toys and to get all their extra shit into the tunnels. Begin draw down for immediate retreat."

The boy nodded in surprise, but put his hands to his lips and blew an elf call.

Craig looked along to the wall to the main force. They were glaring, peering over the wall to see out in the distance. The light show was spectacular. Craig looked out as bits of light lifted into the air. He hissed as he wondered if some of the demons were flying.

"Second wall, light the sky torches and use archers to take out flyers. Inform every one else on the second wall to wait for them to attempt to cross the first and nail them there. Tie them up there." Craig spoke and the elf by him sent the call. *Hold them off for first light so we can see what is going on!* Craig ground his fist into his palm as he tapped into his own call. *'Kuger, you there?'*

'Yeah, like, I'm chillin. Wind is hellatious, the young guns had to cut out. I got them on, you know, remote.'

'I know. I want you to stand by.'

'Drop a clue when you're ready.'

Craig opened his eyes as the front wall lit up with white phosphorescence and heavy smoke grew from the line. A delaying tactic. The second wall suddenly pushed beams of light into the sky.

Smoke rolled thickly, tangibly down the gentle slope and into the river. The enemy was effectively blinded.

"Craig!" Gorn called as he moved along the wall. "You called the evac? Then you heard?"

Craig nodded. "Demons. The little flying buggers can get behind the wall and possibly find the tunnels and cut them off. We have a better chance to take them here."

Gorn nodded quickly in agreement. "They have little equipment. Nothing to smash with, but they have cut trees from the forests to climb the walls. This is the best place to take them."

Craig shook his head. "The flyers will not leave the main battle group. Demons have no command and control. They must stay close to their leader or they break up. I want to wear them out at the first wall and then get them across the field."

Gorn looked at him, almost smiling. "You are planning something."

Craig looked down and caught the archer's face as a sky torch quickly splashed across him. He was loving this. It was his job. War. Anything else was just space filler waiting for war. Like a sleep walker, wandering through motions of life. He was awake now, alive.

"How are the men?"

"Frightened. They don't like demons."

"They should be used to them now."

"What?"

Craig looked at him. "I mean every time I turn around, there are demons on my fucking door step."

Gorn's eyes cocked in surprise and Craig glared at him. The archer had no idea of what Craig was talking about.

"My lord." The elf called, distracting him. "The second wall claims that the first gates are down!"

"Magic!" Gorn hissed, but Craig was ready for that. He pointed to the sparklight by him. The sparklight signaled the catapults and they lit their balls of turkish tar. Craig nodded and ten flaming balls launched into the air.

"The demons are moving quickly. We'll have to pull back soon."

"We have a little time." Craig watched as the balls impacted, exploding into shards of steaming fire, forming for a moment of blazing spiders. "Jose put some shit on the second gates. Their spell casters are gonna get fried if they attempt them." Craig looked back to the archer who watched the fires below. He couldn't wait to get into the fray. He had wanted to lead the first wall but Craig needed him to control the men and organize the Great Wall. Craig wasn't really military. His four years in the Marine Corps was spent behind an accountant's calculator. He knew nothing of war or battles. Roc said that's why he was such a great general.

"The second wall reports activity at the gates." The elf sounded. "They also report heavy masses."

"How long can they hold?"

The elf shook his head. "Not long."

Craig watched as a second volley of tar went down range. He looked to the eastern sky. The sun was taking its dear sweet time. "Tell them to hold a bit longer."

"I've lost my contact!" The elf suddenly panicked as he tried to listen.

Calmly and clearly Craig ordered: "Stand by to evac second wall." Craig clenched his teeth as the signalman waved his torch and his elf sent his call. "Have you another contact yet?"

"Yes! They are being over run!"

"Evacuate!" Craig waved at his sparkman and four ballistas launched fiery missiles that wavered and weaved down into the fray and exploded with white phosphorous and smoke against the first wall. "Main batteries, give 'em some shit!" Catapults shuddered as stones launched into the air. Craig watched the sky as the main wall lit with sky torches. Flyers were coming, silhouetted as the second wall burned with stinging smoke and white fire to hold back the wave of demons.

Craig launched an arrow and Gorn marveled at his distance and accuracy. "Who the hell did we piss of?" Craig asked no one in particular as he launched another arrow.

"Craig!" Onary shouted. "Come down from the wall!"

Craig looked down and them realized that the flyers were coming closer and jumped down. "We are about to lose the city."

"Let us hope that we can hold them here before they get to the homes." Onary looked up sniffing. "The vapors are horrible."

Craig could also smell the flesh of burning demons. "Hey!" He called to the elf by him. "Are we having any affect on them at all?" Craig felt a bit embarrassed not knowing the man's name.

The elf nodded. "Reports are that we have inflicted casualties. But they have a nearly uncountable number."

Craig looked to Gorn. "How the hell did they get an army that big, this fast?"

"They are demons. Magic!"

"Then why didn't they just appear in the back yard instead of the front gate?" Craig scowled. "Or maybe he wanted to go through the hard way?" *Like someone else I know.* "Fuck!" He cursed and launched another shaft and took out another flyer moving dangerously close. "Well Gorn, get ready here they come. Onary! Get below!"

"Right!" The dog answered but didn't move.

"The first of the evacs are coming through. They say we have taken some casualties, fifty or so but that number is inaccurate." Now that Craig was standing on the catwalk beside his communications elf, he was surprised to see he was that tall. From behind him, a human pushed through, from the smell, Craig could tell he was from the front line.

"Let me have it!"

He bowed, trying to catch his breath. "They are coming in a narrow front line." Some one pushed a boda to his lips and he drank quickly, choked and spat it all over Craig's chest. Craig gripped the man, holding him on his feet. The man gasped and Craig took the boda and put it to his lips again.

"A small swallow," Craig coached. "its Slivobitsa."

He rolled it about in mouth, letting it mix with blood before swallowing. He felt it numb all the way down. "We fought very little. They can climb the walls! They over ran us so quickly." He gasped again, and Craig could smell the Slivobitsa on his breath. "We tried to hold, but they care little for their losses. They stack their bodies and climb on them!"

Craig had heard all this before, from a different war. He leapt up on to the wall and walked the line. "Listen up!" He shouted. "They are coming here and they are going to try to overwhelm us. We won't let them! Your swords are good steel and that will kill them! You have to beat on them, but they do die! You must unleash with all of your might! Once we break their initial tide, then we will destroy them at our leisure!"

From below him, a pair of eyes glowered before him, peering over the wall. Craig looked over his shoulder and saw a flyer, crossed in two of the sky torch beams. Craig pivoted, drawing even before the bow of Dragons flashed in his hands, an arrow nocked and ready. He launched it and it flew, unerringly, striking its target with such force that it pushed its flat, horrible face into its thick, fleshy neck. They could hear the sound. It dropped out of the light of the sky torches. Craig turned back to the wall. "JUST LIKE THAT!"

Craig looked out into the darkness, the fires from the second wall blazed and he could see the shadows pushing through. Demons were dying from the heat of the flames and themselves being unburnable, made a path through the fire for others to follow. *Swell.* Craig looked to the sky. The sun was still nowhere to be found. Craig squinted, as the smoke from the defenses swept towards him. He looked at his watch. There was something wrong with the sun.

No! He hissed. *No one is that powerful to alter the sun! Bullshit! I won't believe that!* Craig almost hollered but didn't. He blinked at the eastern sky and remembered what Edia said: Clouds. The bastards put up clouds to block the sun, to delay the sunrise as long as he could. Demons didn't like the sun. *Good.*

"Listen boys, they are trying to pull the wool over our eyes. They are trying to block the sun with magic smoke, it will work for a few minutes, but not long. You have got to hold them! There is nowhere to go from here!"

Craig turned and looked out over the sloping hill. Fires began to appear in the city. Business were going up in flames. In the streets, Craig could see them running, losing their command and control, forgetting what they were supposed to be doing. Looking for loot. *Good.*

Craig bent back his bow and launched. He nailed a large distant shadow and it turned, as if to see where the shaft came from, as he died. "Fuck you!" Craig screamed and turned toward the troops watching him. "We are going to fuck 'em, right? You boys gonna fuck 'em up for me? Would you do that?" They cheered and shouted and banged their shields and clattered their swords and beat each other's helmets and in their own way said yes.

Craig nodded. *Very male, even for the females. Good. Cause here they come.*

He leapt from the wall and went back to his command position where Gorn had been giving orders in his place. Craig clamped a hand on the man's shoulder. "Anything?"

"Their leader is a giant demon. His flesh is black polished leather and he has double bending arms."

"Harroc!" Onary shouted. "The Son of Hate!"

Craig looked out over the wall as if he thought he could see him. He couldn't. "Onary? If he is selling anything, tell him we are convinced and will take a dozen."

"I am under the impression that he isn't selling anything."

"No? Well, shit? What did we do to him? Cross him off the Christmas list!"

Onary tilted his head. "He is not on the list."

"Well, put him on and then scratch his ass off!" Craig leaned over the wall and peered down into the large moat before the walls. He could smell the fumes from the chemicals. *Swim that!* He challenged.

A ballista launched out into the town at some target and Gorn shouted to hold fire.

"What are they shooting at?" Craig asked Onary as he moved forward. They were shouts coming from the main gate forward towers. The demons were massing at the city walls, the last line between the city and the glen that stood before the moat and walls themselves.

Someone was walking down the road.

Craig leapt to the wall again. In the dim morning light, he knew very well it was Harroc, the Son of Hate. "Harroc!" Craig called. "Over here!"

The demon waved. "A pleasure meeting you." The demon bowed with respect. "You have me at a disadvantage. You are…"

"Craig Tyrone."

"Hello, Craig."

"Is there something I can do for you?"

"As a matter of fact, there is something I can do for you."

"Let me guess, insurance. That or home improvement loans. One of the two."

Slowly, all about, things began to grow quiet as the demons found themselves order against the low wall. Behind Craig, the troops along the wall stared silently through arrow slits.

The demon chuckled. "No, nothing of the sort. I can save you a lot of trouble." The demon looked behind him at the burning city. "And real estate." He smiled toothlessly. "Inform Achillia that I am here for her. I have no quarrel with you. Just turn over the Knight of Uko and we will leave."

Craig looked at him in surprise. "She isn't here." He looked about. "Shit, she hasn't been here in nearly a year."

The demon laughed. "I can appreciate your honor sir, but you waste it on a knight. She wouldn't dare think of letting another person die in her name."

Suddenly a figure launched from behind the city wall. A mortal body, elf or human, wriggling and moving, bound in the Dragonslayer's banner impacted against the main wall with a painful crash of bones and slid into the moat which suddenly foamed, hissed and bubbled.

The demon seemed to clench. "Ooooh, you should have that cleaned."

Craig clenched his teeth. This was no longer funny. "You asshole! You shit! I told you she isn't here!"

The demon went unheard as he called into the tower. "Achillia! Come out, come out, where ever you are! Come on out and save Fanrealm. You and I!" He struck a boxers pose. "Fair fight."

"Hey!" Craig shouted. "You piece of shit! I am telling you she isn't here!" The bow flashed in his hand.

"At ease, peon." The demon leveled at him. "I know she is behind these walls. Give her over or I launch another!"

From below the wall Gorn whispered. "No my lord. Those men are as good as dead."

Craig reeled. "She isn't here! I swear to God she isn't here!"

The demon crossed his arms several times. "Prove it. Have you a knight who will swear to it?"

Craig looked down. "No, we don't. You will have to take my word for it. You made a mistake."

"I have made no mistake. For the speaker of the Eye has told me she is here. You have already lied. You say you have no knight, but I say you do!"

Onary put his front paws up to the wall. "Craig! He means Fantista. The two go way back and rumor control says it's a rather nasty affair. He will kill her on the spot."

Craig took a breath and then stopped. Then started again. "Are you a coward? Harroc?"

At the walls, oaths and swears hissed quickly at the shear audacity to ask such a question. On the other side, the demons glowered and snickered at Harroc.

Harroc was speechless.

"I asked you a fucking question. Do you have any fucking balls?"

Harroc's eyes drew into angry slits. "How dare you!"

"Why are you going after women and old ladies? Why not me? I'm right here."

Harroc's jaw dropped and shifted. "You shalt burn with a fire hotter than…"

"Yeah, fucking yeah!" Craig cut him off. "And may the lizards grow healthy sucking the fat from my bones. I am finding it increasingly difficult to appreciate your unique brand of negative attitude, asshole. Answer the fucking question! Have you any fucking balls? Anywhere?"

Harroc's hand shot out and lighting licked from off of his finger and lit the Dragoncaller in blue fire. For an instant, the men along the wall could see his bones.

Craig heard the sound first. Squealing tires and a sudden, expensive car wreck. He felt the pain next. White hot, flash bulbs of pain pushing in a million needles like shards in an ice cube. Craig felt the bow of Dragons slip from his numb hands.

The bow clattered and skittered along the wall in the sudden silence as it fell towards the moat. It flashed out of existence a hair before the fetid water.

Craig knelt on the wall in a little ball. He felt the static clear from his head and eyes. He looked around without moving his head. The men were watching him. *Good.* They would want to see this.

Craig rose, shaking his head. "Not good enough, Harroc. In fact," Craig brushed invisible dust from his armor. "pretty amateurish. I made brighter fireworks with my Mr Chemo, pre-adolescent chem set."

Harroc was truly shaken. The blast should have sent Craig into painful, flaming balls of nothingness, but it barely fazed him. Harroc looked at his finger, then aimed in again.

Craig wasn't about to risk his immunity to magic again—the first hurt too much. He drew, the bow flashing in his stance and with little thought, released.

The shaft streaked down, its black tail could be seen in the dismal light of the morning. Instantly it split Harroc's outstretched finger, pushing its head into the deep of his forearm. Harroc screamed in agony as a thousand demons rushed the walls. They swept from the darkness and dropped from the sky. Demons and monsters crawled the ground and like giant ants scaled the walls. They hovered the sky like dark shadows, dropping and soaring with flames clinging to the spit foaming at their mouths. Big monsters, small monsters, some dragging their hands on the ground as they walked, others, sliding across on their bellies, some slithered through the air with out wings and others flapped their flightless wings as they ran.

Craig went to fire again but a flyer crossed his path and caught the shaft with his ribs. Craig hissed and leapt behind the wall as ballistas filled the sky with arrows at Gorn's command, while the crossbows waited for the demons to gain range. Craig fired again and again at Harroc but the black demon was moving too quickly and other demons leapt to intercept the arrows with their bodies.

There were too many, too sudden. These were beasts unlike anything he could have imagined. He looked about at the things swarming about the walls. This was too much. He wasn't afraid for himself, but his men. He watched as the demons were leaping across the moat, membranous skin between their arms and legs let them glide across to the wall. They climbed quickly only to be foiled by hot tar.

Giant wings of leather zoomed suddenly at him glancing at his face. Craig fell back from the wall onto the lip with a clang of his armor. The beast swept down at him. Craig couldn't really see it, all he could see were teeth and wings. More teeth than wings.

It spun aside and fell over the wall, an arrow buried in its ribs. Craig looked up and saw Gorn waving at him, giving the hand sign of Hammerstrike. Craig waved it back.

He fought to his feet. "Mr Spock, set phasers to well done!" He shouted to anyone. "I've not yet begun to fight." He leapt to the wall. He feared high school delinquents. He forced them to learn Quantum physics, the last thing they would ever need to know for the beach. He mastered them and took the highest grade average for any science major out of the five boroughs of New York. He conquered that fear, so why worry about vicious slobbering flaming, ravenous, rabid pit bulls from hell? There really wasn't much difference.

He dashed boldly along the wall again and took things from the sky with his great bow. He knew that his dashing moves were reckless, but he could think of no other way to motivate his troops and to break the myth of demon indestructibility. If the men knew they could kill the demons, they would fight hard. If they thought otherwise, they would run. He glanced down at the flaming tar dropping down the wall. He saw Shaft, the Dragonguard, on the other side of the sodermen guiding her archers to concentrate their efforts on the battering ram team below.

Craig looked at the giant machines rolling towards the Manor. He hissed at himself. *Where the hell could these things be coming from?* He answered his own question. He bent back his bow and let go its shaft deep into the on rushing army below. This was bad.

Jose Sungazer let loose his magical balls of fire down into the hoard. Rockets launched on the battering ram crew and set it ablaze. Their war machines were useless, as the missiles blasted them to splinters. Napalm hurt the demons as did the flaming tar. The steel in their arrow heads and spears stopped them as well. Craig's magical bow killed them out right. He looked to the far side to a fluid pouring down the wall, splashing in to the moat and someone beside that team waving at him. Craig dropped below the wall and took up his Dragoncall.

'Kuger? Make with the Arclight, and don't toast me.'

'Roger doger.'

The great dragons couldn't fly because of the upper jet stream, but the golden dragon was wingless and didn't need the air to fly. He wormed the sky and mastered Hauge's wicked winds. He glided in and followed the Dragoncaller's signal like a bloodhound on a trail. He bent his nose and aimed straight down. He opened his side gills and felt his lungs ignite and roar with power. He felt warm and smiled to himself as fire streamed from the corners of his mouth.

He plummeted with full force towards the quickening earth. To his right was the last moments of Leatha's night and to his left was the opening shimmers of Kemoto's morning pushing through the clouds. Directly below him was Fanrealm. His target. He lifted his nose and took out some distance, then bent back in, at an angle to where he was gliding almost on his back. The Manor loomed upside down before him.

"HIT THE DECK!" Craig screamed as he saw the fireball of gold streaking down from the dark blue sky upside down.

Dragon's flame erupted in a tidal wall as it splashed against the walls of the Manor. Dragon's fire turned Fikor's cold to Kemoto's sun. Dragon's fire burned back the tide of demon spawn.

The world turned white and the men turned from the heart of the sun. They felt the heat flash against their exposed skin. They felt the buffeting force even through the thick, stone walls. The pressure welled into their ears.

Craig felt the sucking wind as the furious dragon fire subsided. The wind blew by with a hissing whisper as the stink of brimstone was carried away with it. Craig paused, breathing shallowly in the foul air. He scanned all along the line of the wall. There was sudden silence.

The men where afraid to move. They had fought demons from hell before, why on earth were they acting as if they never had? He leapt to the wall and shouted in the air. "I meant, BUDLIGHT!" Heat from the dragon fire came up through his boots. He quickly started to move along the wall trying to play off his hotfoot. "Step up and lock on, they'll be at it again in no time. We have broken their initial assault. Now we hold them and let them die here at the wall! Oh, and watch the wall, it's a little warm." He turned to Gorn. "Stand by!" He shouted. He signaled to Jose and Shaft. They responded.

The men could see their leader preparing to fight and they in turn fell back into their warriors stance. Good. "Hey, Harroc!" Craig screamed below at the rows of burning demons. "I forgot to tell you, These are Dragonslayer's men and we all know that Roc doesn't take **anything** for an answer!" The men were rising quickly, taking to their feet and rearming their weapons. Craig turned to them. "Are you with me?"

A cross bow saluted him. "Aye! I am!" He looked as if he nailed a demon and wanted another. The others began standing in readiness. Craig was on the wall again, seemingly indestructible. The myth of demons was wearing off. They could be killed and they now knew it.

Craig looked along the line. "Then stand ready and we shall see if they are stupid enough to take us on again! FOR THE SLAYER!"

Craig whirled about and shouted below. "Well Harroc, where are your balls? We have yet to see them!" *Where are you now?* Craig scanned the blackened field. Like statues of charcoal, a hundred demons posed across the lawn like a haunting, outdoor horror museum.

As if given a silent signal, more demons suddenly leapt the city wall and inwardly Craig moaned at their number. The shouts of the watch commander's and the squad leaders rose to the air. Catapults launched their fiery balls of Napalm and phosphorous. The ballistas fired their giant spears. The demons kept charging, again leaping the now burning moat and climbing the walls. Crossbows fired at point blank range and they kept coming.

It pranced up the wall on it's short legs. Its gleaming yellow eyes fixed themselves on the lip of the wall, but at Craig specifically. Its tiny wings fluttered as it dodged the tar, and danced through the rain of arrows. It leapt to the top of the wall and smiled as only a demon could.

"Beware!" A swordsman cried and leapt in front of Craig and was quickly burned by the demon's fire.

It bounced too quickly at Craig. Its heavy claws tried to dig into Craig's armor as its weight and momentum took him down from the wall. Craig didn't have to look, he knew the walls were 20 meters in height from the inside. He could calculate that at 12 meters per second acceleration he as going to hit the hard ground with enough force to at least break his neck.

But Craig thought faster as he gripped at the demon's thick fur and held on. It writhed and twisted and clawed and its tiny wings flapped with fury trying to stay aloft and the two hit the ground with a hard thud that rang Craig's dolman.

It quickly pounced at Craig. The high school teacher quickly forced his Bow of Dragons into the demon's throat, but it did little good. The demon's weight pushed down on him. Craig's eyes burned red as he stared past the rows of bleeding teeth, and down the black tunnel of the demon's throat that seemed to go straight to its ass.

"My Master will devour you himself!" As it spoke, the monster's eyes filled with yellow custard and dripped with poison down its cheeks. "But I leave you with this!" The demon opened his great maw and put out his long forked tongue like a black snake slithering over its rows of teeth and through the grill of Craig's helmet. Craig twisted but the demon held him fast. Black acid slid down he demon's tongue and dribbled on Craig's face like burning tears.

He didn't scream, he wouldn't.

The demon's paws grabbed him and slid him along the ground and with little effort smashed the Dragoncaller against the wall and left him there.

Craig rolled quickly to his feet tearing his gauntlets from his hands and wiping the caustic fluid from his face. He felt his skin tear and rip as his flesh melted. His eyes were blurry as the pain tore his sight. He could see the demon running towards the houses on its six, short legs. He felt the acid on his bare hands as he ran at the beast. He leapt and dropped on it and grappled with its flapping wings. Tiny quills on the demon's back cut into Craig's exposed hands but his fingers dug deep into it's fur as he ripped and pulled at it. It screamed as Craig lifted the thing from its feet. It wriggled and tried to claw the Dragoncaller only to glance off on the steel armor.

The strain was incredible. The demon was no larger than a badger, but it must have weighed a hundred pounds as Craig tried to lift it higher. He felt its acid chew into his hands as the beast's long tongue rolled about and licked him.

"Tell you what!" Craig shouted as lifted the screaming demon higher. "Save this for him!" Craig suddenly lunged forward and thrust the beast into the wall. He pulled back and slammed it again and again and black acid dotted the wall as Craig pounded the beast. "And another thing!" Craig shouted as he lifted the beast higher and slammed it onto the floor. "Its not polite to spit on people!" He quickly picked up its tail, giving enough room to avoid the spikes and dragged the beast in the dirt. Craig spun on his heels and like an Olympic hammer toss, he picked up momentum and slammed the monster into the wall again.

It stopped moving.

Craig tried to wipe the pain away from his face. It wasn't going away. He looked though his burning eyes and saw that the guards had finally noticed his battle with he tiny demon and were coming to aid him. He pushed them back. "Return to post. It's gonna get nasty." They turned in unison save one who was a chirurgeon. She took a boda and sprayed his face. Craig tried to fight the pain of acid against acid on his face, but she pushed his hands away and splashed some roughly on his hands and bade him to hold steady.

He blew his nose and felt tears fill in his eyes from the pungent smell of slivobitsa that seemed to push into his lungs. He could feel the slivobitsa numb the pain in his face. He nodded to let her know it was working. She squirted some more on his face and then down his throat. He coughed but let it down.

She pushed his gauntlets at him and folded his arm to hold them. "My lord, rest, I must attended to others."

Craig put her off. "I got somebody's ass to kick." At those words, the bow of Dragons transformed into the sword of Magnum. He pulled on one gauntlet and let the other slide on by shaking his fingers. He pulled his dolman back on unable to remember taking it off. He then turned and took the stairs with a rush. He could hear the sounds of battle raging at the top of the wall. He didn't think about the man who fell from the wall with a wailing winged thing at his throat for he was out of reach to aid. He met the first thing at the top of the stairs and swung with all of his might. The sword of magnum bit with vengeance. A trail of fiery blood dripped from the sword as Craig carried his charge. He leapt to the wall and swung at anything there was to swing at.

He saw demons fighting in the courtyard. They had somehow fought their way through. Craig watched Battle, of the Dragonguard fight with blinding speed. His hands were death as he broke limbs the size of tree trunks. He took up a fallen polearm and used it with expert skill. Blade, chief of the Dragonguard, stood next to him. The heavy Guard planted himself with his giant sword in his hands, suddenly flashing with speed beyond belief, attacked without mercy. Demons fell quickly all about the broad Dragonguard.

Craig looked to the air. He could tell Kugerand was having difficulty with demons flying up at him. The small demons were no match for an adult dragon, but they were enough to occupy the dragon's attention.

Craig looked about. Still no Harroc. His arms itched him as his chest began to burn. He knew where the great demon was.

He glanced to the east and saw that Harroc's clouds were clearing and the sun tipped against the horizon. Suddenly its flames arched off the world and landed right into the courtyard like a burning rainbow. Craig gazed in horror. *What bullshit is this?* The guards and demon's alike, paused as the giant column of flame bent over the wall and fanned in the open court. Craig saw the tiny figures dancing on the great fire. Faster than any horse could run he saw horses at full gallop charging along the great fire.

Fighting continued. A demon leapt at Craig and died at the violent bite of the sword of Magnum. The sword drank the vile blood with want and it wanted more. Craig only locked his teeth and charged at anything moving.

Fist was beside him. The giant Dragonguard held a demon by the leg and tossed it easily over the wall. He then back-fisted one so hard it just broke and crumbled to the ground.

Over the column of fire the two horses charged. Arrows launched over, but burned at the fire. The lead horse was a clydesdale, its coat of dung glimmered like the fire it road upon. Its rider, clad in black armor held his flaming great axe high above his head. Craig recognized him long before he saw the red star of Hammerstrike.

Behind him was a woman. Her black and gold armor matched the armor of her black and white steed. Together they rode their horses over the bridge of fire, across the wall and into the court.

Achillia lashed with her sword from her mount at the first demon she found. Lightning burned blood in its wake as her sword worked deftly. She seemed to glow with power as she attacked the demons about her. Fryto the flame quickly galloped his horse up the stairs and onto the lip of the wall. His great mount stomped and pranced as its master's flaming axe stroked down with the fires of Kemoto himself.

Craig ran along the lip of the wall as Fryto rose in his saddle. Craig held his question as the knight shouted. "In the Name of Meleki, child of Okshiru, I order you to begone!"

With that shout, he burned with white fire and demon's along the wall erupted with flame. Some leapt from the wall to escape the pain in a fall to death while others merely fell to the floor and twitched in agony.

Craig could see, there were others still coming. "Hi, welcome home." Craig said rather off-handedly. "You wouldn't happen to have a howitzer on you?" Fryto said nothing as his great axe leapt with flame and scorched several demons climbing along the walls. "But a flame thrower will do." Craig mentioned. "Stay here at the wall." He said running along the lip. He dashed down the stairs with Fist closely by him. The Dragoncaller headed for the side door and passed it by only to find a small section in the great wall. He pulled his silver four pointed star of Hammerstrike from his arm guard and pressed it against the stone. With a moan, the wall opened, and after Craig and Fist entered, it closed again.

The tunnel was surprisingly cold and damp. Craig quickly made his way along the halls. His eyes burned red with excitement and his sight leapt the darkness to see his way clearly. He felt Fist shuffling behind him. The largest of the Dragonguard had to force his frame through the tight fitting stone.

Craig went his way past two other side tunnels to follow the main lead. It ended abruptly at a wooden door and, with a flip of a simple lever, it slid aside.

"Bush'!" She screamed. "Bushin, yoush spooks! Git outta myes kichin!" Trisha the fat cook swung her pot at two, tiny, giggling demons who danced out of her way. Craig's great sword of Magnum nearly leapt into his hands on its own, its battle lust springing eagerly as it came forward. It cleft pots and racks in twain and sent metal splintering across the tile floor. Fuzzy balls of teeth laughed as they dove and bounced out of the bite of the great sword. Craig divided the counter and chopped the water spigot. A blazing line carved into the cabinets and spice and flour clouded the air as the great sword wouldn't be held back. With the grip of Babe Ruth and the swing of Hank Aaron, Craig Tyrone swung and swiped at two chittering, zig-zagging demons. The main table collapsed as Craig sliced through one of the legs. It knocked into the kettle of steaming water and splashed on the floor.

Craig's fury brimmed and the sword of Magnum screamed in anger as it scored the air itself. He lashed at one of the fuzz balls again but it bounced to the floor out of reach and across the tile. It disintegrated the second it touched the water.

The second fuzz ball clung to the wall, staring at the black, wet spot that had been its brother. It paused a second too long and didn't see the sword of Magnum in time.

The wall shattered in an explosion of spitting rock. Craig had to untwist himself from the momentum of the blow. He looked and could see one half of the little beast stuck to the window sill with its own blood while the other half laid on the table. Craig stepped to the table and looked at the tiny half. "Dry clean only." He said.

Blood curdled in his veins when he heard the Fist's scream from the hall. The big guard had moved past him to check the hall. Craig quickly pushed past Trisha the cook and crossed the dining hall. "Get to the main hall!" He shouted as he past her.

Towards the stairs he saw the blood striping the walls like a mad mural. He quickly followed the trail to the giant body lying by the wall. Craig dropped to his knees by Fist's side and the Dragonguard tried the speak with the last of his breath, but his throat had been torn from his neck.

Harroc's huge hands clamped Craig's arms to his side and lifted him into the air with ease. "Where are your taunts, big man?" He said shaking the Dragoncaller with fury. "Well? I can't hear you. I'm thinking. I'm not going to eat you all at once. I'm going to keep you by the set and snack on you during commercials. Wouldn't that be sweet?" He pounded Craig into the wall, then tossed him spinning in the air and pinioned his arms again so he could face him.

Harroc slammed him into the wall and pinned him there with one hand, waving a bloody finger. Craig could see the hole made by his arrow, tunneling into the black digit. "What say you, my sweet?"

Craig forced air into his lungs and spat the blood on his lips at Harroc. "Snacking on sweets between meals is bad for the teeth!" Craig pulled his legs up and suddenly bucked and some how planted his foot deeply into Harroc's mouth.

The black demon's grip tightened as he felt his fangs moving about on their own. He screamed and shook the Dragoncaller, banging him against the wall. "You're lunch-meat Tyrone! Lunch meat!" He pulled Craig back from the wall and slammed him harder.

Craig eyes began to cloud with gray as blood choked his lungs. "Blow my big salami." He whispered.

Harroc pressed him into the wall, his great mouth opened as he went to take a bite out of the Dragoncaller's forehead. His bloody mouth clamped easily over Craig's helm and head and bit down.

The black demon screamed in pain and threw the Dragoncaller to the floor. He spat out the teeth that Craig had knocked loose. The teeth of the Son of Hate could not push through the steel of Craig's armor. Armor by Max.

His eyes gleamed as he picked up the stunned Dragoncaller like a rag doll and shook him again. He grabbed hold of Craig's helm and ripped it off, letting it drop to the floor with a clang. "You've proven to be a most interesting food. I think I will nibble off your arms and legs first, then I will kill some knights, then I will return and snack on you." He gripped Craig's arm at the joints of his armor, his sharp talons sinking into the flesh. "Go on, scream. I want Fantista to hear you. I want her to know what's going to happen to her, to her children."

Craig whimpered, trying not to cry out. He kicked out, his metal shod feet clanging uselessly against the demon's hide. Harroc drove his thumb deeper, sinking into muscle. "What was that? I can't hear you?"

Craig suddenly screamed and drove his head forward, smashing Harroc nose with a splash of sticky, steaming blood. Harroc bellowed as fire erupted from his eyes. He slammed Craig against the wall leaving a splatter of blood where the Dragoncaller head struck the unyielding rock.

Harroc held the limp body. He sniffed it, but couldn't tell if it was still living. He gave it a shake, but Craig hung limply in his steel shell. His head hung at a twisted angle on one shoulder and his eyes were rolled into his head. Harroc slapped him. "I didn't hit you that hard! Wake up!" With no response, Harroc decided to bite off the arms and legs anyway.

He held Craig against the wall and detached his jaw to easily fit around Craig's shoulder for a clean, single chomp.

Cool and gentle music settled softly about him, stroking the fine quills on the back of his neck, tickling his spine and filling his arousal. He dropped the Dragoncaller without a second thought. Fantista was calling him, and he could not but answer.

Chapter 42

Cold air clung to the dripping walls. Tiny streams of water crawled along the stone tunnels without purpose or direction. Tiny scratches scurried along the rock as Bug Eyed Monsters danced in the darkness.

The solid earth began to warm and tremble. The stench of brimstone rolled like an ominous cloud into the main cavern. The black of the earth began to glow.

Roderhamerdril raised his great head with a sudden start. All of his eyelids were open and his clear, yellow eyes sparkled in the flourescent algae. He felt his hearts pound in his chest—a pounding that made his ear holes ring. He shuddered as he looked about his cave. Fuzzy, Bug Eyed Monsters that had taken up residence by the beast's sleeping body, leapt from their hiding places in response.

He felt his mate beside him. Her white scales didn't move as sleep held her nearly comatose. She was alright, he thought, but he was afraid and didn't know why. His ears listened to the darkness, there was nothing save the sound of dripping water in the far off tunnel. He twisted in his bed of warm sand and nuzzled by his mate again.

She was whimpering.

He shook her. "Alisa!" He cried. "Alisa, awaken!"

The great white lifted her head from the sand suddenly in fear. She gasped and sighed until Roderhamerdril draped a wing over her and held her close with his front paws. "The Dragoncaller!" She shrilled between sobs. "The Dragoncaller!"

Roder cooed her. "Cry not, cry not. There is nothing!" He had never seen a Dragon so frightened before.

"I had a dream!" She exalted.

"A what?"

"The Dragoncaller said that the pictures I see when I sleep are dreams! I had the most awful! I saw a demon kill the Dragoncaller!"

Roderhamerdril had never seen pictures in his sleep and never heard of another dragon having them before. The concept was frightening. "The Dragoncaller?" He muddled slowly in his dim mind. "Dead? Your dream tells you this?" The thought was reeling his mind. The Dragoncaller dead? Pictures in sleep? Roderhamerdril was not a dragon capable of multiple thoughts.

"Yes, my dream says this." She shuddered as she spoke. She looked up to the bronze dragon's eyes. "What will we do? We live for the Dragoncaller!"

Oh No! Another thought for Roder to weigh in his tiny mind!

"I'll tell ya what!" Came the sudden voice from the darkness. A voice worn with age spoke with puffs of gray-white smoke. From the large east tunnel, a gigantic red dragon slowly trudged into the main cavern. His dull red coat shifted in the dim light as he laid aside one of the cavern walls. "I'll tell ya what! You can stop the hideous noises!" The red slouched in his own weight about the floor.

Roder bowed his head. "Forgive us Lord Brezhnev. It was not our intention."

"What all noise?" Came another voice from the lower tunnel.

Brezhnev, the gigantic ancient red dragon moaned. "The lizard is awake." He tilted his head and raised another set of eye lids. Shafts of light poured from his eyes down the hall. "Go back to sleep, Ralph."

"Ralph isn't the only one who can't sleep." Came a voice from the upper hall. Grace slid from her tunnel. The silver dragon made her stand beside Brezhnev. "Kugerand is gone."

Brezhnev's beams of light cast upon her. His light bounced off of her gleaming hide. "Anyone else?"

"I can't find Boxy, Mojo or Windshmere. Not that it matters, my mate is missing!"

Brezhnev sighed tiredly. Grace normally had much more concern for the others, but when it came to Kuger, she lost her head.

"I had a dream." Alisa said timidly.

Brezhnev reared his head rather annoyed. "A what? A dream? Whatever for?"

"I have pictures in my head. I saw the Dragoncaller die!" She suddenly began to weep.

Brezhnev snorted a stream of smoke. "Dragonettes..." He looked over to Grace. "Do I have to listen to this?"

Grace slid closer to the white dragon. "Are you sure this is true?" The white dragon shook her head.

"Humph!" The red dragon said with licks of flame about his maw. "This is foolishness!"

Grace eyed the red dragon. "Perhaps we should call for him."

Brezhnev thought, and then nodded. The big red closed his eyes and opened the dragoncall. *'Craig!'* There was no reply. Brezhnev opened two sets of his lids and looked over to the white who glared at him for a response. "No problem."

"He's alright?"

"Yeah." He lied. "In fact he wants me and Grace to join him and Kuger." The great red dragon slumped towards the cove.

"I come!" Ralph skipped over to the red. "I fly for Craig!"

"Git away from me!" Brezhnev swung one broad wing and sent Ralph rolling back. "How many times do I have to tell you to stay away from me!" He turned irritably and trudged up the steps.

Grace nudged at Ralph to see if he was alright. The blue looked up at her. "He like Ralph, really!"

Grace sighed and nodded her head knowingly. She then turned and quickly dashed up the steps behind the great red, using her wings for more lift.

"Hey!" Brezhnev raised a wing as she came upon him. "One pace behind and to the left!"

She followed.

"I lied." He said.

"I thought you had."

"Alisa is such a spaz and Ralph is just so stupid. Roder doesn't have that much brain either. I didn't want to spook 'em."

Grace stretched her neck forward. "But can't you call the Caller?"

Brezhnev unfolded and folded his wings as he stepped out into the sun. He shook his coat to loosen the Bug Eyed Monsters. Several gold coins also fell from his hide. "Hazards of sleeping in your treasure." He said. "Yeah, I can call him. Comes with age. I remember the first Caller when I was about Ralph's age. He taught me to call and I've waited all this time for him to come again. Most dragons don't know him or have forgotten. But I haven't forgotten, and I won't. After 11,000 years, I'm not ready to give him up again."

"But what can be wrong?"

The red flexed his wings in a pre-flight check. "Don't know. I find it funny that five dragons in dead sleep awaken at once." He crouched and with a spring, leapt, flapping his great wings, the tips pounding into the dirt. He belched a bit of steam to create his own warm air lift as his tail jammed into the ground to push higher. He grunted and gave another thrusting flap and rose into the cold air.

Chapter 43

With a great brush, Okshiru painted his skies with blood. Shegatesu turned her dawn quickly over to Kemoto who flared in brilliant fire. Kugerand's hide of gold sparkled as the wingless dragon wormed and snaked though the air, clawing and flaming the demons that flew. Windshmere, with a daring low sweep, swooped down in from Riles rest, through the gap in 7th and 8th mountain and shot out of the valley. He tore the front line with such speed that the force of his run caused the demons to ball and roll across the field. Most falling into the deadly moat. Before they could recover, Boxy followed his jet-stream leaving a mist of spittle in his wake. Not enough to burn or destroy, but enough to make everything too slippery to hold. The demons below stormed the walls of the Fanrealm manor, leaping over the moat only to slip off the wall and fall in. The guards along the walls fought with their lives to hold the hellish horde at bay. Demons had found their way into the courtyards and fought the guards there. Mojo, the gray dragon and smallest, fought on the ground with the troops. But the demons wouldn't die. Impaled they fought on, decapitated they fought on, disemboweled they fought on. Only near obliteration would they finally lay down and stay there.

Harroc giggled as he watched out the window. This assignment was too easy and too fun. He had worried about the Ninefinger's vaunted power to keep out demons but it seemed to be nothing more than a paper tiger.

He turned from the window and headed casually down the hall. He admired the paintings that adorned the great walls. The polished black wood supports and gold leaf carvings were simple, yet pleasingly elegant. It was a nice place. Harroc weighed the idea of not destroying it in lieu of moving in.

He headed towards the main hall. Following the enchanting music. If the knight was any where, it was there.

Lady Fantista stood at the door waiting, leaning casually against the doors. She wore her fighting robes, thin cotton slacks and a simple blouse. Surly she wasn't to fight, Harroc believed.

"Get out of the way Grandmother." He said flippantly as he came closer.

"I cannot allow that." She said defiantly.

Harroc was surprised. He had actually thought she would get out of his way. She would complain a bit, throw some holy rhetoric that he was not being a nice person, whine about him being a meany weenie, but get out of the way. She was an ancient witch, he thought, ancient witches were smart enough to get out of the way. He had waited for her to get old. Even an elf gets old and she could not outlive a demon. She was young the first time they met, but now she was no match for a great demon like himself. "Look," He sighed. "I'm not in the mood. I'm looking for Achillia."

"She isn't here." She said simply.

He sighed again. She couldn't lie, but 'here' was a relative term. "I went over this with your door man and now he's an hors-d'oeuvre. Get out of my way!"

"No." She said simply as she leaned away from the door.

He felt his arousal again. If she stood in the way, he had no choice but to fulfill his contract by going through her. He could eat her arms and legs and leave her, find Achillia, eat her and then come back and play with Fantista. Oh, what fun they would have.

He grunted and went to pass her.

He saw three blows: a punch, a kick, and a reversal kick, but yet he felt pain in five places. He leapt back. Her hands hurt him. A grandmother! With no weapons, she hurt him. He suddenly remembered the first time. She was still delivering the same blows with the same speed.

"I give you one warning." She warned him. "Leave or die."

He grit his teeth and charged at her. He felt her foot sink into his hardened stomach forcing him perpendicular and her elbow crack at the back of his neck. Before he knew it, his face was into the stone floor.

He heard her leaping over head as he rose from the floor. He reeled around to see the old witch leaning against the wall. Smiling. "Leave now." Her head motioned towards the door.

He charged at her again. His great fists went swinging as he tried to pommel her, but she sidestepped and let him crash into the wall. He spun at her again, but only felt her foot sink into his teeth. Warm salty blood rose to his lips and pain bored into his gums as his several of his teeth laid at his feet. He put his hands to his face to catch the spilling blood. "You bith!" He shouted a spray of blood. "You will pay for that!" His body swelled like a great bellows and fire spewed from his mouth. Brimstone flooded the hall and set the air to flame.

He paused his fire. His bloody eyes shifted about as beams of light poured out from them; roving search lights pushing back the smoke.

She wasn't there.

There was a click.

The sky tore asunder as the great demon roared his agony. He danced around in a circle chasing his tail and acidic tears flooded his eyes as he caught hold of his tail and held it up to see; it was bent at a 90 degree angle. "YOU BITH!" He roared through his broken teeth. "YOU BROKE MY THAIL!"

His arm extended and fire shoot out from his fingers. Fantista danced like a marionette between the shafts of flame and leapt towards Harroc. The great demon reared back and brought his hands up to his face to protect his teeth but Lady Fantista planted a kick into his ribs.

The demon reeled. These were no mortal blows she was delivering. Her speed was immeasurable, her punches went through him. It is not like before, accursed Trid, she is better! More effective! It cannot be! She is too old for this! It is a knight's trick somehow! He looked up and she seemed to float above him, her right fist cocked above her head bringing it across and down like thunder rolling across the hills. Her fist cracked at the side of his heavy head twisting it completely around. By time he had brought it back around she was ready to do it again; and did.

He felt sudden blackness envelope him as pain flashed with white pops in his head. He felt his will go numb as he crashed to the floor. He could see the cracks in the floor shifting around him through a blurry cloud. Something was whispering, don't get up.

Mortal steel could not hurt him—not plant or rock of all Mortalroam could harm him, yet this grace of Okshiru, this knight of power, was kicking his demonic butt all over the place. This was not to be! The legends will not write of his death this way! He would not let her kill him.

He called Hauge to his will and bent the winsome god to serve. The great winds swirled in the room with sudden fury. He saw her lift to the air and fling towards the wall, but her lithe body twisted and bounded to the floor safely. But Hauge's winds swirled around the Son of Hate and the monster of darkness rose to his feet.

His eyes of blood cast down at her. She seemed frail. The winds pulled at her garments and her wispy bones were clearly exposed. Her long black hair was wired with gray lines. She seemed so small before him. He could crush her with a single blow, smite her from existence.

She was sweating, panting in Hauge's winds. It was evident to the great demon that she was using all of her might, all of her strength to fell him as quickly as possible before her age caught up with her.

With a wave, Hauge was free and he quickly swept from the hall. The black demon charged at her, but the Grandmaster of Knights was already in motion. Her hands flashed as she punched again and again with sudden power and fury at the black demon. Harroc ignored the pain and with a blurring back hand slapped the will from her. He lifted her and tossed her like and rag doll into the wall. Her tiny wire limbs grasped and clawed for balance but the demon hammered into her ribs and she curled into a tiny ball on the floor.

The great demon bent to pick her from the floor, but the wench shot out like a snake and slithered between his legs and quickly crawled to the wall by the window.

"You are beathen gwandmothther." Harroc growled around his broken teeth. "Look out thhe window. Thee my demonth wip your thoy tholderth tho peithes. They pile the bodith at your window. Thuwwender to me and I thall eat you quickly."

Fantista moved slowly and painfully, uncurling, her weary frame. "You are a fool, thing of hate." She rasped.

Harroc dropped his head back and laughed. "Ith ith you who are the fool! I am Hawwoc, thon of Hate!"

"I know who you are." Lady Fantista sat on the floor, her arm, laid limply across one knee. Sweat glistened on her ivory skin. Her lungs rattled as she forced her self to breathe. "I blame myself for this." Her words grated as she rose to her feet, sliding smoothly and slowly up the wall. "Years ago I tried to teach you a lesson. I failed in my teaching." She stood in the window's light. Her robes were transparent as she stood there and Harroc could see her thin muscles flex and tighten as she hissed like a snake.

She stood as the sweat rippled from her body and stained the floor at her bare feet. He felt the air twist as licks of power swept about her. Power of might given by Okshiru, power of strength brought by Sho-Pa, power of will brought by herself.

"I haven't felt this way in a long time, Harroc. I curse you and thrice damn you for bringing it back to me. You hurt me Harroc." She looked up at him with her pained, angry eyes. The demon matched her gaze, trying to think of what to hit her with next. He had depleted his arsenal and was desperately trying to think of something new. By all rights, she shouldn't be standing—she shouldn't be alive. "We are knights, to protect, to nurture, to uphold, but we were made to destroy the evil we could not save. I have turned from destruction, I have turned from hate. You have woken it again in me…" She smiled faintly and cold struck Harroc. "Do you remember the lesson, Harroc?"

Harroc flinched and in that space of time she was upon him. His magic formed a shield before him that webbed like shattered glass from her first blow. It gave way on the second. Her leap carried her above him and she rained blow upon blurry blow. Her speed was beyond sight for she had thrown eight blows before she touched down again.

He felt the sight in his eye explode in a burst of white light, but he wasn't sure which one it was. He whirled around blindly, hoping to catch her with a wild swing, but she eluded him. He felt her thin arms and body wrap about his extended arm like a boa constrictor and her feet plant into his shoulder. He forced open his remaining eye. Before he could think, before he could react, he watched her holding on to his arm with her legs and right arm. With a sudden jerk, she brought her left arm down at one of his elbows and snapped the bone in two.

He howled and felt his right side leave him. She was underneath him suddenly and a kick thundered into his body. His ribs moved about on their own as pain was his only breath. Another blow cuffed him and filled his only eye with blood. Another blow pulverized his jaw.

Through the black blood he could see her, smiling like a demon herself, her eyes shining with the glow of Hiran elves. He felt other blows, elbows, knees, feet and hands hit him like steel and lightning. She was alive now, a sleeping dragon dragged from slumber. She whirled like a dervish as she drove a blow to his temple that stood him upright.

It stopped. The pain was beyond feeling. She could hurt him no more, she could only kill him.

He was standing, teetering like a tree swaying in the wind. Only habit held him at his feet. She was still before him. Smiling.

She flexed her body, drawing on her power. Her arms moving in synch, the delicate spider in her web. She screamed, a charming note Harroc numbly thought, and her fist went ripping through the air with a sudden strike into the black demon's chest. Her force didn't end until her fist cleared past his spine.

She held her arm there for three, long heartbeats—each beat, wheezing out its last. She suddenly jerked free and Harroc fell to his knees. He could feel the breath suck though the hole as the blood flowed out. He looked up at the light shining on him. He looked up at Lady Fantista glowing with the light of Okshiru.

Harroc, son of hate, closed his eyes and died.

Lady Fantista felt Arru, god of anger stand beside her. She watched him as he walked from the hall and out of reality.

She looked at the black demon curled into a fetal position with his arms across his chest. She watched the black blood spill from his heart and pool on the stone floor.

She saw it. For the first time she actually noticed it, hidden among the other fetishes and totems that he wore about his neck. She reached down and took the silver chain from the demon's neck and pulled until it snapped. She took the silver star of Hammerstrike into her hands and with out looking, knew it to be Denice's.

Suddenly, ten thousand screams sang to the new day. Demons wailed in agony as each suddenly burst into white fire. Fantista knew it was Dwayne's white fire.

Craig bounded up the stairs to the window. He casually leapt over the black demon and peered out. He paused as the sunlight fell upon his exposed flesh. The open scars on his hands and face burrowed pain as light touched them. He reached for his cloak automatically, but it wasn't there. He pulled away, but then couldn't see anything out of the window. He finally shadowed his face with his hands and took a quick look. He watched the guards standing about in awe watching the smoking remains of the demons scattered about the courtyard. He scanned the wall. There was the same confusion there; men wondering what they should be doing in the light of this new event.

Gorn waved. Craig waved back.

Kugerand turned and made a lick in the air and spiraled higher. Craig could sense that Brezhnev the big red and Grace the silver were also circling over head.

Craig stepped back from the window and out of the sun's glare. He turned to find Fryto standing behind him looking just as confused as he was. The Dragoncaller looked to Lady Fantista but Fryto cautioned him with a gentle hand. The Grandmaster of Knights stood there, with her arms wrapped around her body, tightly clinging to herself. Her head was bowed and her long black hair was undone and draped over her face and shoulders. She shuddered, and Craig knew she was crying. Craig looked to Fryto hoping for a little guidance in what to do, but the fire knight seemed to be equally lost. He slowly stepped closer to his mother, lowering his great axe to the floor as he did. He paused and waited, trying to peer under the curtain of hair which hid her face.

Quickly she looked up at him. Her face was white and with out warmth. Her deep brown eyes were drenched with tears and over flowed as they looked up into his. She sniffled and tried to speak, but only coughed. Slowly her arms reached out and wrapped tightly about her son. She buried her face into he steel of Fryto's arm and prayed to be forgiven for her anger.

"This battle had such potential." Achillia trotted up the stairs. "Ended all to quickly. Does a knight's soul good to…" She paused as she looked to Craig. "Lord Tyrone, are you alright?…"

Craig waved at her casually. "Yeah, Harroc banged me about and rattled my brain box but good. Put me right out." He winced as he touched the back of his head. "Fryto found me a few moments ago."

Achillia pulled off her gauntlet and reached out to touch him. "Your face." He instinctively pulled back. She clutched his hand and held him steady and touched it again. Craig winced even to the light touch. The flesh had been eaten and torn. Muscle and bone had been bored though by demon's acid. She left his face and took up his hands. The scarring was extensive, but not as bad as his face. With a touch of magic, the cosmetic scars began to seal themselves closed. "Keep these clean. I'm going to have to dress them. How does your face feel?"

"It only hurts when I laugh." He said grimly.

The doors to the dining hall opened, and Onary poked his head out. He pulled his head back and a moment later Neeko poked her head out. "Craig!" She rushed out of the hall and tossed her arms about him. Craig looked rather blase to Achillia as if to say, '*Women do this to me where ever I go*'. When Neeko pulled away, she placed her hand to where Craig's cheek had been. The Dragoncaller hissed and pulled away. "Okay, no more of that."

"Lady Fantista." Achillia called to the Grandmaster while Neeko cooed and pampered over Craig's face. "I have done what I could." Achillia explained as Lady Fantista came closer. "But it seems the Dragoncaller needs you."

Lady Fantista wiped her face with the back of her hand and took up her role as the Grandmaster of Knights. She took Craig's right hand in her own and closer examined Craig's face. "How bad is it? Can you move this side?"

Craig blinked and winced. "I really can't feel it, is it moving?" Lady Fantista shook her head. "Then is my tongue sticking through my cheek?" Lady Fantista nodded.

"Come." The Grandmaster guided him. "Let us go to the kitchen."

The word food popped into Craig's mind almost instantly, but something still nagged at the back of his mind. "What happened?" He said as they entered the stairs. "I mean one second, the gates of hell have opened on the lawn and the next, it's a demon barbecue." Craig stepped into the hall and paused at the sight were Fist had been killed. He sensed Lady Fantista, still holding his arm, clench at the sight. She turned and quickly led him into the kitchen. She sat him down on the bench and stepped over to the cupboard.

"Does it really matter?" Lady Fantista said as she pulled table linen from the closet. "It is over." She dropped the linen into Craig's lap and took up a sheet. With her teeth, she started a tear, and then tore the sheet into two, handing half to Fryto. "Donald, tear this up." She then looked to Achillia. "Diane, go out and help the wounded." Achillia nodded and headed to her task. "Neeko, I will need you here."

"Find Gore!" Craig shouted after Achillia. "Have him secure the walls and account for the remaining men. Send five horsemen to Cornerstone and get Max to send Corpsmen, uhh, chirurgeons!"

Neeko sat beside the Dragoncaller. "You must relax now."

Craig shook his head. "I can't, there is something unfinished here. I want to know what happened!"

"Donald, Go upstairs and take charge of the children, have them help with the wounded." Lady Fantista set a bowl of water before the Dragoncaller as she spoke. "But Blessid! Be sure they leave alone the demons lying around. Let the soldiers do that."

Fryto nodded as he set the bandages before the Dragoncaller. As he left, Trisha came in through the other hall.

"Ohhh Lawdy, Lawdy!" She howled. "Looket whats theyses dones ta mes kichen!"

Fantista pumped at the sink and filled it with water to wash her hands. "Trisha, We'll need hot water. Get a fire started and get some children to help you. We'll have many wounded and they'll need to be cleaned and feed!"

"I'ls do dat." She said. "But Its snot bees easy, cause day done tore up mes kichen!" She waddled out to the smoke house.

"Actually," Craig said from under a sheet where he was hiding. "I did most of the damage." He pulled the sheet away. "Put it on my tab."

Lady Fantista took up a towel and dried her hands as she came closer. "It is we who owe you. And besides, it takes time to wield a sword." She reached to the counter and took up a jar. "My children learned to walk with a sword. You will learn in time." She sat beside him and opened the jar of brown paste. Craig immediately recognized the Thatch that was used for cuts, burns and belly aches. She scooped out an large mound in her fingers and worked it in her palms until it was soft. Then she went to apply it to Craig's face.

The Dragoncaller pulled back and glared at her. "What happened?"

The Lady held back and then reached to his face. "If it really means that much to you...It was Dwayne's barrier of magic."

Craig grit his teeth to bar the pain as she rubbed in the Thatch, mixing it with the blood oozing from the cauterized wound. He could feel his wife holding him down. "But then..." He spoke through his teeth trying not to think of the pain. "why the heck did it take so long to kick in?"

Lady Fantista wet her hands in the bowl beside her and set them to Craig's face. Pain drilled deep into and he felt it strip down his right side and curl his toes. He felt Fantista's strong arm and leg brace him into the bench she use the power within her to heal him. He felt his own hands grip the seat as he feet clawed the ground. "Ohs shit." He mumbled as she took her hands from his face. "Ohs shit." escaped his lips as his hands instinctively went to his face. Lady Fantista pushed his hands away and whispered don't touch, as she folded a bandage.

Neeko leaned forward and looked him over. "Its different colors, but its there." She looked at Lady Fantista apply the bandage. "How can you put back his face like that? You make it look so easy."

"It is the will of Okshiru." She said simply. "You will learn in time."

"I'm glad he remembered me in his will." Craig mumbled as everything grew quiet. Fantista's touch became lighter and lighter and the pain began to fade. Craig's ears began to ring from the quiet. He opened his eyes and found he was alone in the kitchen.

Craig rose from the bench and glared at the quiet kitchen. Onary sat on the floor before him and Edia snoozed on the counter. He looked at his hands. There were no scars, no bandages. He touched his face and it was the same. "I am dreaming." He told Onary.

The dog nodded. "It happens every time you come in contact with Thatch. I think its an allergy."

Craig thought about the correlation. "But I have had dreams with out Thatch."

"Ahh, but you haven't had Thatch with out dreaming."

"True. Now the question is, is this the Past, Present or Future?"

A rabbit materialized on the tall boy.

"Do not be alarmed," The rabbit spoke. "I am a talking rabbit."

Craig started with the rabbit's sudden appearance. He glanced at Onary who only regarded the rabbit. Edia still looked asleep. Her bottle brush tail lazily swung back and forth like a clock pendulum.

Craig looked back at the rabbit, and then back to Onary. "Don't be alarmed." He told the dog. "Its a talking rabbit."

Onary called to Edia. "Edia, its a talking rabbit."

The cat only stopped her tail swinging. "Alarm, alarm." She said tiredly."

"Don't be."

The rabbit glared in astonishment. "Goddess Meleki! A talking dog and cat!"

"Alarm! Alarm!" Edia sounded almost convincing in her panic, her tail swinging again.

"Don't be." Onary cautioned.

"Actually," Edia spoke up no longer pretending to be alarmed or asleep. "The dawg doesn't really talk, the cat can throw her voice."

"Edia, you couldn't throw a rug."

"Why would Ah want too?"

Craig put up his hand and the two quieted. "Is there something I can do for you? Is there a reason for this dream?"

"Yes," The rabbit answered quickly. "I must speak to you. This whole mess with Harroc was partially my fault."

"What?"

"He had orders to kill Achillia. We calculated that his arrival on Mortalroam would...is there something wrong?"

Craig was looking around. "You said 'we'. Who else is here, Bobo the wood mouse?"

"No one else is in this dream."

"So who is 'we'."

Chritchfeild paused. "I'm not at liberty to disclose that."

Craig folded his arms. "Sure."

"Well, if Harroc found her out on her own, with the litter that he had with him, she and Fryto would be dead."

"So you and your forest friends couldn't handle that so you decided to endanger a castle full of children!" Craig stepped closer. "Children!"

Chritchfeild rose on his hind legs in panic. "Oh no! That was not our intention when we deceived Harroc into thinking Achillia was here. We counted on Frito's barrier of magic to work."

"And what happened?"

"The demon had the Star of Hammerstrike. The one you hold in your hand."

The star was not there before, but was when Craig opened his hand. He hadn't realized that he had been clenching it. "The star allowed him to pass? Is that how Thumber passed? And then gave it to Harroc?"

"I do not know about Thumber or how Harroc got the star."

Or you are not telling, rabbit. Craig shook his head morbidly. "I know that there are many men dead and more wounded. I hope you and your friends choose your demon dumps a little more carefully in the future." He looked at the star in his hand. The name Denice was scrawled on the back. "Where is Denice now?"

"The house of Ura. A house by the sea, near the town of Brewster. Will you go to find her?"

Craig looked sideways at the rabbit. "'We' don't know." He looked about and then back at the rabbit. "How is it..."

The rabbit was gone.

"How is what?" Fantista said looking at him as she finished his bandages.

Neeko recognized his far away look. "Twilight Zone again?"

Craig nodded and rubbed his eyes.

"It happens every time you come in contact with Thatch." Onary concluded. "I think its an allergy."

Craig wanted to smile, but his face wouldn't respond. "We went over that already." He rose to his feet. "I'll take it up again when I have time."

"Sit down." Fantista ordered. "You have plenty of time."

Craig shook his head. "Got work to do."

Neeko pushed to her feet, leading with her stomach. "You're in no condition to go anywhere!"

Craig touched his finger to his numb lips and then to hers. "You're right." He quickly snatched up a bottle of Slivobitsa and forced four big gulps. "Now I am!" He gasped already feeling his face warm. "I gotta find Frita and bring her this." He looked up and knew where to find what he needed. He reached out and gently took Denice's chain from Fantista's neck, separating it from her own and then allowing the star to fall into his palm and the chain pool over it. For the first time he noticed that his Star and Frita's star were different than Fantista's.

"Do you know where she is?"

Craig nodded. "Brewster, in the house of Ura."

Neeko gasped. Craig gently rubbed his free hand against her cheek and she grabbed it, holding it there. "I gotta go fast and that means by dragon."

Deep inside, Neeko knew it to be true. "Be careful." She whispered. *May your Lord watch out for you.* She didn't say.

"No sweat. I have a feeling I'm going to meet Frito on route. I'm not gonna mix it up with anybody. I'll be back soon." She kissed his hand and held it a beat longer before letting it slide from her grasp. Craig turned and stepped out of the door, with Onary close behind.

Chapter 44

Kemoto finally leapt from the hills of the world and took flight. High into the blue bonny blue, the great god of the sun glided a straight and steady line across the above. His golden light beamed, causing Mistang to flee from the stone mountains to hide in the valleys. From his vantage above the world he could see the god of winter and the god of the wind.

Fikor ran through the mountain trails with Hauge close behind him. The capricious god of wind, still angry from what had happened earlier that morning, sprinted ahead of the Snow Dog. Across a frozen pond the two ran, only stirring up the frost into tiny swirls of white. They ran up the side of the bank and along the hardened road.

The two ran along the edge of the road; on one side a spiraling mountain, on the other, a sheer cliff. Swirling left and right along the twisting path the two gods raced. Fikor took the lead then pulled farther ahead and as the road bent to the right, the Snow Dog went on, leaping across the sky and higher into the blue.

The wind god stood at the edge panting. His cheeks stung and his caramel skin became as ash from the lick of Fikor's cold. His brown eyes bled tears that lined his tender face. He howled after the Snow Dog, but the answer was only his echo.

He stepped to the edge, and in a bluster, he raced down the steep face whipping up the dead leaves behind him to follow him over the edge. He gusted through the woods and followed a still flowing river. When it forked and split, so did he, parting each way to follow where it took him.

Past a glade of grass and fields dried and frozen, past farms and homes boarded up for the chilling season ahead, past a string of hills following each other in a trillion year game of 'leap frog'.

He finally arrived south, several clicks from anywhere in particular but not as far as others. The trees were black and drove black shadows across the brown earth. Their leaves of green were stripped from their boughs by Fikor's vicious bite and the talons of his wind. The moss had tried to creep back into the earth but was too slow and lay dry and brittle on the rocks and trees. Beyond the small group of trees was an open field covered over completely with giant bramble. Thick branches of looming thorns twisted painfully and mindlessly each way. Hauge

346

drifted gently through the razors and pikes that pushed from the reddish, bruised plants writhing in agony. He found a hole in the midst of the mess and bent his godish ear to lend a listen.

It was at this particular point in time and general placement of space, that a rabbit, with gray/black fur, poked his tiny head through the thicket, peered into the hole and also gave a listen.

Friska lay in his place half asleep. His eyes fluttered as his head rolled back and forth on the pillow. He cried, and then sobbed, moaned and then sighed. Sweat beaded his brow and pain swept his head. The leathery winged woman still sat at his side, pampering him, protecting him. She listened to his ravings and answered them. She felt his symptoms and fed them. She did what little she knew and the rest she invented from what she thought was right.

But Friska could not be calmed. His anguish was unsolvable. There was a weight pulling in his centre. There was a pain tugging at his head. There was a shadow across his bed.

His eyes opened with a sudden start and suddenly burned green as his race. The tall gaunt silhouette loomed over him, laughing quietly to itself.

Thamrell.

"How are you Friska?" He asked cajolingly as he drifted around the small hovel. "This place is a dump." He said dejectedly as he looked it over. "Hardly a dwelling for one of your great status." The thin flesh covering his skull pulled back to show a toothy smile.

Friska fought to rise from the bed but the sheol tried to hold him there. She glared back over her shoulder and hissed at Despair. "Get out!"

Thamrell looked contemptuously at the demon. "Sheol, what do you think you're doing? Protecting him?" He leaned his head back and laughed. "He doesn't love you, you're just a hot fuck on a cold night."

Her face wrinkled as her fangs bared. "You lie!"

"I do? Then why hasn't he taken you to Fanrealm to meet his Mom? Taken you shopping in town?" Thamrell slowly turned in a circle. "At least bought you a house?" He looked at her. "He has given you nothing."

"He has given me a name!" She hissed and flapped her wings. "I am Cassandra!"

"Of course he has." Thamrell drifted about the room looking at her collection of baubles and the other shiny things that she adorned her home with. "You have a very poor sense of reality. He is using you, as he uses you now to protect him."

Friska rolled from his bed. Cassandra tried to hold him back but he fought to a sitting position regardless. "Despair, begone! You speak lies and spread death like the plague. GET OUT!"

"By the will of Okshiru? You have fallen little angel—right on your holy face."

Friska glared with blurry eyes and a head still muddled from the powerful vision he received. "You used me. You lied to me. You deceived me. You tripped me and made me fall!"

"Did I? I am the god of human introspection. I can't lie. But I suspect that I am the only one in your life who hasn't. Oh, holy knight, you've been deceived since the day you were born. You have been blind since you were a child and I showed you the truth!" He sailed right at Friska. "Your older brother has always had the light and what was left fell on you. He was the choice of your father and mother. Okshiru's special child he is, the Archknight. Not you. You are just a living abortion."

"Liar!"

"Am I? You want me to spell it out for you? Frito took the glory of Hel and stormed the world in such carnage as to make the reawakening of time turn her head! And when he fell from Worldsend, his mother, your mother, ran breaking strides to kiss his feet and forgive him. But Frito felt his guilt and went into penance. Okshiru used you to redeem Frito, to force him to live in his light, to return to Knighthood to save your life, and now that Oks' done with you, he's cast you aside like the morning's trash to live here, wallowing in your own sins with this whore! Okshiru forgave your brother for beating his mother, raping his wife, breaking his cousin's bones and enslaving his brother. Okshiru forgave him and reestablished him to his former rank—and you? Humph. You're not even on his list to be redeemed. Frito was the chosen one. You, you're nothing but another step in the Ninefinger's staircase to Worldsend. A staircase that spirals to nowhere! Okshiru has sacrificed you to save Frito. But why? Why the Hel him?" Thamrell floated around in a circle. "What makes him so great?" He weighed the idea. "I will confess, he does love you like a brother. What a great guy he is."

"You son of a bitch." Friska hissed as he found his feet. "Frito deserves to be Archknight. He always has. He's mastered magic and the Sho-Pa. He trained me."

"But not as well as himself." Thamrell answered quickly. "He taught you the basics and put you in your place."

"I was too impatient to learn. My sister learned the magic, not I. I was too headstrong."

"Or the Ninefinger's just didn't bother to impress you. Perhaps he was frightened of you. Chances were Donald was going to immolate himself before he came of age and Denice was a woman, no threat there, or so we all mistakenly thought. You had to be put in your place. One pace behind and to the left. You'll clear out the trash to glory so he won't get dirty as he strolls through to claim it." Thamrell's eyes of emptiness gazed at Friska. "He's got you trained like a dog." He drifted closer. "But its not really Frito's fault. It was Okshiru's. Frito is Okshiru's insurance against your father the Supergod. He controls Frito and keeps the Supergod in his place. But like his father, Frito is too hard to control on his own, so the god of sky and sea uses you and your siblings to control him. To do his will and make him look good. You build his power and when you're no longer any use, you're history. Cast aside from his sight.

"You still think I'm making this up? Did you see how fast Okshiru changed sides? He was with you that night you went to kill your brother. But the instant that he knew you were going to lose, he dropped you and went to your brother. If he didn't want you to confront Frito, then why didn't he drop you before? Why wait for mid-fight? I'll tell you. He wanted the fight. He wanted the Ninefingers and he was willing to risk you to do it. If you didn't die and stayed a knight, all the better. You can still be a knight, of course Ok' will accept you. But his real prize is Frito.

"And why does he want Frito? Frito was destined from the reawakening of time. He was the son of the Supergod. We were pulling for Dexter, but he was a mistake. Frito shined like Kemoto's light. Don't get me wrong, Dexter was a brave son of a bitch, but only the precursor, Frito was the one. And now, above anything, after Hauth, Okshiru walks around Worldsend bragging that he has the great Ninefingers, son of the Supergod, Lord of Lightning, Devilslayer and Trid Dreath the Third in his back pocket; and you, you my little piss pot, you're the stain that is easily covered up. You were expendable and no more than that. But there is hope. Not much hope, but a little. It all depends on you. If you're strong enough to resist the leash of Okshiru.

If you're man enough to claim what is yours. You can succeed where even your brother failed."

Friska turned away from Thamrell's stare of nothing. His ears rang in his stuffed head. It was hard to think. He ducked down and pushed from the bed. "You're filling my head with your lies."

Thamrell put his hands in the air. "Then I have wasted my time." He floated towards the hole to leave. "I cannot lie. I can only say what you yourself are thinking. You know what I say is true for I am only pulling it from your head. But you are truly a slave to Okshiru, just as your brother is. I underestimated his chains. Take up your knightly vows again and bow your head with your tail between your legs. You disgust me. You are not a man, but a worm." Thamrell turned his back and floated up.

Friska's head spiraled and he only heard Thamrell's last sentence. He blinked, suddenly forgetting what they had been talking about. "I am a Man!" Friska screamed after the god of despair.

Thamrell stopped and with his back still to Friska, smiled.

"Don't listen to him!" Cassandra wailed at him.

"Women." Thamrell sighed. "Is she your master?" He slowly turned.

"I am my master." Friska said proudly. "And I am a knight!"

Thamrell laughed dryly. "Sounds like you are a slave to this sheol bitch?"

Cassandra bared her fangs at the haunting god. "Tell him!" She shrieked. "Tell him why you are doing this! Tell him your motive. Is the Lord of Depression doing this out of the kindness of his nonexistent heart?"

"Shit no." Thamrell answered easily. "I have my motive like anyone else. I want my revenge on Okshiru. I want to walk in Worldsend, and drink coffee with my toast in the morning and play golf all afternoon. I want to be able to skip over to a Circle K and buy fucking M&M's. I want what he's got. I want freedom! I don't want to be controlled by any one. The chains of Okshiru are just as strong on me as anyone else, but I don't want anyone's chains on me. That's what I want 'Cassandra', I want to live like the bodiless god that I am and not in Oks' shadow." His hollow gaze fell heavily on the fallen knight. "Is that wrong? Friska?"

Friska grew dark as he thought, slowly shaking his head. "No, Thamrell, it is not wrong to want that."

"No Friska!" Came a voice from nowhere.

"What was that?" Thamrell reeled about. "Who else is here?"

Chritchfeild the rabbit put his paws to his mouth. He had listened at the hole's entrance in silence until now. He could hear Thamrell drift closer to him. The little rabbit panicked and ran into the bramble. Thamrell lifted out of the hole and watched the little puff tail duck out of sight.

<u>Chapter 45</u>

"Raw cod, special deal for today only!" Shouted the fish man from his stand. From his little cart he selected a choice catch and held it by the gills. "Cod milady?"

The woman pulled back slightly as it was difficult to see the thing under her nose. "Fresh?"

"Fresh, fresh, caught this morn I did myself." His fingers pulled open the gills to show her. "2 coppers for a fish of this weight."

"I'll need salted too. Can you salt it?"

"I have already salted ones. You see?"

The woman bent over his barrel and examined his dried, salted fillets. The crowds merely shuffled around her and continued on. The shepherd brought a few of his sheep through the crowds to the slaughterhouse. The wood carver finally opened his display. He produced a toy of a wooden dancing clown and the child cried until her mother bought it. Someone with a drum stood beneath one of the Nightglows and shouted banging his drum. 'Boom boom boom'. "Tis high sun!"

The crowds went on. Fikor's winter seemed a little farther away as the heavy crowd pushed their way about.

A dark figure made his way quietly through the side street. His cloak was draped over his entire body and his broad, straw sun hat shielded his head. He darted about, keeping closely to the shadows as he did. He watched the main street with curiosity for a moment and stepped out into the midst of things. He shuffled quickly and smoothly through the crowd, pulling his hat lower and heading directly for the main hall.

"Halt there you!" A burly sergeant with six troopers following made their way through the crowd. The dark figure ignored him. "Hang on!" The sergeant bellowed at him. "I order you to HOLD!"

The dark figure stopped and waited. The burly sergeant strolled right up to him. "What business have you here? Where is your writ of entry?" The fat sergeant poked at the man as he spoke. The man held up his papers for the sergeant, but he ignored them. "Hey?" The sergeant exclaimed. He suddenly balled the man's cloak and held him, poking his chest with his other hand. "He's wearing armor!"

Steel spears suddenly lowered. The people gasped and mumbled about themselves as they did. The sergeant stripped the man's sun hat, his glasses coming away with it and let the sun fall on his skin. They could almost hear his flesh crinkle. The man shielded his eyes, blinded. "Look at him." One of the troops exclaimed. "He's an elf...a NIH! Almost as black as Milo."

The spears came closer and the man looked up at the crowd. "Uh, look, lets not get touchy okay. I'm not a Nih elf, I'm a Keebler elf. I make cookies." Through squinting eyes he tried to see around him.

The sergeant shook his head in disgust. "You're Nih. A dark Nih." He accused. "Never seen a dark Nih before. A lying one yes, a dark one, no." He spat and wiped his chin with the back of his hand. "A dark, lying Nih."

"Hey, at ease, it was a joke." The man stepped backward and a spear poked him in the small of his back. "Hey! Watch it, I'm allergic to spears. Look, here is my writ. It is from..."

"Were not talking to Nih." The sergeant said abruptly as he planted his fists into his hips. "Where does scum like you get armor plate like this?"

"Sears layaway. Look Bud, call off your boys okay. Before I get hurt."

"I asked you a question!" The sergeant nudged him with a thick finger.

The dark man stepped back. "Hey lay off! Look, I'm not armed. Just let me be and give my back my hat and glasses and we can talk." The man reached out for his hat, but the Sergeant moved it away. It was obvious the man was blind. "Okay, then give me my glasses, please. They dropped off when you snatched my hat." The sergeant stepped sideways playing blind man's bluff. "Look, here is my Writ." The man held out his paper. "I'm Craig Tyrone, envoy of Roc The Dragonslayer." Craig could tell they no longer cared about his writ so he pulled out the silver star of Hammerstrike.

"You Lying THIEF!" The sergeant suddenly snatched his wrist with the star. "Thief! Seize him!" Spears suddenly thrusted through but Craig stepped forward, back-fisting the sergeant's jaw with a quick left and driving down with his right to break the hold. Craig side stepped, putting his leg behind the sergeant's knee and pushing him off balance, spun him around. Craig's K-bar flashed in his left and pressed tightly to the fat man's throat. "I'll spill him!" He threatened. "Okay, you're right, I am a Nih elf and that means I can hear any move you make. The wrong one and he learns to talk through his neck." Craig put out his right hand. "My glasses!" He demanded. A soldier stepped forward and reached down, afraid to touch a Nih thing. "Pick it up with your Damn Hands!" Craig jutted his hand out again and felt his glasses set in his palm. Craig flipped them open and put them on. "Okay," He scanned the crowd around him, his eyes blazing red through the smoked lenses. "Now hear this! I am the envoy of Roc The Dragonslayer. I am to deliver a message from Lady Fantista of Fanrealm, Grandmaster of Knights!" Craig moved his knife away and tripped the sergeant. The fat soldier fell face first to the ground. "Now what Nih would dare speak her name in his lie?" Craig kicked the feet out from under the sergeant trying to scramble to his feet. "Now, direct me to Roc before I get pissed off!" The fat sergeant only glared at Craig in astonishment. "What, too many moving parts for you? Where is Roc?"

"Leave him alone." The crowd had parted to allow another man through. He wore silver plate armor with a black surcoat over it. His surcoat was embroidered with a pattern of the pierced silver crescent. Craig looked to the sergeant and let him up. As the sergeant crawled away, Craig sheathed his knife and lifted his hood over his head to shield the sun. "A half billion apologies my lord. I recognize the sight of a Knight. I am…"

"CRAIG!" A boy pushed through the crowd and right into Craig's arms.

"So Orrin," The knight said pulling loose his helm. "I see you know this Nih."

Craig looked at the knight. "I'm not a Nih elf, I'm a Santa's elf. I make toys." Craig re-adjusted his sunglasses. "If I had brought my American express card with me, this whole scene wouldn't have happened." Craig took Orrin's hand and walked over to the knight. "Craig Tyrone, High school teacher, and you are?"

"Milo." Milo said smartly and stuck out his left hand.

Craig paused for a moment's confusion before suddenly realizing, Milo was missing his right arm. "There is something missing in this picture."

Milo warmly gripped Craig's left wrist in welcome. "Lost in a battle with Tarspat, the black dragon. I apologize for my men."

Craig waved his hand to forget the whole thing. "My fault. I get it all the time. You should have seen the problems I had at the front gate. That's why I snuck in."

"Come." Milo gestured. "I know that the Nih hate the sun."

"I'm not a Nih elf. I'm a shoemaker's elf." Craig looked about the crowd and they all looked back with despite. "I hate Nih." Craig whispered under his breath.

"How so? You must not hate your own people."

"It isn't my race. I wasn't born a Nih. I'm mostly West Indian with a little Native American Indian from Canada to make things interesting." Milo stepped under the awning of a store keep and Craig pulled off his hood. "I don't even know what a Nih is supposed to do."

Milo paused and wondered. "So how is this?"

"An incredibly long story, lets just say a serious mistake in the time/reality spectrum. Or the butt end of a really bad joke."

"Are you from another country?" Milo asked.

"No, another time. Somewhere so far in the past there is no history or record."

"There is, like, the red Bar-chet-ta!" Orrin announced. "It was, like, an ar-ti-fact, eh?"

"I've been meaning to talk to Roc about that." Craig spoke to Orrin leaving Milo on his own. "The Red Barchetta was one of the first Ferrari. A small Italian motorcycle with doors built in the 40's. The car we have is a 55 Lincoln Futura four door custom. I didn't know they even made a four door." Craig suddenly paused and looked at Milo. "Did I lose you anywhere? Do you still think I'm a Nih?" Milo dumbly shook his head. "Good." Craig went on. "I don't think RTD would have a Nih on the payroll and speaking of the worst thing to happen to anyone, Where is he? You know, big guy, about the size Buick, eats anything not on fire, more fun than electroshock therapy with the personality of a mugging? You know, a face that could waylay a moose at thirty yards? Likes the taste of veins wiggling in his teeth?" Craig waved his hand in Milo's face. "Hello, NASA? Negative on orbit trajectory."

Milo looked away and then looked back. "You are a jester!" He announced laughing.

Craig didn't like the idea of jester. "No, actually I'm crazy. Now, where is Roc?"

"I shall round up a party and seek him out." Milo said turning to street. Most of the crowd had stepped on to go their way, but the guards and a few spectators stayed by. "Hear me, Men!" He called to the guards. "Here is Lord Craig Tyrone, envoy of Roc the Dragonslayer. We must gather and find the Dragonslayer!"

Craig dashed out after the knight pulling his hood over as he did. "No! Milo, there isn't time." Craig shielded his eyes as he looked up a the towering black man. "Just tell me where he is or point me in the right direction."

"My lord, I…" Milo started but Craig cut him off.

"Look, shit's been going down and I've got to find him." Craig looked around at the crowd forming again. Someone looking almost apologetic handed him his sun hat. "Thank you." Craig acknowledged, then to Milo: "I know you mean well, but I don't really have time to explain." He glanced at his watch. "Shit, maybe I do have time…No not really. Where is he?"

Milo took a breath and thought. Then he stooped to the ground and made a rough sketch in the earth. "Its a days ride, my lord. Take this road to the coast line and follow it." He leaned back on his haunches. "How will you travel?" He looked about the square. "Have you a horse?"

"The Red Bar-chet-ta!" Orrin exclaimed.

Craig shook his head. "Na, I wouldn't have made it this fast if I did."

Someone shouted from the crowd. Milo looked about and people were scattering from the street. Slowly, about double a man's height above the ground, Kugerand the gold, wingless dragon slithered through the air. His whiskers from his wide head brushed lightly against the permanent dwellings as he made the tight fit. People pulled under awnings and out of the street as he lowered down. He arched his back forming a huge loop that was a rest for his upper body as it too looped. From his towing height, he looked down at all the people and smiled.

"Orrin, you've met my gold before, haven't you?" Orrin's wide eyes of bewilderment said, 'No'. "Oh, well, what do you think of him?" Orrin gave a stiff nod. He gripped into the Dragoncaller's side and never lost sight of the dragon. "C'mon," Craig encouraged. "You've seen dragons before."

Craig and Orrin took nervous steps towards the dragon. "Yuh, your blue dragon isn't as big!" Orrin exclaimed from a dry mouth. "I've never been this close, eh?"

Craig stood at the gold dragon's side and the beast knelt to offer his neck to ride on. Craig took Orrin's hands to guide him where to hold before giving him a foot up to the dragon's paw. From there, Kuger slowly lifted the young elf towards his neck. "He has no wings! Eh?" Orrin said looking around.

Craig swung up in one smooth motion and settled easily behind Orrin. "Neither does a frisbee."

"Huh?" Orrin wondered not knowing the term 'Frisbee'. But he let it go. It was always best not to ask about fifty percent of what ever Craig said. "Does he, like, have a name." The dragon's head swiveled around above the height of the buildings and looked down at the boy. Orrin tightened his grip on the dragon's mane.

Craig knew that a dragon's name was never to be spoken to mortals, with the exception of Ralph, who never really knew his own name. "This is, Uh, Frisbee."

"Okay then, Frisbee." Orrin squirmed about. *To ride a dragon! Wait until Rob hears about this!*

Craig looked down to the knight on the street. The town was deserted, not a soul around save Milo. "Good luck Craig Tyrone! Next time, you will be more welcome."

"Next time I'll take a cab." He spurred his dragon, "Hi ho bullion! Away!" Kugerand, The great golden dragon leapt to the sky and bounded on the air. The brilliant sun flashed against his hide as he slipped like a giant snake through the sky.

"Does this, like, hurt you?" Orrin shouted in the wind. "I mean, you know, the sun."

Craig shook his head. "No, its strange, while I'm on dragon back, wind, sun, rain, altitude, nothing bothers me much."

"It is, like, the will of Ok-shi-ru, eh?"

"Yeah sure, whatever."

Chapter 46

High in the azure blue of Okshiru's spacious sky, Kemoto, god of sun, flew. His wings of flame glided gently on the highest of Hauge's winds. Fikor the dog of winter stood on the crest of the white mountain and looked into the brilliant glow of the sun bird. It was now his season of winter. He had slept too long and it was time for him to hunt. His breath rolled down the mountains with vapors of ice and clung to the rocks pushing from the earth. He laughed and great clouds puffed into the sky. He watched as the cold he commanded swept across Okshiru's sky, until even Kemoto felt his cold. The sun bird folded his wings to protect his heart from the ice of winter.

Two horses far below made their way slowly through Meleki's forest. Wild colors in the shades of a setting sun were burned into the leaves as they flittered and floated from the trees. Horses hooves shuffled their way through the carpet of yellow, red, and brown leaves.

One was a horseman of war. His armor of gray dull steel was adorned with spikes. Magic had been melded with steel and iron to form the adamantine skin, wrought and shaped to fit his body and move as he moved. A hammer of might at his side and a great sword of power at his saddle. His horse of brown plodded along as horses do, occasionally puffing or snorting and stirring its mane.

Riding beside the man of war, was a knight of the gods. His armor of grey was intricate, yet plain and made from the same metal of magic. It was not as bulky nor as imposing and the knight wore his tunic and pants over it. Robes of black covered his head and shoulders and continued over his entire frame. At his side was his fabled blade-spear. A staff of life and a blade of death. A knight's weapon to be used to smite the evil, right the wrong and preserve the American way.

"The what?" Roc grunted.

"The American way, like Mom, apple pie, and the video pirate next door."

Roc looked back to the trail. "You've been paying attention to Craig. It isn't good." Roc looked to the sky.

"I don't think so." Frito answered knowingly. "Craig is a genius. He did build the Red Barchetta."

"Rebuild." Roc corrected. "Genius yeah. Crazy, that too." Roc looked back to the road. "Fikor came suddenly this year…" Roc blew a long cloudy breath. "and late. I wonder who put Mescaline in his Alpo."

"And I listen to Craig too much?"

"I use moderation."

Frito leaned his head back and laughed. "You...moderation?"

"Quench it bucko." Roc snorted.

Frito looked about for a moment and looked back to his cousin. "Are you sure about this short cut?"

"I'm the Dragonslayer." He said weakly. "Short cuts are what I do best."

"I thought you preferred hacking to cutting." Frito looked behind him and then to the trail. "I don't know about this. I've been lost before and it looked a lot like this."

Roc sniffed the air. "Smell that." He looked to the sky again. "Freezing rain. Tonight, everything will be ice!"

"You're changing the subject."

"I think its best we find shelter." Roc ignored his cousin. "Don't want this stupid rent-a-horse dropping dead on me."

"Rent-a-horse?"

"Yeah!" Roc said proudly, "Thought of that myself."

"Regardless, we are still lost."

"We are not. Roc doesn't get lost."

Frito's horse whinnied at the thought.

"Shut him up."

"You know Roc," Frito said skeptically. "Horse here is smarter than I am."

"That isn't saying much." Roc pointed ahead. "I bet you a coin, there's a river up ahead."

"I have ears too."

Roc spurred his horse into a light trot and skipped into the brush. Frito followed close behind. They both paused at the river bank. Roc eyed the swift flowing river. It was a stones throw wide and seemed to be too deep to cross with armored horses. He looked up and down the banks hoping for a easy way to cross. There were none.

"Well Roc," Frito said riding over. "I am quite sure that it is your turn for a good idea."

Roc held up an armored finger. "I do not believe that this would rule as a perilous situation; however, I know exactly how to do this."

Frito glanced around for a moment, then leaned closer. "Yeah?"

"You get us across." Roc said with certainty. "Make with the spells." Roc pointed a finger. "This shouldn't be too tough."

"Okay…" Frito said slowly. "Do you want me to part the river, or just dry it up?"

"Actually, I want you to lift the damn thing and we ride under." Roc said harshly. "Look, nothing big, just across."

Frito glared at him in silence. Roc looked over at him. "What?"

"Nothing."

Roc shifted on his horse annoyed. "Look, you've been glaring at me like that for days. What is it?"

"Why did you wait two years to piss me off?" He asked simply.

For a moment, Roc had no idea what his cousin was talking about. "Time wasn't right."

"You're afraid of me, still."

Roc glared at him as if he were crazy. "Nah!"

"You are too." Frito sounded almost like a child. "You flinched when I said about splitting the river. You almost believed that I could. I still frighten you."

Roc clenched his teeth. "And who wouldn't be! Drying up a river to get across would be a Hauth thing to do. Yeah, I'm still a little spooked 'cause you keep doing shit. 'Fuck Okshiru' you say. You said that before."

"I said it long before I went to Hel."

Roc nodded, "Yes, but now its different. It tells me that you are still not in sync with the big guy."

"I never was and you know it!"

"Perhaps."

"I can never become Hauth again."

"I know, just give me a little time, okay?"

Frito nodded and looked at the river in front of him. Roc watched him for a beat and wondered: *and where did you learn to lie so well?*

Frito looked across the river and whispered words of magic. He called for Hashu, god of the river. He shouted at the river and ordered it to carry him across. Then he leaned forward and whispered into his horse's ear.

Suddenly, Horse bolted forward. His hooves skidded across with tiny splashes in the running water as he galloped across the river to the other side. Safely across, Frito waved back to his cousin. Roc grunted and kicked his horse forward.

The horse halted and refused to budge. Roc shouted at the beast and kicked it again, but the horse refused to step into the raging water.

"Roc!" Frito called from the other side. "Your horse has to be lead across the water!"

Roc growled and grunted as he swung himself from his horse. He took up its reins and stepped to the river bank. He paused as he looked into the water rushing at his feet. It didn't look any different. But Frito had made it right across, so why couldn't he?

The Mighty Dragonslayer took one step into the water and sank like a rock straight down.

Frito leaned back in his saddle and laughed loud and long. To see his cousin just sink right down below the water was truly funny.

Frito suddenly remembered, Roc couldn't swim.

Frito spurred Horse and the two sprinted across the river to the other side. Frito leapt off his horse and dropped to his hands and knees at the river bank for any sign of his cousin.

There was only bubbles.

Frito pushed his hands into the cold water and felt for him. Suddenly giant arms of steel seized him and quickly pulled him in. Steel wrestled steel as the two splashed about in the water. Roc gripped Frito's ankle and flipped him backwards under the water. Roc stood there and laughed as Frito found his feet and stood up in the four foot water.

"Next time, I'll let you drown!" Frito shouted.

"Next time, find deeper water for me to drown in. I'm not afraid anymore." Roc laughed as he reached up and took the reigns of his horse and lead it into the water.

Frito looked after him. "What brought that on?"

Roc didn't look back as he made his way across. "If Hauth was anywhere in you, you would have left me in the water a little longer."

Frito shrugged and looked to his own horse and waved it on. The black horse stuck one hoof into the water and splashed it about. Horse looked up and whinnied.

"I'm sorry." Frito apologized. "But the spell doesn't last that long." Horse shook his head as if he wanted Frito to cast it again, but Frito shook his head. "Sorry, I can't spare the energy, but if its any consolation. I'm wet too." Horse looked about the bank and stepped out of reality.

Frito waded across the river and Horse stood on the other side for him. Roc gave his cousin a hand and pulled him out of the water. "Well, that's my bath for today." Roc poured water from his gauntlet. "Explain to me again how your horse just walked over here like that."

Frito walked over to his horse and looked about in one of the saddle bags. "Horse can transverse the multiplanes. He just can't take people."

"But he can take horses right?"

Frito paused suddenly and looked at his horse. "Yeah, that's right. Why didn't you take Roc's horse across?" Horse just looked away. "What do you mean you didn't think of it?" Horse looked at him again. "True," Frito mumbled. "I didn't think of it either." Frito pulled out a dry cloak and pulled it on.

Roc shook his head as he poured water from his boot. He paused suddenly and fixed his eyes on a target. "Frito." He hissed. "I spy something with my little eye." Roc dropped his boot and took up his hammer. "Something that starts with 'splat'!"

Frito looked up as he stuffed his wet cloak into his saddle bag. "What are you doing? Is that a rabbit? Leave it alone, you don't eat rabbit."

"I eat anything." Roc growled as he slowly stalked the rabbit. "And besides, he's looking right at me, daring me to pound him." Roc came closer and it suddenly turned and dashed under a bush.

Frito laughed. "Not this time. Lets go."

Roc looked at the bush and could see the rabbit's puff tail. The rabbit twitched its tail and disappeared into the bush. "Did you see that!" Roc stormed at the bush. "No rabbit mocks Me!" Roc gripped at the bush and tore it away. The rabbit stood there on its haunches glaring right at the Dragonslayer. Roc raised his hammer and quickly brought it down. "Ha! Now your dead! Now what are you going to do?" Roc lifted his hammer to pound again, but the rabbit was gone.

He paused with his arm cocked over his head looking about. There was no way that he could've missed. It just couldn't have happened; he couldn't have missed.

He lowered his arm slowly and looked about, then he called to Frito. "Come see this."

"I've seen enough rabbit guts for today thank you."

"No…" Roc said soberly. "Come here and see this."

Frito was up on his horse and trotted over. Roc cleared away a few scraps of bush and dead leaves and exposed thirty two stones set about in the shape of the four pointed star of Hammerstrike.

Frito swung from his horse and knelt beside the Dragonslayer.

"Any idea? It seems that this has been here awhile." Roc ran his hand in the center of the star as he spoke. "Who could have put it here?"

Frito shook his head.

Roc suddenly stopped at and started to dig his hands into the hard, cold ground. "There is something here, I can feel it." He said as he went deeper. Frito pulled out his knife and started digging as well. "Can you feel it?" Roc stopped and watched as Frito stabbed at the ground and Roc dug away the lose dirt.

He found a chain and pulled on it, a moment later he pulled free the silver star of Hammerstrike and handed it to his cousin.

Frito wiped off the dirt with his thumb and read the name engraved beautifully on the back. "Denice." Frito said. "And...Stephanie. Look see, the name Stephanie was scratched in."

"Well..." Roc said looking over the pendant. "Explain this."

"Its Denice's. That's obvious, why she would scratch Mom's name on the back is beyond me."

Roc leaned in closer and glared at his cousin. "How long has this been here?"

"I would guess about 7 years. I remember that I made the one she wears now when she disappeared and ascended."

Roc cocked his head. "She said she lost it?"

"I never asked. Weird things happen when knights ascend. You know that. I noticed she didn't have one so I made another as a surprise. That was six or so years ago."

"And how many Stephanie's do you know?"

"One." Frito said simply. "My mother."

"You sure?" Roc half accused him.

Frito paused and thought again. "No...Oustrand's child."

"How common is the name Stephanie?"

"As common as mine and yours. It isn't."

"I've never heard it anywhere else either." Roc stood up and looked around as if to organize his thoughts. "Your mother used her knight's name Fantista most of her life. Who knows her name other than us?"

"Its not something we share too often."

"Yeah," Roc fixed his jaw trying to push out an answer on the edge of his mind. "A now this." Roc pointed to the stones. "Then why is this here? An alter? And what of the star?" Roc glared at the spot. "Its as almost if…This is a grave, isn't it?" Frito nodded. "What did Frita bury here?" Roc scratched his chin. "Something small I would imagine. And the star as a headstone, or a…Then Frita…" Roc's eyes suddenly grew wide. "And you knew!" Roc shouted.

Frito found his feet quickly. "No…I did not know this…blessid I did not know this!"

"Is it her's?"

Frito took up his thousand click stare as he thought. "There would have been enough time."

"But why? How? What happened?"

"I don't know. It might have driven her to ascension."

"Filled with sorrow and probably guilt wrapped she went willingly and they took her!" Roc stepped away and paced for a moment. He pointed his finger at his cousin but said nothing. Instead he chewed the inside of his lip and then asked. "How?"

Frito answered. "The answer was in the beginning, we were just to blind to see. Child of the gods."

Roc turned in fury and snatched up Frito's blade-spear. With all of his great might he hurled it right at Worldsend. "TO HEL WITH YOU ALL!" Roc then howled with a bellow and looked about for something to destroy. He took up his hammer and suddenly lunged at a large boulder. He pounded again and again with his magic hammer of war until the rock itself burned red with fire. White sparks flew from each blow as a crack crawled along the burning surface. Roc raised higher and higher and higher and hit harder and harder until the stone burned white with pain and magic. He screamed as he delivered his final blow and shattered the boulder to hot sand.

He stood there breathing harder and harder, clenching the hammer in his hands. Sweat slowly began to cool on his shoulders and lift into steam.

Frito sat calmly by the site fondling the chain in his hands. "You done?"

Roc turned at his hotly. "I hate being manipulated!"

"Your not being manipulated. I am."

"How can you stand it?"

"Have you seen much choice for me?"

Roc paused and thought about it, then dropped to a squat. "What are you thinking?"

Frito put his hands together, touching his fingers to his lips. "I'm thinking, of what Okshiru is thinking."

"And?"

"I can't guess…I feel I am on the edge of the answer…looking right at it…yet, it escapes me."

"And Okshiru? Isn't he supposed to be looking over his knights?"

Frito rose to his feet. "He is. He is watching this whole thing. Probably letting Ura get away with this." Frito mounted his horse.

"What?" Roc snatched at his leg. "Explain!"

"I do not know. But he has not abandoned us. He leaves us clues. Like that rabbit."

Roc took up the reigns to his horse and mounted. "And what will you do?"

"I will see this through till the end. I will bring out my family if I can and damn anyone to Hel if they try to stop me."

"I'm with you, lets burn down the first place we find."

Frito looked back to Roc. A characteristic act of random senseless violence. "Deal." He whispered. He turned his horse to the woods and looked at his blade-spear before him embedded into the ground. One of its many powers is to the return to his hand, but now it stood before him. A weapon of Okshiru to his knights. An oath in the body of a sword. To break that oath is to break the sword. For a knight to regain his status, he must quest and prove himself. But the sword will never be found again, but born anew in a new form as the knight himself has been. Fryto's great axe and Frito's blade-spear.

But now it loomed before him like a reminder of his promise to his god, himself and to his father. He quickly snatched it up. "And such is my lot." He swore under his breath.

"And mine is as tightly woven in the same fabric." Roc said as if he could read his cousin's thoughts. "I can't ride away, but in."

Frito nodded. "We've wasted enough time."

Chapter 47

Fikor ran across the great breathing sea of Okshiru. The Snow Dog leapt over the wet hills and the chopping waves until he reached the end of the sea. From there, he howled to the great god of sky and sea for the rain of Danshu to fall. Okshiru raised a mighty hand and with a touch to his white sky let Danshu fall.

Fikor laughed with glee and ran towards the shore with Danshu behind him. The great Snow Dog out raced Danshu and leapt up the banks of the beach and on to Mortalroam.

Frita licked her horses again and drove her cart a little faster. She could hear the howl of Fikor getting closer. Although elves were immune to the cold of Fikor, it was not wise to travel while he roamed about.

She followed the road about the rim of the cliffs and around to the large manner itself. The old manner looked poor and burned in the frame of the white sky. The house sagged upon itself and stared out over the sea with dark empty windows. The gate before it, pulled and pushed to Hauge's winds like a ghost, testing its hinges. Dead leaves clicked and hissed on the over grown walkway that led to the rotted front door complete with a rotted old door mat that said 'Welcome'.

Welcome to the Home by the Sea.

Frita quickly brought her horses over to the stables. She found a corner that was still covered by a roof and secured her horses. She fed them some fresh oats that she had brought with her in the cart. She brushed them down and gave them water. As she secured the tack and harness, she heard Danshu tapping on the zinc sheet roof of the stables. She covered the horses with blankets, took up her things and hurried to the back door that led to the kitchen. She quickly dashed up the three short stone steps and stopped at the open door. She called for Kathreen as she pushed her way in. The house was cold and silent. Frita slowly turned about. The kitchen was a mess with pots and pans piled on the stove and plates and bowls stacked in and about the washbasin unclean. There was a wicker cage on the kitchen table that had not been there before.

She closed her eyes and held still, letting her elven ears listen about the house. She listened past the moans and creeks of the old house and shut out the dance of Danshu on the roof. She listened past the running of rats chasing the bats in the attic and the bats chasing the rats in the cellar.

There was no sound of Kathreen, nor Buffet.

There was a man snoring.

The man's scent was strong. He had been recently in the kitchen. Frita allowed her senses to go on, go deeper, into the cracks of the wood and faded carpets and curtains where essences crawled away to hide.

Frita moved across the old wooden floor with the silent footfalls of elves and dashed up the stair with ease. She stepped into the hall and the top of the stairs and poised like the marsh hare or red squirrel, listening to the new silence of absent snoring. She let her senses breath the fetid odors that assailed her.

It was a human stink.

She could feel the magic around her. She had foolishly set off an alarm and now, who ever was around, knew she was here.

At the top of the stairs she could clearly see the hall to the end in both directions. To the right were three doors, all open. At the closest door, swords, axes and clubs lay at the sill. To the left were also three doors, all open. The closest was the room they used for baths, the second was were Buffet slept while the third was Kathreen's room. The door to Buffet's room lay in shards of wood on the tattered carpet.

Frita held her breath and counted the beats. The snoring had stopped before she reached the top of the stairs. The only sound was coming from the house itself moaning in complaint to Fikor's winter. But the odor was unmasked. Its trail lead boldly to the right. Slowly she turned and silently crept over to the first door on the right, her feet carefully stepping between the weapons on the floor. From a crouched angle, she peered into the room.

Blues ran in the shape of broken pentacles across a marble white wall. Crimson reds ran across fields of yellow in cryptic words of Hate. Thrice damned chants of Vulgar scripted in Envy green blazed across the floor and ceiling. Magic in symbols and spells in color meshed into an assailing wretch of human evil. A nightmare, in the middle of the day.

The Knight of Okshiru suddenly flared in her centre. It pulled her and tried to push her away from the room of blasphemy, but there was more.

Kathreen laid on the floor.

Frita rushed in and dropped to her knees. Her centre suddenly screamed in pain as she pulled at Kathreen's unmoving body. Frita wrapped her arms about Kathreen and tried to give her elven warmth. Kathreen didn't move nor respond.

Frita sobbed and cried aloud as she shook at Kathreen to hear. Words of Okshiru sprang from her mouth and her voice pleaded to Worldsend. They were automatic words that were inbred in all knights of Okshiru, words of healing, words of strength, words of life, words of debt.

Frita wept as she chanted and her tears splashed on to Kathreen's face like Danshu on the roof above. She gripped Kathreen's wrist and held it close to her breast. She could feel the white fire in her centre grow like a tree, with branches reaching through her arms and into her hands of healing. The stump of Kathreen's arm slowly began to mend itself in answer to Frita's calling.

The white fire burned hotter and the healing went on. Frita's body began to glow with Okshiru's power. So consumed she was with her chant, that she failed to notice Paradox standing behind her.

Outside, Danshu danced faster as Fikor howled with glee. Hauge the wind chased the white dog around the house. At the cliffs below, the sea of Okshiru crashed into the rocks with a trembling roar. Frita only held Kathreen tighter and let the white fire of Okshiru flow through her.

Slowly the white fire began to wane as the tide pulled from shore. Frita tried to flame the passion again, but her fire was exhausted. She only held Kathreen and rocked back and forth as a mother with a tiny sleeping infant. Outside, Danshu slowed his dance and the race between Fikor and Hauge carried on elsewhere. Paradox uncrossed and crossed his legs.

Frita gasped and turned her head, her hands still clutched tightly about Kathreen. Paradox stood at the door with a small crossbow in hand. "Hi, Denice. Fancy you being here." He raised the crossbow and calmly shot her.

Frita tensed and twisted her arm forward to protect Kathreen and caught the bolt in her forearm. Pain shot from her elbow to her fingers with a rush. Tears blurred her vision as magic came to her lips. She tried to speak the words of power, but lacked the strength to call on her own voice. So exhausted from chanting for Kathreen, she had nothing to save herself.

Paradox laughed as Frita clenched Kathreen's limp body to her chest as she crawled painfully towards the wall. "Denice...You rascal." He slowly came into the room, limping slightly on one foot. "I really wish I knew you were coming." He sat beside her and watched the knight of Okshiru bleed sweat against the wall. "The poison on that bolt will kill you, but only after 20 beats of surreal agony. That was really off the cuff, and if you had only let me know you were coming, I would have had something a little more dramatic. But any port in a storm, right? I mean, you are way too dangerous to have walking about. Even if I were not in this condition, I would have been no match for you." He watched her for a moment longer. "You have to consciously remember to breathe, you'll live longer that way." Paradox shifted closer and touched her sweating face. "You were so beautiful...you still are. I really did like you. More than her." He glanced to Kathreen. "Why did you join the order? What possessed you to do that?"

Frita gasped and swallowed and gazed with silver elven eyes at Paradox.

"Don't bother trying to talk, you'll find it impossible. By now, the ants you feel crawling behind your eyes should begin to bite. The pain will grow in intensity in a little bit..." He gazed out the window then looked back. "It was the child wasn't it? You thought that I was going to destroy the child. I guess you were right...I would have had too, fate screamed that my own son would have killed me. If you had given me the child I would have forgiven you. Instead you ran off and took my son. You left me alone...Denice, why did you leave me alone? How could you? And now you've come back, but it's too late for forgiveness." He stroked her face again and peeled her black hair from her wet face. "I could still like you. You are so pretty. Too pretty for any of Okshiru's knights. Tell me Denice, where is my son? I've been racking my brains for all these years trying to find him. You hid him well. Where is he?" Frita gasped and moaned but said nothing. "Why wasn't it a girl? I would have raised her in the image of Ura. She would have been a goddess on earth. I would have taught her all I knew, I would have raised her as a son! That would have been wild and you would have been the mother! But you had to have a son."

"It..." Frita gasped. "Was not...ah a sson."

"What? It was a girl? Then where is she?" Paradox sat on his haunches. "You had a girl and didn't tell me?" He grabbed the knight and shook her. "Answer me! Don't die yet!" He back fisted her with all of his waning strength but she only felt the poison in her body. "Why did you take my daughter from me? Speak!"

Frita said nothing, she didn't try.

Paradox grabbed Kathreen and yanked her limp body away from Frita then held her against the wall. "You bitch...You bitch! I will find her!

"Nh, nh, no...yyyou wwon't." Frita suddenly slumped as she felt her strength wain.

"Where? Where is she? Tell me!" He sat back down as he realized that she was giving no more answers. "It would have been great." He shook his head and watched her a little longer. "Right now it should feel like your eyes are about to explode. Does it? Good." He sighed and looked out the window again. "Well, I gotta get some sleep. I'm still racked out from the cacodemon." He leaned in close and kissed her lightly and for a moment he felt her pain. He found his feet and stepped over Kathreen as he headed for the door. He stopped and looked back at Frita, her eyes staring into space. "Denice? Before you pass on. Tell me something? What do you see? Is there a name for what you see? Can you cry? No...not from those eyes, they are dry and have cried their last. Shall I cry for you?" He shook his head and stepped out of the room.

Frita's eyes of pain watched him leaving. Her voice couldn't call after him, but she didn't want too.

"So..." Thumber said standing by the door frame. "Can you see me? Frita. I'm brought to you via complements of the son of Hate. Actually, he had little to do with it, but it's his fault non the less." He strolled lightly in the room and stood beside her. He stooped down and watched her die for a moment. "Actually, I'm really here because you called me. I don't even think you know you called me, but you did. Believe it or not, you summoned me to torment you for your sin. You gave me my power. And as sort of a thank you, I can help you. Paradox said that you were in pain and I can see it. I can end that pain. Would you like that? Yes, I see you do."

Chapter 48

The howl of winter swept in the trail of the mighty snow dog as he ran boldly across the face of Mortalroam. He stopped suddenly as something caught his eye. He leaped up, landing on a cloud, and peered down for a look. He saw a rabbit, gray and half frozen with ice-rain, running with great determination. This was indeed something odd for fragile rabbits to do. He thought a moment, and then another. His collar jingled as he shook his fur to free the clumps of forming ice. He often did this while thinking. Without an idea coming, the great snowdog slid down from his cloud and laid along the side of a mountain with his head hanging over the top and his long white tongue hanging out. This was another thing he did while thinking. This rabbit had a mission, his frantic pace and steadfast course proved that. He looked to the great white sky of Okshiru that loomed above him and by the natural sense of correctness, he knew it to be true.

He watched a while longer from his mountain top and finally came to a decision. He would hold off, for a while, at least until he had a clearer understanding of this rabbit. He called for Hauge the wind, to still his rivers of air. It was not time for the storm as yet.

Danshu, oblivious to Fikor's revelation, danced in the trees of the woods and along the long winding road that ran the edge of the cliffs that slipped into the sea. His rain slid slowly down the long hanging fangs of ice that dangled from the boughs of the barren trees. The rabbit dashed along the trail avoiding the stalactites of ice in fear of one falling. He ran with his fur wet slick with rain and his bones frozen with ice to the road that went along the edge of the cliffs. He didn't pause as he ran directly up the walk. He leapt easily over the sagging fence and up the crumbling path towards the old house. The rabbit ran directly to the rotted old door complete with door mat that said Welcome.

Hooves suddenly loomed about him. He was too small to be seen by the great armored Clydesdale that trotted almost on top him. He dove instinctively into a pile of wet leaves to hide.

"Welcome to the Home by the Sea." Roc said sliding from his horse.

Frito brought his horse closer and looked up the second story windows. "Is this the wrong house?"

"That sounds like a thinly veiled insult on my trail blazing skills."

"I had no intention to veil it." Frito said with a frown. "However, it is a place. Knock, if we get no answer, then we will camp here until Fikor's storm passes."

Roc grunted his approval and raised a heavy gauntleted arm to pound on the door.

"What is it?" Frito sat up taller in his saddle. Roc only stood there with his arm raised in the air. He turned from the door slowly lowering his arm and his eyes lifting skyward.

"Dragon." He growled as he went to his horse. "Coming this way."

As a reflex, Frito's blade-spear leapt into his wanting hand. "Here? Now? Aren't they asleep."

"Not always." Roc pulled free his great sword from his horse's saddle. "A dragon can awake hungry at any time." Roc slapped his horse and sent it towards the gate out of danger.

Frito dismounted with his blade spear in hand. His own horse, Horse, stepped out of reality. "And it's coming here? This very spot?" Frito followed Roc as he moved towards the front fence. The knight kept searching the sky. "This isn't right Roc, are you sure?"

"I am the Dragonslayer." Was all he said.

Frito adjusted his dark glasses as he searched the sky. "Is it hostile?"

"What dragon isn't?" Roc twirled his sword in his hand. "Are you up to battling a dragon?" Roc shoot a look back to his cousin. For the first time in a long time, Roc was happy. The great fighter swept his sword about as if to test what he already knew.

Frito squinted as he looked to the sky. "There it is." He pointed his blade-spear to the tiny dot a click above them.

"Move over, he'll go for one of us, the other will have him." Roc said as he gestured Frito to move back.

Roc watched the dragon lowering from the sky, still only a tiny speck knowing full well that a dragon could cover the distance in the time he could draw a single breath. He had to plan this correctly. He had to wait for the dragon to lower for the kill then run like Hel to cover. The dragon would be forced to land to fight. On the ground Roc The Dragonslayer and Frito, Knight of Okshiru might have a fighting chance. If the dragon soared...rose back into the air and spat his fire...well, as Craig would say, shit happens.

Frito moved closer to the tree line. Roc was a better target, more heavily armored than himself. As the dragon came in, he could call forth lightning and charge his blade-spear to full power, launch his weapon and strike the dragon at the arch of his swoop. The dragon would have to land and charge after him, allowing Roc a chance to make dragon fritters.

Hopefully.

Frito whispered and felt tingles in the haft of his spear. He was ready. Roc, a stone throw way, waited cocked, directly in the dragon's path.

Frito watched the speck grow and circled over head. It was a gold dragon, erratic and unpredictable. Adult in size and might. This was going to be tough. *What is it doing? Deciding to attack?* Music suddenly came to his ears. The sounding call of elven wonder floated down from the air and rested about him.

Roc looked around in surprise for the elfcall was coming from the dragon.

"ORRIN!" Frito screamed as the dragon came lower. The knight waited for the gold dragon to set down and Craig to dismount. Frito and Roc both came at the great gold beast while Craig helped Orrin dismount.

"That was like, wild! Eh?" Orrin exclaimed. "Really Fes-tive!" Roc stopped short as he came close and the giant beast looked down at him. Roc growled and feinted with his sword and the beast reared back slightly. "Hey," Craig called to the dragon. "Leave him alone. You know Roc doesn't like that." Craig looked at Frito as the knight came closer. "Hey, big guy, you're looking good."

"So do you." Frito said sarcastically, looking over Craig's face and hands.

Craig touched the side of his face. "Never try to shave with a case of the hiccups." Craig nudged his dragon to stop him from staring at Roc and then turned back to the Ninefingers. "The shit has really hit the fan back at Tarra."

"What is it?" Frito glared at the dark elf.

"Harroc, son of Hate, you know him? I think you do. Well, he wasn't selling Avon. He came a knocking with a few thousand of his hell rasing buddies. Relax, every one is fine, almost. Fist, Shaft and about a sixty men were killed at last count. About a hundred are seriously wounded and might not make it. The rest are in care of Lady Fantista. Your mother is a miracle with healing people, I think we'll have a good survival rate."

"So my mother is alright?"

"Is she? I'll say. She kicked more ass than Bruce Lee. I'm gonna start taking lessons. She punted Harroc for the game winning field goal. The woman's got more moves than Exlax, and smoother too…why I bet…" Craig looked up to his dragon. "What are you looking at?" The dragon only looked down at the Dragoncaller.

Craig looked back to Frito. "Were being watched, from within the house."

Frito looked up to the second story. Roc only grunted as he made his way to the gate.

The huge elf kicked the sagging gate to wooden splinters and stomped up the crumbling walk. He stepped up on the rotting mat the said Welcome and without much ado, went to smash down the door.

With a heaving spiked gauntlet, he raised up, seizing all of his power to powder the door and stopped in mid swing.

There was a rabbit, with one paw on Roc The Dragonslayer's foot. The rabbit's large brown eyes glared up at the masked armored fighter as if to ask a question. His gray ears were slicked back and his head slightly cocked to one side as if it had nothing in the world to fear.

Fifty thousand, seven hundred and thirty nine ways of how to prepare rabbit, crashed with seven hundred forty seven thousand, nine hundred and two, ways to kill a rabbit without using a siege weapon, forming a giant collage in Roc's head as his mind reeled.

He suddenly went to stomp the tenacious rabbit, but it dashed and dove and evaded Roc's tromping feet. Roc paused and the rabbit, balanced on its hind legs looked to Roc, stuck out its tongue, and wiggled its ears in a most insulting manner.

Roc The Mighty Dragonslayer, stood pointing at a tiny rabbit.

"SEE WHAT IT DID?!" He screamed.

The rabbit suddenly took off and full speed around to the rear of the house.

Frito dashed quickly after the rabbit. It waited at the corner of the house before darting up the stone steps and into the kitchen. Frito followed suit, to the rear of the house and up the stairs into the darkness of the kitchen. His elvish eyes burned red as they pushed back the shadows lying on the floor. Dark shutters were pulled tight against the windows. The air was heavy with stink and drifted lethargically in the room.

The rabbit was gone.

Roc made his way up the stairs and halted at his cousin's silent command. Frito slowly slid through the mess and into the dinning room. A stripe of light spilled across the floor from a leaking window blind. The long shadow of a rabbit slid across the line of light for a beat before hopping up the stairs.

Frito tasted the magic that hung in the air about him on his tongue. Wires of power strung like a spider's web across the floor. Threads as fragile as silence. Trip wires, hooked to an alarm.

The Ninefingers made a sign in the air. He made large steps and signaled for the others to follow in the same way. They slowly tipped up the stairs in silence. Frito's armor was muffled by his heavy robes as was Craig's armor, hidden beneath his tunic and pant. Only Roc's monstrous armor clinked slightly as he moved. Frito waved for him to hang back as he slipped up the stairs.

Frito crept lower as he reached the top. His blade-spear pushed into the shadow of the dark house. Tiny green flecks of earthen green suddenly splashed onto the blade as it summoned power to itself. Charging power to fight.

Knives cut the darkness with a scream. The blade-spear dashed before him and blocked them away. A shadow faded across a wall as the Ninefingers leapt to the top of the stairs. His blood filled eyes beamed back the dark.

He was thin, cadaverous, worn and exhausted. Frito could feel the emptiness of his soul, drained by a spell greater than his own body. Frito knew him. He was Paradox.

In his left hand, was a dried, shriveled hand of a woman and in his right, was a long sword. He clenched them both as his last grip on reality.

Flecks of light pushed from Frito's blade and leapt into the ceiling. With a brilliant flash the hall exploded with light. Frito stood like a silhouette, backlit with his own glow, his blade twirling in his fingers, its edge, cutting the shafts of white into dots flashing against the wall. "Give it up." He said in a voice long and low. A tall shadow with bleeding holes were his eyes should be. "You've failed Paradox. Look at yourself, you're nothing!"

The frail man held out the withered hand, but it only crumbled to dust.

Frito stepped closer. "You cannot raise a hand against me." He slowly swept his great blade about. "Stop this, lower your sword."

Paradox clenched his teeth and lunged for a door. It sprang open from his weight and he tumbled in. Frito followed after. The room was empty save a bathing bin and a bucket beside it. There was smoke from a smoldering fire in the place, and the back of the place closing shut.

Frito dashed across the floor, walking across beams where there was no floor and crouched beneath the mantle. He pounded the back of it and it responded as solid. He pulled and pushed and twisted at the hanging rack dangling over the fire and it opened to a small dark tunnel going down.

An elf's size and bulk is much smaller than a man. Even Frito who was large and thick for an elf was smaller than most men, but he was in heavy robes with equipment and armor. He wasn't going to fit.

"ROC!" He shouted. "Outside! Don't let him escape!"

Frito stepped carefully across the room again and out into the hall. Orrin stood at the top of the stairs. "This way." The boy whispered.

Frito pushed through and followed the boy to the room where Craig was waiting. The dark elf was crouched over a human woman with his hand on her throat. "She's alive." He said twisting her body so she would lie flat. "But that isn't saying much." Frito swept to her side pulling off his gauntlets. He pulled her hair from her face. "Who is she?"

"Your guess is as good as mine." Craig said.

Orrin perked his ears. "It is Roc, eh? He has Para-dox!"

Frito looked to Craig. "Go see. Keep Roc from killing him. I want him alive."

Craig turned and headed down the stairs. He paused for a moment as he passed through the kitchen and then out the back door. Less then 3 meters from the door, Paradox laid on the ground with his own sword pushed through his bowels and into the dirt. He tried with fleeting strength to pull the sword free, but failed. His hands tore and bled as he tried to grip the bloody blade.

Roc leaned against a tree. "You're dying pal," Roc said to Paradox. "The worst part is, you're dying slowly. Blood is spilling out of your guts and into one of your lungs. You'll drown in your own blood before you bleed to death." Roc yanked a dry reed from the ground and twirled it in his armored fingers. "Sucks don't it?"

Craig crouched at the side of the body. He loomed close to the dying man's head and whispered, "What is going on here? Harroc goes door to door, Frita and Friska are on the backs of milk cartons and there is a rabbit monkeying around." Craig's elven eyes burned red. "Tell me what is going on!"

Paradox looked up. His flat pale eyes bleed sweat and tears, but glinted as he recognized Craig. His yellowed stained teeth bent to a smile as he whispered back. "You have made it far in this world." He swallowed the blood rising in his mouth. "When you first arrived, I spared your life knowing you were going to get yourself killed anyway." He chocked and wheezed and made a face as pain flashed across his face.

"You call that sparing? I think Webster's defines that as 'leaving someone to die'."

"But you didn't." Paradox went on, trying to fill his lungs with enough air to speak. "When I did decide to kill you, I thought it so fortunate that I failed—letting you suffer on with this life. But you didn't suffer. Congratulations. You are the only one to foil me this many times." He swallowed, tasting his own blood. "What's going on? You ask as if there is an answer." He wheezed a laugh at his own joke.

Craig rose to his feet. Paradox was still trying to pull free the sword. His grip on life, the hands that killed so many others, refused to let it go regardless how the sword carved into him. Roc was still leaning against the tree watching intently.

Craig looked at the sword. Suddenly he grabbed the handle and jerked it free. Paradox screamed as it was torn from him. Roc pushed to his feet. Paradox rolled over with his hands over his wound chanting an ancient call for healing. Craig watched him for a moment and raised the sword. Paradox looked back, his eyes filled with terror as the steel came down at his head.

Paradox made a whimper, and then died.

Roc towered over Craig in surprise. Craig didn't look at him, he merely tossed the sword to the ground and stepped away.

Frito came from the back door with the woman in his arms. Orrin followed behind with a box in his arms. Frito stood over the bloodied mess. "I wanted him alive." He hissed at Roc.

Roc glared back. "He wouldn't come quietly!" Roc growled back.

"Don't yell at him." Craig said as he slowly eased to the ground. "He didn't do it. I did."

Frito looked down at the dark elf in surprise. "You?"

"PMS is not just for breakfast anymore." Craig said to no one in particular. Just then, Kugerand, the gold dragon, slipped to the rear of the house. He bowed his great head and nuzzled Craig in the side. The Dragoncaller mindlessly reached back and scratched the gold beneath its chin. "He was Paradox. He got his kicks off of killing."

"You knew him?" Frito asked.

"When I first arrived. He was working for the Witch Queen." Craig looked at the blood that stained the white bandages on his hands. "He wasn't going to help us." Craig sighed heavily. "I keep asking 'Why me?' and someone keeps answering, 'Because we care'." He looked up to Frito. "Is she alright?"

Frito nodded gently passing the unconscious woman into Roc's arms. He turned, holding up his Blade-spear and lightning shot from the tip striking the house. Another bolt sprang forth and tore through the kitchen with a tremendous roar. A third slashed the second story windows and smashed them all.

Light rose from inside the broken windows. Fire quickly crawled along the walls, and drapes. The old brittle furniture was kindling for the uprising fire.

Horse stepped into reality pulling Roc's horse and two others with him. The other horses were pulling a cart.

Frito didn't look twice at the house as he secured the wagon properly. Roc and Orrin gently placed the woman in the cart and wrapped her in cloaks to cushion her."

"And where did Horse find this." Roc asked as he tied the woman in place.

"Probably from the stables over there." Frito answered as he finished. "They probably belonged to Paradox. Which reminds me." He took up his blade-spear and a bolt of lightning fell from the white sky and set the barn afire.

Craig mounted Kugerand and watched as Orrin took command of the wagon and followed Roc down the road. Frito rode in the wagon with Horse ambling behind. Craig turned and looked back to the house. It was alive with flame roaring within its walls. He sighed as Kruger leapt into the air.

Chritchfeild the rabbit hopped from the burning house and stood on his hind legs at Paradox's head. The Rabbit watched him for a moment with his ears slowly twitching. "So, dead man. What do you see?"

Gozoo, the rabbit god walked up beside Chritchfeild. The rabbit god's long bony arms reached under and scooped up Paradox's body. He then slowly turned and walked into the burning house. The rolling waves of flame crashed against the walls like the tide of Okshiru's sea. The sea of fire parted from the rabbit god as he made his way to the main dining room. The god paused, then tossed the limp body onto the dining table where it burst into flame from the heat. The god then turned and walked out bidding: Farewell.

Farewell, to the Home by the Sea.

__Chapter 49__

Blood slid from the great cracked skull of the stone idol. It slowly crawled along the cheek and hung for a long tenuous moment before dropping off into the river of Therd. The empty, dark eyes of the great, cracked skull stared at the sinking sun dipping below the southern continent. They gazed intently at the black shadow of thundering dead buffalo sweeping across the plain. The buzzards swirled overhead, counterclockwise, about a half click from the crest of the stampede. A vicious growl blitzed in from the east as seventy demon bikers from Hel, mounted on their iron machines, charged head on at the giant heard of stampeding dead buffalo.

The resulting crash, directly under the buzzards circling counterclockwise, was nothing less than spectacular.

The great skull turned away and looked to the rising moon in the north. From his mountain height he could see the evening star flare in hues of blue and green. Across the wide sandy desert he could see a demon. His size and color was distorted by the moon's white stare, however, it was evident, that he was carrying something.

The great skull cocked a bony brow and watched, as the demon paused to allow a herd of White Wolly Waddits, trying to escape the press of the Slothering Hothering Wanderblest Beast complete with Horro-shred option, pass by. The White Wolly Waddits ran a furious criss cross pattern trying to evade the 25mm explosive rounds from the mounted, fully automatic, electrically operated, air cooled, duel belt fed gattling gun, capable of firing so many rounds per second that the dirt they impacted ignited from the friction. Any White Wolly Waddit that escaped the rain of steel jacketed death, but failed to leap in time or became confused and paused, discovered savagely exactly what a buzz-pressor could do.

The White Wolly Waddits ran for the cover in the tall swaying grass, but the Slothering Hothering Wanderblest beast complete with Horro-shred option activated its Rip-mower attachment and made short work of any White Wolly Waddit in the tall swaying grass.

The demon shook his head as the Slothering Hothering Wanderblest beast complete with Horro-shred option drove past him using a patented Blast-o-grind cannon to seriously overkill the smaller White Wolly Waddits to protonic vapors.

Thumber, The Beast Under the Bed and Keeper of Nightmares followed in the track-gore treads of the Slothering Hothering Wanderblest beast complete with Horro-shred option, for it had cleared a path through the tall swaying grass. The White Wolly Waddits left in the path, slowly shook their heads, pulled closed their avulsed bodies, and went off to find the Slothering Hothering Wanderblest beast complete with Horro-shred option for another agonizing round. Thumber shook his head again and went on.

Things were really fucked up in Hel.

After quite sometime of trudging through the slimy swamps of goo and traversing the floating mountains of coral, he finally boarded the asphalt road that lead to Madagar. At his left was the Argra, or Mef as he called it, and directly before it and to the right of a furious sandstorm was a truck stop where he was not welcome. Not one of the Demon bikers were there. *All out on the buffalo hunt*, the beast thought to himself. *Won't The Trid Dreath be surprised when his personal guard don't come home.* He chuckled to himself and headed along.

Night had covered Hel and the white moon cast a wicked light across the land. Crooked black cracks of shadow fell from the dead trees that lined the road to the walled city. The gates were open and a tiny candlelight poured from the window of the guard house. Thumber stopped just short of the gates and set Frita's still unconscious body down. Thumber took the cloak from his shoulders and draped it across her. Once she was concealed, he picked her up again and strolled boldly into the city.

"Haly Whoa! Unmush! Retract and Haltamundo Amigo!" Shouted Mally the gate guard as he leapt from his house. "Haly rue! One untrue gesture and I'll dice you slice you and perforate you with great and rapid expedience!"

"Don't bother." Thumber said as he pushed on by.

Mally the gate guard watched the large demon basically ignore him. He smiled and waved a friendly hand. "Have a nice day."

Thumber was ready for this and whirled on his heels. "Don't YOU tell me what kind of day to have!"

Mally stood there teetering in speechlessness as Thumber pushed hurriedly down the street.

A handful of decadents loitered in the street before him, passing about a bottle of Bitterspice. The women were allowing the men to handle them in any way they saw fit, and the men were doing so.

Thumber pulled back and waited, hoping they would pass. He could boldly walk through them, breaking a few bones to prove a point, but he was carrying Frita, A knight of Okshiru. They would attack her, or word would get around that she was in Hel and others would most certainly come. This was a case of discretion being the better part of valor. This idea went down easily with Thumber as he had no valor to speak of.

Thumber pressed himself against the alcove of a door and waited. He counted the beats, then the tics, and finally the tocs. Something had to happen. Something did.

Wounk, the God of stubbed toes walked like a zombie down the street directly at the rabble. His giant skeletal feet shuffled in the dust and his face still held a look of terrible surprise.

Thumber quickly dashed across the street as the rabble's attention was caught by the skeleton with giant feet. He quickly dashed up the steps to someone's apartment and tried to cross over and down the other way.

Teddy, the god of innocent lost stood at the top of the stairs. "Hi!" It said with a cheerful grin.

Thumber was paralyzed with fear. His eyes darted down to the street below at Wounk who was reduced to little more than a skeleton at the stuffed god's touch. "Hi." The beast said weakly.

The bear smiled delightfully and blinked it's black button eyes. "Wanna hear a joke?"

Thumber was lost. He couldn't go down stairs with Frita in his arms. Perhaps, he could humor the god of innocence lost and the little creep would go on his way.

"You see, there were two guys named Nate and Never and they were in a wagon...no, it was Late and never...No, No, It was Nate and TATE! Yeah, Nate and Tate, Are you with me so far?"

The beast found himself sweating. "Yeah." He answered nervously.

"Well they were in a wagon in the woods and like, there was this lever they found. Nate said: 'Tate, go to the house and'...No, Tate said 'Go to the house'...Uh, there was a sign at the house...No...wait...Umm, okay, there were these two brothers right?"

"Right." Thumber said hoarsely. The beast was feeling an uncomfortable pain in his side. He shifted his load slightly and waited for the joke to end.

"And they went in the woods one day and found a sign, that's it, and it said 'Who ever shall pull this lever...' There was a lever there. 'Will

382

destroy the worlds.' So Tate sent Nate to get...Nate sent Tate to get the cart and bring it back. No, fill it with stuff to hide the lever so no one will find it, yeah, that's it, and come back. So Nate, no, Tate went back to the house and got the cart and filled it with stuff to hide the lever with while Tate stayed behind. No, Nate stayed behind and Tate went."

Thumber's uncomfortable feeling was stretching into unbearable. He swallowed and shifted his load again.

"So Tate got the cart and filled it with stuff and came back, and like, he was coming down the hill and, uhhh, wait, Yeah. He was coming down the hill and he saw Tate. No, Nate, Is it Nate?"

Thumber had really no idea what this little god was saying. "Uh, Yeah." He answered. The pain in his side was excruciating. It was the little god's joke. A cruel torture from Okshiru. A joke that will knock 'em dead each time. The beast shifted his load and hoped for the best.

Frita's arm swung free and hung down in plain sight, but Teddy didn't see it as he tried to remember his joke. "And Tate saw Nate and couldn't stop cause he was on this hill and he ran over Tate. No, That's not it."

Thumber's side was aflame and the beast was sweating profusely as he tried to nonchalantly flip Frita's arm back where it belonged. "Okay, so Nate was standing by the lever, the one that would destroy the worlds and he couldn't hit Nate so he hit the, wait a minute. I got it, so he hit Nate! Ha Ha Ha Ha Ha!" The bear laughed at his joke and slapped his soft knee. "No, that's not it." The bear paused and thought ignoring Thumber trying in vain to flip Frita's arm in place. "I got it, the moral is, Never Tate than later, Better Tate...Better Nate than lever!" The bear went into hysterics as Thumber finally got Frita's arm to get where it belonged. The Bear wiped a tear from its black button eye. "You wanna hear it again? I could tell it better."

Thumber was bleeding sweat. The pain in his side was inconceivable, he would never survive another joke. His eyes searched the steps and across the way. He needed an idea. "Uh, I hear your mamma callin'"

The little bear turned to see. "Yes Mamma?"

Thumber quickly turned and dug his toe-claws into the wall and climbed straight up the wall in a desperate escape. With one hand around Frita's body, he gripped the lip of the roof with the other. His claws were chewing the soft clay as he flipped his way over. He felt the pain in his side ease but his gratitude and relief turned to horror as the ceiling gave way.

A thatched roof of molding straw and sticks passed by Thumber as he fell through. The floor slapped him in the rump with a sudden stop as the final bits of roof bounced off of his head. He shook his beast like head and brushed off bits of roof from Frita's face. The fall had done her no obvious harm. *About time something went right*, the beast thought.

"Sanna Claus! Sanna Claus!" A little boy's voice chirped happily. "Sanna Claus!"

Thumber shook his head. "Out of the fire." He mumbled as he picked up Frita in his arms. He looked about the demolished shack and the six peasant children dancing around him singing a rousing chorus of 'Santa Claus'! Thumber, the Beast From Under the Bed and Keeper Of Nightmares looked at the array of red and green tinsel and wreaths for the season. A scrawny tree with home-made decorations stood humbly in the center of the shack. The children ran about the Keeper Of Nightmares in delightful glee. Thumber looked for a clock or some way to tell how late he was. He only made a face and looked at the kids dancing around him. "Look, I'm not Santa," He said to the ring of smiling faces. "Uh, he's on his way." But the children failed to hear this and continued their prance. Thumber had no time for games. He looked for the youngest child and timed the dancing circle and waited for the child to be right in front of him. At that moment, he swelled and let out and tremendous bellow right at the child. "Santa Claus is dead!" The beast shouted and the circle derailed and stopped. "Picked off with a Stinger while cruising over restricted air space!"

Suddenly the children broke into tears and ran about the room. Thumber smiled and pushed his way through a crumbling wall and back out into the street. He looked about for signs of anyone noticing, or caring if they had noticed, and went on his way.

Down a dark street and left at a brutal mugging, over a short bridge and around a cemetery, past some burned cars and a condemned,(what in Hel wasn't condemned?) rat infested building, past the 'Out of Service' elevator and up the stairs. Eleven flights of stairs and counting thirteen at each landing to his apartment. With a kick, the door was open.

He stood at the threshold with the knight in his arms. Sweat stained his body and the breath in his lungs ran raw through his pipes.

Cublatack sat in bandages reading for the seven hundred and forty fifth time the August issue of McCalls. "Is this the only thing there is to read?"

Across the room Formor stopped his digging through old socks and screamed at the other monster. "YES!"

"What are you looking for? You've torn this place to pieces?"

"Ah ha!"

"What? Did you find what you were looking for?"

"No, but I found the remote control. I was looking for that last week."

"Its things like that," Cublatack reflected. "You only find what your looking for when you don't need it. While your there, flip the set."

"Can't." Formor said as he began to tear apart the fridge. "I tossed the set."

"What! You tossed the set because you couldn't find the remote control! Why couldn't you just get up and turn it on?"

Formor stopped and pulled his head from the refrigerator. "What good is a remote control set if you don't use the remote control?"

This train of logic was enough to satisfy Cublatack, The Small Mouth Monster That Hid in the Basement. "So, what are you looking for?"

Formor pulled a plastic container from the fridge. "Is this good?"

"What is it?"

"It looks like a cake of snot in gravy."

"Save it, I'll get hungry and eat it." Cublatack replied.

Formor made a face and tossed it back in. From the corner of his eye, he noticed the Beast From Under the Bed standing in the door. "Thumber!" He said with glee as he slammed shut the fridge and headed over. "Is that her? Frita?"

Cublatack leisurely turned a page of his magazine. "Lo' Thumber."

Thumber stood still with an expression of shell shock. "Fuck." Was all he said as he stumbled in to the room.

"By the way Thumber," Cublatack said off handedly, "We caught the man who kept adding stairs. He's hogtied in the corner." The Small Mouth Monster That Hid in the Basement pointed to the corner where sure enough the worker, in his heavily starched, bleached white coveralls, was bundled painfully with his wrists lashed to his knees and his ankles tied to his elbows. "We caught him just as he finished putting in another step." The monster went on reading his magazine. "Did you find it?"

Thumber tromped over to the bed where Formor was quickly clearing it of all trash. "Yeah, I did." The beast said as he laid Frita down. "Fourth floor, second landing." He grumbled over his heavy panting. "I stumbled and bashed both of my shins and had to limp the remaining seven flights. I tell you, limping on both legs is impossible!" The Thumber adjusted Frita so that she was lying comfortably.

"Is this her?" Formor said excitedly, scurrying up Thumber's back to peer over his shoulder. "I've never seen a knight so close before. She is pretty."

"What is this?" Thumber said as he reached under the pillow. "A candlestick?"

"Gimme that!" Formor suddenly lunged at it. "I've been looking all over the place for that!" He quickly dashed down Thumber's arm but Thumber changed hands.

"Don't give it to him!" Cublatack screamed.

Thumber reached over to the mantle and put the candlestick on a high self. "Leave it there. Now listen you two. I gotta find Thamrell and get things rolling so keep an eye on her. Formor, don't you touch her, and keep Cublatack away."

Formor saluted in acceptance of orders. Cublatack went on reading his magazine. "Hey Formor, is this the only thing to read?"

Formor didn't answer, he only leaned closer to Frita's sleeping face. "She is pretty."

Chapter 50

Darkness swept Mortalroam with the cloak of Leatha, goddess of the night. Hauge, the fickle god of wind swept through with tremendous fury, bringing with it the stinging cold of Fikor's wintery breath. Danshu's freezing rain had encased everything that it touched. Fikor, the Great Dog of Winter, shook his coat and snow fell from Worldsend. It mixed with Danshu's freezing rain turning the weather to a hard sleet.

J'son twisted in his sleep and J'cob watched him. It was too wet and too cold for a fire. Its light would have been nice, but that was not to be. He only sat in the darkness and plucked lightly at his lute, trying to make music from the rhythm of the rain.

The wind of Hauge tangled itself in the trees and bristled furiously to free itself. Flakes of ice fell down and bounced on J'cob's head. The elf looked up and his eyes began to glow green as his elvish sight came into play. For a moment, he could see the great wind god caught in the branches above, or was it?

J'cob slowly took his hand from the neck of his lute and reached for one of his swords. With it, he poked his twin in the side. J'son awoke with a start and a bit annoyed. "What are you doing?"

J'cob didn't answer as he slowly took the lute from his lap and reached for his other sword. J'son looked to where his brother was looking. His eyes also began to glow with green as he looked to the trees. He saw nothing.

"I saw a woman in the tree." J'cob finally answered. "She was up there."

J'son pulled his wet cloak tighter and rolled back over. "Stay away from the wine. I'm having enough trouble sleeping without you annoying me."

"But she was up there, I saw her!" But J'cob was ignored as his brother rolled back over to sleep. J'cob poked him again. "Don't sleep." He hissed. "Look there!" He pointed to another tree.

J'son glanced that way then glanced again. He tossed back his cloak and snatched up his staff.

"Hello." She said rather politely.

J'son looked to the woman in the tree. Her leathery wings were apparent as she used them as a shield from the freezing rain. It was a Sheol. "There isn't time, Friska needs you." She said pleadingly.

J'son eyed his brother who eyed him back. It was apparent that neither trusted her. Sheols were beautiful nude women who did one of two things, entrance men with their charms and enslave them, or kill them outright and rip the flesh from their bodies.

But she wasn't beautiful, she was homely, but not ugly. She was also wearing clothes—very uncharacteristic of Sheols. "I am Cassandra." She said. "Friska has been taken by Thamrell. I don't know where. You have got to help me find him."

J'son didn't take his eyes from Sheol above him. "Cross patten?" He whispered.

J'cob answered. "One, two, three!" Suddenly the two turned and ran into the woods. They criss crossed and headed in a wide circle only to criss cross again with one doubling back, the other heading out.

Sheols were lower demons and not to be challenged. She was trying to trick them, she had to be. Sheols had no other purpose. J'son looked above, his green eyes searching about the trees. Could she follow through the heavy woods? He was an elf, lightly armored and swift as the wind. He leapt from rock to tree and over streams with the speed of Hauge. He had only to worry of the Sheol's net of capture. A net that no mortal could escape.

His elven ear listened to the rain and wind. He tried to pinpoint the sound of the Sheol to no avail. *Where was she?* He thought as he kept running through the wet, ice slick woods. *Could she have gone after J'cob?*

A lashing rope entangled him into a ball. He was suddenly lifted into the air and in moments above the trees. He felt the rain of Danshu sting his face with ice as the Sheol swept him higher. He sawed at the net with his dagger, but only blunted its steel. There was nothing to do save enjoy the ride.

She circled high above and then came back to the ground. She set J'son down and sat up on a rock.

"You'll never find my brother." He shouted as she set him down. "And I'll never be a slave, so just go ahead and peel off my skin."

"I don't want your skin." She said as she pulled up the rope and set him free of the net. I'm not going to hurt you." She held up the star of Hammerstrike that hung from a chain about her neck. "Friska gave this to me."

J'son looked at the star. It was a trick. If she didn't want his skin, then she wanted him as a slave. He slowly made to his feet pretending to weigh her words in his head. "Why would my brother give that to you?"

"It was a present."

J'son leaned back against a rock. "How can I trust you?"

She looked about and then back to J'son. "I have nothing," She said ruefully. "But I set you free, isn't that something?"

J'son looked past her. "What do you think?" The Sheol was confused as to whom he was talking to.

J'cob stepped out from behind a bush. His great bow was in his hand with an arrow knocked. "I don't know yet." He said aiming in his bow. "Be warned Sheol, an elvish arrow will kill you!"

The Sheol rose up. "Then kill me, for without Friska I am doomed back to Hel and there I shall not go. Without your help, I am lost."

J'cob relaxed his draw but kept his arrow knocked and at the ready. "Very well," J'son said. "We're not going to kill you as you did not kill me. We need to find him too."

She nodded, and J'cob put away his arrow.

Chapter 51

Danshu's rain slowly began to wane and Fikor's snow slowly thickened to large flakes falling like goose feathers from Leatha's starless night sky. Hauge the wind had finally found someplace warm to sleep that night and his winds had stilled. Soon, Danshu made his way back to Worldsend and gave up his dance of rain. Fikor stopped his snow only after the ground was covered in white.

"I'm, dreaming of a white Christmas…" Craig sang to himself. "My next re-invention will be marshmallows for these nights at the campfire."

"What is a marsh-mel-lows, eh?" Orrin asked.

"White things you use to keep the ends of sticks from burning."

Orrin wondered about the practicality in such a thing. Craig could read the boys wonder in his face. "Hey Orrin, Remember the ice cream I made last winter, it was an indulgence. That's what marshmallows are. A warm indulgence. Something to give your dietetic conscience a run for it's money."

"Oh, I see." Orrin said not completely sure. "Will you, like, make more ice-cream this year?"

Craig nodded. "I'm going to try a fudge twirl." Craig looked about at the snow all around them. He sighed and then looked to Frito. "So, what's the story, Cory."

Frito looked up from Kathreen's body. "She is alright. Frita used her power to heal."

"Are you sure it was her?"

"I can smell her."

Craig thought about it nodding in agreement. "So where is she now?"

"That, I don't know. I would dare say she vanished again. But this time, I have my ideas."

"So what are they?"

"You say that Harroc used the star of Hammerstrike to pass my barrier?" Frito abruptly changed the subject. "A flaw on my part. I never thought of the stars doing that."

Craig leaned forward. He could tell that Frito was holding back information, purposely changing the subject, but he didn't press it. "What are the stars? I know they represent the clan, but…,"

"What makes them special?" Frito asked for him. "My father made the first set for all of us. As the Supergod, his mere handling of them gave them a touch of magic. That touch made them distinct. Since then, Frita, Friska and I have either lost or misplaced our stars. I tried to recreate them in exactly the same manner."

"And you attempted to imitate your father's touch." Craig went on. "It leaves a magical signature. Anyone who wears them has your signature. Any magic that you set up, is fooled by the star into thinking it's you and lets him past?" Craig concluded. "That's how Harroc walked through the barrier? And when it was taken away, the barrier suddenly kicked in." Craig leaned back and thought for a moment letting it all sink in. Then he touched his chest. "You made mine, and Neeko's as well?"

Frito nodded.

"But we have all of the stars!" Craig exclaimed. "Right?"

"No, we don't. And to make matters worse, after dwelling on the idea of why my magic can't tell me from anyone else wearing the star, I am under the impression that anyone of my immediate family can disrupt my magic. I was not careful enough to teach my magic how to differentiate between me and my siblings."

"Well, this means that as long as your brother and sister are unaccounted for," Craig wondered out loud. "Then any barrier standing is in jeopardy. What other barriers do you have standing?"

"The gates of Hel." Frito said simply.

"What?" Craig's eyes grew wide.

"When Hauth returned, the gates were open, I used the last of the "Poer Ther Of", to seal them shut. I also put one at the Wove of the Worlds."

"What exactly is the Wove of the Worlds?"

Frito rearranged his position and tried to think of the easiest way to answer. "Between all the different worlds, there is a buffer zone, or space between them. I sealed it so no demon could leave or enter another world. To get from one place to another, you need both passages open at the same time."

"Well, isn't that lovely." Craig said pulling his robes about him. He suddenly looked worried. "Shit."

"What?"

"I had a dream before, the kind that comes true." Craig said quietly. He rolled up his left sleeve and looked at the dragon tattoo on the inside of his forearm. "The dancing dragon. You know what that means. Shit rapidly approaching fan."

"What was this dream?" Frito said leaning closer.

"I saw Ferris, The Iron Dragon."

"No," Frito shook his head. "He is gone."

Craig disagreed. "You wanna hear this? Good. He was standing at what looked like the gates of hell."

"Hel." Orrin corrected.

"What's the difference?" Craig looked to the boy.

"The spel-ling." Orrin said quietly.

Craig rolled his eyes. "Whatever. But he opened he gates of hell and an army spilled out."

Frito took a deep breath and slowly let it out. "I was afraid of that."

"That's not all. There was a ringing. At first I thought it was a bell, but I heard it before at Max's shop. Hammer on anvil. Heavy construction."

"An-other Iron Dra-gon!" Orrin exclaimed and Craig nodded.

Frito gazed into the fire shaking his head. "That will take years. Meanwhile we have got to find my brother and sister. Two portals, two keys. There isn't much time. Someone is up to something and I have an idea who it is. Ferris is just a part of it. There is too much involved just to get Ferris back on Mortalroam." Frito's eyes began to glow red as he thought. "There is only one reason that I can think of to open the gates and the wove of the world." He looked at Craig, his eyes steady. "War."

Craig sputtered. "What? Why?"

Frito shrugged. "Its what demons do." His eyes cooled as he looked in the fire. "Ura would do it for kicks, but Thamrell?" Frito looked up. "He would not be doing this unless there was a plan. Sneaking one or two demons out is no big deal, but to get an army, a really big army, you need to open the gates."

Craig looked to the dark sky above and then all around. "You hear that?"

Frito nodded. "Its an elf call, J'son and J'cob." Frito said as he reached into his pouch and took out a cloth satchel. "They say they have found Cassandra, Friska's lover."

"Good." Craig said.

"Bad." Frito said unwrapping his white gold flute. "They say that Thamrell has Friska." The Ninefingers fell silent as he assembled his flute.

From over the hills and across the way came another tune to the Ninefinger's ears. "It is Fryto, he has heard and asks what we should do." The Ninefingers looked towards Worldsend and then into the fire. He slowly put his flute to his lips and began to play. He played pipes of war and a call to arms.

"Is that our only choice?" Craig asked when the Ninefingers was done. "I mean, how is it like, we have had two demonic invasions in two years? Is this like, an bi-annual thing?"

Frito shook his head. "No, in fact the only times the gates have been thrown open like this was at the reawakening of time, and Hauth, Me. According to prophecy, that was to be expected. This one however, is unusual, and my fault."

Roc suddenly leaned forward. "What?!" He growled.

Craig jumped with a start. "I thought you were asleep or dead or something like that."

Roc shook the snow from his hair. "Did I hear correctly? This is your fault?"

Frito looked into the fire. "I set up the barriers, I should have…"

"No!" Roc cut him off. "Not so!"

Craig put his hand on Roc's knee. "Hold it Roc, Try this." Craig turned to Frito and pointed a sharp finger. "Bogus, Ace! We all know the shit came down like Niagara falls and you were left holding a bucket with a hole and expected to catch it all." Craig motioned to Roc. "Go a head, try that."

Roc looked at him and then to Frito. "What he said. How could you have known?"

"He's got a point." Craig went on. "From what I see, you're holding back the China sea with a whisk broom and can't figure out why you're getting wet."

Roc gripped Craig firmly on the shoulder. "By the Beard of Okshiru, I understand him! Frito, was it not you who said Okshiru is purging his knights. You also said that guilt is just as destructive as sin? You blaming yourself for the folly of gods will do you in just as it has Friska!"

Craig reached back and grabbed Roc's arm. "Suffering succotash, the Sultan of Slaughter is making sense! Stop being the scapegoat for wannabe deities."

Frito put his hands up. "Alright...Alright." He sighed. "Let us work at the problem at hand. War is inevitable."

Roc looked forward anxiously. "What kind of army will they have?"

Frito shook his head. "I would imagine a smaller force than Hauth had. I don't think any one, not even the Trid Dreath could unite all of the armies of Hel."

"You forget." Roc leaned forward. "That my army was pounded in the process. We no longer have the strength we once had." Roc glanced to Craig. "Half of them would still be ten times us. Our only advantage is that my men are seasoned and very disciplined." Roc brushed the side of his nose. "Demons are tough and hard to kill. We will need the dragons."

"They will have dragons." Craig put in. "I've seen them. Ferris will be there."

"Ferris? Ferris is dead." Roc spoke quickly. "I did it myself."

"Look, I don't know, maybe he had an engine rebuild and a new paint job. Regardless, he will be there."

"That will be a problem." Frito said.

Roc shook his head. "He's mine."

Craig put his hands up. "Hold it, according to legend, stop me if I'm wrong," He looked to Orrin for confirmation. "it is only the bow of Tc-mock that can hurt the Iron dragon." Suddenly, as if to respond to its name, the black compound bow appeared in Craig's lap. "Well then, I'm elected. I'll take out the red baron. Me, Snoopy."

Roc grimly frowned, and then slowly nodded his head. "Very well."

"Hey," Craig spoke coolly, "Put the boy down as spare parts. I'll get a can opener or something."

"You don't know what you're dealing with." Roc cautioned.

"How is that any different from anything else?" Craig laughed. "Everything is out to punch my time card. I'll think of something, I always do."

Frito nodded in agreement. "Roc, what do we have for an army?"

"Not much. Hauth did a hurtin' on us." He brushed his nose. "I can rally, maybe about 170,000 strong in a week."

"We don't have a week. I don't think we have more than four days and we will need seven times that number."

"Then I will think of something." Roc imitated Craig. "I can send word to Monsterbelly the Uptyfrats and get reinforcements. We'll send an elfcall tonight and spread the word." Roc looked to Craig. "We have the Dragons."

"And they have theirs." Craig answered. "I think I can effectively negate them. I can also send word to Dormoth." Craig watched the reaction on the faces around him. "We will need him and he will help if I ask." Craig said defensively to Roc who said nothing.

"Craig," Frito began quietly. "From your dream, what can you tell us about them. Their size, equipment?"

Craig looked rather grim. Then thoughtful, then went to speak and then stopped and then started again. "We are on the wrong side."

Roc grimaced. "That bad?" Craig nodded. "What can you tell us?"

"Dreams are hard to pin point for reliable details. I can, however, safely say I know everything there is to know save five things." Craig held out five fingers.

"And what's that?" Roc spoke anxiously.

Craig's eyes wondered about before he answered. "I don't know."

Frito shook his head moving on. "Next, thing to evaluate is where. Our advantage can be the battle field. If we know where they are, we can prepare."

"I do know," Craig spoke up. "Their goal is Cornerstone. One of the corners of Magic."

Frito took a stick and drew a sketch in the snow. "This is Cornerstone. This is the Wove of the World." He drew a sharp line across the map. "They can be at any point on this line. A lot to cover."

Craig put his hands up to form a 'T'. "Wait a sec, time out. How can the Wove be this big?"

"Its not that." Frito answered. "The Wove of the Worlds can appear at any point along this line. The edge of the world. Craig nodded understanding, then he waved his hand over the map. "This can be covered by dragon easily. Anyone shows we'll see them."

"Outstanding!" Roc exclaimed. "This is turning out to be a war to remember!"

Frito pushed to his feet. "Craig, fly back now and organize the troops. Take Orrin and this woman with you and start to rally. Roc, take the wagon to Brewster. Set up your headquarters with Milo and rally there. Build what you can and wait for word."

Roc slowly rose to his feet. "And where are you going?"

"I'm going to Hel to get my sister and brother. If they are being used to open the portals, that is where they will be. I also believe that I can find another ally there."

"What...wait!" Craig stood with a start. "You're going to hell alone?"

"You see anyone else?"

"Yeah, Me." Roc grumbled.

"Me too." Craig said. "I've been to that weird place. I know what to expect."

Frito shook his head. "No, there isn't time. Roc, there is no one who can rally better than you. There is no better general. Craig, there is no one who can handle a dragon."

"They will be waiting for you." Roc cautioned.

"I know."

Chapter 52

Darkness twisted in spirals of heat. Sweat and dirt seemed to breathe the air through the tunnels. Beneath the earth, below the world, in a place were time itself was as confused as everyone else.

Somewhere, somehow, a spark of light hung by itself in the darkness. It was a beacon, a leading light. Through the misty, humid air it shined dimly, flickering, magically.

"So, Thumber," The Small Mouth Monster spoke as he shuffled the cards. "Are you going to show us how to work the soda machine?" The monster began to deal. "You did say that if we helped lug her down here you would show us."

"I'll think about it." Thumber said as he took up his cards. "What's the ante?"

"Wait a tic." Formor spoke up. "I have two Jacks of Hearts!"

"Yeah, I know. I had two incomplete decks so I combined them." Cublatack tossed out two cards. "Dealer takes two."

Formor tossed up his cards and rolled his eyes. He got up and walked in a circle making a long howling noise as he did.

"I hate that noise." Cublatack mumbled. "You want?" He motioned to Thumber.

Thumber tossed down his cards in disgust.

"What? No body wants to play?" Cublatack said as he picked up his cards.

"No!" Formor shouted.

"Well you don't have to be such a child."

"I'm not a child! I'm not, I'm not, I'm not!" Formor cried.

"Are too."

"Are not!"

"Are too."

"Are not!"

"Are too."

"Stop it!" Thumber shouted. "Both of you."

"Are not." Formor whispered.

Cublatack stuck out his tongue.

"What was that?" Formor jumped to his feet peering into the gloom. "That was her, she's awake...I think she fell."

"That's okay." Thumber said leaning against a wall.

397

"Why did we leave her down there? I'll go get her."

"Nope." Thumber ordered. "All part of the plan. You can sit right there."

Cublatack shuffled his cards. "Formor has a crush on a Knight."

"I do not!"

"Do too."

"Do not!"

"Do too."

"Do not!"

"Do too."

"Do not!"

"Do too."

"Do not!"

"Do not."

"Do too!"

"Do not."

"Do too!" Formor stood on his back four legs and waved the other four. "I do too and that's final! End of sentence, period!"

"Exclamation point." Thumber snickered. Cublatack leaned his head back laughing.

Formor looked baffled and realized what he had said. "You tricked me!"

Cublatack wiped a tear from his eye. "I did nothing of the sort."

"Stop laughing at me!"

"As soon...as I catch my breath." Cublatack burst out into gales of laughter. He pointed at the Monster of the Attic and laughed some more.

"Okay, Cubly." Thumber said. "Joke's over."

"Ohhh, but you see his face!" The Monster From the Basement laughed. "Hey," The monster suddenly stopped laughing. "Where did you get that candlestick?"

"Formor!" Thumber shouted. "You can stop beating him now. You have got to learn to control your temper."

Formor pushed the candle stick into his belt. He reached down and picked up the small mouthed monster's deck of cards. "Hey, I'm a monster. I don't have to be personable." He sorted through the cards until he found the King of Clubs and tossed it on the body.

"What's that for?" Thumber asked.

"I couldn't find the Ace of Spades." The monster answered as he tossed the rest of the cards into the air, letting them flitter down on Cublatack's unconscious body. "Well now what?" The Monster From the Attic spoke as he took a seat on Cublatack. "You still haven't..." Formor's words trailed off as he looked down the tunnel. Frita stood there, leaning against a wall. Her elvish eyes of silver shone plainly in the dim light. Her tunic was torn and exposing. Her flesh was bruised and bleeding.

Thumber pushed to his feet and swept over to her. He took her hand and guided her down the tunnel. Formor popped up and darted quickly behind the Beast From Under the Bed.

"Where I'm I?" She asked in a voiceless whisper. "Why do I know it so?"

"Shhh, my little knight. All will be answered." Thumber cooed as he took her around the bend to the great heaving door. "Welcome to the gates of Hel."

Frita stood there for a moment gazing up at the emaciated, shriveled body of Weishap, god of answers. Cruel twisted spikes pushed through his thin frail limbs and nailed him to the door. "Why are..." Frita spoke slowly as she tried to think. "These doors called gates?"

Weishap's head bobbled on his thin neck and his eyes fluttered. "An advertizing ploy." He spoke in his high, squeaky, irritating voice. "Sounds more fearsome than 'The Doors of Hel'." His head bobbled again as the doors began to push out. They stretched the limits of his limbs and held him there, agonizing, threatening to draw his arms from his sockets for several beats before easing back again. "I know your unspoken questions my mother," He spoke once again. "And I see that now you are ready to hear the answers to them."

Frita stumbled back and Thumber's strong arms caught her and lowered her gently to the ground. She sat, her arms weakly gripping into the Beast's legs for support. Her silver eyes never strayed from Weishap's glinting eyes of black. "My baby?" She whispered.

"Is here." He answered.

"She is in Hel?"

"Yes."

Frita's eyes slowly wandered as if she had finished asking her questions. She slowly scanned the room as if to understand what was Hel.

Thumber stood still behind her. He had never before heard Weishap give a straight answer with no embellishments or hidden innuendos. This was something of interest.

Frita looked to the god of answer's once again. "Why?"

"Because y is a crooked letter and if you cut off the tail it becomes a v." The god answered with a toothless smile.

Thumber suddenly knew the god's plot. He was forcing her to think things through. He was giving her enough time to understand what he wanted her to understand. Thumber was quite aware that the more a person thinks, the easier it is to trick them.

Frita blinked to the god's response. She paused and thought again. "Why is my baby in Hel?"

"She is unblessed, disborn, denounced and not wanted." Weishap lifted his head and looked to her. "That is all the reason needed."

Frita shook her head as her elvish brows pulled low on her eyes. "No, I think not."

Weishap suddenly lost his smile. She was thinking on her own too far. That would not do. "So you say my brother, but what truth I have spoken, you have heard lies fall from my lips. I shall not be misrepresented, misinterpreted, and misunderstood. No more answers shall I give until you hear them."

Frita looked at him. "You speak lies..." She said in an almost pleading moan. "My baby was none of those things."

"So is that which you have said. But, my blossom, she resides here in Hel for the reasons so stated above."

"I don't understand."

Weishap looked away from her. "I cannot ask a question, I can only state the answer. I can spew answers all day but they are nothing but invisible bookmarks with out the proper questions to tag them with. For as a man without a wife, what am I but a answer waiting to happen."

Frita looked up to Thumber hoping he would have a bit of input that might clear things up, but he was still dwelling on the concept of y being a crooked letter.

The knight squared herself away and tried to pull her frayed wits together.

Weishap looked down at her with angry eyes. "I have given you the questions and you did not wish to believe in them. Then if that is the case, it is as if I had never said them at all!"

"You gave me no questions." Frita answered.

"And so you have accused me my Mistress. Truly I haven't spoken at all. In the wake of havoc and all that was shattered in disarray, what was there before no longer exists, so therefor in case referring onto the first and former half, then there was not any in the first at all or in the case where there was any in the original plans, then it might have well not been there at all!" The god of answers gave an angry 'hrumph' and looked away.

Formor sat on four of his hind legs drawing in the dirt. "So I erase the bottom part and what do you get?"

Thumber scratched his head. "A 'U'?"

"A 'U'?" Formor exclaimed looking at his drawing. "Yeah, it is a 'U'!"

Frita looked away from the monsters and back to Weishap. "I heard what you said. And I am quite sure that you said it. But...How do I do it?"

"Break it down in your marbley mind my son." Weishap prompted her to speed things up.

"You said my child was Disborn? How is she disborn?"

Weishap smiled. "If that is what you heard then that is what I said. You baby was disborn, as life is taken, it is so given, and taken again and so on etcetera etcetera ad infinitum. Life is only given and taken by God. Not even Okshiru can give life, but he can exchange it. Any one can exchange a life. That is disborn. A life was exchanged."

Frita took this as fact. Her head lowed and her eyes flashed back and forth as she searched her mind. "What is unblessed?"

"Unblessed is a double bladed meaning." Weishap answered quickly. "Each as equally sharp and cutting; however, only one is needed for a sword to be just as effective. A blessing is a request to Okshiru, or anyone really, to live a life in its form. A blessing is also the love of one to another. One of these, then it lives. Both of these, then all the better, none of these is unblessed and disbirthed."

Frita looked hard at the god of Answers. "But I loved my baby. Why was it disbirthed?"

"Now my love you mustn't accuse yourself of that things which you are not certain."

"I say I am certain!" Frita felt her heart rising in her centre. "Are you saying that I did not?"

"You are asking what I have said as if I had not said it before!" Weishap shrilled. "You are not hearing what is said and to say it again would only result in a repeat of what I just said which would only result in a repeat of what I just said which would only result in a repeat of what I just said, which could easily throw us all into a vacuous void of repetition of a non-going time swirl."

Frita licked her dry, split lips with a dry tongue. She caught her breathing and cooled her centre. She fixed on his words and thought them through. "How could I not love my baby?"

Weishap smiled but bent his head low as not to show it. "Oh, wholly grace of dreams and visions of Meleki's quainting forests. From the beginning of the reawakening of time until the actual second it lays its head in the embrace of the spectral analysis which is the total sum of the historical distortion of what was, and what went wrong, and mostly whose fault it was, I Weishap, know the answer to any question that falls within the space of reference in the above paragraph and by the blessing of Okshiru whose mightiness is beyond regaling I am graced with the choice of what questions I want to answer."

Frita felt herself falling into the hole that sucked open in her centre. So fixed on Weishap to answer her question, that it stunned her when he didn't.

Formor scratched into the dirt a gain. "Okay, so this is a 'y'."

"It should lilt more here." Thumber scratched with his fingernail.

Frita caught herself and fixed on what Weishap had not said and spelled it out. She knew she loved her child yet he said otherwise. "Must I show you?" Her silver eyes searched him over.

"Showing me, oh breath of Shegatesu, oh daughter of Kemoto, is a present tense and that is improbable."

"I didn't show love before?" Frita argued. "I showed her all of my love."

"Again my sweet you contradict the occurrence, and that is as detrimental as an unstoppable force striking 147 pounds of creamed spinach."

"How could I not show love for my baby?"

"You don't want me to answer and when I did you wouldn't believe so there for I won't."

Frita suddenly found her feet. She clawed the walls for balance and staggered closer to the door. "I remember! I remember I loved her so much! She was my body, my soul, what I had given my life for!" Frita slipped and her knees buckled. Thumber's reflexes caught her and helped her to her feet again.

"Again you go against the grain. You have exchanged nothing for her."

Rage flooded her eyes. "I gave my LIFE!" She screamed with dying strength that echoed over the moaning din of the gates of Hel.

Weishap went unimpressed. "I, is a questionable term."

Frita paused and reshuffled her thoughts. "I wasn't what he wanted." She whispered, her spirit draining. "He wanted the child."

"Yes."

She grew quiet, staring at the floor before her as if she could see the scene again in the dust at her feet. "He wanted the child. I loved her so much, I had to save her." She said without a voice in her throat.

"I heard you not. A question unheard is filed with unspoken!" Weishap shrilled quickly.

Frita quickly stared up at the god nailed to the door with power. "I saved her!"

Weishap raised his hairless brows. "Confused you were, Paradox was in your head. You could not go home for he would find you. He would wait for world in and world out and take away your child. You could not hide her enough, so you gave her away."

"I gave her to Frita." Frita said with her strength leaving her.

"And Frita exchanged her life and disborned her to save her from her father, my concubine. Because you could not exchange your own daughter's life."

Frita swayed as if she were going to fall and Thumber put out his giant hands to catch her, but at the last moment she caught herself. "Yes," She said finally with lacking strength. "Frita took the baby."

"And Denice, you my sweet Denice, tried to exchange your life, but it was lost in the shuffle to a place so complicatedly baffling that I will mercifully spare you of the intricate notations and I will take the liberty and edit my answer for you and conclude simply; that Frita took your life to her own." Weishap said grimly. "And she moved on with your life, your memories, your name. It was not her child, and so she had no guilt. Guilt all went back to you and your bubbly mind." Weishap bobbed his head from side to side as he tried to balance his head on his spindly neck. "And so now," Weishap said loudly. "You ask of questions whose answers are better given by yourself..." Weishap finally balanced his head straight up. "Save one." He said and his neck gave away and his head flopped again.

Frita found herself leaning heavily into Thumber's arms. She looked to the god nailed to the door before her. "I know the question." She said softly. "And I know the answer." She paused and raised her eyebrow. "But a question not asked, is not a question in the least, and an answer is posted as its same value." She found herself speaking words that the god put in her mouth for her. "So then, to put worth in what has not been said, I must go ahead and ask the question."

Weishap hung silently on his door and waited.

"What must I do to free my daughter?"

Chapter 53

Hauge's winds settled to rest in the quiet moments before the dawn. Danshu's dance of ice and rain had ended long before. The Great Dog of Winter settled in the center of Mortalroam, curled into a ball in the light sleep of all snow dogs. The face of the world was covered in a thin blanket of white, frosty snow with only the specks of trees pushing through.

Shegatesu, child of the dawn never arrived that morning and her father, bird god of the sun, slept in as well. The great wide sky of Okshiru was as white and plain as the snow below.

Only the giant floppy foot prints marred the snow of the early morning as the god of rabbits made his way through the forests of Meleki. He sniffed the frosty air and headed west, deeper into the woods. He found a boulder in the center of a ring of trees. He brushed off the wet snow from the boulder and sat on it to wait. His hairless hide shivered in the cold and he blew on his forepaws to warm them.

His ears twitched and tuned as sound came to the air. He rose when he smelled her perfumed fragrance and turned to her. It was Meleki, stepping from the trees. The goddess of forests and animals was not happy. "I think we're in trouble." She said grimly. "Okshiru knows about Chritchfeild."

Gozoo the rabbit god looked around and listened with his giant ears for any spies in the area before speaking. "Is he mad?"

Meleki shook her head. "I don't know, I haven't seen him. I just know that he took Chritchfeild."

"Took him?" Gozoo exclaimed. "Then he must know that we both broke the law!" The great hairless rabbit god put a forepaw over his eyes. "I'm Hosenphefer! I know it."

"Stop that!" Meleki said sternly as she reached up and took the rabbit's paw from his face. "I don't know what he's going to do yet."

Chapter 54

The span of the galaxy went on in the chronological plan that had been laid out since the reawakening of time without the slightest flux or change. Hand over hand it pulled itself along the gigantic chain of events with a steady, effortless motion in the very same way that it had been doing since the restart of creation. The great white sky of Okshiru began to break and gigantic holes in the fabric of the clouds began to appear. High above, Kemoto, great bird god of the sun peered through, and cast great warm light down to the face of Mortalroam. The chill of Fikor's winter began to leave the air as Hauge swept the warm winds of the south through the valleys.

The white cloth of snow became worn and patches of earth poked through. The Great Snow Dog opened one eye and then the other. His winter still had more time to go for full effect. He raised his great head and let out a wintery howl that set Hauge fleeing south with fear, bringing cold winds from the North nipping at the brown wind god's heels.

The white snow dog sat up and looked to the sky above. Kemoto was flying high above. The dog knew that he needed more time for winter to start. The days belonged to Kemoto and Chinook, the dog conceded, but the nights would be his.

Brass horns trumpeted from the valley below the Great Snow Dog. The dog of winter looked over his shoulder and down below. He could see the Manor of Fanrealm, home of some of Okshiru's knights. He could also see a line of men, an army marching like ants from the walls of Fanrealm across the wet earth.

A war? The dog wondered. *How could this be?* Didn't they know that it was his season? No mortal could as foolish as to hold a war in his season!

He howled again and the Northern winds swept with stinging sharpness down across the hills. The men pulled their tiny coats about them and went on. The Great Snow Dog mustered a tempest and prepared for a wintery assault. He summoned Hauge to return and bind his winds to his plan. He called to Okshiru to let Danshu dance again, but this time not of rain, but of snow. There will be no waging of war in his season!

The Great Snow Dog barked with cold and winter and shook his coat. The bells of his great collar giggled and clumps of ice and snow fell to the earth below.

Tiny tracks beyond the sight of the Great Snow Dog leapt and hopped a line across the land and up to the mountain where the dog stood. A black and gray rabbit, small and timid stood on its hind paws and spoke to the snow dog. "Excuse me oh Great Snow Dog."

Fikor looked below. It was the little rabbit he had spared before. Surly a rabbit on a mission from the gods. All of the rabbit family was asleep for his winter, save for this one. "Speak little one." The snow dog bade. "I am indeed listening."

"Hold off your great wintery anger against the men you see."

"Why?" The dog lowered its great head to the rabbit. "Suppose you tell me."

Chritchfeild wiggled its ears and brushed snow from its nose. "Is not Frita, the knight of Okshiru placed in your charge? As the knight Friska is in the charge of Hauge and the knight Fryto in the charge of Meleki?"

The great snow dog nodded.

The rabbit went on. "And I am here to plead for her life. I ask not of you to interfere as gods have been bade not to interfere. Yet, I ask you not to hinder. These men are the Dragonslayer's men. He summoned them through an elfcall and prepare them for battle in the name of your knight Frita."

The dog sat down and looked thoughtful for a moment. "I hear you." He said finally. "I have not been blind to my knight and her concern has weighed my centre. I held back my paw to aid her as Okshiru bade me. I shall do as you ask. I shall send my winter on the other side of the great hills, far to the west of here if that will aid my knight."

"Actually, oh Great Snow Dog. Sending it east right now would be great. If you could freeze the great river of Four Moon that stretches between here and the Tam-ber so that the men can cross over it two days from now, it would be much appreciated."

The snow dog raised his great head. "What are you planing?" He growled at the rabbit. "I've always known rabbits to be a sneaky lot."

Chritchfeild placed a paw on his furry chest. "Me? Plan something? Sneaky? Perish the thought oh Great Snow Dog. I'm just doing my job."

"Mhmmm" The dog hummed and leapt from his mountain to the east and took most of his winter with him.

Chapter 55

The snow crunched beneath their swift feet. The earth spilled beneath in white blur as the two elves dashed quickly in pursuit of the leather winged demon. The Sheol looked back, hovering in the air as she did, to be sure not lose her compatriots. She was impressed by their speed and endurance to keep up with her for so long.

She took off again, following the scent of the air and tracking her lover like a hound tracking a coon.

"Hold Cassandra!" J'son called ahead as he quickly came to a halt. J'cob, his twin, stopped looking back at his brother. The elf's sweat lifted from his shoulders into steam and his breath made clouds before him as he panted. "What is it? Are you tired?"

J'son shook his head. His eyes burned green as he scanned about. "Something is amiss." He looked ahead and Cassandra was gone. "Blessid."

J'cob stepped back to his brother, drawing his blades as he did. "You think that the Sheol leads us astray?"

"No…" J'son waved his hand to his brother to put away his blades. "This is Friska's trail."

"Then what?" His brother motioned.

"You didn't hear it?"

"Hear what?"

"What I heard!"

J'cob held back his answer as the Sheol swept over head. "What is wrong?" She landed gently on a rock.

"Ask him." J'cob pointed to his brother.

J'son became cross. "Listen!"

J'cob paused for a moment and listened. "An elfcall!"

"Well, imagine that?"

"I hear nothing!" Cassandra said sniffing the air.

J'son and J'cob looked at her sniffing for a moment and then let it be. J'son looked to her. "Only elves can hear a call. It is Orrin. He is seeking us out." J'son put his hands to his lips and blew an answer.

"I heard that!" Cassandra exclaimed.

"Yes." J'cob nodded. "Your standing right here, how could you not hear it. The big thing is, what did it mean?"

Cassandra's brows lowered. "It meant something?"

J'cob nodded. He then turned and looked to his brother. "He is telling Orrin where we are."

Cassandra lifted back her head and sniffed again. "I still can not tell."

J'son took his hands from his lips as his answer was finished. "Why does her sniffing make me nervous?" He whispered to his brother at a volume that only an elf could hear.

"Because you don't trust her." J'cob whispered back. "Just ask her." J'cob turned back and looked at her. "What are you sniffing?"

"I am losing Friska's trail." She turned and hopped into the air, her leathery wings lifting her above their heads. "If we are to find Friska, we must go now."

J'son nodded. "Let us go."

The Sheol lifted higher into the air and sniffed as she did. "What are you sniffing now?" J'cob asked as he gave a hand to J'son.

"Your guard!" She shouted as she bared her fangs. She circled quickly and pushed out her talons.

J'son withdrew his bow and a shaft with a spin as J'cob pulled his twin swords. Both elves could suddenly smell the acrid stink of demons sweeping in on them.

Circling from the air. Two Nude Sheols dove in with fangs bared. Cassandra soared upwards at them snarling as she did, her flailing talons clawed the air. The two Sheols flanked her and swirled about her and the three collided in the air with a tangle of arms.

Cassandra spiraled from the air and smashed into the dead leaves. J'son's bow was drawn with the nock to his lip. J'cob swept around the fallen Cassandra to protect her from the Millymen rushing from the woods.

"You forsake us, you abandon your kin." The Sheols spiraling above spoke to Cassandra in unison, with one sultry voice. "You abandon your power, you abandon your strength, you abandon your beauty." They laughed as one and spread their nets.

J'son held his shaft and watched as the Millymen surrounded them. J'son had seen Millymen when Hauth had brought them. Foot men, the only thing from Hel with a standard uniform. They were all six feet, at least, with bold chests and thick arms. They were a woods unit, equipped with glistening broad swords and small, square shields. They wore their war belts with small pouches wrapped their waists. These war belts were not only useful for carrying small items, but (according to rumor control) was also good for holding in their bowels after heavy battle.

"Forget it J'son." Said one of the hovering Sheols. "Your brother has delivered you and his whore to us." Said the other in the same voice.

J'cob paced a circle with his back to his brother and standing over Cassandra. They were surrounded. The Millymen had made a circle less than twenty paces from the elves and waited anxiously for the command to attack.

"Put down your weapons men of earth." The two spiraling Sheols sang. "Embrace despair. It is your hope."

J'son felt a hand against his boot. "It is the song," Cassandra whispered, pretending to be unconscious. "Don't listen."

The song of Sheols could entice men and draw them into their power with no hope of freedom. Only the knights of Okshiru could resist, but they weren't knights. "Embrace this!" J'son shouted disrupting their song. "Cassandra! Take 'em high!" His shaft left his fingers and took a Millyman in the throat. Cassandra dug her talons into the frozen earth and clawed a rock the size of her head and with a grunt, hurled it into the face of one of the Sheols knocking her from the sky. She had lost her strength, but not all of it.

J'cob whirled his twin blades against the on coming rush of silver blades. His brother gripped the upper limb of his bow and swung it like a club with a sudden broad swing that caused the Millymen about him to stop short from the sweep. One buckled from the surprise move and slipped. With his arms flailing, he plopped onto the hard ground. Faster than the eye could follow Cassandra reached down and snatched the fallen Millyman's ankle. Her claws dug through his winter boots into his flesh for a better grip. Her other hand latched onto his chest, her talons pushing easily through the leather of his cuirass and into his ribs for a more secure hold as she lifted him effortlessly into the air. She bolted forward with him as a ram and shoved back the other Millymen with him.

J'son took up a second shaft and with elvish dexterity knocked and drew at the one swirling Sheol above him. She dove and tried to evade through the trees, but J'son felt the low humming vibration in his bow as the string launched his arrow into the air. An elvish steel arrow head punched through her creamy white thigh and pushed out of her buttock check. She screamed as her black blood ran a line down her leg. She

411

dipped losing altitude but regained her height and composure quickly as she tried to maneuver again. With deft speed she deflected J'son's second shaft with a glancing arm, but lost her net. She roared like a tiger as she lifted rapidly up and soared down with a sudden swoop. The Millymen ducked and J'son dove from her path as Cassandra tried to hit her with a dead body. She swept passed without resistance.

"J'cob!" J'son screamed as he rolled. "YOUR BACK!"

Long too late was his brother's warning as he felt the talons slice through the chain mail on his back and into his flesh. He rolled into the hard earth from the strike, writhing from the pain. Millymen quickly mustered around him, their swords ready to put through him.

Cassandra threw the Millyman she had used for a shield and bowled the others over from the force. J'cob brandished his sword while his other hand was reaching to his back to check the damage.

J'son let loose another shaft at the Sheol and she deflected it with a angled wing. It roared and swooped back over head. J'son let loose again and the shaft splintered as it pushed through the bone near her shoulder blade.

The Millymen had regrouped and faced off with Cassandra. She had another body, this one screaming, and fended them off. J'cob found his feet and with one sword clashed steel with two of the Millymen. He kept back stepping from their press, glancing behind him to avoid stumbling over any rock that were there. He wasn't doing well. "J'son! Take off!" He shouted as he felt the heavy blood flowing from his back. "Were losing!"

J'son knew that. He had unloosed one shaft into a Milly face and knocked another for the Sheol limping in the air somewhere.

His eyes looked up to the trees above. The red and brown leaves that still clung to the trees had hidden her from his elven sight.

A roar from behind him rattled his ears and shook his bones. J'son whirled and saw the second Sheol standing three paces from him. Her face was bruised and bled slightly from the rock that Cassandra had hit her with. In her arms she held J'cob above her head. The elf tried to find the right angle to stab her with his sword but he failed to pull enough strength to damage her seeming invulnerable skin. She heaved him simply into the air.

In flight, J'cob watched the ground flying away from him and his earth bound brother growing smaller. The trees and leaves swished passed him as he now sailed above the height of them all.

The gray sky above was clearing and the air about him was brisk and cold. Hauge pushed passed him. J'cob was trying to swim in the air, reaching for the tides of the sky that swept around him as he was now falling.

Below, the second Sheol lifted a few feet from the ground and suddenly knocked the body, no longer screaming, from Cassandra's hands. The Sheol made a sweeping wave and slashed Cassandra with such force that she spun and fell to the ground. J'son drew his bow but in a blur, the Sheol punched him in the head and sent him flying off his feet.

Falling through the trees again, J'cob trying to snatch a branch that was far out of his reach, began to re-live his childhood past. At first he was surprised to find that it really took a long time to fall to his death. He remembered his mother training him in the way of Sho-Pa. Her favorite saying was to always take a tactical advantage of any situation.

With grim determination he twisted suddenly in the air, and gripped firmly into a passing white ankle.

A Sheol can easily fly with a man's weight. In fact, they are known to take off with plump cattle, but with a arrow through the bone of her tiny wing made keeping herself aloft difficult let alone with J'cob trying to stab her with his sword. She was quickly losing altitude as J'cob kept stabbing her. He lacked the power and proper magic to hurt her badly, but he was still making small nicks.

She kicked out and J'cob lost his grip. Falling three paces to the frozen ground, he stumbled and pushed to his feet. He whipped his sword about and blocked the two Millymen rushing at him. He blocked a pass and clipped a Milly in the fleshy part of the leg. The Millyman fell back, but two replaced him.

"Stop!" One of the Sheols screamed. The Millymen stopped obediently but J'cob's momentum carried over with a deep slash that cut a Millyman's belly. The Millyman stumbled back, dropping his small shield and instinctively readjusting his war belt a little higher.

Over head the Sheol lifted. In her net was J'son, balled into a neat little package. "I know not how you lived." The Sheol spoke no longer in her sultry voice. In fact, her whole beauty had transformed into a horrible thing. "Man cannot fly as the Sheol." She held up J'son. "Shall we see if he flies? Shall we see how far I can throw him?"

J'son's face was pushed into the net. He was panting too hard and had to swallow to slow it long enough to speak. "I love you, J'cob. Tell Mom I love her too."

J'cob frowned as his breath flared from his nostrils. Ironically, during his fall, he remembered that too. "I love you too." And with that said, faster than anyone could react, he took off like a shot into the woods.

The Sheol paused in aghast amazement. "I'll throw him!" She screamed into the woods. She looked around and saw her wounded sister flapping nearby and the Millymen standing below waiting for orders. "Well! After him!"

J'son only snickered to himself.

Chapter 56

Leatha filled the sky with night and stars. Hauge filled the air with crisp winds at Fikor's bidding. Far below, Mortalroam slept wrapped in cold shadows. Patches of frost clung to the barren fields that rolled gently below the stars. The great river that ran north of Modo and Cornerstone still ran. Torches burned into the night where the drole gnomes worked their shifts on the new site for Dragonslayer's castle. Trudging the heavy stones along the scaffolding to the great cranes to lift the blocks to the higher towers, four golems walked like zombies with loads of mortar and brick. Each walking stone behemoth was escorted by a gnome to point it where to go. These were the last of WARCO, Wreck and re-build company. They were to sure up the construction, then make way to the call to arms.

Following along the river and up out of the valley, the watch fires of Fanrealm could be seen. Tiny glistening specks of light in the black fabric of the land sparkled like orange stars far below. Beacons, like a candle in the window waiting for him. Kugerand circled above and Craig could hear the elf call singing to him. Craig shook his head. He was not born an elf so he could hear the elf call but couldn't understand it. If they wanted him bad enough, he reasoned, they would send a runner for him.

Kugerand headed into the gully and soared smoothly toward the cave opening. His feet touched down lightly on the grassy field nearby and skidded to a stop. It was normally a dragon's manner to hover and drop, but this time the great gold dragon had passengers. The dragon raised a paw and Craig slid down to it like a step ladder. The dark elf then reached back and nudged the sleeping Nihra elf. Orrin moved only enough to slip from the dragon's back and into Craig's arms.

'*Craig.*' The dragon whispered.

Craig looked up to where he was pointing. By the mouth of the cave a woman stood. The light winds of Hauge tugged at her cloak exposing her well covered feet. Kugerand lowed his paw to the ground and Craig set Orrin on his feet. The dragon and two elves made their way over to the entrance where the cloaked woman was standing. Craig reached out and embraced her. Her hands wrapped about his neck and clenched him tightly. Her tears ran like ice on Craig's exposed skin.

Craig pulled her away and held her. She was ice cold. Her face was dry and stained with lines of frozen tears. She was Ne-arri, the cat people, they felt the cold. Craig turned her and led her towards the cave. "You'll catch pneumonia out here. Lets get inside!"

"Right!" Onary said brightly as he trotted ahead after the gold dragon.

"I knew you were coming." Neeko shuddered in Craig's arms. "The dragons told me. They didn't speak in words, but I could tell."

"And did they tell you to freeze to death?" Craig said half annoyed. "My God, Neeko, why?"

"Master, dog relations!" She said fully annoyed. She twisted from his grip and lumbered ahead of him as fast as her belly would go. "You were wounded and burned, and you hopped on a dragon and swooped! Shoof! Like the wind." She stopped and whirled about. She leaned back with her hands on her hips trying to imitate a man. "So long dear, I'm off to drop the mob." She spoke in a deeper voice.

"Drop the bomb." Craig muttered to himself.

Onary sighed. "This way Orrin." And the dog and young elf moved ahead.

"Bomb, mob, what difference does it make? I was alone with a hundred burning demons stinking up the place!" She caught her breath and punched at her cloak with tiny balled fists. "You took off! Can you get it through your head that I love you? I wanted you with me? You took off and my centre went inside out. I wanted to help you, go with you…" Her fist brushed under her nose. "I wanted to at least kiss you goodbye, send my love…pack a lunch, I don't know." She turned and lumbered up the stone cut steps. Craig dashed after her and reached out to touch her but the Ne-arri smacked his hand away. "No!" She hissed. "I'm still mad at you." She faced him pulling her cloak about her almost as a shield. "And why aren't you arguing?"

"I have no idea of what you're mad about." Craig said simply.

Neeko's face filled with rage and her cat eyes filled with anger. "You…You!…" She balled her fists and shuddered. "Ohhhhh!" She turned on her heel and waddled below the sub tunnels. She stopped at the entrance to the pit. The warm stink of Brezhnev filled the hall and made her eyes water. She stormed by and up towards the higher tunnel where the natural winds would keep back the dragon odor. In the hall to the main intersection she paused and faced him again. "Is this how you're going to fight?" Craig nodded. "You should have been here!"

"When I left, you didn't say anything."

She bit her lip. "I didn't think I had to."

"I'm a rock, you should spell these things out." Craig took her shoulders and held her. "What was I supposed to do?" Neeko gasped in anger and punched him in the armor. "Look, Neeko," Craig said quietly. "I would cross the span of time for you."

"You already did that."

"I'd do it again because I love you that much. But Jesus, I'm a hero, You said it yourself. My job is to do bone headed things. I'm the Dragoncaller." Craig caressed her hot blushing face and wiped a way the tears that she was trying to hide. "You're not mad at me, are you?" She shook her head no. Craig's eyes lowered as he glared at her. "Then what?"

"You were hurt, I wanted to help you but when I saw how bad it was...And then you took off. How could I help you then? How could I say anything?" Craig looked down and brushed her cheek. She took his bandaged hand into her own. "You're bleeding!"

"It's not mine. Its Paradox's. I killed him. Now don't get into a dither, it was a really lopsided fight. If you could call it a fight." Craig brushed his hand on the soft ears at the top of her head. He kissed her forehead lightly. "Are you still mad?"

"Yes." She said tightly.

Craig winced and pulled away. "My face..."

"What is it?" Neeko suddenly took his arms and tried to hold him as he was stumbling back to the wall. "Craig, what is it?"

Craig fell into the wall and clumsily slipped to the floor with a clang. "What is my face? Is that what you're asking?"

Neeko deftly unworked the bandages on his face. She took her hand and laid it gently against the side of his head and began to cast. Craig tried to resist. He desperately tried to hold onto the reality that was around him. On one side, the side that Neeko was touching, he could see the walls of the cave melt. Okay, he thought, that can melt, that's okay. But when he wasn't looking, everything else went out like the light at the end of a tunnel. He broke through the clouds of ack-ack that were exploding black puff balls all around him. He caught that one too close. The stick was fighting him and his Corsair was bucking like a bronco. Oil was sliding up his canopy and he could hardly breathe from the smoke pouring out of the manifold. Below him, the tiny speck of the Japanese island exploded in hellfire as the rest of his squadron dumped their loads down below.

He turned and peeled off. Diving down, the gull-wing sailed smoothly, he knew that was going to happen. Down was easy. Getting back up really wasn't his problem either. He wasn't planing on that.

"Grampa…Grampa, zeros on the rise bearing three o'clock!"

"I'm on!"

"I'm behind ya!"

"V formation and hold, Dragon! Get up here!"

Get up here he says. I'm busy! He screamed in his own head. He dropped his landing gear to slow his speed. He let loose his load and his spare tanks. He wasn't going to need them. They were serving liver back at the mess hall. Tyrone hated liver.

"No No!"

"What the hell?"

"Grampa, I'm hit, I'm hit."

"Ski! Your manifold's on fire. Get out!"

"Oh, no! You rice sucking bastard!"

"He's on your tail Dragon! Get The hell out of there!"

Tyrone knew that. He was gunning for the bunker.

"Dragon, they're swarming you! Pull up!"

I'm busy. He launched his rockets. Two plowed into the coral reef with trembling roar. Two buried themselves into the jungle, but one bounced off an embankment and careened into the bunker. Japanese soldiers dove out of the way as the bunker went to kingdom come.

"Bank right, Bank right!"

Tyrone pulled hard right. It was the only thing he could do. He knew he was in trouble when the light from his landing gear went out and he didn't feel them slide back in place. Either his plane was shaking too much, they didn't raise up and the stupid light failed, or the damned things fell off. Slowly his crippled plane crawled back up into the sky.

Right there. *Pay attention rice ball, this wounded fighter still bites.* Squeeze and fire. He could feel the six 50. caliber machine guns shudder his already shuddering plane. Release the trigger. Don't over heat 'em and melt the barrels, you may need them later.

Something screamed at his ear. Static howled and Zero parts went past him. *Stupid zipper head, shouldn't have been worrying about the bunker and stayed in the air where ya belonged.*

Tapping, tapping at my fuselage door. A jap on his tail, too close and not enough power to dance with him. A lousy way to go.

Hell fire swarmed about him and another piece of the rising sun fell into the sea.

Gipper.

"Dragon, nobody could have sunk a bunker but you, you cocksucker!"

Fuck you and thanks. The marines were storming the beach. *Good God no! The transports are stuck on the coral, those crazy fucks are running on the coral, the Japs are tearing them apart.* He banked left and felt the plane lose control. He forced it to work and laid down cover fire for the devil dogs to storm the shore. Gipper took his wing and laid in also.

"Oohrah!" Gipper screamed.

"Grampa! Grampa!"

"He's on me! I can't shake him!"

"I can't stop him!"

"Good God!"

"Hold on, I'm on him."

"He's on you!"

"AHHHHHHHHHHHH!"

"Gipper! Dragon! Get up here!"

Can't I leave you guys alone for a minute? Tyrone looked above. He couldn't count his squadron for there were so few. He jerked his stick and pushed his throttle forward. His engine screamed in defiance and shot a glob of oil at him for good measure. Tyrone climbed the sky but there was no one there. His squadron, was gone. The japs were gone.

What the hell?

A shadow running across the sky, a zero on his tail. Tyrone pulled and banked. Rounds tore his broadside and peppered his tail. Tyrone folded and looped hoping to at least catch a glimpse of him, to slip him. He was there. Ten times the size of any plane. Not just a Zero, but a Zero to the tenth power. Rounds peppered him again. Something was on fire. Oil was covering the stick. Not oil, blood. *Whose? Mine? Fuck.*

He dove, it dove. The giant silver monster swarmed down on him with guns a sparking into his tail. His canopy splashed glass against his face. He was done.

It let off. Something frightened him. Something scared him. The giant plane, the size of a bomber but the speed of a fighter turned in fear from the tiny corsair hounding his tail. Gipper.

The fear didn't last long and the giant bird turned on itself and dove head on with Gipper. The Gipper faced off, his tracers were bouncing off the hide of the giant zero. *God, its indestructible!* But Gipper was undaunted as he turned on the juice and plowed into the giant rotor blades and the thing ate him alive.

His mission to take out the bunker was done, he couldn't cover the grunts down below for they had already rushed the beach and were now in the jungle. He looked to the sky. He barely had enough rounds to fight with. Black smoke spewed from his manifold. He had to run. Something that big couldn't be fought. *But how can that thing fly?*

He had to run.

He banked to a west heading to a smaller island clump, a landing strip the seabees had set up a little while ago. He could make it.

Something pushed out of his manifold—something important. He wasn't going to make it. Fire was all around him. The canopy wouldn't pop. He was going down trapped in his plane. Dead marines laid slashed on the coral bleeding into the sea. This wasn't good at all. *Fuck me.*

Lips wrapped with his and warm breath laid lightly on his face. His eyes opened and Neeko's dark green cat eyes glared back at him. With blurry sight he looked at his hands. No scars, only a little redness. His face only tingled when he touched it. "It took some time." She said. "But I am a healer." She kissed him again, but he didn't react. "I admit that I'm not in Lady Fantista or Frito's class, but I'm right up there. I know you did that on purpose. You do everything on purpose. I love you." She kissed him again then searched his face for a response. "Craig? At least Onary will wag his tail."

Craig suddenly looked at her. "Neeko?" His voice was sore and hoarse.

Neeko searched his eyes. "You had a dream, didn't you...the kind that come true." She knew for certain.

His heart was pounding as he began to sweat. "Hold me."

She did.

In the cavern below, the dragons nestled in their own beds and tried in vain to sleep.

In the darkness of the shadows, Thamrell stood beside Thumber watching Neeko and Craig.

"Will it work?" Thumber prodded.

"Of course it will work. He is no knight, only human, or elf, or something. He is already lost before the battle has begun."

Thumber shrugged his shoulders and lumbered off. Thamrell watched as Neeko helped her husband to the house. The cat and dog swarmed about them as they reached the door. The boy Orrin was with him. Thamrell shook his head. Craig was just mortal. Strong willed like the Dragonslayer, but more dangerous—too much of an unknown factor. Craig had to be taken care off.

But he's strong. Perhaps, too strong.

Chapter 57

A hollow rumble echoed from out of the depths of Argra. A belch from out of oblivion. It wasn't often that the eternal shadow made any noise and then it was never for any apparent reason. No one really knew why and made up spectacular stories of what was in the world of nothing. In truth, there was a lot down there in nothing.

Not wanting such damaging information to leak out, it was kept a great secret by the Trid Dreath that the eternal demon of demons known as Kiupquixdaviduom, The Moaltoian Meca demon—Dave to his close friends—lived in oblivion. He had been set free by Hauth during his conquest of Mortalroam and enslaved again by Frito on his return from the god's god. He wasn't coming out of there. Trid Dreath IV made sure of that.

Trid Dreath was the devil. He wasn't really the proverbial devil, but when Trid Dreath the first, declared himself the devil at the re-awakening of time, no one disputed him for eons until Frito came to Hel and killed him. Since then, there had been two other Trid Dreaths, one killed and one resigned, sort of. He was the forth in sudden succession and had all intentions of having a long and prosperous reign. The Trid Dreath was a position not granted but earned by being the most powerful, ruthless, and sneaky son of a bitch in all of Hel. Dave the Meca demon was only a demon, but a big fucking demon that Trid really didn't want to mess with.

Trid Dreath slid lower in his chair and eyed the buxom wench as she served him wine. Her knowing eye and seductive wink was only meant for the Trid Dreath. Her tight, wasp-waisted corset and short dress was meant for everyone else, for the Trid Dreath was above ogling at women.

His long fingers stroked the stem on his wine glass. It was chilled and he felt the condensation on his finger tips. Dave wasn't going any where, he thought in his devilish mind. The Meca demon was asleep. Regardless of this comforting notion, when the beast rumbled loud enough to be heard above the sand storm outside, it made the devil nervous.

He glanced slowly about the bar. He had it built especially at the edge of Hel to keep an eye on Argra. The Paradise Lost Truckstop was empty this late afternoon. Geezer, the bus boy, scrubbed his mop at the floor with effort as Wally restocked the bar. It wasn't often the place was so quiet. It was best to take advantage of the moment.

Geezer paused his mop and listened for a moment. The boy looked out of the window and watched for about a minute before he turned to the Trid Dreath. The devil hadn't moved. He had a tendency to sit for hours like a statue and this was one of those times.

The devil finally moved and looked at the boy. The tall bony kid only shrugged his shoulders and said nothing.

The doors swung open and light flashed into the room. Geezer shielded his eyes from the light and tried to see into the silhouette that was standing in the doorway. The man stood there soaking in the dim atmosphere of the bar before walking boldly into the room and slipped onto a bar stool. He slapped his red, white, and blue helmet on the counter and pulled off his wire aviator glasses. His plastic/nylon red and blue riding suit clicked and squeaked as he leaned over the bar. "Gimme a light!" He then turned, leaning his back against the bar. "I heard this was the most, the jazziest place in all of Hel. Hey, kid!" He flipped a coin to Geezer. As he did, the words, 'Easy Rider' that had been embroidered in white and black on his arm, could be seen. "Play something on the box will ya?" The Easy Rider turned around and his beer was there waiting. He nodded to the bartender and took a sip. "So…Off night? I mean its kind o' quiet." The Easy Rider suddenly whirled about on his stool. "What is that? Don't you have anything good at that thing?"

Geezer stood a little dumbfounded at his selection. "We got Lynard Skynard if you prefer that to Hank Williams Jr.?"

The Easy Rider shook his head and turned back to his beer. "Kids." He mumbled and sipped at his beer again.

The Trid Dreath watched him causally for a moment before he turned his thoughts elsewhere. He could hear thunder again, but it wasn't coming from Argra.

The boys were home.

The door exploded and they suddenly piled in hooting and hollering and storming the bar. Wally had heard the thunder and was already lining rows of beer on the bar. An instant crowd filled the room brandishing their buffalo heads and hooves and hides. One went running about with a set of buffalo wings. They were demon bikers and there was no mistaking them. They were mostly hairy, save the ones that weren't hairy. Mostly big, save the ones that weren't very big. In fact, the only thing that any of the bikers had in common with one another was the fact that they were all mean and wore the insignia, 'Demon Bikers From Hel' embroidered on their jackets of denim or leather, except for those with neither denim or leather, and just had it embroidered on their backs.

And they were all ugly, save one.

He stood in the middle of the room. Unlike the other demon bikers, he was human, standing a bold five feet eight inches in jeans and 'Holiday Greeting from Ted Nugent' tee shirt. A baseball cap with the word 'FOG' printed smartly on the front covered his dirty blond hair. He was rather heavy set with a strong, squarish frame. His full face was unshaven and proud whiskers bleakly pushed their way from the end of his chin. A frown was bent into his face. As the room ran wild with bikers drinking and partying brandishing their Buffalo parts, he stood alone tapping his foot impatiently. "THERE IS SOMETHING QUITE WRONG WITH THIS PICTURE!" He suddenly announced in a voice loud enough to cover the bar room din. He stood tapping his foot impatiently with his left arm stuck out with all the fingers wriggling. His right hand was jammed into his jeans pocket as he stared intently over his right shoulder. Then he glared at the floor before his right foot before glaring at the ceiling. Then he suddenly glanced at the wall over to his right before glaring at the ceiling again. All the while during this dramatic display, he continued to tap his right foot impatiently. From out of the crowd, a beer emerged and found its way to his left outstretched hand. He gasped and looked rather surprised at his left hand. "For me?" He exclaimed. "Thanx!" He took one long pull and finished it off. "Wait! Take this back. Its defective!"

"What's wrong with it?" Asked Mortar Round, the short wide biker with his teeth on the outside of his mouth.

He looked at him and smiled. "Its empty!" He tossed the mug and looked around to the corner of the bar where the Trid Dreath sat. Boldly he walked up to a place none of the other bikers had dared to go. "It was a Blast!" He announced as he took a seat. "You should have been there."

The Trid Dreath looked at him. "Kevin, I bought you a present."

Kevin's face lit up as his broad face grew broader. "A Blond!"

Trid Dreath made a face. "I gave you a red head last week."

"I know." Kevin leaned closer to whisper to the devil. "She's gorgeous and I love her, but ya gotta watch em'." Kevin suddenly looked about to insure no one was eves dropping. "Never, ever go to sleep before a red head."

The Trid Dreath smiled and pointed to the table. Kevin leaned back and saw his present. It hadn't been there before, but that didn't matter. It was there now. "A six pack of Molsen Golden!" Kevin cooed as he took one out. "And frost chilled! Thanx boss."

Trid Dreath IV watched as Kevin opened his present and took a swig. "You and red working out?"

Kevin wiped his face on the table cloth. "Oh yeah, she's hot, and swallows. At every stop, she fills the tanks and buys me my smokes."

"Checks the oil too I bet."

Kevin glared at the Trid Dreath with astonishment. "Oh, Heck No! Checking the oil is a man's job. She just reloads the shotgun and changes flat tires." Kevin took out his cigarettes and popped one in his mouth.

"So I see." Trid said reaching for the pretzels. "I think this gentleman is here to see you."

Kevin turned around and looked up at the Easy Rider in the red and blue riding suit. Kevin lit his smoke and took a toke. He blew a steam of smoke of to the side as not to offend the stranger and stuck his hand out. "Hey dude! C'mon and have a beer!" Kevin's hand hung out but the Easy Rider wasn't shaking.

The Easy Rider took a finger and pointed it into Kevin's broad chest. "You drive that truck right?"

Kevin seemed pleased. "My fans." He said to Trid. "Hey like an autographed beer cozy?" He asked the Rider. "Or an autographed copy of my new book, 'To Hell and Back Without a Toll.' In book stories now. Hardcover edition."

The Easy Rider seemed to grow with anger. "You ran over my bike!"

Kevin seemed mortally wounded as he suddenly placed his hand over his heart. "Are you sure?"

The stranger's eyes widened. "I can see parts of it under your truck!"

Kevin leaned back towards the Trid Dreath. "College grad." He mumbled before facing the stranger again. "You sure it was my truck?"

"There is only one truck and you're the only truck driver." The stranger concluded.

"Boy Genius." Kevin mumbled to Trid. "Well that's okay." He told the Easy Rider. "I'm not going anywhere for at least an hour so you can climb under there and pull it out. Meanwhile have a beer." Kevin rotated a finger above his head and a beer came passing through the rabble of the bar. Kevin resumed his seat and waved at the bar wench to bring him some more Hawaiian bread and cheese.

The Easy Rider clamped a hand on Kevin's shoulder. "I'm not through with you!"

Kevin slowly stood up and turned around and glared into the man's plastic/vinyl chest. Kevin then looked up. The Easy Rider was rather built and rather tall. "Look dickcheeze." Kevin started quietly, now annoyed. "You parked your japshit riceburner in my space." Kevin took a toke from his cigarette and went on. "But I'm not mad, really. The amount of damage to my truck was insignificant so I'm willing to let you slide if you hiaku outta here real ric tic."

The Easy Rider suddenly grit his teeth and hauled off to swing at Kevin. Kevin blocked the blow with his left and brought up an axe handle into the Easy Rider's crotch with his right.

The Easy Rider hadn't seen the axe handle before, but it really didn't matter as he rolled and writhed on the bar floor at the feet of the demon bikers. Kevin walked a circle around the man on the floor with the axe handle over his shoulder. "You had your chance, but you don't hear too good." As if on cue, the bikers suddenly picked up the man and plopped him down in a chair in the center of the room. They held him fast in place while Kevin stood behind him. The stranger tried to see what Kevin was doing, but couldn't. "We're gonna play a game. I'll make a sound and you tell me what it is. Ready?"

The stranger sat in fear of the demons holding him down. He felt a vibration at the back of his head and a buzzing roar in his ears. "A motorcycle?" The Easy Rider guessed.

"No!" Kevin shouted over the revving noise. "It's a chain saw!"

The Easy Rider's screams and blood splatter were almost drowned out by the horrendous laughter from the demon bikers. In no time at all the bikers had the Easy Rider naked, his body scarred and bleeding from where Kevin used the chain saw to cut off his plastic/vinyl jump suit and was strapped across the bar with his body bent at a ninety degree angle and his feet tied to the pole at the base of the bar. With great effort the Easy Rider could see Kevin in the mirror, pulling on a pair of rubber surgical gloves. "What's about to happen." Kevin announced as he smoothed the bubbles from his gloves. "Makes even me shudder." Suddenly Kevin froze and an instant later, he quaked violently for nearly a second making a squealing noise as he did. When it was over, he stood there with his arms out stretched as if to hold back a crowd. "It's alright, just a minor attack of the heebee jeebees." Kevin looked at the face of the stranger in the mirror and smiled cynically with healthy, clean teeth for a half second. He then held out one rubber hand and someone gave him a live hamster.

"That is enough!"

The bar suddenly froze at the sound of the order. Kevin whirled towards the Trid Dreath who was sitting still not really paying attention to what was going on. He hadn't said it.

"Says who?" Kevin demanded.

"Says me." A man stood from his table. He was dressed in robes that draped to the floor. A low hood was pulled over his head that hid his face in shadows. A gnarled crooked staff was clenched tightly in his right hand.

Kevin seemed to weigh the man's words as he weighed the hamster in his hands. "You're no fun." He said. Quickly he reared back as if to throw the hamster but thought second of it and didn't. Then he thought thirdly of it and wailed the hamster in to the bar. Kevin pulled off his rubber gloves with a snap as a couple of the demons untied the Easy Rider and let him gather up the parts that Kevin had cut off.

"And who might you be, stranger?" The demons around Kevin began to snicker. The hooded man stood a little taller than Kevin, but still much shorter than the average demon biker. The hooded man looked around the bar, at the twisted mangled faces of the demon bikers who were slowly crowding around him. The hooded man looked to the devil in the corner. The Trid Dreath was staring at him. His dark eyes sparkled in the lamp light. "I am the Walker, the Wonderer, The Stranger." He began. "I am the Ninefingers, The Lord of Lightning, Archknight of Okshiru. I am Trid Dreath," He matched the Trid Dreath's gaze. "The third." He pulled his hood from his head. "I am Frito, son of Lord Hammerstrike. I am the Devilslayer."

"Yeah well that's real good to know." Kevin said as he stepped in between Frito and The Trid Dreath in a declaration meaning simply, 'You gotta go through me first.' "He's busy right now, come back next Tuesday." The demon bikers snickered again.

Frito leaned his gnarled staff against the bar then pulled the cords holding his robe and let it slip to the floor. His dull gray armor was clearly seen by all. "I think I should make myself clear." Frito loosened his equipment belt and let it fall to the floor. "I'm here to see Trid." Suddenly Frito jousted a finger into the crowd of bikers around him and pointed at the largest one present. "Do you have a problem with that?"

It was a challenge. It had to be made. Basic demon protocol expressed that to petition the devil, one had to be worthy. Frito also had to be careful in his challenging. If Frito was to challenge Kevin, he would have to go through all of the demon bikers first because of even more protocol. But this was an even fight, more or less, and as all of the demon bikers began to back away making an area for the fight that was evident they all knew that as long as it was a reasonably clean fight, it was between Frito and his opponent.

The biker Frito had chosen stood a little under eight feet when slouched over. His long arms swung like tree limbs as he flexed and unflexed the tight network of muscles. His thick leathery hide was covered with heavy chainmail. Retractable ivory spikes pushed from his shoulders and arms as he circled the room sizing up the much smaller elf. His great horns that were attached to his helmet waved around as he shook his head with a snort. He was ready.

Let the battle begin.

Kevin took his seat beside the Trid Dreath. "And welcome to the action here at Ring side." He announced using his beer bottle as a microphone. "I'm Kevin bringing you the oncoming slaughter. And speaking of the devil, here with me is none other than Trid Dreath the Fourth. Sir, what can you tell me about our two combatants circling the squared ring?"

"Well Kev," The Trid Dreath began. "Martin Mangla is a powerhouse, however, the Ninefingers is no slouch by any means, but this is going to be a no magic brawl with old navy rules, 'First guy dead, loses'."

"Well at the jump its Mangla on the press, wailing eye blurring blows with enough force to waylay a cargo ship, but the Ninefingers is dancing out of range."

"Frito is an elf, Kev. That dexterity will save him."

"Frito is on the inside and mixing it up. A pure power upper cut to Mangla's jaw. Frito is aiming for small areas and avoiding Mangla's body."

"Well Kev, Mangla's body is too armored. His head is his only weakness."

"So it seems. Good tail sweep by the Mangla. Frito dodges the spikes by a hair. Isn't the armor Frito is wearing cumbersome?"

"Not really. That's armor by Max. True Dwarvish steel with enough magic to run a Cadillac with power windows. Look! Frito throws that brilliant side kick to the Mangla's open kidneys. His armor actually flexes, bends with him. Ohh, good blow by Mangla. If it wasn't for that armor, Frito would be floor wax right now."

"Frito moving on his feet again. Duck and weave pattern to avoid Mangla's haymaker punches. Frito is in again already, his threshold for punishment must be outrageous!"

"Well, Kev, he's a knight. Knights are stronger here in this part of hel. Another feather in the Ninefinger's cap."

"Well he's gonna need it. Mangla caught him with a flat chop and sent him plowing into the bar. Frito is dazed and it looks like Mangla's going early for the longhorn gorge and is heading horns first at the downed paladin...And its One...two...whoaaa like a snake the Ninefingers wriggles under the oncoming charge and through the Mangla's legs. Mangla's horns first into the bar. Frito is up and Mangla's having trouble freeing his head. Frito has got the tail and...CRACK! There it goes. Ohh, that looked painful. Where have I seen that before?"

"Well Kev, Mangla is paying for over confidence in going for an early gorge. That tail crack was perfected in the early demon wars by none other than Lady Fantista. It seems that a demon's center of balance is in the tail and with out it they are hurtin'."

"And pissed too Trid. Mangla's screaming and wood has flown everywhere as he pulls that head out. Frito springing on his feet and Pow...a chop to the side of the neck. It seems that Mangla is hurt."

"Frito went for a ganglia of nerves. Part of his Sho-Pa training from his mother."

"Good table action by Mangla. He's swinging that around keeping Frito at bay."

"He's got to keep him away. Frito can finish him off from the inside. Technically Frito can now use a weapon."

"I lay odds he's going for that staff he brought in...No! He's gone Phantom walk. The table swung through his immaterial body and Frito is on the inside and delivers another blow to the neck. Frito drops back down and jumps again and…Ohhh right above the eyes…Mangla's blind and whirling about. Whoops. Frito's has hit the deck, the tail caught him unawares from behind."

"Although broken Kev, it still works."

"Works it does but Mangla's bleeding from that blow above the eyes and the big brute is having trouble seeing. Frito is finding his feet and…no! Bad oil technique on the part of the audience. Frito has gone face first in to the base boards and that hurt. Trid, what's the recovery time?"

"Frito is tough but knights feel pain. Frito can't win by attrition and he has got to be running out of tricks. No points for audience interference."

"Mangla's on him and Wham! That had to hurt. Wham again! Frito is stunned and Mangla picks him up and whoaaa Fly By Knight Okshiru Air Lines. Frito sails across the room and crashes into the glass behind the bar. Mangla isn't letting up and dashes over to the bar and Hello! Frito is already on his feet. He's got Mangla by the horns and One…Two…Three times a lady into the bar with the face technique. Frito still has him by the horns and jumps up on to the bar and Yes…Yes…OhhhhhhhSLAM! Mayhem here! The Myanise face smash! Incredible! Mangla is reeling! What action!"

"Note here Kevin, Frito is bleeding severely from the glass. The knight is going to have to take him out now."

"Frito is on him and Mangla's stunned; it looks like Frito is setting up for a flying…oooops, Frito buys it in the leg, good table toss by Mangla. A blind hail Mary throw but effective. Frito is staggering and back in the oil. Mangla is on him already with a chair and Pow he…No! Frito has opted for the Phantasm again and the chair goes through him. Again the blow to the neck and Mangla is reeling."

"Kevin, every time Mangla uses a weapon, Frito is going to use his only physical Kamri for that extra defense. Mangla's just to dumb to figure that out."

"Mangla is hurting. It seems that he can't lift his right arm from the blows to the neck. Mangla is still whirling about blind with blood. Frito is screaming obscenities at him. Mangla is homing for the voice, Frito ducks low and holy Carrier Landing! The Ninefingers dives and skids across the oil slick floor and jumps behind the Mangla. The Ninefingers rolls up and grips the Mangla's horns and, YANK! The Mangla goes backward off his feet and in a classic judo flip over the Ninefingers.

430

Slam! Into the deck. Frito is now dragging the stunned Mangla by the horns and Wham! Face to Knee! Wham again! And again. Frito does a roll and Mangla's head follows along with the rest of his body and slam into the deck! And slam again! Where is the referee? This has got to be stopped! Wait? No! How? Mangla is stumbling to his feet, Frito nails him again to the head but Mangla is still standing! He shrugged and the Ninefingers releases his horns. Here comes that left from Mangla and Frito opens the envelope, reads the telegram and evades. Frito steps past and drives a kick to the spine. Oh, that has got to hurt. Frito has got the demon by the tail and is a pullin'. He's dragging the boy back and Lordy Lordy he's spinning him around. Mangla is pawing for the floor but it is too late and he's airborne. Caaaarash! Through the window and into the bikes. Mangla's out…eight, nine, ten! What a fight!"

The cheers of the Bikers flooded in Frito's mind as he stood in the middle of the floor teetering slightly. Blood dripped freely and quickly from beneath his arm guard. He looked around at the hideous faces shouting at him. He watched money passing about and fists shaking in the air. Frito dis-concerned himself with the demon bikers who actually were rather thrilled. The knight of Okshiru stood gazing at Trid Dreath who only smiled back at him. Frito slowly walked over. His steps were unsure and shaking. He sat in the seat that was provided for him and remained quiet.

"That was a fight." Kevin exclaimed as he ordered a beer for Frito. "Hand to hand, mano y mano, with a demon the hard way. Hey, you know that is a good way to get AIDS?"

Trid passed the M&Ms and sat them before Frito. "Mangla has AIDS?" The Trid asked quite surprised.

"Got AIDS?" Kevin started cutting chunks of cheese. "Heck no, he just gives it to people." Kevin offered some cheese to the Ninefingers. Frito hadn't moved since he sat down. In the dim light of the bar Kevin could see a faint aura around the Frito. His bleeding had already stopped.

"You know, Frito." Trid Dreath IV began. "I feel it is quite an event when any one can predict you."

Frito looked at him. "If you know why I'm here, then why did you put me through that?" Frito stopped glowing.

Trid smiled. "The devil made me do it."

431

Frito slowly closed his eyes as a sudden want to moan came over him. "Then your answer?" The Knight slowly opened his eyes.

"Maybe."

Kevin slid a plate of Hawaiian bread before Frito.

"How many of them?" Frito asked as he took a fist out of the bread.

"Ten times more than you got. About a eighth of Hauth's." Trid sipped his wine. "Ferris is with them."

"Old news." Frito fingered the M&M's trying to decide what they were. "Where?"

"They're in the Wove now. I can't tell you where they'll pop out."

There was a crash from behind. Mangla fought to his feet and climbed through the window. He flung off his helm and for the first time, Frito realized that Mangla's horns were not attached to his helm. The demon stumbled over, gripping into Frito shoulder for balance. "Slomph Skeelles." He mumbled and headed off to the bar.

Frito took up his beer and drank deeply letting it dribble down the corners of his mouth and run down his neck. "Gotta go." He said and slapped the mug down. Frito stood to his feet and turned to leave. His staff leaning on the bar slowly balanced itself and then leapt into the air. In midair it transformed into the Blade-spear and landed properly in Frito's hand. Someone handed him his robe and belt as he walked through the door.

"Hey!" Kevin called after him. "Thanks for not destroying the place." He looked at Trid. "He's such a nice guy. A little bi-polar, but a nice guy."

Trid Dreath listened carefully as Frito mounted his horse and trotted out. The jukebox was on again. Outside, the Argra belched, but no one heard it. No one save Trid. *Not good* the devil thought. *Not good at all.*

Chapter 58

Danshu fell softly from Okshiru's gray afternoon sky. Light drops of rain splashed on Meleki's wet blanket of leaves. Hauge had either found himself a cave to sleep in or ran ʃo play with Fikor elsewhere. The barren trees with scant leaves still hanging from their limbs stood as sentinels guarding the woods. Standing thousand year posts, watching the seasons of the gods come and pass—Armies of man rise and fall. Sentinels that watched the demon war of two years ago. They had seen the hordes of Hel pour from gates thrown open wide. They watched them crawl back, humbled and beaten, and the gates closed once more. Only the mountain majesties has seen more than the Sentinels of the trees. They watch Meleki's forests and all that live within them.

They watch the rain fall.

J'cob sat at the base of a tree staring blankly at the leaves of gold, yellow, red and brown that sprawled before him. It didn't really matter to him that Fikor's cold snap had ended and the day, although miserable, was a little warmer. He only dripped with Danshu's rain.

His feet sank into the blanket of snow as he jumped from the cart. He pulled his hood lower to keep the chilling wind from his face. His brother Dwayne drove the cart on into the barn and when he emerged, the two pushed the doors closed. He walked with giant exaggerated steps to cross the knee deep snow as they crossed to the house. He could smell the stove and warm bread wafting out of the small farm house in gray smoke against a white sky. Father stood on the porch. A tall man, human, wrapped in several layers against the cold. He watched with steel eyes as they came from the stables and up the stairs. Dwayne gave him a nod as they stepped inside.

Lamp light pushed back the darkness and cast jumping shadows along the walls. Dexter stood in the kitchen hunched over a large pot, stirring what seemed to be supper. His thin pale frame looked deathly in the fire light. Denice worked on the counter rolling dough for bread. Donald pushed in the back door. Walking backwards with his arms filled with lumber he dumped them in a neat pile by Dexter's fire. Daniel followed closely behind pushing the door closed with his foot. He struggled to balance the pail of water until Dwayne caught it and steadied it. Dwayne's dark skin was hard to see in the lamp light, but his eyes of Nih shone like blood.

"Here." He said handing the parcel to his older brother. "The medicine." Dexter's long bony fingers took it and he nodded. He was nothing like Dwayne's wide stocky powerhouse self. As elves go, they do not mix when they breed out of species. They remain pure to a race. With enough out breeding (although rare) one family could easily cover the range of elves. Dexter was Nihra. They tended to be thin and either pale or olive in complexion. As for Nerin and Hiran, their only difference is their elvish sight. Nihra eyes glow gold. Nerin, most common breed of elves, are green. Hiran, the second rarest breed have eyes that glow silver. Nih elves are easily recognizable. Like the Hiran and Nerin they cover the entire spectrum of complexion, size, and build however, elves do not need to see their eyes of red to know the evil breed. They just knew.

Michael pushed in the door. Frost clung to his cheeks and his brown eyes suddenly blazed green as they hit the darkness. His eyes cooled as he set his shearing axe in the corner. He stepped over to Denice's fishbread and seized one. "This lunch?"

Denice's eyes suddenly flared with silver. "That's dinner!" She said as she snatched at Michael's arm.

Michael moved too quickly and used his unusual height to hold the bread above her head. "The mouse roars 'Hickory, Dickory, Dock, but she must learn, not to touch the Roc." He went to shove the bread into his mouth when his eyes caught a glimpse of father. "Uncle…" He said handing the bread back to Denice with a gentle pat on her head.

"Eat it." Father said quietly.

With a swipe it was gone.

"At least chew!" Denice cried.

Father looked to Dwayne. "And how was the trip?"

Dwayne leaned the hand and a half sword in the corner. "Town, I guess. Everybody knows. They all send their love." Dwayne sat down at the table and Denice quickly went to set food before him. He and J'cob had missed breakfast that morning. "Come J'cob." Dwayne motioned to the table.

Father laid a large gentle hand on the youngest. "Go eat."

J'cob looked up at his father then around the room. The whole family was there save mom and…"I'm not hungry daddy. Can I go see him?"

Every one in the room slowed to a stop and looked at the little boy. Daniel's eyes of green glared at him. Father smiled a little and stepped over to the stove. He took up a potcloth and lifted the ring of the small steaming kettle. "Bring this to your mother and tell her we have his medicine."

His little hands reached out and took a death grip on the handle of the kettle. He turned slowly and plodded carefully out of the kitchen to the small parlor. He then walked slowly down the short, unlit hall. His eyes grew green with elven sight as he stood before the door to his father's bed room. The handle loomed over his head. With both hands on the kettle, it would be quite difficult to open the door.

It opened by itself. Mother stood there with a warm smile. The room rolled with heat and little J'cob felt it roll about him like a wall of warm fog. The air was moist and steaming. His elvish senses were young and undeveloped and could not help but gag at the stench of sickness. He was paralyzed. His mouth dried suddenly and his words clung to his throat. His hands, on their own, held out the steaming kettle. She took the kettle from him. He held on to it for a fraction longer to make sure she had it before letting go. "Daddy...daddy said the medicine is here." He somehow said. She knew that. If he was here, then the medicine had to be here. He felt his mother's firm hand guide him into the room. He coughed on the thick air. He prayed that he wasn't sick and swallowed another cough only to have it explode up at him.

"I need someone to watch J'son while I go and show Dexter how to make the medicine." Mother said to him. He nodded quickly as he accepted his mission. She watched him turn and plod over to the chair in the corner and drag it over to the tall goose feather bed. He hopped up on to the chair and sat by his brother's side.

"Hi me." J'son's eyes of green glowed through the thin slits of his eye lids. He was sweating and his face was swollen.

"Hi me." J'cob said sharply. The twins stared at each other for a few moments with nothing to say. "J'son?" J'cob asked ever so timidly. "You gonna die?"

"I hope not." He said slowly. "It would ruin my day..." He laughed pitifully at his own joke. J'cob managed a dry, fake laugh and a small smile. "I don't want you to die...I don't want to die."

"You're not sick."

"But you are." J'cob leaned closer. "And if something happens to you, it happens to me."

The older twin nodded. "Your right…It does. But you can't die. It wouldn't be right."

"But how can I live without you?" J'cob found himself gasping in the thick air.

"You just gotta. We're so good they need two of us." J'son coughed in a wheeze. He reached out and took his brothers hand. "J'cob, promise me that you won't die if I die."

"I'll try not to."

J'son tried to hold his brother tighter but wasn't sure if he was. "You gotta promise that you won't die for me. Not now, not ever."

A lump suddenly leapt up into J'cob's throat. "I promise…"

"Cross your heart?"

"Cross my heart and hope to…" Tears suddenly spilled from his face and splashed on the bed. "Don't die, me."

He sniffed and wiped the rain from his face. His back was sore from his wounds and leaning against the tree. He looked to the gray sky above him and felt Danshu's cold rain mingle with his warm tears.

"Why are you crying?"

J'cob leapt and rolled. His sword was drawn and clenched tightly in his hand by the time he found his feet. He blinked quickly to clear his eyes of tears and rain and looked to the forest around him. His eyes burned green as his elvish sight beamed a circle around him.

A gray rabbit suddenly pushed from the leaves. "I didn't mean to startle you."

J'cob didn't relax his stance. "You talk?" The rabbit nodded. J'cob's eyes flashed back and forth and then back to the rabbit. "Who are you?"

"Chritchfeild…rabbit at large."

J'cob slowly relaxed his guard. "So the gods are involved." He concluded.

"Actually," The rabbit said thoughtfully. "They've been pulled out. Okshiru is quite upset. I'm sort of left on my own."

J'cob paused a moment and let his ears listen to the woods for a moment. Only Danshu dancing about. J'cob then sheathed his sword. "And what is it you want?"

"Want?" Chritchfeild shook his head. "I don't want anything. I'm on your side."

"Why?"

"Why?" The mortals ask too many questions. "Why? Two reasons, one, I've nothing better to do. Two, logistical reports indicate a big war. Wars rip up forests. That's my home. If I can stop it, or minimize it, I will." Chritchfeild scratched the back of his ear to brush away the rain. "Which brings us back to my initial question. Why were you crying? Is it because of J'son?"

J'cob's eyes widened as his heart leapt up. "War? What war? And what of J'son? Have you seen him?"

"You will find out about the war soon enough. As for J'son, he lives. The Sheols have him prisoner." Chritchfeild could read J'cob sudden loss of hope. "I'm sorry, but I have more bad news." Chritchfeild hopped a little closer and stood on his hind feet. "Friska has fallen in with Thamrell."

J'cob dropped his head. "Blessid." He mumbled. "Blessid." He said louder and looked around the woods to see who heard. There was no one. He spun suddenly and looked to Worldsend. He clenched his fists as if to punch the sky. "DAMN!" He screamed hoping all of the gods had heard him. He paced in a circle and then stopped. He knew that there was nothing he could do.

Chritchfeild hopped over to him. "Don't despair!"

J'cob pointed a finger at the rabbit. "You do not bode well with me rabbit. You've done your helping, now begone."

The rabbit didn't move. "I can take you to him. I know where the armies of Hel are coming into Mortalroam. J'son and Cassandra the Sheol are at the main camp."

J'cob glared at the rabbit. There was more. "You have to get there and stop Friska. The hole in the Wove must be closed before the whole army can get through."

"Stop him? How?" J'cob glared at the rabbit. "You mean kill him!" The rabbit glared back. "I will not raise my hand against my brother!"

"And J'son?"

"I will rescue him. Where do I go?"

"The Sheols have flown him to the Forests of Dacova. It's several days north and to the east. You'll never make it in time on foot."

J'cob felt rage and frustration raise in his centre. "Then why are you telling me this?"

"I must take you." Chritchfeild said quietly and precisely. "But you must promise me that you will stop Friska."

J'cob's centre suddenly howled. His sword flashed from his scabbard with a sharp ring. "You manipulating rabbit!" Chritchfeild hopped back. "Don't bother to run, I can kill you before you get away."

Suddenly the thought of a second death loomed at Chritchfeild. Could he die twice? Would it hurt the same? Two deaths in one lifetime would certainly be unfortunate.

"You're asking me to choose." J'cob waved the blade at the little rabbit.

"I'm not asking you to kill him..." The rabbit said carefully. "I'm asking you to stop him. Perhaps you can sway him from Thamrell."

J'cob shook his head. "I'm no knight."

Chritchfeild cocked his head and stared at him accusingly. "Are you going to give up on both of your brothers so easily? Are you not going to at least try?"

J'cob stood in silence as the Danshu danced about him. "Rabbit..." He said quietly. "When this is over." He looked at Chritchfeild. "I'm going to kill you."

Chritchfeild only shrugged his ears. Par for the course.

Chapter 59

The wolf of the night howled, and the bay carried through the winding, maddening tunnels buried below the blackened Mountains of Anguish. Tunnels dug into the bowels of Hel by the running fingers of the river Therd. The river ran viciously up in straight lines, defying (more like ignoring) the laws of gravity for no apparent reason, and then back down in cascading waterfalls, ending in brown murky foam in pools of black water. The river ran on along the halls of Malice and washed away the blood that spilled from the twelve dead guards that laid there. The river flowed deeper down, and dragged with it the corpse of a sentry beast. The gigantic fire breathing beast had been decapitated and its head was nowhere to be found. The river flowed into the great lake Destitute. There at the shore, the detachment of guards, twenty five in all, including two captains and one major were all ruthlessly slaughtered, along with two members of the ferry crew who had done something funny after being directly told not to perform anything of that nature. The ferry boat rested in dock at the other side and its captain nervously watched his watch and his crew waited as ordered.

The guard detachment on the other side, although reinforced, also lay dead and butchered at the mouth of the Caves of Darkness. In the cave itself, the notorious wizard, Zot!, lay partially disintegrated, partially burned, and partially decapitated in the corner.

Further down the winding caves a set of thick oaken doors lay demolished on the floor and further beyond them a little monster stood bravely with a candle stick clenched tightly with four of his paws. "Another step!" The monster screamed. "Another step and POW! Your toast!"

The man stepped from the shadows. His robes trailed in the dust behind him. He leaned tiredly on his gnarly staff and sighed before he spoke in a soft voice. "Get out of my way."

The monster braced himself and tightened his grip. "No way, Jose!"

The stranger sighed again. "I've just killed several sets of guards, ferry boat crew, a fire breathing beast and a wizard. Must I kill you too? What is it that you guard so preciously that you can't let me by?"

The little monster didn't change his pose. "And what is so important that you must get on the other side of me?"

The stranger brandished his staff and it changed into Harbinger, the Blade-spear. Two eyes of bloody crimson flared from beneath the stranger's hood. "I seek my sister. Now my tolerance is just about over." The stranger pointed his Blade-spear. "Last chance, get out of the way."

The little monster lowered his stick. "You're here for Frita?" His face drained of anger and filled with sadness. "You're here to take her?"

"Take me to her."

The monster nodded his head as he stuck his candle stick in his belt. "Yeah, c'mon, I'll take you." The monster turned. "I knew you'd be here eventually."

"You know me?" The stranger said as he followed.

The little monster looked over his shoulder. "I have an idea…but who cares right? By the way, I'm Formor, Monster From the Attic and Thing That Goes Bump In the Night."

"Hello Formor. I am Frito."

"Yeah…Hi. Hey, how did you get in here? I waited by the gates but you didn't show. Is there another way?" Frito remained silent.

The little demon hung a right and then another left. Due to the constant physical changes that occur randomly in Hel, Formor had to double back on himself twice to find his way. It had been a long time since Frito had been to Hel and the place had changed beyond all recognition. Formor turned four times in the wrong direction and wound up back at the gates of Hel.

The gates of Hel were just as Frito remembered them. Frito paused when he saw them thrown wide open. He felt his centre fill with the acid of anger. Anger at Thamrell, anger at himself, but mostly, anger at the little giggling god sitting by the open door.

"Weishap." Frito moaned. "If there were a way to kill you…"

The god lifted his head and smiled brightly. "The answer lies in lieu, want of a question but since the question is unknown my son, then the answer is as elusive as the morning fog. If there is no question, and therefore no answer, then my lovely tool of destruction, there is no way I can be killed." The god crawled higher on his rock and looked at the Ninefingers from there.

Frito stepped closer. "Where is my sister?"

Weishap waved a passing hand at him, then peered through the hole in his wrist from where he was nailed to the door. "You ask to inherit the wind, to see into the blank stare of the dead, to hear the roar of

440

silence and feel the wires of tension. I thought you smarter than that my master, your sister is, out of sight, out of mind." The god beamed a brilliant smile at the knight.

Formor tugged at Frito's robes. "He's an asshole. Forget him. C'mon, she's this way." The little demon led him beyond the doors into the pits of The Abyss.

The howl of night echoed louder for this was the source. The scream of a thousand pains filled the air. A black cloud of winged things fluttered around the Ninefingers with a quick frenzy before they passed to the higher catacombs and clung to the higher ledges above him. Creatures of lower forms oozed piteously out of the way of Frito's steps. Things turned from their fires and watched the monster leading the knight past. They paid them little mind and returned to their fires. A crier sounded a warning, but no one was there to care. Formor made a strange path through the piles of rotting dead and dying that cluttered the place. He stooped under the rancid meat hanging from black chains and stepped over or around the looming bottomless pits that randomly opened and closed in the floor. He stopped when a scaly monster suddenly popped out of one and quickly dived into another.

To a secluded section, in a darkened corner, the little monster lead the Knight of Okshiru. Formor snatched a torch from something that hovered around it for warmth. The monster feigned to slap the thing when it moaned at the loss of its light. Down a dark tunnel the two went. Frita sat at the end, balled tightly to herself, clutching her legs tightly to her chest. All about her, were tiny demons.

Formor ran at them brandishing his candle stick in one hand and his torch in another. "Git outta here!" He shouted at the little demons swinging his torch at them. "Go-wan! Git!" He singed the rump of one to send his point home. "And don't let me catch you around here again!" He turned to Frita and lit the torch beside her as he did. "I told ya not to let this go out."

She didn't answer.

"Its okay." He cooed. "You didn't eat any of your pizza?" He pointed to the dried, cold, wrinkled slices sitting in the open box. The little demons had been nibbling at it. "It was the only good thing I could find."

"I know." She said in a tiny whisper. "Thank you."

"Hey, it's okay." He looked at the pizza. "It isn't too bad, you can eat it later. When you're hungry or something." Formor looked over his shoulder at Frito staring at him. "I got a friend here. He wants to be your friend okay?" Getting no response, the little monster stepped back.

Frito crouched down and looked at her. Slowly, her gaze lifted and looked at him. Her eyes of silver searched slowly over his face. "Do I know you?" The words stumbled over her cracked, bleeding lips.

Frito leaned closer. "Yes, you do." He reached into a small pouch on his belt and pulled out a small silver necklace. The silver star of Hammerstrike dangled from the chain. The torch light sparkled and its reflection sent tiny beams of light that played on Frita's battered face. Slowly Frito placed the star about her neck and the pendent rested comfortably on her chest.

Her eyes flashed at him. She seemed to be filling with new life. "Will you hurt me?" Tears filled in the rims of her dark brown eyes as they cooled.

Frito shook his head. "No. I will not hurt you." He took her fumbling, quivering hands in his own. Her hands were stinging with cold and his were warm. He felt in his touch the light of Okshiru's healing flow into her as slowly and softly as Shegatesu's dawn. She was quivering almost violently and his arms wrapped softly about her and pulled her cold body to his own. He cooed her and called her sister and kissed her stinging tears away. "You are Denice." He whispered. "I am Dwayne. Your brother. You are the Daughter of Lord Hammerstrike. I will take you home."

She suddenly pushed from him. "No...I must get my baby. She is in this place." She looked over Frito's shoulder and then all about him to see if the baby was there.

From the back of his mind, Frito could hear the bloody cackle of Weishap. "She is only here in your mind." Frito took a firm hold of her shoulders. His eyes burned crimson as he glared at her. "Set her free in yourself, and she shall be free. Okshiru took her and now you must see it in yourself to free her."

Her eyes wondered as the world for her rolled. Her hands reached out to her brother and grabbed on to a piece of reality. With that as an anchor, she pulled herself back. "Stephanie?" She said painfully as more tears lined her face. "My baby?"

Frito pulled her close and held her until she had stopped crying and fell asleep. The knight removed his robes and covered her with them. He then scooped her up in his arms. Formor stood before him holding his torch. The little monster turned and led the way out of The Abyss.

Past the gates, Horse was standing there waiting. Frito set his sister in the saddle of his Clydesdale. He looked at Weishap still sitting on his rock. Smiling. "Why?" The knight asked him.

"Because we like you." The god of answers, answered.

Frito nodded. The god was correct. "Why do you want Worldsend?"

"Something to live for, oh wreaker of havoc. We had the means and the way. When Hauth left me here, I made him believe in what he wanted to believe and that his way was infallible and the gates could never be thrown open again and like the sick puppy you were, you followed in what I wanted and you paved the great road to Worldsend for us in our second coup."

"You knew that I could not stand up to my father in Worldsend!" Frito shouted at him. "You set me up just to plan this?"

Weishap smiled. "To plot, to plan, to think, to change, to improvise, to overcome," The god shrugged his tiny shoulders. "What works might have been accidental and our plan all along."

Frito nodded. "Ura helped you?"

"Ura did to what her own ends met." The god said hoarsely. "As all the players jockeyed for position, oh great stomper of the masses, I merely guided and followed, advised and devised."

"And Stephanie?" Frito asked.

The god of answers looked away. "Things unforeseen and answers left unquestioned. I can only answer what is asked, and nobody asked."

"I am asking." Frito seemed to remind him.

"Oh, fragmenter of the realm, so you are. Stephanie was reblessed, rebirthed, reborn, reloved and rewanted. Through a tangled chain of haphazard and random accidents committed on purpose by the big 'O' himself, she was dropped into play and like mad dogs over meat, the bishops, pawns, rooks and Knights all scrambled wildly o'er the game field to control her, only to find in the end, that no one could posses her. But in the bowels of the muck dwelling mind, it is unnecessary to actually posses, only maintain control."

Frito nodded. He had dealt with he god of answers before and understood him too well. "Thamrell and Thumber took their power from Frita and Friska?"

The god looked at Frito in astonishment. "You are the son of the supergod! You are the possessor of the "Poer Ther Of"! You ask the questions of a rank amateur fumbling blindly in a bowl of razors! To ask questions that you know the answer to wastes the time that you saved solving them yourself." The god squealed like a pig as he shouted at the Knight. "Frita unknowingly gave her power of magic to Thumber as self penance for her sin. She summoned him from the start. Friska did the same to Thamrell. We only used that to our advantage. You accuse and believe that the gods stick their fingers into the soup and stir and stir until they are satisfied, but they only lay their odds on the happenings and on the now, vice trying to lower the river and bet their money on the soon to be."

The god was quite correct as he always was. Frito was reasonably satisfied and needed only one more answer. Formor stood below Horse and watched intently what was happening.

"I need another answer." Frito said calmly.

"This is what you tell me Oh, masher of landscape, but I am the god of answers who's ears are only bent for questions. Declarations are down the hall and to the left."

"I need to have these gates closed again when I send Thamrell's armies through here. Closed again for all of eternity." Frito went on ignoring the god.

"To dream the impossible dream, to fight the invincible foe," The god began to mutter.

"I want the "Poer Ther Of". Again."

Weishap stopped and looked up at the knight, his eyes wide with wonder. Out of all of the answers that he had to possible questions that there were, this was what he was not expecting. The power of Hauth.

"I don't want it for my self." Frito explained. "I want it for you. You see, as Hauth, I had the power of the whole world and nothing to do with it, so I took over the world. It was the thing to do. But this time. I'm going to give it a purpose, specific orders on what to do and how to do it. Then I'm going to give it to you and all you can do is carry out the orders of the "Poer Ther Of". That was my mistake. I used the Poer through me to close the gates. That way, all any one had to do was unrest my magic. This time. I'll let the "Poer Ther Of" do it. To open the gates again they must unrest the universe.

"But I need two things. I need a question to ask to properly form the concept of the Poer and its task in my head. And I need an answer to my question."

Weishap shook his head. "Oh raper of will, I am entitled to question the answering that I choose and I shall answer no such questions."

Frito smiled and looked over his shoulder to Formor sitting beside Horse, then back to the god sitting stubbornly before him. "You might answer this question because I already have the answer. But as a question unasked is nothing as an answer unfound. Am I right?"

"Right is in the eyes of the sovereign body and none other." The god said angrily. "There is still a question that you have left to ask oh piler of the dying."

Frito nodded. "Yes, why give the Poer to you?"

"You ask what you know, so I shall not answer the known."

"Because you cannot wield power. You cannot hold it or touch it, or keep it, you can only answer questions. If I give you the Poer, then you will only release it again. If I give the Poer a specific task, it will perform and then leave you. I will not take it as absolute power corrupts absolutely. But you oh great baffler of the confused. You cannot keep the Poer."

"Ask your question already!" The god muttered in a hiss.

Frito stood to his tallest height and then glanced back to Formor who was still sitting there. Then Frito spoke to the god of answers in the language of Thest, ancient tongue of magic and something the little monster beside him didn't know. "Tell me oh great god of answers, did His feet get wet?"

Then the head of the god of answers bobbled slightly and then broke into a full nod. 'Yes.'

Chapter 60

Hidden in underground catacombs the dragon division of Hammerstrike International based their operations. Buried in the center of the dragons' caves, slightly elevated above the wind tunnels (To keep away the dragon stench) Craig Tyrone had built his home. It was a small dwelling for himself and Neeko. Craig had designed ducts for heating or cooling and Neeko had arranged and decorated their little home. Onary had his place by the fire and Edia had hers in the rocking chair. It was always unusual to find a dog or cat willing to talk to people let alone live in the same house, however, this household was quite unusual.

Neeko stood in the kitchen supervising the brewing of vats of healing thatch. Steam filled the air as she hummed contentedly to herself over her task. The elfcall had sounded. War was coming. The front was going to need as much thatch as they could handle. Four girls from Fanrealm did the mixing mashing and measuring the raw thatch leaving Neeko, who had to use her powers of healing, to actually make the stuff work.

The door to the kitchen rolled open and Onary stuck his head inside. "My lady, a wagon is here."

Neeko nodded and took up a rag to wipe her hands. She motioned for one of her helpers to keep stirring her bubbling pot and stepped out of the kitchen. Edia was standing by the door. "What is it Pus-Pus?"

"It's the master, Mum." Edia replied as she hopped in to Neeko's open arms. Neeko opened the door a little wider and there was Craig arguing with someone.

"Wait a minute." Craig began. "You're here for what?"

Neeko gently tapped him on the shoulder and Craig glanced back at her. "Honey?" He asked her. "Did you order something?"

Neeko stepped in front of him and spoke to the men. "Take it to the kitchen. Just follow the bouncing cat." She said as she set Edia down.

"This way, boys." Edia called as she trotted across the living room into the kitchen.

Neeko took a gentle hold on Craig's wrist and lead him towards the bedroom. "Roc is sending the calling song for war and they will need Thatch. Seems like somebody totaled the kitchen in the Manor and most of Fanrealm is in disarray. So I kinda volunteered to help out."

Craig looked back at the men carrying barrels out of the kitchen. "Am I losing control here?"

"Not at all, dear. You're still in charge." Neeko confided to him as she lead him to the bed and sat him down.

"Then how am I doing?"

"Absolutely outstanding. The enemy is retreating, the general is pleased and the men all love you." She laid him in the bed and pulled the covers over him, tucking him in. "Especially me." She kissed him lightly on the lips and smiled. "You should sleep some more. Healing and thatch will wear you out."

"I've slept too much." Craig said with a yawn in his mouth. He pulled his hand out from under the blanket and took his watch from the night stand. "Look at the time!" Craig rolled out from under the covers before his wife could catch him. "I'm gonna shower."

Neeko watched him dart into the bathroom. "How is your face?" *No sense in arguing with him,* she thought.

"Fine." Came Craig's voice. "I can't feel it."

"Mum?" Edia leapt onto the bed. "The ladies in the kitchen ask what to do. The kettle is beginning to simmer."

"Cat." Came a voice from the Bathroom. "Off bed."

"Edia, tell them I'll be right there." Neeko watched the cat leap off the bed and into the kitchen. Neeko could hear the furnace firing to heat the water for his shower. She shook her head. Elves…she thought…no, him.

In the kitchen she set aside the simmering kettle and put on more water to boil. She directed one of the girls to fetch more water from the well and two others to help her with the lifting of the gunny sack. It was only fifty pounds but it was quite impossible for her advanced pregnant state. Together, the two began to lift.

A scream tore through the house. Neeko dropped the gunny sack and it split open, spilling grain at her feet.

It was Craig screaming.

She bolted to the door and flung it open. A small black Bug Eyed Monster, the size of a fist, bounced into the living room from the bedroom and neatly into a flower pot. She could hear armor crashing to the floor in the bedroom. "WHERE'S THAT FUCKING BEM!" Neeko dashed to the bed room but Craig came barging out with the sword of Magnum in his hands and a towel wrapped around his waist.

Neeko could feel the room vibrating with the power that Craig could invoke from the sword. With each slice into the air she could feel the room scream in agony. Craig was wild, screaming after the BEM swearing damnation and death if he could find it.

China on the shelf exploded from the shock. Books flew into the air and crashed around him. Craig lashed out thinking one of the books was the BEM. His wild swing only clipped the cover, but the book was suddenly engulfed in flames from the power he was wielding.

The BEM panicked as the flower pot suddenly gave way from stress. The fuzzy little Bug Eyed Monster leapt up quickly seeking a new hiding place. It bounced from the ottoman to the rocking chair.

The chair suddenly erupted into a shower of splinters and was dashed to the four walls of the living room. The BEM riding the waves of the explosion, was tossed towards the mantle place where it quickly ducked behind a pile of collapsed books. Craig's swing carried on and took out part of the wall. The rock suddenly spat fragments of stone in his face from the blast. Craig paused, startled at the rocks audacity before realizing, he had taken a chunk out of the wall.

"CRAIG!" Neeko screamed and Craig paused again. His heart was pounding in his ears. The sword was vibrating through his hands into his arms and straight through his chest like an anvil dropped in soft earth. She moved quickly at him and her cooling hands of healing reached up and touched his heated hands of pain. His fingers numbed and the sword suddenly became quiet. Her hands took the sword from him. It's weight pulled it to the earth and even with both hands, she was unable to keep it from falling. But she really didn't want too. It pinged lightly on the floor. Dragging the sword with her she wrapped one arm around Craig's waist and guided him gently to the couch and sat him down. She set the sword down and crawled onto the couch to keep her husband from shivering. The shivering stopped as she pulled the blanket from the couch and covered him. His elvish eyes blazed red as he stared intently at the fireplace. Neeko's eyes of green watched him intently. The black slits in her eyes widened automatically as she watched him.

The door to the kitchen opened slowly and one of the girls put her head out. Neeko fanned a quick wave and the door closed again.

Edia was no where to been seen. Edia was a cat and their standing policy is 'When trouble strikes, don't be anywhere near by and prepare a suitable alibi just in case.' Onary was a dog and their standard policy is

'When trouble strikes, be the cause or close to it.' Onary stepped in existence right beside Craig and took his faithful position at his feet.

Craig never liked to have BEM's pop out of his shower-head while showering and today was no exception. But he had never gone after them before. He had suddenly lost his unflappable cool. Craig had laughed in the face of the Demon Dragon Witch Queen and heckled Dave the Meca demon. Craig was dependable, reliable. He could juggle cotton balls in the middle of monsoons while tap dancing on a bowling ball. Attacking anything unless in immediate self defense wasn't normal for him. There was something wrong.

She didn't want an answer. She knew that he had secrets that had to be kept. Secrets that no mortal should know. She only wanted to make sure he was alright.

Nothing was right.

He looked back at her. He had to concentrate to cool his elvish eyes. With his quivering hand he reached up and brushed Neeko's whiskers with the back of his hand. She took his hand in her own and kissed it and caressed it, slowly sliding it along the side of her silken cheek. She reached over and held him as much as her swollen stomach would allow.

"I had a dream." Craig finally spoke. They had sat in silence and the fire in the fireplace burned down to angry coals. Edia had once poked her head from under the couch only to pull it in again. Time had passed and Craig really didn't care how much had. He had to think, and what he was thinking, he didn't like. "The kind of dream that comes true."

Neeko knew the dream.

As the fates go in the spectrum of man, anyone who could see the future, would one day see his death. Neeko prayed daily to Craig's God, that Craig would only see his death far into old age. That dream had come too soon.

"It...was an abstract...scene." Craig spoke in sudden bursts of words, selecting each one carefully. "But the message was clear. Roc will win the war."

Neeko felt her centre suddenly lift. The word 'WIN' filled her quickly. Win was a good word. But something pushed at her from inside. Craig wasn't happy with the word 'win'.

"We're gonna buy it." Craig cleared his throat. "Me, the dragons...We're gonna buy it."

Buy it? Neeko thought. *Buy what? Die? Blessid, Jesus, no.* Neeko could feel Craig's heart through his chest. He was calm now. She could also feel her unborn child squirm about within her. She could feel her own heart. It was pounding. She tried not to say it, she tried not to let the words from her mouth. "Don't go." She whispered. *Stay here and be with me and your baby*, she screamed within her self.

Craig shook his head. She knew he was going to do that. He did it with Hauth. He went off to the front lines with Roc and she stayed to heal the wounded. She knew what he was going to say. "How long can a man run from his destiny, before he finds himself running to it?"

She bit her lip. *Where the Hel did he get that saying? Did it come in one of his dreams?* He had a dream with Hauth too, but he didn't know the outcome before it began.

She only held him tighter, and watched as the fire died and eased the room into darkness.

Chapter 61

J'cob walked. He followed the little hopping gray rabbit north through the forest valley. J'cob had little idea where he was in the first place and now was putting his faith in a rabbit. He looked around but recognized none of the woods about him. Mistang, the morning mist covered the forest in a gentle blanket of fog. Shegatesu didn't light the sky that morning, and her father didn't follow behind. Okshiru's sky was gray and solid like a marble wall covering the heavens. To the north, the wall in the sky grew darker, angrier. He now knew that the forest walk was in effect and that he had traveled many clicks in scant hours. He also knew in his centre that he was headed in the right direction.

Alone, walking directly into the arms of the forces of Hel.

The rabbit showed no weakness, no pause for rest or wind, merely hopped a steady pace, sure of his course and direction. Only occasionally the rabbit would suddenly stop and twitch his ears for sound and then move quickly on. He had no time to waste.

J'cob followed, eating his breakfast on the move. Dried fish, soaked from Danshu's rain was his meal and a swallow of water from his wine skin was his drink.

Through the break in the trees he could recognize the back side of Eighth Brother Mountain and beyond it to the north was Cornerstone. But the rabbit was bending east and away from home. The great mountain that he and his brothers climbed in their youth quickly faded into the fog behind him. He could feel the forest walk still in effect. It was hard to see, walking in heavy forest, but when he crossed open areas and fields, he could see the motion around him slip quickly past him.

Okshiru loomed above him. He could feel Hauge's wind at his back as if the fickle god of wind could push him that much faster. He felt the howl of Fikor's breath much stronger now. The gusts of Hauge blew the brown leaves at his feet into billowy clouds flittering around him. It was getting colder as he quickly pushed north and east across Dragonslayer's territory and beyond Monsterbelly's former northern province, Thunderkeep. The abandoned garrison flashed quickly past J'cob as he walked by. The garrison was the last outpost before the end of Mortalroam. Beyond lay only the great woods of Dacova. The garrison had been originally set by king Monsterbelly to watch the woods of Dacova and as an early warning as to what ever came from out of there. The blackened woodlands were the final slice of Mortalroam before the great distortions that led to the land of Hel.

Monsterbelly, the obese king directly south of Dragonslayer's realm had held the garrison in the time before Hauth, and Roc never concerned himself with it until word from the garrison had stopped. By time Roc could react, the kingdom of Monsterbelly had fallen to the march of Hauth, the beast with backward knees.

Two years had passed and the garrison was remanned under the Dragonslayer's banner.

J'cob had already lost sight of the Garrison as his mind bent back to remember. He wanted to tell them, warn them what was coming. Tell them to evacuate, to pull back, but they were gone.

The black trees loomed around him and as if a curtain had fallen over him. His elvish sight pushed back the shadow and he walked on. The rabbit as his guide found a trail and made his way quickly through. J'cob suddenly felt the cold around him. It almost burned him with its suddenness. He wrapped his cowl tighter around him and followed on. His thin boots suddenly filled with tiny needles of ice. He was an elf and elves did not feel the cold, so why dress for it? He was now freezing. A shudder ran quickly through him. He decided that he didn't like the cold at all.

His pointed ears began to burn as did his fingers. His face began to deaden and his lips were numb. He glanced back but there was no light, no sign of a way out. He had never traveled the forest of Dacova, no one ever did. There were too many things that had slipped through the cracks of the Wove and roamed the dark and sinister woods. There was no treasure or glory there, only the land where the monsters ruled. He was now totally dependent on the rabbit to guide him. To guide him in, and to guide him out.

He suddenly remembered, he never made a deal for the way out.

Drums boomed around him as the rabbit came to a final halt. The rodent listened and J'cob crouched beside him. He could hear far in the distance the clanking of brass bells ringing off key. Shouts and horns sounded in the darkness and J'cob could feel sudden waves of heat buffer his exposed cheeks. A horrendous acrid smell assailed him. The wove was open and the stink of Hel was polluting Mortalroam.

"You're on your own." The rabbit said.

"What? Wait!" J'cob whispered in an urgent rush. "I need a way out!"

The rabbit was gone.

Chapter 62

The gray sky of Okshiru crossed the land of Mortalroam. Hauge's winds pushed steadily. Danshu held his breath and waited above for the right moment to fall. Uko's thunder rumbled and rolled about the eight mountains that surrounded Valleyveiw. Fikor's cold had waned and lifted from the world, holding off his winter a bit longer. Meleki walked the perimeter of Dragon's Bane, following the forest line with Gozoo close behind. Mistang had crawled back to her lowlands and waited there.

The gods were taking their seats, some nervously awaiting the outcome and others placing their bets on the spectacle that was forming.

Fanrealm stood proudly with its burned and blackened walls at the crest of Tashwalk, rising on the gentle slope of Valleyveiw. From the spyeye, the high tower of Fanrealm, one could see the low valleys and the spires of the City of Cornerstone, lying quietly on the other side of Seeda Gully.

Craig watched Okshiru's great sky from the spyeye with intent. Hauge tugged at the banner beside him. The fire pot beside him crackled and smoked in the wind. The guard standing at Craig's side watched over the lands around as was his job and Craig paid him no mind other than to be sure he wasn't in the man's way, for as the spyeye watched the lands, Craig watched the sky.

Moxy turned on a wing and brought his blue body about in a snapping turn that defied physical laws of flight and motion. The 25 meter blue dragon dove and snatched at a grazing steer before it even had a chance to run. In flight, he shredded the beast and stuffed it quickly into his open gullet. He was the last to eat. The cattle that had been slaughtered during Harroc's raid had been left unfit for human consumption, however; dragons were a different matter. The beasts feasted on the cold meat with indifference. Craig had to stop Brezhnev from gorging himself and grumpily, the big red complied.

Eat my children. Be ready for war. Craig pulled them out of the tunnels and got them into the air. They had been sleeping and needed the flight time. Moxy was in prime shape as a younger adult. Boxy and Windshmere although a little younger, also performed well. Alisa floundered on take off, but once air born did well. Dore, Mojo, and Punjab, merely leapt to the air and swarmed over the feeding grounds.

Only Roderhamerdril had any difficulty. He took to the air and sailed off quickly in the wrong direction and ate out of someone else's heard. Roderhamerdril was smarter than Ralph, but that wasn't saying much. Craig made a mental note to find out who he was going to repay for his dragon's meal.

Brezhnev, the oldest by far, sat and stretched in a ritual pre-flight check, then flapped and flopped and thundered and tore soil and gravel as he steamed and huffed and flamed and heaved his gigantic mass into the sky. Once there, he flew loftily like a cloud or a manta ray gliding over the ocean floor. He spotted what he wanted from the warm meat and positioned himself in the sun. His death black shadow fell upon the field and the sudden cold loomed over the cattle. They looked up in unison, paralyzed with awe. The ear crushing sound swarmed over them moments after the mighty Brezhnev plucked his meal from the grounds, one in each forepaw and lifted into the sky again. The cattle, confused and dazed only lowed and mooed trying to figure out if they should run or not. Their noses twitched for lingering traces of the immeasurable lizard, but Brezhnev was already above the height of the sky and gone from sight with one bovine already devoured.

Grace now made her final approach. She was three times the size of Moxy and half the size of Brezhnev. In flight, she was known for her namesake. But this afternoon, she seemed to labor and flounder a bit and took her time selecting her meal. By the time she was ready, the heard was stampeding.

Craig signaled to Kugerand who quickly headed off the cattle from the river and sent them back towards the grazing ground. By that time, Grace had taken her meal and the cows were quieted. Craig watched her. She had dropped on the beast using her weight to crush it, and ate it there on the ground. That was unusual for a dragon.

Craig felt the wind and then the rumble. Brezhnev soared over head and covered the sky with his gigantic body with Boxy gliding below him. Boxy's full wingspan fit easily beneath the giant red's single gliding wing. '*The bitch must be hungry.*'

Craig looked to the red as he sailed off and curved around the valley climbing in height with Boxy still under his wing. '*Why do you say that?*' The Dragoncaller spoke.

'*This is her second time.*' He growled. '*If she gets seconds, I get seconds!*'

'*You had your seconds with your firsts.*' Craig argued calmly as he watched the silver dragon on the fields. As Kugerand the gold dragon approached her, she snapped and protected her kill. This was wrong. Kruger and Grace were mates. Craig tried to dragoncall, but only heard sounds of her eating. She didn't want to talk.

Craig watched her closely as she quickly and savagely tore her kill. Brezhnev was quite right, this was her seconds. She had been the first on the fields and ate her fill of the cold meat. Now she was at it again.

Craig looked back and noticed the spyeye had been watching in awe, the dragons looming about. A year ago Craig started his harem of great beasts and keeping them in the tunnels near by. Until then, dragons had never been seen anywhere near Fanrealm. Their dwindling numbers due to age, and rapid decline in births had seen to that. The great dragons were more of a fairy tale than legend. Their unbelievable size and ability to defy gravity and soar above the skies of Okshiru seemed to only be stories of far off adventures. Minstrels sang of Roc the great Dragonslayer, but minstrels tended to exaggerate and fantasize more than anything and Roc himself wasn't one to boast about anything but himself.

But now the dragons were out. Flashing their brilliant and colorful scales. The spyeye was trying to do his job and watch for enemies, but could not resist watching Mojo and Windshmere romp and play about him as if they were nature, part of the world.

Craig smiled as the spyeye looked to him. Craig only shook his head and jumped over the lip of the high tower.

The spyeye paused in astonishment. The Dragoncaller had just leapt off the high tower! It was fifteen paces to the nearest anything from that side.

An instant later, Craig sailed easily across and up with one foot braced on a spike and his back supported by the main dorsal fin on Punjab's back. Craig waved and smiled and so did the big green as he circled the spyeye and headed off. It looked as if the guard said something, with his jaw slowly opening and closing, but Craig couldn't hear anything. He didn't even wave. Craig was rather impressed that he didn't drop his spear and horn.

One by one each dragon fell into formation with Brezhnev in the lead. They took a holding pattern around Hendle's Hump, a large rocky mesa between Mount Rile and Mount Bran, and one by one touched gently down. Craig dismounted and each dragon huddled close together to hear him.

'*Quit shovin'!*' Brezhnev pushed Dore.

Craig raised his hands for silence and got it. *'Okey dokee, this is the drill. We can't use names over the dragoncall, at close range Ferris can hear them.'*
'Can you hear him, is my question.' Brezhnev interrupted.
Craig looked back at the biggest dragon. *'I know everything he does. I know where he is right now.'*
Dore looked around in sudden realization. *'Then lets take him now!'* He said with sudden bravery. *'We can all take him!'* Kruger, Brezhnev and Grace said nothing, but the younger dragons all nodded their heads.
Dragons in nature only worked in groups up to one year old. Once they learned to fly, they separated quickly, or killed each other. The only exception was during mating, and even then, the male skedaddled as soon as conception occurred, or he was devoured by the female. Only through the presence of the Dragoncaller could these dragons be together in one place.
Next, Ferris was invulnerable and Craig knew it. His dragons would be slaughtered unnecessarily when only one could do the job that he was planning. *'Who's in charge?'* Craig looked at all of his dragons and then at Dore. No one challenged him. *'Then we will do it my way.'* Craig wanted to explain, but there weren't enough days to waste to get it clear to the slower ones and at this point, it was unnecessary to understand.
Brezhnev rustled and asked politely. *'And what is your plan?'* The great red wasn't being rude or defiant, just curious.
'I'm getting to that now. They have several yearling black dragons...'
'Ralph downed twelve!' Ralph announced cheerfully holding up eight fingers to illustrate.
Craig knew that Ralph wasn't boasting. The blue dragon just couldn't count. *'They have more left. Dore, Mojo and Windshmere, you're going to be Brezhnev's wing men. Clean it up for him.'*
'Bullshit!' Brezhnev argued using Craig's magic word. *'I'll snuff yearlings and eat them!'*
Craig shook his head. *'We're going to be racing against time. I need you to do the heavy bombing. The odds are they'll have their best troops in the front line. Bresh, you can set fire to things just flying overhead. Your flaming breath is irresistible. I want you to lay down a heavy line of fire, code name will be 'Hiroshima'. Unless I give word to the contrary, and you think you can do it, then you will make a second run, code name, 'Nagasaki'. Your fire blast will do almost as much damage as your scaring the piss out of them in the first place.'* Craig looked to Roderhamerdril. *'Roder, you will fly above Bresh and watch his back.*

When he tells you too, drop below and flame anything that moves until Bresh tells you to pull up. You'll be the back door.'

'And Ferris?' Brezhnev said impatiently.

Craig waved his hand as he turned to Grace. 'I'll get to that. Grace, you're the ground assault leader. Keep the kids in line. Use your magic, the enemy won't expect that. Flame them on the way out.' He then turned and pointed to Moxy, Alisa and Punjab. 'Come in low over the tree line and go for machinery, ballistas, catapults and such. Get their crews especially. Hel has a finite number of engineers. If you see a command tower, come in close, but do not attack. I say again, do not attack. You boys and girl are important to draw fire and attention from Boxy.' He then pointed to Boxy. 'Come in low below the tree line and sweep the command towers. Take them out. That's your sole job. You're my best flyer for that. There may be more than one tower but the odds are against more than three. They should be reasonably close for communication. If you get them all, then go back for machines, but stay away from the front line or Brezhnev will roast you.'

Boxy looked about and then to the Dragoncaller. 'What exactly does a command tower look like?'

Craig resisted the urge to massage his forehead. It was a good question. 'A command tower...' Craig said carefully, 'is a platform or scaffolding riding on wheels being pulled and pushed by big beasts of some sort. It's surrounded by banners and everybody around it and on it has the shiniest shit on their armor.'

Shinny. Dragons could follow the word shinny very easily. Craig was using the same logistics and tactics that he encountered with Hauth. Roc had said that Hel was very little for strategic change and he was right for Hauth. There was no need to change this time around. They won the last time.

'Remember with these low bombing runs,' Craig coached. 'They will have spell casters. Mortal magic can hurt and if they tag team you, enough of it can kill a dragon! That's why time is so important, if they catch on and pull together, it's gonna get hot real fast.

'Our advantage will be the dragon call. Communicate with it, talk to each other. You see something interesting, someone is close by, let him know. Fighting is exhausting. You'll be flying out from Sugartown and then back. That's a healthy distance to start with. Any closer and the bad guys might try to pre-emtive our butts so its best to be absent from the front until curtain time.' Craig looked at the dragons unasked question. 'Chiron has been informed and will be waiting for you. Sugartown is the only safe place for a base between here and target.'

'But Ferris can hear.' Brezhnev reminded him.

Craig nodded. '*He can only tap in when we are on the line. I will have to keep it open for you all to communicate. I can jam him from this distance. But at show time and we're close, we will have to use the code-names—Use them. We can't afford it if he learns your real names. Let's run them down.*'

Brezhnev looked to the others and decided they were waiting for him to begin. '*Backfire.*' He said.

'*Sopwith Camel.*' Dore said.

'*Corsair.*' Moxy said.

'*Frisbee.*' Kuger said brightly.

'*Blackbird.*' Boxy said.

'*Phantom.*' Windshmere said.

'*Tomcat.*' Punjab said.

'*Mustang.*' Mojo said.

'*Zero.*' Roderhamerdril said.

'*Thunderbird.*' Alisa said.

'*Spitfire.*' Grace said. Craig looked at Grace. Her voice bubbled in his head with a strange stress to it. She was not scaled like the others but was smooth silver and reflected things about her like chrome. She was normally brilliant in the sun light, but even now with gray sky above, she was gleaming.

'*You're pregnant!*' Craig suddenly realized as he half accused half asked her.

Brezhnev clocked an eye. '*You're just noticing?*'

Grace suddenly looked shy and turned her head rather coyly. Craig looked at Kruger and the gold dragon had also been shining a bit brighter as the father. Craig paused a moment and then went back to the business at hand. '*Change of plans. You stay home sweetheart. You are too valuable to risk losing the baby. Punjab, you're ground assault leader. Keep open com with Brezhnev and do what he tells you.*'

'*Great, but what of Ferris?*' Brezhnev pressed again.

'*Kruger and I will deal with him.*'

No one moved and no one spoke for what seemed to long. Then Brezhnev glared at him. '*Alone?*'

Craig nodded. '*Kruger is the fastest and most maneuverable. He is my choice. Next, only the bow of the Dragoncaller can hurt the Iron Dragon, which means I have to be the one to do it.*' No one could dispute that. '*My plan is to ride up, near the edge of space. In the thin air we will be able to outmaneuver him.*' Kugerand the gold was wingless and didn't need air to fly.

The red dragon looked grave, but nodded his approval.

459

Ralph the blue dragon looked about and stepped forward with his small paw raised. Amazingly he figured out that he had nothing to do. '*And what of Ralph?*'

Craig was ready for this. The blue could fly, but the rip in his wing couldn't handle the stress or turbulence they would find in battle. '*Ralph, you have a very important job.*' Craig approached him and spoke very clearly and carefully. '*You are to remain here and guard the rear. You are the last line of defense that we will have. You've got to hold up Cornerstone and Fanrealm. Lady Fantista will need you here.*'

Ralph looked up. The other dragons who knew, shook their heads in approval that Ralph was the only one to do such an important job. The others who didn't know, wondered how the heck Ralph of all dragons, got such an important job. '*And Ralph's code name?*'

Craig forgot about this part but quickly recovered with little floundering. '*You're...pah, fah, Gipper!*' Gipper? '*You are Gipper!*'

'*Gipper!*' Ralph chirped and looked at the others and they nodded and shook their heads in approval. '*Gipper.*' Ralph nodded again.

Brezhnev thought for a moment, then the big red looked up with his head cocked slightly. '*You're positive that Ferris is going to follow you to near 'space'.*' Brezhnev had no idea where space was being that he himself had never flown that high. '*What if, suppose mind you. he goes after these three,*' He pointed to Dore, Mojo and Punjab. '*They wont last against him.*'

Craig shook his head. '*He's gunning for me.*' Craig's mind filled with the dream where he had seen the iron dragon standing over the gates of hell. He saw the dragon's eyes. '*He'll be coming for me.*'

Brezhnev took the Dragoncaller's words as gospel. '*And the kid?*'

Craig looked about quizzically, '*What kid?*'

'*That kid.*' Brezhnev motioned his head towards the edge of the plateau and Craig could see fingers grip the edge in an effort to scramble up. A moment later Orrin crawled over. The elf paused and stared around in wonder at the gigantic dragons standing calmly around him. Each one nodded to him save Ralph who waved gleefully and Brezhnev who snubbed him. 'G'day...' He said in a awed whisper.

Craig pointed to Dore. "Okay, Orrin. This is Sopwith Camel." Dore stepped closer getting a better sniff at Orrin without the looming odor of the big red beside him. The elf took a nervous step back at the dragons approach, afraid to be snorted into the vast nostril. "You know the mission, patrol the perimeter." Then he spoke to Dore in silent Dragoncall. '*Remember, first sign of anything, no mixing it up. You 'Hiaku' right back home!'* Dore nodded. He understood completely, even the word, 'Hiaku.'

The Dragon crouched down and extended a paw for Orrin to climb on. When the elf climbed on his paw, the dragon lifted him to his back. Orrin climbed on, settling comfortably on the dragon's shoulders. Dore took a leap, flapped once and took to the sky.

Without warning, Onary stepped into reality.

The dragons were startled and shifted about. Brezhnev was the only one who didn't bristle, as he was used to Onary's trick. The springer spaniel paid them little heed as he spoke to his master. "Lady Fantista calls." Normally they would have used an elf call, but Craig wasn't normal. He was born human. When he arrived at Mortalroam, he was cursed by the Demon Dragon Witch Queen to be a Nih elf. Since then, he had mastered the elves tongue and dragon's tongue, but was yet to catch on to the elfcall.

'Okay…Backfire, you got the helm.' He said as he mounted Boxy. *'Keep running the bombing drills with the exception of Grace and Ralph. Ralph, head out to 'Riles rest' and nest there. Keep guard.'* Craig watched as each dragon took off to their task with Brezhnev the last to take to the air. *'Blackbird? Take me down to the house and you head back to the drills.'* Boxy nodded. Craig looked to his dog. "Wanna ride?" Craig slapped his lap invitingly.

Boxy looked down at the dog and smiled exposing all of his teeth at once. Onary knew the gesture as a dragon's polite way of saying *'I can eat you in one bite'.* But Onary was a dog of a higher class and only glared back at the dragon. "No bother, I'll make my own way down." Having said that, Onary stepped out of reality.

Craig stared at the back of the dragon's head listening to the beast whistle innocently. Craig only shook his head. "Home James." Craig leaned back as they took to the air.

Chapter 63

The heavy horses leaned into their harnesses and pulled their loads. The Thundercracker, the Bonemasher, the Mountain Quaker, and the Brain Banger all lined up, one behind the other waiting. Wagon loads filled with rocks, Turkish tar, bramble, shot, and barrels of stuff that Craig had made with the word 'Napalm' stenciled neatly on the side, made their way to the formation behind the great war machines. The Helsender, Flesh Remover and the Thwacker followed behind that. The gigantic Painshowerer and the even bigger Regimental Decimater Overbiter, known lovingly by its crew as the RDO, (known unlovingly by the enemy as 'Oh no, not that!) were already there.

Meleki watched intently from her forest seat as the great entourage lined along the road. The men waited by their machines, setting their little camps off in the woods and posting their guards by the road. Patrols were long ago sent out to secure the area.

She watched one of the patrols chasing and trying to corner a brown hare. The men had their own portable mess wagons and had no need to forage for food, but boredom had the men frantically trying to herd the hare in order to catch it. The little rodent was elusive and out maneuvered them—ducking over a low hill. Undaunted, the men followed and were quickly lost from sight.

A vicious roar sounded through the woods and the patrol came running back over the hill in deathly fright. Moments later Gozoo the rabbit god sat beside Meleki, goddess of the forest. "You should have seen their faces." He started.

"I could imagine."

"They thought they had her, closing for the kill and wham! I jumped out!" His huge eyes bulged and his front teeth bared like fangs to demonstrate. "I love it."

"Never go rabbit hunting with you around."

"Okshiru can't take that from me." The god suddenly became introspective. "Can he?"

Meleki smiled to herself. "He hasn't yet. Gods have to have some fun."

Gozoo looked at the troops still arriving. "You should see the stuff they got." He said in awe. "They've got this thing called the Person Pounder, and another thing call the Meat Maker!"

Meleki shook her head, amazed at mortal ingenuity. From her seat, she could clearly see the command post and something was going on. "Can you hear them?" She asked pointing.

Gozoo's giant ears turned and tuned. "They say an incoming elfcall from Dacova."

Meleki silently held her breath. Dacova, the only forest on Mortalroam she did not rule. What went on in there, she had no say over. "They have an elf in there?" She said in astonishment. Gozoo suddenly became quiet and Meleki could see it on his face. "What is it? Do you know who?"

Gozoo looked at her. "Its J'cob Hammerstrike. The youngest of the children of the Supergod. He says a rabbit brought him in! It had to be Chritchfeild!" He whispered urgently.

Meleki looked around suddenly to see if Okshiru heard him. There were only larger, more frequent patrols roaming about ignorant of two gods sitting invisibly nearby. "What are you doing? Isn't one warning enough?"

"I'm not doing anything!" He said defensively hoping Okshiru heard him. "He's acting completely on his own accord." He bowed his head and whispered in her ear. "To tell you the truth..." He looked around to see that no one was listening in. "I think ol' Okshiru is doing the rabbit shuffle."

Meleki pulled back with her hand over her mouth. "You think so?" She said through her fingers.

Gozoo nodded. "Not, uh..." He gestured with his big paws trying to grope the word from the air. "Overtly, or directly."

"Like we were." She reminded him.

"Right, Chritchfeild may not even know it. Okshiru is in charge not just for looks you know, he can be one sneaky old coot."

There was more shuffling in the headquarters and Gozoo listened in. "They're 'Bugging out.'" He looked at her curiously, hoping for a definition, but she could only shrug her shoulders. "See that human?"

"The big one talking to the Gnome?"

"Yeah, That's Gorn. He's 'Field Commander'. He's got the exact area of the enemy in Dacova from J'cob's elfcall."

"It will take days to reach there." Meleki reminded him. "A fortnight with those machines to drag around."

"No..." Gozoo pointed to the gnome. "That gnome, he's Hosay Sungazer, a spell caster."

463

"That's Jose Sungazer." She corrected him.

He looked at her, but didn't say, *but that's what I said.* "Anyway, they are dividing forces. He going to make a Transport Spell."

"Everything?" She exclaimed. "Jose can't be that powerful. No mortal can lift this whole army!"

Gozoo shrugged and watched. Jose Sungazer walked away from the camp and two other men followed behind. They carried his pots of incense, book stand and carpet bag stuffed with parchments, glass tubes and dead snakes. They were dressed as he was, simple long black robes with gold belts. They set up quickly and the three began chanting, humming, gesturing and invoking.

The heavy horse teams came pulling their machines towards the magic gnomes. "Oh, The three are combining their powers and then only taking certain heavy pieces to the battle area." Meleki said knowledgeably. "Very smart. They'll rest a day or two and then do it again. In fact..." She said rising slightly from her seat for a better view. "They might have other spell casters performing the same thing."

Gozoo listened. "Yes, I can hear more chanting back that way." Gozoo pointed towards the rear of the camp. He paused momentarily when he noticed something. "Isn't that one yours?"

She quickly looked over. It was Fryto, galloping boldly on his horse White-fire. She nodded. "He's mine alright." She nudged the god beside her. "Isn't he a dream?"

Gozoo wrinkled his nose. "What is he doing?"

"He's going to try to Forest walk some troops." She knew that automatically. A knight's powers were given to them by their god. Friska's power of wind from Hauge, Frita's power of cold from Fikor, Achillia's lightning from Uko, and Fryto's forest walk from her.

"Will you allow him to take the whole army?"

She looked at the rabbit god. "And why not? He's mine! I can do what I want with him. I'm not interfering, just granting a boon that is allowed me. Ura gave whatshisface a cacodemon!"

"And she got in trouble for it." Gozoo reminded her.

"That was out and out interference." She reminded him.

"But this whole army, that really is out of the ordinary." The rabbit god argued. "Normally a forest walk is a small group of mortals and animals."

"Whose side are you on?" Meleki seemed angry. "He's been good and deserves a little bigger boon from the goddess he serves. Serves well I might add." She spoke the last part of her sentence for any one who might be listening.

There was.

Gozoo nudged her and pointed. Standing upright on her haunches about a stones throw away was the brown hare that the men had been chasing.

Meleki's mouth suddenly went dry. Through the hare's eyes she could tell that Chritchfeild wasn't the only rabbit Okshiru was using. "A regiment. Only a regiment. I'll let him do that." The rabbit glared at her. "A battalion." The rabbit didn't move. "A company..." The rabbit came down to all fours. "A small company...a couple platoons?" The rabbit slowly turned and began to hop away. "Really big platoons!" She shouted after it and the rabbit suddenly turned and looked over her shoulder at the goddess of nature. "Not really, really big..." She corrected herself. "Just, just plain big." The hare turned and hopped quickly away and the goddess of nature and god of rabbits breathed a little easier.

"Well," Gozoo said watching the army muster about. "Glad we got that covered."

Chapter 64

The city of Brewster lay quietly beneath Okshiru's glaring white sky. The banners of Dragonslayer and the banners of Brewster billowed frantically in Hauge's winds, as the god of wind ran through the streets. The god paused catching his breath, looking at the boarded shop windows and doors bolted tightly. The streets seemed much wider in the absence of the tarps and tents of the seasonal merchants. Thick lines of hemp rope lashed about the water tower to secure and reinforce it.

The god of wind suddenly took off and flashed quickly to the end of the street. The people moved urgently through the streets hoarding supplies from anyone who would sell. They carried pails of water, sacks of grain and planks of wood. They sold and traded livestock quickly at record prices. The animals brayed and mooed and clucked nervously not understanding the urgency that went on around them as the people readied for a storm.

The storm of war.

At the end of the street was the citadel and beyond its bold walls of stone, voices could be heard. Hauge dashed over and quickly ran the circumference of the wall. From outside and through the thick walls of stone, he could hear Dragonslayer's caterwauling.

The god leapt over the courtyard to the balcony and peered through the glass.

Roc hovered over the large table that dominated the room. Out of arms reach stood the generals of his armies, plotting and scribbling notes. Milo walked about the round room, looking at the plain, simple paintings and sculptures that ornamented the walls that he had seen a thousand times before. He paused at the window and looked out over his city. In the back of his mind he could hear the pounding war drums. His right shoulder throbbed to the beat that thrummed in his head. It wasn't a good feeling.

He turned and for the first time, actually listened to Roc's plans.

Roc jammed a finger at the map. "With full mobilization we will be in these hills in time. The bad guys will come through here."

His general pointed to something on the map. "And why not cross through here?"

Roc looked at him incredulously. "'Cause there's a mountain here. They can't move a full army over this range. They can't go south of us because of this river. They don't have any ships or water monsters at hand so we can use naval bombardment." Roc suddenly glared at his admiral. "Right?"

The admiral stood a little taller. "Sir? The new catapults and ballistas that the Dragoncaller designed have that range sir, but Hauge will have to cooperate."

The wind god standing out on the balcony peered in closer.

"What ever…" Roc mumbled.

"Sir?" The general spoke again. "That still gives them this whole area. Why not go through the heavy trees along here and only break with us with light contact?"

Roc nodded. "I'm sure that is what I would do, but they have an army ten times bigger than us. They consist of blood sucking, light hating, human eating, elf despising demons who are not going to walk past a mortal army with light contact. Also, this leaves their flanks wide open for us to slice our way through and go for their leaders. No, they aren't going to walk past us."

Another general spoke up. "My lord. How sure are your intelligence reports?"

"One from Frito and the other from J'son and J'cob." Roc left out the part that J'son had been captured. He twisted his lip in a Roc like way and swallowed the bile that was filling up his centre. He didn't like the idea that J'son was surrounded by the bad guys and J'cob was dancing around them. What bugged him the most was that Friska, little Daniel, was leading the armies of Hel. He knew Friska. He knew exactly every logistical move that the pompous, bold, cocky fool was going to use. Roc should know them. He was the one who taught them to Friska.

"Look." Roc balanced himself nervously. "They are going to use the same damn battle plan as they did the last time."

"With Hauth leading?" Said one of the lower colonels.

"Heck no!" Roc growled at him. "That's our advantage. Demons are undisciplined. Their leaders have to be right on top of them or they go for personal gain and desert. Demons can't see in terms of long range goals. That's why they'll have such a narrow war front. That's why they're coming through here. On the other side of these mountains and this river is just too much damn room for them to control troops effectively."

"And what is the plan?"

Roc looked up to Milo who was now standing by the table. The tall dark human was only a few inches taller than the tall elf. Roc knew Milo. They had fought a three man triangle with Frito during their younger years when Frito was the Knight of Uko. They had chosen their titles and defended them—The Devilslayer, the Dragonslayer and the Demonslayer. All the knight wanted was demons to kill, and was beginning to fidget with the holy power that was filling his centre. Milo was a gentle, reserved man, but when it came to monsters, he was a knight, and this knight lived for the purpose of killing demons.

But Roc had to play him in session. He had to orchestrate his game against the forces of Hel, and move his chess pieces to the places were they would operate most effectively.

Roc nodded and waved to his crew. "Gather round my children. For this land we'll defend. I'll smite the demon horde, for I swear upon my sword and that you can depend." Roc pointed to his map. "We take the 103rd Kossack Horses and the 25th, 35th, and 45th, infantry lined up here. They're gonna be bait and on this signal, pull back. Directly behind them, the engineers have already dug trenches designed to stop those giant machines they have. They'll be bogged down here. I've got a dragon that is gonna heat it up for them.

"We'll pull back to the woods. The faster they move, the less communications they'll have with their leaders and they will start to scatter. Keep them scattered. The 103rd Kossacks and support divisions will join with Hurgay's Spitznats, go for light contact and fall back here. This is the main battle field and the real game plan in this area." Roc stopped suddenly and looked to one of his Colonels. "Am I going to fast?"

"No sir, but there is a slight problem. The engineers are having difficulty with their trenches."

Roc looked startled and puzzled at the same time. "What? They're engineers, digging frigging holes is what they do. Enlisted Engineer is a nice way to say, ditch digger."

"They haven't dug the trenches yet."

Roc seemed to grow as anger swept his centre but some how managed to quietly speak. "Why haven't they dug the trenches yet?"

"Because they haven't arrived on site yet." The Colonel failed to notice that every one in the room was backing away from him.

Roc slowly advanced towards the Colonel. "Why not?"

"The wind sir? The ships are having a hard time carrying the troops South."

Roc paused and looked out of the window. In the fading light he could see the flags billowing across the square. "The wind is at your back. Unless you're going in the wrong direction."

The colonel looked out of the window. "What? Just a second ago..."

"Captain." Roc said massaging his forehead.

"Colonel," The Colonel corrected.

No one breathed. No one moved. Roc stopped in mid massage.

Roc suddenly struck at him and seized the man's shoulders, balling his uniform in his fists. With a quick, brutal tear, removed the man's uniform. "Private." Roc corrected him.

Roc turned and glared at his admiral. "Colonel..." He started.

"Yes sir." The admiral now demoted and transferred to a new branch of military replied.

"I want my engineers out there. I need bridges, and pit falls built and dug. They have full priority. I don't care if you swim them out there."

"Yes sir." And the man quickly turned and left the room.

Hauge pulled away from the window and glanced at the flags now blowing in the opposite direction. He wasn't interfering, he thought as he dashed over the wall and down the road towards the river. *I'm fickle.*

Chapter 65

Leatha, wife of Okshiru, goddess of the night spread her cloak of darkness over the world. Ovam the moon perched at the edge of Third mountain and from his post could look across the world as his sister Neathina danced along the rim of Ronnie, the sixth brother mountain. The second youngest of the gods played her panpipes and carefully placed her stars in the threads of mother Leatha's long, black, silken hair. The child god paused and admired her own work of art. The goddess looked across the night sky from her perch and into the dark valley bellow. She stopped playing her pipes as a chilling air came about her. It wasn't the winds of Hauge or the cold of Fikor. It was Dru, the goddess of Death. She was marching along with the armies of fire heading off, out of the ring of the eight mountains of Fanrealm, across the lands of Dragonslayer into the forests of Dacova. The little goddess looked closer into the parade of red angry lights from below. It was like her stars spread across the shadow of the mountain. They were the torches of men marching. This was not general policy of men and their wars. Only under the bright banner of Kemoto did men go about their business, not in the disguise of her mother's night.

But that was a thing of men she thought, and until they could climb the great mountains and reach her stars to steal them from the sky, she wasn't going to worry over them.

Ovam dipped and settled lower and readied himself for bed. He had watched his sister dancing on the other side of the world, caring only for the placement of her pretty, pretty stars. He shook his head and felt sympathy for the knight who had been assigned her. Every god had one knight save Shegatesu, the dawn and Neathina. The twin goddess shared the same single knight. Ovam watched little Neathina dance with out cares and decided that her knight must be all alone...Or doesn't need her.

Ovam shed the final shaft of his clean white light on the pass of Tashwalk and the land of Valleyview, where the manor of Fanrealm stood. He could see mortal light pouring out of the windows into the dark shadow of Leatha's night. Ovam could see Fantista, standing in the cold she couldn't feel, watching Neathina dance at the edge the of mountains, reaching up to the sky to set her pins of light. Lady Fantista was the oldest living knight of Okshiru. She had earned the title of

Grandmaster, Mistress of the Sho-Pa. She was the mother of seven, now six. She is the Knight of Neathina, goddess of the stars and Shegatesu, goddess of the dawn.

Fantista looked below her tower into the courtyard. The children of Fanrealm moved beyond their bed time stacking supplies, loading wagons and preparing for war. There were thirty seven in all. Each was an orphan of war and death, left for wardship in the welcoming walls of Fanrealm. Whole families of children now resided under Fantista's guiding hand. The knight taught them, nursed them and cared for them.

Fantista's eyes raised from the court yard and watched her most delicate child play against the sky of night. She could feel the chilling wind of Dru, the goddess of Death marching with the troops below. Through clenched teeth Fantista whispered a tiny prayer for the children. The halls of Fanrealm would soon be crowded.

"Blessid..." Fantista whispered. "And you shall map the sky without a single note to the children below?"

Neathina paused her playing and looked below. "You are the knight. What am I to do?"

Fantista smiled to herself. "Give us a guiding star through out the night and into the day. That our dragons and men might follow and come home by. So that its light can set my working children to sleep without Thumber's nightmares to frighten them. To show my little Daniel, J'son and J'cob the way home." *To lead my little Denice back home to her mother, and to her daughter.*

And above, the night whispered to the sky. "She knows."

And the sky whispered back. "Is she not my greatest knight?"

Neathina looked at her pail of stars. She gathered up several of her stars and burst into speed down the face of the Seventh brother mountain, across the valley and up the side of the third brother mountain, and with a sudden leap, the child goddess of stars leapt across the space of the sky and placed a single bright light high above.

"And it is done." The sky said to the night.

Ovam set below the edge of Mortal roam thinking about what he saw. He could now see the wisdom of Okshiru. He wasn't quite sure what it meant. *But surely, it was filled with wise judgement.*

Fantista smiled in her own way and looked down to the children who had paused from their labors to look at the newborn light in the sky. 'A blessing!' One called out pointing to it. Another, older, told him not to point at blessings. A sign from the gods said another. It

471

looks more like a bright star argued a younger. A miracle, a very young one cried. Fantista shook her head and whispered to her self: "There are no such things as miracles, my son."

"And why not My Lady?"

Lady Fantista was not surprised, she had listened to Neeko waddle up the stairs. The Grandmaster of Knights turned to the Ne-arri healer and shook her head. "I'm sorry. I have spoken out of text." The Lady took Neeko's hand and lead her up the steps to the balcony. "The lesson of old goes, 'There are no such things as miracles, save the ones you make yourself. Do not believe in miracles, only count on them."

Neeko gazed into the elvish woman's eyes. "So that's how you knights do it? Make your own miracles." Neeko smiled when Lady Fantista did.

"I think its designed to keep the knights from whining at there gods all the time." Fantista's eyes sparkled from the light of the new star.

"So I see." Neeko said then spoke on. "I've put some of the younger ones to bed."

"And Stephanie?"

"I had to put her to sleep." Neeko spoke of her magic. "It is her soul that is in need of healing. That is the job of a knight."

Fantista shook her head. "That is the job of her mother."

A sudden shout came from within the chambers. Neeko bit her question and quickly waddled to the stairs. It was Craig's voice that she had heard.

Fantista caught hold of Neeko's upper arm. The elderly knight's hand was a sudden anchor of hidden strength. Neeko stopped and looked defiantly at the Lady who only glared back with commands of obedience to wait with which Neeko complied with little choice.

Lady Fantista dashed down the steps and into the room as Neeko waited on the steps. The round study hall was brightly lit with magic glow balls. Craig stood on one of the huge oaken tables with Onary growling ferociously by his side. Fantista could feel the air tingling with the tension from the Dragoncaller. She could hear the dark elf's heart pounding with fear in his centre. She could easily see the cause.

It sat calmly in the center of the room. Its shining black fur rippled with muscle. Black talons pushed from out of its huge paws. White Fangs and hand and a half in length hung from its maw. It's black leathery wings were folded neatly at its back. Its green jungle eyes glinted as it took interest at the Ne-arri waddling down the stairs several paces behind The Lady Fantista.

"Hold it." Craig said with one hand held in a halting way. "Just give me a second to get my heart to slow down." Then he spoke to it with a dragon call. '*Who are you?*'

It reared its head slightly. '*You speak to us? You speak?*'

'*Yes I speak, now answer the question.*'

'*I am Reginald.*' It said simply.

Suddenly in the back of his mind he heard Brezhnev rumble. '*A Dragon-panther? Forget it. They're no use at all.*'

'*Get off the line.*' Craig ordered. He then stepped off the table. "Sorry about that." He said aloud to Lady Fantista keeping his eye of the three meter beast. "I've been a little hyper of late."

"Quite alright." Fantista folded her arms and eyed the beast carefully. "I've never seen one."

"I summoned him from Dormoth. Roc is calling in old markers. I didn't know that my summoning would let him through the magic barriers, and into reality right behind me."

Neeko stepped closer.

'*Dragon-panthers aren't real dragons!*' Brezhnev bubbled in Craig's head. '*They have no memories, no mothers, no upbringing, no soul. They are not dragons.*'

'*What did I say?*' Craig said harshly.

'*Sorry.*' Brezhnev suddenly fell quiet.

'*I asked him here. I am the Dragoncaller, and he speaks to me. In my book that makes him...*' Craig didn't want to upset his dragons too much. An outsider was a confession of weakness. A blow to a dragon's delicate ego. '*It makes him a dragon-panther.*'

Craig looked to Reginald who was looking at Neeko. '*Very well, I'll brief you on the plan.*'

Reginald took his eyes from Neeko and looked to the Dragoncaller. '*We are at your command.*'

'*We?*'

Neeko tried to bury a shriek in her throat. Ten dragon-panthers stepped into reality about the room. From the many off shoots of the library came larger white tiger dragons. The new white tigers stood five meters at the shoulder and had to squeeze into the room.

Reginald looked to each one and spoke their names to the Dragoncaller. *'Clock wise is, Archabald, Winston, Bertram, Sabastian, Alexander, Leopold, Leonard, Godwin, and Melville. Of the White tigers are, Moppy, Floppy, Buffy, Muffy, Biffy, and Tiffy.'*

Craig looked at each one in name and then to the last one. He was clearly the tallest and having great difficulty in standing in the room. But oddly enough, he didn't seem to mind the crouched space. His white stripped tail wagged back and forth and his tongue hung out of the side of his mouth. Craig then realized, that Reginald had failed to mention his name. *'And him?'*

Suddenly all of the Dragon-panthers and White tiger-dragons glared at the misfit. *'Abacromby!'* Reginald hissed. *'Go Home!'*

'Abacromby?' Craig asked.

The White Tiger-dragon seemed to drop and the command and looked to Reginald with hush puppy eyes.

'Go Home!' Reginald command more sternly and the White Tiger Dragon bowed his head and went to step out of reality.

'Let him stay.' The Dragoncaller said quietly.

Reginald looked at Craig. *'I am sorry sir, but Abacromby is a little…defective.'*

'So who isn't?' Craig looked at the White Tiger. *'You will stay out of the way!'* Craig ordered to him. The white tiger nodded in frantic understanding bashing his head into the ceiling several times with his long, black tongue slobbering up and down like a flipper. *'Ho boy.'* Craig moaned to himself before calling to Reginald. *'Have you eaten?'*

Reginald nodded yes.

'Good, this is the plan. You boys are the support group for the ground and air. You're going to fly low, as in four meters, I mean, paces off the ground low to give tight bombardment for the troops and take out enemy magic to allow my dragons to do the big stuff.'

Reginald nodded.

Craig felt Neeko at his side. The Ne-arri didn't want to interrupt immediately, but had to. "Can you speak to them?"

Craig frequently forgot that he was the only one who could speak to Dragon. "Yeah, don't sweat it." He confided in her.

"Could you ask them why they are all staring at me?"

And indeed they all were. Whispering back and forth to themselves. *'She is a cat? She is a fat cat. Is she a little dragon cat? Like a Dragon House*

Cat? Perhaps she is a baby dragon? Dragons only come in one size. Why is she so fat?'

Craig could hear far off in the distance Brezhnev the big red snort in disgust.

Chapter 66

Shouts of anger rose into Leatha's night from the dark patch of Mortal-roam called Dacova. The warm, putrid stench of rotting flesh, filtered through the woods, riding on the ice cold air for Fikor's winter. Drums of war sounded, echoing with the cries of pain. Lashing whips ripped against sweat. Beasts pushed into yokes. Demons danced to songs of anguish.

Friska tightened the reigns on his mount. The two legged what ever that he had been given to ride was suddenly assailed by something. Friska patted its neck reassuringly and continued to survey his troops.

"You're making a mistake Daniel!"

Friska turned his beast about and looked down to the cart. The two wheeled cage pulled about by an eight legged demon contained his second youngest brother, stripped naked and bound. Friska sighed sympathetically and shook his head. "No, J'son, it is you who are making a mistake. You just don't see do you?"

J'son twisted about to stand on his knees. "See? All I see is another army from Hell! What are you trying to do?"

"Heading to freedom. To Worldsend."

J'son's eyes widened. "What? Worldsend? Hauth couldn't take Worldsend, what makes you think that you can?"

"Because Hauth ascended alone. I'm taking all of them with me."

"And Worldsend is going to resist." J'son cautioned.

Friska nodded. "I know, I've been listening to your brother's elfcall. He is here in Dacova." Friska looked about the woods around him.

"And what when they defend? Roc will be there."

Friska looked down with a scowl. "I'm not afraid of him."

"And mother, will you fight her?"

Friska paused and then shook his head. "She will not raise her hand against me. And I'll not raise my hand against her."

J'son banged his head on the top of the bars and winced until the pain subsided. "And you will be able to keep your dogs at bay?" J'son motioned to the troops moving about him.

"Yes." Friska smiled. "They love me."

J'son's eyes grew to circles and burned with green. "What?"

"They love me." He repeated.

J'son looked to the floor of his cage in disbelief. "You can't be for real!"

He looked up and saw himself.

"Hi Me!"

J'son's breath caught for a half beat in his throat as he looked his younger twin over. "Hi me."

J'cob turned and looked up to Friska. "Dan ol' boy."

"J'cob, a pleasure to see you again." He said pleasantly. "How did you...Uh,"

"Get in? Not too hard. Hey, you might want to call in those patrols that are out looking for me before they get really lost." J'cob drew his sword and cut open J'son's cage. "So Daniel..." J'cob began, not turning from his task. "I missed the first half of this. What are you trying to do?"

"Conquer Worldsend. Uh, I don't think you should be doing that."

J'cob reached into the cage and stared to cut away his brother's bonds. "Yeah, like we're escaping. Okay, I got the part about taking Worldsend." He looked up to his older brother. "What I'm asking is, what for?"

Friska paused and his beast shook and stamped underneath him. "Look around you."

J'cob did as J'son shook the blood back into his hands. "I don't get it." J'cob finally answered. "All I see is a lot of wretches."

"Yes!" Friska suddenly exclaimed. "And these poor souls are all creations of Okshiru. Created to improve himself. So he could rule them and abuse them. They are innocent examples to any one who disobeys, goes against the will of Okshiru."

J'cob looked to J'son, then back to Friska. "I thought they were created by the other Supergods and Dad created Hel."

Friska shook his head. "Not Hel, just some place to put them. Okshiru made it Hel and punished them for crimes they didn't commit."

"So what you're saying," J'cob started to put together as he gave his twin a hand up. "Okshiru created all of Hel as an incentive to obey. Do as I say or else this will happen."

Friska nodded enthusiastically. "Partly. Okshiru maintains all of Mortalroam as his personal play toy. They whole system is a giant game for him to play. I will unrest that game."

"And so you are going to lead them triumphantly across Mortalroam. Stomp any and all opposition against you, burn

Cornerstone to the ground, use the magic forces there to ascend into Worldsend and kick out Okshiru."

"Yes!" Friska shouted triumphantly.

J'son gripped his younger brother's collar firmly. "What are you doing?" He whispered.

J'cob ignored his twin and looked up to Friska. "Well I think that is wonderful!"

"You do?" Both J'son and Friska exclaimed simultaneously.

"Yeah! This is a triumph for the underclass. I say we should celebrate! Lets get some wine!"

J'son's grip suddenly tightened as he raised his fist to hit his brother. J'cob caught his arm and held him. "Hey, relax."

Suddenly, a frightening wave swept over J'son's centre. His younger twin had an idea.

J'cob released him and looked around. "Is there someplace to sit?"

Friska looked around. "Yes, but we are on the move..."

J'cob waved a hand. "You're in charge, tell every one to take ten. Its not like Worldsend is going anywhere."

"I see lovely seating for three over here." J'son added still trying to figure out what J'cob was up to.

Friska dismounted and watched his to brothers head over large rock and kneel at it. Friska looked to a short demon standing by him. "Give the order to halt."

The demon's eyes widened slightly and then complied. He took up an ivory horn and gave a single blast. The sound was echoed by other horns all across the woods.

J'cob pulled the cloak tied to his knapsack to cover his brother's nakedness. He smiled as Friska came closer. "I think we should all be together at a time like this..." J'cob began. "Brothers again. Just like old times!"

Friska nodded a little confused. "I am surprised that you are this receptive. I figured a bit more resistance."

"Receptive? Daniel! I see it in your eyes!" J'cob glared at his older brother's eyes as if he was trying to pick it out directly. Not being able too, he went on. "I mean...it must be frightening for you Daniel."

"Yes..." J'son agreed taking a boda that someone had handed him. "Simply terrifying." He said going along with J'cob.

"I mean, the sudden realization that every thing that you've ever learned in your whole life is garbage." J'cob went on. "All those lies that Mom and Dad taught you."

J'son took a swig and suddenly gasped for air. "Yeah lies." He said breathlessly as he handed the boda to Friska.

"All that time, training to be a knight, converting Cassandra..." J'cob paused. "Hey, the old girl should be here for this! Bring her about!"

Friska pulled the Boda from his lips looking confused. "Cassandra? Here?"

"Yeah, I saw her back there a bit." J'son motioned with his head as he took back the boda.

"She is here?" Friska suddenly jumped to his feet. "Bring me the Sheol!" He ordered.

"Sit down..." J'son motioned breathlessly as he handed him the Boda. "So what you're saying, is that the entire population of Hel are all victims of circumstance?"

Friska suddenly noticed him. "What?"

"These demons are basically decent people." J'son said motioning for him to drink. "A little twisted, but decent."

"You proved that with Cassandra." J'cob carried on.

"No, no, no," J'son corrected. "That was a lie."

"Oh, I'm sorry." J'cob apologized to Friska. "What you're saying is that decent people are bad, and bad people are decent."

Friska shook his head. "No, you're twisting it all around."

J'son tagged Friska on the shoulder. The knight looked at where his brother was pointing. Cassandra was being dragged to him.

Friska jumped to his feet and dashed over to her. She was bound tightly and stripped of her clothes. Her flesh was hot and sweaty. Her face was burned and blistered. She reeked from smoke.

Her dark eyes locked with his and somehow she managed to smile. "My love..." She whispered.

Friska knelt to her and propped her up. He looked to the two stumps that pushed from her shoulders. Her wings had been amputated. Anger swept his centre. "Who did this?" He snarled at the demon who brought her. The demon only shrugged his shoulders.

Cassandra coughed. "If this is right...then I will do it."

"Talk about dedication." J'son said as he knelt at her side.

"No no no." J'cob corrected her. "You don't want to do what's right. Every thing that you have been taught is a lie."

Friska's eyes suddenly howled as they burned green. "NO!" He shouted at the twins. "Shut up!"

"What is going on here?" Thamrell floated from out of the woods. "Who ordered this?"

Friska looked up. "You? You ordered this?"

Thamrell paused confused as to what was going on. He looked at the demon with the ivory horn. "Sound march."

"No!" Friska countermanded. "Did you order this?"

Thamrell looked at him and realized what he was talking about. "Her? Friska, you rate much better than that."

"Sorry kid." J'son looked sympathetically to the Sheol.

"Back to the mud pits for you." J'cob finished.

Her eyes widened at the horrifying prospect. For her, a slow, agonizing death was a much better choice. "No...Friska! Please!"

"Now, now, none of that." J'son started again. "You see, everything that you've learned was a lie."

"Except for the lies you were taught, they were the truth."

"What are these two doing here?" Thamrell snarled at the demon with the horn.

"And why can't we be here?" J'son threatened.

"Who the Hel are you anyway?" J'cob questioned.

"Friska," Thamrell floated lower. "They are here to disrupt you, to confuse you."

"We're his brothers." J'son said.

"And how can we confuse him?" J'cob went on.

"He knows the truth." J'son continued.

"And how can we distort the truth?" J'cob finished.

Thamrell put up his hands as a shield. "Get them out of here!" He ordered.

J'son gripped his older brother's arm. "Why? Tell me Daniel, why can't we stay?"

"We love you Daniel. You're our brother..." J'cob paused in mid thought and then looked to his twin. "Or is that a lie too?"

J'son nodded. "Of course it was. You think that it was real? Just like Hauth. He had the same reasons too."

"Friska..." Thamrell leaned in. "Don't listen to them."

480

"And why the Hel not?" J'cob quickly countered. "What do you have to be afraid of?"

J'son gripped him tighter. "Lies, Daniel, be afraid of lies." He whispered.

"And why are you afraid?" J'cob pointed to Thamrell. "Who are you?"

"I am Thamrell." He said simply.

"Pleased to met you." J'son said without a glance as he squatted down to Cassandra's side. "So you understand Cassandra, that you must die to love Friska."

"What?" Friska looked at him.

"I'll die for you Friska." Cassandra said quickly.

"You can't die for him," J'cob countered. "That's a lie."

"Daniel..." J'son started. "You've got this girl thinking lies!"

"Get them away..." Thamrell chanted. "Don't listen to them."

"All we want to know is..." J'son looked to Thamrell. "What is going on here?"

"Look around you Daniel and tell me what is truth." J'cob asked him. "Are these the demons you want on Mortalroam?"

"They'll bow to you." J'son whispered. "Hail Friska, Hail."

"They'll be your servants, your slaves. You'll rule." J'cob whispered into his other ear.

"These basically good demons who gleefully cut off your lover's wings will be the right..." J'son said.

"In the light," J'cob went on. "Working side by side. Mom will have new neighbors to invite over for dinner."

"Get them out of here..." Thamrell ordered to other demons.

"How proud she will be." J'son smiled. "Her son brought them to Mortalroam."

"No, J'son..." J'cob argued. "If the demons are coming to Mortalroam, then every one on Mortalroam must be going to Hel."

"I see," J'son said thoughtfully. "Then Mom will be so proud at the son who sent her to Hel."

"ENOUGH!" Thamrell's voice roared over the woods and the sound of the army fell into sudden silence. "It is over. Friska come here."

Friska didn't move.

Thamrell's wrinkled face wrinkled more. "Get them out of here." Large demons suddenly seized J'son and J'cob and lifted them roughly off their feet. They grabbed Cassandra from Friska's arms. "Take them away." Thamrell said heatedly. "They will be the first in our body count." Then to the knight, he said: "Friska, come here." He ordered.

Friska rose slowly to his feet. "No…Thamrell. It is alright. Let me handle this." He turned to the demons. "Let them go." They dropped them. "J'son, J'cob, Cassandra, get out of here. I want you to run back to Roc and tell him to surrender. Tell him what you have seen and that he doesn't stand a chance."

J'cob shook his head. "No Daniel, not without you."

"If Dwayne can come back, then so can you." J'son finished.

Friska smiled. "It is too late for that my brother. I see now how Hauth was fooled. I will not be so tricked. I have one course that lies before me and to end this nightmare, my part must be played out. But you and J'son have a part yet to play." He nodded to the woods. "Now go before that choice is closed and I am naught but failure."

The two stared at the errant knight and found themselves for the first time in their lives, with nothing to say. J'son looked to J'cob and J'cob looked to J'son and the two took off at full tilt. Cassandra stood there quivering. "I will not leave you…" She whispered, trying to hobble toward her lover.

J'cob bounded back. He caught her still bound body and pushed his shoulder into her stomach and lifted her up. Friska could hear her screams of love as they made their way into the woods.

"Why did you do that?" Thamrell asked him.

"I need a sword." Friska announced. "I will need a sword to fight with."

Thamrell regarded the knight carefully, then nodded and a sword was brought.

Friska snatched it and held it up. It was crudely made and improperly balanced, but in his hands, it suddenly gleamed and shined. He thrashed at the air and the sword responded as a blade of craftsmanship. "No knight should be without a sword." He said. "Amazing isn't it?"

"What?" Thamrell slowly glided away, trying to guess what was going on in the head of the knight of wind.

"A knight that has fallen will lose his sword. If he is regained, he will gain another weapon." Friska looked at his sword. "Yet I have a sword."

Thamrell stood a little taller as hair suddenly climbed on his neck. "Put the sword away, you will use it soon enough."

"Hauge…" Friska whispered.

Waves of wind suddenly swept up and scattered the smaller demons about. The large ones stood strong fighting the great waves of turmoil. Thamrell stood about ten hands above the ground. The wind only tugged at his cloak. "Friska, what do you hope to accomplish?" In the center of the maelstrom Friska held up his sword and the great white light of Okshiru burned from it. "Friska, you have betrayed us…" Thamrell went on. "You will lose."

Friska swung his sword in a circle over his head. Again and again he twirled his sword. The wind around him moaned and cried as he did. The sword hummed a single note, higher and higher in pitch as the sword flailed faster and faster. Demons tried crawling on the ground, grasping at plants and roots for hand holds as they dragged their way toward the whirl wind only to find themselves flung away as they grew close.

In the center, Friska the wind, laughed at the power around him, his elvish eyes blazing a brilliant green. His laughter turned to a cry of anguish as tears trickled down his face.

Slowly, purposely, he brought the white flashing sword lower and lower and with a sudden snap of his wrist, cut off his own head.

In that instant, the whirlwind exploded into a cone of white fire and heat and was gone. The winds dropped suddenly. Demons suddenly lurched forward, stumbling. The forests of Dacova grew suddenly silent.

Thamrell sighed slowly and then shrugged his shoulders. "Oh well." He then looked to one of his demons picking himself up from the ground. "Blow your horn. Let us get moving."

A great crashing noise tore through the night. Shouts and screams quickly followed.

"What was that?" Thamrell ordered. "Go find out what that was!" The god of despair floated higher with the hopes that he could see what was going on. He couldn't. A winged demon sailed towards him and squealed piteously at him. "The wove is CLOSED?" Thamrell shouted. "Are you sure? How many of our forces got through before it closed?

Don't shrug your shoulders at me, find out! I want a list of equipment and troops right away. GO!"

As the little demon sailed off, Thamrell looked to the bloody, headless body lying in the dust.

Chapter 67

Hague's winds had started sweeping in from the north. Fikor ran next to the god of wind with blistering cold through the fields and valleys. The great dog took quickly to the top of The Eighth brother mountain with the wind god close behind. At the crest, the dog of winter stopped and looked above to Leatha's night sky and the new star that Neathina had planted in it. The great dog howled at the star with a freezing cry.

Hauge sped past him into the valley below. He swept the tall grasses and raced across the barren wheat fields. He dashed over the cattle grounds of Seeda Gully and up over Tashwalk.

Craig pulled the blanket over his wife a little closer. She nudged him and rubbed her ears against his unshaven face. She rumbled with a cat like purr.

"You're not cold?" Craig asked her.

"I'm leaching your heat." She answered in a low voice.

Craig smiled weakly and pointed to the sky. "That is Ursa Minor, right next to Ursa Major."

Neeko's arm wormed from under the cover and pointed to the brightest light in the sky. "And that one?"

Craig had been hopping to avoid that. "To be honest, I really don't know."

She pulled away and glared at him. "What? Something you don't know?"

"No fair. That star wasn't there yesterday. I can only assume it's a nearby star that super novaed a half billion years ago and its light has finally reached us." She looked at him quizzically. "Actually, its quite a phenomenon." He went on. "It must be about million light years away for us to see it with the Human...Uh, Naked eye. Quite a find. If I had a radioscope it would be quite a study." He looked at her and smiled. "Also, we have to give it a name."

"A name?"

"So our kid can study it."

She nodded in agreement. "We will call it Krisanna." She said readily.

Craig looked at her and waited. When she didn't answer he prompted, "Why Krisanna?"

"In honor of our daughter." She said simply.

Craig looked down to see if Neeko had given birth while he wasn't looking. "What makes you so sure it's a girl?"

Neeko looked at him surprised that he didn't know. "Because I'm the mother. You think I can be this close to my own child and not know what she is?" She took his hand and placed it on her belly. "Besides, nine months ago you said it was going to be a girl."

"Oh, yeah...I did." He smiled to himself as he remembered. He then looked up at the new star. "Then, the new star will be Krisanna." He looked at her. "And by the light of the new star, I would like to ask you something."

Neeko could feel Craig trembling. He was actually nervous. He doesn't get nervous. "What?"

Craig took her hand into his. "Will you marry me?" With that, he slipped a ring on to her finger.

Her eyes grew wide as the light of the new star caught in the diamond stone and it sparkled like it was alive. Her breath left her and her mouth dried.

"Just say yes." Craig encouraged.

It was several beats before her mouth could find a voice. "Yes..." Her eyes lifted from the cool white stone to his red burning eyes. Her heart had fallen into her centre and bounced around before it came to a rest. Her arms flung themselves about him. Her lips found his readily. She felt his heat warm her and filled her centre starting her heart again.

Hauge dashed quickly by and the heavy blanket was swept off in his wake. The god of wind stopped suddenly as he realized that they two lovers paid little notice to the blanket. The brown god of wind watched the two for several beats.

"I love you I love you I love you." Neeko cried as she gasped for air. Tears were spilling down her cheeks. "Don't leave me...Don't die." Her voice suddenly broke and she held him tighter.

"Don't think about it." He said quickly. "Only think about now. There is only now." Craig could feel his own tears mix with hers as they locked in kisses again.

Hauge watched for several more beats. Then the god of wind picked up the blanket and slowly made his way over to the couple. With gentle, calm winds, the god wrapped them back in the warm blanket. Then the god turned and soared up to Second brother mountain.

When they finally broke, Neeko's green eyes were lit with the light of the new star and she gazed lovingly at him. "There is only one problem." Her voice bubbled.

Craig eyebrows dug deeper. "What?"

"We're already married."

"I've been meaning to talk to you about that. I don't remember getting married. Only one morning you said we were and I accepted it."

Neeko nodded understandingly. "I'm sorry, since you were the Dragoncaller, I thought you knew dragon tradition."

Craig cocked his head. He knew that Neeko had been orphaned as a child and raised by Ameri, queen of dragons. She was raised on dragon traditions but Craig wasn't. He waited. He wanted to hear this.

"Once the female has decided on her mate, they take the secret marriage vows and they're married."

Craig raised an eyebrow and took a very calculated deep breath. "Hokay." He said letting out his deeply calculated breath. "One problem. The vows are so secret, that I don't know them."

"Neither do I," She smiled impishly. "That's what's so great about them."

Craig nodded as a smile slowly crawled across the half of his face that was working. "A rat in cat's clothing." He kissed her. "Okay, were gonna do this one my way. First comes the engagement ring. That's this thing." He pointed to her finger. It didn't fit right and only passed the first knuckle. But that was to be expected in her advanced pregnancy. "This is to show the world that were going to get married."

"Then what?" She said anxiously.

"Then comes the ceremony in which we exchange rings to show the world that we are married."

The smile slowly slid from her face. "So when are we going to do the ceremony?"

Craig smiled. "Right now."

She giggled and hugged him. She pulled away and her smiled left her. "What's the matter?"

Craig's face was suddenly wrought. He looked behind him, and felt his heart stop. '*ABACROMBY!*' He shouted in a Dragoncall instead of just screaming in surprise. Craig pounded on his chest to start his heart again.

Neeko smiled at the tallest White Tiger Dragon. "I think he's cute."

Craig shook his head. "He's not supposed to be cute. He's supposed to be a vicious, snarling monster."

"He looks like a puppy with his tongue hanging out like that." The white tiger dragon seemed to smile at her. "What is his name?"

Craig had to be carefully. Dragon's did not like their names to be known. He wasn't sure of the ruling on White Tiger dragons, so he made one up. "Mitten." He mumbled. "Now Mitten, Go play in traffic." Craig couldn't help but smile at the beast as it walked out of reality.

Something clicked in Craig's head. White Tiger Dragons could not shift about reality by themselves. They could only go when lead by a Dragon-panther or by a mortal who could speak White Tiger Dragon. There were only two who could, Dormoth, and himself. He had to speak to Reginald about this little twist.

Something came to his ears and broke his thought.

"What is it, now?" Neeko could tell that Craig had heard something.

"An elfcall." Craig said ignoring it. "I don't speak elfcall."

"You don't even try." She said motherly.

He sighed and gave it a listen. "Its something…Friska, I recognize that name. Dead. I recognize that word and that's about it."

Neeko's eyes dawned with horror. A beat later, Craig realized what he said.

A scream filled Leatha's night. Neathina tripped on the crest of the fourth brother and her pipes fell into the valley. The little goddess looked up in fear. Fikor bowed his head and Hauge's winds stilled. Dru only shook her head and Ura leaned back her head and laughed.

Craig and Neeko stumbled to their feet. His elvish hearing and her cat ears listened to Lady Fantista crying from the manor. Craig could tell that the Grandmaster of Knights was trying to compose herself. To hold the pain torn into her centre within herself. But the damage was too great and her turmoil spilled out of her. Craig knew that all of her children where far from home and could not come to comfort her. He could hear the elfcalls coming in from all around him. Elfcalls to her from hundreds of places all sending what comfort they could.

Craig and Neeko would be her children for this night. Her children for life.

Chapter 68

Shegatesu peered above the horizon and looked down to the black valleys bellow. She reached up and painted Okshiru's sky with gentle water colors. She stained the clouds with gold and frosted the land below with silver.

Kemoto boldly leapt to the sky and fanned his great fiery wings. His warm light shed across the world. Shadows crawled away and followed Mistang to the lower lands.

Meleki and Gozoo watched the hoards of troops continuing their procession, marching into holes in the neighplane opened for them by Dragonslayer's spell casters. The troops marched from the neighplane a little confused, disoriented. But the sergeants' barking voices quickly pulled them into line and marched them into place. Roc the Dragonslayer watched intensely as his dwarves directed the entrenching. The dwarvish engineers planed and pointed, built snares, pits and booby traps. Hornton Roquechuqur was the lead dwarf. He stood on a little platform and directed the troops of men and elves given to him in building what was needed.

Men shouted and then scattered. A whistle pierced the air followed by the sound of tearing linen. A boulder the size of a man's chest fell from the sky above.

Elfcalls sounded. Answers came. Gorn trotted over to Lord Roc as the giant elf only rubbed his temples. Beside him, a signalman reported. "The Colonel reports that the ships have catapult range from the river— This was an accident and he is sorry."

Roc nodded slowly, letting the information sink in before answering. "Tell the admiral, now Colonel, he is now a Lieutenant and I'm sorry too. Also tell him to report to me when this is all over and remind me to inflict upon him a head injury of some sort." The elf raised his horn to his lips and sounded a reply.

Roc listened for the reply of confirmation and nodded to his second in Command. "Is the RDO in place?"

Gorn turned and watched a young lieutenant make his way down from the hill. "In a moment my lord," Gorn spoke without turning around. "We shall find out."

The lieutenant peered brightly and clean shaven before his Commander in Chief. "Regimental Decimater Overbiter is ready for testing, Sir!" He brightly overemphasized the sir and Roc squinted at the noise as he nodded and turned to his map.

"With the RDO up here supported by the Meat Maker up here in Alpha, we'll have covered Alpha, bravo, and Echo." Gorn nodded in agreement.

"Signal!" Gorn called out. "Signal to Bravo to start the test!"

The signal bearer took up a bright green banner and waved to the west. The young lieutenant politely tapped the signalman on the shoulder and told him that he was signaling in the wrong direction.

Roc quickly stepped in and took the banner away all together. Gorn pulled the lieutenant by the upper arm and turned him around. "What are you doing?"

The lieutenant lost his smile. "Well sir, the RDO is that way." He pointed to the south. Roc moaned and looked at his map. Gorn shook the lieutenant and roared. "WHAT?"

The lieutenant quickly reached into his satchel and retrieved his map. He opened it quickly and showed Gorn the bright red circle were the RDO was.

Gorn took the map, turned it right side up and handed it back to him. "Is that easier to read?"

The lieutenant's eyes widened. "Oh."

"Oh?" Roc said turning from his maps. "Oh?"

Gorn put up a restraining hand to hold back Roc. "What did you think you were doing all the way out in this sector?" Gorn said trying to keep his body between the lieutenant and Roc.

The lieutenants eyes fixed on Roc and didn't move. "Well sir, there was nothing out there...I thought it was perfect."

"YOU Thought!" Roc howled. "Who gave you permission to think?"

Gorn kept his calm demeanor as he continued to speak with the young soldier. "That is because we have a dragon sweeping up there. Tomorrow the RDO will be charcoal." Roc's huge spiked arm shot over Gorn's shoulder and fell within inches of the young lieutenant. Gorn held him back. "You are relieved of command." Gorn went on quietly. "Now run up to the officers head and be shit on for a quarter day then come back here...and stand down wind."

The lieutenant nodded and ran off to be shit on.

Gorn turned and signaled to the Dragonguard. "Blade!"

Blade's wide frame turned. "Yeah!"

"The RDO is in Gamma. It is to be in Bravo."

"Check." The leader of the Dragonguard lumbered off.

Gorn turned to Roc with a shrug. "My apologies my lord. I take full responsibility."

"When he is done getting shit on, give him a head injury."

"Is that today's punishment?"

Roc nodded looking off in the direction to the lieutenant went in. "Can't give them broken limbs, they will need that for later. Seems that their heads are the only part that they can do without. In some cases, it's a marked improvement." Roc looked at his second. "I knew not to trust him. He was clean shaven."

"It's the old story, Roc." Gorn replied. "The most dangerous thing in a war."

Roc looked at him. "Even I fear a lieutenant with a compass."

Chapter 69

High above and far below, past the borders of man and on the outskirts of thought, lie the great unscalable mountains of Worldsend. Great mountains of black indestructible obsidian reach far above sight and simply vanish out of comprehension. A great cloud of brown earth rises into the air forming a storming wall of flying dirt in which the great mountains are nestled in. It is a little known fact that the great mountains are actually floating a 1/1000th of an inch from off the face of Mortalroam and actually move about. It hovers, on the will of Okshiru himself, because the great mountains, and they are truly great, should not have to touch the lowly earth.

The remains of a gigantic escalator lie in a giant metal and rubber heap at the foot of the great mountains as a cruel but educational reminder that the great mountains are not only unscalable and indestructible, but it is also seemingly unescalatorable. Its dizzying height is also unreachable by dragons for the air is too thin for their gigantic wings to ride upon. This was always a great comfort to the great gods that lived upon the great mountains until it was discovered, quite by accident, that the gold wingless dragon could fly to that height if it had such a mind to. But dragons rarely got such an idea, and the rare occasions that they did, it took such a long time for the beast to get that high, that it forgot what it was going up there for in the first place (which in actuality was quite lame to begin with) and headed back down the great mountains, much to the great relief of the great gods.

As time went on, it was then decided that the Dragoncaller, the mortal appointed by the gods to keep dragons in check and linked to mortals, could inspire a gold dragon, if he had one, and simply ride into Worldsend perched greatly upon its great mountain and visit for tea, or whatever. But he never did and 11,000 years ago he died an agonizing death at the paws of Ferris, the Iron Dragon and that was that. The great gods were once again greatly relived and lived quite greatly in their great world.

But then he came. The physics teacher from Brooklyn. He was smart, fast on his feet and not really impressed with greatness, which he displayed in his encounter with the Demon Dragon Witch Queen and Dave the Meca Demon. Now the great gods were greatly worried as it seemed that this stranger, (and he was strange), was quite capable if he knew, (and he did), that the gold dragon could reach them, (and it could), and if he had one, (which he did), and could stop in for tea, (which he might). Fortunately for them, the physics teacher was not impressed by greatness, (as was said before) and wouldn't waste the time to stop in. The great gods knew, that if the physics teacher knew, that Worldsend at the top of the great mountain where the great gods roamed, was the only place in the entire universe were there was a shopping mall complete with a Circle K's, Domino's, Dunkin Doughnuts and Baskin Robbins, that the wayward, misplaced teacher from Brooklyn would pack up his Wife/child, dog, cat, and big red car on the gold dragon and move in. But he didn't know and the great gods kept their great secret to their great selves and lived in great contentedness with little concern for the new Dragoncaller.

Now the bigger secret lies in the fact that the Dragoncaller does know that the last mall is in Worldsend, but has no desire to move in simply because having stuck up, immature, quasiomnipotent wanna be gods for neighbors was about as much fun as having a hot cinder jammed under the nail of his ring finger. Ergo, the Dragoncaller had little concern for the gods and the gods had little concern for the Dragoncaller.

All save one.

Thamrell was a god. But he was never issued a body. He rated rather lowly amongst gods and was generally shunned when they even remembered him. It was a depressing idea for him as the cold treatment of his fellow godlings drove him out of Worldsend. He roamed aimlessly about Mortalroam, moaning over his plot in life and from that, depressed the mortals that he encountered, thus the name Despair. He discovered some pleasure in despair and became proficient with it as he built up a reputation. Unfortunately, this reputation caused his fellow gods to shun him further and this idea drew him deeper still into the chilling embrace of oblivion.

He didn't even rate a knight. Even Neathina had a knight. Ura's knight, Paradox, would soon be replaced. Dru got Frito back and yet himself, the god of despair, who could easily cause men to suicide, mothers to kill their children, Kings to destroy their kingdoms, didn't even rate a locker at the racquetball court. He could destroy lands with war, inspire pain, deliver death, grow deceit, harbor greed, and build loneliness in cities of people. He could control every human trait that was worth something on the open market and he didn't even have a

493

body, let alone his own knight. Knights were a social status among these great gods, and to not have one, or to be without was a cold slap in the face from Okshiru himself.

This fact alone distressed the god of despair into deep depression.

So he waited, and he plotted for what seemed for all of eternity, saving and storing his power, (which wasn't much), planning his evil Machinations, (which were quite evil), and deceiving those who actually remembered him into thinking that he was quite harmless, (which he was).

Hauth came from the bowels of the earth unexpectedly. His legend was foretold generations ago how a Knight of the gods would bring the great mountains of Worldsend down about their ears and sure enough, Hauth had done it. The great indestructible floating black obsidian mountains crashed into the earth against the will of Okshiru and Hauth rolled in on his escalator.

But this was rather helpful to Thamrell, for he saw for the first time since the reawakening of time the gods truly let out with all of their powers and resources, favors and loans, cheats and deceits to stop Hauth's unstoppable advance. It showed Thamrell clearly what the gods could and would do if forced into a corner, (which Hauth had done). He knew all of their weaknesses, their limits and loopholes. He knew how to destroy them all. He now knew, without question, that millenniums of saved power, all of his planning, all of his amassing tides of hate that he stood no chance in Hel of ever conquering Worldsend and dethroning Okshiru. This depressed him greatly.

But the god of Despair was not to be so easily undone. If he could do anything, it was hate.

And he hated.

Then he came, from the ashes of Hauth's burning path. The great beast of the backward knees was yet to ascend Worldsend and he spoke of his defeat at the God's god. It was a god whose reason to hate the great Okshiru was just as infinite as his own. The god of answers had the plan to topple Okshiru and throw the universe into his palm without troubling the all powerful god's God. A plan that would win. He could lead the forces of Hel into Worldsend and take Okshiru by the great godly balls. It would work. Hauth's mistake was avoiding Cornerstone and then challenging the Supergod. But as fate would have it, as if the gods had predicted the prophecies and made plans to quell it long ago, they made the destroyer of the great black mountains of Worldsend, the son of the Supergod. No matter how twisted he had become, how he destroyed his best friend and cousin, humbled his brothers, beat sister and mother, the beast with the backward knees could not destroy Cornerstone and use its untapped power against his father, Lord Hammerstrike.

Perhaps that was the plan. The great gods attempt to force prophecy. *Let's get an enemy that will shake things up, but leave them intact and the prophecy will be fulfilled, and that'll be that. Or perhaps we'll stage the whole thing and the real conqueror of the realm will get lost in the shuffle, give up and go home.*

Gods think this way.

Perhaps, Thamrell thought to himself, perhaps, Hauth was only a precursor to the then and now. It was because of a planned error, misinformation fed to Hauth by the god of answers that made his whole plan possible. To leave a key, in which the gate could be opened. Was it a sheer coincidence that the knights of Okshiru would be so vulnerable? Frito serving his self penance in the mountains, out of contact, Friska still in shock by his defeat at Hauth's hands, Roc's great forces broken, Frita's sin of…What was Frita's sin? Thumber called it *'Professional Courtesy'* and *'to tell you would blow it'*. All the god of despair knew was that the girl knight was completely bonkers. What a coincidence!

Thamrell had to think of hope or he would fall into despair himself and simply cause his own small black hole to implode about himself.

This was going to work.

"Then why are you brooding?"

The god of despair turned about in the air. Ura, the goddess of chaos laid on her couch. Her silk dress spilled to the floor but not before splashing over her large melon like breasts. Her golden blonde hair flowed down the arm that propped up her head like a water fall before pooling on her pillow.

Thamrell floated mindlessly about the circumference of the room. "If I we're not brooding, would that make you feel better?"

She shook her head no. "That wouldn't make me feel better." She whispered in a voice of honey pouring from her crimson lips.

"There has been a problem."

"I know…and I want you to solve it."

Thamrell looked out the window and Mortalroam spiraling below. "Something that we haven't counted on."

"I'm counting on you." She hung on the world 'YOU' pursing her lips as she did. Her tongue quickly lashed out and liked her lips of blood so they shined with spit in the light. "Come over here and fix it."

Thamrell looked over his shoulder. The goddess was on her back twisting her poking nipples. "That isn't the problem." He said coldly and then looked outside of the window.

She looked over the edge of the couch arm and could tell he was paying absolutely no attention to her bump and grind show. She sat up pulling her flimsy robe about her as she did. "Well, I'm listening." She said testily.

"One..." Thamrell started as he turned and sailed smoothly towards her. "Friska had a sudden streak of morality and killed himself."

Ura, who just knew this was going to be dull suddenly perked her head up with her wide blue eyes. "Really? Is that how he died?"

"Cut off his own head." Thamrell said grimly.

Ura paused for a moment as she put long out of service parts of her brain to thinking. "So what is the problem?"

Thamrell sighed and let it go at that. "It closed the Wove. I've lost a third of my forces. With out guidance, they will wander lost in the Wove for at least a thousand years before they're found and led back to Hel." *Why aren't you watching what's going on?* Thamrell thought to himself.

"Cut off his own head?" She exclaimed with a gleam in her eye. "Is that possible?"

Aren't you listening? Thamrell screamed to himself. *I've lost a third of my forces!* "Yes, he did." He instead answered.

She smiled suddenly and tried to hide it with her hand but it spilled over just the same in spits of giggles.

"There is another problem." Thamrell went on. "It's the Dragoncaller. I had hoped that he would back down with Thumber's illusion, but he hasn't."

She looked at him as her smiled melted to bother. "Ferris will take care of him." She waved a flimsy hand at him.

Thamrell shook his head. "And what of the prophecy, the Dragoncaller will kill the Iron Dragon?"

She laughed breathlessly. "Tc-mock was the Dragoncaller 11,000 years ago. Remember how long that fight was? Four beats!" She snapped her fingers, One, Two, Three, Four. "Four beats and he was torn to shreds and eaten."

"That was Tc-mock, this is not." Thamrell argued.

"And the same will happen…" She said rather snottily. "He will be no problem."

Thamrell soared higher into the room. "Roc has planted his army right in our path. There is no time to deviate and avoid him."

"SO?" She glared at him angrily. "This is nothing new. That is why you have an army a thousand times stronger! They are not ornamental. Demons verses mortal steel!" She laughed as she envisioned a sand crab attacking a bear. "Swat him! Pow!" She slapped her hands together. She leaned back in her couch. "Walk over him."

Thamrell lifted over the surface of the pool that sat in the center of the room. She wasn't getting the point. He had to go for the big one. "Frito is gone." He said dreadfully.

Her eyes twisted in disgust. "Good."

Thamrell soared about the ceiling as his anger swelled. He passed harmlessly through the stanchions and curtains as he flew about. He slowly lowered to the couch and hovered over her. "Good?" He whispered. "Good? You say, Good?" His empty eyes fell upon her and her white china skin began to crawl. "I'm talking about Frito, The Knight? The Devilslayer?" *Does that name ring a bell? He was given that for a damned reason.* "Lord of Lightning? THE THRICE DAMNED NINEFINGERS!"

Ura sank into her pillows. Her chin touched her heaving chest as she tried to pull away. She flicked her fingers at him hopping he would 'shoo'.

He lifted higher. He was angry and wasn't afraid to show it. "Frito is too bloody sneaky to have wandering around unchecked." He snarled.

She sat up and like a child thudded her fists into her hips. "To Hel with him!"

Thamrell froze in mid glide. Slowly he rotated and beamed at her. "You're not listening, are you?"

"I'm listening. I'm listening to all of your paranoid bullshit!"

"Paranoid…" He blinked quickly and nodded his head. "Oh, paranoid am I?" He floated lower. "It seems that I've got to do some thinking for you. There are suddenly too many variables all of a sudden. Too many things are going wrong."

Her red lips folded into thin tight lines. "Perhaps you need a little thinking." Her little turned up nose wrinkled as she leaned closer. "You have the army, I gave it to you." She was hissing. "You have the Iron

Dragon, I gave it to you too. No Mortal army can face you...If Craig kills the Iron dragon, then what? He is nothing but another man. His dragons can be shot from the air with your magic. Roc has not enough men to stop you. The knights are in total disarray with Frito gone to boot. We all know that Frito will not and cannot become Hauth again, so he is nothing. The gods have been warned to stay out of this one so you'll have no interference from us. All you have to do is march a thousand clicks into Cornerstone, that little stupid mortal city with the lines of Poer running conveniently beneath." She leaned back in her couch and planted her elbow into the rest with her fist to her head again. "Take your worst case scenario, Ferris is killed. As we speak, Another is being built. Roc's armies slays ten thousand demons, No...twenty, no Fifty! Fifty thousand demons, you still have another million. What can Frito do? He is still only one knight. And say, just say that by some great eternal miracle happens and your defeated, the gates of Hel are open and only the Poer can close them, and nobody has the Poer to close them. Demons don't die, they only go to Hel and regroup. You can waltz right through the doors again.

"Thamrell, I can't see the problem." She smiled ever so sweetly. Thamrell waved in the air. She didn't care whether he won or lost, it was all how she played the game. She was the goddess of chaos, win or lose, her chaos was caused. She won anyway.

Suddenly her beauty was gone. Her glamorous aura was stripped away and her clear sharp lines were shown. She was no woman. She was nothing soft or tender, warm and consoling, supporting and wanting of support, she was only a whore in the worst way. She had used him. Used him to wage this war of chaos. Almost mindless and pointless reasons for anyone but himself, thus creating the most chaos in itself. She had used him with nothing to lose, while he would lose a lifetime of power that he had stored. Wasted possessing a knight, wasted with solidifying enough so that his army could see him long enough to lead them. Wasted! A life time effort wasted on what was promised to be a sure thing! She had used him...Behind his back she had used him, just as he thought he was using her.

She reached up and brushed his tattered robes. "Come down here." She said warmly. "Don't sulk up there." She was warm and fuzzy with softness again. Switching it on and off like her chaotic self.

"I need more." Thamrell whispered.

"What?" She leaned forward. "What else do you need?"

"A guarantee!" He hissed. "I want to walk into Worldsend. I will have my revenge on Okshiru." *And you.*

"You have it all ready lover..." She cooed playfully. "You have it already. What else can I give you?"

"Give me Dave..." He said quietly.

She suddenly sat up. Chaos is chaos, but Dave was out of the question. "I can't." She lied. "I simply can't." She suddenly relaxed in her lie as she eased into the couch again.

"I've spoken to him." Thamrell set his bony jaw. "Right under Trid Dreath the IV's nose." More wasted power. "He is willing. I have sent an agent of mine to infiltrate the Demon Bikers and monitor Trid Dreath and Dave. I can have my boy contact the Meca Demon at once. Give me the word."

Her eyes darkened as her sultry smile broadened. "I can't...Okshiru pulled out the rug." She reached beneath one of her pillows and slowly pulled out a blue silk scarf. "He gave the order, and he is the boss..." Slowly she wrapped her wrist in blue silk. "My hands are tied." She cooed and suddenly snapped the scarf into a tight knot about her creamy wrist. She let the dangling end drape as she twisted across the couch and writhed like a snake. The tether of silk caressed against her other wrist as she crossed them. "You can tie me up, if you like." She whispered.

Thamrell looked at her. White film robes flowing like a fog over her china smooth skin, a bright blue tie streaming from her wrist. Her red satin lips blew kisses into the air.

Thamrell had underestimated her too many times. He had underestimated too many things, too many times. Dave would bring him Worldsend. It was guaranteed. He brought it to Hauth the first time. She wasn't going to give it to him because of Okshiru—they were too close to a coup to suddenly start obeying the rules. She could give him Dave, but Dave was too much. The Meca demon would bring her down with the rest of Worldsend. Can't have that.

Was this a precursor to losing the war? If he lost, and she had cheated and helped him against the will of Okshiru, the penalties would be too great to risk. If she did interfere, would Okshiru counter and keep it even, or tip the scales as an example?

It was too late regardless of the consequences for him. He was in too deep. It was only onward for him. He had the power, only a fool would hesitate and fail knowing for the rest of existence that he had failed with the might of Hel behind him. Frito went into hiding from a family who understood that it wasn't his fault. Thamrell had nothing save his great pit of despair. He could do it, he could take Worldsend. Even if the entire thing was Okshiru's plot to purge his sin riddled knights, Thamrell could not fail. The god of despair had the might of Hel against a limited and quickly assembled army of Roc. Even with the Dragoncaller and the Ninefingers, there was no possible way that Thamrell could fail unless Okshiru blatantly crossed his own word and interfered. If Okshiru did, and the whole pile of wax melted before his eyes, he could quietly live out the rest of time knowing that Okshiru had to cheat to beat him.

Regardless of that, he would still tromp on Mortalroam. Roc would die, Craig would die, Frito would die…Somebody would die. Somebody would pay. He was going to take his revenge on somebody. Who ever was in the way, was going to buy it, plain and simple. Cornerstone; the bright shining peasant city of Cornerstone would be crumbled and the mortals will sing in legend a thousand years from this day how the great Thamrell, God of Despair, humbled the Dragonslayer, destroyed the Dragoncaller, enslaved the Devilslayer and leveled Cornerstone. Mortals sang that way. They would remember him.

Thamrell smiled as he lowered gently to the couch. The silk band tied itself at his command, binding her wrists. He could feel her hot damp breath on his dead cold cheek. His hollow eyes smiled at her— smiled with the teeth of the great Meca Demon from the pits of oblivion. Once he gained Cornerstone, he thought, once he tapped it's Poer, he would do the opposite and not attack Worldsend. The god of despair thought to himself. He would use the magical might in Cornerstone and free the Meca demon.

He hadn't thought of that until the very moment that his dead lips fell upon hers.

Then you'd all be fucked. He thought. *Wouldn't you. I can't lose.*

Chapter 70

Kemoto looked from the great sky of Okshiru at Mortalroam spanning below him. The golden sun bird watched as Fikor and Hauge dashed quickly across the land. It was Fikor's season, but the face of the earth was still covered with Chinook's Autumn. It was dried, browning but it still breathed with life.

The great god looked to the rivers and watched the war ships of the Dragonslayer sail with full sails through the narrow rivers bringing with them troops and supplies. Kemoto looked ahead to the west and from his height he could see the battle fields. A series of battle zones, each one mapped and orchestrated to give the Dragonslayer the most advantage in the up coming war. He watched Gorn, a human, Roc's number one, give directions to the preparations. Beside him was Fryto, the flame, Knight of Okshiru complemented to Meleki. Fryto was directing a special team to prepare hoses to squirt a concoction that The Dragoncaller had whipped up. Napalm it was called.

Roc stood on a high tower preparing his command signals. Standing beside him unseen was Dru, the goddess of death. "Getting a good seat?" Kemoto called down to her.

She looked at him coldly. She looked at everything coldly. "Tell me sun god. Have you seen my knight?"

Kemoto shook his head. "No."

Dru looked away coldly and waited for the mayhem to begin.

Kemoto sailed on overhead watching as other gods stepped in to watch the festivities. Ura was nowhere to be seen.

He looked around, and far below he could see the dark forests of Dacova and pushing out from it were three beings. Two men and one Woman. He recognized the two men as the Hammerstrike twins. The woman he knew not.

The bright wings of Kemoto blinded J'son's dim eyes and pained him. He raised his arm in defense but he could feel the warm light bathe his thinly clothed skin. In the forests of Dacova elves can feel the cold. That was over, Dacova was passed and Kemoto's warm glow was welcome.

"We're out of the Forests already!" J'son exclaimed pausing to let Cassandra rest. "That was fast."

J'cob nodded. He knew why. "Forest walk." He said simply. "Rabbit at large."

J'son looked at him but let it go. He tended to Cassandra at his side. He set the boda to her lips and let her finish the last of the demon wine. "You'll be alright." He whispered to her.

She nodded feebly and attempted to smile. J'son and J'cob were the only two people other than Friska to be nice to her.

J'cob used the last of his water to wash her burns and blisters and then used the last dabs of Thatch to take out some of the pain of her wounds. "Never a knight around when you need one." He muttered. "What happened to her any way?"

"They were roasting her on a spit when you showed up. I was going to mention it to Friska, but every time I opened my mouth I got the butt end of a pole-arm in the teeth." J'son glared at his twin. "Why did you do it, me?" He said suddenly serious. "Why did you break our pact? You could have been killed!"

J'cob shook his shoulders. "Because you would've."

J'son looked away as a grin pushed past his efforts to hide it. "Besides that."

J'cob smiled and tossed the finished tin of Thatch over his shoulder. He stood up and scanned the sky. "Lets go, Me." He pointed to the star above.

"Why are we following that star?" J'son helped Cassandra to her feet.

Again J'cob shrugged. "It led us out of the forest."

J'son moved on and J'cob followed. The mountains flashed about him and the forest walk bent distances around them. They both knew that by the time Kemoto had finished his flight they would be at Roc's reported front lines.

Kemoto sailed on to the west and watched the shadows stretch into black lines below him. He flew out over Okshiru's great sea until its edge and set down below it. He knew that before he rose again, Mortalroam would be at war.

Chapter 71 (Whew!)

Soft quilted sheets caressed her cheeks with warmth. Her elvish ears listened to Leatha quietly pass outside of her window. Neathina played her pipes with one hand and with the other stroked her head with gentle fingers of starlight. Hauge was tranquil and his winds had settled.

A chilling fang filled the air as the fire in its place shrank into darkness. The child of the gods rolled in her bed. Her little legs kicking out as her head bobbled on the pillow. Tiny whimpers filled the dark room. Frost, like thin puffs of clouds, curled about on her lips.

Her eyes flashed open and silence thundered in her ears. She lifted to a sitting position counting the rasping breaths in her lungs.

Her eyes flared silver and glared into the room. Two eyes stared bleakly back at her. A chilling finger of ice pushed into her centre. Her knuckles wrung tightly the quilts of her bed. Her voice was gone. Her glowing eyes of silver trembled behind the soft white cheeks of her face.

The eyes came closer. They told her not to fear and her fear was gone. She could hear the giggle of winter loom closer as the eyes came upon her. Her hand pushed out before her. Her bone china skin was a dead white, bathed in the light of Neathina's star. Her fingers pushed into the chilling fur of the snow dog's coat. It was coarse and itchy as she caught a firm hold on his heavy collar. His snout pushed gently into her belly and with a gentle roll, she landed firmly on his back.

Hauge suddenly leapt to the sill and the windows were flung open. Outside there was only the silence of the night and the cold of Fikor's winter. The child of the gods turned and lay her belly flat on the snow dog's back. His scratchy fur tickled her chin and she held with both hands to his heavy leather collar. She felt the snow dog shift and step to the window and with a heaving leap, dashed quickly into the sky.

Fanrealm quickly fell behind as did all of Mortalroam. Her head suddenly rose to the height of Neathina's stars. She could see the round disk of the earth below. Ovam, the obese moon god hung just slightly off the lip of the disk. She could see him wave with gentle beams of moon light. The child of the gods waved back.

Hauge had found a cloud and pushed it near. Fikor gently set down in the great waves of cloud. He bowed and the child of the god slipped off the white snow dog into the white snowy cloud glowing with white radiance from the white light cast down from Neathina's bright white star.

A black rider on a black mount stepped into reality from the black cloak of Leatha's night. Black hooves pushed down the fluff of the white cloud and it silently moved closer. The child of the gods held tightly onto the leg of the snow dog. She watched, with the eyes of a child, the black rider. The black horse took slow purposeful steps towards her. The child of the gods recognized the black rider as the Devilslayer. She didn't fear the Devilslayer.

A woman slid out from behind the Devilslayer and dropped down from the horse to the cloud. Her bare feet sank into the white cloud. She wore tattered clothes that couldn't hide the bruises and scars that adorned her. Her short black hair was matted with dried mud and blood. Her body was rank with days of sweat and urine. She had the stink of Hel about her. This woman, the child of the gods was afraid of.

The woman came forward. Her eyes of silver glared like stars at the child of the gods. Fikor bent and nudged the child at his leg forward. First with a gentle push, then again with a bit more. The girl took a few steps forward and looked at the woman that stood above her.

Fikor gently howled with a cry into the night. White skirts of ghosts swirled to his command. Tiny figures of humans, lifelike in every detail, took shape and performed for the great god of winter. Their flesh was as the snow, white and unblemished. Their costumes were ice and flowed like white silk as they pantomimed their review.

The child's name in the elven tongue was Northern Sun. In the ancient tongue she was Stephanie. She took to the elvish art of Sho-Pa and ascended as Knight of Lord Okshiru complemented to Fikor, god of winter. Her knightly name was Fantista. She wed and loved the Supergod known most commonly as Lord Hammerstrike. The lady fought beside her Lord for almost a thousand years, through the great demon wars and was appointed the Grandmaster of Knights. She finally grew old and retired. She and her husband settled down and bore seven children. Six were boys and one a girl. The girl's name was Denice.

Denice was thought lost at the age of eighty. For years the family of Hammerstrike searched for their little sister. During the search, the eldest son was killed, the second, lost a finger and earned his right as a Knight of Okshiru and was complimented to Uko, god of lighting and his knightly name was Frito. The Supergod ascended into Worldsend.

Denice was returned and the Supergod was never seen again. Denice had also ascended to the order of knights and was complimented to Fikor to replace her mother who was now complimented to Neathina and Shegatesu. Denice's knightly name was Frita. Since Denice had returned home as a knight, it was assumed that Okshiru had taken her and no questions were asked.

The third and fourth brothers soon ascended to the Order. The third to Kemoto and the fourth to Hauge. Fryto and Friska.

Fikor the Snow Dog blew at the performers and they scrambled like the mist and reformed. Their story was turned back to the disappearance of Denice. While her brothers set out to find her, she was taken by goblins off to the sea and sold as a slave. She was immediately purchased for a high price by a witch woman who then gave her to the Knight of Ura. His knightly name was Paradox. Paradox loved her and she bore him a child. But Ura hated the child. She feared that Paradox would love the child more than herself. So she drove Denice out of the House by the Sea. The god of Chaos swore to take the baby but Denice outsmarted her when the child was born. Denice held the newborn child in the river and drowned her and buried her so Ura would never find her. Denice named the child her after her grandmother, Stephanie. But the snow dog had been watching and took the child from the cold ground and took her to the house of Oustrand. He swore the farmer to secrecy and laid the belief on the people of the town that the child was in fact the daughter of Oustrand.

Denice wandered the land believing her child was dead and went to throw herself from a mountain into Okshiru's sea, but the great god of the Sky and Sea took her made her a knight.

The dancers faded like the mists they were and were gone from the cloud. Slowly the little child walked from the gods that had kept her until now and went to her mother. The child was swept into strong arms and her cold face was pushed against her mother. She could feel dirt and grime on her flesh. The warmth of her mother's embrace filled her with life. She could hear within her mother's centre the anguished wail of a mother lost and the joyous cry of a child found.

The black horse snorted and Denice looked away to the rider. Denice then looked at her child and she smiled at her. She then looked up to the snow dog who was looking down at her. She lifted her child and placed her on the white dog's back. The child didn't want to go but her mother bade her. The child of Denice watched as her mother mounted in front of the Devilslayer. The horse then turned and stepped out of reality.

Fikor leapt from the cloud and fell to the earth with the child of Denice clinging tightly to him. She looked to the east and saw Shegatesu preparing for her dawn. With a single leap, he was in her bedroom and gently lay her in bed. He bade the covers to tuck her in and touched her white cheek with his black wet nose to bid her Goodnight and Goodbye. Then the great snow dog leapt out of the window and it closed behind him.

The door opened and Lady Fantista glided into the room. She quickly and gently came to her bed side. She pulled the covers closer about her.

"I...saw my mommy." Stephanie said finally.

Fantista looked at her and smiled. "It was a dream." She whispered knowing that it wasn't.

Stephanie glanced out of the window and then back to Lady Fantista. "She is coming back soon."

Lady Fantista nodded. "Yes, she will, and now you must sleep."

Suddenly the little girl's eyes wanted nothing more than to close. She gave a final look out of the window. She felt the gods that had watched over her for her whole life lift away to another land far away. Her centre pushed out, for part of her wanted to go with them, but she knew that this was now her home, and this is what she wanted.

She drifted quietly and quickly to a sound sleep. Thimbra, Mistress of Dreams and Thumber's despised half sister, gave the little child of Denice lovely dreams through out the night.

Chapter 72

Ovam, the obese moon god had slipped quietly below the lip of Mortalroam. Neathina danced her dance along the rim of Okshiru's sky. Her stars were set all along the edge of the sky and the brilliant cluster that she set high above gleamed brightly. Hauge swept past her and into the valley below. The god of wind brushed over the crisp grass fields and frost covered lands through Seeda gully and along the trail of Tashwalk. He climbed the steep sloping hill towards Fanrealm.

The big red dragon lifted his head when he felt the wind rush by him. Brezhnev didn't like the cold. He didn't like it at all. The red dragon sighed a long patient breath and looked above. Boxy circled over head. It was rather unnecessary to have Boxy as a watch. Brezhnev was one of the few dragons who could initiate a dragon call instead of waiting for the Dragoncaller to call him. He knew exactly where Craig was.

But he had to give the young black dragon something to do. Black dragons were always bad at waiting.

Boxy turned and fell from the sky. He swept and pulled at ten paces and licked back into the air. 'He's here!' He announced in growling dragon tongue.

Brezhnev grunted and settled lower. He knew that long ago. The red looked to the sky. He could see the silver glinting shine sparkling in the star light. The scaleless silver dragon glided gracefully down to the tall, dried, grasses and slowed to a stop. She crawled on all fours towards the big red. On her back, Craig Tyrone, the Dragoncaller, was nestled and sound asleep. Grace turned her head and nudged him. Craig stirred with one eye half open and looked about the dark field. Glowing eyes of Dragons all looked back down at him. 'Toto?' He mumbled. '*I know this ain't Kansas.*' He rolled up, folding his legs as he did. '*Okay, the Barchetta is in place. All we have to do now, is do it. Hit the runway boys.*' He slid from Grace's smooth back and gave her a light pat.

Moxy and Windshmere were the first in the air and Roderhamerdril was next.

Craig looked to the giant red. The great dragon glistened in the star light. He was oiled. Probably just took a bath. The first thing dragons loose with age was the ability to keep their own hides smooth. The red looked at him.

'*What?*' Craig asked as he pulled on his leather pilot's cap.

'*Two things.*' Brezhnev grunted. '*The first, take a look at my right rear.*'

Craig tossed his white silken WWI Flyers scarf theatrically over his shoulder as he passed to the dragon's rear. From the narrow of the tail, Craig could see over the dragon. '*What's with your wing.*' Craig pointed over Brezhnev's tail. The wing was draped across the ground.

'*My rump if you please.*' The red grunted.

Craig looked up and saw that Alisa and Dore were in the air before he looked over the dragon's rump. He ran his hand over the oily scales. '*There's something here.*' Craig lifted under the large scale and slid his hand gently underneath. Suddenly Craig yanked his hand out. '*Yeow! How long has he been up there?*'

'*I don't know, but get him out!*'

Craig shook his head. '*You should have done this earlier.*' He said as he reached under again with both hands.

'*I tried, but the oil bath didn't work....Ahh, you got him. He's digging in.*'

'*He's putting up a fight. My god he's huge!*'

'*Hurry!*'

'*Stop your crying. I hate it when dragons cry.*' Craig gave a sudden pull and the black fuzzy BEM came sliding out. Its little claws dragging on the red dragon's thick hide. It was the size of Craig's head and writhed in his grip with more flailing legs than he cared to count. Craig dropped it into the grass and it took off like a shot.

'*Thank you.*' Brezhnev said quite relieved.

'*I didn't know they got that big.*' Craig mumbled as the fuzzy BEM made its way through the grass. '*Okay...What's two?*' He said looking up.

Brezhnev folded his dragging wing and crawled towards the take off run way. Craig looked at the giant heated trough where the red dragon had been laying. His wife, dog and cat laid in a bundle of blankets where they had been hidden under the red's wing. Craig dashed over and her head lifted slowly as he approached her. The cowl of her robe slipped back and her beautiful face seemed to glow in the starlight. Dried white tracks of tears lined her face. She leaned and lifted and gripped his arm for balance as she stood. With out a word she wrapped her arms about him and kissed him very deeply. She then pulled her robes closer and waddled towards the manor. Craig caught her shoulder and turned her about. She was crying again. "We never had our wedding." She said in a small voice.

"We'll have it soon." He whispered.

Her eyes widened. "But your dream, your dreams always come true."

"I'll be back." Craig said in a low voice. "Or I'll die trying. Remember our motto. Impossibility is our specialty." He kissed her again and then pulled her robes about her. "Miracles at half price." He turned and looked at the silver dragon. *'Take care of her.'* Grace nodded.

Craig quickly mounted Kugerand. The gold watched as the Dragonpanthers and White Tiger Dragons stepped out of reality. The big stupid White Tiger Dragon was now standing next to Neeko. Kugerand looked back. Craig zipped up his leather bomber jacket over his armor.

'Are you aligned about this? I mean, are you cosmic about this scene?' The gold dragon asked.

'When have I not been sure? I'm always sure. Even when I'm not sure, I'm sure.' Craig looked up at the gold dragon.

Kruger shook his head. *'Dude, you are too cool for school. Here I am shaking in my scales like a newbie and you're set for a tool in the park.'*

'Yeah? Well, right now I'm so cool I don't know whether to piss or go blind. My question is, are you sure? You know what's going to happen.'

'Hey man, that's all part of the game you know?' Kuger looked to the sky. *'Like, I guess it would be, you know, major bonus points to die with the Dragoncaller himself.'*

Craig nodded thoughtfully as the dream flashed like a kaleidoscope his head. It didn't sit with him as other dreams did. With his dreams, he had to interpret them. Although there were no right answers, he felt comfortable with an interpretation if he was on the mark. He wasn't comfortable, but he never saw his own death before either. *'I have never run scared and I won't now.'*

'But the dream?'

'What of it? Its funny, when I first came to this world and decided to stay, I had a dream where I saw my daughter. That's how I knew she would be a she even before Neeko was pregnant. So now, I have two conflicting dreams. No, avoiding it is not the way, only controlling the outcome.'

'Can you do it?'

'What can I not do? I am the Dragoncaller! Twenty four hours a day, seven days a week and twice on Sunday's. Now lets hit the air before I realize what I am doing.'

'Then lets jam!'

"Hi Ho Bullion!" He shouted into the star lit night. "Awaaaaaay!"

Neeko watched the big gold dragon raise on his haunches with his fore fists pawing the air. The dragon suddenly leapt into the air and took off over seventh brother mountain. Neeko leaned on Grace's giant fingers. The silver dragon had clasped her hands about the Ne-arri healer to keep her from rushing the Dragoncaller. Grace could tell that Craig would not have gone if Neeko lost her composure. Grace knew that Craig had to go.

Neeko wept openly against the dragon, her tears steaming in the cold.

She gasped. Pain tore through her as something opened from within her. She looked to Onary with horror. "What is happening?" She cried as pain swept over her again. "What is wrong with me?" Her hands crossed her belly and pain waved again. "Ooops. This is the proverbial it. What timing!"

Grace gently swept around and lifted Neeko into her paw. The silver dragon lowered her wing as a ramp and Onary the dog and Edia the cat quickly dashed up the silver wing onto her back. The dragon took easily to the air and sailed towards the manor. Abacromby, the White Tiger Dragon, pulled in his tongue, spread his wings and followed close behind.

Chapter 73

Shouts and hoots broke Leatha's night. Fires blossomed in the cold, dark air where the mortals took their military stand. Horns sounded and flags waved. Men stood at their posts, some in fighting holes and some behind shield walls. They rubbed their weapons for warmth and comfort as they shifted about nervously waiting. The old timers counted the moments with casual passing. The new recruits trembled, listening to every sound as the word to go. Elves and humans could clearly see the fields before them from the gentle star light that fell from Neathina's new star.

Shadows fell from the night flyers in the sky, backlit by the new star. Spell casters pointed and the demonic scouts suddenly gleamed with magic and archers pumped magic tipped shafts into them until the fuzzy furry flyers dropped from the sky. Gorn's great magical bow hummed and a bloody streak rocketed the sky and a flyer burst into flames and crashed into the earth.

"More flyers." Roc grunted leaning against the rail of his command tower. "They're here."

Gorn nocked another shaft and kept it at the ready. "Yes. They'll attack at any time."

Roc stood up. "You'll have the helm and give the signals. Remember, light contact..."

"And fall back." Gorn recited. "I know the plan. They'll over run us if we let them. They'll have enough trouble crossing this field with all the traps we've laid for them."

Roc shook his head. "The traps in this field are for their machinery. It will slow them up long enough for a dragon to toast the place."

"Is Craig going to show? I don't see any sign of..." A flyer suddenly light up with magic. "Excuse me my lord." Gorn said and he drew to fire.

The flyer suddenly ignited in brilliant, pale green flames. It screamed with its unearthly voice and dropped from the sky. A giant beast of black swooped under the flaming fuzzy furry flyer and with a swat sent it back up into the air. A second black flying beast appeared into reality over head and caught the flaming fuzzy furry flyer and with its big black paws, tore it to shreds and sent its burning bits to the ground below.

Gorn watched the horror. He could clearly see the beast in the pale green light. Giant white fangs hung from its grinning mouth and silver whiskers pushed from its snout. Giant black leathery wings held it in the air. "Are these the Dragon-panthers you ordered?" Gorn looked to Roc as he released the tension on his bow. The Dragonslayer nodded. "Then the Dragoncaller is near by."

"And so is Ferris." Roc said quietly looking to the lightening sky. "Good luck, Craig." Roc then turned back to his second. "Shegatesu is coming. We will be starting soon."

Along the battle field. Dragon-panthers and White Tiger Dragons stepped into reality. The men had been warned to expect them, and they stepped from the horrible beasts to allow them all the room they wanted. The newbies feared them because they knew nothing about these monsters. The old timers feared them because they knew everything about them.

Horns sounded and Roc listened to the elfcalls. Gorn saw the magic lights. A lone demon walked, slowly and unarmed, across the battle field. He didn't break stride when the magic lights fell upon him.

Gorn leaned over to Roc. "An envoy?"

Roc nodded and stepped from the tower. His frame swung over the railing and slowly stepped down the ladder. A runner quickly pushed his weapons at him and helped him strap them on. Roc took his dragon helm and pulled it on. He cracked his knuckles with a crisp staccato and then pulled on his gauntlets. The runner held his mount steady as he swung into his saddle.

He looked out over the men looking up at him. His eyes burned with a comfortable green. He took a deep breath of the Fikor's frosty air. As he let it out, he watched the mist float before him. He reveled in the thought that Hauge didn't dare cross the battle field. Roc the Dragonslayer smiled under his mask. It was going to be a good day.

"From Dawn's rising light,
A star shining bright.
Through Dru's house a flood,
of dying mortal's blood.
A ringing call from Hel,
Sounding out a bell.

Harper sing and piper sound,
Give the call for men around.
Time to fight the demon foe,
Dragon fly and soldier go!"

Roc's mount set to a trot and headed to the front line, watching the illuminated demon walk casually closer. Roc waited. Beside him, a Dragon-panther stood.

The demon stopped at a stone's throw and waited. Roc dismounted and stepped forward. "Come closer, I'm not going to shout." Roc said in a voice loud enough to be heard.

The demon came closer. He was a spindly thing, with his head perched upon a thin crooked neck. His spectacles of wire and glass, probably a prized possession, were perched on his long thin crooked nose. His thin eyes sparkled in the star light and flashed as they shifted back and forth. He stood boldly at the height of the slayer's chest.

"I am Outh, the ambassador from Hel."

"So?" Roc said simply.

"I have been endowed with a message from Thamrell, the commanding general of the United League of Monsters, Demons and Things From Hel." He spoke in his whinny voice.

Roc folded his arms and drummed his fingers impatiently.

Outh went on. "He has mercifully granted you this opportunity to surrender your armies on the conditions that: the men will be executed in a totally agonizing way and eaten, the children enslaved and raised as beasts of burdens and the women impregnated with demon spawn."

Roc waited, but Outh was finished. Roc paused and mulled the option in his mind and carefully selected the proper diplomatic words to use. "You're out of your fucking mind, Right?"

Outh bowed slightly. "His greatness Lord Thamrell expects an answer promptly."

With a graceful, fluid motion, Roc's gigantic armored hand reached out and gently plucked Outh's glasses from his face. Roc regarded the artifact perched in his finger tips as he mulled about on a proper answer to send to Thamrell. The lenses caught the light of the Neathina's star as Roc held them, turning them back and forth.

Roc smiled as he balled it up in his gauntleted fist. The sound of glass crushing in his palm were clearly heard. He then reached out and dropped the wad of wire and broken glass into Outh's astonished outstretched hand.

His answer, not yet done, he turned slightly and called over his shoulder. "Uh, Rellik?"

Rellik, who was standing by a weapons rack stood taller. "M'lord?"

Roc draped his hand casually over his shoulder. "My number four answer." He said decidedly. Rellik quickly selected the number four answer and placed it into Roc's hand. Roc tested the weight of the large hand ax, waving it casually while his softly glowing green eyes took in the demon. He looked at his answer. He twirled it and its chipped but keen edge caught the star light.

"I am the Envoy..." Outh began. "Of the commanding general of the United League of Monsters, Demons and Things From Hel..." He reminded the slayer. "You wouldn't da-"

With a thin whistle and a slight metallic ring, Outh's head rolled about in the dirt gagging on his own demonic blood. Roc looked at the dripping, smoking, demon blood on the blade of his axe. After determining that his ax hadn't been damaged, he held it out for Rellik. "My whips." He said in a low voice. Rellik quickly exchanged the ax and placed Roc's special three lashed whip in his hand.

With a sudden crack the Dragonhide whip came to life and wrapped itself about the demon head on the ground and pulled it into the air with a spin. Roc cracked the whip again and lashed the spinning head into his arms.

Roc held up the head by its thin, stringy hair. Stripes lined Outh's face. "You'll rue this act!" The demon whined in a harsh whisper.

Roc seized the demon's body and pulled it closer. He spat into the bleeding neck and shoved the head into its mid-section. "Take that to Thamrell."

The demon stumbled back fumbling its head. It held the head higher up and it shouted back. "You'll rue this!" It whined and stumbled again.

Roc cracked his whip and Outh suddenly jumped back with quick jerky steps. The demon took faster steps backwards afraid of turning his back on the Slayer. It stumbled again and fumbled its head. It quickly grouped for it, found it, and headed back to the forests of Dacova. "You'll Rue!" It turned its head around to shout back as it ran at full speed and fell into a pit trap.

"And watch were you're running!" Rellik shouted after it. The men were laughing. Laughing loudly. Roc knew it was good to laugh. Laugh the fear from their centres. He watched as Outh tossed his head out of the pit and then pulled himself from the hole. The thin demon shook a fist at them before gathering its head and running off, this time carefully watching were it ran.

Roc smiled. "Here it begins."

<u>Chapter 74</u>

'Stand by for target acquisition.'

Okshiru's great sky began to lighten as Shegatesu mixed her colors of blush to paint the sky.

'Target...target...who's got the Target?'

The wind pushed about him like the tide, surrounding him, tugging at his silk scarf. The fur on his jacket tickled one side of his face, the other side was still too numb to feel.

'Four minutes to FEBA. We're looking a little hot. All calls will be early, I say again. All calls will be early.' The Red Dragon's deep resonating commands came clearly through the dragoncall.

He could feel the muscles of the gold dragon sliding beneath him as he slid across the air. It was comforting, a natural thing.

'Pull it tighter, there might be one who can count.'

He looked to his watch. Soon.

'Klingor Klingor, I say again, we got Foldrop.'

'Wait a minute, who is that? Sopwith?'

'He's making stuff up!'

'Get off the line.'

Craig smiled.

'Morning boys and girls!' He announced cheerfully. *'We have clear skies in our viewing area this morning. As we check the Acuxy for the weekend with only slight patches of early morning fog that should clear up. Our Barometric pressure is steady and our wind chill is at negative 20 for a brisk morning so cover up. Taking a look at our five day forecast, we see clear but cold skies so you elves can plan those picnics for the weekend at the beach. Try to avoid large fields because of rampaging hordes from hell. As for Monday on through, we hope there is one. This weather forecast was brought to you by SunSigns Horoscopes. Aries: Get out and meet new monsters. Pisces: plan that long siege and for us Geminis: Avoid fire breathing 747's.'* Craig looked below. It all looked peaceful from that height. The snow capped mountains were only white lines below. To the east before him he could see the dawn. Shegatesu, youngest of the gods. According to myth, she paints the sky every morning. He wondered how many dawns has she painted over the bleeding battles of man. He quickly shook his head. He didn't need to get poetic. Not now. The beautiful dawn was reminding him of Neeko.

'*Batman, Batman, this is Blackbird, request confirmation on Target acquisition.*'

The black dragon's voice boomed in his head and swept it free. He felt the logic circuits, already warm, kick in and thousands of orderly numbers filed in at his command. Air speed, altitude, time and distance ratios. He plugged into his calculating mind and worked physics formulas in his head and patched them through to his Dragoncall. '*Confirmation on target acquisition.*' He said. He could pick up the enemy like a radar. Sixteen Black dragons. Yearlings. He triangulated, formulated, and calculated to gain their exact position.

'*This is Backfire.*' Brezhnev spoke clearly and slowly. '*By the numbers. Go to weapons free. Patch the dragoncall and pick your targets. Roll 'em and smoke 'em.*'

Craig let Brezhnev do his job as he looked to the sky. Where was he? Craig pushed his dragoncall further out. Where was he? He wasn't immune to the Dragoncall. Craig could feel him. He was somewhere. Where?

'*Stand by, stand by.*' Boxy called.

'*Frisbee,*' Craig said quietly. '*Take to Seven Zero, bearing three zero One. He is close.*'

The gold dragon lifted his nose and sailed to 70,000 feet. The thin air didn't bother Craig. Nothing bothered him while on Dragon back.

'*Where are you Ferris?*' Craig called out. '*Olly Olly Oxen Free!*'

'*I'm right here.*'

Craig whirled about but there was nothing. He adjusted his goggles and tried again. '*Laying quiet or laying scared? I ain't got all day rust breath.*'

'*You are too anxious to die Dragoncaller. You do know that I am going to kill you.*'

Craig smiled. '*I take it then you haven't read the story, Oh, I'm sorry, you can't read. Well it goes like this. Once upon a time the Dragoncaller killed Ferris the Iron Dragon and used him for spare Barchetta parts and lived happily ever after.*'

'*A mortal's story for a mortal's mind. I killed the last Dragoncaller. I ate him. Whole. I'll eat you too.*'

'*What is this fascination with eating mortals?*'

'*Have you ever eaten a monster? Tastes horrible.*'

Craig shook his head. '*Forget I asked.*' Craig looked about and still couldn't see the Metal Monster. '*You wouldn't mind sticking your head out for a second so I can get a clear shot.*'

'*You don't seem to understand. You can't kill me, I am invulnerable. You can't win.*'

'*And yet, here we are.*' Craig looked up. In his mind he could see the beast. His eyes could see a tiny fleck in the sky, his brain could see something at least three times the size of Brezhnev. '*Climb Frisbee. Eight Zero.*' He whispered. '*Fast.*'

'*Since my creation all I've heard was how the Dragoncaller was going to slay me.*' Ferris began his story. Craig could feel him coming closer. '*So I sought him out and the fool challenged me on the ground. There wasn't much of a contest.*' Craig pulled tighter to Kuger as the gold flew higher. '*Where are you going? Dragoncaller?*'

'*Down wind, your breath stinks.*' Craig said casually. '*So you were saying?*'

'*Then after his death, all I heard was how another Dragoncaller was coming and he was going to kill me.*'

Ferris grew closer. His speed was unimaginable. Craig's mental calculator pulled up numbers that couldn't be right. Mach 1.4 had to be a wrong number.

'*Tuck and Duck, Frisbee!*' Kuger banked and dove. Ferris was there suddenly, bigger than life. Kuger slipped like a golden snake beneath him. Craig could see the great inter-working plates on his underside. No chinks, no holes, perfect.

In the sudden pass it was over. The two dragons soared passed each other in the blink of an eye and faster than thought, Ferris was almost out of sight. Craig watched as the Iron dragon lifted and turned as only a tiny dot in the sky. He was coming back.

Tail wind dragged at him suddenly. It was a lions roar as sound caught up with him. He felt it pierce his ears and grip his leather jacket with a tearing force. Kuger was sucked into a sudden whirl wind of backlash. The gold dragon clawed but only leveled in the vacuum.

'*Straight up Frisbee!*' Craig screamed. '*Through the eye. You don't need wind to fly.*'

The Iron Dragon was already there.

The gold dragon twisted like a screw and bored his way higher. The Iron Dragon slashed below them. Kuger climbed higher, pulling out of the backlash all together. '*Higher!*' Craig screamed.

'*Climb as high as you like Dragoncaller!*'' Ferris taunted as he circled around again. '*I thought I had you in the first two passes. You are clever.*' Ferris came about and lifted higher. '*Where are you going now?*' Ferris called after him. '*Don't run away.*'

'*I'm not running, I getting a better view to kill you with.*' Craig said in total honesty.

'*Well then I will join you.*' Ferris called as he pointed his nose straight up and began to climb.

*No...*Craig thought. *This is physically impossible. The altitude is to thin, nothing with wings can lift on it. Dragons are gliders, they can't fly straight up! He can't be flying straight up!*

Craig looked behind him. The Iron Dragon was gaining. '*Faster Frisbee! Faster!*' Craig forced himself to think. *I am flying on a wingless dragon, why am I dwelling on physical impossibilities?*

'*So for eleven thousand years...*' Ferris went on. '*I've waited for you. Even Roc, the mighty Dragon slayer couldn't hurt me.*'

'*But he did put your ass on ice Amigo.*' Craig called as the Bow of Dragoncaller formed in his hand.

'*A minor set back that shall be rectified once I kill you, and I am going to kill you Dragoncaller.*'

'*Yeah? Come get some!*' Craig looked below. He was still climbing too fast. He wasn't going to make it high enough in time.

Kuger flipped over, rolling like a hook straight back down. Craig drew his bow to fire and Ferris was there.

Craig's shaft bounced harmlessly off of a transparent pink disk that popped into reality right before it and vanished again after it was done.

The world exploded with sound as a thousand teeth tore into Craig's flesh. His leather jacket went to the wind. He felt warm water splash up at him, blinding his goggles. Through red lenses he could see sharp teeth of stainless steel.

The earth loomed below. Kuger was twisting in the air trying to level off. Craig's ears rang to loud to sound through the Dragoncall.

'*Did I neglect to mention my new anti-arrow shielding device?*' Ferris hummed in a half sing-song voice.

'*Craig! I mean, Batman, he's got too much juice!*' Kuger called as black dragon's blood ran an thousand lines down his golden scaled coat. He could feel flesh flapping around him. '*Craig what do we do?*' Kuger looked around and could only see the sharp lines of claws upon him. He spun again, turning on himself as he did. His bloody, slippery body slipped neatly through the metal dragon's grasp. He spat his fire at full blast. It erupted like a tide of Kemoto's sun on the metal hide. Mortal armor would melt at a gold dragon's fire, castle walls dried into dust, lakes boiled into steam, but it did nothing to Ferris. Nothing at all.

Craig thought about seat-belts as he fell away. He wiped the blood from his goggles so he could watch as the gold dragon slipped out of Ferris's claws. The Iron dragon's scream could be heard even as they shrank away from him. *That scream*, Craig thought, *At least some laws are working. If we had been at a lower altitude, that sonic scream would have killed us. He's moving so fast he has to be right on top of us for it to work. Perhaps that might have been a better way to die.* He looked to the earth below. Still no recognizable detail yet. He imagined what his body would look like when he hit. He had already reached maximum acceleration and all that was left was to enjoy the ride. He knew that even if he hit water, from that height, he was still going to go splat. He looked up and could only see the red feather of Kuger's fire. He was still fighting to get away from the metal dragon. Who ever built that thing was good. Very good.

He looked to the north. Far below he could see Nagasaki. *Good job boys.* He didn't bother to call them. He knew fully well that at full speed no dragon could reach him. He knew that a Dragon-panther could, but lacked the manual dexterity to catch him at his velocity without shredding him. He was going to die and that was about it.

Why didn't it work? He wondered. *I was too damn certain of physical laws in a world were laws were over ruled in the higher courts by magic.*

He gave a last thought to Kuger as the gold was heading towards mountains trying to use his maneuverability to get away from Ferris. *Good luck Kuger.*

"I love you Neeko."

Gravity was arrested. Air suddenly sucked from Craig's chest in the sudden vacuum. Blood balled and floated around him as giant steel blue hands enveloped him.

"RALPH!" Craig would have screamed had he air in his lungs.

'*No...*' Ralph corrected, hearing his name in the dragoncall. '*Gipper!*'

'*You son of a Bitch!*' Craig screamed in anger and joy. '*I told you to stay home!*'

'*I did...For a while!*' Ralph steadied his flight and raised his fore paws so Craig could climb on his back. '*What Craig do? Craig cannot fly like Gipper. Is falling Craig's plan to fool Ferris? Gipper does not like falling plan.*'

'*Nice catch.*' Craig mumbled. *An air vacuum with his wings*, Craig wondered. *Ralph isn't that smart. It must be instinctive.* '*Frisbee, do you read?*'

'*HEEEELLLP!*'

'*Hey Ferris!*' Craig screamed. "*You big wuss! Leave him alone! I thought you wanted me? I thought you had some guts in that chassis.*'

'*You Live?*' Ferris rumbled as he turned in the air. '*How?*'
'*My God, you must have the Nash Rambler for a brain. I'm the Dragoncaller. We're made of studier stuff.*'
'*I will kill you.*'
'*Hey, Ferris? Bring it on!*' Craig challenged.

He watched the tiny fleck in the sky coming closer. He told Ralph to dive. He watched Ralph's wing. It was holding. He couldn't put to much pressure on it or it would snap. He had to be precise on his next plan.
'*What is next plan?*' Ralph asked.
'*Quiet. I'm thinking.*' Craig looked back. '*Dive faster.*'
'*Dive is easy. Dive is much like falling.*'

The trees were swelling below him. This had to be good. '*Follow that grove,*' Craig pointed. '*Keep it close.*' Craig looked behind. Ferris was at Mach 2.3 in the dive and coming too fast. *Damn-it!* Craig couldn't calculate him. There was always more to him! '*Pull Up!*' He screamed and Ralph took to the sky. Ferris plowed into woods and trees and snapped aside like tinder. Craig watched the Iron Dragon rearing into the sky again, blasting chinks of dirt and rock from his snout with a fiery blast. His metal wings slid with plates and unfolded like metal fans to cup and scoop the wind like the wings of a sweep wing fighter. The Dragon's tail opened with sheaves like an oriental fan.

With a smile, the Iron Dragon screamed again.

The world exploded again. Craig and Ralph were out of range from the dragon's scream, but his skin shivered tightly as if it were shrapnel. The wind tore at his open flesh as Ralph fell to a tail spin. His blue wing was shattered.

The blue dragon didn't scream. His teeth were clenched as he held on to his pain. '*Frisbee!*' He cried as he fell faster trying to pull out of the spin. He arched his tail and planed out but couldn't hold altitude. '*Take Craig! Take Craig now!*'

Craig's ears cleared in time to realize what they were doing. Ralph suddenly bucked and bounced Craig into Kuger's waiting paws. Craig could only scream his orders for Ralph to run as he hung in the gold dragon's grip. Craig's eyes flashed with the dream.

Ralph the blue dragon dove straight at the Iron Dragon. Flaming balls of static belched from Ralph's lungs as lines of white fire danced around Ralph and struck the on rushing iron beast with a flurry of sparks.

Ferris didn't blink.

The two collided head on and Ferris ate him alive.

"No…" Craig whispered. "No…"

'We're outta here.' Kuger turned north and poured on the speed.

Craig knew how he was supposed to die in the dream, running like a coward. *'Bullshit.'* Craig whispered in a daze as the Marine Corps Hymn started to play in his ears.

'What?' Kuger looked down at him.

'Bullshit!' Craig looked up at the gold dragon. *'I'm gonna kill him.'* Craig tore off his shattered goggles. *'I'm gonna murder the bastard!'* Craig twisted and climbed on to Kuger's back. Human and dragon blood made the scaly hide slippery. Craig latched tightly on. *'Climb.'*

'Craig, Man, he is indestructible! Like, look what he did to Ralph!'

'And his sacrifice will not be wasted. Climb, full throttle.'

'We gotta run!'

'We kill him now.' Craig said. *'I'm not running this time. I will not die a coward. This one's for the Gipper!'* He shouted enthusiastically then moaned not believing he said that.

Kuger climbed.

'You don't give up.' Ferris said amazed as he licked his paws clean of Ralph's blood with a hose sucking device. *'I mean, really…'*

'Hey Ferris…' Craig answered. *'You made a mistake, pal, 'cause now this is personal. I am pissed! Just lay down 'cause you're dead.'*

'I'm tired of this Dragoncaller. Give it up.'

'I've been meaning to talk to you about that negative attitude of yours, asshole.'

'You're insane.'

'And you're dead.' Craig could feel Kuger panting beneath him. The gold dragon was exhausted. He wasn't going to make it. Higher they climbed. Ferris didn't grow tired, he grew faster. *'Everything Frisbee.'* Craig whispered to his dragon's ear focusing to block out Ferris. *'They're serving liver back at the ranch. There is nothing to live for! You expected to die…this is it!'*

'My heart is going to like, explode,' The dragon answered as he climbed on. *'You didn't tell me that dying was painful.'*

'Then fight to live.'

'Just to check the current events bulletin board, this plan didn't work before, dude.'

'I was right. Why did Ferris have to open his wings at lower altitudes when he can fly with them closed? Simple, to conserve energy. At higher altitudes, he has to

exert more energy or magic just to stay aloft and I bet if we get high enough, it will drain those Mr Scott mother fucking shields of his. He is weakest up there. Plus, I can use gravity against him.'

'*Man, this had better click!*'

'*It will.'* Craig answered. '*Higher, we have to get above eight zero. Much higher. Beyond one six zero, into the Mesosphere. We have got to use the time Ralph bought for us.'* He said.

Ferris was getting closer.

'*I, I can't man.'*

'*You can. You must. Gimme that turbo-boost. Anything you've been saving, pour it on now. Fly up into the night, you can do it. You must do it.'* Craig could feel the temperature suddenly plummet. A cold that pushed into his elven bones like a thousand needles.

Kuger's eyes rolled into his head as the sky around him suddenly grew dark and the stars of Neatha appeared. '*Is this like, glory?'*

'*The stuff legends are made of.'*

'*Then, let's make history.'*

Kuger flipped and charged head on at the Iron Dragon. The bow flashed in Craig's hands and he drew back. Blood was frozen against his face. His eyes were squinted and all he could see were steel teeth looming at him.

The bow of Dragoncaller sang loud and low. A black stripe lined the sky. A plate of transparent pink flashed before the shaft and shattered as the shaft punched through pushed into the Iron Dragon's eye. It roared and Craig felt the wall of sound hit him but the air was too thin for much of an effect. He was already in motion as bow changed to sword.

The final pass.

Ferris, the Iron Dragon soared upward. A hole in his left eye like a fat black spider nestled in the center of his web. Kuger rolled and twisted like a screw beneath the Iron Monster. The gold dragon dashed by the flashing steel teeth and claws of the Iron Dragon. Craig lashed out with his awesome sword. Without magic shields, power sliced into the invincible hide like paper. Plates of torn metal littered the air.

It was unnecessary to do that, and Craig realized it as he grabbed on to his dragon again. His arrow propelled not only by his bow, but also by the added velocity of Kuger and sucked by the gravity of mother earth without the friction of air, had bored into the Iron Dragon's heart. Ferris was dead.

The metal monster's wings locked. The dragon began to tip to one side and slowly arc away from the sky and sail to the ground. Smoke poured out of his torn belly leaving a thick, gray, puffy tear in the sky as he headed down.

"Just Like That!" Craig screamed as he released his sword and it vanished. He looked to the earth spinning at him again and flicked the frozen blood from his chin. *'Uh, Frisbee? I don't want to pry, but, why are we still diving?'* Craig waited politely for an answer but there was none coming. *'Hey!'* Craig patted an armored hand on Kuger's neck. *'Anybody home? Frisbee? That is earth and it is coming up at a really bad rate. Come on Frisbee, don't be dead. It would be a major bogey for both of us if you were dead. Frisbee, oh, Frisbee, we're not done yet.'*

Craig pulled his head and held it tightly to Kuger's neck. *'We gotta write the story. We gotta tell the world about Ralph, and how we…we kicked metal ass.'* Craig looked ahead to the earth below. It seemed that gravity was going to finally have its way with the law defying dragon.

Craig smiled. In spite of himself, he smiled. He was going to die this time on the back of his faithful gold dragon. Appropriate, he thought. The legend would have the gist of the story. Dragoncaller slays Ferris the Iron Dragon. But beyond that, Craig predicted, the story would be distorted beyond recognition. *'They will probably have us fly off into the sunset.'* Craig said as he looked to the raising sun. *'Or close to it. Something glorious. Something that your son, or daughter, will look back on with pride. They'll name a constellation after us. Kugerand, the gold dragon forever flying the night sky.'*

Kuger belched and his eyes flickered. *'What are you like, talking about man?'*

'Kuger?' Craig looked down at the dragon's head and could see the dragon's eyes moving. *'You son of a BITCH! You're alive!'*

'Who said other wise?'

Craig looked down below. It was no longer earth, but a forest. He could easily make out terrain features and the hard rocky surface they were going to hit into. *'My apologies oh great gold dragon.'*

'You want something. Like, you only call me oh great gold dragon when you, you know, want something.' Kuger replied.

'Yes…' Craig said urgently. *'I don't want to alarm you, but we are still diving and we are about to make our last impressions in this world. I thought you might want to fix your hair or something.'*

524

Kuger had noticed the ground rushing up at him before, but he really didn't pay it any mind. '*Oh.*' He said.

'*OH!*' Craig repeated. '*Do you mind if I ask what you meant by "OH"?*'

'*Uh, like, no, I don't mind at all man.*'

Craig banged his head against Kuger's neck for lack of anything better to do. '*Okay,*' He said to the dragon's neck. '*What did you, Kugerand the Gold Dragon, mean when you, Kugerand the gold dragon, said, "OH"?*'

'*I can't pull up.*' Kuger said quickly and desperately. '*I can't pull out of the dive man.*'

There was a long pause in Craig's brain. In spite of everything, killing of Ferris, the war, and now, threatening to crash into the ground, his brain found it a perfect time to dwell on the idea of "can't".

'*Can't...You can't.*' Craig said very slowly and very carefully as he brain started working. '*Can't is a frame of mind Kuger.*' Craig was almost cooing to the dragon. '*You can't because you think you can't.*' Craig closed his eyes to avoid looking at the world below him now larger than life. '*Things are done on wanna's...*' He opened his eyes because he was getting sick with them closed. '*Gold dragon's have no damn wings, but they fly, you know why? I bet you don't. They fly because they "Wanna". "I wanna fly!" They say as they leap into the air, so they fly. Kuger, Put your fucking nose in the god damn air and soar like a bird or pal...*' Craig let go and his sword appeared in his hands. '*Your gonna be fritters before you hit the ground just because I "wanna"!*'

'*Okay man.*' Kuger grit his teeth and folded his brows back. '*Hold on cause, I don't "wanna" be fritters.*'

Craig's sword vanished and he gripped Kuger's mane with both hands. He could feel through his legs as the gold dragon open his gills and fill his lungs with rushing air. The gold dragon let his eyes close and thought flying thoughts. Craig buried his face in the furry gold mane and also thought flying thoughts.

Kuger grunted. He fluttered his tail and balked his head suddenly in the steam of rushing air. He balked again but this time with less effect. The gold dragon looked below at the rising earth. '*I...Man, I can't do it!*' Kuger screamed at the ground. '*I'm too weak, I'm exhausted!*'

'*You'll be dead in a minute, that will take care of any exhaustion.*' Craig looked up but not at the ground below, but to Kuger's head. '*The stuff that legends are made of.*' Craig hissed. '*Tell your own damn tale. You can walk away from this. Fly away at any rate. Brezhnev can't even boast that.*' Craig now looked to the ground below. '*Remind Brezhnev every time he calls you young pup just who dispensed with the Iron Dragon.*' Craig leaned closer and whispered. '*For Grace. For her unborn pup.*' *For my unborn child.* '*You wanna see if?*' *I do.* Craig smiled and felt his teeth dry in the quick air. '*Last chance at glory.*'

Kuger opened his gills and let air fill not his lungs, but his blowholes. He felt sudden dragon fire roar in his heart. He snorted and flames licked at his squinting gold eyes. He pulled suddenly and balked at the air, his great tail thrashed at the air with a whip and a snap and the great gold dragon suddenly defied the law of gravity and pulled from his sudden dive with a billowing, flaming roar!

His eyes were white and a giant smile was etched on his snout that showed all of his teeth. Fire spilled from between the spaces of his razor sharp fangs like water and ran down his golden belly.

Kugerand the Gold Dragon had pulled from his dive and in doing so, formed a sudden vacuum that sucked the wind from his lungs. The sudden loss hit his tiny brain like a smithy's hammer and slammed him into unconsciousness. The gold dragon fainted again.

Craig looked at the ground again rushing at him and only shook his head. "fuck." He mumbled.

Warm wind suddenly swirled around him. Giant pillows of the air suddenly buffeted and tossed him and his dragon like toys. Craig's legs clamped tighter to Kuger as he tried to ride out the sudden turbulence. Kuger's eyes suddenly flashed and opened as the abrupt arrest of his fall brought him back to his senses. The gold dragon pawed the air and caught hold. He pulled himself and the Dragoncaller back into the air.

Craig could feel the sudden warm air around him. The sun was suddenly shadowed around him. Brimstone made his eyes tear.

Brezhnev's great sweeping wings curled around them forming a gentle pocket of air for the gold dragon to fly upon. '*Well young pup, mind explaining just what are you doing?*'

Kugerand shook his head to clear it. In the lower atmosphere his bloody wounds were bleeding again. '*Hey man, you're like, stressin' me!*' Kuger felt blood filling his mouth and evaporating into black steam that trailed from the corner of his mouth. '*Man, We dissed Ferris! Like, crash and burn man!*'

'*So I guessed.*' Brezhnev rumbled. '*You'll be an absolute delight to live with for the next millinium.*' Brezhnev looked down at Craig who was huddled tightly on the gold dragon's back. *'I heard Ralph go down. I'm sorry. Damn my age, there was no way I could have reached in time.'*

'I know.' Craig mumbled into Kuger's neck. *'I know...Damage report.'*

'Backfire is unscathed but low on fuel. A few scratches with the yearlings,'

'Backfire ate a yearling!' Punjab announced brightly.

'Whole.' Dore commented.

'Hey!' Brezhnev grunted. *'He was flying right at me!'*

'Go on.' Craig said without raising his head.

'Tomcat got a little roughed up with the yearlings. Blackbird had a pretty bad run in and Corsair had to pull him out.'

Craig slowly lifted to a sitting position and looked over to the black female. *'What happened?'*

'I hid a hommand dower.' Boxy answered. *'Whid by dose.'*

Craig shook his head. *'Anything else?'*

'Gold star for Phantom. The Silver terror. If it didn't belong in the air, He took it out.'

Craig looked at the small Silver dragon. Windshmere tried to hide a smile.

'Hope you don't mind me saying boss.' Brezhnev spoke. *'But you look like Woffda.'*

Craig looked over head at the red dragon. He could see pockmocks and black spots where ineffective demon magic tried to penetrate his impenetrable hide. Brezhnev had spent most of his energy defending himself and the others from magic. *'What is, woffda?'*

'When a dragon takes an air borne crap, it's the sound it makes when it hits a dwarf below.'

'Woffda.' Craig mumbled wondering if dragons aimed specifically for dwarves.

'What I am asking,' Brezhnev went on. *'Is do you want to continue with part two of the plan?'*

Craig nodded and then buried his face in Kuger's mane again.

Brezhnev shook his huge head with doubt. The Dragoncaller was much to weak to go flying about, let alone driving into battle. But he was the Dragoncaller, and he called the shots. *"Phantom, On me. The rest of you hiaku to the sweet city and rendezvous. I'll be along shortly.'*

The red dragon banked slightly to the left and watched the others lift to higher altitudes. He looked below to Kuger. The gold dragon was merely worming through the air half asleep, riding on the air currents that Brezhnev laid down before him. Windshmere took the lead and watched the forest below.

'*I see the clearing!*' He announced.

Brezhnev circled and watched as Kuger slowly lowered to the ground and made his landing. Windshmere simply arrested in the air with a slight swoop and drifted gently to the ground. Brezhnev dropped like a giant red rock and hit the ground with a rumbling thud.

Craig slid from Kuger's back and crumpled into the dirt. Kuger didn't move. He laid flat on the ground panting as rings of steam pushed from his snout into the air.

Craig rolled over. He tried to stand, but only fell back on Kuger. He closed his eyes and tried to rest.

'*Come.*' Brezhnev rumbled, '*I'll take you back.*'

Craig shook his head slowly. '*Negative. Just give me a sec.*' Craig could feel the ground beneath him vibrate, his muscles still accustomed to Kuger's wriggling back.

Weakly he waved at the big red. '*Come here. Come closer.*' The big red did and Craig reached up and took hold of a lock of chin whiskers and pulled himself up.

Like a drunken man, Craig stumbled to where the Red Barchetta was hidden. He yanked back some of the bramble that hid the car and fished about in the glove compartment.

Brezhnev watched as the Dragoncaller pulled out a metal cylinder. He unscrewed the top and then yanked out a plug. He poured a brown, murky liquid into the top and Brezhnev could smell the coffee laced with Slivobitsa.

Craig breathed easier as the coffee slipped down his throat. He looked up to the gigantic red dragon. '*Just get to Sugartown, rest and I'll see you in four hours.*'

Brezhnev nodded and with a huge paw, nudged Kuger. '*If you live that long.*' Craig said nothing as the red dragon half lifted the gold dragon to his paws. Kuger sluggishly lifted to the air and sailed off. Windshmere gave a slight hop and pulled into the air.

Brezhnev rose to his haunches and looked down at Craig. '*I've waited too long for your return Dragoncaller. I'm not ready to see you march off and get killed.*'

Craig smiled and felt his face tingle. '*I'm not rushing anywhere until after my coffee break.*' Craig sipped at it and regarded the awful taste of the slivobitsa. '*Would you rather see me crouch out of the way like a BEM?*'

528

Brezhnev looked away. From his height over the trees he could see the flares of magic shoot in the sky from the battle a click away. '*Maybe.*' He growled.

'*Roc needs me.*'

Brezhnev nodded and looked down. '*You're just too damn mortal. That's all.*' Brezhnev leaned forward and cocked his wings. He leapt into the air and took to the sky. He made a circle and disappeared.

Craig watched him sail off. He actually wanted to go and hide in a corner, but he couldn't and he knew it. "Bone head." He mumbled as he pulled back the rest of the dried bramble. "Standard stupid stuff that makes up heros." He said mindlessly as he slid into the leather seat. "The Craig Tyrone's school for stupendously foolish stunts and half cocked ideas." He reached to the steering column. "Are you ready?" He spoke to the Red Barchetta.

"Yeah!" It rumbled as its engine came to life. Its bright shining chrome grill with missing teeth smiled into the sun. Its cherry red paint seemed to glow with warmth. It front bumper was twisted slightly, giving the Barchetta a grim, curled, gritting grin.

Craig let it idle as he sipped his coffee. He took a deep breath and watched the needles dancing in their gauges. He let his hands slide around the simulated wooden wheel. His hands were stinging and his face was burning but he didn't care. He smelled like a dragon. It was all over him and it's pungent, acrid odor was assailing him, making his brain swell. It was a euphoric feeling. Craig wondered if it was also an aphrodisiac.

He shook his head trying to clear it. He took another deep breath of cool air and finished off his coffee. He was feeling very good. He reached into the glove compartment where he had stashed bandages and more Slivobitsa. He uncorked the bottle and let a bit trickle into his hands and rubbed it around on his hands, face, and anywhere else he was bleeding. He then took his bandages and wrapped his hands carefully.

When he was done, he stuffed the rest back into the glove compartment. He looked to the road ahead of him.

"Atomic batteries to charge!" The Barchetta said. "Turbines to speed. Seat belt on?"

Craig mindlessly looked for his seat belt and fastened it. He wondered what had made him remember it.

"Ready?" The Barchetta asked.

Craig revved the peddle. He was ready.

"Lets go to war!" The Barchetta roared and tore down the road.

Chapter 75

Kemoto sailed higher into Okshiru's great sky. The bird god flew past the swelling clouds that hung in the air. Younger, lesser gods all sat upon the clouds watching the spectacle below. He could see Fikor curled around two mountain ranges watching carefully for his knight.

"Have you seen her?" The snow dog of winter asked the sun.

Kemoto shook his head. Peering over the field, he watched the probing attacks and preliminary battles. He was able to account for every knight in Okshiru's care save two. He could immediately see Uko's knight, Achillia was fighting side by side with Ovam's knight, Milo. Chinook's knight, Pul, in a reserve unit was about to engage the enemy. Danshu's knight was being carried out with the dead, but not without covering himself with great glory and courage.

He could see every knight either fighting or ready to fight save three; Fikor's knight was missing, Dru's knight was missing, and Shegatesu and Neathina's Knight was home, where she belonged.

Neeko's voice filled the halls of Fanrealm. It was a piercing cattish cry that did nothing but irritate Onary. The Springier Spaniel sat out in the hall. He laid on the floor with his head on his paws and his tail beating back and forth in a steady beat.

The door opened and he felt the full blast of Neeko's very powerful voice. He flinched at the sound, pushing his ears forward. Trisha the cook rushed out and headed down the stairs and Onary watched her go. He could smell that Edia had stepped through the door with her and was sitting behind him. He ignored her.

He watched the children push past down the hall. Each looked at the door and then quickly looked to the floor. They could hear the screams. For the younger ones, mostly boys, who didn't have any idea of what was going on, looked very guilty and didn't know why.

"Is this ah great event." Edia said brightly.

Dictionary the dog suddenly thought that if Encyclopedia the cat went out side and skinned herself, that would be a great event.

"The master should be here." Edia went on even though the dog was ignoring her. "This is his place!"

Onary thought about that. Several months Craig had made the factual statement that a man's rightful place during the birth of his child was in the waiting room. "Craig is in his rightful place." He said without lifting his head. "He's fighting for his child's life." He suddenly looked at the cat. "Should he be else where?"

The cat suddenly realized that the dog, pompous and snobbish as always, was uncharacteristically correct. But she wasn't about to admit that and turned up her tail and strutted back into the room following Trisha.

The smell inside the room was of birth. Edia knew it well. She bounced up onto a chair and then to the dresser where she could see.

Neeko was braced facing the wall, her hands clutching sections of moldings. She was naked, save for a large white blouse that was gathered under her breasts and above her belly. Her legs were spread over a trough to catch the fluids of her body. Crouched behind and below her was Fantista peering up between the Ne-arri's legs. Trisha stepped around her, draping a sheet over Neeko's waist to cover some of her nudity. She tucked the ends about her, letting part drape in front and leaving her backside exposed.

Neeko was glistening with sweat. Anita, oldest of the children of Fanrealm, had an arm around Neeko, holding her up against the contraction that threatened to double her over. With her free hand she was dabbing the balls of water from Neeko's forehead.

Neeko was clenching her teeth. Spit was bubbling about her tiny fangs. Her claws dug into the wood moldings as the pain continued. She was feeling tired, then hungry, then thirsty, then the thought of food made her sick, then she wanted to go for a walk, then she wanted to sit, then she didn't, then she wanted the baby to be born right there and now, then she wanted the baby not to be born for at least another month.

Her legs were bent and quivered and the heels of her bare feet bounced up and down on the wood floor when the shuddering contractions hit her. She kept rocking as if she was trying to put her head between her parted knees.

"This is going well." Fantista said calmly lowering the sheer. "You're doing fine."

Neeko's eyebrows bent and pain clenched her again. Lady Fantista put a soothing hand on the Ne-arri's lower back and calmed the flashes of pain that she knew was there.

"I'msoglad!" Neeko said in a sudden burst. "That I am...doing so well!" She sucked air through her teeth. "Foramoment I thought I wasdoing somethingallwrong!"

Fantista cooed her. "Think past the pain. I know how you feel. I've gone through it myself seven times."

"Seventimes! Ohblessid." Neeko moaned.

"Think past the pain. Relax."

"Relax!" Neeko shouted as if she just stumbled on the answer. "I've got to relax! I'll take up needlepoint!"

"Don't hold your breath like that." Fantista coached. "Breathe." She said letting out a long breath to demonstrate.

The door bolted open. A boy stood in the way looking almost as surprised as Neeko. His tiny, thin frame panted with breath as if he had just run up the stairs from the courtyard. He suddenly looked away, hiding his eyes.

"What is it, Drake?" Fantista said urgently.

Drake kept looking at the ground ashamed at what he had seen. "Uh, M'lady, we need you outside." He said in his small voice.

"CAN'TYOUSEESHE'SBUZY!" Neeko screamed through her teeth looking back over her shoulder at the boy. Anita tried to comfort her.

"I can't come right know, Drake." Fantista told him gently. "It'll have to wait."

"But it can't wait Mum." He said looking up and then away again. "It's a dragon. There's one right now a-flying over head!"

"What kind is it?" Fantista asked turning to Neeko again.

Drake looked up at her incredulously and then away again. "What kind, Mum?"

"Yes what kind. Go on the balcony and see what kind."

Drake looked to the doors and quickly dashed across the room. He stepped outside being careful not to let the dragon see him. "Its a big silver one!" He shouted in.

"It's one of Craig's." Neeko said rather annoyed for no reason as she looked back to the knot in the wood of the wall that she had been staring at. "It brought me to the house."

Fantista nodded. She had suspected as much. "Drake? You stay right there and keep an eye on it."

Drake nodded and crouched beside one of the stanchions so the dragon couldn't see him.

"How am I doing?" Neeko asked panting.

"Perfect." Fantista smiled warmly. "You're doing everything perfectly."

"Are you sure?" Pain swept her again and she bonked her head against the wall. "Have you delivered a Ne-arri before?"

Fantista smiled. "I've delivered Gnomes, dwarves, elves, humans, Wozits, Huphelups, Wuzzls, one goblin and one dragon."

Neeko's eyes widened. "Ah, ah, Dragon!" Neeko exclaimed.

Fantista nodded. "A hundred and eighty six years ago." She said matter-of-factly.

Neeko had forgotten about the life-span of elves. "Any one I know?" Neeko panted.

"Craig's little male grey. He nested up in the hills until Craig came."

Neeko was rather impressed and the thought took away her pain. "So, just how many of these have you done."

Fantista beamed with pride. "Three hundred and fifty five." She looked at Neeko with her gentle brown eyes. "And I've never lost one."

Edia suddenly rose. *Not one out of three hundred and fifty five! That has to be a record among people. Why, even I could lose three or four in a litter of eight.*

"There's another Dragon, Mum!" Drake shouted from the balcony. "He's gray and a bit smaller than the first!"

"Another of Craig's?" Fantista asked.

"I think so." Neeko suddenly couldn't remember.

"There are a two blues!" Drake announced.

"Ralph and another." Neeko remembered. "Craig has two blues."

"Two gold." He then announced.

Neeko suddenly looked to the window. "Craig only has one gold."

"There is a white thing, and it ain't a dragon. The whole sky is a swarming!"

Fantista ignored him. "Okay Neeko, it is time. When I tell you, I'm going to need you to push." Neeko glared at her spot on the wall while Anita adjusted her grip to prepare. "Just let it come. Give me a little push."

Drake suddenly dashed into the room unconcerned with Neeko's pregnancy any longer. "M'lady! There are a four gold and a silver so big it takes up the whole sky!"

"Mother!" Neeko screamed still staring at the wall.

"Concentrate, Neeko." Fantista coached as she rested one hand on the girls lower cheek. "I need you to push just a little more."

Drake watched trying to decide what was more important, a hundred dragons swarming around outside, or Neeko giving birth.

"Don't worry about the dragons." Fantista said over her shoulder to Drake. "If they wanted Fanrealm. They wouldn't need a thousand dragons to do it."

Drake thought her right. He glanced back at the window, then to Neeko.

Neeko was bucking, her knuckles clenching white holding onto Trisha and Anita. Drake stood wide eyed and wondering.

A woman stood beside Drake. Her long, flowing, silvery gown of spider's silk brushed his arm. He jumped back in startled surprise. Neeko's wet, pained face turned, her green eyes were mere slits behind her tan cheeks. "mommy." She squealed.

·Fantista didn't looked from her task. "A little push…a little more…A fine day your majesty." She said off handedly. "Pardon my lack of respect…"

"Please continue." The woman in silver said as she replaced Trisha at Neeko's side. She took a hand and stroked Neeko's forehead, brushing a lock of hair from her eye.

"Get ready for a big push Neeko." Fantista spoke very calmly and coolly, one hand still resting lightly on Neeko's lower cheek. "Trisha? Anita? Drake? This is Lady Ameri. Queen of Dragons. Neeko's stepmother."

Drake stood with his mouth hanging open.

Neeko clenched and pushed at Lady Fantista's direction. Drake felt himself clenching. His toes made little fists in his boots. "Drake?" Lady Fantista went on not taking her eyes from her task. "You should learn to spot her majesty who is white gold dragon."

Drake tried to answer, 'I'll learn that Mum.' But his voice was trapped in his body.

Neeko's green eyes shifted over to her mother. "How am I doing?" She whispered.

"Beautiful, my little kitten."

"Neeko…another push…" Fantista went on. "Not so much…Did you want a girl, or a boy?"

"Uh…a girl." She said breathlessly. "A girl."

"Do you have a name?"

"Krisanna…Krisanna Muh Muh Mari Tyrone."

Fantista suddenly snatched up towels. "By the almighty Grace of Okshiru the god of Sky and Sea, I name you Krisanna Mari Tyrone." The scream of a baby suddenly filled the room as Lady Fantista held up a tiny bundle and gently placed it into Neeko arms. "356" She whispered. Ameri had to move Neeko's arms to hold her baby. The women lifted Neeko and laid her on the bed covering her with sheets. Neeko and baby cried for what seemed to be different reasons.

Outside, dragons roared.

Chapter 76

From above, the gods peered down. From the sidelines, the gods peered in. From spying pools and crystal balls, the gods watched, placed their bets, and argued on the outcome. The odds were poor. The hope of Worldsend was in the hands of mortals. Okshiru had given the word that there would be no interference in Mortalroam. Simple enough. The lesser gods argued that Thamrell was a Worldsend problem and they should do as they pleased, pulling all of their mighty resources together to fight the common foe in a spectacular burst of symmetric power and cunning that would cause grave doubts and second thoughts to any other challenger thinking of cresting the panicle of the universe.

Most gods agreed to this line of thinking.

Sharpe, the god of deep and involved thinking, argued that Okshiru was wise in making his decision. Gods, like dragons, with their immense egos to stumble over, can not work together to save their own lives, which was clearly demonstrated when Hauth came knocking. Bengal, god of ferocious beasts, fought Thang, god of natural disasters for control of leading armies of Worldsend. Danshu fought everybody while Dru counted the bodies and Ura changed sides so fast at one point she found herself fighting herself. This left the gods of dawn, fog, stars, forests, all things bright and beautiful, sugar and spice, butterflies, hayfever, Spring, Winter, and rabbits to make up the defending force for Worldsend against the ravenous, horrendous, bone marrow sucking, light snuffing horde of Hel. The rest of the gods, when they got around to it, fell in their appropriate places and at best, argued themselves to a standstill. Hauth was kind enough to wait, but eventually became bored and pounded the entire lot without mercy or difficulty. If it were not for Hauth's own inability to face the supergod, Worldsend would have crumbled and been sold as driveway gravel.

Sharpe's argument was swaying, if not convincing. But all the gods were still firm in the thought: of all the mortals on all of Mortalroam, why did Roc The Dragonslayer have to be the one chosen to defend Worldsend?

Sharpe only shook his head and said he'd give it some thought.

Roc the Dragonslayer's armies took a line against the tide. They dug in and built bunkers and walls. The Monks of Artus with direction from the Dragoncaller had brewed and supplied Napalm, white phosphorous, and smoke grenades. The ancient Druid had sent down several of his zealots to aid with he healing of the wounded and to string their P.T. Bushes where directed. P.T. Bushes, (Pain and Torture) where comprised of sharp, intertwining thorns that could cut through a demon's hide if he tried to push his way through. They were used as barriers to funnel the demons through choke points to allow Roc's War Machines to work to their best effect.

From the guild of Stonegaut, ten spell casters of S.H.A.M.O.S.S. (Science, Holistography, Arts, Magic, and Other Strange Shit) came in a puff of smoke. Not to be out done, they were joined by a team from the school of Quisiputmoun who pulled each other out of a hat and a fraternity from the college of Hokus who came in on a flying carpet.

Ships from the south, north and west sailed the rivers with supplies, food and weapons of war. Men came from the farms, fields, cities, mountains and valleys. Elves came from the woods, gnomes from their holes in the earth and dwarves from the mountains, moving to the sound of the Dragonslayer's calling song.

Troops marched from the newly allied councils of the west. Cavalry came from the steeps in the south. Worgs came from the north and sailed in with a Battalion from Duke Monster on Fourteen great warships of stone. Allia sent her Warrior and Bowmen leagues 409, 849 and 732 who were escorted in by Wendell who also brought the rest of Dragonslayer's Wreck and Rebuild dwarf company (WARCO) with his entourage of survivors from the Crystal Spire.

Roc the Dragonslayer was the undisputed commander in chief, and he quickly coordinated his forces. He took the untrained farmers and put them in the rear for supply and support. He took the spell casters and intermingled them with the forces at key points with a squad assigned for their protection. Elves and their bows in the high points, Dwarves and Gnomes to dig their trenches across the fields. His armies and Dragonguard stood in the front lines and the Barbarians of the lost nation of Faraway were ten paces in front of the front lines. Roc the Dragonslayer stood five paces in front of the barbarians, picking his teeth with a knife.

The dark curtain of the night faded to blue as Shegatesu prepared the sky for morning. Far away, like a black scab on the earth, Roc could make out the front lines of the demon forces. His elven hearing wasn't sharp enough to hear the distant horn that sounded the hellish forward march. The first wave of demons rolled in like a black stampede and Roc tried not to smile.

The first wave of demons stopped short in mid field as the sky suddenly grew dark. Trees and grass still wet from morning dew, steamed with fog moments before suddenly bursting into flame. Hauge's wind suddenly stood still and a wave of fear rolled across the armies of Hel.

Hiroshima erupted and Roc turned his head from the rolling blast that turned the sky to a scarred gold. Dragon fire tore, billowing, angry, a tsunami a hundred paces high into the demon lines. Charred silhouettes stood still, silent, frozen in ferocious pose, until a quick breeze from Hauge scattered them to dust.

The demon's second wave swarmed with equal strength and enthusiasm. Thamrell had put his most devastating, desecrating, top line troops in his first two waves with the hope that they'll over run the Dragonslayer and end his foolishness. The second wave made it three quarters of the way.

Nagasaki happened. Rising twice as high, twice as hot. Swords and axes turned to dull grey pools of slag on the black smoking ground.

Black walls of billowing smoke assailed the Dragonslayer. Even he had to crouch down to breathe. Heat suddenly assailed him. He turned his back using the heavy cloth in his war cape as a shield from the heat.

He tossed the smoldering cloth theatrically back over his shoulder as he stood again. Hauge was with him. The god was subtly using his winds to blow clear the smoke and drive it towards the enemy.

There was silence.

Then, there were drums.

Roc held a fist in the air and whistled an elfcall. The pipes began to cry for war. His hot blood was running in his body. The acrid air and stinging smoke filled his senses. The stench of burning demon stung his eyes. Drums and pipes filled his head, his heart. They were coming.

They were coming.

The lead demon banners suddenly broke the smoke wall. Hauge quickly snatched back the cloak of smoke and revealed the armies of Hel coming out of the woods of Dacova. Dragons suddenly charged over head, fire spitting from their mouths. Their wings dipped and swept with natural grace. They were swift and brilliant. Magic popped like balls of light about them leaving black spots in the sky. Dragon-panthers suddenly leapt into the fray and went after the casters of magic.

Bodies were torn, broken and burned as Dragon-panthers stepped into reality beside a spell caster, roasted him, stamped out the pieces, ate them and stepped out of reality before any of the demons assigned to protect the spell caster could do anything.

They were coming.

Great demon war machines pushed from the woods. Painfully they made their way past the fields of P.T. Bushes only to sink helplessly into the preset traps. White Tiger Dragons suddenly leapt into reality and spat their brilliant white fire at the machines and crews.

They were coming.

Their magic was gone. Their machines were burning. Demon flyers were swatted out of the sky with magic and elvish arrows. Spotters counted that Hiroshima claimed thirty one thousand, five hundred and eighty nine demon lives while Nagasaki took another seventy two thousand, seven hundred and forty five. *They had to have felt that kind of loss*, Roc thought. They had seen his might in the first twelve tics of battle and he hadn't even raised a sword.

They were coming.

Walls of shields lined the fields. Spears like a thousand twigs poked from spaces. They lifted and took a step forward and set again. Again they lifted, took a step and rested. They were in clumps of thirty, moving to the sound of the war drums. Moving in a uniformed wave of armor slowly across the field.

Roc hissed and called back his Dragon-panthers and White Tiger Dragons. The moving armies only pulled in their shields like armadillos and glanced off the blasts of fire from the retreating beasts. Balls of Magic followed suit, chasing the Dragon-panthers out of reality. Roc couldn't risk them. It was still early.

They were coming.

Roc waited.

They were coming.

Roc raised an arm. Signalmen raised their banners, sounders brought their horns to their lips.

They were coming.

Spears were raised and poised. Men wiped the sweat from their hands and re-gripped their swords. Helmets were pulled down and shields were set.

They were coming.

Roc could see their faces. Cruel and twisted eyes glared back at him. He had seen almost one hundred thousand of them die before him and still there was more.

They were coming.

The word was given. Roc and the rows of barbarians charged forward with a cry of war. Horns sang and drums rumbled. Anger filled the air with passion. Human will rose up against demonic power.

The demon rows suddenly braced and waited for the charge with their spears planted for the attack.

Roc ran madly with the barbarians in suit for fifty paces before he turned and ran after his own fleeing army.

The demons lowered their spears and shields. Their shock and astonishment was obvious. They watched as the Dragonslayer ran madly into the woods before them. They were turning! They were running! Roc was Running...AWAY!

There was a call and the orders were sounded. The demons charged after, breaking their walls, some of them dropping their giant door shields and dashed into the forest after the running Dragonslayer.

Roc broke the tree line with a maddening dash. He paused for a fleeting beat to see the demons running after him. Lumbering as quickly as his armor would allow, Roc tip toed past the nearly invisible wires woven in the dead fallen leaves and underbrush, trying not to inhale too much of the head spinning fumes rising from the chemicals that covered everything.

They came running after. Their feet tearing into wires. Some tripping into the beds of spikes while others set off traps of wailing arrows, spears and spiked druid-stones.

Roc and the barbarians leapt from their nests and charged. Roc jumped to a fallen tree and dove into a clump of shields. "Mighty cry, from blood red banner," His hammer wailed with clashing might, sparking against steel. "Raging war and fighting clamor," Shields suddenly yielded, burst asunder by the tremendous blows. "Leads a life of war torn manner." He suddenly pushed out with his bladed buckler, sinking its spike into flesh. "Yielding to my awesome HAMMER!" He drove forward whirling his hammer like a dervish. Bones shattered and bodies fell. Shields were cast aside like so much planking. It was a field unit, armed with large shields and spears, now useless in the cramped spaces of the wooded growth. Roc and his barbarians armed with small bucklers and axes, pushed past the oaken shields to the soft demon flesh behind.

Battle stood behind Roc. The dragonguard twisted like a coiling snake and struck with the wrath of Sho-Pa. His sudden blows shattered clusters of nerves and sprawled demons before him. Roc pounded like a mad man. Driving his hammer forward with nothing made hard enough to stop it.

More demons came forward. A woods unit armed with short swords came bounding in. Their lighter armor took them easily over the trip wires and P.T. Bushes and into the heart of the battle.

Roc drove an upper swing home, a blow so sharp that the demon stood for several beats before crumpling to the ground. A woods demon suddenly came falling from above at the Dragonslayer but faster than the eye could follow, Roc drew his bloody magic stone and roasted the demon in flight.

"Can you see, of what you've been shown, the magic might of my Firestone!" Roc quickly stashed his magic crystal and pulled back suddenly realizing how stupid that impulsive act was and fled from the woods. The demons quickly re-grouped and gave chase.

Roc broke the shade of the trees into the open glory of Kemoto. Friendly shields parted and he quickly pushed through. Roc shouted for the ready call and the ready call was sounded. He turned, his natural height bringing him over the height of the wall of shields and watched the tree line as demons stumbled out of the woods quickly in pursuit.

Roc raised an arm and shouted. Horns sounded and gnomes in their tunnels below the ground cranked their pumps. Hoses suddenly came to life in the hands of dwarves crouched behind the shield-men. Green water suddenly gushed out under pressure blasting at the tree line and the demons rushing out.

They stumbled in the slippery solvent. It burned their open flesh and stole their breath. They gasped and gagged for air that was denied them. Their blinded eyes bled yellow demon custard as they scrabbled about on the ground.

The Dragonslayer's archers came into play, launching their flaming arrows into the woods.

Roc smiled and the troops cheered as the tree line erupted with the heart of Kemoto. Demons writhed and curled in the burning roar that suddenly claimed them. They had never felt Napalm before. They would never forget it now.

They were coming.

Still demons pushed on. Some with hides thick enough to ignore the Napalm that clung to them moved forward with slow steps, trying to see through the flames on their faces. Roc watched intently as they came closer, setting the ground they plodded on aflame in small patches behind them. He counted seventeen. Arrows whistled and thudded in their flesh. The juggernauts pressed on, as more arrows pushed into them and one by one, they fell to the ground.

They were coming.

Shields set themselves. Roc had planned for the demons to be stopped by the intense heat of the fire. But some just couldn't get the hint.

One fell. Suddenly falling into a pile of flames and remained burning. Another collapsed and then another. Each one immune to fire, but not its heat. Napalm roasted each one in their respective skins.

They were coming.

Suddenly the great curtain of Napalm fire fell with a sucking wind. Demon spell casters finally found a way to knock it down. Roc's troops prepared for the next phase as the demons slowly made their way through the woods and reformed just beyond the tree line. Slowly they mulled and gathered and pulled together behind their shields and pointed their thin spears and prepared for command.

Roc shouted for the ready call and it was sounded.

A demon general, mounted on his horse came plodding out of the woods line. His glistening sword was raised as a symbol of command as the Dragonslayer's archers fell short from distance or bounced off the magic shields all around him. The general shouted with a waved arm, and sent his armored men to motion.

A Dragon-panther suddenly stepped into reality beside the general. The winged jungle cat snatched him from his horse and tossed him into the air. A White Tiger Dragon flew into reality above and caught the general in flight and raked him to shreds. Shiny bits of his armor fell like tinsel to the ground where the Dragon-panther quickly set them to flame. The two then suddenly ducked out of reality.

They were coming.

Roc and his shield wall stood their ground. Fifty one clumps, in an alternating, staggered line, braced for attack. Each clump was filled with four hundred warriors surrounded by shields. The demons across the way lifted their shields and started to march forward. The wide line of shields, were walking a slow and steady pace, keeping their tight formation, getting closer to Roc's armies.

Roc waited. He was the crab on the shore. He and fifty other crabs were waiting on the beach to stop the tide of the sea. The tide of the great sea of Hel was coming in. Roc waited. He waited some more. He tried to count the front line but he couldn't. He watched as the wounded barbarians were dragged towards the rear. The conscious ones swore to return to battle as they were removed from the field. A bottle of Slivobitsa was being passed around and someone thrust it at Roc's chest. He dropped his hammer and let it hang from its strap as he drank two deep gulps and passed it into the crowd around him. They were huddled together within the circle of the wall. Shoulder to shoulder on their knees, they tried to peer though the thin forest of spears that surrounded them at the line of demons coming closer.

They were coming.

Roc could see the shields, flashing like mirrors in the sun. Scrawled and engraved devices of twisted heads and writhing tongues decorated the moving wall. He could see their tiny bleeding, hating eyes peering over the rims of their shields coming closer.

They were coming.

There in the huddle of armored steel, as sweat rolled smoothly down his spine, with the taste of Slivobitsa still tingling on his tongue, Roc the Dragonslayer smiled, and began to rhyme.

> Closer they come, to take their part.
> Wanting to take, the Slayer's heart.
> Bold is bold, and a dare, a dare,
> But the winner this day, will be the Dragonslayer.

Grenades suddenly popped and clouds suddenly swelled on the fields. Walls of billowing opaque smoke rose from the earth covering the land in shades of brilliant blue, orange and violet.

Horsemen suddenly sprang into the fray. The Dragonslayer's Spitznats battalion, who had held their horses crouched and hidden behind the shield walls, leapt over the protective shield walls and charged. Barbarians sprang from the walls and followed Roc as he charged into the clouds of color.

The demons were blind and cut off from command. The Spitznats horsemen bounded over the demon shields trampling all underneath.

The barbarians followed into the breaches like flowing water, separating the shield men and breaking them apart.

The Dragonslayer's drums quickened their pace, and his shield walls picked up and marched forward, holding their formations as the demons scattered. Demons fell apart in panic. Roc bellowed and a thousand arrows filled their air with the whisper of death. Demons fell to spears, trapped against the oncoming crush of Roc's shield walls. They ran scattered in bewilderment as the Barbarians moved through them keeping them confused.

Blood filled the air in a fine, red mist. Demons gagged on their own hellish, black spittle. Roc's hammer sang with a whirling thunder, and monster and beast fell with shattered bones.

Roc paused, watching the melee. Demons, like gods and dragons, could never work together in groups of two or more. They were too filled with short sightedness, quick gain and treachery to trust each other. If it were not their fight, and they couldn't see the goal then and there, they didn't fight.

The demons were lost, scattered aimlessly about the field. Without direction they were dropping their weapons and running off. The tiniest of wounds would cause them to fall to the ground wailing and crying for mercy.

Roc shook his head. It was too early.

Horns sounded from beyond the woods. Growling howls rose in a deafening cry over the battle din. Demons rose, suddenly motivated to fight, took up their weapons enraged, suddenly brought to a furor. As if they were listening to an elfcall, they understood their commands. They were reforming, gathering again, fighting back.

Gorn sounded the call and trumpets cried in response. Banners shot into the air and the Dragonslayer's armies responded.

Fall back boys and girls, fall back.

The Spitznats horseman gathered up the stragglers, snatching up the wounded from the field to the staging area. Roc was the last one, himself, carrying a female warrior over his shoulder and her husband under his arm. The two fought bravely at Roc's side, and he was going to see to it that they would not die beneath the feet of the demon horde.

Roc glanced back. Plumes of smoke still lingered from their cans. It crawled across the field covering the dead and soon to be. The demons were not charging after, but re-forming their walls, re-grouping their strength. They could understand the signal horns from the woods. Roc hadn't counted on such communication. He was hoping to use their lack of it to his advantage, to keep them off guard.

Demons began to ooze from the woods like sap from the bark of a tree. Roc couldn't count them. It was too many to bother. They had been sending them into the woods to set off the traps and throw their bodies onto the P.T. Bushes. Demons were walking on the bodies of their brethren, using them as carpeting for their war machines, for their command tower.

The demons were waiting, reforming, organizing. Roc didn't want that, but there was nothing he could do about it. He needed a bit more time to assemble in the next staging area. As long as his traps in the woods held back their main forces he'd have time.

He didn't.

They were coming.

The trees suddenly dropped. Magic snapped them to splinters and tossed them aside like twigs. A hundred slaves pulled thick ropes—their moans of pain and lashing whips came quickly to Roc's ears. He knew he was out of time. It rose from the woods beyond the height of the trees. Kemoto's firelight sparkled on its gleaming armor. Its great banners waved and caught Hauge's winds. Trumpets and drums filled its many levels and tiers. In the spaces of the armor plating, Roc could see them crawling about like ants. They were the think tankers, spell casters, and signalmen. They were the leaders.

They had sacrificed much to get it forward over the traps and impediments as quick as they did. Roc marveled at their ability to move something that big.

Against its armor plating, Roc could see the impact where something big had smashed into the tower. *Damn Dragon.* Roc hissed to himself. *He was supposed to burn it to the ground, not eat it.*

Six Dragon-Panthers and eight White Tiger Dragons suddenly popped into reality about the tower. The gigantic tower lit up with flashes of power. The glare of the magic was so thick it filled the air and Roc had to turn away. A Dragon-panther dissolved instantly. Three suddenly swooped off. A White Tiger Dragon suddenly fell limp and dropped out of the sky. Two Dragon-panthers appeared beneath him, caught him and took him out of reality.

They were coming.

Reginald and Muffy stepped beside Roc. Muffy bowed and Roc tossed the wounded he was carrying onto the beast's back and then quickly mounted. Muffy trotted quickly over to a staging area.

Reginald only stared at the tower, his eyes, glared to slits. It snorted and broke into a charge. Buffy and Floppy joined him in a full flying run. At four hundred yards they leapt out of reality.

Buffy and Floppy suddenly flew into reality at ten yards to the tower, soaring upwards with and arching pull. Magic flashed about them as they flew out of reality. Reginald flew in low. With the all the attention going to the larger, White Tiger Dragons, they failed to see the Dragon-panther soar in and set the slaves pulling the ropes to fire before soaring out of reality.

The tower itself was undamaged, but it was stopped. Roc couldn't calculate how that was going to affect things, but it was something. The main pull of magic for the demon army was in that tower, out of range of his lines.

Roc slid from Muffy's back. He pulled down his wounded and hands came up to aid him. He watched as they were carried to the rear. About him, men were moving, carrying equipment and fresh bottles of Thatch. A boy stepped to Roc and offered him a cup of Slivobitsa. Roc waved it off, his eyes fixed on the tower rolling forth.

He glanced down at the boy stepping off and snatched his shoulder. "What are you doing here?" Roc had seen they boy before, but couldn't place him. The silver star of Hammerstrike hung from a chain around his neck and Roc knew him to be one of Fantista's orphans. "Are you trying to get me killed?" Roc roared.

The boy suddenly floundered. Dirt and blood clung to Roc's mask. Bone and sinew stuck to the tiny spikes that adorned his broad shoulders. The stench of Slivobitsa burned his nose. He had never been this close to the Mighty Dragonslayer. He was tall, big enough to shadow the boy from the sun. He was bigger than life.

"If Lady Fantista finds out that I had you out here, she'll kill me!" Roc shouted at the boy shaking his thin arm. "What is this to you? A game? A boy's dare? You see this as fun? Is that why you're here? Well its not. Its pain, and hurt and death, death that you can spread thick across the sky and have more left over. That is what is out here! Do you like it? Well do you?"

The boy wavered, trembling in Roc's stone grasp. A shudder passed through him, but his lungs filled with air and his voice somehow found him. "I...I wanted to help." He whispered.

"What?" Roc suddenly stumbled on his own train of thought. "Wanted to..." The boy was from Hammerstrike. An orphan. His father had probably ran off to some war and left him as the man of the house. Now, it was his turn to run off to war.

Roc turned him lose. "Help with the wounded in the rear." He mumbled and pushed the boy that way. He turned and looked at the demons still amassing not to far away.

"Wode?"

Roc turned and looked at the Druid. His dress of simple woven stitches of cloth and a bit of rope for a belt seemed natural to be roaming about a crowd of armor. Druids never fought physically, shunning violence as a rule, but frequently found themselves on battlefields healing any wounded they found regardless of side. This one was holding a blue finger at the Dragonslayer.

Roc nodded and pulled off his dolman and lifted his mask. The excitement of battle had caused Roc's face to twist and fix in a gripping war grimace that gave the druid a slight pause. The druid recovered quickly and put a single blue strip of paint from the center of Roc's forehead to the end of Roc's long, and slightly bent nose.

"May you die without pain." The druid said as he smacked Roc with a twig of mistletoe. Roc grunted and turned away. He could see the burning remains of the Meat Masher and the Thwacker out on the field. They never did have much of a life expectancy on the field and he hoped they only did the damage they were made for. He shook his head as Rellik came running.

"Roc...glad I caught you. They bad guys have only this one main tower and several small machines, mostly ballistas, left. There is a large group of Golems and one great worm."

A great worm. Roc wondered. *Could the Dragoncaller speak with a great worm?*

Rellik went on. "They've got their forces amassed in one great column coming this way. There are a few attack squads snaking around on our flanks but the main column is there." He pointed to the tower on the other side of the field. "They have nothing air born and very little magic spread amongst the troops."

Roc nodded. "Tell Gorn to stand by to burn our command tower and pull back. They are running faster than I had hopped. They are too good and too coordinated for demons. I was counting on Frito to show up some time this morning. Inform the RDO and Pain Showerer to stand ready, their moment of glory is at hand. They are to dump their load, burn the marchine and join the line to fight. Everything else is still according to plan. Anything else?"

Rellik seemed to think before answering. "Yes, Craig is the father of a baby girl, six and a half pounds. The name is Krisanna Mari Tyrone, born this morning."

Roc nodded. A birth, some good news for..."What?" Roc's eyes glistened in heavy green. Rellik was human, he wouldn't be able to hear an elfcall from Fanrealm. "Where are you getting your information from?"

Rellik's eyes wandered as he slowly sucked air. Roc eyes cooled to brown as he slowly closed them to a squint and held a hand for Rellik to be silent.

"Orrin?" Roc said quietly, "Where are you?"

'With Gorn.' Came a small voice in Roc's head. 'I'm like, really help-ful, I can see with my Kamri ev-ery-thing the de-mons do and re-port it to the field com-man-ders, eh?'

Roc still didn't open his eyes. "And does Max know?"

'No.' He said timidly.

"BLESSID!" Roc bellowed. "I'm going to catch it not only from the demons, and Lady Fantista, but Max as well!" Roc turned and took wide strides to the front line.

Rellik looked after him. "My Lord, where are you going?"

"To fight the demons. I have a better chance against them!"

'Roc?' Came Orrin's Kamri. 'About the squads that have sneaked by...'

"Jose should be back there. He can handle them."

'Jose went down, eh? He is with like, the woun-ded.'

Roc stopped abruptly in his tracks. "Went down? Sungazer?"

'He isn't like, too bad, most-ly magic drain, but he's gon-na be out of it, eh?'

"What happened?" Roc grumbled.

'Magic, eh? That's all the wit-nes-ses say. Ap-pears to have been like, a pri-vate duel. I tried like, to reach him with Kamri. All I could get was, "You should have seen the other guy!" eh?'

Roc smiled.

'And an-other thing. Like, Wen-dell is here. He's got a whole band to-ge-ther, eh?'

Wendell! The last person he thought he would see was Wendell. Good news, very good news. "Tell him to guard the rear."

'I'm already here.' Roc heard Wendell's Kamri kick in. Roc would have wanted Wendell in the front with him, but he need someone to hold down the rear and Wendell was the choice.

They were coming.

The far off demon shield walls were moving. Roc had caught them unaware in the first rounds, but now the full forces were coming forward. He could see giants, towering over the wall. He could also see stone golems of magic marching mindlessly to the resounding beat of the war drums. Roc could hear the horns playing their wailing doom cry. Roc waved to his signal men and far off he could hear his pipers play their songs of glory to match the hellish songs of despair.

He had only slowed them down. The tower was moving again. As long as that tower was moving, they could move. The Dragon-panthers would never get close enough again to do any damage to it. He grit his teeth in anger. He had nothing to throw at it. Nothing to stop it with. He looked to the tower and squinted his eyes to its glow. If he couldn't stop it, he couldn't stop the demons.

They were coming.

Roc pushed to the front line and waited.

They were coming.

A section of their shield wall suddenly disappeared below the ground as one of Hornton Roquechuqur's patented pit traps sprang. The breach in the wall was easily patched with more troops as eager to do battle as the rest.

Banners waved into the air and dropped below sight. Roc eyed the oncoming tower. It was glowing with its magic barriers of protection. He watched as the inhuman slaves dragged it along to the task masters whips. Runners dashed before it to search for pit falls and traps. Roc watched as most of the runners found the traps accidently and died painfully. The others found the traps and gleefully sprang them with their bodies. They impaled themselves on giant oaken spears and fed themselves to pits filled with voracious, poisonous larvae. The tower was creeping slowly onward, unhindered and unafraid while the forces of Hel marched before it, around it, and behind it, carrying their flags and banners of victory. Roc watched the oncoming procession of shields, spears, fighters, pipers, drummers, and flagstaffs, marching steadily across the gigantic yellow 'X' painted onto the field.

They were coming.

As the great tide of Hel swept across the pre-painted 'X', Roc heard the RDO fire. He felt the earth shiver a beat after. He listened to Hauge's screaming wind and the sound of tearing linen as the light of Kemoto's sun suddenly eclipsed.

Demons paused and looked to the darkening sky. The great RDO poised over head, blooming above them. They watched as it slowly unfolded like a parasol umbrella. They pointed at it. It was all they could do save whisper, 'oh, no, not that'.

A steel cage 100 yards in circumference bit into the earth with a rushing boom. Demons caught inside and not crushed by the rim of the cage, shrieked in terror at being trapped in the confines to the huge steel cage. 50 feet above them, the ceiling of the cage waved and tilted. Razor sharp spikes attached to the sixteen ton sheet of steel ceiling prepared to fall. Demons closest to the rim of the cage pushed and tried to squeeze through the bars to avoid the horrible fate that dangled above only to find the Scalpel web made of wire so thin and keen that when thinner demons slipped through the bars, they wouldn't notice that they had been sliced to pieces until their fifth step.

Roc heard the lashing sound of the Pain Showerer. A thousand, thousand mechanical spears filled the sky. Each spear opened in flight with four off shouting spears and moments before impact the spears suddenly blazed to flame and turned the sky to gold.

Those outside of the RDO, tried to push their way in.

A thousand spears didn't open from malfunction. A thousand more didn't burst to flame. Yet a thousand screams were torn from the shredded demon's throats. The air was thick with blood and sound. Rivers of sticky black monster blood poured along the ground, forming into steams and rivers.

There was a wave of wind and a cry of demons as the sixteen ton spiked ceiling of the RDO dropped to the dirt with a sickening thud.

They were still coming.

Rockets and rocks from the warship's bombardments pounded the earth filing the air with choking dirt and smoke. Demon body parts hurled themselves into the air while other parts were impressed into the earth. Fire exploded into beautiful rainbow arches as the Dragoncaller's munitions exploded above ground.

Roc wasn't surprised. This was nothing for them. They marched steadily around the RDO cage and the forest of metal spears still flaming with Turkish tar. They stepped over the crying wounded, only occasionally putting the livelier ones out of their misery.

They were coming.

Closer.

Closer still.

Roc was pressed against others. The wall compacted itself with bodies pressed upon bodies as the demon shield wall came into range. Spears poked at each other testing the distance. The forces exchanged flurries of arrows as magic bounded between one and another. Long pikes poked at shields and hook men tried to grab hold to drag down the plates of the walls. Shouts exchanged and orders were given. Yards became feet, then feet became inches, inches became blood.

The meat grinder began. The demons pushing, Dragonslayer's forces holding on. Spears lashed back and forth, each trying to find a hole, a chink in the armor. Bodies died and were held in place by the tight pushing. The dead wormed their way to the front as an extra cushion for the enemy to poke though.

Roc gripped his hammer as the meat grinder went on. He was three rows to the rear and compressed to the point that with even his great height, he couldn't see over the wall of fighting.

He could, however, see the banners of the Demon tower standing over him.

Doth ye hold? The banners asked him.

Roc shouted, "HOLD!" and the cry was repeated. Slowly the lines shuffled backwards. Groans and grunts were heard along the line as the walls reversed themselves against their grain and set space between themselves. Human and demon had dead piled up to the point that no one could fight around. Bodies were lifted and passed hand over hand over head. Roc had no room to avoid the rain of spilling blood as a dead shield man was passed over him. Roc watched the limp body go past and red lines ran through the impressions of his mask. He tasted the salty brine. It wasn't his first taste.

The demon tower's banners changed. They asked: *Art thou ready?*

"Step up!" Roc shouted and the call was repeated. Roc suddenly realized that he had passed from the third row to the second. "Stand by!" Sweat rolled in beads on his face. His eyes grew blurry as he blinked it away. He sucked on the sweat that rolled on to his dry cracked lips.

"LAY ON!"

The lines clashed again. Magic flashed over head and into the crowd. Roc sought a foot hold. He looked back. Blade had a hand on his shoulder waiting for the signal. Battle was crouched beside him to the right. Bloc was to the left. Roc's three most valued and trusted Dragonguards, sworn to defend the realm.

"Now's the time." Roc whispered. "Here's the plan, we take this fight, in our own hands."

Roc suddenly sprang up. He pushed along the heads and shoulders and dove into the forest of spears ahead of him, shrugging the hafts aside. His hammer whirled and cracked armor to the soft flesh below. Black blood spat at him and he pounded for more. He felt Battle beside him and Bloc pushing though. Blade leapt last with his thick short sword and sliced effortlessly through the first shield he found.

The Firestone roared in an arc of fire from Roc's left hand. He sprang forward and pounded a flaming demon that much faster to death. Steel was flashing past him. Demons tried to wield their weapons against him to no avail. They couldn't maneuver in the tight cluster of their formation without stabbing one another. With each swing of his magic war hammer, regardless of aim, he hit something critically. He reached out into the mass of fanged faces with his bucklered hand and latched on to something. He pulled it forward as he climbed on the pile of bodies he had broken. He could feel his fingers sink past the cuirboillied leather that protected its throat while he raised his hammer to the sky. He looked down at the brilliant white row of teeth clenching at him. Perfect square lines locked together. Two tiny slits of eyes were poised above the white rows, beaming the demon's anger and pain. Spittle bubbled through the demon's perfect blocks as it tried vainly to breathe. Perfect white teeth.

Teeth? Meet Hammer.

"HOLD!"

Roc's arm tightened and held. Hot demon blood dripped and ran the length of his up raised arm. He suddenly looked up. The tower's banners were calling for a hold. He looked back to his own forces. His banners were calling for a hold. Gorn had called it.

He looked down to the teeth in his grip again. Eyes replaced with white balls glared back at him. Roc released his grip and the demon held it's throat as it coughed up blood. It looked at the Dragonslayer, surprised he had let it live.

Roc glared back hoping his stare would kill it, but it didn't. He turned and pushed his way through the sea of demons to his own lines. He had lost track of his forces, a mistake that Gorn had saved him from. He had planned that when he broke the shield wall, his forces would follow and disrupt the wall altogether. But the hold of the tower over its demons was too great. They reformed and plugged the hole Roc had made and continued their slow pressing advance.

Roc's shield walls opened like a mouth and swallowed him safely behind his own lines. The dead flowed to the rear. Roc couldn't see where they were coming from. They were just expelled from the line. The dead raised limp and unmoving out of the crowd and slithered over the armor capped heads to the rear, their arms dragging over the metal stubble.

He had to pull back. He was losing too many in the meat grinder. He needed more time to pull back and a hold wouldn't grant that. He chewed the inside of his cheek as his eyes looked to the rear. "Stand by." He called to Orrin and pushed back to his front line. He stood pressed shoulder to shoulder behind his first wall. He looked along his first two lines and bid them all goodbye.

"Do as your asked, do as your told.
For sake of the war, you must now hold!"

He looked to the enemy line before him. They were snarling hounds on leashes, baring their foam dripping fangs in anger. They were pounding their shields with the flat of their short swords making a clattering applause.

Roc eyed the faces with an evil stare of defiance. His eyes fixed on a set of perfect white teeth glaring in ungracious contempt back at him.

Roc cocked his hammer arm.

And the banners raised: "Lay On!"

With a screaming heave, Roc's magic hammer spun from his hand and chewed into a set of perfect white teeth, snatching the whole head from the wall.

They were coming.

Shields clashed again as spears pushed and passed through. Great axes and halberds fell past each other. The demons pushed one step. Roc's line fell back one step. The shield bearers could feel the weight of the sea pushing against them. Blades slashed though the spaces as hooks were pulling whole shields into the mass of monsters and were devoured by the line.

Roc drew his great sword from his back as he felt his forces behind him lift away. He was sacrificing his first two lines to hold back the tide long enough for the rest of his forces to pull back and regroup for a better place to secure.

The shields suddenly collapsed, spilling to the ground like falling cards. Roc plowed through the line, his armor ignoring the spears about him. His great sword sliced cleanly through wood, flesh and bone. He drove his great biting blade before him as his dragonguards protected his flanks. His shield walls broke into small clusters and circled themselves as demons swelled around them. The demon shield walls couldn't bend about and had to break up to get around. Pikes were dropped and swords were brought into play. The clusters fought back as the demons tried to push past. Roc challenged as many as he could. His voice screamed to a brittle rattle as he hollered obscenities. He felt their steel cut into his magic armor. He felt a arrow in the pocket of his shoulder. He felt the push of a hundred demons about him, enraged by his presence. His great sword lifted and fell again and again with out mercy while more and more demons, obsessed with the honor of killing the Dragonslayer raised against him.

He risked a quick glance to the rear. His remaining forces were still pulling back. They needed a little more time. His eyes returned to his sword already in motion. It splashed into the raging ocean of monsters around him. His own blood mixed with demon blood. There was an endless supply of demons, cutting at him, wearing him down. "Bite the blade!" He screamed as he wailed. "Eat its sheen!" He lifted his sword and a head shot into he air. "Taste the edge!" He spun about on himself and chopped three neatly in half. "Know its keen!" He glanced to his rear again and could see they needed more time. He raised to his great height and bellowed to his troops fighting vainly at the bee hive swarming about them: "Use your will, hold your ground. Wait until, the dragon sounds!" He couldn't count his own men for there were too few. They were sinking into the havoc around him. There wasn't time.

He needed time. His forces were still retreating, if he couldn't hold the demons, his men would be caught on the run and slaughtered.

He roared as he whirled his great sword about. The dead had again piled itself at his feet and now stood to the height of his waist. He felt something at his back and with a shrug and a twist brought his sword around. Blade bit through bone and demon's blood spat in his face. He spun about again, and demons were thrown aside from his might. Dead lay strewn about him like some bazaar carpet. He was standing on dead. Skulls cracked under his weight and ribs gave way. He couldn't fight this way, demons couldn't get past the line of dead to reach him. He reached with his buckslered hand and pushed into the pile of dead and climbed. His foot sank into soft flesh and his hand slipped off blood slick armor throwing him off balance. His teeth clenched tighter as he regained his center and his eyes looked to the sky. Something landed on his back and with a sudden snap he brought his elbow about and knocked it free. He jammed his great sword into the pile of bodies and with a monstrous scream, pulled his heavy frame to the top of the pile of dead. He stood, catching his balance and eyed the field. Arrows bounced from his armor as spears whistled past him. Roc the Dragonslayer pulled off his mask and drew his sword from the pile of dead. He looked to Worldsend, flashing his blade at the sky. "Here's my cry, I will make my prayer, deliver to me, the Devilslayer!"

Lighting dashed around him with a tremendous roar. Blinding sheets of white hot lines cracked the air about him. His skin shimmered and burned from sudden heat. Clods of dirt bounced as black dots before his blinded eyes. Acrid wind assailed him and swept suddenly about him. Mortalroam suddenly shifted below his feet and threw him to the ground. Demons dashed about him, tripping over him as he found his feet.

Roc's bloody eyes looked up. He could see demons dance macabre steps as the were flung into the air and knocked to the ground. Lines of tight, tiny fires erupted about him as lightning burned the earth.

The metal skin caught Kemoto's light and flashed it brilliantly around. The metal monster wielded its 25mm electric explo/merc rounds and demons fell before it. It's patented Rip Mower buzzed and blood showered the sky. It was the Hothering Slothering Wanderblest Beast complete with Horro-shred option and standing tall on its upper quarter deck with his blade-spear held above his head was Frito.

The knight dropped from the metal monster as it turned to circle again. Frito wielded his great blade spear to cut down bewildered demons as he carved a way to his cousin.

Roc found himself falling into Frito's arms, but Roc gripped him, holding himself to his feet. "Buy me a breather." He whispered.

Frito raised his blade spear. "By the power of Dru and the might of Okshiru, I command you all to DIE!"

Brilliant white light erupted along the field. Demons suddenly broke into blinding white fire and screamed to cinders. Others pulled back stumbling, clawing on each other to get away from the light of Okshiru. Roc found his feet and looked at his cousin. From behind a shroud of grime, Roc's floating eyes settled on the blood covered knight. "Where the Hel have you been?" He growled between pants, his lips twisting into a snarl. "You're late!"

"Your gratitude is overwhelming!" Frito barked back. "I've been working while you're out here playing around." Frito pointed to the pile of demons that Roc had made. "Will you just look at this mess! Who's going to clean this up?"

Dirt showered them both. Roc dropped his shielding arm as he looked to its source.

"You call for a Taxi?" Craig beamed from the driver's seat of the Red Barchetta.

Frito half lifted Roc into the front seat. "Watch out," The knight cautioned. "He's in a bad mood."

"Fuck you." Roc mumbled as tires spun in the dirt as Craig turned the car around. Craig had to drive slowly and carefully around the dead and Blade and Battle bounced in the back as he went by. Bloc jumped into the lid-less trunk searching the sky. "INCOMING!" Frito instinctively cast a spell over head and shafts the size of posts were deflected away.

Roc suddenly glared at Craig, his eyes beaming. "And where have YOU been?"

"Hey, I had to drop off Mrs Karlyle's kids at school. Seems her husband's a bit under the weather." Craig answered simply. "Here." He reached over and opened the glove compartment and took out his thermos. "Drink that. You look like Woffda."

Roc uncorked it and sniffed what was inside. "What is it? Slivobitsa?"

"No…" Craig said a little bothered, swerving to avoid something. "Its rat poison. Drink up!"

Roc leaned back his head and drank deeply.

Craig looked back to Frito moving beside the car, piling the dead and dying into the car where Battle helped to stack them. "What the hell happened back there?"

"I threw every thing I had, that's what." Frito looked back to the smoking scalded earth. "They are still coming."

Craig frowned. "Why don't you cast one of those killer barriers of yours." He glanced back at the knight. "They do work."

Frito half lifted a pikeman onto the hood. "Sure, give me about a year and I can block off a quarter click circle that no demon can pass." Frito stopped to check someone, then left him behind with a sad shake of his head. "Last time we took on Trid Dreath I had to prepare for six months. I've had about 45 minutes and I haven't had breakfast."

Roc tossed the empty canister over. "Our plan isn't working." He leaned back and looked up at Frito. "I thought that with out Hauth they would lose interest and go home. But that damn tower." He turned and pointed a metal finger towards the glowing structure.

Battle hopped out of the car and ran ahead of it, he scooped up a still living body and carried him to the car. Craig stopped as Battle laid him on the hood. As they started moving again, Frito climbed over the front seat to tend to the man.

"Frito, Craig." Roc called. "We're going to have to make a press. We're going to have to make a straight run at the tower. We stop the tower, and its all over."

Craig shook his head. "My Dragon-panthers tell me no dice. We'll need a small tactical nuke and I don't have one."

"If you were not so damned stubborn about giving me shit when you first came from your world, I would have had a greater arsenal by now."

"I had my reasons!" Craig barked harshly. "I gave you what I could."

Roc let it go. "Dragons?" He leaned closer.

Craig pulled back. Roc wasn't wearing his mask and his face was twisted. "Exhausted from all that demon magic. They won't make the flight. They'll need to rest. They took a lot of magic drain." Craig looked at him. "And back off, or unscrew your face or something, your giving me the ickies."

Roc leaned back offended. "Oh yeah? And when was the last time you saw a mirror? You look like shit!"

Craig looked to where he was driving and then back to Roc. "I look like shit?" Craig looked at the blood and dirt caked on Roc's armor. A disembodied hand was stuck to the spikes on his left shoulder. White sinew clung to his eye lashes. Craig looked ahead. "I look like shit?" He said quietly.

Craig drove slowly and steadily through the lines and Gorn stood waiting to receive them. "I sent Orrin to the rear." He said calmly as he gave an arm to pull Roc from the car. "We haven't the force to hold much longer."

Roc shook his head as he climbed out. "Don't worry about that. Mount for a charge." He said somberly turning to Frito. "You had best come up with a way to smash that tower."

"ME?"

"Look around!" This is a perilous situation and it's your turn." Roc anticipated Frito's retort and cut him off. "You were not here when I pulled us out of the last one. Your turn."

"Can be done." Frito said matter of factly as he watched his patient being carried off to the rear. "The spell they are using is similar to the one I have around Fanrealm only it keeps us out." He looked to his cousin. "I also have someone on the inside of the tower. I need Fryto and Frita and we'll crack it."

Roc gripped Frito's arm suddenly. "You found her? Does that also mean that you got us allies?" Frito shook his head. "Then you best have something because I don't have the forces. They have us in sheer numbers let alone the fact that they don't die unless they've been completely mauled. The out look of this isn't very good." Roc looked out to the line of demons reforming to march again. Roc let his mind roll about. Frito's blazing appearance was wearing off, but Thamrell was playing it safe. The tower was stopped, but that wouldn't be for line. After losing so much to the first waves of battle the god of despair was going to keep a short, tight leash on his troops. *I'll be damned if I can't use that to my advantage.* Roc thought as Fryto limped over and hugged his brother.

The Flame held him at arms length. "You succeed? Frita?"

"She's around here somewhere." Frito looked at his brother's leg. Fryto dismissed it, but Frito's hand was already glowing. "Roc is going to need you. Its glory time."

Roc watched as Fryto winced in pain from his wound knitting itself closed. He looked to Gorn and then Craig. The Dragoncaller was looking at the ground. "Alright, this is the plan." Roc stood up on the running board, letting his voice carry. "The last thing they'll expect is a frontal assault in a narrow, wedge formation. I'll need to get a sudden burst from the Spitznats and a full all out charge with the Barchetta as a ram to smash their lines. We'll need order and to keep in line to insure they don't pinch us off. I'll need as many knights as we can muster. We'll have to head away from the tower about forty paces and cut in to the side because they will be strongest in the front. Frito, I need you in the front with all your magic to cut us a hole as long as you can. Then you and I will take out their golems. Achillia will take the point."

The Knight of Uko stepped up after hearing her name. Her sword was clenched tightly in her shaking hand and she reeked of Ozone. "What are we doing?"

Gorn answered: "A suicidal charge. You're in front."

"Wonderful! Its about time. What of Milo? We were separated. Shouldn't he be in on this?"

Frito looked up. "I think he's in that crowd over there." Frito pointed deep into demon territory.

"By Ovam's belly! Should we get him?"

"You know him. He's happy were he is. I guess it is best though."

Craig looked up. "Allow me."

Suddenly two White Tiger Dragons appeared over the knight of Ovam, set fire to anything around him, picked him up and flew out of reality. An instant later, Milo was dropped beside Craig. The knight was ablaze with holy fire and looking for something to kill as Fryto lifted him to his feet. He looked about uncertainly, wavering in his stance.

"Milo!" Craig piped cheerfully, "Glad you could make it. We're charging the tower."

Roc pointed to him. "You and Achillia are in front. Don't go berserk until she says to."

Milo took a boda of Slivobitsa and sprayed it on his head, face, then down on the inside of his armor. "And what if Thamrell rushes our line." The black knight looked across the wall reforming again. "They won't hold a full press."

Roc nodded, surprised that the knight was capable of rational thought. "I have already summoned Wendell from the rear to take over the line. He will hold it together. In addition, Thamrell will be aiming for us." Roc looked to the knights and warriors around him. Craig was looking down again. "He will not go anywhere if we are threatening his tower. He will take us out before dealing with the line." Roc continued with his plan. "Craig, you and your Dragon-panthers make a straight line to the tower after Achillia. Gorn, you Fryto and Frita will be with Craig. Frito and I will fall in behind. Craig, you've got the important part in this. They're gonna shit on you and the Dragon-panthers and we need them to keep the magic off of us. You're gonna be jizz if you don't watch it. Gorn, Battle, Blade and Bloc are going to be your arrow stoppers. Don't use them up too quick. You're the Dragoncaller and I need you alive and Thamrell needs you dead, dead, dead. Hopefully, Achillia will be the lure for us...What in Worldsend are you looking at?"

Craig didn't look from the ground. "This is asphalt." He said pointing to the ground. "Real asphalt...With yellow lines, and reflector bumps." Craig reached down and touched it.

"Blessid!" Frito suddenly gleamed. "We got allies!" He said with raised eyebrows.

"Who?" Roc countered.

A wailing horn sounded into Okshiru's sky. Roc looked to his pipers, but they were silent. Craig looked to the rear with astonishment. "An air horn?" Craig slowly lifted to his feet. "A truck?"

"Roc!" Frito suddenly took action. "Get ready, we go now. I just hope our allies play the game."

Roc climbed back into the Barchetta. "Who the devil did you get for an ally?"

Frito climbed into the back seat.

Roc grunted and pounded a mailed fist on the door of the Barchetta as he tried to think. He didn't like to depend on magic, but he needed it to break the force around the tower. He looked up at the tower starting to move forward and laid out before it like a crawling swarm was the forces of Hel. He gritted his teeth. This wasn't good. He watched intently as his own motley rabble of an army prepared to charge.

Roc looked to Craig who was looking at the ground. "What are you doing?"

Craig looked up from the ground rather bewildered. "This is asphalt."

Roc pointed to the wheel. "Get ready to drive!" He growled and Craig jinked.

Frito laid a hand on Roc's shoulder. "Keep the men off the road."

Roc waved to Gorn to carry on the order, then waved at Craig to get moving.

High above Mortalroam, Kemoto the magnificent flaming sun bird poised at his highest point. His light shone down pulling out every detail of the blood red sea of devastation. He watched with awe as Milo slashed his way through the tide. The black, one armed knight was easily recognized as the single greatest threat to demon kind. The Demonslayer's fury was undiminished by the numbers as he brilliantly carved his way in.

He watched as Frito pulled in riding on the Hothering Slothering Wanderblest Beast complete with Horro-shred option and, unknown to mortals, *Duel Turbo*. Dru had to be thrilled. In his first thirty beats of battle, Frito and the Hothering Slothering Wanderblest Beast complete with Horro-shred option and, unknown to mortals, *Duel Turbo*, had totaled more dead then all the knights combined save Ovam's knight, Milo. However, Kemoto was willing to lay wages that when Klitac, the god of numbers, had totaled the war dead, they will find that pound for pound, the Dragonslayer will put all of the great knights to shame. However, the battle was still young.

He watched as Roc's forces collected and pulled about. The men were gearing into a great shaft to pierce the demon lines like a great spear. Roc's forces looked diminutive, scant to the oncoming volume of hate before them.

Klitac's number's had drastically changed and gambling was turning sour. The gods were forbidden to interfere and now their favorite sport was losing its flavor. Even with the sudden appearance of Frito, Knight of Dru, the odds changed very little in Roc's favor. The Dragonslayer was the long, long, way out there, shot and few were foolish, or hopeful enough to go with them regardless of the pay off. A tactical natural disaster suddenly happening and swallowing the entire lot into the earth had better odds than Roc winning this war.

But this new gambit was something to watch at the least. Ura was nearly drooling, squirming in her seat. Dru only stared, coldly as always. Meleki chewed her nails while Hauge rooted. Klitac's slide-ruler only flashed bone white adding his numbers. This was a spectacle to behold.

Far below, Roc was out of the car and pacing now. He looked to Worldsend and hissed into Hauge's wind. He licked his dry lips with a dry tongue. He looked to the east at the shining tower looming towards him. Its height and brashness was mocking him, scorning him. He could feel his face twisting again. His muscles were knotting with hate. The water bag came past him and as it did, he knelt at it and let it pour into his mouth and down the inside of his breast plate. The water was cold and so was the air and it felt smooth and comforting as it slid into his shorts. He looked up and nodded his thanks to the water bearer.

"Thou art quite welcome, Michael." She answered.

Fantista? Roc suddenly looked at the bearer. It was Frita. She was wearing borrowed armor and it fit her rather badly. Her face was clean and untouched by the days fighting, yet it was bruised and scabbed from other recent tussles. Her hair was braided tightly and hung in a single rope over her shoulder. She smiled sweetly and tenderly and for a moment and looked so much like her mother, Roc was paralyzed.

"Off your knees, Roc," She chided as she gripped his arm. "People would think you're bowing to me." She heaved him to his feet, snatching a still moving disembodied demon hand from his shoulder as she did.

Roc's mouth was hanging open and it took a bit of effort to close it. She was smiling, joking. He hadn't seen her show an emotion since Dexter died. Roc suddenly realized that his younger cousin, although adorned with scars, was beautiful.

A smile swelled on his face as his arms swept around her. He lifted her, spinning about as he bellowed a shrilling whoop. He dropped her and held her at arms length. She was still laughing! Laughing at pain, laughing at anger, laughing! This was the girl he had grown up with.

"My lord," She beamed at him. "Save your enthusiasm for the battle."

Roc suddenly looked up and realized that every one had seen his uncharacteristic display and was gaping at him. Roc twisted his face in return and made a tortured sound and they all turned back.

He relaxed his face and looked to Frita again. "Frita I..." Roc paused as he found himself speechless.

"Denice," She corrected him. Her smile only faltered for a moment. "It's Denice now."

Roc realized that she had lost her knighthood and he only nodded in understanding.

A mourning cry suddenly filled Hauge's winds as the funeral precession came closer. She looked at it. Roc could see her white face suddenly darken as if a shadow fell upon it. She looked away and was smiling again. "We have work to do."

Roc nodded grimly. "I will fell that tower for you." He pledged.

She shook her head as her smile faded away. She said with determination: "We will."

She took his hand and they walked to the front.

Craig stood tall on the hood of the Barchetta. "It's just as I feared." He said grimly, taking the spyglass from his eye.

"What is it?" Frito asked anxiously.

"Dual turbo." Craig answered dramatically.

"Is that serious?"

Craig looked down at him. "Serious? Serious? Lets just say I'm glad he's over there."

"Is it that bad?" Frito asked skeptically as he helped Craig down.

"Bad?" Craig again echoed Frito. "Bad? Let's put it this way, if bad was looks, Roc would be pretty."

"What's this I hear?" Roc said coming closer.

"The Hothering Slothering Wanderblest Beast complete with Horro-shred option has *Dual Turbo*." Frito answered simply.

"So?" Roc glared at the Dragoncaller.

"So?" Craig repeated him. "So, he says." He looked at Denice. "He says 'So?'." Craig suddenly turned at Roc. "Let's just think about this for a minute. It means that there is someone out there in hell with enough knowledge and technology to attach one. Or even worse, the Hothering Slothering Wanderblest Beast complete with Horro-shred option and *Dual Turbo* is not only capable of independent thought, but self refinement, or even – shudder – self replication!"

"Frightening." Frito mumbled sardonically.

Frita showed no concern for the matter as she pushed over and took Craig's hand warmly. "Congratulations on your daughter."

Craig suddenly looked around but no one seemed to have any concern about the Hothering Slothering Wanderblest Beast complete with Horro-shred option and *Dual Turbo*. Roc climbed into the Barchetta while Frito took Craig's other hand. "Neeko delivered?" He said patting Craig's limp arm. "That's great!"

Craig looked to Roc in the passenger seat. "But the…"

Roc cut him off with a wave. "As long as its munching on demons, *Dual Turbo* is rating little concern on my list. Now get in and drive!"

Craig slowly climbed over the door feeling foolish about bringing an important, but rather irrelevant discovery to light. He sat in the driver's seat taking a hold of the wheel. "Drive where?"

Roc pointed with a wave of his heavy hand. "We're going to ram their front shields and push deep into their lines."

"Oh." Craig said simply, then raised his hand. "May I be excused?" Roc sneered. "No."

Craig whined. "But don't you have like battering rams and stuff? Don't you have respect for such a classic car?"

"Nothing is going to give us the punch better than the Barchetta." Roc looked around. "Now get ready. On my signal, I want everything you got."

Craig drummed his fingers on the wheel. "Wait a minute!" He turned around and looked at Frita. "How did you know my wife gave birth?"

Frita smiled. "Orrin is broadcasting the news."

Craig suddenly wondered why he was deaf to the broadcast. Another irrelevant thought, he said to himself as he wheeled the Barchetta into position.

They were coming.

Two White Tiger Dragons stepped into reality, flanking the red Barchetta. Pikemen raised their halberds and stood ready. Pipers took up the tune following the drummers tempo. The banners waved proudly in the steady wind. Frita looked suddenly around. Fikor was on the field. She felt his crisp fur push past her with a breath of ice at his snout. The god of winter kissed her and blessed her and quickly stepped out of the way.

Frito touched her arm, "Are you all right?"

She quickly nodded. "Fine." She looked ahead at the tower. "Let us do this."

Frito could feel heat from her arm. Heat billowing from her centre. White holy fire. "You heard the lady." Frito said to Craig.

Craig revved the engine the Barchetta answered him. "Wanna Drag?"

Craig pushed the button to arm the Atomic batteries. A whine poured from the engine. "You said everything, right?"

Roc had a firm grip on the dash board. He bared his teeth like a front grill straight ahead. "Everything!" His lips twisted around his teeth as he spoke.

Craig shrugged his shoulders. "The man said, 'Everything'." He casually flipped the turbos to standby. The vibration of the twin turbines suddenly shook the car. The Barchetta smiled. "Turbines to speed." It said.

Roc suddenly looked at the car then at Craig. "Hey! What are you doing? You never showed me this!"

"Oh?" Craig said amazed. "It must have slipped my mind." He said trying to sound truthful.

They were coming.

The air horn sounded again from the rear, this time with more urgency. A deep throaty roar came billowing from out of the woods. Craig sat up in his seat, as far as his seat belt would allow, to see. Frita's strong hand slapped him down again.

Arrows passed each other in the sky. The incoming volley shattered and bounced in the air at Frito's wave. The Dragon-panthers suddenly leapt into the fray dragging enemy spell casters out of the melee and into their stomachs. White Tiger Dragons laid down sudden lines of glowing fire on the ballista crews.

The air horn sounded again. Craig knew it was a truck. A truck from Hel.

The twenty two wheel, black Kenworth screamed out of the woods with a tremendous roar. The Barchetta heaved from the backlash as the truck monstered past. Its' horn blasted an ear bending noise as it thundered on.

"It's a twenty two wheel Kenworth from Hel," Craig mumbled in disbelief. "With Pennsylvania plates."

Behind the black monstrous truck was all seventy five of the demon bikers.

"GO! GO! GO!" Roc roared and pounded the dash board. Craig suddenly nailed the pedal and with a snap that pushed Roc's head into the rest, the Barchetta poured after the Demon bikers.

The Spitznats horsemen leapt after the red gleaming car followed by a giant throng of blood heated Barbarians. The rest followed in a charge that drowned out the pipers's cry.

The devil's Kenworth plowed into the demon front lines without pause. Oaken shields suddenly flipped and floated in the air like giant paper cards. The glowing white flames laid down by the Dragon-panthers seemed to part and the procession pushed on through. Parts and shafts and splinters fluttered past the Barchetta. Demons caught in the blast of the Kenworth, now fell beneath the wheels of the Barchetta. Craig kicked the car into four wheel drive and kept his foot to the floor.

Blood was flowing on the asphalt track beneath them and the Barchetta was bogging down.

The Kenworth flinched as it clipped something hard. A stone golem rolled along the side of the truck before flinging itself in the bikers path. They revved their engines and powered around or over it. The stone golem pushed its face from the black tar surface and glared at the quad head lights of the Barchetta.

Craig swerved, spinning the wheel violently to the right. The Barchetta responded quickly, fishtailing as it changed direction. Its left bat wing went to the winds as it clipped the golem's arm. Craig suddenly found himself plowing head on into demons.

They bounced over the hood. They bounced off of the door. Roc flung them from out of the front seat. Lightning leapt from Frito's blade spear and carved a heated line before them. The twin White Tiger Dragons kept the flanks clear with the assistance and guidance of three Dragon-panthers flying overhead.

Frita looked to the rear. The Spitznats, Barbarians and Dragon guard were behind. The rest had followed slowly behind the great truck.

Craig felt mud splash up in his face. He felt heat swelling from around him. He could only cling to the writhing steering wheel and hold the car steady.

The right wheel exploded and the car swerved hard. Craig fought the wheel and made it conform. The four wheel drive, now three, automatically compensated for the loss. Craig couldn't see ahead of him. Roc was standing in the front seat swinging his great sword with lust. Frito was in the back also swinging with fury. Craig grit his teeth. Neither Slayer could see the car was being over whelmed.

"Stand BY!" Craig screamed as he reached up and gripped Roc's belt. The Dragonslayer's heavy armor toppled into Craig's lap. Frita threw her arms around Frito and he fell back with demons leaping at his throat.

The atomic jet turbos exploded with power. The barchetta suddenly leapt over the pile and plowed bumper first into the demon mob. A long billowing streak of fire trailed behind the car as it bounced and rocketed through.

Things threw themselves past. Craig ducked below the dashboard and closed his eyes. He felt bodies rolling over him. He could hear the paint on the Barchetta shrill and peel as armor cut into it. He could feel the wheels sink into yielding bodies as they rolled over them.

He could hear that damn truck horn.

Craig took a peek. They was traveling head on at the Devil's Kenworth at 200 miles an hour.

His feet sank the brakes to the floor and the wheels tried to lock on the blood slick grass. Twin chutes popped automatically.

They stopped.

Craig opened his eyes and all he could see before him was a chrome grill. The Barchetta looked through its broken head lights and spat through broken teeth. "Git outta my way!"

Roc gripped the dashboard. He blinked several times to get his eye balls to stop rolling in his head and focus.

Demons suddenly sprang at the Barchetta with vengeance. Roc reached for his great sword too late as a thousand hot sweaty hands overwhelmed him.

With a roar Roc was on his feet and pushed at the pile jumping into the car. Two Dragon-panthers stepped in and tossed demons aside while another White Tiger Dragon laid a barrier of white fire. Lightning flashed from the backseat, throwing demons from the car.

The devil's horn sounded again. Demon bikers rolled by clearing out the stragglers with little trouble, their maces and morning stars rose and fell with practiced rhythm.

Roc tossed a demon over board and looked to the truck in front of him. Arrows streaked around him as he walked out on the hood of the Barchetta. His left foot skidded on blood but he quickly regained his balance and glared imposingly at the devil. "You're in my way." He said.

Trid Dreath opened the passenger door and leaned out. His pale white face looked deathly in the bright sun. He wore no emotion that any one could see.

"I said," Roc stepped a bit closer. "You're in my way!"

Trid cocked a dramatic brow while peering at Roc.

Craig pushed forward with an assisted paw from the Dragon-panther named Archabald while the rumbling motorcycles circled about the car. He looked to the Kenworth. The driver, wearing a Philadelphia flyer's shirt, was standing on the front fender. "The boss wants'cha to move." He said quietly.

Roc stuck out his chest and it nearly touched the front grill of the Kenworth. "You're going the wrong damn direction." Roc said defiantly. "We need to take the tower."

"I'm am here to show a presence of power." Trid said simply. "Get out of the way.

Craig ducked as a spear passed by him. With a slight glow, the Bow of Dragoncaller came to his hand. In one fluid motion, he rose up, drawing shaft to cheek and letting fly. It pushed into the line of demons with a whistling snap.

"Mighty fine shooting, Tex!" Kevin shouted as Craig drew again. The devil's driver only smiled at him. "Neat!" He said pulling a pack of Marlboros out of his rolled sleeve. "How many pounds? That's a compound! You don't see them around here."

Craig relaxed the draw. "Its up to 250 now. I brought it from home. Its magic gets stronger as I get stronger." Craig drew again and fired. The black arrow streaked a tearing line in the air and struck a giant, who was about to lob a big rock, in the forehead.

The driver nodded as he lit his smoke with a zippo lighter nodding. "Nice. But check this out." He pulled a huge Colt 454 Casual out of his waist belt and aimed it into the mass of demon with one hand. He frowned as he aimed down the barrel and squeezed the trigger. With a resounding boom a demon head exploded like a zit. "There you go!" He exclaimed. He looked at Craig and stepped down from the fender to the hood of the Barchetta. "I know you." He said pulling a memory out into the open. "You're that guy from Brooklyn." Craig nodded. "Yeah, that's cool. Kevin." He announced himself sticking out a hand and giving a firm shake. "York P.A."

"Kevin!" The devil was standing on the front fender of the truck.

Kevin turned and gave a quick wave to Craig. "Later dude!" Kevin quickly climbed into the cab of the truck and began to back up. Roc snorted and stepped from the hood. Craig didn't ask what he said to the devil, there were more pertinent things to worry about.

"Roc the Barchetta's lost a wheel. We ain't moving." Craig said taking up his sword.

Gorn, who had been clinging onto the trunk but got flung off when Craig hit the golem, came running up. "Roc! The demons are paying us little mind, the tower is still rolling on. Obviously, Thamrell is assured that you can't break his barriers and he is rushing the line. Even if we reach the tower and knock it out, there are too many of them to stop!"

Roc twisted his face and thought loudly for Orrin. "Tell Wendell to pull back and don't stop until Aelph area three."

'We're not far from there now.' Wendell replied directly.

They were already pulling back. Roc looked at the tower still moving forward. Thamrell's strategy was simple. Push on.

Roc looked around sharply for Frito and Frita. The two were missing. Roc snatched at Craig's arm and pulled him close to shout in his ear. "Thamrell is just going to crush us. We take it out, we stop the forward push!" Roc looked around again. A large giant was stomping towards him followed by a gaggle of demons. Roc turned and squared off with the giant.

Light flashed and Craig spun around. Archabald the Dragon-panther, tossed a limp body over his shoulder and looked. Lightning sprang from out of the sea of demons like a white thin twisted tree. A small ring of smoke puffed out in its wake.

"Roc!" Craig screamed. The demons didn't care about the Dragonslayer or the Dragoncaller. "They're gunning for the knights!"

Roc whirled about turning his back to the giant. He could barely see the white holy glow that Frito was giving off. Roc grit his teeth and sprang easily over the Barchetta. "Drat! Thamrell is more resourceful than I thought. Take care of him." Roc motioned to the giant as he dashed by. "I'm A Commin' I'm A Commin'!" He shouted as he plowed into the fray. Demons suddenly turned and formed a wall of swords and spears. It was evident that the tower was indeed capable of multiple commands. Roc needed his cousins. Thamrell didn't.

Roc pulled back his great blade over his shoulder and with a rolling growl brought it about like a woods man's axe. Demon steel and bone yielded quickly the awesome might and fury that only Roc could wield.

Craig stood looking up at the giant. The giant stood looking down at Craig. Around them, Gorn and two of the Dragonguard, Blade and Bloc fought against the Giant's entourage. The giant seemed confused, rocking its head first to the right and then to the left. Its numb expression and sharp glinting black eyes searched the Dragoncaller as if looking for something, wanting something.

The giant smiled as he seemed to have figured it out.

And raised his club.

Craig's bow flashed, changing to a sword.

Craig clenched his sword in both hands and raised it over his shoulder. He spun and twisted to the right, barely dodging the swinging club and the huge spike that protruded out of the wood. Craig swiped his sword back handedly as he passed and only cut air. The giant raised to swing again but Craig easily danced out of the way. The Dragoncaller feinted, stepping back then suddenly springing forward with a curving upswing cutting the flesh in a long black line. The giant stumbled back and Craig bounded forward. The Dragoncaller swung again but the giant shifted and the blade merely glanced him. The giant suddenly kicked out, catching Craig in the side with a toe the size of a fist. Craig rolled and quickly found his feet, but the giant seemed faster and was already in the air for a rousing stomp.

Craig could feel the sword guide him. Pulling itself forward in a thrust. The huge blade aimed its edge for the lower abdomen and pushed its way through with a howling hiss. The giant fell, dragging Craig with him as he tried to free his sword. The Dragoncaller rose quickly pulling his blade with him. He reared it back over his head and brought it down quickly on the Giant's neck. With a second blow, the head rolled free of its body.

Craig didn't pause, he turned quickly following after Roc's demon strewn trail as Blade and Bloc flanked him.

Demons lunged at him and Craig only swiped back. He muscled through the running spears, pushing and grabbing at the wooden shafts. He ducked, swinging blindly, letting the sword guide itself. The Sword of Magnum took advantage and screamed with joy. It pulled into what flesh it could find. Arms and heads quickly fell to its burning bite. Hands leapt free and weapons clattered with little resistance. Craig pushed on, following the sword's lead as Max had taught him. He didn't fight it for control, only lending his skill to it. He went with its motion, he could tell what it was going to do, what it wanted him to do, so he did it.

He could hear Roc and feel the vibration of his magic sword of Dragons. He could see its flaming arch rising above the blur of demons. Steel blinded him and Craig pushed on. The Sword writhing in his hands pulled him on.

Roc was shouting about his flank. Watch his flank the sword told Craig in its own way. Craig followed and brought it about clearing out the demons trying at Roc's wide back giving the Dragonslayer one less thing to worry about.

Something bloody and unattached flew by. Craig could only see the blade rising over the Dragonslayer's frame and coming down again. Craig couldn't hear over the din. He felt steel slashing at his armor, hands grabbing at his feet, claws lashing at his face. The sword swung up and took and arm with a bloody ring. *Watch what you're doing* the sword reminded him.

Hot blood poured from his face. Demon blood was making his hands slippery. He could feel his knuckles turn white as his hands clenched tighter. He could see Frito fighting toe to toe with a large, multi limbed demon. Frita was lying at his feet.

Roc sprang straight up and cut a bloody smile into the upper arm of the demon. It howled and tried to jerk its arm back. Frito swept in from the side and caught the demon with the man catcher hook of his blade-spear. He pulled the demon forward and off balance while Roc removed its spine with two bold strokes.

Craig rushed to Frita's side, half pushing, half cutting his way through. He threw himself over her as Archabald soared over and laid down cover fire. Craig scooped her up looking for a wound. Blood was every where he touched, pooling in the creases. He could find no large points of entry, only a few random nicks and scrapes. It wasn't her that was bleeding. Craig looked at one point where his hand held her and traced where the blood was flowing. He then looked at his arm. Demon blood mixed with his own and burned into the newly cut grove in his arm. Craig's fingers continued their search and found another that creased his bassinet. He didn't remember being wounded. *Minor.* His sword told him. *You call this Minor? My head is puking out my brains and you call this minor? Sombody just bust me upside the head and I don't know who.* He argued. *And what is worrying going to do you? Are you dead? No, like you can do something about it. You know, worry is going to be the first thing that kills you.* The sword answered. *Besides, you wacked the guy who hit you. He got the worst of the deal.*

Craig fixed a snarl on his face as he lifted Frita to a sitting position. The one thing that he hated more than magic was magic that was smarter than he was.

Frita shivered uncontrollably as her eyes reeled in her head, crossing and uncrossing. Craig could feel the magic. It made the tatoos on his arms itch. He slapped her quickly and sharply twice leaving a bloody smear where his hand had touched her.

Her eyes focused on him. She bolted upright and forced her head to think. Over her, Roc and Frito fought back to back. Black blood rained on her white face. Craig raised a hand to shield the blood from her eyes. It fell to her lips and its taste burned her.

Her lips were in motion. Her hands went to her head as she tried to shield out the havoc around her and concentrate. Static shot along her arm to her fingers and light exploded in a ball before her. Her hands pushed out and pure white light poured from her ball with the night cry of Fikor. A sudden whirlwind sprang about them. Ice drove in blinding sheets, freezing demon blood in their veins. They fell, they stumbled, they pulled back.

Frita's magic of cold suddenly shot out from her silver eyes and beams of blue turned a monster to frozen stone.

Frito suddenly released the lighting to play, and it rained down with fury. Demons locked in ice shattered and crumbled to the ground. Others leapt into the air convulsing with licks of power falling away with their flesh.

Pain shot through Craig's mind as Frita's cold hand of healing unexpectedly touched his head. He felt his scalp cool and his mind clear. He instinctively touched the same spot and he could feel the closing wound on his skull. He looked at his hand as it came away. There was four colors of blood streaking his fingers. One of them was his own. He didn't even want to think about where his helmet had gone.

She touched his arm and it's wound also closed quickly to her command.

"Thanks. And here I was coming to help you." Craig mumbled.

Frita said nothing as she took his hands and placed them on the breast plate of her armor. "Get me out of this thing!" Her hands were already in motion, snatching at the leather thongs and popping the rivets. "Don't argue." She said without looking at him. "This suit will kill me."

Craig gripped and pulled. The cuirass came off in his hands. He pulled at her arm guards while her fingers danced, unlacing her thigh guards. The metal shell peeled from her and fell away. "The tower is getting closer!" She had risked a brief glance to the east. "Its bearing down on us! Hurry!"

Craig took up the Sword of Magnum and with a touch, her war belt and ass guards fell away. She suddenly sprang out of her shell to her feet. She took up her sword and held it threateningly in her hands. It was cold and unresponsive. It was heavy and abandoned. She cast it aside and left it behind.

Craig called for Moppy and Floppy and twin columns and flame fell from the sky at his command. Demons were being frozen and roasted between breaths. They pulled back again into the sky with demon magic chasing them. Craig scooped up his fallen helm.

Frito shuffled back with his blade-spear wavering before him. "The tower is coming after us."

"Good!" Roc rumbled. "Let it come."

"The closer to it we get, the harder the demons get."

Roc shook his head quickly, "And what does that change?"

The Devilslayer looked to the Dragonslayer and smiled.

Roc took the lead plowing with heavy armor while Frita followed him. Frito raised his blade-spear and a weaving stroke of lightning waved over Roc and cindered a line before them. Demons closed about them. Axes fell and spears pushed through. Frita, out of her armor, brought her mother's Sho-Pa to play and blocked their sharpness with kicks and punches. Her snapping blows cracked chitinous shielding while her blinding kicks shattered marrow. She was alive now, glowing as white as her brother who rolled behind her.

Craig held up the rear poking and hacking at the mass as they tried to close in on the flank. Milo from out of nowhere, kicked a demon and pushed him on Craig's blade. Craig hardly had an instant to thank him before another followed behind. Craig pulled back his blade freeing it from their hollow bellies but another drove itself home.

Craig twisted the edge and drove it out of the demons side. He raised to bring his sword down when another demon crumbled before him as Achillia brained it in the head. The Sword of Magnum screamed at them to wait until it cleft them before they died, but it went unnoticed as a head was suddenly flung at him.

Fire rolled at him in a tremendous cascading ball. Demons fell to it being crushed beneath its flaming body. Craig brandished his sword with an instinctive but vain attempt to split the element when it suddenly split itself and obliqued to the sides. Craig was mad now. If things were going to be like this, he could have stayed at home and phoned the war in.

Fryto came running on the charred groove of ground with Achillia close behind. Beside them were four of the Demon bikers from Hel. Frito moved to the front while Battle, Blade and Bloc circled Frita. Craig and Fryto held up the rear.

The tower loomed before them. There was a line of the Spitznats and Barbarians augmented by the Demon bikers from Hel who had followed the Kenworth, now branched off under Gorn's command fell in behind Craig. Support came from the sky as Dragon-panthers and White Tiger Dragons controlled the air, weaving in and out of the flashes of demon magic.

A giant head suddenly popped from the earth. Its flashing fangs and giant mouth quickly opened on Frito and swallowed him whole, taking the patch of dirt he stood on with him. Roc screamed and dove in the worm's gaping mouth after him, leaping over its front line of teeth and diving with a swords thrust down the beast's gullet. The great worm raised up with a terrible screech, its eyes went rolling as smoke, thick and black, crawled from its mouth. Blood spat from a hole in its throat as it teetered like wheat in the wind before crashing to the ground like a felled tree.

It rolled to its back, crushing three slower demons as it did. Roc's spiked gauntlet erupted from the carved hole in its throat. His head and shoulders quickly followed as he pushed and twisted free. His other hand came out dragging his sword along. He buried it deeply in the worm's thick hide and used it pull himself free. He pushed his bloody hand back in and pulled until Frito's arm followed. Blade, the Dragonguard, had scrambled, with help from Battle and Bloc, up the worm's side and was running along the worm's stomach to lend aid to his Master. Roc pulled harder while Blade hacked at the hole to make it larger. Frito's head broke the surface with a gasp and a pop. His body quickly followed as Roc and Blade pulled him clear.

"It's getting nasty." Roc mumbled as they slid from the great worm's belly. Below, Fryto had built a semi circle of fire, using the worms body as a wall, to hold the demons back.

"Frito!" Roc had to hold up the coughing knight. The smell from the giant worm's innards was overwhelming. "We need some hot shit right now!" The demons were more coordinated the closer they came to the tower. They bathed in the direct glow of its controlling influence and responded without hesitation or care.

Frito leaned back trying to catch his breath and trying to find a bit of unpolluted air. He cocked his eye as he held his breath and let it out. "Right." He whispered. "Where is Trid?"

"Holding up what's left of our front lines with the Hothering Slothering Wanderblest Beast complete with Horro-shred option." Roc answered.

Frito looked along the body of the Worm. Its three hundred pace long body proved to be an excellent wall. "We'll use the worm as a shield to keep the fighting to one side."

"I know that!" Roc bellowed. "I was hoping for a little creativity!"

Frito turned to Fryto. "A fire bridge!"

Fryto didn't turn from his concentration. His face was a glow from the burning wall he maintained by channeling his power of fire given to him from Kemoto, through his magic axe. "I can't hold this wall and a bridge!" He shook his head. "I've only got so much power."

"Frita?"

She nodded. "It will take all my magic, and we still will have to get closer!" She reached up and touched his arm as if to get his attention. "It's Denice." She reminded him.

Frito wiped worm's blood from his face and blinked the sting from his eyes, smiling. "You're telling me my business, Frita? Am I not the Archknight?" He then looked to Roc. "Well, that's all I have, I used all my magic at the front. Save for a few card tricks. We have to get closer." He suddenly ducked as arrows wiped by him.

"Then I will get her closer." Roc swore holding up his sword.

They readied and the wall fell at Fryto's command. The demons had been waiting for it to fall and charged when it did. Achillia commanded them to hold in the name of Uko and the charge was broken. Roc and Frito clashed with shield and steel with a crunch and groan.

With wide eyes Craig looked into the masses of demons before him. They were not going to make it to the tower.

'*Backfire to Batman. Arclight in twelve.*' Rumbled in Craig's head.

Craig pulled behind Fryto and concentrated on the dragoncall. '*What? You said...*'

'*Hey!*' The big red grumbled. '*I'm dying up here so don't argue, I got one pass and I'm gonna make it good.*' Craig could hear Brezhnev's lungs rattle with exhaustion. The dragon was wheezing, with each flap of his sweeping wings more spittle foamed his maw. The great dragon had shrugged off demon magic, but at a price. He was flying by sheer will. '*So where do ya want it?*'

'*Clear us a path to the tower*'

'*You're too close*'

Craig stepped quickly beside Fryto and lashed out with his blade, killing the demon the knight had been dealing with. "Fryto...I'm gonna need a big fire shield in a few seconds. The strongest you can muster."

"Fire shield? To protect us from fire? Do you have a plan?" Fryto asked without breaking his concentration.

'Arclight in Nine. I can't change course now. Tell me you have a plan' Through the eyes of the red dragon Craig could see the swarming ants of the battle below.

"Just can you do it? Shield dragon fire?" Craig shouted letting his sword do the fighting for him. Fryto nodded but his face was filled with uncertainty. Craig looked to the sky. Blood misted around him and he squinted to clear it. Two sets of tiny black wings poised in the sky. Backfire and Phantom, Craig mused. They both hung awkwardly in the air barely aloft.

'Arclight in seven.'

"Get ready Fryto!"

Fryto turned to his sister. "Frita! Take my hand. I need you!"

'Arclight in five.'

Craig could feel the dragon open his blowholes and flood himself with air. He felt the dragon's lungs swell, awash with circling spheres of fire, orange to yellow to white.

'Arclight in Three!'

"Now Fryto!" Craig shouted.

Shimmering in patches of gray and fog, an opaque wall rose suddenly about them. Frito and Roc stopped unexpectedly in mid swings as the shield sprang before them, closing itself in a circle on top.

'Arclight! Now, Now, NOW!'

They saw the light spill from the sky as their shadows were thrown to ground pooling at their feet. They felt the heat pour around them in a deluge as everything became white. They heard the roar only after it flooded about them in brilliant gold and scarlet. The great wave of fire heaved and splashed with a great rippling circle across the field sending everything in its swelling path into instant smoke.

The tide subsided and the waves pulled back. Fryto's barrier was gone and the slick grass around them steamed with evaporating blood. If they had been in the direct blast of the Red Dragon's anger, despite Fryto's charge of fire control, they would have been as crisp as the charred demon remains that lay about them.

"Fucking A mickey skippy." Craig whispered in astonishment.

"Now that's what I call an Idea!" Roc hollered pushing forward with a fast trot. Frito quickly followed behind moving along on the hot ground. The wave of Dragon fire left a clear, steaming path to the Tower itself. The structure built with wood and covered with plates of metal seemed rickety close up, almost straining to collapse under its own weight. It moaned piteously. Creaking louder than the horns it was sounding. Its magic shield rippled from the dragon's blast.

Below, slaves from the rear rushed to replace the slaves that were incinerated as bolts of magic rained from the tower. The Tower trembled as Frito combined holy might with his fellow knights to send their cursed magic ricocheting back on itself. It shuddered, changed its tactics, abandoning the orders to the front lines to directly control its surrounding vassals.

Demons harkened to the call and ran to intercept the Dragonslayer's party. Magic was failing as Frita, surrounded by the Dragonguard to protect her, used her skills to knock it down. The tower sent fists and sword against them, controlling each blow and swing of the demons at its call.

The attacks were clumsy. The demons tried to fight for control of their own bodies. Frito's reflexes and reactions were blurs to them. His blade-spear was a brilliant flash, slicing bone and sinew like a windmill through the air. Roc was dramatically ruthless but wasted no effort or stroke as he hewed anything that stood before him. Craig released his blade, much to his stygian sword's disliking, and summoned his bow, sniping from the sides. Achillia, Fryto, Milo, Gorn and the Dragonguard hacked, slashed and stabbed what was left.

The tower spat three combatants from its walls. Looming giants with flesh like raw meat grasping gold flaming scimitars in their silver taloned hands. Fire bled alternately from their ears and nostrils as they charged.

Frito arched back with blade-spear in hand and let it fly. Brilliant light marked its trail to the red titan's heart.

It hit solidly. The Titan was too thick to penetrate, so the blade-spear began to burrow, twisting and writhing to push its way through. The titan's bloody hands slid on the shaft trying to free it. Its brothers loomed over him, torn in conflict between wanting to help their brother and obeying the will of the tower to leave him to die.

Frito turned about and took his sister's hands. She had been mentally scrounging the strength within her to cast an ice bridge and now she cast it through her older, stronger, brother, adding his strength to hers.

She heard Fikor howl and Hauge sweep to her side. Ice rode the winds as blue white blocks suddenly grew from the forming pool of winter magic. It struck the face of the tower with half an arc of flow.

Roc was already moving up the path. Steps were already carved to accommodate them. Flyer's soared from the rim of the tower and fell to Craig's relentless supply of magic shafts that leapt into reality on the string of his bow as he drew. Fryto brought up the rear. With each step he took, the bridge crumbled, falling away, leaving the earth bound demons shaking their fists and futilely throwing their spears.

At the top of the stairs the wall of magic suddenly loomed before them. Roc felt his skin crawl with ants standing before it. It was blinding and Roc had to look away. Frito didn't bother to look as he commanded his fellow knights to join, surrounding the others, forming a barrier of knights.

Below, his blade-spear listened to the call of it's master and gave a spinning heave to push its way through the fallen carcass of the titan and fly to his hand. The knights touched sword to shield and hand to shaft in a circle. Frito stood at the front, walking slowly, stepping easily though the shield.

Darkness consumed them. Heat swam through a hideous odor that blinded their eyes with tears. Craig was gagging as he mistakenly breathed too deeply. He easily found the floor with his knees.

Fryto raised his axe and it flared hot with fire, casting a brightness that filled the room they were in.

Little fuzzy monsters dashed from the illumination, jumping through holes and cracks to escape the light. Roc stood hunched over in the low ceiling. He snorted as if to reject the hideous stink that tried to infiltrate his lungs. "Looks like a little slice of Hel." He snarled turning to his cousin. Frito was sagging, leaning on his blade-spear for support. In Fryto's light, the Ninefingers look drained. "Who's got the slivobitsa?" Roc looked accusingly at Achillia and reliably, she had a full boda.

"Worked like a charm." Frito tried breathing through his nose as he spoke, his nostrils flared. Achillia set the boda to his lips and he drank deeply. "Its just like Thamrell did to me. I found a chink in his armor. A subversive in his flock and penetrated his barrier." Achillia gave him another swallow before passing it along. "Seems the communication doesn't extend on the inside like it does the outside." The Archknight ⋅

commented looking at the cleared room. He looked at Roc and waited for him to take his swig of Slivobitsa before continuing. "I think you're right, Roc. This is a little slice of Hel. If that's so, then we knights have a bit more influence but the demons that we find here are also stronger in their own element. It won't be as easy as it was outside."

"Easy?" Craig blurted out before Frita poured a third gulp of the plum brandy down his throat. The Dragoncaller wasn't used to combat so intense around him. After fighting with Ferris and now against the tower, he was worn the worst of them all.

Roc tilted his head toward the two main entrance ways to the small room and Battle and Blade leapt to respond. The Dragonguards stood in crouched positions listening to any sign of movement. Roc then turned to Frito. "We move on and up. They know we're here by now, they just don't know what to do about us."

Achillia was peering through the spaces of the metal plating at the war far below. "The front line isn't moving." The light of outside cast a sharp line against her face. "They are getting troops to start moving the tower again."

"Well that answers that." Frito said grimly. "They're hoping to crush our lines and then do away with us at leisure."

Roc stiffened and then relaxed. "Hels bells, I've lost Orrin. Wendell is on his own. I don't think they can hold."

Frito shook his head, he had no ideas. Craig found his feet reading the consensus of gloom about them. The Dragoncaller smiled.

Roc glared at him. "And what are you smiling at?"

Craig put up his hands in a shrug. "You know?" He reached and drew his sword into reality, much to its delight. "I volunteered for this!" The others readied themselves in response.

Roc took the lead. The left corner led to a wide hallway that faded into shadow. Torches were held in place on the stone walls with black iron brackets. The thin layer of dirt and dust on the floor had been disturbed recently by the tiny prints of minor monster feet. There was no debris, no scattered trash in the length of the hall.

Craig looked around. He stood up straight nodding his head casually. "Hold it." He said calmly. "Reality check."

Frito paused and looked back at him. "This isn't right."

"When you said slice of Hel…" Craig started.

"It's the barrier." Frito explained. "It has brought a entire section of Hel in the body of the Tower. That's how its so powerful. It must be a source of energy."

"Ahhh so." Craig said with a slow nod of his head. "And what happens if we drop the barrier on the tower? It goes back or does it just go pifft."

"We have no way of knowing." Frito answered.

"With or without us?"

Frito shrugged.

Craig smiled in spite of himself. "Lets go kick some ass before my common sense gets wind of this concept."

Roc was standing further along the hall with Battle. Bloc and Blade had moved beyond them. The Dragonslayer gave a go ahead wave and the two Dragonguards moved on. The party made their way as quickly and as quietly as they could down the seemingly endless hall.

After some distance, Roc paused and shook his head. "Something is wrong." He grunted.

Craig looked to his feet and cursed. "This shaft is giving us the shaft!" Everyone looked to their feet at the thin layer of dust recently disturbed by the tiny feet of minor monsters and heavy armored clogs. Frita took her bare foot and placed it into the print in front of her. It was her print.

"Delaying tactic!" Frito hissed at his own stupidity.

"Illusions, mind games, good drugs." Craig quipped with a thin lipped grin. "So what is reality?"

Bloc and Blade suddenly took defensive stances, crouching into springing positions with their weapons ready. Frito dropped Craig's question to scan the hall for what the guards had sensed. The dragon tatoos on Craig's forearms and chest began to burn as the bow of the Dragoncaller was replaced by the Sword of Magnum "Somebody doesn't like us thinking so much."

Frita stepped forward, her lips were trembling as her centre was drained of heat and filled with fear.

Bloc and Blade suddenly began to sway. Their weapons fell from their numb hands and clanged on the floor as their eyes rolled in their heads. "Where am I?" Bloc cried in the voice of a child. "Mommy, come find me!"

Battle gripped the wide guard and shook him. "You are here! I am here with you!" But the Dragonguard was deaf and his heavy frame dropped to the ground sobbing. Battle fought vainly to keep the Dragonguard to his feet, but Bloc was boneless and pooled at his feet.

Blade was even worse as he held an invisible dead father in his arms and mewed piteously.

Frito suddenly screamed as he's knees buckled. Roc's strong arm grabbed him and tried to hold him up, propping him against the wall. Roc looked at the Archknight's legs. Frito's armor flowed like clay as shin guards twisted themselves around backward. Frito's eyes flashed at Roc from behind the face of Hauth, the beast with backward knees.

Achillia screamed as white wolves chased her through the woods of the white mountains. Snow laden branches lashed at her with black talons as she fled with the sound of howling wind flooding her ears. Uko hadn't come to save her this time.

Fryto stood in a barn ablaze with fire. Bales of hay roared and crackled and sparks filled the air with red speckled strokes. Through the heat, his voice screeched. He could see Dwayne by the house with father. If they turned, they would see him and save him. He was trapped and the heat pressed on his cheeks. Why couldn't they hear his screams?

Craig stood beside Frita. His bow was glowing in its dull black light and his eyes were flaring with a nih elve's red. Frita was paralyzed, unmoving with a blind stare down the endless hall. Battle tried in vain to aid his fellow Dragonguards while Roc wrestled with Frito. Roc raised a huge gauntleted fist and back fisted the boar's snout of Hauth. Blood curled at the beast's lips but nothing more. Hauth grabbed at Roc's arms and strained to reach his ear. "Its Thamrell and Thumber...don't give in!"

Roc glared at him. "You don't give in! Pull out! You are not Hauth!"

"But he is!" Thamrell's voice roared in the hall. "He always was! He was destined from day one to day last. Why not accept his fate?"

Craig tightened his grip on his bow. "Bullshit." He spat though his teeth. "Big time bullshit!"

Thamrell looked up at the Dragoncaller. "You amaze me." The god of despair lifted higher over Roc's frame for a better view. "Really amazing. But now the game has ended. You failed. You see, in this trap, time isn't on a one to one. For every passing beat in here, a day has past outside. We have already conquered Mortalroam and are now boldly approaching the great mountains of Worldsend." His shadowy eyes looked to Craig. "Would you like to see your daughter. She's already walking and talking. We had to pry her out of Neeko's cold dead grasp."

The bow of Dragoncaller roared as a shaft leapt across hall. Thamrell waved his hand slightly and the shaft veered and impacted with the wall. "Futile waste of effort and time." He said dismissing the attack. "Each second passing your daughter gets older." A beautiful woman stepped out from behind Thamrell. Her cat ears pushed out gently from her black hair that flowed in gentle curls from her head. Her eyes flashed a bleeding red that caught with the sparkle of her shimmering lips. Tiny dragon wings lifted slowly behind her back cowling her shoulders. Her unformed breasts were only proud nipples and her hairless genitals were only guarded by her prensile tail. "Of course without a father…" Thamrell explained while the girl stroked his leg with a purr. "We had to raise her the only way we know."

The girl looked up and smiled. Her tiny fangs glistened white in the light. "Daddy." She whispered in Neeko's voice.

Craig laughed breathlessly and sighed. "Right." He said as he quickly drew another shaft and fired.

Thamrell went to deflect the arrow, but he wasn't the target. She was.

In a wisp of a shadow, she was gone.

"Cut the shit." Craig cursed as he pushed closer. "I got you beat."

"How?" Thamrell said in disbelief. "How can you do this? Its impossible."

Craig smiled. "Impossibility is our specialty."

Thamrell turned his back and slowly floated away. "No matter. There is nothing that you can do any way."

Craig drew again and fired. The arrow careened and hit the wall. Flustered, Craig fired an arrow at the wall and it missed the wall and hit the god of despair in the back with a dry cracking sound.

Thamrell spun about with fury as Craig fired again at the wall. The god of despair didn't move as the approaching arrow slowed in its path to a crawl and Thamrell simply stepped out of the way. "Again you lose."

Hauth stood on his backward bending legs and shouted through his boar's snout. "You're fighting the wrong man, Craig!" Hauth turned to Frita and took her arm roughly. "Take back your power. Take it from him!"

She looked at him. She didn't see Hauth the beast with backward knees, she saw Dwayne, the second son of her father. She looked down the hall at Thamrell and the Monster that stood invisibly beside him. She felt her centre open and fill with the magic he had stolen from her.

Frito screamed as he fell to the floor when his knees reversed again. Achillia blinked several times while Fryto looked for where the flames went.

A monster of scales and bleeding eyes suddenly came into view. He looked about in surprise as it dawned on him that he could see himself and ergo others could too. He looked at Craig and Craig looked back with a pointing finger.

"I know you!" Craig said accusingly.

"Who? Me?" The monster placed a heavy clawed hand on his chest.

"Yeah, you! You were under my bed when I was a kid!"

"Hey," The monster protested. "There was a lot of us about in them days. Are you sure it wasn't Ivan? Did you have dreams of Communist takeovers and Stalinism?"

"No. No. No." Craig shook his head stiffly. "It was you…" Craig pushed his mind to work. "Thumber!" His brain spat the name through his mouth in exaltation.

Thumber suddenly cowered at Craig's words and stepped back. Thamrell swept behind him. "He can't hurt you!"

"Oh yeah?" The monster realized. "Yeah! You can't hurt me!"

"But I can." Frita said simply, the knuckles in her fist popping as it tightened. "You have united us." She smiled at the thought. "Me, Frita and Denice. I know who I am now. I am Denice, daughter of Lord Hammerstike. I am Frita, Knight of Fikor."

Sweat could be seen rolling from beneath Thumber's scales. He looked for Thamrell, but the god of despair had abandoned him.

Frita smiled. "You've taken something from me, Thumber. Now I will take it back." She closed her eyes as the air filled with white light. Her long hair slowly began to fill with wind. With a sudden, hissing breath, a flash of heat and light pulled from Thumber's centre and into Frita's.

Thumber shimmered, and faded quickly, sucking from memory like a bad dream.

The walls of the hall fell and the inside of the wooden tower, its structure creaking and moaning was revealed. Craig fought for balance and Frita had to hold him to keep from falling as the tower suddenly lurched forward. Bloc and Blade quickly recovered their weapons and took to the ready.

They were standing in the same room they had first entered. Achillia again peered out between the armor spacing. "We're moving. If we're going to do anything, we must do it now."

Without hesitation, Roc made his way through the thin slit of an entrance way that lead to a set of stairs. He was crouched and had to squeeze his way through the narrow flight of stairs. His eyes of green peered into the darkness. The others below could hear an undaunted Roc grunt and his armored spikes dug into the walls around him. Blue and white light flashed above him. They could see Roc's hulking black silhouette in the intense light and hear the warrior scream with pain. There was a shuffling, and grinding of trapped metal on wood and a bone crushing sound. Roc's grunting and pushing began again as the broken body of a spell casting imp rolled limply down the stairs.

From the top of the stairs, they could hear Roc's voice call back down: "Frito? These guys are here to see you!"

Bloc and Blade emerged from the stair next. Although they wore little armor, their human size made it difficult to push up the narrow space. Achillia was next, her female human frame found little trouble. She paused abruptly at the top. Her eyes fixed on two meat fleshed Titans standing side by side against the far wall. The tips of their golden scimitars rested on the deck as they waited like two statues, unmoving.

Before Achillia could speak, Roc barked at her. "You're blocking the stairs."

Achillia held her sword at the ready as she slowly made her way from the stair, her eyes fixed on the pair. They weren't moving.

Battle and Frita popped out next followed by Frito.

The titans sprang to life, their blades flashing with glints of sunlight as they twirled them, almost causally, to a fighting pose.

Craig poked up and quickly caught sight of the two Titans coming closer. "How the heck did they get up here before us?" He felt Fryto push him from below and he stepped out of the way.

Frito quickly side stepped, twirling his blade-spear in a similar fashion, eyeing his two opponents. Blood dribbled from their gleaming eyes as they fixed on the Archknight. They were honorable, as demons went, waiting patiently for Frito to show, choosing a room with adequate fighting space; although small enough that only few could participate without slicing each other. They were probably upset at the loss of their brother, Frito figured.

Frito looked around quickly, there was no other door or entrance to the room.

Roc was standing beside him. The armored fighter cursed at the loss of his hammer for fighting in close spaces. He jammed a think armored finger under his mask to scratch his nose as he sank into a fighting stance with his cousin. "Armies built of evil horde, bow to the might of the Roc's sword. Devils and demons have all paid, to the biting strike of Frito's blade. The two shall join and heaven will sunder, for one is lighting, and the other is thunder!" Golden blades clashed and clinked as they danced in and danced out with smooth synchronicity, each side coming away with more knowledge of their opponents than they had before. They clashed again, Roc ducking beneath a sweeping blow, tried to thrust forward with his giant sword, but air was his only reward.

Achillia and Fryto stood by, looking for a way in. The room was too small for a round house melee and both Frito and Roc were using large weapons to fight with. To enter the fight would only aid the Titans.

Bloc shouted and Fryto turned. Demons were flooding up the stairs. Quickly the knight of fire took up his flaming axe and laid down a shimmering column of fire and covered the narrow stair. But the demons didn't stop their charge as a giant beast, covered in flames, leapt from the hole and grappled with Fryto for his axe. Battle turned quickly, driving a snapping kick to the flaming creature's spine. The flaming beast buckled and Fryto pressed him, bringing about the hook end of his axe and catching the beast's burning head and twisting until its skull broke open.

More poured from the hole, Achillia with the help of Bloc and Blade held the stairs.

Frita suddenly leapt into motion. She touched Craig for his attention as she sprang to the far wall. She ducked almost casually below the sweep of a Titan's blade. A door had opened in the wall and in its arch, an eight legged monster waved. She knelt beside it and whispered to it. She then waved for Craig to follow her.

Craig didn't try to figure it out as he ducked low and dashed across the room to the hole and the little monster. "Hi! Formor." It stuck out a small paw and Craig shook it.

"You're the thing that goes bump in the night, aren't you?" Craig asked as he sank to a crouch.

Formor seemed impressed. "You've heard of me?"

Craig nodded, bafflement etched on his face. "Yeah, some how I have."

Frita touched Craig's leg. "He will take us to Thamrell."

"Can we trust him?"

"You got another offer?" The monster said sardonically as he looked around to see if there was another monster offering a better deal.

Craig shook his head. "Guess not. I'll get Frito." He mumbled reluctantly.

Frita's eyes widened to ask him 'How?', but he had already turned his back. The Dragoncaller stood up, drawing his bow quickly. He paused and waited and fired.

A black shaft appeared in the foot of the left Titan, pinning him to the floor. The giant waved, swimming his big arms, fighting for balance. Frito pushed forward quickly, pushing his blade-spear smoothly through its ribs with little resistance. The titan grabbed the shaft and gained his balance, bringing his scimitar down like a guillotine' but Frito was faster, twisting his blade-spear, and spreading the titan's ribs apart with a dull, muffled, cracking sound that stopped the Titan's falling arm. His gleaming scimitar fumbled from dumb, dead fingers. Frito braced his foot on the giant's belly, and dragged his blade-spear free with a plume of flesh dragging with it.

Demons filled the room, fighting with claws and teeth and great perseverance, but Frito pushed past them all with little contact to the door where Craig was calling him.

"Its a delaying tactic." Craig said turning to the door. "This way!"

"Do you know what you're doing?"

Craig turned on him. "Why do people keep asking me that question?" Craig turned his back on him and headed up the stairs, "Look here, these stairs come from the bottom of the tower straight to the top. That's how they beat us up here." Craig didn't bother to try to conceal his voice or presence, the din outside was enough. "I am beginning to regain radio contact with the Dragon-panthers, if we don't act now, there won't be a later."

Frito followed behind quickly, dragging his blade-spear behind. "Can we get the Dragon-panthers to strike the top?"

"Negative, even though there is less shielding at the top, its still too rough for them. I can barely reach them as it is. They're flying as close to the tower as possible to stay in contact."

"We'll need them!" Frito found himself shouting over the roar around them.

Formor spun about on himself with a stinging hiss. "Quiet!" The monster reared slightly on four paws. "For Nih elves, you sure are the noisiest pair."

Craig stuck his tongue at the little monster.

"We're almost there!" The little monster whispered harshly. "They've got lots of guards, but real pussies. You two can trash them." Formor motioned at Craig and Frita. "And you! Big guy!" Formor looked at Frito. "Just jack in the box and trash the floating corpse. No hello's or by your leave, or how's the wife and kids, just fuck his day for all of eternity."

"Wait!" Frito stopped him. "Thank you for all of your help. We would have never gotten this far with out you. But why are you doing this?"

Formor looked down at him. His head bobbled from the shifting of the tower as his black mica eyes only glared back at the Archknight. "Suppose you tell me." The monster said as he turned and passed up the stair.

Craig and Frito squeezed past Frita and made their way higher. Formor was at the top of the stair with four paws braced at the trap lid and the other four held a firm grip on the top stair. "Ready, Freddy?"

Frito nodded and Craig swallowed.

The trap sprung open with a bark as the little monster pushed with all of his might. Sunlight flooded the stair as dirt and dust rained in. Craig bounced as high as he could, swinging his voracious sword with all his strength. Its length and weight chewed rapaciously through a cuirboillied leather breast plate and into the soft flesh beneath. Arms fluttered in the air as the head and shoulders popped off from sheer might quickly leaving a four foot stump spewing blood like a fountain.

Craig followed his swing, twisting his body about until its energy was spent and then reversed direction for a howling back swing. His target feigned, raising his arms and pike in a vain attempt to evade the blow but the Sword of Magnum passed through the haft as easily as it did its wielder.

Frito reared back out of the hole and launched his blade-spear the moment he fixed target. Thamrell was floating wistfully above a small platform, his head only beginning to turn.

Red, blue and white plastic/vinyl suddenly leaped in the way, catching the blade-spear with his chest. The polearm pushed through, tossing the Easy-rider backward. He fought for his balance as the blade-spear twisted and pushed. Thamrell could see his loyal agent fighting with the shaft, trying desperately to pull it free. Thamrell could also see the glistening blade pushing its way through the Easy-rider's back and coming right at him.

The rider's spine gave away and cartilage tore like wet rice paper. The Blade-spear now free quickly leapt to its original target.

With a flick of a Thamrell's hand the blade-spear swerved from its course, sailing harmlessly over the side of the tower.

Craig found himself viciously swinging his powerful Sword of Magnum at random, trying not to cut too deep in fear of his weapon slowing in the heavy thickness of someone's chest.

Frito watched in stunned surprise as his blade-spear began to circle the tower unable to penetrate the magic shielding.

"You Lose!" Thamrell shouted as demons swarmed them. "You dare to attempt me? A god? How dare you!"

Frito's Sho-Pa leapt into play as he punched and kicked. A stiff sword thrust through, and Frito snatched it with a simple disarming blow. With sword in hand Frito blocked and parried the porcupine of steel before him.

Frita lashed out suddenly with a furious kick that gave her room. She spun around quickly throwing a punch that to Craig sounded like a gun shot. Frita was glowing in the white light of knights. Her blows rained in fury, buckling chests, snapping bones, cracking shields. Her power was suddenly flaming within her. She had found her weapon again. Her weapon was herself.

She pirouetted, turning a jaw into paste with an invisible kick. She didn't pause in her Sho-Pa technique as she punched out twice and came down with her elbow. "Frito!" She shouted without breaking concentration. "Go phantom!"

Frito suddenly thrust out. His skill as a swords man had not waned since his taking up the blade-spear. "No! I'll not leave you!"

She suddenly turned to him sending up a blind back fist as she did. "You're telling me my business? Frito?"

Frito looked at his sister, sweat glistening on her holy glow. He had no choice.

Demons suddenly tossed and tumbled in the air as the trap door sprung open and Roc bounded out. "KOWABUNGA!" Roc's great heavy sword came down splitting a demon and the wood at his feet. "You thought I'd missed the fun," His sword mowed at shin height and demons either jigged or fell out of the way. "But don't you ever fear." Roc wasted no time piling a row of bodies before him. "Now the party is in the sun, And Roc the Dragonslayer is here!"

Thamrell hovered over the pile rising to the top of the tower. "You are all too late! The lines are broken, fallen and crushed. Even now your vaunted forces are falling on their weapons! You've lost!"

"Wrong Thamrell."

The god of despair spun in the air. Frito had phantom walked his way unharmed through the crowed and now stood in a battle stance on the general's podium. The general lay in a broken ball at the Archknight's feet.

Frito jumped and latched on to Thamrell's tattered robes. The god of despair sank slowly, and then began to rise again as he compensated for the weight. "You can't kill me, Ninefingers!" Thamrell spun about trying to shake him free. "I've been promised my sweet revenge! I've killed Friska with his own hands, and if you kill me, this tower will be destroyed with you on it. You'll be dead for real and I'll be back in Hel. I'll gladly go back knowing that I killed the Ninefingers. I killed the Dragonslayer and the whole house of Hammerstrike. Unhand me!" Thamrell tried to paw with Frito to make him lose his grip, but Frito latched tightly on Thamrell's bony hand and crushed it into dust. Thamrell screamed and suddenly dropped to the deck. He was trapped in reality, using his very limited power to stay solid enough to command his forces. He had to hold out for only a few moments more. He brought what little magic he possessed into play, fading in and out of existence, but Frito came with him, countering with his own, physical Kamri. Quickly, Thamrell phased out again, hopping the Ninefingers wouldn't, but Frito felt the air tingling and went phantom with his Kamri and held on. The god of despair slowly fought for height as he chanted on. "I'm in a no lose! I have had my revenge on you! On Okshiru! I've won!" He shook his bony stump like a wagging finger. "Don't you understand that? You've failed! Take your thrice damned hands from my neck! You can't kill me! I will have my sweet revenge!"

Frito gripped tightly to Thamrell's neck and pulled himself until he was high enough to whisper in the god's ear. "But it will be my vengeance!" Frito suddenly let go.

The knight fell into the swarm of demons while Thamrell, free of Frito's weight, soared high above the tower and unknown to him, its shield. "I've won!" He screamed. "I've won!" He turned to Worldsend, floating higher. "I've won!" Thamrell's dusty bones creaked as he drew air into his withered lungs. "I've…" Thamrell's empty eyes filled with fear. His concentration had been broken and the blade-spear, free of the tower's shield soared through Thamrell's hollow chest with little resistance, its blade drilling violently, sending broken, brittle, bits of bone and dried, dead flesh in a spray out of the god's back.

A blinding pulse of light flashed and the barrier lifted. The tower screamed as its joints leapt free. Fire swept in red satin sheets from the walls as the armor plates slid from the skeletal grid work. The tower shifted and started to collapse.

The top deck turned sideways, like a ship tossed in a stormy sea, and every thing slid toward the side with an invisible rush of water. Some demons bounced into the rail and plummeted to the fires below, while others failed to make it that far and impaled themselves on the protruding splinters of wood. Craig spun about on the deck like a fish out of water trying to grab the rail as he tumbled over it. The tower lurched again and the rail was snatched that much further from his hand as he began to fall for the fourth time that day.

Fuck

Black wings swept around him and talons hooked into his armor. Craig felt his skin pinching and tearing as black paws grabbed him and held him fast. The tower suddenly shrank below him as he was lifted above the war to where he belonged. Quickly Craig climbed onto Reginald's back. The Dragoncaller only glanced at the sun and realized that the same 'Gift' that allowed him to ride Dragon back in the sun allowed him to ride Dragon-panthers. He looked below and watched his fleet of rented Dragon-panthers latch on to each member of the party and lift them above the exploding tower. He watched as a White Tiger Dragon soared into the swarm at the top of the blazing tower to fish out one of the party and accidentally rescue a demon. A Dragon-panther flew by, politely informing his feline cousin of the mistake and to put it back, which the Tiger did.

Craig tuned into his Dragoncall and the first words he heard roar in his head were from Floppy. *'Tell the Nasty One to sit still.'* Craig almost laughed as he watched Roc fighting and squirming in the White Tiger Dragon's grip.

'Just hold on to him, Floppy.' Craig said before crouching lower to Reginald's ear. *'How's it going at the front?'*

'Melville is at the front.' Reginald informed him.

Craig sent his call and Melville responded. Craig could hear the sound of the battle raging around the big black cat. *'There has been an explosion!'* The Dragon-panther reported. *'I can see the tower. It is in flames!'*

'Yes Mel. What are the demons doing?'

'They're stunned and unsure.' There was a pause as Mel cut off and cut on again. *'Sorry. Even the front lines have stopped fighting. They don't know what to do!'*

Craig looked over the landscape before him. The masses of demons swarmed like of bugs below him. He could see the tiny spots of color that was Roc's final stand of men. Jesus! They were holding! Roc's troops had set up barriers and archers picked off demons bogged down in tangle foot wire. The ragged and torn front line pulled into a tight 'V' formation with PT bushes to their flanks and used the natural hill incline to their position. Jose was conscious and Wendell and Tristan were now grouping the last line of troops to hold.

The demons had no idea what to do. The second and third lines looked to each other for guidance while the front line held off attacks.

'There, Floppy!' Craig pointed to the center of the fracas. *'Set the Nasty One down there!'* Craig waved for the rest to set back a bit farther behind the front lines. Craig ordered Reginald to circle higher as he fired a rain of arrows into the crowd.

From his height, Craig watched as Roc pushed away from Floppy four meters from the ground and dropped right into the front line of demons. Craig called in two White Tiger Dragons for assistance. The three Dragonguards joined with four others and leapt into the fray. Wendell and Tristan called for a frontal push and soon fought beside the Slayer. Roc was the spear head of the front line press. The demons recoiled and pulled back. The black Kenworth sounded its air horn and slowly rumbled forward while the Demon Bikers from Hel pressed on, following the spearhead.

The demons out numbered them ten to one, but without leadership to guide them, without reason a to fight, they just didn't. One rose up, quickly giving orders, trying to rally the demons to hold back the spearhead, but a black shaft from the Bow of the Dragoncaller, dropped from above, silenced him and discouraged any other demon from trying the same thing.

The horn of the Trid Dreath howled again and the demons cringed. Roc knocked them around like gnats. The Hothering Slothering Wanderblest Beast complete with Horro-Shred option and *Dual Turbo*, suddenly clicked on its Trac-shredder and demon parts went flying in gobbets of meat. The demons weren't having fun any more. They weren't fighting. They were losing.

They had lost.

The war was over.

<u>Chapter 77</u>

They danced and drifted, sailing this way and that, floating like white goose down. It was unorganized and disorderly, bouncing into one another on occasion as they made their way down, landing softly on the white blanket that covered the land. It piled on the tower and the steps and made white pillows on everything it touched.

Through mist frosted windows Craig watched the snow fall. *Fikor,* he thought, *god of winter made snow, not…uh, god of rain…oh jees, whoever.* He rubbed on the glass with his sleeve to clear the condensation. The white sky before him touched the white earth below. The mountains before him were swathed in a white curtain. The New York City snow was nothing like this. The city was still the city, stone hard and unyielding, not noticing the snow until it was slush and then it was despised. Here, it was beautiful.

He watched the horse drawn sled as it was pulled over the bridge that spanned Seeda Gully towards the manor walls. Max and Orrin had arrived for the dinner Feast of Fikor's winter and the spy eye announced them. The gates were opened and the sled drew in. Kathreen, bundled in her coat and boots and Frita, bare foot, dressed in her thin cotton tunic and pant stood together, hand in hand, to greet the new arrivals for the feast.

He smiled, and then wondered why he was smiling. His hands itched and he rubbed them. They were still scared, but not as they were before. He was healing, as were all the others. Magic had gotten them through the war, now months behind them, and nature would take them on further.

The snow seemed to cover over the hurt and torn land before him like white gauze and bandages. He knew that come the spring, there would be nary a trace of the war at all. Trid had opened the Wove and led the demons back to hell…Hel and Frito had said that the gates were closed forever.

"Forever?" Craig had pressed.

Frito shrugged. "Put a dike around the ocean. How long can it contain the tide?"

Craig nodded.

He was still smiling and still didn't know why. He was never happy in Brooklyn without a reason. Now he was.

He could smell the cold rising from the window. The wet frost and water smelled refreshing and made him thirsty. He took a deeper breath to take more in and could smell the feast cooking on the lower floors and it made him hungry. He had taught Trisha to make sweet potatoes just right and its aroma was making his mouth water. His new elven senses were good for something.

He listened to glasses clinking with laughter down stairs. Frito's flute sang with J'son's guitar and J'cob's pipes. Roc's tuneful voice, (Shock!) sang low and smoothly with harmony as Orrin brought out the melody.

He heard Stephanie's voice of the angels rise. It was captivating, shifting and moving with the snow falling outside. Filling the halls of Fanrealm with warmth.

Still looking out the window, he could hear his dragons snore and rumble in their sleep. They too were happy.

Craig was still smiling, but he knew why.

He looked around the room. He was in Lady Fantista's bed room and it was decorated with a collection of gifts from her children both natural and adopted. Quilts and spreads, rugs and tapestries, baubles and trophies, jewels and gems filled each space with life, history and love. Neeko looked up at him. In the gray lighting from where she sat, her green eyes sparkled. She was smiling at him because for the first time in a month, he was smiling.

She sat on the edge of the bed rocking back and forth gently with Krisanna in her arms. His little daughter was suckling at her mother's breast intently, with one hand braced on her mother's chest. Her eyes were closed tightly as she drew her milk. Craig could see little tiny ears, like nubs poking out from the top of her head through the faint, fine lines of hair sprawled on her head in disorder. She was only a head and an arm in a bundle of cloth. She had her mother's beauty, but her father's eyes.

Sunlight glared at him as the room swept away. The ground trembled and he fell back, his legs spilling up above him. Sound overwhelmed him as he landed in the soft cushion of leather. He tried to cry out but couldn't, his voice piling up in his throat. Sight was a smear of light and darkness that came to focus with stunning quickness. A dream, someone in his head told him. The kind that come true.

He looked around the inside of the Barchetta. He looked up and Fryto was looking down. "You okay?" Fryto reached down and gave him a hand up.

Craig looked around as he balanced himself on the door again. "Fine." He said a bit confused. It felt odd to be in armor after such a soft dream. "I uh,…I nodded off. Its that thatch."

"You're tired. We all are." The knight said. "You rate the sleep."

"Yeah," Craig laughed breathlessly, as he looked across the battle field. Bodies lay strewn everywhere, the stench, staggering. Scattered demons straggled and dragged themselves doggedly picking up bits of things that they owned as they went on their way back to Hel. Trid Dreath's orders were for several demons to hang back and clean up their battle. Craig watched one straggle up to the Barchetta, past the leery eye of the White Tiger Dragons who had set themselves up like bed posts around the car and toss a war hammer into the back seat. Craig looked at the demon and it looked back with sullen, swollen, defeated eyes. His mouth hung open and bits of white teeth, like chips of a broken plate, pushed from his gums. Craig watched as the fellow wandered off, back to hell.

Craig lifted the bottle of Molsen Golden that was in his hand, to his lips. It was empty and he couldn't remember finishing it off. He leaned back and put the empty bottle into the glove compartment. He wanted to keep a hold of the gift that Kevin, the devil's driver had given him. *Nice guy, that Kevin.* Craig thought to himself. *Even helped me fix the wheel.*

Frito and Roc moved towards the car. The two moved arm and arm like a four legged beast that couldn't coordinate its feet. The two shifted to the left and then the right as the made their way closer. Blood and mud caked their armor, hands and faces. Even their teeth. They flashed with smiles of victory.

"What a war!" Roc gripped Craig's arm for balance. "Too bad it only lasted a day."

"Roc…" Craig said softly. "I got a note from my mommy saying that I can stay home for the next one."

"There won't be a next one." Frito said with confidence. "And when there is, I'm staying home with you."

Craig toasted his idea with an invisible glass of champagne.

Roc made his way around the Barchetta, holding on to it for balance. "You two are no fun." He grumbled. He looked into the back seat and then closer for identification. "Hey! My hammer! They brought it back!"

Craig nodded. "And from here it looked like he had quite the time prying it out of his mouth." Craig lifted a hand to shield the setting sun from his face as he turned away. He pulled his cloak closer to block its painful stare as he reached into the glove compartment for his spare set of dark glasses. "So are we done?" He adjusted his glasses.

Achillia walked slowly and painfully to the rear of the car and sat herself in the trunk and said nothing.

"I am." Frito said looking at Roc.

Roc rolled into the backseat with his feet hanging over the front seat. He looked to his cousin and then around him.

Two demon bikers rolled up slowly, their bikes grinding and bubbling as they made their way closer and pulled beside the car.

Frita slid from the back of one of the bikes. She gave a pat of thanks to the driver and he snorted a welcome. The bigger biker looked up at Frito, his splinted tail waved at him. "Slomph Skeetles." With a twist of a throttle, they sped off.

"I'm not going to ask." Craig said as he fell behind the drivers wheel.

Horse, Frito's horse, stepped into reality at his master's side. Frito pulled a blanket off of Horse's saddle and pulled it about him to shield off the sun. He set a heavy foot into the stirrup and with a heave and a groan, swung into the saddle.

Frita slipped over the door into the back seat. "Roc? You have a hand on your shoulder."

Roc held up his hands and looked at them, one at a time like an inventory. "How about now?"

She nodded.

"Is it moving?"

She nodded.

"Closer or away?"

"Closer."

Roc smiled. "I like that! Determined little bugger!" He yanked it off and looked at it. Since it wasn't anyone he knew, he leaned over the side of the car and placed the hand in front of the back wheel. "Well?" He said looking to the back of Craig's head.

Fryto slipped quickly into the front seat between Roc's legs while Craig looked for the keys. "I just hope this thing starts." He said as he slipped in the key. A painful screech erupted from under the hood that made him jump. He twisted it again and the engine shrilled as it turned. Another twist and it whined and sputtered and cranked once, twice, a third time with effort and a forth with more. Craig let go of the key and shook his head. "C'mon." He whispered. "I'm ready to roll." He pumped the pedal and gave the key another twist. The engine turned slowly, then faster. Suddenly, with a cough it filled with power that trembled with a roar. Craig felt the eight hundred or so fiery horses stamp and shake their flaming manes before him.

"Lets Roll!" The Barchetta spoke through its broken grill, spitting out bits of demons as it did.

Craig shifted into gear and turned the car west, towards home. Towards the setting sun.

The End.

Acknowledgments

Not in any particular order

Orrin Ailloni-Charas. The Fool that Did.
"There was this termite that walked into a bar and asked, 'is the Bartender here?'"

M. Dwayne (Diablo) Herron. Peace love and Chocolate Chip Cookies.
"No shit, there we were"

Scott L. Raymond. The expert.
"This is the part where Scott's head explodes."

Michael F. (Roc T. Dragonslayer) Francis.
"Let it not go unsaid that your stark terror was unappreciated."

Kevin (Land-Waster) Glatfelter
"Do what again? Lose?"

Donna S. Francis
"No Pity! I don't want your Pity!"

Hilary (Lady H) Neckermann
"I am not a witch"

Dexter C. Frodo Herron. The First, the Last, and the Only.
"Aw fuck, here we are."

Robert (Rob) Wilbarg.
"I have blonde hair and a red beard, I just don't understand it!"

George Christopher (Christopher George) Marion
"I was there, remember? I was standing right next to you!"

Jan-Erik S. (what's the S for Jan?) Krous
"How come I don't get a quote?"

Jason (Jay) Cloit
"Of course I know where the First Aid kit is, I'm the only one whose ever needed it."

Ann (Ann) McFadden
"The term you're looking for is 'Differently sane', not 'Crazy bitch'!"

Special thanks to Hickey Pimpleton for his outstanding performance as Thamrell, the god of human introspection.

About the Author

Dexter Herron was born and raised in Brooklyn, New York and began his writing career at the age of twelve, scripting fantasy episodes for his favorite TV. programs. After joining the U.S. Marine Corps and traveling the world, he settled down in Connecticut and works full time as a police officer. If or when he ever grows up, he hopes to continue his passion for writing full time. He is married and has three cats, two which like him. He is a member of the Society for Creative Anachronism and has been for quite a long time. His favorite authors are J.R.R. Tolkien, Kurt Vonnegut, Anne McCaffrey, Walt Simonson and Frank Miller.

Printed in the United States
1529200005B/13-21